Unity Hall has been writing ever since she joined a woman's magazine as a tea-girl, aged fourteen and a half. She is the former Woman's Editor of *News of the World* and now the paper's Agony Aunt. The author of four previous novels, she has also written several Royal books.

She began a love affair with France in her late twenties and has a house in the South, near Grasse.

She lives in London and Kent.

The House of Secrets

Unity Hall

HEADLINE

First published in 1989
by HEADLINE BOOK PUBLISHING PLC

First published in paperback in 1990
by HEADLINE BOOK PUBLISHING PLC

ISBN 0 7472 3376 4

Typeset in 10/10½ pt Plantin
by Colset Private Limited, Singapore

Printed and bound in Great Britain by
Collins, Glasgow

HEADLINE BOOK PUBLISHING PLC
Headline House
79 Great Titchfield Street
London W1P 7FN

For Pamela Doyle,
my girlhood friend I found again,
then sadly lost again

BOOK ONE

Chapter One

'I wouldn't want you to think –' the girl on the bed faltered, swallowed and then said: '– I do this all the time. It's only with you.' Then she added with a touching simplicity that might have moved him had he cared one way or the other, 'You see, I love you.'

She was leaning up on one elbow, the pillows piled behind her head, the skin of her shoulders and slender arms almost as white as the linen which she had pulled up to cover her full breasts. Violet blue eyes, black-fringed in a broad, snub-nosed Irish face, watched him anxiously. Her black bobbed hair was tousled, and the kiss-curls that she stuck to her face with spit on her little finger were standing away from her cheeks. As he moved back to sit beside her on the bed, he thought she looked like some kind of delectable small monkey.

'I know you do,' he said soothingly, stroking her shoulder. 'And I know you don't do it all the time.'

'You don't think I'm cheap?'

'No, but I do think you're beautiful.'

There was no harm in showing her a little kindness. He knew how to please. He had been brought up to please.

'And do you love me?'

'Questions! Questions!' he said, lightly brushing his lips over the square, strong fingers that clutched the sheet near to her chin. It never ceased to amuse him how women, once it was far too late for modesty, concealed their breasts.

'Oh, Pierre,' she sighed, her startling eyes filling with tears. 'I wish you loved me like I love you.'

'What makes you think I don't?' he said, but added a small chuckle so that she could not take him too seriously. 'Now

3

come along. Time to get up and dress. I'll get you a robe.'

Barefooted, with just a towel round his waist, Pierre Dupuis padded to the bathroom of his apartment and took a heavy white velvet bathrobe from behind the door and tossed it to her. She put it on, making some play of hiding her nudity, and then said, her voice eager, 'Can I use the tub? Is there time?'

'Sure,' he said, knowing that the South Boston slum that this extraordinarily beautiful girl called home boasted no such thing.

She sang while she was in the water, and her voice in song held the lilt of old Ireland. Her speaking voice had some melody but was spoilt by the ugly flat vowels of the Boston shanty Irish neighbourhood that she came from. Her name was Mary O'Flanagan, but she called herself Feathers and insisted that everyone else did. It had taken him three weeks to extract from her the name her parents had given her. By then he was in the habit of calling her by the one that was her own ridiculous choice. But not sufficiently in the habit that he did not feel a fool whenever he did so.

'Why Feathers?' he had asked the night he had enjoyed her virginity. She had cried that night, too, begging the Virgin Mary to forgive her. Eventually the question distracted her from her tears. It was simple, he had discovered, to distract Mary O'Flanagan.

'Because feathers are beautiful, shot with lovely colours. They can be strong like cock feathers, all black and shiny and fierce, or they can float delicately like tiny white angels as if nothing could hold them to the earth. Feathers are glamorous and I want to be glamorous,' she had told him dreamily, her head on the shoulder she had dampened with her remorseful tears.

He did not love her in the slightest, but she had qualities that appealed to him. He had picked her up one evening six weeks previously walking along by the River Charles where he had gone to clear his head after a day's studying. Her looks attracted him. In her Irish way, she was quite beautiful. She reminded him of some bright and enquiring little animal and he liked animals more than he liked people. She was as unformed as some wild species, ignorant and uneducated. Always hungry, she ate greedily when food was put before her as if she feared it might be snatched away.

She worked behind the drapery counter at Boston's smartest

department store, Jordan Marsh on Washington Street, and made it clear she wanted something better. Therefore she was quick to learn. He suspected that her aim in walking by the Charles had been to find herself a Harvard scholar. Having achieved this, she was learning as much from him as she could. It was a fair bargain. She had given him her virginity in return. But he was aware that she was a little frightened of him. Sometimes this worried him when he remembered how so many women had been frightened of his father, and how frightened he had once been of his father himself. He did not wish to resemble Jean Paul Dupuis in any way.

While she was in the tub, he dressed himself in casual trousers and a button-down collared shirt, then went to knock on the bathroom door.

'Come along, Miss Mary Feathers O'Flanagan,' he called. 'It's nearly eight o'clock. You must hurry unless you want my uncle to catch you in my tub.'

She squeaked and there was loud splashing of water. A few seconds later she came back into the bedroom, wrapped in his robe. She gathered up her clothes from where she had flung them almost instantly after he began to kiss and caress her. For all her piety and moans to the Virgin to forgive her, Feathers O'Flanagan required little rousing.

'Why is he coming?' she asked.

'To see me.'

'All the way from California?'

'No. He's been in France with my father's family. My father is French. He came here when he was in his early twenties but he went back to Europe a few months ago with my Uncle Peter. My uncle is only here for the night. Tomorrow he'll go back to New York and take the train for California.'

'He makes champagne? Like your father?'

'Feathers, no one makes champagne in America any more. Not since Prohibition.'

'We do,' she said giggling. 'Well, not champagne wine. Poteen. Dada makes it in an old zinc bath. It's horrible stuff. And, my, it sure makes him horribly drunk.' She was slipping into a shiny peach garment that skated over her curvy body. She had beautiful breasts and a neat waist, but her behind was too heavy and her legs were built for standing. Since her skirts

5

showed little more than her ankles and they were neat enough, the legs did not matter too much. She was, he told himself in his detached way, a peasant. Still, it was pleasurable to watch her pull on silk stockings and anchor them with frilly white garters. She had good taste in clothes, probably from working at Jordan Marsh. He never minded being seen out with her as long as she didn't say too much.

'Anyway, if they can't make champagne any more, what are they doing?' she asked him. 'Or doesn't it matter if they don't work? Are you that rich?'

Pierre shrugged.

'Rich? What's rich?' he said.

'Well, we're not. You could put our whole place into this one room and there's six of us in it,' she said. And she sounded angry.

'Come on,' he said, changing the subject. 'It's time you went.' He did not wish to discuss his family finances with her. He had his own anxieties about the family finances since Prohibition had become law in June 1919, the previous year. The cablegram from Peter announcing he would be arriving had not been encouraging. It merely said he had something important to say. Somehow the message had carried an air of doom.

Feathers' little pointed shoes with bows on the front were on, and her dress with the dropped waistline and the bow at the hip had been pulled over her head and wriggled down into place. The rows of dime store pearls were strung round her neck. She was inspecting her face in the mirror, dabbing a little rouge on her cheeks, and spitting on her finger to glue the kiss-curls on her cheeks. She looked delectable and a touch flamboyant. He found himself wishing that there was time to undress her again, but the doorbell rang.

'Gosh!' She turned to look at him, her lipsticked mouth a round O of anxiety. 'I am sorry.'

'Just put your coat on,' he said as he went down the hall to open the door.

Uncle Peter was standing outside, his overcoat on his arm. Pierre found he was inordinately pleased to see him and then with a pang realised Peter was getting older. The blond hair was becoming grizzled, and the bright blue eyes were now surrounded by a few light wrinkles. He had aged even since last summer.

Peter opened his arms, letting his coat fall to the floor, and the two men embraced.

'It's good to see you,' Pierre said, bending to pick up the abandoned Burberry. 'Come in.'

He stood back to inspect Peter again, and was troubled to see that the older man looked as if he was about to burst into tears. Once through the door, Peter stopped in his tracks when he saw Feathers standing uneasily in the hallway.

'Uncle Peter,' Pierre said easily, 'let me present Miss O'Flanagan, a friend of mine who called for tea. Miss O'Flanagan, this is my uncle, Mr Peter Brunner.'

'How'd you do,' Feathers said nervously, edging for the door.

'Miss O'Flanagan was just leaving, weren't you?' Pierre said smoothly, taking her arm and gently propelling her through into the communal hallway. 'You know your way down, don't you? I'll be in touch.' Neatly and tidily she was outside, the door was shut and she was gone from his apartment, leaving only a faint scent of the cheap face powder she used.

'Who was that?' Peter asked suspiciously.

'Just a girl.'

Peter's face showed what he thought of girls.

'Nothing serious,' Pierre assured him. 'Come in and sit down. There's a bottle of champagne in the icebox. I've still got a few tucked away. We'll crack it together.'

He went into the kitchen, leaving his uncle to look around the book-lined living room. Pierre had found this apartment on Commonwealth Avenue when he first went up to Harvard. He decided that since he had his own car it was not necessary to live at the college. Pierre was a loner. He could do without the company of other freshmen. And he liked the large, roomy apartment with its long windows overlooking the wide street below. He liked watching the parade of people passing; it was so different from the remoteness of his Californian home where a stranger was hardly to be seen. He had furnished the apartment himself, filling it with books, good pieces of New England furniture and some paintings in the new Impressionist manner.

The champagne was a pre-Prohibition bottle from their own Champagne D'Or vineyard in California where he had been brought up. It opened with a satisfying pop. He filled two

7

champagne cups and put the bottle back in the icebox before going back into the living room.

'What we'll do when it's all drunk, God only knows,' he said, handing a glass to Uncle Peter.

Peter was not really his uncle, but he regarded him as such. He was his father's partner in the Californian champagne business that the two men had built up since the turn of the century. Pierre's mother had died when he was born and the two men, his father Jean Paul Dupuis and Uncle Peter Brunner, had brought him up with the help of a succession of nannies and, later, governesses. Peter had been like a mother to him and therefore Pierre considered him as family – certainly the nearest thing to a family he had ever had. He felt the pang again, seeing how Peter was beginning to age. His childhood would have been intolerable without his 'uncle'. He was the only person in the world Pierre had ever loved. But Peter still looked as if he was about to burst into tears.

'What is it?' Pierre asked gently.

Peter put down his glass and took a deep breath.

'Your father has disappeared,' he said, his voice choking.

'Disappeared?' Pierre did not grasp what he had said. 'I don't understand.'

'He's disappeared, I tell you.' Peter was having difficulty speaking.

'How could he disappear?' It was inconceivable that his tough, self-sufficient, cunning and totally dishonest father could do anything so careless as to disappear.

'How long is it since you heard from him?' Peter asked.

Pierre considered. 'Some months, I believe. He wrote and said he was going to France on a trip. I've heard nothing since.'

'You weren't worried?'

Pierre shrugged. He knew he was the apple of his father's eye. The feeling was not reciprocated.

'Do you know why he went to France?' Peter asked.

'To find his long-lost family. Did he find them?'

'Your family, too, Pierre. They're your family!' Peter said violently. His hands were shaking. 'Did he tell you why he went?'

'No, but I guessed. I suppose the law caught up with him.'

'Pierre, it was terrible.' Peter sunk his head into his hands. 'The Yugoslav tenants tipped off the enforcement officers that your father was still making wine. They came to Champagne D'Or and they smashed every bottle of champagne on the estate. They emptied all the vats, drained years of work back into the ground. They left nothing. Absolutely nothing. Every bit of machinery was smashed, the vats hacked to pieces. Nothing, nothing is left.'

Pierre felt regret for the good wine poured into the ground. For the machinery and the artefacts of the business he found he felt nothing.

'The Yugoslavs would have had it in for him,' he said thoughtfully. 'He did use them as slave labour for years.'

'Pierre, don't you care? There's nothing left. The business has gone.' Peter's voice was frantic. 'You don't seem to understand.'

'There's still the land and the vines surely?' Pierre said. 'You could make raisins.'

Peter was silent. He had put his head back in his hands again.

'Oh, I see. There isn't any land or any vines?' Pierre suggested. He found he wasn't surprised.

Peter groaned. 'Jean Paul sold off the land to Gino Angelino. It seemed like a good idea at the time. We couldn't get rid of the tenants, and they were threatening to get unionised. It would have hit the profits seriously.'

The picture was becoming clear.

'So Father sold it all to one of the biggest mobsters in the United States so that the tenants wouldn't dare get unionised. Is that it?'

'Only the land. Your father held on to the winery and the house. It was to be for you. You know he wanted everything to be for you. The deal was Gino would sell him the grapes cheap and he'd sell Gino the champagne cheap. It was a perfectly reasonable business deal. We couldn't guess that Prohibition would come in and he'd lose the winery, though God knows we should have thought it through. It's all worthless now. There are other fields that he hasn't planted yet. He hadn't told Gino about them when he made the deal, but it'll be some years before they're producing. Even when they do, what can we do with the grapes? California is up to its ass in grapes no one wants.'

Pierre was silent. There didn't seem to be much to say. If he had said that he never wanted the winery, never wanted to make champagne, it would only hurt Peter. The winery had been his father's and Peter's life. All their energies had gone into the impossible dream of creating champagne as fine as the best France could produce. Now the dream was finished. But it had never been his dream.

'He went to France to claim his inheritance there,' Peter was saying. 'He knew that his twin brother, Clovis, and his mother had a fine vineyard and a thriving champagne business. It was his right to go and take it over.' He suddenly sounded defensive. 'He is the eldest son. So that's where we went. I hated it. It was all right for him, he'd been brought up there. I couldn't even speak the language. I came back here to sell their champagne to people like Gino Angelino, and when I got back to France, your father had just disappeared. Nobody knew where he had gone. His things weren't there, only his automobile. His family said he'd sent his trunk back to the States. I suppose it will be at Champagne D'Or when I get there, but your father isn't there. I've called and called. Nobody's heard from him. God knows where he is.'

Pierre was aware he should be feeling more, but the only distress that he felt was for Peter. Poor, unhappy Peter.

'Did he cross Gino Angelino?' he asked. 'People who cross that gentleman do disappear, I believe. Not,' he added dryly, 'that I have much experience of mobsters. But if you feast with jackals . . .'

'That's what I believe has happened,' Peter said, and sounded a touch too eager to embrace the theory. 'What else could have happened? It has to be Gino. But Gino swears he knows nothing about it.'

'Well, he would, wouldn't he?' Pierre said. Covertly he regarded the 'uncle' for whom he had been named. Peter still had his head in his hands, as if he did not wish Pierre to see his face. Did Peter know more than he was telling? Was he keeping something back, thinking to save Pierre from hurt? That would be in character.

'So what happens now?' Pierre asked. 'We must surely tell the police.'

'The French police say it's nothing to do with them as he had left France for America. I wanted to talk to you before I did anything.'

'Then we must go to the police and report him missing,' Pierre said.

'But which police?'

'Californian, if that's where he was headed.'

'But we don't know if he was.'

'New York?' Pierre suggested.

'I don't know.' Peter's voice was without hope. 'I don't know what to do. It's all so complicated without him. How can we touch any money if he's reported missing? Everything will be frozen. Not that there's much left anyway. Jean Paul was a big spender, and without the business . . . There's been no income for a long time now.' He paused and said abruptly: 'Is your allowance still coming through?'

'As far as I know.' Pierre felt the twinge of alarm that he had felt for some months when he thought of the effect Prohibition could have on their lives. This time it was not so simple to push the thought aside.

'It may not be for much longer,' Peter told him. 'Not without income. I don't know whether it's best to keep quiet and see if he comes back or to report him missing.'

'Do you think he'll come back?' Pierre asked quietly.

'No.'

A bleak silence fell on the room and Pierre felt certain that Peter knew more than he was telling.

'Then the police must be told,' Pierre said firmly. 'We can't simply ignore his disappearance.'

'You don't really care, do you?' Peter sounded both bitter and defeated. 'Sometimes you're so cold, Pierre. You don't feel anything. I care very much.'

'You loved him,' Pierre said, surprised to hear himself speaking in the past tense. 'I did not. Never. I hated him. He was bad.'

'I know.' It was no more than a mumble and the thought crossed Pierre's mind that perhaps Peter was somehow responsible for this extraordinary disappearance. Had his father betrayed his long-time lover one time too many? For Pierre was certain that his father and his uncle had been lovers in spite of the many women in his father's life.

'Drink your champagne,' Pierre ordered and went to the kitchen to fetch the bottle. He refilled both their glasses and then sat down himself. 'And now tell me about France.'

'It's difficult to explain,' Peter said reluctantly. 'The estate is called Les Hérissons – it means The Hedgehogs. It's run by my sister Rosie –'

'Your sister Rosie? I didn't know you had a sister!' Pierre was so surprised that he slopped his champagne down the front of his clean shirt.

'Didn't you? Well, I hadn't seen her for gone twenty years, any more than your father had seen his twin brother, Clovis, for twenty years or more,' Peter said uncomfortably while Pierre mopped his shirt with his handkerchief. 'I guess I never thought to mention her. You see, she was married to your Uncle Clovis . . . '

'She was married to my father's brother?' Pierre said, astonished. 'Just wait a minute. Let me get this straight. Your sister *is* American?'

'Yes.'

'You *were* both brought up in California?'

'That's right.'

'And she married this extraordinarily named Frenchman, Clovis, and he's my father's twin brother?'

'That's right.' Peter said almost apologetically. 'But Clovis died just recently. You did know your father had a brother?'

'He mentioned his mother and a twin brother last time I was at Champagne D'Or. I gathered they had never left France. He said he'd lost touch with them.'

He had an instant of total recall. Reluctantly he had gone home for the summer vacation, wishing he could stay in the East. Prohibition was already a fact of life but Champagne D'Or was exactly the same. The wine still bubbled in the vats, the golden liquid was bottled and turned daily until the time came to rid it of sediment. The whole complicated process continued. His father could not bring himself to pour away his life's work. Defiantly he had announced that he would break the law until they caught him. He was going to hide what he could of the stock and keep going for as long as possible.

It was one of the few times when Pierre had felt some admiration for his father. For once his dishonesty had a certain nobility, if not a spurious honesty of its own. It was at that same dinner Pierre had told his shocked father that he had no intention of making champagne and that he wanted to be an entomologist. And had to explain that an entomologist was someone who studied insects. His father had not been pleased.

And then later, for something to talk about, he asked about his father's family. The answers to his questions were sparse. And then his father had said, full of treacly sentiment, that one day they would go together to France to find this long-lost family that he had not seen since he was twenty years old. Pierre knew that his father had not intended any such thing at that time for when, out of devilment, Pierre then said that he would take French next term, his father's expression had jerked into momentary alarm. For this reason alone, Pierre had taken French anyway, hopeful of annoying his father further.

'So my father did go back to France?' Pierre asked.

'Right.'

'And your sister runs the winery?'

'They don't call it a winery, but yes.'

'But how did your American sister get to marry father's brother and run a French champagne house?' Pierre was doing his best to take in and sort out these unexpected but riveting family revelations.

'Luck, I guess,' Peter said, making a feeble joke. Then seeing Pierre's expression added quickly: 'Rosie left home and went to France to get away from our pa when she was just a girl. Our pa was pretty mean. He drank a lot. Our mother died when we were young, but she came from France, too. I guess Rosie went to find our folks in the old country. I never really knew. She just went. I met your father when he came to California and she met Clovis when she went to France. It's an amazing coincidence when you think about it,' he said eagerly, pleading to be believed.

'It sure is,' Pierre said dryly, thinking that Peter should really have thought up a better story.

'You've got two real cute French cousins over there. Girls. One your own age called Allie, and a little one called Rosanne. Allie and Rosanne Dupuis. And a grandmother Dupuis as well.'

He was obviously doing his best to divert attention from the impossible coincidence.

'I have a grandmother,' Pierre said, shaking his head. 'Well, well, well. Perhaps I should go visit her.'

'I don't know that that would be a good idea,' Peter said quickly. 'They weren't too pleased to see us. It didn't work out too well.'

'I suppose Father took over.'

'Well, you know how your father is.' Peter was definitely uncomfortable. 'But what else could he do? We'd lost our livelihood here. And Les Hérissons is rightfully his.'

'And if something has happened to Father, it's presumably rightfully mine?' Pierre asked.

'I don't know about that. I don't understand French law.' Again he was defensive. 'But you wouldn't like it there anyway. No one speaks English.' He finished his champagne in a gulp and held out his glass for more which he drank at equal speed. 'Let's go eat someplace,' he said. 'We've got to decide what we're going to do. I suppose you wouldn't consider coming back to Champagne D'Or with me?'

'Leaving Harvard?'

Peter nodded his head and Pierre shook his.

'Oh, God!' Peter said, and burst into tears. 'I can't bear the loneliness. How will I live with the loneliness?'

Pierre wanted to comfort him, but did not know how. Instead he refilled both their glasses.

'Come,' he said, 'we'll drink to Papa – wherever he may be.'

The toast caused Peter to sob like a woman, and then Pierre knew without doubt that his father was dead. The only question was, could he be bothered to find out how and why?

He hadn't even given her time to put her hat on, she thought resentfully, looking back at the closed door. He didn't care how much he hurt her. She pulled on the little cloche she had stuffed in her handbag, careful not to disarrange her kiss-curls, and then went slowly down the marble stairs of the apartment block to the street.

She had hoped he'd take her out to dinner. She had wanted to spend the whole evening with him. Being sent away after they had made love made her feel like a whore. But at least he had been telling the truth when he said that his uncle was coming.

14

She had wondered at first if it had been an excuse to get rid of her after the lovemaking was over.

He didn't love her. She thought perhaps he liked her because sometimes he was kind. He took her out for meals, and he explained things. He didn't seem to mind that she didn't know too much about anything. But he didn't love her, and she loved him. She thought about him all the time when she was at work, at home, squashed in bed with her sisters, everywhere – he hovered at the back of her mind and he wouldn't go away. And when he touched her, she was lost.

The memory of that, of him on top of her, panting and excited – the only time he ever lost control – brought back the guilt. The awful guilt. The guilt was as painful as an abcessed tooth, and she dare not lance it by confessing. If she confessed she would have to stop, and she couldn't stop. When they made love, it was the only time she felt that she was really close to him. When he wanted her that way, she was in charge. He might be taking her from above while she lay on her back under him, but the reality at those times when he rode her frenziedly was that *she* was on top. And when he came and collapsed sweating on her, she felt an overwhelming triumph.

But the guilt was terrible to live with. She had taken to sliding into churches to beg forgiveness and to explain why she couldn't confess and why she couldn't say no. But what troubled her was that since the Virgin was a virgin, how could she possibly understand the terrible need, like a desperate thirst, that love created? It wasn't fair of God to give such pleasure and make it a sin as well. She knew it wasn't a sin in marriage, and she would much rather have married than burn, but she knew in her heart that Pierre would never, never marry her. First-generation Irish girls from South Boston did not get to marry wealthy Harvard men. That was an impossible dream, and another good reason for saying no to him, but she did not know how to say no once he had kissed her.

It took her nearly an hour to get home to the wood-frame house on the mean street where she lived. It was her grandfather's house. He and her grandmother lived upstairs with two unmarried sons, and her parents had the two downstairs rooms and the scullery. The privy was out the back and the scullery was living room, kitchen, dining room and bathroom to her,

15

her two sisters, her brother and her parents. The four children slept in the back room, her parents in the front. Sometimes her father worked, sometimes he didn't. Mostly he was drunk, and when he was drunk it was best to stay out of his way.

She hated the house. Once she had gone into the scullery in the middle of the night, carrying a candle. As she opened the door, a startled black sea of cockroaches vanished back into the walls and cracks of the filthy old building. She had never walked barefoot in the house again.

There would be no food by the time she got home. Her mother cleaned for a rich woman on Beacon Hill, and was allowed to bring home leftovers. The woman was kind, but by now the food would be gone. The larder was always bare. Her father took her mother's money. It was meant to be for the rent and for gas and food. It mostly went in the saloons around Scully Square. Sometimes Feathers suspected on the Scully Square whores. Her mother, married and pregnant at sixteen, now forty, was a worn-out drab. Feathers at seventeen wasn't going to let it happen to her. She lied about her earnings, and kept a secret savings account. One day she'd get away. Her terror was that she might get pregnant, too. So far she was safe.

Before she went into the shack she called home, she walked to the church round the corner.

And kneeling in its quiet, candle-lit depth, she prayed that Mary Mother of Christ would forgive her, knowing that Mary Mother of Christ never would.

Champagne, July 1920

Allie Dupuis was sitting, knees under her chin, on the hill high above Les Hérissons. From the time she had been a tiny child she had come to this spot together with her father, Clovis. He had liked to stand there regarding his kingdom with the pride of a simple man who had created something good. Now it seemed all wrong that even though he was dead the vines in the fields still grew in orderly rows and the grapes peacefully ripened in the sun of high summer. The neat outbuildings and courtyards where the Les Hérissons champagne was made were as spick and span as he would have wished. The cellars were bursting with champagne that they had not been able to sell throughout

16

the war. Cruelly, the estate continued to blossom without Clovis Dupuis, yet at the same time its fecundity was a fitting memorial to him. Somnolent in the July sun, Les Hérissons had already shaken off the violence of the recent past.

Allie missed her father all the time. He had died in the most terrible circumstances just a month ago, and her grief had not yet begun to subside. And as the long days of summer passed, she found she remembered him more and more as he had been in the good times before the war when she was a child. Childlike himself, he had been as much companion as father – until the dreadful war that had ruined both his life and hers.

She sat on a grassy slope, dark-haired, blue-eyed, and aged just twenty, mourning her father while she watched the Épernay road below. Her mother was coming home, and Allie yearned to see her. Rosie Dupuis had been away for three weeks. She had left Les Hérissons abruptly only two days after Clovis's funeral, and when Allie had complained at her desertion of them at this time, Madame Dupuis, her grandmother, had told her to hush. It had, she said, been a hard time for Rosie, and Rosie needed – indeed was entitled to – some time to herself.

But was it time to herself? Or time for someone else? Allie wondered, fretting again that never, never did she seem to come first in her mother's order of priorities.

Below in the distance she spotted the old red Léon Bollée automobile with its long bonnet snaking gently round the bends on the soft hillside. Creaky old Henri who had been with them for ever was at the wheel. He had taken the car into Épernay to fetch her mother from the Paris train. From this height Allie could not see if her mother was alone in the back seat, but hopefully she would be. Pleased, Allie grabbed her bicycle from against the tree where she had propped it and pedalled madly back down the dirt road to the house. She wanted to be home ahead of the car in order to join Mimi, her grandmother, on the porch where they would welcome her mother. Henri never drove fast. Even though he had learned to drive in the early days of the motorcar, at heart he preferred the old-fashioned horse and carriage.

Allie's young legs beat his careful driving and Madame Dupuis was able to greet her daughter-in-law from the front porch of Les Hérissons with both her granddaughters, Allie and Rosanne, flanking her. Allie held her grandmother's arm. Her much-loved Mimi was frail these days and welcomed a little support. At her other side, five-year-old Rosanne bounced up and down with excitement, ignoring the new English nanny's attempts to calm her.

Rosie was alone. She jumped from the back seat of the car, careless of the amount of leg that she showed, and ran up the steps of the house. As always, she looked beautiful. Her soft pink dress in some kind of fine, clinging fabric skated over her body and fell in uneven folds above her neat ankles. She was laughing, holding her hat in her hand. She had had her hair cut much shorter and it waved neatly around her head, making her amber eyes look enormous in her fine-boned face. Allie felt the old familiar pang of admiration and envy combined. But the admiration and envy were tinged with anger that her mother could laugh when Papa was dead.

'Mama! Mama!' Rosanne was calling, and running to jump into Rosie's outstretched arms.

Rosie grabbed the little girl, lifted her high into the air and brought her down for a smacking kiss, and then with the child on her hip, moved to kiss both Allie and Madame.

'It's good to be back,' she said breathlessly. 'I've missed you all so much.' Then in order to hug Allie to her, she put down Rosanne. The child's lower lip immediately quivered and she began to cry.

Ignoring Rosanne's tears, Rosie was suddenly serious. 'Darling Allie,' she asked tenderly. 'Are you all right?'

'Just about,' Allie said.

'Still hurt?'

Allie nodded.

Her mother made no attempt at words of sympathy. She just took Allie's hand, squeezed it and led her inside. As they walked, she placed an arm round her mother-in-law's shoulder and asked how she was. Rosanne, still grizzling, trailed behind, one fat little paw clinging to the hem of Rosie's dress.

Rosie had been in Cannes for the past three weeks but she said little about it. They settled themselves in Madame Dupuis' small sitting room and after Rosanne was taken off to the nursery for her tea Marie brought in a bottle of the *douce*

1913 vintage and a plate of fresh cream pastries that Cook had prepared specially. The sight of Marie surprised Rosie; she jumped to her feet to give the maid an impulsive hug.

'You're back with us, Marie!' she said. 'How marvellous.'

'Yes, Madame,' Marie's broad grin showed her pleasure at the hug. 'And very glad to be when Madame asked us.' She gave a twitch of her white apron, asked if that would be all, and slipped out through the door.

'You asked her back and she's forgiven us!' Rosie said with a smile to Madame.

'Yes, and so has her Robert,' said Madame. 'I asked them to come back after the funeral. They were content enough working for the Pommery's but glad to come home again.' She sighed. 'It feels better with them here.' She took a handkerchief and dabbed at her eyes. 'But my sons will never come home again.'

No one spoke. Allie felt her eyes fill with tears too at the thought of her father, but the other one, his twin brother, Jean Paul, who'd sent Marie and her Robert away, she'd shed no tears for him. She was glad that he was gone and would never plague them again.

'Have you heard from Peter?' Rosie was asking.

'No word, thankfully.' Madame Dupuis' back had stiffened again. 'Perhaps he is out of our lives for ever.'

'Perhaps,' Rosie said, but she didn't sound certain. 'What will he do? He has no livelihood any more. He may come back.'

'I think he knows he will not be welcome.'

'But, Mama, he is my brother,' Rosie said. 'If he comes back I cannot turn him away, any more than you could turn Jean Paul, your son away when he came home again.'

'This is still my home, Rosie,' Madame said, 'and he is not welcome.'

Allie had liked Peter when he had been living at Les Hérissons. He was a silly soft old thing, and none of the horrors had been his fault. He was a victim in a way, just as she herself was. Was that why she had liked him? she wondered. He had also been good company. She wouldn't mind if he came back. She was so often lonely now. Rosanne was too small, Mimi too old, and her mother too occupied to make good companions. Her father had been the one who had had time for

19

her – except for that dreadful period when he had been shell-shocked, but she didn't want to remember those bad times.

Rosie had gone very quiet, and Allie knew that she wanted to continue to argue with Mimi but had judged it unwise. Then her mother put down her champagne glass and said: 'Mama, I have something important to tell you.'

'Yes?' Her grandmother sounded not exactly indifferent, but as if she knew what was to come.

'It's not easy to say,' Rosie said, and Allie had never seen her mother so ill at ease. 'But I am going to get married. To Philippe Lefevre.'

Allie could not believe her ears. Her father not cold in his grave in the little churchyard at Chigny les Roses and her mother speaking of marriage again!

'I thought that was what you were going to say,' Mimi said calmly, sipping her champagne. 'It's something you have wanted to do for a very long time, isn't it? I have known for years.'

'I tried to do my best, tried not to hurt anyone.' Her mother's voice was almost a whisper. 'Are you angry with me?'

'Not angry. Disappointed. You could have waited a little longer.'

'No.' The spirit had returned. 'I cannot wait. He needs me. You must see he needs me. We will wait for the wedding if you wish, but I must be near him.'

Allie could no longer control herself. 'Papa needed you,' she shouted.

Rosie shook her head. 'The truth is he would have been better off without me.'

'Maybe that is the truth,' Madame Dupuis said. 'But we would have been worse off had you not come here. We have all needed you and leaned on you for many years. No doubt we shall continue to do so. But I would not wish you to live under this roof with Philippe Lefevre. When I am gone, you can do as you wish. But not yet.'

Rosie looked stunned.

'But Mama,' she said, 'this is my home, too. It has been for twenty years now. And the business –'

'The business is most certainly yours, Rosie. You created it, and whatever it makes is yours. If you wish to continue to run it, do so. If not, I shall close it down. We managed without it before you came and we can manage without it again. This house, too, will always be your home, but not that of Philippe Lefevre who cuckolded my son.'

Allie, who was boiling with anger at the idea of her mother's remarriage, heard the word cuckolded and realised that her grandmother had forgotten she was there. Sometimes her grandmother did forget things these days, and sometimes she was a little unreasonable and even not rational. Her mother had gone very white, and made a little chopping movement with her hand towards where Allie sat.

'She is grown now,' Mimi said placidly. 'She is old enough to know these things.'

'But I would rather she did not, Madame,' Rosie said, her voice cold as charity. 'We will discuss this later when we are alone. Allie, will you take a little walk with me? My legs are stiff from the train.'

'No. I would rather not,' Allie said and her mother's face set.

'Go with your mother,' Madame Dupuis said sharply. 'And mind your manners.'

Bewildered by her grandmother's change of attitude, Allie got to her feet, leaving her pastry uneaten. Her mother was already leaving the room, back straight, head up. Resentfully Allie followed her as she walked through to the back of the house and out into the paved rear courtyard. There she turned and waited for her daughter to catch up with her.

They stood facing each other for a moment, Rosie's face sad, Allie's deliberately showing defiance.

'Let's walk through the vines,' Rosie said quietly, and held out her hand.

Allie hesitated. She did not want to take the hand, but she could not bear to see her mother's face so sad.

'I'm sorry, Allie,' her mother said, her voice very low. 'Please let us talk about it.'

Allie half sobbed and Rosie sighed, took her hand and led her along one of the gravelled paths that bordered the vineyards nearest to the house. There was a stone seat at the end of the path and they walked in silence towards it. There they both sat, Allie carefully not looking at her mother. If she saw her mother was hurt, she would melt, and she still needed to feed the anger she felt.

21

'Was what Grandma said true?' she demanded.

'Yes.'

'How could you!'

'Because Philippe and I love each other.'

'I can understand all sorts of things now,' Allie said bitterly, remembering so much in the past that should have alerted her to this betrayal of her mother's. 'Grandma said it had been going on for a long time. Is that true too? Was it going on when you took me to America with you and him that time?'

'Yes.'

'What about my father? Didn't you love him?'

Rosie was silent for a moment and then said: 'I loved your father very much – once.'

'Until you met Philippe, I suppose?' Allie put as much contempt into her voice as possible, but in a way her mother's answer had been a relief. She had always feared that her mother had never had any real feeling for her father.

'Yes. But I still felt warmth and affection for Clovis,' Rosie said, almost humbly, but as if she was carefully choosing her words. 'Oh, Allie darling, these things shouldn't happen but they do. I never intended to do anything about it. Never would have except for –' she faltered '– all the horrors we have lived through. But remember Philippe is blind. He needs loving eyes, and now I can be those eyes.'

'I need you, too,' Allie said passionately, wishing her mother's lover dead as well as blind. She turned to look into Rosie's stricken face. 'I've always needed you, but I've always come second. You've always lived your own life, gone away and left us all. Now you're going to go for ever.'

Her mother's eyes filled with tears.

'I'm not doing any such thing, Allie,' she said distractedly. 'I am going to marry Philippe. If Madame won't let us stay here, we will make a new home, and it will be your home as much as ours. And Rosanne's, too. It is cruel of your grandmother to take this attitude to Philippe, a man who lost his sight fighting for France. I don't understand it. She always liked him so much.'

'It is because he is taking Papa's place and Papa lost his mind fighting for France,' Allie said. 'I know how she feels.'

'But you always liked Philippe.'

22

'Yes. But I know now why I was always jealous of him. I had good reason to be.'

Her mother was now crying. Thinking about it, Allie could not remember ever having seen her mother cry with such abandon before. At that moment she felt she was the grown-up and her mother the lovesick girl. A young girl so foolishly in love that she could not understand the hurt that love was causing others.

'Allie, one day when you fall in love with a man you will understand,' her mother was saying through her tears.

'I shall never love a man, never,' Allie said vehemently.

'You don't think so now, but I pray that when you do fall in love it will be for ever. It is so easy to make a mistake . . .'

'Are you saying Papa was a mistake?' Allie was outraged.

'Not exactly, but we weren't right for each other. He'd have been much happier . . .' She stopped, sighed and shook her head. 'Might have beens,' she said softly. 'No point in might have beens.'

She had dismissed her tears, her head was up again and she was calm.

'One day you will forgive me, Allie. You are the most precious thing in my life, but the love between a man and a woman is precious, too. Philippe and I will delay the wedding, but tomorrow I must go to Paris to see him to explain all this. He will be hurt, but he will probably understand better than I do. He has an understanding nature. We will make some arrangements so that he and I need not live in this house. But you will have to choose where you live, Allie, because where Philippe is, I will be. I would like to think that you will be there, too.'

She rose to her feet, leaned to kiss an unresponsive Allie on the forehead and hurried back towards the house, her heeled shoes scrunching on the gravel path.

Allie watched her go, torn between anger and pity. And only when her mother was out of sight and hearing did Allie cry too.

Philippe Lefevre lived in what had been his father's house on the Ile de la Cité. Once, when he had been married, he had owned his own establishment in the wooded parkland of Neuilly. When his young wife had had their marriage annulled after he had been blinded at the battle of Champagne, he had returned to live with his father and his valet, Georges, who had been his eyes since he lost his sight.

It was Georges who let Rosie in when she arrived at the house on the Ile de la Cité, informing her that Monsieur was in the little study.

He was sitting by the open window, a Braille book on his lap, and her heart turned over as it always turned over when she saw him. His blindness was not immediately obvious. There were slight scars around his eyes, but it seemed to her that he had not changed since she first met him and fallen instantly in love twenty years ago in this very room. His hair was perhaps a little thinner and a little less blond, but his tall, spare frame remained the same, as did the smile that greeted her.

'So soon,' he said, getting to his feet and waiting until she walked into his arms. 'Can't you stay away from me?'

'You know I can't stay away from you,' she said after he had kissed her. 'But I've come because we have to talk.'

'Ah,' he said, 'your family are not pleased with your news.'

'I might have known you would guess,' she said ruefully, settling herself on a small sofa. 'No, they are not at all pleased. Allie is distressed and feels that I am letting down her father. In a way Madame is more reasonable, but says –' she paused – 'that married or not, we cannot live together under her roof.'

'I see,' Philippe said.

'I wish I did. She says she has known about us for ages. She says she is disappointed that we did not wait longer. She doesn't seem to appreciate how long we have already waited . . .'

'But how could she?' Philippe said gently. 'You were married to her son.'

'I know. I'm being unreasonable. It's just that I thought that at last we could be happy.'

'But the happiness has come about because of her son's death.'

Rosie felt a deep pang of guilt. 'You're right. I know you're right, but it's just going to be so complicated. I can tell she wants me to go on running the business, though she's too proud to say so. But where are we supposed to live?'

Philippe was settled back in his chair, looking remarkably unperturbed.

24

'Would it surprise you if I said that I don't particularly want to live at Les Hérissons?'

Rosie stared at him.

'Why not?' she asked.

'Because it is where you lived with Clovis. It's a house of unhappy memories and secrets. I'd much rather we lived somewhere else. In fact, I was working up to telling you. I was afraid you'd be disappointed. I know you love the house.'

She had started to laugh.

'Not as much as I love you,' she said. 'Heavens! What an insensitive clod I am being. It just never occurred to me that we wouldn't live at Les Hérissons and carry on with the business and that nothing would change. But you're right. We don't have to.'

'I was thinking of Reims,' he said. 'It's a pity the Germans bombed our secret little apartment. Now that was a place of happy memories.'

'It's not just our apartment they've bombed. There's hardly anything of Reims left to live in,' she told him. 'That's one thing I'm almost glad you can't see, the devastation is so terrible. And they've hardly started rebuilding yet.'

'Then Épernay. You choose. You have eyes and will have to look at wherever we live. I no longer need a room with a view. As long as you are there, I'm content anyway. But there's nothing to stop us spending most of our time right here in this house. I won't be falling over the furniture all the time, and you can become *une vraie Parisienne* while I get on with my work.'

'That sounds good,' she sighed. 'But if we keep Les Hérissons producing, I shall have to spend a lot of time there.'

'Perhaps not if we can find a good manager,' he said. 'You'll need some help now that Clovis is gone. Perhaps we can find someone who not only knows the land but knows about wine as well to take some of the responsibility off your shoulders.'

Rosie was silent for a moment.

'I know I've been insensitive,' she said sadly, 'but it'll be hard. Madame made it clear that it was her home, even though I've lived there for so long. She even said that if my brother Peter came back she would not have him under her roof. If he does turn up, what am I going to do with him?'

'From what you've told me, he'd have to be desperate to come back,' Philippe said.

'He might well be desperate. What does a wine salesman do for a living in the United States now Prohibition's in force? The old homestead won't be producing any income, and the old homestead is half mine if I wanted to be bothered with it.' She sighed. 'I wonder what it's like now? Maybe we could visit it one day.'

Philippe's mind was still on her brother.

'We could probably employ Peter in England if you felt you had to do something for him. But a good salesman should be able to sell anything. He doesn't have to stay in wine. I suggest we cross that bridge when we come to it.'

'Why don't we?' she said. 'I'd really much rather talk about when we're going to get married.'

'And so would I,' he said, beckoning her to come and sit nearer to him. 'Perhaps we had better just do it very, very quietly and not tell a soul. How do you feel about that?'

'I'd rather make an occasion of it,' she said. 'But there I go, being insensitive again. No. I guess you're right. As long as we have a long, long honeymoon. But it is a pity,' she added regretfully, remembering long ago and the misery of what had been her enforced marriage to Clovis. 'I do wish Madame understood.'

Allie gradually began to come to terms with the fact that her mother was going to remarry, mainly because no one ever mentioned it. Things weren't so very different. Her mother had always been away a lot, in Paris, in Reims, and now it was obvious why she had gone away so often. She'd been cuckolding her husband. Poor Papa, Allie thought bitterly.

Perhaps Rosie was away even more now, but it appeared as if she was making a real effort to spend more time with Allie and little Rosanne. Allie herself would have liked to spend more time with Rosanne if the five-year-old had not been so naughty and so difficult to control. In an attempt to calm the child, an English nanny, aptly named Miss Shepherd, had been hired and it was agreed that the little girl should remain under the nanny's discipline until she quietened down. Miss Shepherd had laid down her orders and they were to be obeyed. She had pointed out that Rosie and Madame could not resist spoiling the child. They gave in to her every whim. Allie did the same – but only when no one was about to see her snatch up Rosanne for hugs and cuddles and to ply her with chocolates and sweet biscuits. It was not surprising that Rosanne was confused, Allie thought guiltily, for in company she ignored Rosanne's existence and then the child cried.

Her mother's forthcoming wedding was less of a problem than her father's death. She could not come to terms with that. She still woke in the night, sweating, having suffered the same nightmare. Her father was striding up the hill on the estate to where the entrance to the Roman chalk pit was, and as she ran behind, screaming for him to stop, suddenly he vanished. In her nightmare it was she who was falling, falling, falling the dizzy depth of the pit. But she always woke just before the ground received and broke her, as it had received and broken him, leaving her to mourn him.

Her mother had been home about ten days when Allie's depression became almost unbearable and her grandmother said it was time she got away from Les Hérissons if only for an hour or two.

Henri drove her into Épernay where Mimi told her to buy herself some new clothes. Clothes were not Allie's first priority. Her mother adored wearing the latest fashion, but Allie had not inherited the passion. Still, she thought as she set off, perhaps something new and pretty would lift her spirits.

She was passing the town's *salon de thé* when through the window she saw a familiar face, a chubby, snub-nosed face heavily powdered and with a painted rosebud bow of a mouth. It belonged to a woman who was dressed in powder blue, with a little powder-blue cloche of feathers that let a few bright blonde curls escape below the ears.

It was Madame Claudette – the woman who had brought her father home the day he was shell-shocked during the war. And it was she who had then helped nurse him back to health. Allie had often seen the woman after her father recovered his memory, but they had never spoken. She always scuttled away, even though Allie had been curious to talk to her. But now Madame Claudette was anxiously beckoning to her. A little reluctantly, Allie went into the tea room.

'Forgive me for calling you in,' the woman was saying as she half rose from her seat at the table, her cheeks flushing pink.

She was ill at ease. Allie remembered how she had been equally uncomfortable at Les Hérissons when Clovis was ill.

'It's Madame Claudette, isn't it?' Allie said smiling and holding out her hand, hoping to relax the woman a little.

'Yes, it is. Will you join me?' Madame Claudette made ineffectual movements with little fat hands at an empty chair. 'I called you in because I wanted to say how sorry I was to hear about your father's death.'

To Allie's astonishment the round baby blue eyes in the tired made-up face opposite filled with tears. The woman immediately began fumbling in her handbag for a handkerchief, apologising all the while.

Embarrassed herself, Allie sat down. 'Please don't apologise for crying,' she said, 'it's kind of you to care.'

'It's been very difficult,' Madame Claudette said, wiping her eyes. 'I wanted so much to talk to someone, but I didn't want to intrude. I was,' she hesitated and then said, 'very fond of your father. We were old friends.'

'Oh, really?' Allie said politely.

'We . . . we were at school together.'

'Yes,' Allie nodded. She was a little uneasy about where the conversation was going. 'I remember how much he relied on you when he was ill,' she said. 'He only remembered you. He didn't even remember me.' She recalled the terrible day in the summer of 1915 when they had come home to find this woman on Les Hérissons' porch. Her father had been beside her, curled up into a ball like the hedgehog after which the estate was named. And he had not recognised any of them. Not his wife nor his mother nor his daughter. 'I was too young to realise what had happened to him. I didn't understand about shell shock,' Allie said staring down at the table. 'It hurt me very much at the time.'

The woman ignored what Allie was saying.

'It's not knowing what happened that is so terrible,' she said, twisting her handkerchief between her fingers. 'Please, can you tell me how he died?'

Allie took a breath and shut her eyes. 'He fell down the Roman chalk pit on our land.'

'Was it an accident?'

'Yes.' Allie said it with conviction, though she did not know if what she was saying was true.

28

'It was just that he was so strange that day.' The woman might have been talking to herself.

'Which day?' Allie asked.

'The day he died.'

'You saw him the day he died?'

'Yes. He just came for a chat. To my premises.'

'Oh, yes.' Allie remembered her mother saying that this woman had a dressmaking establishment. 'You're a dressmaker, aren't you?'

The woman looked at her doubtfully, and then nodded. 'You see,' she went on, 'he seemed unhappy. Resigned to being unhappy. He told me things I'd never known. Sad things. It made me afraid that perhaps –'

'He had killed himself?' Allie asked before the woman could voice her own terrors. She was trying to stop her voice rising. 'No, he did not kill himself. It was an accident. And what sad things did he tell you?' She knew she sounded belligerent, but Madame Claudette did not seem to notice.

'I can't really remember now,' she said, her voice vague, 'but it worried me so much. I thought I could perhaps have done more to help him. He wanted things, promises . . . But it would have been impossible.' Her voice sharpened. 'You've put my mind at rest. You are certain it was an accident?'

'I saw it. I was behind him.' Now Allie knew her voice was rising too loudly. 'It was an accident, I tell you. An accident.' Aware that people were staring, she jumped to her feet. 'I must go now,' she said, forcing her tone back down to a normal level. 'It was kind of you to be concerned.'

She muttered a goodbye and rushed out of the tea room, disturbing people's chairs as she went by. Outside in the street she found she was near to tears and that she had lost all interest in shopping. She would go home. Henri would be waiting outside the station. He could take her home.

Once back at Les Hérissons she went straight to the kitchen to find Marie. Marie was the source of all local knowledge and gossip. She was sitting by the table, peeling potatoes while Cook, a fierce, raw-boned lady, chopped up beef for the night's supper.

'Can I have a coffee, Cook?' Allie asked.

Cook, a woman of few words, poured her one.

29

'And drink it here?'

'It's your kitchen,' Cook said.

The three women sat in silence for a moment, and then Allie asked: 'Marie, did Madame Claudette go to school in Chigny?'

Marie shook her head. 'Not that I know of. I believe she comes from the Auvergne.'

Allie digested the answer. 'What exactly does she do?'

Cook gave a cackle of laughter.

'Runs the local brothel,' she said as Marie, too late, threw her a warning look.

Slowly the awful implications began to sink in.

'I see,' Allie said dully.

'Why do you want to know, Miss Allie?' Marie asked.

'No reason. Just wondered,' Allie said. Very carefully she put her coffee cup down, hoping that her hands weren't shaking, and as slowly as she could manage she left the sudden chill of the kitchen and went upstairs to her bedroom.

There was a lot to digest. Including the possibility that her mother, too, had lived with unfaithfulness.

As she took her diary from the drawer, where it was always hidden, she found herself wondering which of her parents had broken their marriage vows first.

Chapter Two

Boston, July 1920

Pierre was almost wishing that he had gone with Peter to California for the summer. The vacation loomed ahead with nothing exciting in view. He found he could not bring himself to study for the next semester. The only positive thing that he was doing was to continue with his private French tuition. Time dragged. He was bored and restless even though by nature he was rarely bored. And out of boredom he was seeing more of Feathers than he knew was sensible.

His uncomfortable state of mind had come about due to sudden and unusual reluctance to spend cash. Peter had alarmed him with the thought that the dollars, which had always gushed as liberally as the champagne which provided them, might dry up just as the champagne had. In fact, thinking about it intelligently, the money had to dry up. With no winery and therefore no income from Champagne D'Or, the only question was how much money had his father saved over the years?

Presumably only his father knew the answer to that, but where was his father? Not that Jean Paul Dupuis' whereabouts troubled Pierre deeply. He did not dwell on his father and his mysterious disappearance. He did not care if he was dead or if he never saw him again. Sometimes when he had climbed into his big bed he would wonder briefly what could have happened to him and how he could have died (if he had died), but the questions would be lost in sleep.

Pierre had never been particularly extravagant but money was something he had taken for granted. It had always been there for anything he wanted. Now he found himself anxious about it. And because he was anxious, the windows of Brooks

Brothers on Boylston Street seemed filled with the most desirable clothing, and he had a ridiculous urge to treat himself to a brand new Single 6 Packard automobile. However, he bought nothing, even though his allowance was still being paid – so far – and his bank balance was comfortable enough.

He had taken the trouble to read up French inheritance law and found that he and his unknown French cousins were certainly heirs to the Les Hérissons vineyards and wine business. It seemed to him that even before the death of his father's mother and Peter's sister he could claim a living from the estate if all else failed. But he doubted if he would be any more popular with the French Dupuis than his father had been if he just appeared on their doorstep. The cousins must be praying that he did no such thing.

Then reading the last term's copy of the Harvard magazine he had spotted an announcement for scholarships offered in France. Sponsored by the American Field Service, the scholarships were available to American citizens aged between twenty and thirty. The degree was equivalent to a Ph.D. Pierre thought that he might apply just to assuage his restlessness, if for no other reason. The offer could not be taken up until July 1921, which would give him another year to work on the French language, and by then he might need the financial benefit of a scholarship if he wanted to go on studying. He had a nagging presentiment that he might be forced to visit his father's family's champagne business, where presumably the cash had not dried up.

He mentioned the scholarship scheme to Feathers one hot evening after they had listened to jazz at the Hampden Café near his apartment. She was in a strange mood, both defensive and aggressive at the same time, and she was boring him. He watched her tucking into a plate of fried clams and french fries as if her life depended on it, and then he told her that he was thinking of taking a scholarship to a French university. As he could have foretold, she instantly pushed her plate away, all appetite gone.

'But why would you want to go to France?' she asked, staring at him, her voice dismayed.

Why did he want to go to France? It was a good question, particularly as he didn't really want to go to France at all. Nor

32

did he wish to tell her that lack of money and need of free tuition might be the reason.

'I have family there,' he said briefly.

'What sort of family?'

'A grandmother. Cousins.'

'But do you know them?'

He shook his head. 'No, but I believe I am an heir to the property,' he explained, aware of sounding a little pompous.

'So you have property in California and in France,' she said, a note of bitterness in her voice, and he knew that she was thinking of how little she and her family had.

'I don't have anything yet, but I might inherit it one day,' he said, not wanting to talk about it any more.

With her fingers she picked up one fat brown clam by a string of batter and slowly put it in her mouth. She chewed for a moment, thinking, and then said triumphantly: 'But you can't go to college in France. You don't speak the language.'

'I'm learning,' he told her. 'It's not difficult if you've learned Latin.'

The news crushed her and he felt a mean little flicker of triumph at being able to make her unhappy so easily. Then she said sadly: 'Nothing's difficult for you, you're so clever. It's better to be a man.' She was not flattering him, he realised. She was envious.

'Well,' he said, now trying to please, 'they're admitting eight girls into the Harvard educational school this year for the very first time. Things are changing for women.'

'Only some women,' she said.

'Anyone, including you, can do anything they want to if they're determined enough,' he said, again feeling pompous, but irritated by the trend of the conversation.

'Oh, yeah!' she jeered and snorted loudly. She obviously thought he understood nothing and maybe he didn't. Not liking her or himself very much he called for the check.

He liked her better when she was back in his apartment. They had walked back silently, and he knew that she was aware she had annoyed him. She kept giving him quick little birdlike looks from the corners of her eyes and did not speak until he spoke to her. The feeling of power and triumph came back and shamed him. He was, he knew, behaving like his father and that

33

was something he tried never to do. He wondered if this girl would let him blindfold her and tie her to the bed, legs wide apart, while he then pretended to rape her. That was what his father used to do to the women who were misguided enough to think that they might become his wife and Pierre's stepmother.

He knew there wasn't anything that poor Feathers wouldn't do to please him. That was confirmed the moment they were inside his apartment. Right there in the hall she dropped to her knees as if she were begging and began unbuttoning his trousers. He stood quite still while she reached inside for him, then rubbed his flesh along her soft cheek before covering him with lightweight kisses and taking him into her mouth.

He stood with his eyes closed, aroused and surprised at her daring, but unable to resist what she was doing as she rolled her tongue round him, breathing exciting warm puffs of air deep from her lungs. Had he let her continue, it would have been all over for him. Reluctantly he reached down, and drew her to her feet.

'No more,' he said. 'Wait.'

Her enchantingly pretty face was turned up to look at him.

'I just wanted to make you happy,' she said.

'You do,' he told her. 'Now come to bed.'

She undressed herself in her eagerness to please, and then helped him with his buttons, peeling his shirt from his shoulders. She stood before him naked, mute, and he took her into his arms and kissed her, something he rarely did. He felt bad that he had been unkind when she offered him so much and cared for him so much while he felt so little for her.

He bent to kiss her nipples which stood red and proud from her heavy breasts, and then he guided her gently back towards the bed. He placed her in the way that his father had placed his women, but there were no thongs, no blindfolds. Just his hands, pleasing a beautiful girl and making her moan as he kissed along the length of her thighs and ran his tongue over her black-clad mount of Venus before he gently lapped the rose between.

She was making little crooning sounds. When finally he drew himself up over her body and entered her, the sounds rose to soft panting cries. Then, as he rode her, she began to talk, an incoherent snatched jumble of words: 'Oh, yes, yes! Please. It's

34

good, it's good. Please love me! Please love me! Deeper, in me deeper!' until she gave the loud incongruous cry: 'Oh Jesus!' that always told him she was there. He pushed the last of his strength into her, and then fell panting on her soft body. They were both silent and he thought that perhaps he slept for a moment or two.

'Good?' he asked drowsily, again wondering at her abandonment, and wondering, too, if he could really have been the first man in her life.

'Umm,' she nuzzled into his shoulder, and then looked at his face anxiously to make sure that he didn't mind. Sometimes he pushed her away when it was finished. Other times, like now, he felt a deep post-coital affection. It never lasted very long. She recognised the affection and her relief was tangible.

'Pierre . . .'

'Umm?'

'I've got something difficult to tell you.'

He felt the hairs at the back of his neck stiffen. Whatever it was, and he thought he knew what it was, he didn't want to hear, but it had to be got over with.

'I suppose you're pregnant,' he said coldly.

'I'm not sure. I think so.'

'How long is it?'

'A week.'

She was crying silently and her tears irritated him yet again, but he tried to be kind.

'A week's not long enough to be sure,' he told her. 'I expect you're just late. Girls are often late when they first make love.'

'How do you know?' she asked.

'Biology,' he said, trying desperately to remember if that was biologically the case, or if he was just making it up to console her and, indeed, himself. 'Give it a few more days.'

'You're not angry?'

He considered the question. 'No. Not angry. But I wouldn't marry you, Feathers. I'm twenty and not ready to marry anybody.'

'Oh.' The bleak little sound hovered in the air. 'If you were ready, would it be me?'

'Who knows. Maybe it would,' he said, making one of his swings from cruelty to kindness. 'You're the most beautiful girl I've ever met.'

'But you don't respect me because I let you make love to me?'

'Nonsense!' he said stoutly, while suspecting that what she had said was true since basically he did not respect women at all. He had felt only contempt for every single one of his father's many women, but he had not realised until he was older that not all women behaved as they did. All his father's women were lacking virtue, but that was not the reason why he had not respected or liked them. Even as a small boy he had understood that they let his father do those things to them only because they wanted to be the mistress of Champagne D'Or. Love did not come into it.

But what was Feathers' reason for succumbing to him? Was it just because he appeared to have money and because he was a Harvard scholar who could take her away from South Boston? Was she just like his father's women? Or was it because she loved him? Unfortunately, he decided, she loved him. That made it all the more difficult, because even if she were pregnant, he wasn't going to do a damn thing about it.

For the next few days he deliberately refrained from meeting her at Jordan Marsh when she finished work. In the time he had known her he had never made a positive date with her. When he wanted to see her, he just picked her up when the store closed. He knew she always hung around the staff exit, hoping to see him, but he thought it better to stay away for a while.

A week later he found a little hand-delivered note in his cubbyhole in the hall of his apartment block. In round, girlish handwriting it read: 'It was a false alarm.'

The news barely moved him but he smiled as he tore the note into shreds. Now he would be able to see her again and that would save him the trouble of finding another girl who would be prepared to sleep with him.

He did ponder whether Feathers had really believed she was pregnant. His guess was that she had not. He reasoned she had lied to him to find out what his reaction would be if there really was a baby on the way. And now she knew the answer. Even if she did get herself a baby she wouldn't get a husband as well. His lack of intention was out in the open. If she had lied and tried to alarm him he was glad. From now on, as long as she continued to let him make love to her, knowing there was no future in it, that small frisson of anxiety she had momentarily caused him had been well worthwhile.

Luke West was whistling as he walked up the dusty road bordered with fields of fast-ripening grapes. His professional eye told him that they were coming along nicely. The weather was cool for August, but the grapes looked of good quality and were healthy. He wondered if the fields belonged to Les Hérissons.

He had left the train from Paris at Rilly-la-Montagne and decided to walk the rest of the way in order to get the lie of the land. The battered old suitcase he carried swung easily from a muscular shirt-sleeved arm. It was warm so he held his dark jacket over his shoulder as he covered the distance with long strides.

The station master at Rilly had been bursting with questions at the sight of a stranger but managed to restrain himself from asking any while he gave precise directions on how to reach Les Hérissons. It was not far – a few kilometres from the little station town which was still being restored after war damage. As he walked, Luke looked about him, noting with interest how different the terrain was from Cognac where he had been working since the end of the war. Here the northern hills were gentle, the air cooler, and the villages prim, almost austere, but he liked the way the poppies bloomed at the sides of fields and marvelled at how little evidence there was of the terrible fighting that had taken place on these chalky fields.

The ring of trees the station master had described was now in view and he headed for them, knowing that the house was hidden behind. At the crown of the road and through the trees he came to a small gatehouse set at the beginning of a long drive. The door to the gatehouse was open and inside a very small, very old man slept in an ancient armchair with his mouth wide open. Grinning, Luke decided not to wake him and continued on up the drive.

Round a bend he came upon the turreted house ahead and stopped to look at it critically. It was large but not particularly grand with its wooden porch and big windows. From where he was standing there was no sign of the vineyards. Only the rather quaint, rambling house could be seen. The house didn't matter that much, he thought, though he was used to working on grander properties. It was the champagne itself and the way they produced it that mattered. Philippe Lefevre had assured him that Les Hérissons made some of the best champagne in the area and that if he really wanted to become an expert, it was as good a place as any to start.

He put down his suitcase, put on his jacket and continued on up the drive. He had just reached the flight of steps that led to the porch when the front door burst open. The young girl who came out was in a hurry. She began to run down the steps, saw him and stopped dead.

'Can I help you?' she asked, her voice full of suspicion.

She had, he thought, the most extraordinarily interesting face – not exactly beautiful, but memorable. Her skin was clear olive, her features were even, almost too strong for a girl, the eyes brilliant blue with strongly marked black brows that formed two question marks. They were hostile eyes, but the mouth was soft, red and vulnerable.

'I'm looking for Madame Dupuis,' he said easily.

'Which Madame Dupuis? There are two.'

'Are you one of them?' he asked.

'No, I'm the daughter. Do you want my grandmother or my mother? My mother's out. Tomas, at the gate, should have told you.'

'If Tomas is the old, old chap who's having forty winks down there, I didn't disturb him. He looked ancient enough to have earned an afternoon nap.'

A smile twitched at the corner of the daughter Dupuis' lips.

'He is old,' she said, as if it were a confession, 'but he's always been with us.'

'That's nice,' he said gravely. 'Nice that you don't get rid of people just because they get old.'

'Everyone here is too old or too young,' she said gloomily. 'If you want my grandmother, she's having an afternoon nap too.'

'I think I probably want your mother,' he said. 'She's the boss here, isn't she?'

'Very much so,' she said. 'But she's out. What did you want to see her about?'

'A job.'

'A job?' She looked puzzled.

'A job. Sort of her job.'

'Is she expecting you?'

'I think so,' he said, though he wasn't entirely sure. Philippe Lefevre had said that Rosie Dupuis was resisting taking anyone on and wouldn't make up her mind.

'You'd better come in,' she said abruptly and swung on a pretty shoe below a peach-coloured skirt to go back up the steps.

Inside, the house was as stiffly formal as French houses tended to be. He left his suitcase in the hall and she led him into a little side parlour that had a cosy feel about it. She motioned for him to sit on a small sofa. He sat down gingerly. He was not built for small sofas.

'So Mama's going away, is she?' the girl said accusingly.

'Not that I know of,' he said, wondering what it was that made this one so angry.

'Then why should you be "sort of" after her job?'

My word, he thought, she is belligerent.

'Because I'm led to believe that she's looking for a deputy – someone to help about the place, to take the load off her shoulders. Your father died recently, didn't he?'

She turned her head away from him.

'Yes,' she said stiffly.

'And he was responsible for a lot of the work?'

'Who told you?' she asked fiercely.

'Philippe Lefevre.'

'Him!' Her voice was full of scorn.

'You don't like him?' It was a funny sort of conversation to be having with the daughter of what might be his future boss.

'I hate him,' she hissed, and he found himself smiling.

'He seemed like a great chap to me,' he said, cheerfully. 'Brave and good.'

She pursed her mouth in the way his governess used to do when she disagreed, then asked: 'How well do you know him?'

'I don't know him well. I've only met him once. He's a friend of my family. They have run a small sherry business in Spain for generations. Philippe Lefevre handles the sales for them.'

'But you're not Spanish. Your accent isn't Spanish,' she said accusingly, looking up and down his big frame and taking in his

39

fair hair that was beginning to lose its colour and his light grey eyes.

'As you see, I am not,' he grinned. 'I'm English.'

'How very curious. The English don't drink wine, do they?'

He laughed. 'What makes you think that?'

'I once stayed with an English family and they didn't have any wine with their meals.'

'What sort of family were they?'

'He was a vicar.'

'Ahh!' he said so drolly that she laughed.

'I still don't really understand,' she said. 'Why would British people make sherry?'

'A lot of British families make sherry,' he informed her, 'and cognac in Cognac as well.'

She looked as if she didn't believe him, and then asked: 'But do you know anything about champagne?'

'Not much,' he told her. 'But I know about growing grapes, I know about clarets and I know about cognac. I don't have much to do with the family business. My elder brothers run it. I'm just fascinated by wine, and now I want to make champagne. I wanted to get here some years back, but the war got in the way. They don't grow a lot of grapes in Flanders.'

'You fought in the war?'

He nodded. It wasn't a subject he liked talking about, but the mention of it seemed to have softened her.

'It was the war that killed my father. He was shell-shocked. He was never the same again.'

Her eyes had filled with tears, the toughness had gone; he saw her childlike vulnerability but he couldn't work out how near to being a child she was. She could have been any age from fifteen to twenty-two with her sudden mood changes. Probably about eighteen, he decided. Just a kid.

'Listen,' he said, 'you were going somewhere in a hurry when I arrived. Am I holding you up from anything?'

She shook her head. 'I wasn't going anywhere much. I just wanted to get out of the house. I'd been trying to write something but the words wouldn't come. I thought if I got out and thought about it, it would help. Mama will be back in about half an hour. She went into Reims this morning, Henri's gone to pick her up. You'd better wait for her since you've come all this way.' She stopped to draw breath and then asked: 'Would you like to see the place?'

'I'd like to very much,' he said.

She nodded and set off out of the room, calling back over her shoulder: 'I'm Allie Dupuis. Who are you?'

'Luke West,' he told her retreating back.

He assumed he was meant to follow her and she led him through the back of the house and out of a door into a stone-paved courtyard bordered by well-kept buildings and barns. Beyond were the vines in orderly rows, carefully tended, stretching as far as the eye could see.

'We'll start here,' she told him, leading him towards a small walled vineyard guarded by large wrought-iron gates. The gates were half open; she pushed them back and beckoned him in. 'This is how Les Hérissons got started again after that terrible insect phylloxera killed all the vines. Before I was born, Mama came all the way from California to here with a great big trunk full of American wild vine cuttings and she and Papa grafted Chardonnay cuttings onto the American roots. They grew and lived because American wild vines resist the phyl-loxera. Mama had defeated the wicked phylloxera – well, here at Les Hérissons anyway.'

'Indeed,' he said mildly, amused by the drama with which she delivered her lecture and her assumption that he would not know about phylloxera.

'Of course,' she went on, 'the trouble here is that the vine-yard owners are so old-fashioned. Mostly they've still got phylloxera killing their vines and in some places it's getting worse. They're still trying to kill it with carbon disulphide. It smells absolutely disgusting, costs a fortune and doesn't work anyway. Sometimes they blow themselves up with it.' She gave a little giggle. 'Mama says they're mad when they can see with their own eyes here at Les Hérissons that using American roots works. But the vineyard owners are always difficult. That's why we like to grow most of our own grapes.'

He thought it might be time to indicate that he did know something about the subject.

'But surely most growers are changing over to American stock now? They have long ago in the south.'

'But the south got phylloxera first, and here they left changing

41

over to American stock too late,' she said decisively. 'It'll take ten years while they're changing over before there'll be a really big crop again in Champagne. Mama says there will be the most awful shortage of grapes – but that can only be good for us. We've been phylloxera-free ever since I was born.'

'And these are the original roots your mother brought from America?' he asked looking round the neatly walled vineyard.

'Yes,' she said, her violet blue eyes glinting with what looked like mischief or even malice. 'I love this place. I love it for all sorts of reasons. And just think – bringing vines all that way all those years ago and look how many grapes they bear. Do you think maybe there is something special about the soil? Are they not beautiful?'

'Beautiful,' he agreed, thinking the drama was becoming a little excessive.

'Grandmother had never bothered to make champagne, but Mama got it all going. She built the barns and put the place in order. I'll show you the tasting room later. Mama herself does all the blending. She is the *chef de cuvée* here and it's acknowledged that we make very fine champagne at Les Hérissons.'

'Your mother must be a remarkable woman,' he said, and the girl tossed her head.

'I suppose she is,' she said grudgingly. 'In some ways, anyway,' and he wondered about the mixture of pride and resentment that the girl showed when she spoke of her mother.

Allie gave him a guided tour of the entire premises. He was impressed by what he saw, except for the fields on the other side of the mountain. These, she explained, had been ripped apart in the war by the fighting.

'But they are all replanted,' she assured him. 'The Government paid out lots of compensation and they paid it quickly. Mama built a little hothouse for grafts with some of the money so that we needn't buy new stocks from the nurseries.'

Les Hérissons was obviously well run and profitable. He liked the feel of the place, liked the sight of the one-armed man working in the cellars, delicately turning the upturned bottles to shake down the sediment in the wine. Allie said that the man's name was Robert, and that like old Tomas at the gate, he had been with them for ever. Robert, it seemed, had lost his arm in the war.

'But even with only one arm, he can still perform the *remuage* faster than most men with two,' she said.

The tour over, she took him back to the house and into the small parlour. She had just rung for tea when an ancient but still handsome Léon Bollée automobile drew up outside the windows. An elderly chauffeur climbed out to open the back door for his passenger and Luke West had his first glimpse of Rosie Dupuis as she slid out of the vehicle, showing rather a lot of pretty leg. She straightened, stretched like someone tired of sitting, twitched her clothing back into place, and his thirty-five-year-old heart bounded as it had not bounded since he was twenty. He had been right. At first sight he could tell that Rosie Dupuis was a remarkable woman.

It wasn't just that she was beautiful, he thought, even though she was, with her thick dark hair in a modern short cut that highlighted amber eyes. It was the vitality that emanated from her that was so attractive. The life force in her was so apparent that before he had even spoken to her she made him feel more alive himself as if her energy were contagious. He could not hear her voice, but he could see that she was thanking the chauffeur, and then she ran up the steps to the porch, creating waves of activity around the hem of the soft green skirt that she wore teamed with a simple white blouse. Her hat was in her hand, and she looked carefree and happy in a way that few people had since the war.

The front door was open and she came straight into the house, calling: 'Marie, Marie.' He heard her brisk positive footsteps heading towards the parlour where he sat on the too small sofa. She stopped dead when she saw him sitting there, spotted her daughter across the room and, lips smiling, eyebrows raised, waited for an explanation.

Allie had jumped to her feet.

'Mama,' she said, 'this is Luke West. He wants a job. He's English and he knows all about claret, cognac and sherry. He doesn't know anything about champagne, but he wants to learn. Isn't it amazing an Englishman knowing about wine?'

'Amazing!' the amazing woman said, and stepped towards him, her hand held out. 'Welcome,' she said. 'Philippe told me about you, but I hadn't expected you today. I'm sorry I wasn't in.'

She was much smaller than he was. Her head just about

reached his chin and her hand was small but workmanlike in his. He liked her voice. It was a trifle husky and there was a faint, undefinable accent which he knew must be the last vestiges of her American English. A musky perfume floated about her.

'I think he thought you wouldn't let me come if he told you,' he said. 'You haven't made your mind up about what you want to do yet, have you?'

She shook her head slowly, and considered him with her dark amber eyes. He felt she did not dislike what she saw, and once again was surprised. He was always surprised that his effect on women was good. He did not understand what they saw in a big, clumsy man with the ugly battered face that nature and life had given him.

'Philippe said that you hadn't made your mind up about what you want to do either,' she said.

'That's true.'

'So you're inspecting us, are you?' She was amused.

'Your daughter has just given me a tour of your property.'

'And how do we measure up to your standards? Philippe tells me your standards are very high.'

'So far, so good,' he said.

'Thank you,' she said lowering her eyes demurely so that he wondered if she was flirting with him.

She flung her small hat on the sofa beside him, then she smiled a smile that turned his heart over again and said: 'Your French is very good – for an Englishman.'

'And yours is very good – for an American.'

'I've lived here most of my life,' she protested.

'Me too,' he said with grin.

They had both forgotten the daughter and he saw she was standing with her mouth drawn back into a disgruntled pleat. She had sensed a current between him and her mother and she did not like it. The daughter, he realised, was jealous of the mother.

But Rosie Dupuis settled herself on a chair across from his uncomfortable sofa, sighed and looked at him consideringly.

'Since you're here perhaps we'd better talk about it – when Madame Dupuis, my mother-in-law, comes down. We can do nothing without her approval. Perhaps we should talk over a glass of champagne? You really ought to taste the product.'

He agreed he really ought to taste the product, and as she gave instructions to the middle-aged maid whose head had come round the door, he decided that without doubt he would work for this woman. But he hoped that with luck and chance it would be more than a working relationship. This was someone he wanted to know very well. Very well indeed.

Allie went up to her room while her grandmother and mother were still talking to the Englishman. No one noticed her go, not even Luke West who had been so friendly and warm when she first found him. The same had happened as always happened. He had taken one look at her mother and she had been forgotten under the powerful spell of Rosie's charm and attraction.

Allie liked him, and she was pretty sure that he would come to Les Hérissons because she could tell that he liked her mother and her mother liked him. More important, her grandmother had taken to him. It was touch and go at first, though. When the old lady had come down from her nap she was bristling. Madame did not care for anything going on that she had not been previously told about. The beaky nose and pointed chin were pushed forward in the pugnacious manner that denoted to all the household that Madame Dupuis was not pleased.

But as she came into the room, swishing the skirts of her old-fashioned black gown, the big man had lumbered off the sofa and taken her hand, bowed and escorted her to her chair, murmuring that he hoped he had not disturbed her rest. She was, it was obvious, quite charmed.

He had natural manners and an unusual face, Allie thought from where she sat opposite him. He wasn't ugly, but no one could call him good-looking. His hair sprang from a forehead sloped back to make a strong bony bridge above his eyes. His eyebrows were fair but very wiry. The eyes under the bridge of bone were deep-set and light grey but there was more light in them than was usual in grey eyes. His nose looked as if someone had once hit it and his skin was weatherbeaten. In fact, if she had been describing him for one of her stories, she would say that he looked like a sturdy building that had been under siege. Or was that a bit pretentious? Perhaps just better to say that he had an uncompromisingly masculine face, and add that it was a good, likeable face.

Madame settled herself like a bird unruffling its feathers and said: 'My daughter-in-law tells me you are English.'

'That is true,' he said.

'What does an Englishman know about champagne?' Mimi asked him, her nose now in the air.

'Very little, but a great deal about wine. I want to work with champagne, the finest wine of all – and I am told that Les Hérissons is the place to discover the finest.'

Allie could see her grandmother relax again.

'And what do you think of our champagne?' she asked, nodding towards the glass that he held in his hand.

'It is, as I expected, excellent. Small bubbles and many of them, gentle nose and the colour is good. I prefer a champagne to be golden rather than honey.'

Madame acknowledged his expertise and then said: 'Personally, I don't think that we need any more help here,' but her voice lacked conviction.

'If we are to expand . . .' Rosie said, which meant that Mama had definitely decided to take him on.

'Why do we need to expand?' Madame asked.

'Because it is bad to stand still?' Rosie made it a suggestion rather than a statement.

'True. That is true.' Mimi delivered one of her sayings for all occasions: 'When the fire is at its height, it is beginning to go out.' She then nodded gravely. Both the Englishman and Rosie solemnly nodded back. Mimi looked pleased with herself. She twitched her skirts and said: 'Come, tell me more about yourself, young man.'

Allie listened while Luke repeated to her grandmother much of what he had already told her about himself on their walk around the property. When they started on their second glass of champagne, Allie slid away, telling herself that probably Luke West was just another horrible man really, while admitting to herself that she had liked him better than most. If he took the job, Mama wouldn't be here most of the time and maybe he would become a friend. He was a lot older than she, but younger than Mama and Mimi. And maybe better company than the naughty little Rosanne.

It was true that Rosanne's manners were improving under the firm guidance of Nanny Shepherd, but Allie needed someone grown-up from the outside world to talk to. Sometimes she felt that Les Hérissons was stifling her. But where else could she go? She did not feel any urge to be independent and live alone as so many girls of her class now did. She could go back to New York and stay with her mother's friend, Lizzie Webster, but she had made a terrible mess of that the last time she was there. They might not want her back. If she could be more normal with Rosanne – spoil her and love her openly – it would be easier, but there had always been good reason why she could not show Rosanne the love she felt for her.

She sighed, and went back to her desk to try again to get on with the short story she was writing. She was determined to be a writer. When she was young, she had wanted to be an actress, but that was when her personality was more outgoing and before she suffered the dreadful fits of depression which plagued her now. Her temperament seemed more suited to that of a writer these days.

There was a discreet tap on the door and Marie's greying head appeared.

'Your mama wants you to go downstairs,' she said.

'What for?' Allie asked.

'She didn't say. Something to do with that man, I think.' Marie looked around to make sure no one was near. 'Who is he?' she whispered.

Allie and the maid were companions in curiosity; they had always shared information.

'He's coming for a job.'

'What sort of job?'

'What Papa did, I suppose,' Allie said miserably. 'Isn't it awful to think of? He's English, too.'

'English!' Marie's tone told exactly what she thought of the English. 'Your mama has to have some help – but English . . .' With a toss of her head she sped back downstairs, with Allie close on her heels.

Both her mother and Luke West were standing when she came into the parlour and her mother was smiling.

'Darling,' she said, 'Mr West thinks that perhaps he might join us, but before any of us decide, he's going to stay for a few days and get to know the place and our methods. While Marie gets his room ready, would you like to have another wander around with him, and show him anything that he hasn't yet seen? I want you to look after him because I have to go to Paris in the morning.'

'Of course, Mama.' Allie found herself pleased, her spirits lifting. 'I'll show you the vats,' she said to Luke, and he could not know how great a favour this was. 'We missed them last time.'

He followed her out through the back of the house again and they walked side by side across the courtyard towards the building that held the huge vats of new wine.

'Are you involved in the running of Les Hérissons?' he asked.

The question surprised Allie. She had never actually thought to involve herself in the business, though she always helped out at the *vendange* and knew as much about what went on as anyone who worked there. The business had always been Mama and Papa's province and no one else's.

She shook her head.

'Oh, no,' she said, 'I don't have anything to do with it at all.'

'But you know a lot about it. Wouldn't you like to run it yourself one day?'

Allie looked at him suspiciously. Was he already thinking to the future and taking over because she and Rosanne were just girls? Her suspicious look was wasted. She could see by his open expression that he had nothing of the kind in mind.

'I hadn't ever thought about it,' she said. 'I love the house and the land and everything, but I want to be a writer.'

'A writer,' he said, sounding genuinely impressed. 'It's all I can do to write a letter.'

She took him literally. 'Aren't the English schools very good then?'

He threw back his head and laughed.

'They think they're very good,' he said. 'The one I went to prides itself on its academic results, though they never did very well with me.'

'Where was it?' she asked as he helped her push open the big heavy door into the building that housed the largest vats. She hesitated at the entrance. It was a building she tried to avoid

48

and she could not help a quick look at the spot where all the horror had happened.

'A public school, which in Britain, oddly, is a private school. The one I went to is called Winchester. Then for a while I was at Cambridge University,' he said. 'How about you?'

'I had a lovely English governess until the middle of the war and when she went home I had to go to the village school. I liked it. It was good. Then I had a trip to America that was meant to be educational. I suppose it was in a way.'

'You didn't like America?'

'Oh, yes!' she said. 'It's exciting.' She stopped and added lamely: 'It was just that things went wrong.'

He didn't push for the reasons as they walked slowly round the vats. He merely said: 'Things have a habit of doing that, but you mustn't let it get you down. Tell me about your writing.'

She felt herself brighten.

'I've been trying to write short stories. I've written dozens, but the one I'm working on now I like better than the others. I really think that it might work.'

'What's it about?' he asked.

'About a little girl who falls in love with an older boy, but he gets killed in the war before she even has a chance to grow up.'

He looked at her in the grey light. 'Personal experience?' he asked.

'Sort of,' she said.

'Who was it?' he asked.

'Just a boy,' she said, feeling guilty that she should call Sebastian just a boy and remembering again that she had lost both of the men she loved, her father and Sebastian. She shuddered looking round the vats and the stone walls and wanted to get out of this sinister building.

'Seen enough?' she asked abruptly.

He laughed. 'Sure,' he said, taking her arm and leading her towards the light as if he sensed her uneasiness. 'A vat is a vat. They mostly look much the same. It's what's in them that counts. Just like people,' he added with a grin and she felt for sure that at last she might have found someone to talk to.

'What did you think of him?' Philippe asked. They were together in the big bed in the room that had once been his

49

father's. Rosie had her head on his shoulder and he had his hand on her breast in their familiar, reassuring after-love position. The afternoon sunshine crept through the shutters that covered the windows and from outside came the sound of two pigeons softly cooing on the sill.

'Nice,' Rosie said, her voice both drowsy and muffled. 'He looks as if he'd be competent. I'd feel safe leaving him there while we went away.'

He chuckled. 'What does he look like? Am I safe leaving you there with him?'

'Look like?' Rosie thought before she spoke. 'Big – as tall as you but much bulkier, clumsier. Squashed sort of face. Ugly in a way. But strong. I liked him. But not as much as I like you.'

She had indeed liked Luke West and he had liked her. She had seen that look in his eyes, the one in men's eyes with which she was familiar. The naked lusting they could not hide when they saw a woman they wanted. Luke West wanted her, but she would not mention that to Philippe.

It was perhaps dangerous to take the man on but he was the answer to her prayers. She was desperate to be with Philippe, yet she would not leave her responsibilities at Les Hérissons without someone to take her place. Dangerous or not, Luke West could do most of what she did and give her the freedom she needed. She would be back well before the *vendange*.

'He says he's only met you once,' she said. 'Is that true?'

Philippe's fingers were playing with her right nipple, and she felt that old deep tingle and sighed contentedly.

'I know his father and elder brothers well. They're old friends. They have a very successful sherry business in Jerez. I used to sell it in cask for them before the war. Matthew West, his elder brother, came to see me a couple of weeks ago to ask if I'd resume business with him. He also mentioned that his younger brother wanted to work with champagne and asked if I knew of anything. Luke has never had much to do with the sherry world. Apparently when he'd finished university he decided there wasn't enough work in the business for three brothers and a father. So he chose to go off on his own.

'He was working with one of the big châteaux in Bordeaux but he went back to England and enlisted when the war began. He was in Flanders the whole time. According to his brother,

50

he won the Military Cross, and you had to do something pretty good to get that.'

'Medals!' she snorted. 'Everyone who was in that bloody war deserved a medal. You most certainly did.'

'Don't defeat your own argument,' he said lightly. 'Anyway, when I brought it up at first, you were so adamant that no Englishman could possibly know the first thing about wine that I told him to arrive unannounced. I knew you'd like him.'

'He seemed a happy man,' she said thoughtfully, reaching down to stroke him.

'I thought so, too. He seemed like someone that nothing would get down.'

'And Allie liked him,' she said.

'Thank God for that. How is she?'

'Up and down. She spends a lot of time in her room writing. I think that must be good for her. I even thought Luke West might be good for her.'

'He's a bit too old surely?'

'Not that way. Just because he is happy. Happiness can be catching. Anyway, how old is he?'

'Thirty-five.'

'Maybe she would be better with someone older,' Rosie said thoughtfully. 'Lizzie said she nearly broke Alexander's heart.' She sighed remembering how both she and Lizzie had hoped for a match between their children. 'But talking of Lizzie, I have a good idea.'

'So have I,' he said, sliding his hand down over her rounded stomach and between the soft thighs below.

'No, listen, just one moment,' she said while letting her legs part so he could gain entry. 'I thought we could go to New York, stay with Lizzie and Mr Webster, get married very quietly there, and go to California for our honeymoon. I want to see my old home again. I want to see if Peter is all right. I want to lay ghosts. If Luke West will stay at Les Hérissons, we could go almost immediately and be back before the *vendange*. What do you think?'

He was kissing her neck and his fingers were unbearably insistent.

'Could we just have a taste of the honeymoon right now?' he whispered in her ear, and his breath was warm and tempting.

'I'm not going to be able to think straight unless we do.'

She closed her hands over her own breasts and felt how her nipples were tight little hard columns; she savoured the damp, warm glow below and she rolled over onto her back, pulling him over her and spreading her legs so he could lie between.

'Well, get on with it then,' she said huskily, half-laughing. 'Since you mention it, I'm in a bit of a hurry myself.'

Rosie spent the night in Paris so that she could begin organising her wedding trip the following morning. Georges was sent to the Bureau de Poste just before they closed to send off a cable to Lizzie Webster in New York. All Rosie said was: 'May Philippe and I come and get married from your house, please? Rosie.' She was certain that Lizzie would say yes and Mr Webster would be in his element arranging the whole thing.

It turned out to be a hot and humid morning with a grey leaden sky, but she was at Thomas Cook's at the Madeleine the moment they opened. There she sorted out Le Havre–New York sailings leaving in a fortnight's time. She felt as excited as a young girl instead of a mature woman of nearly forty.

She longed to book herself and Philippe the biggest and most luxurious double cabin, but caution prevailed. With different names on their passports, they would be the talk of the ship. Coming back, though, it would be quite, quite different. She would be Madame Lefevre. An impossible dream would have come true. Without even stopping to look at the shops, she returned to Philippe's office in the Bourse district to tell him that everything was arranged.

'It will be all right? You will have time to leave the business?' she asked.

He was sitting at his desk, alone, his hands idle.

'You flatter me, my darling,' he said with a rueful smile. 'It's hard to run a business when you're blind. You know how much I have to rely on others.'

It was an unusual touch of self-pity and it alarmed Rosie, but she merely said lightly: 'I intend to do a lot of relying on other people in the future. Starting with your friend Luke West. I hope he's going to stay. It'll ruin all my plans if he finds us wanting and declines to take the job.'

'He won't find you wanting,' Philippe said. 'And I want to rely on you for the next half hour. I want you to read the latest figures over to me. Then I've some tasting to do. That I can do on my own and you can go off shopping if you like.'

'For a wedding gown?'

'For a wedding gown,' he agreed.

She moved to stroke his head, something that made him content since he frequently suffered from bad headaches.

'Darling,' she said cautiously.

'Umm?'

'Would you be hurt if I didn't tell anyone at Les Hérissons that we were going to be married in New York – if Lizzie will have us, of course? I just think it would be better somehow. For Allie's sake, really. I have a fortnight to find an apartment in Reims or a house in the country, or both – whichever you prefer so that we have something to come home to.'

'Small apartment in Reims, big house in the country,' he said promptly. 'But you haven't got just a fortnight. You have as long as you like. We can live here for the time being, and you had better wean yourself gently from Les Hérissons. As you say, for Allie's sake.'

She took his hand from where it lay on the desk and squeezed it, their own signal for 'all right'. She had learned long ago that it was not enough to nod or shake her head. Philippe needed tangible evidence of what she was thinking.

'But I did want to be with you,' she sighed.

'Rosie, I've lost count of the years we've been apart. You can wait, I can wait, and our happiness will be all the better for it.'

'Why are you always right?' she said plaintively.

She visited her favourite designer, M. Poiret, later that morning, but found nothing that she wanted to buy. His clothes suddenly seemed theatrical and over-extravagant to her. Perhaps she was growing up, she thought, smiling to herself. She went then to the rue Cambon to look at the work of the new designer, Chanel. Poiret had been unknown when Rosie had first been dressed by him. Perhaps it was time to find a promising new talent.

Madame Chanel, monkey-faced and full of forthright charm, was excited by the idea of making a wedding gown, and promised sketches in two days. While she was there, Rosie bought several outfits of lightweight knitted jackets and skirts which would be perfect for travelling. She then returned to the house on the Ile de la Cité where she and Philippe were to have lunch alone. They had just settled themselves in the dining room when the front door knocker banged imperatively.

'It'll be the telegraph boy with Lizzie's reply,' Rosie said, pushing her chair back to run into the hallway.

He heard the slithering noise the chair made on the carpet, and held up his hand.

'Wait. Relax,' he said. 'If it is, Georges will bring it in.'

Georges did, the envelope placed dead centre on a small silver salver.

'Will there be any reply, Madame?' he asked.

Eagerly Rosie tore open the envelope. She read the message out loud: 'She says, "Yes yes yes stop. When when when query." ' She turned to Georges. 'There will be a reply. Can you write it for me? It's just "Soon soon soon stop. Will let you know dates in a few days stop." '

' "Soon soon soon stop," ' he repeated. ' "Will let you know dates in a few days stop." '

'That's it,' she said. 'Thank you, Georges.'

After lunch she rang Henri at Les Hérissons, arranging for him to meet her from the fast train to Épernay. She promised to ring Philippe in the morning and Georges drove her to the Gare de l'Est. The leaden sun had disappeared, the air was cooler and it was beginning to rain. Her *vignerone*'s instinct noted it would be good for the grapes. The weather had been cool and dry. They needed both sun and some rain.

She half dozed in the train, and went over all that was to be done if she and Philippe were to get away in a fortnight's time. It was a good time of year to be away. There was little to worry about until the grapes had to be picked; then the whole estate came to life. Her only problem was to work out some story to tell Madame and Allie about her disappearance so soon after the visit to Cannes. With Prohibition having wiped out the wine trade in the United States, her reasons could hardly be business. But Philippe had said that there was money owing from some of their American customers. Perhaps the excuse could be that they were going debt collecting.

By the time the train reached Épernay, the rain was falling

in stinging cords and Henri, carrying a large umbrella, creaked his way from the car to meet her.

'I fear we are in for a storm, Madame,' he said as he held the umbrella over her head.

'Keep yourself dry, Henri,' she said absently, not minding the cool feel of the rain, her mind still on Allie. 'You know getting wet makes your rheumatism play up. Anyway, we need the rain. Just as long as it doesn't hail and ruin the grapes.'

He gave a practised, countryman's look at the grey sky.

'No, Madame,' he said solemnly, 'it won't hail. But with your permission, I shall drive home very slowly, just to be sure.'

'But of course,' she said, smiling to herself since Henri always drove very slowly.

They had just driven up the hill to Champillon and come to the wooded country beyond when in the fading light Rosie saw something small and grey hurtling along the middle of the road.

'Careful, Henri,' she warned. 'There's something in the road.'

'It appears to be a dog, Madame. A very wet and frightened mongrel dog.'

Slowly they overtook the animal. Looking at it from the car window, she saw it was young and ran in terror of something, its ears back against its head, thin legs pounding the rough surface. On impulse, just after they had passed it, she said: 'Stop, Henri, I'll get it. It could cause an accident.'

His back displayed disapproval of stopping in all this rain for a mongrel puppy, but nevertheless he drew up the car. Telling him to stay where he was and heedless of the downpour she jumped out into the road. The animal was streaking towards her and she bunched her skirt, bent down on her haunches and whistled gently to it. Seeing her in its path, the puppy stopped and in panic headed off the road towards the woods. Fencing blocked its escape. The car was just behind, Rosie in front. Terrified, the animal stood shivering in the road, brindle coat soaked and plastered flat along bony ribs.

Slowly and gently, making soothing noises all the while, Rosie neared the animal. As it stood quivering, slowly, slowly she reached it and very carefully put out her hand for it to sniff.

It did no such thing. It cringed and rolled onto its back in an attitude of supplication.

'I won't hurt you, you poor old thing,' she said. 'You'll get yourself killed if you're not careful.'

Her voice seemed to reassure it, and very gently she was able to pick up the wet, trembling body and stroke the pointed foxy little face that looked at her with scared eyes.

Unaware of how wet she was and the muddy marks that the puppy's paws were making on her dress, she went back to the car and climbed in, putting the puppy – which was a bitch – firmly on her lap.

'That's that,' she said.

'Where to now, Madame?'

'Why, home,' she said, surprised.

'With that?'

'Of course.' She laughed out loud. 'Oh, come on, Henri, don't be a misery. We couldn't leave it to get run over.'

'Just as you say, Madame,' he said, making it clear he definitely disapproved of picking up stray dogs.

She stroked the wet fur on her lap, noticing that the animal was flea-ridden, and thinking that its timidity reminded her of someone. She said: 'It's a nice little thing, Henri. I think we might keep her.'

'Just as you say, Madame,' Henri said woodenly, his eyes firmly on the road.

When he let them out of the car the puppy, as if it sensed his disapproval, made a brave stab at a growl and showed baby teeth. Henri merely sniffed as Rosie ran up the steps to the front door with the bitch still in her arms. Marie was there to open it. Like Henri, the maid gave the animal a disapproving look.

'Where's Miss Allie, Marie?' Rosie asked as she turned into the small parlour.

'Upstairs in her room, writing, Madame,' Marie said.

'Ask her to come down.'

Madame Dupuis and Luke West were comfortably installed in the parlour, Madame looking flushed and pleased with herself and obviously enjoying the male company. As Rosie came into the room, the bitch saw Luke West and began to struggle violently in Rosie's arms, teeth showing, but eyes terrified.

56

Rosie put the puppy down, and she immediately tried to bolt out of the room but finding the door shut behind her, vanished under the sofa.

'Would you believe, I think she's afraid of men,' Rosie said in wonderment and realised who it was that the puppy reminded her of.

'What are you up to, Rosie?' Madame Dupuis asked sternly. 'Your dress is in a terrible state. And where did you get that dog?'

'Bitch,' Rosie corrected. 'She was running down the middle of the road, away from Champillon. I've never seen a more timid, terrified animal. I thought she might make a pet for Allie.'

'Ahh,' said Madame, nodding sagely. When it came to anything to do with Allie, Madame and Rosie were entirely in tune. Words became unnecessary.

'And if it's afraid of men . . .' Rosie turned to where Luke West sat relaxed and watching. 'Mr West, would you mind going out of the room for just one moment?'

'Not at all,' he said. As he walked past the sofa a scuttling noise came from beneath and a muted growl. Rosie shut the door behind him, saying to him: 'Don't go away.' She then got down on her knees in front of the sofa and made coaxing noises until a black nose appeared, followed slowly by a pointed face and a wriggling brindle body.

'There's a good girl,' she said soothingly and picked the puppy up again as Allie came into the room. The girl stopped and peered at the wet bundle in her mother's arms suspiciously.

'What's that you've got?' she asked.

'A puppy. I found her on the road,' Rosie said. 'She's in a terrible state. She's frightened, wet and I should think hungry, as well as being covered in fleas. Could you look after her? She's gentle enough, but I've got an idea she doesn't like men. She seems to be terrified of them. I suppose she must have been ill-treated by one.'

Though it sounded a touch contrived even to Rosie's ears, she had said exactly the right thing. Allie came instantly and took the bitch from her mother's arms. It made no attempt to escape but trembled a little, soft ears still flat against the collie-type head.

57

'Come back in, Luke,' Rosie called. 'Let's see what happens.'

As the man appeared, the bitch became frantic again, trying to escape from Allie's arms.

'It's all right, he won't hurt you,' she said, stroking the wet coat. 'He's a nice man. Try and stroke her, Luke,' she suggested.

He put his hand towards the animal, and its head shot forward and the small teeth sank into his flesh.

'Ouch!' he said, inspecting his hand ruefully. 'She doesn't like men, does she? No harm done. She's too young to do any real damage. But her teeth are like needles.'

Allie was giggling.

'I'm sorry, Luke,' she said, 'but it was funny.' Another giggle escaped. 'How old do you think she is?'

Luke West inspected the dog from a safe distance.

'About six months,' he said.

'Very sensible animal, this, for one so young,' Allie said chirpily. 'I'm going to call her Jessica.'

'Well, if your mother is right and Jessica is covered with fleas,' Madame said, 'perhaps you would get her out of my parlour. Go and bath her or something.'

'Right,' Allie said. 'Sorry, Luke,' she said again as she went. 'She didn't draw blood, did she?'

Luke, Rosie thought. She was calling him Luke, and had said he was a nice man. And she had taken to the bitch. And she had giggled. She looked at Madame and raised her eyebrows. Madame nodded. 'That was a very good thought, Rosie,' she said. 'A very good thought indeed.'

And Rosie noted the quick look Luke West gave the pair of them as if he were trying to work out exactly what they were on about.

Cook made a bit of a fuss about Allie washing the puppy in the big stone sink in her kitchen. Eventually she produced some carbolic soap and inspected the animal where it stood shivering as Allie poured kettles full of warm water over it.

'You'll need something to dry it,' she said. 'I don't want water all over my kitchen floor.'

She found an old towel, but too late. Jessica shook herself

and gave them and the floor a shower bath. And when Cook shouted, the dog crouched in terror and made a large puddle.

'I'll mop it up,' said Allie, not wanting Cook to be cross.

Cook let her do it and stood watching, hands on hips.

'Wouldn't make two sous' worth of bones, that dog,' she pronounced. 'I'll see what I've got it can eat.'

She produced the remains of a beef stew from her larder, found an old cracked dish, filled it and put it down on the stone floor. The bitch, almost crawling on her belly with fear, moved towards it and began to eat hungrily.

'That's better,' Allie soothed, hoping that if she talked to this new pathetic pet it would get used to her voice.

All would have been well if Robert hadn't come in from the cellars, looking for his wife.

'Where's Marie?' he asked, and at the sound of his voice Jessica instantly bolted out of the kitchen door and back down the hall to the parlour. Allie followed in hot pursuit. 'She doesn't like men,' she shouted back to Robert as she ran.

Only Luke was left in the parlour and the puppy hesitated in the doorway, growling gently. Allie scooped her up and went back to the kitchen. Robert had gone, and the animal subsided back into quivering again.

'You show 'em,' Allie told it as she gave it a last towelling. 'You bite 'em if you want to. That'll teach 'em.'

She picked the puppy up again and it whined softly, and licked Allie's ear. It had definitely relaxed. It seemed to Allie that the meal and all the attention had given the animal some confidence. Pleased, she went looking for her mother in the little laboratory where she blended different champagnes for each year's *cuvée*.

'I'm just taking Jessica for a walk,' she said. 'I'll be back in time for supper. Mama, can she sleep on my bed?'

Rosie looked up from her notes and raised her eyes skywards.

'When you've got rid of the fleas,' she said, 'and as long as you don't let your grandmother know.'

'I won't,' Allie promised and headed for the front door, whispering into the puppy's fur as she went: 'But you'll have to stop biting Luke. He's a nice man.'

* * *

59

Luke West watched the girl run down the steps from the house to the drive, encouraging the brindle pup to follow her. It did so reluctantly at first, but seemed to gain confidence as they left the house behind. It was his third day at Les Hérissons and Allie was puzzling him. From things she had said he realised that she must be older than he had first thought. By his reckoning about twenty. She was bright and intelligent; extremely well read and articulate, but she seemed fixed in a childhood mould, almost as if she were retarded in some way. But whichever way it was, it was not intellectually. He suspected that she was probably very clever indeed, and he would have liked to have read some of her writings. Yet her reaction to the puppy had been that of a ten-year-old.

Her attitude to him was puzzling, too. At first he thought she was making a set at him, and then it had dawned that this wasn't a flirt or an attraction. She was treating him as a little girl might treat an older man. There was nothing sexual about her approach in spite of a tendency to sit very close and almost nuzzle him. She was, he realised, lonely, and was looking for affection and a masculine figure to replace her father. He was beginning to like her very much, and had decided that she probably had no experience of men at all. But her ingenuousness could be dangerous and give quite the wrong impression to a man younger than himself.

He had remained in the parlour at Madame Dupuis' invitation after she had gone to her room to change for dinner. He was reading the morning paper when Rosie's head came round the door, and stupidly he felt his pulse quicken. Every time he saw her he was aware how remarkably attractive she was.

'Shall we talk?' she said.

'Why not?' He told himself he must not flirt with her.

'Good.' She came into the room and settled herself in the chair by the fireplace and crossed a very neat pair of ankles. He found it difficult to tear his gaze from them.

'What do you think of us?' she asked, her smiling eyes making no attempt to hide the fact she knew he was looking at her ankles.

'Do you mean us "us" or us Les Hérissons?' he said cautiously.

'Us Les Hérissons,' she laughed.

Now he could tell the truth without embarrassment. 'I think it's a marvellous place,' he said. 'Very well run, very professional, and charming into the bargain. I'd like very much to stay – if you're prepared to trust an Englishman with your vines and your wine.'

'Good,' she said briskly. 'That's settled then. Now we must find you somewhere to live.'

'I said to Madame Dupuis that I would have to do that, but she suggested I stay here,' he said, wondering how Rosie would react.

She was surprised.

'You have made a hit with Madame!' she said. 'But do you want to stay here? You don't have to. Wouldn't you prefer somewhere with more privacy?'

He realised she longed for privacy herself.

'I've been a wanderer all my life,' he said. 'Boarding schools in England as a kid, lodgings in small wine towns once I started work. I've never had any inclination to marry.' That was not quite the truth, but he had managed to convince himself of it. 'I think I'd like a home atmosphere for a while, if that doesn't worry you. This house felt welcoming from the moment I came in.'

She looked pleased.

'Some people say it's sad,' she said quietly. 'A sad, secretive house.'

'Not to me,' he said firmly. 'Maybe there are some mysteries, but mysteries are there to be solved.'

'There are no mysteries.' Her smile had vanished.

'Okay,' he said easily. 'If you say so.'

She was silent for a moment.

'Allie likes you,' she said and it was almost a question.

'I like her. She's very young for her age, isn't she?'

Rosie nodded. 'Yes. It was the war. It disturbed her so much she seems to have retreated into childhood.'

'It was bad here?'

She nodded again. 'Her father was shell-shocked and didn't recognise any of us. Then the house was occupied by the Germans and we had to live with them for what seemed for ever. It wasn't good. No worse than anyone else's war, I suppose, but it affected Allie badly. She's always been imaginative and sensitive, but before the war she was so outgoing. Now you'll find she suffers from terrible depressions occasionally.'

He was listening intently, but felt somehow that even if there were no mysteries, this was not the entire story.

'I've seen no sign of these depressions,' he said.

'We always hope that one day they will go away. I do think the gaps between get longer. Has she been looking after you?'

'Admirably.'

She hesitated. 'Sometimes when she likes someone she can give the – well, the wrong impression.' Her voice was low and she was looking at her hands folded in her lap. 'I wouldn't want you to think that . . .'

'That she was reacting to me as a man?'

'Exactly.' She looked relieved that he understood. 'Her manner led someone astray once, and she had only meant to be good friends. But she does . . .' she hesitated.

He laughed. 'Snuggle?' he suggested. 'Like a puppy? Don't worry. I'd worked it out. In matters of that kind she is still a little girl.'

Rosie nodded.

'Did you hope that the dog you found might help her?' he asked abruptly.

'Yes, I did.'

'And what's the significance of it being frightened of men?'

'No significance,' she said stiffly, and he knew that wasn't the truth. 'But if you can be her friend it might help. I've never been the perfect mother.' She seemed almost to be speaking to herself. 'I love her more than anything in the world, but there were always so many other things that had to be done.' She sighed regretfully. 'She relied more on her father than me, and she misses him dreadfully.'

He wanted to ask more questions, but sensed he would get no answers.

'You see,' she went on, 'I'm going away again for a while. Not too long. About six weeks. To America. We're owed a lot of money there, and I want to get it all sorted out. I'm glad that you've decided to stay, because I'd like it if you took charge. I'm not going for two weeks yet, so we can work together until then. I'll be back for the *vendange*. We can decide on your salary with Madame, and I thought you should have a share of the profits if she agrees. Will that be all right?'

He could tell by the anxiety in her voice that it was important that he said yes.

'I'll look after things,' he said soothingly. 'At the moment this is like any other vineyard. The routine's the same. Don't worry.'

'I'm not worried,' she said, back to her blithe self again. 'I don't know if you had time to get to know Robert, Marie's husband?'

'The chap with one arm?'

'That's right. I was thinking of making him a sort of manager to work directly with you. He's been with us for ever and he knows the land and the wine-making process as well as anyone. Do you think that would be a good idea?'

'Excellent,' he said. 'As Allie said, he seems to operate as well with one arm as most men with two.'

She smiled. 'It'll please Allie. Particularly as I haven't yet told her I'm going away.' She dropped her voice and confided, 'I'm praying Jessica turns out to be a mother substitute.'

Privately he thought that Allie with her curiously ambivalent attitude to her mother would not, in her heart of hearts, be too displeased that Rosie was going away. Mama stole Allie's thunder.

'Still, enough of that,' she said. 'We have to decide which room you should have. In a month or two, it would make sense if you had mine.'

'Yours?' She had startled him.

'Yes,' she was suddenly ill at ease again. 'I shan't be living here eventually.'

'Why not? Where will you be living?' He was aware of sounding peremptory, but was thrown by the disappointment of hearing that they would not be living under the same roof.

'I think it's time I had a home of my own,' she said, a little hesitantly. 'That may sound odd to you, but this is very much Madame's house and I've been living under her roof for over twenty years now. I would like to find a small apartment in Reims, and buy a house of my own near here in the country.'

'I see.' He wanted to know more, but could hardly ask. 'And Allie and Rosanne will go with you?'

Her face clouded. 'Rosanne, certainly, but Allie will have to

63

make her own decision. I hope she will come with me. But perhaps it is time to cut the apron strings.'

Allie, he thought, wouldn't leave Les Hérissons. This could be her chance of escape from the mother she adored but resented.

'So Madame Dupuis will have plenty of room for me?' he said ruefully.

'I'm sorry. It will be less of a family home. But I expect we will all be here a lot of the time.'

'I hope so,' he said smiling, hoping that his disappointment didn't show. But Reims and a house nearby in the country were not a million miles away. With luck he would still get to know her – and as well as he wanted to.

Jessica was disinclined to go for a long walk. She lagged behind, and began to look nervous again, stopping to make frequent small puddles. What was needed was a collar and lead, though Allie thought it would be better to let the puppy become a little more confident before she tried to tether her in any way. Once at the gatehouse, where as usual Tomas was sleeping, Allie turned back and the puppy seemed relieved and even began to sniff a little and make small forays onto grass at the side of the drive. Allie then tried a small experiment. She stopped, clicked her fingers, and called softly: 'Here, girl. Here, Jessica.' The puppy stood still, knowing something was expected of her, and then cautiously made her way to Allie's outstretched hand.

'Good girl! Good Jessica!' Allie enthused, and the dog rolled over on her back while her tummy was rubbed.

They went back into the house by the rear door, and going past the parlour, Allie could hear the murmur of her mother's voice, answered by Luke's deeper tones. She would have quite liked to listen in the hopes that they were making arrangements for Luke to stay, but if she did, with her luck someone would only come along and catch her with her ear to the keyhole. Instead, she went up to her room, taking Jessica with her.

She locked herself in as was her habit and settled the puppy under the counterpane – in case her grandmother came by. She was just about to get her diary out of its hiding place to record Jessica's arrival when there was a gentle knocking on the door.

'Allie, Allie,' entreated Rosanne's piping voice. 'Let me come in.'

Allie instantly opened the door and the five-year-old shot through and pushed it shut behind her.

'I escaped,' she confided, half whispering. 'The witch is asleep with her mouth all open.'

'Rosanne, you are naughty,' Allie protested. 'Nanny Shepherd is not a witch.'

'Oh yes she is,' Rosanne said. 'You don't know. You don't have to put up with her.'

'Well, if you were a good girl you wouldn't have to put up with her,' Allie admonished, but couldn't resist picking the child up for a hug.

Rosanne bore the hug stoically, but then wriggled free. Her blue eyes were bright with excitement and her long curly black hair looked as if an electric current was running through it.

'You've got a dog,' she said. 'I heard them say you've got a dog. They think it will cheer you up. Marie says it will do you good.'

Allie grimaced. She had guessed something of the sort was in their minds when they were all so accommodating about her keeping Jessica. In the normal way she would have rejected whatever it was that would 'do her good', just to show the world that she couldn't be influenced and pushed about. But Jessica was different. She decided to ignore what Rosanne had told her and pretend she had never heard it.

'She's not a dog yet. She's only a puppy. And she doesn't like men.'

'Just like you,' said Rosanne. 'Where is she?'

'Here.' Allie drew back the counterpane. The puppy was curled up underneath, and waved her tail gently as Allie stroked her.

'Can I stroke her?' begged Rosanne.

'Only if you're very gentle. She's very timid.' Rosanne could be heavy-handed.

'She likes you already,' Rosanne remarked. 'Will she like me?'

'Only if you're very gentle and kind.'

65

The little girl heaved herself up onto the high bed and cautiously put out her hand towards the puppy, who waited equally cautiously. Rosanne then scratched between the animal's ears, and Jessica shut her eyes in bliss.

'She likes you, too,' Allie said.

'Oh, good! Can I have her? Can she be mine?'

'No,' said Allie firmly, aware it was the first time she had ever refused Rosanne anything.

'Why not?'

'Because you'll tease her and frighten her.'

'I won't.' It was a wail of protest.

'You say you won't, but you will.'

'I won't!'

'You will!'

'Allie.' It was her mother's voice from the hallway outside. 'Are you two quarrelling?'

'No, Mama.' Allie hastened to open the door, and Rosie came in and settled herself on the bed. With one hand she scooped Rosanne onto her lap, and with the other she stroked the puppy's head.

'Does Nanny know you're here?' she asked the little girl. Rosanne wrapped her arms round her mama's neck and said coaxingly: 'She'll guess.'

'I expect she will,' Rosie said, 'but you will go immediately and tell her where you are and apologise for disobeying her. Then you can say that I gave you permission to come back because I want to talk to you.'

'She's asleep. She looks funny when she's asleep.'

'Then wake her,' Rosie said firmly.

With a theatrical sigh the child ran off. Rosie grinned. 'Impossible!' she said. 'She gets more like Sebastian was when he was a little boy every day. Do you remember, after he was killed and before she was born you wondered if she would have his soul? I'm beginning to think she has.'

Her mother wasn't looking at her, but Allie felt herself flush. These were things she did not want to remember.

'Sebastian was so naughty when he was little,' Rosie went on. 'But he had all the charm in the world. Just like Rosanne. He grew up all right, and so will she.'

'There's not much wrong with her now,' Allie said stiffly.

'Of course there's not! And when Miss comes back to teach her, her behaviour will improve no end. Look how good you were when Miss was in charge of you.'

Allie thought she must have misheard.

'Miss! Miss is coming back?' Allie could not believe it, her old governess from when she was a little girl coming back.

'Umm.' Rosie said. 'Rosanne has to have a governess now she is getting on for six, and who better than Miss?'

Now Rosie was looking at her, but her expression was hard to read. For a moment Allie felt panic. Miss was another one who knew. But surely Miss wouldn't say anything? No one who knew *could* say anything. And she did so love Miss.

'I wrote to her,' her mother was saying. 'I asked if she would come back and teach Rosanne. She was thrilled. She says she longs to see you again. There's not so much difference in your ages now. And since you're grown-up you might even be able to pronounce her name.'

'Thoronson,' said Allie twisting her face into a grimace. 'What a terrible name it is.'

' "Miss" was always sufficient,' Rosie said cheerfully. 'I expect that's what Rosanne will call her, too.'

'When is she coming?' Allie asked eagerly. Things were looking up. Jessica, Miss and Luke coming into her life all at once. Maybe she wouldn't be so lonely any more.

'She arrives just after I go to the States.' Again her mother wasn't looking at her.

'You're going to the States?'

'Not for long.'

'How long?'

'About six weeks.'

'With Philippe, I suppose?'

'Yes, he's coming too.'

Allie glared at her mother. 'Will you stay with Mrs Webster?'

'Yes. Shall I give Alexander your love?'

'No!' Her mother was too much! But the exchange, angry on her part, patient on her mother's, was forced to a halt. Rosanne came back into the room.

Rosie picked her up again and sat her on her lap.

'We have a governess coming for you,' she said, rocking the child up and down.

'A what?' The child was suspicious.

'A nice English lady called Miss who is going to teach you to read and write and speak English properly. The same lady who taught Allie.'

'I don't want to learn to read and write.'

'Well, I want you to. And I want you to surprise me when I come home from America by being able to write your own name.'

'You're going to America?' Rosanne's face crumpled.

'Yes,' Rosie ignored the signs of tears. 'Nice Luke West is going to look after everything, Allie's going to help him. Robert is being promoted to a manager, and you're going to learn to read and write.'

'Robert's being promoted?' Allie was delighted.

'Yes. I gather from Mr West that you say even with only one arm Robert is as good as most men with two.'

Allie nodded. 'Is he pleased?' she asked.

'I haven't told him yet. As the young mistress of the house, would you like to do it?'

'Can I?'

'I wouldn't have suggested it if you couldn't.'

Allie gave her mother a quick impulsive hug, picked up Jessica in case Rosanne appropriated her, and ran off towards the cellars.

She knew exactly what her mother was up to with all this placating but even so, with so many nice things happening, whatever the reason, maybe it didn't matter too much that her mother was going away again.

Chapter Three

Pierre had spent a relaxed morning walking on the Atlantic beach out at Lynn, north of Boston. The city had been unpleasantly hot, but the long sand-covered spit of land was cooled by a gentle breeze from the ocean. He had intended to observe the minuscule wildlife of the sands but he came across a small group of his fellow students who had also driven out of the stifling atmosphere of the town and found them more absorbing. Freed from the lecture room they disported themselves in the latest striped bathing tunics which gave them the look of some wallowing misplaced jungle species.

He sat in his white trousers at a distance from them feeling alone and yet superior. The men had buried beer in the sand at the edge of the surf and lit a flickering blue-flamed fire with driftwood. Around this they toasted frankfurters and marshmallows on sticks and engaged in unseemly horseplay with the girls who accompanied them.

Inspecting them with a critical eye, Pierre decided that none of the girls with their upper-class Boston accents were a patch on Feathers when it came to looks, and he found himself idly wondering what her future might have been had she been born into a decent background. The humane side of him that he had to cultivate so assiduously felt a fleeting pang for her circumstances. Beauty set in such a tawdry frame was a sin and a shame.

The Back Bay girls were shrieking now as the boys chased them into the sea. One large muscular blond lad was carrying his woman slung over his shoulder in a fireman's lift as she beat impotently with small fists on his broad back. He flung her into the sea and she came up spluttering, water streaming from her black rubber bathing hat and down into her eyes.

Extraordinarily, she did not appear to be angry. The large blond man must be either rich or the son of a rich man, Pierre decided, smiling cynically to himself. And it was as well that these girls' snob Back Bay parents could not see their daughters now. It was obvious that another couple in the sea up to their waists were exploring each other under the cover of the water. That made him think again of Feathers.

The noise of the students and their vigour made him feel very grown up, yet he could not help wishing that he could be part of such a group. But his bizarre isolated childhood had done for that. He knew he was old beyond his twenty years. He could perform perfectly adequately and with charm in the company of others if it was strictly necessary, but he had no taste for groups, gangs or gatherings. There were few people with whom he was content to spend his time. Uncle Peter was one, but Uncle Peter seemed to have become so old even though there was only a seventeen-year age difference between them.

The absorbed expressions of the couple standing so close and with their hands hidden underwater were giving him stirrings of his own. He decided that he would drive back into Boston, freshen up, and pick up Feathers. It might be amusing to bring her back out here. If they arrived when it was dark, the danger involved in being caught on the beach would add some spice to the lovemaking, though he had to admit that once Feathers was naked and open before him, little spice was needed. Her own heavy musk was appetiser enough.

He left the beach to the young frolickers and drove back to Boston, his thoughts briefly lingering on the Packard 6. He wondered if perhaps he could afford it after all, and thinking of money, realised that he would have to take Feathers to eat if he wanted to wait until dark before they went to the beach.

It was gone three o'clock when he let himself into his apartment block through the stained-glass front door. In his cubbyhole there was a letter with a Californian postmark, addressed in Peter's precise handwriting. He took it out reluctantly. He had figured that no news was good news, and had almost begun to lull himself into a false sense of security regarding his financial position. Would this letter justify any complacency? Pierre was no optimist. He decided it would not.

Once in his apartment he quite deliberately made a cup of

coffee before opening the letter. A glass of champagne would have suited him much better, but his stock was getting low. Soon he would need to find a bootlegger just like everyone else. If, of course, he could afford one.

Eventually he lay on his bed in his dressing gown and steeled himself to open the letter.

Dear Pierre,

I am so sorry that I have not written before but I have been trying to find out exactly what the situation is here, and work out what is best to be done.

I fear there is no word from your father and I miss him dreadfully. It is lonely here without either of you. The house is far too big. I could almost wish it back to the size it was when I was a boy, but I could never bear to be alone in it even then. I have paid off all the servants and already the house is becoming sad and dusty. I miss Jean Paul so much that I can't seem to find the energy to do anything about it. Most of the time I am in despair, not knowing what to do for the best. I can see no future for myself. But once I have come to terms with the new situation, maybe things will improve.

I have done nothing about reporting your father's disappearance, mostly because I don't know what I should say after all this time. All his things have arrived here from France, but they give no clue to his whereabouts.

We can manage for a while if I do not report your father missing. All the money that he and I had is in a joint account and either one of us could sign cheques. It may be that the bank will find it odd that he never presents one now, particularly as he always handled the financial arrangements. So far nothing has been said.

I am very sorry to tell you that there is very little cash remaining. Your father was a very heavy spender, but then, of course, there was no need not to be. Champagne D'Or made a great deal of money in its day. But now there is absolutely no income whatsoever, just this huge house which costs a fortune to keep up, and the useless land I told you about. There are vines planted on it, but as I said to you, they will not bear fruit for a long time yet, and when they do, who will want the grapes? Others are turning their land over to fruit and walnut trees, but that requires workers who have to be paid. There is so little land left as part of the estate that I can't see much point in it.

The other serious problem is that I cannot even sell this land as I find your father put it in his name and any deeds of transfer would require his signature. Nor can I sell the house as it only half belongs to me. Of course, if your father does not reappear, his half becomes yours. But before this can happen, we will have to report his disappearance which I am reluctant to do.

Therefore, I am afraid that we are both going to have to face some harsh and unpalatable facts. If we share what is left in liquid cash, there is sufficient to pay your allowance for another six months. Also, we might be able to scrape together enough for you to stay on at Harvard for another term if you think it worth doing.

I shall stay on here for a month or two in case your father appears. If he does not then I will be forced to shut up the house and get some work – though I don't know what a thirty-seven-year-old wine salesman does in Prohibition America.

I may have to do what I am going to recommend you do. And that is to go to France.

In your case you have every right to be there. Les Hérissons is a very good, highly profitable business and would quite easily support you and there is no doubt that you are a legal heir. I did actually know this before and should have told you, but I selfishly hoped that you would return to Champagne D'Or with me. It must be said that your father caused problems while he was in France, but initially your grandmother was overjoyed to see him. She might feel the same way about her long-lost grandson. If you do decide to go, Les Hérissons is near the village of Chigny Les Roses, not far from Reims.

I cannot think that you would have any problems with your cousin Allie. She is a nice girl who I believe would welcome the company of someone of her own age.

My sister Rosie may not be so easy. She has Allie and

another much smaller child and undoubtedly would prefer that the inheritance should not have to be divided between the three of you instead of just her two. She is strong and clever but she has a loving heart. She was always my champion when we were young. Maybe she will be yours. Who knows.

I think she will be my champion again. I am sure she will find me something to do if I return there, though I would prefer not to have to do so since I do not speak the language.

In a way yours is the more serious situation and I am sad that you should be forced to make such difficult decisions so young. It seems to me that your choice is to eke out your allowance and any savings (hopefully) that you may have and stay on at Harvard for as long as you can and pray for a miracle. Or you must find some paid work in Boston, or, go to your inheritance in France. No doubt all three appear bleak prospects to you at this moment.

I would suggest you came to California and that together we tried to find some way of saving the situation here, but it is a selfish thought on my part. Maybe the house would make a hotel, but I do not see either of us as hoteliers. And I know you have unhappy memories of living here. This wretched Prohibition has smashed so many lives; not just ours by any manner of means. I wonder if those who fought so hard for it realise how much misery they have caused.

It has taken me a long time to write this letter, and I can think of nothing else to say to you. I wish we could sit and talk together, but perhaps for the moment we should conserve what money we have.

Dear Pierre, please let me know what you plan to do. You know I love you and that you are always in my thoughts. And I promise I will do anything that is possible to make things better.

   Peter

Pierre put down the letter on his bedside table. He was dismayed at how unhappy his uncle sounded, but there was little he could do about it. Under no circumstances could he imagine himself returning to the lonely splendour of Champagne D'Or ever again. But it was almost a relief to have the situation made so dismally clear. He looked at the scientific books lining his walls, and the microscope on his desk with the carefully labelled specimen boxes. Here ended his career as an entomologist – unless, of course, he could get a scholarship.

The French one would be the thing. He did not fancy trying for one at Harvard itself. His fellow scholars were a snobbish lot, and he wasn't popular because of what was regarded as his stand-offishness. The apartment itself would have to go as well – it was far too expensive. Maybe even his automobile.

He was quite calm now the truth was out. He was also intelligent enough to realise that at twenty it was not the end of the world for him. He knew he wasn't the type to go down. This could be an adventure. He could change his whole life if he wished. Anything was possible.

Though Uncle Peter had said different, it was in fact Uncle Peter who had the real problem. What *did* a thirty-seven-year-old champagne salesman do in the USA circa 1920? Pierre hoped that Rosie Dupuis would come to Peter's rescue. Indeed, he hoped that, if necessary, she would extend a hand to him as well. He felt convinced that his father was dead; the one thing that puzzled him was Uncle Peter's reluctance to report him missing. Apart from causing their funds to be frozen, this would be the obvious and most sensible thing to do. He was now certain that Peter must have had a hand in the mysterious disappearance and was afraid of police involvement. Since he would not wish anything bad to happen to Peter, Pierre thought it best to play it his way.

He made up his mind quickly, almost as if he had known what he would do since the day Uncle Peter told him that Jean Paul had disappeared. He went to his desk and settled down to reply to the letter.

He began with a few generalities and words of good cheer and then went straight to the point.

I think it would be madness for me to arbitrarily decide to live in France without even knowing what sort of place France is. There is a scholarship that I can apply for to a French university, but I might dislike France so much

74

that I would not want to take it up even if I got it. I am convinced that the thing to do is pack my bags, arrive at Les Hérissons and see what the place is like. I might as well claim my inheritance. And if the French relatives turn out to be hell, then I'd rather come home and get a job of work in Boston. I'm sorry, Uncle Peter, but I don't want to live in California ever again.

He paused, and thought that perhaps he could be happy in France. It would be pleasant to have a grandmother and girl cousins and a strong but goodhearted aunt. There had never been any women who had had any influence on him or shown him real kindness in his entire life; now maybe there could suddenly be four. He discovered that the thought appealed to him. He continued his letter.

I shall write to the Dean and tell him that I will be late returning next term due to family problems. It's better not to close any doors just yet. Then I shall leave as soon as possible. All I need is a passport, to lock up this apartment, buy the tickets and pack. I shall travel first class. When the money runs out – well, that will be that. But for the moment I shall continue as if everything is just as it has always been.

He signed himself with love and affection and put the letter in an envelope ready for posting. His bedside clock said four thirty and there was no reason to change his original plan. He still had time to catch Feathers as she left the store. And even if he were late he had no doubts that she would be hanging about, hoping that he would turn up.

He whistled as he tied his cravat and looked for his least expensive suit. He'd have to leave his clothes on the beach if he could persuade Feathers into the water after it was dark. He'd better take a couple of towels, too. He planned to try to make love to her in the sea – if it were possible, of course. And even if it wasn't it would be a lot of fun finding out.

She had just decided that he was not coming. She was hot and sticky from standing in the heat of the street and about to set off down Washington Street for home when his red Buick skidded round the corner, raising dust from the road surface. It stopped where she was standing with a screech of brakes and engine panting.

'Hop in,' he said, leaning across to open the door for her.

She climbed into the leather seat as quickly as she could, relief flooding through her, fanning her hot face with her lace-edged handkerchief. He hadn't appeared for four days. She had been beginning to fear that she would never see him again, though she knew perfectly well that she should stop seeing him altogether.

But it was no good. She was in love and that was all there was to it. She hadn't the resolution to end the affair, and with a wisdom older than her seventeen years accepted that their relationship would go on until he himself, or fate, took a hand to finish it. She never would.

'I was just going home,' she said as he roared off down Washington Street in the direction of the Common. 'I thought you weren't going to come. It's been four days . . .'

They had seen each other and made love three times since she left the note and its contents had never been mentioned. She longed to know if he realised she had made it all up just to find out what would happen if she really were pregnant. It had hurt dreadfully when she found out that he would do nothing, and now she wished she hadn't lied. She was sure to be punished for that lie in some truly dreadful way. But at least knowing there was no future with him left her free to choose whether or not to go on sleeping with him. She knew she would go on. And maybe he would grow really to love her. There was always that hope.

'I've been real busy,' he said, his eyes on the road as he manoeuvred round a plodding horse and cart.

With another girl? she wondered, giving him a sideways look. He seemed remarkably cheerful. There were times when he was moody and silent, but not tonight.

'I was a bit late because I stopped to make a reservation at the Copley Plaza,' he said.

'My!' she said, thrilled. The Copley Plaza where Back Bay held its proms and society dinners was one of the grandest, if not the grandest, hotel in town. He couldn't be ashamed of being seen with her if he was taking her there. Hope sprang again, and she thanked Mary Mother of God that she had put on her newest pale green crepe dress. The one she should not have bought at all since the purchase had chipped dangerously into her precious savings.

She began to rummage in her purse for her compact to make sure that her nose was not shining and that her small matching green hat with the feather was at the correct angle.

'You look fine,' he said, and she marvelled again as he drove into Copley Square, stopped and waited until a liveried doorman came to open the door to let her out.

He tipped the man to take charge of the automobile and led her into the tall elegant building where more liveried men rushed to be of help. It was suddenly cooler, the heat left outside. She held his arm, looking neither to left nor right as they went through the lobby, though she longed to have a good look around. But it seemed better to act as if she walked into the Copley Plaza three times a week and twice on Tuesdays.

The dining room with white linen, flowers everywhere and black-coated waiters overawed her at first, but the menu sparked her familiar hunger and she studied it rapt and intent since there was so much to choose from. She asked for turtle soup because she had never had it followed by steak for her main course. Steak was filling and would last her through tomorrow if there was nothing at home. She could see the most marvellous desserts on a trolley and hoped that he would offer her one.

'I've been on Lynn beach all morning,' he told her while they waited for their food to be served. 'It was marvellous there – cool and fresh, right out of the city heat.'

'I've never been there,' she said. 'It's too far away.'

'It takes no time at all in the Buick,' he said. 'I thought we might drive up there after dinner. It's real pleasant after this scorching weather in town.'

She was doubtful, thinking it would be so late when she got home that her father would kill her.

'I get into trouble if I'm too late home,' she said.

'We won't be late.' His deep blue eyes were beguiling her. 'Afterwards I'll drive you right home to your front door.'

But then her dada would see the automobile and want to

know who she was out with and what she was doing. It could all cause trouble.

'I don't think I should,' she said doubtfully. 'If you want to walk on the beach we could just go down to Dorchester. It's much nearer.'

'Dorchester's ugly and spoilt. But Lynn is a proper, real wild beach,' he said. 'If you've never seen it, you should.'

'It'll be dark when we get there, won't it? We won't be able to see it anyway.' She could see he was getting annoyed and she said quickly: 'All right, we'll go if you want to. But we just mustn't stay long.'

'Okay,' he said, smiling again.

She was enjoying her steak which was definitely the best of the very few she had ever had when he suddenly said: 'Did you really think you were pregnant?'

She started, and felt her face go hot. She hesitated over her food and said: 'Of course I did.'

'I sort of wondered if you were just testing me.' He was still smiling, but there was that touch of cruelty in the smile that she had come to recognise and dread a little.

'Why would I do that?' she said carefully.

'I would if I were you,' he said. 'Anyway, you know now, don't you?'

'Know what?' she asked woodenly.

'Know that I wouldn't marry you.'

'I don't think I ever flattered myself that you would,' she said, finding a bit of spirit.

He was looking at her searchingly.

'What would you have done if you had been pregnant?' he asked.

It didn't bear thinking about. It was a question she had tried to avoid even asking herself.

'I don't know,' she said slowly. 'Killed myself, I guess –' she quickly crossed herself – 'if my father hadn't done it first. What else could I do?'

'Have the baby?' he suggested, and she asked herself if the man was raving mad.

'There's enough mouths to feed in our family, let alone the shame of it. I don't want to talk about it,' she said firmly.

'Then why do you take the chance?'

78

For God's sake! What a question. He must be baiting her. She put down her fork, sat upright and stared at him.

'Why do you think? Because I'm foolish enough to love you and I can't help himself.'

He looked down under her steady gaze, and she could only see his forehead and the winged eyebrows below the curly black hair. With one of his disconcerting changes of personality, he suddenly seemed ashamed. He looked up, and his expression was rueful. He leaned across to take her hand.

'I'm sorry,' he said.

'You don't have to be sorry,' she said with dignity. 'The position is perfectly clear. It's entirely up to me, isn't it?'

'I'm very fond of you,' he said. 'I wouldn't spend so much time with you if I wasn't. But I don't need people very much, Feathers. I'm used to being alone. It makes you selfish in the end, being alone.'

It was the most personal piece of information that he had ever given her. She was tempted to say that she knew why he saw so much of her – it was because she let him make love to her. He was young, handsome and hungry. The sort of man her mother had warned her about. Her view of the situation was unclouded. But she wanted to change the subject. It was a sin even to talk about killing oneself. She would be punished for that, too.

'There's no chance to be selfish when there's too many of you,' she said lightly, thinking of the crammed apartment she would go back to tonight. 'But let's not talk about it any more. It's bad luck to talk about these things.'

'Then we won't,' he said. 'Eat up your steak. It will do you good.'

She did get to eat one of the amazing desserts – little tiny éclairs full of cream and covered in chocolate sauce. He saw how much she enjoyed it and ordered her a second portion. She ate it quickly, not caring if she did look greedy.

'It's sad we couldn't have wine with our meal,' he said as he watched her eat. 'I'd have bought you champagne if the idiot law didn't forbid it.'

She looked at him with big eyes over a full spoon and began to feel that maybe he did care a little for her.

Once back in the Buick she was content and sleepy with food

as he turned the automobile towards the north and drove out of Boston. As the light began to fade she dozed a little, her head dropping forward with sharp little jerks that woke her and made her worry if perhaps she had been snoring. He was driving fast and skilfully, and every now and then he put his hand on her knee and stroked up to her thigh. He was making her nervous. Surely he didn't want to make love in the back seat? She began to worry about the effect this would have on her dress let alone the terrible embarrassment and consequences if a policeman should catch them.

It was a long drive and when he stopped there was only a narrow dirt road with sand beaches on both side. The sun was just slipping away and she saw what he meant about Lynn beach. It was deserted and beautiful; a golden expanse of endless, rippling sand rapidly turning silver-grey in the disappearing light and merging into a vast sea that seemed more like swaying molten steel than water. Little wavelets barely disturbed the surface, and fluttered into a small flurry of white foam at the edge of the water. A sea bird cried overhead and a few late-up sandpipers scuttled comically for shelter. There was nothing and no one to be seen.

'It's lovely,' she said, her voice awed as she stood looking about her, her hand in his. 'So peaceful. There isn't anyone. Such space. At Dorchester beach there's other land to be seen all around. It doesn't feel like the open sea.'

'That's what I told you,' he said, giving her hand a squeeze. 'Leave your shoes and your hat in the automobile and we'll walk awhile.'

She took off her stockings as well while she was at it. She didn't want to ruin them and, glory be, it looked as if he didn't want to make love at all. She didn't mind making love, but she didn't want to do it anywhere where someone might see them. She had an idea that you could go to prison for doing that and she had enough troubles without going to prison.

They walked along the beach hand in hand, not speaking, as the sun slid behind the horizon like a dime in a slot. Suddenly it was night, a thin sliver of a moon rose high in the sky and stars, brighter than she had ever seen them before, glowed above their heads.

'It's so quiet,' she whispered, not wanting to spoil the silence.

'Ummm.' He did not speak, but turned her gently to face him and, while she stood there, her toes digging in the sand, he took her in his arms and began to kiss her in a way he had never kissed her before.

First he nibbled gently at her lips, parting them with the tip of his tongue, and then he sucked gently on her bottom lip between tender little bites that didn't hurt but made the hot warm feelings grow in her. Then his tongue was deeply in her mouth as she clung to him, pressing herself along the length of him, and feeling how he, too, wanted her.

But in spite of her excitement and ardour, one part of her brain was asking herself where they were going to do it. There was no way he wouldn't want to do it, not now. But Holy Mother of God, surely not here on the beach?

'Let's go in the water,' he was whispering in her ear, and he was breathing very hard.

In the water! She had never set foot in the sea in all her life, and the idea of doing it now in the dark terrified her. Things might bite her toes. It would be full of horrible slimy monsters in the black depth. And what about her new dress? It would be ruined.

She tried to pull away from him.

'I can't swim,' she said.

'You don't need to swim. It's shallow. We'll just go in up to our waists.'

Did the man want to make love in the water? This time she did pull herself from his grasp.

'I've never been in the sea,' she said. 'It would frighten me.'

'Surely not with me to hold you.'

'Yes, even with you to hold me,' she said firmly.

'Oh, come on,' he said, sounding like her little brother sounded when he couldn't get his own way. His hands were fumbling to find how her frock came off, but it had no fastening. It just skated over her head.

'Don't you dare tear my dress,' she said fiercely.

'I'll buy you a new one,' he said. She could hear him panting as he tugged. There was a horrible ripping sound.

'Oh Mary, Mother of God!' she cried. 'What have you done? My father will kill me. Oh, you've done for me.'

She wrenched herself away from him and began to run

81

wildly along the beach, not certain in the dark which way she was going. She could hear him behind her, calling her to stop, but she just ran on blindly until suddenly her feet were in cold water. She gave a piercing scream, turned, and fell at the water's edge into the damp, gritty sand. She lay there, sobbing, knowing that now her dress was completely ruined.

He was picking her up, and amazingly he was murmuring apologies, but she was too distraught and angry for apologies.

'You don't understand. You don't understand anything at all,' she sobbed, battering his chest with her fists. 'You're rich and spoilt and you don't know about real life. You can't begin to know what you've done. My dress is ruined, it's torn and dirty and if I walk into my home like this my father will beat me black and blue, and I won't be able to work tomorrow, and I can't afford to stay off. Would you go to work with black eyes and split lips? That's what you'll have caused with your wicked ideas. I know what you wanted. You wanted to make love in the ocean, didn't you? You wanted to do it to me in the water. Well, you're not going to, not in the sea or anywhere else ever again. You'd have forced me if I let you. God, oh God, to think I thought I loved you – now I hate you for what you've done. It was disgusting, what you wanted to do. Out in the open where anyone could have seen us.' Her voice rose to a hysterical wail. 'Mary Mother of God forgive me for what I've done. You – you think I'm just a whore. Someone you can do what you like with. I'm not good enough to marry if I get pregnant, am I? You don't want any responsibility in it. You'd leave me to manage all alone. You're cruel and wicked and I hate you, I hate you . . .'

He had managed to imprison her fists, and then he put his arms round her and held her very close to him. 'Shhh! Shhh!' he kept saying as he rocked her just as her mother had done when she cried over some childhood injustice.

'I'm sorry, please, I'm sorry. I'll buy you a new dress. I'll make it all all right.'

'But you can't buy me one tonight, can you?' she said through her sobs. 'I have to go home like this and it'll be murder if my father sees me.'

'Oh, God,' he said softly. 'Oh, Feathers. I'm so sorry. Look, let's get back to the Buick and see what the damage is. Do you want me to carry you?'

'No thank you,' she said stiffly. 'I can walk perfectly well.'

But he held her arm tightly as they walked in silence back to the car through the still, hot darkness that felt as if it was coming down on her head. She tripped on a stone and cried out again.

'I don't like it here,' she said with a little sob. 'It's scary.'

Without speaking, he scooped her up into his arms, and strode along carrying her. His closeness now felt so loving that she was left defenceless. She gave a little hiccup and put her arm round his neck and her head on his shoulder. He had never been so nice to her before and her anger was slipping away, leaving only the fears of what would happen when she got home. She could tell from the slight breeze that her frock was split down the front. One breast was cooler than the other. Her father would definitely kill her, and as she let herself be carried away from the beach, she murmured her prayers, hoping that somehow the Holy Virgin would get her out of this terrible, terrible mess.

Feathers might have screamed that she hated him, but Pierre was ashamed and hating himself as he carried the girl to where he had parked the Buick. Yet again he had behaved like his father. And he felt a sort of despair that he would never eradicate the seeds of Jean Paul's sins. He didn't want to be his father's son, but the old Adam persisted in coming through.

She did not seem particularly heavy and her sobs were subsiding into small hiccups. He could hear her muttering and knew that she was saying her prayers. And much good that would do her! Far better that he did something to put things right. She had more chance that way than by praying.

When they reached the Buick he put her down and went to turn on the headlights. Then he came back to inspect her where she stood dejected and miserable in the glare of the two beams. One side of the front of her frock hung loose. He could see the peach satin of her underwear beneath. It was hard to tell just how dirty the frock was; the light was too bright.

'It could be worse,' he said, lying.

'Oh no it couldn't,' she said, one hand trying to hold the torn fold in place. 'It's wet. It's crepe. It'll shrink up.'

'There's only one thing to do,' he said. 'We must go back to the apartment and see if we can repair it and clean you up a bit. Or you can stay the night and I'll go out and get you another dress as soon as the shops open.'

'Stay the night!' He'd shocked her. 'What if someone saw me going in the morning? And what could I tell my father? Whatever I said, he'd never believe me.'

'Well, let's get back and sort things out from there,' he said, his inventiveness drying up. Perhaps on second thoughts she'd better pray.

He was sweating as he cranked the automobile with the starter handle, and when it caught and spluttered into life, he hurried round to his seat and drove as quickly as he could to Boston. There he headed straight for his flat. Before getting out of the car, he made Feathers put his jacket over the torn frock. But it was too late for anyone to be about and no one saw them enter his apartment block.

Inside in the electric light he was able to see the extent of the damage he had done and guilt washed over him once again. Her face was tear-streaked, her hair rumpled, the dress was wet and filthy as well as torn and it was indeed riding up. She was looking at herself in the mirror, her face set.

'We'll have to mend it and wash it,' she said. 'Do you have some needle and thread and a flatiron?'

He had some trouble finding the needle and there was only white thread. She said that would have to do.

'If he's drunk enough he won't notice,' she said. 'Mama will, but she won't say anything in front of him.'

He watched as she sponged the frock with the expertise of someone who was used to taking good care of their clothes, and then she sat and sewed it back into shape with tiny, neat stitches. He had the flatiron on the gas. She cleared the kitchen table, placed a blanket he gave her over it and carefully spread out the dress. Patiently she ironed it, judging the correct temperature of the iron by spitting professionally on its base. She seemed to be able to tell the difference in heat by the degree of hissing it made. Then the iron would cool and have to be heated again.

She was intent on what she was doing and took little notice of him as he watched her, feeling a sort of admiration for her expertise. But it all took a long time. It was gone midnight

84

before she had finished and the dress was back on looking, if not as good as new, reasonably all right.

'I'm going to drive you home,' he told her.

She looked doubtful. 'I don't know,' she said. 'If Dada sees you . . .'

'I'll drop you near your house.'

She nodded. 'Perhaps it would be best. It would take for ever if I waited for the trolley at this time of night.'

He could see she was worried.

'Won't your father be asleep?' he asked.

'He might. But he always wakes up when I come in. I'm in trouble anyway because of the time.'

'He won't really hit you, will he?' He could not conceive of anyone hitting Feathers.

She smiled ruefully. 'Oh yes he will,' she said, 'if he feels like it.' Then she added, as if consoling him: 'It might be all right. Don't worry.'

He tried to give her $5 for a new frock, but she laughed out loud at his naivety.

'If I come home with five dollars in my purse, my father will know I've been whoring,' she said bitterly. 'I don't want your money.'

As he drove through the dark streets of South Boston with her silent and apprehensive at his side he made the decision to cause her no more pain and to tell her the truth. When she told him to stop and that she would get out here, he said as gently as he could: 'Feathers, I am going to France, and very soon. It's probably the best thing that could happen for both of us. You won't have to see me again, but I want you to know that I did care for you in my own way. I never thought of you as a whore. I did understand that you loved me. I just wish I could have loved you back in the same way. But it wouldn't have worked between us. I'm too cold for you to bruise yourself on.' He paused. 'Most of all I'm desperately sorry about tonight. I wish our last meeting had been happier. The only thing I can say is that I did it because I desired you very much. It was wrong of me, and I apologise.'

She did not speak, but when he turned to look at her he could see the tears glistening on her cheeks as she looked resolutely ahead.

'Do you forgive me?' he asked, and it was important that she did.

'Yes,' she said, and he could barely hear her voice. 'Goodbye. I must go now.'

She opened the car door and, leaving it swinging for him to close, ran down the street of sagging wooden houses and disappeared out of his life into one of the wretched doorways.

He did not drive off immediately. He sat in the Buick, his headlights illuminating the mean street where Feathers lived. He had known that parts of South Boston were little more than slums, but he had not realised quite how ugly and derelict the area could be. In Feather's street, rubbish lay rotting in the gutters and the houses had not seen a coat of paint in years. He felt he could smell poverty. Feather's street was dark and noisome. He now understood exactly what shanty-Irish meant. He thought of the beauty of Champagne D'Or and remembered how he had longed to get away from it. Feathers would think him insane. And he appreciated the wonder on her face when he had led her into the Copley Plaza earlier. The small treat of the meal at the hotel he had given her merely to soften her up for what he wanted to happen later was light years from this street and the realities of her life. He had understood nothing except the urges of youth.

A light burned above the transom of the house she had entered. As he watched, hoping that it would go out and all would be well, he heard the scream. One long, anguished scream full of pain, and then silence.

He buried his face in his hands and vowed to himself that though he did not wish to see her ever again, he would make it up to her somehow.

Feathers turned the key in the lock with her heart in her mouth. The gaslight in the passageway burned low. She gently tugged on the brass chain and the blue flame flickered, spluttered and was gone. Still crying silent tears, she crept on tiptoe in the sudden dark towards the far room, praying that her father would not wake, but as she reached the door of the room she shared with her sisters and brother, a square frame of gold light flooded round the rickety door of her parents' room. It opened, and her father appeared, tall and menacing as he stood clinging to the door jamb.

'Mary O'Flanagan, where in the name of God do you think you've been?' he shouted.

'Out, Da,' she said as expressionless as possible.

'Out is it?' he said, and took an unsteady pace towards her, one meaty hand upraised.

Before he could bring it down on her face which was where he always aimed and never missed however drunk he was, the frustration in Feathers exploded. Normally she took her punishment in stony silence. This time she screamed, a long, banshee, wailing yell that encompassed all her pain and anger against Pierre, against her father and against an unjust world.

The sound startled and frightened him. His hand dropped and he stood swaying, staring her at drunkenly. His once handsome Irish face had spread into a blotched potato. His eyes were red-rimmed and bloodshot, but the curly dark hair of the Donegal lad he had once been still covered the few brains, now sodden by drink, he had once had. She felt nothing but contempt and a tinge of pity for him as they stood staring at each other, both surprised by their own reactions.

'Don't you touch me,' she said quietly, her back straight and her eyes fierce, the tears still on her cheeks. 'You just dare touch me, Da. I've been hurt too much already.' There was no fear in her, none at all, and he saw it and fell back. 'There is nothing you can do to hurt me ever again, you understand. Nothing.'

Her mother had come to the doorway of their room. She wore a hand-me-down nightgown that had belonged to her employer. Once it had been fine white lawn, now it was grey, the neckline fraying. Her mother had been as pretty a colleen as her daughter, but her skin was as grey as the nightgown, her arms sticklike below the short sleeves, her face puffy with sleep.

'Leave her be, Pat,' she said quietly, 'and get yourself to bed before you fall. She's grown now.'

With a snarl he turned on his wife.

'Don't touch her, Da,' Feathers warned. 'Do as she says. Get yourself to bed.'

He stood looking at them, one shoulder on the wall to keep himself upright. The two women stood firm, daring him to raise his hand. He shook his head slowly as if somewhere in his addled brain he was beginning to understand that something had changed. Then he lurched back into the room and there was a noisy creaking of springs as he fell back onto the bed.

Feathers' mother moved out into the hall.

'Are you all right?' she whispered, one rough hand coming to touch her daughter's cheek. 'You've been crying. Some man?'

Feathers nodded.

'They're all the same, Mary. All want one thing.' She paused, looked back into the bedroom and leaned to whisper even lower: 'Are you pregnant?'

Feathers shook her head.

'Try not to be. See what happens . . .' She indicated over her shoulder to where her husband was already beginning to snore. 'You ought to get out of here,' she added. 'It's no life. Use your looks. Don't waste them like I did on him. Looks can take you anywhere if you use them right.'

Without saying goodnight, she drifted back into the room, and the springs creaked again, more gently. She was back in bed and her husband hadn't woken. Knowing she was safe, Feathers went on down the passageway and quietly let herself into the room where she slept.

Her two younger sisters were sitting up, their silhouettes hazy in the faint light from the window. It seemed that their brother, Kevin, had not woken. There was no movement from the truckle bed where he slept.

'What happened?' Eileen, the fourteen-year-old, whispered, eager for information. 'Did he hit you again?'

'No,' Feathers said. She was in no mood for midnight conversations.

'Why did you scream then?' Kathleen, who was nearly sixteen, asked.

'To stop him.'

There was an impressed silence.

'If it works, I must try that!' Kathleen said, her voice awed.

'It worked,' Feathers said briefly. 'Now go back to sleep.'

She crept into her place up against the wall with Eileen next to her. She lay on her back in the darkness, staring straight up, tears gone, eyes wide open, listening to the gentle sound of her siblings' breathing. That was the end of it, then. Pierre was going away. She'd never see him again. Her life might as well be over, for she'd never love again. 'Get out of here,' her mother had said. 'Use your looks.' Perhaps the answer was to go whoring properly. She'd done it for nothing and look where it had got her. Now she might as well do it for money. She sighed into the darkness and crossed herself, trying not to make too much movement. Now that was a thought for which the Virgin would most surely punish her – and rightly so, too!

But before she fell into troubled sleep she remembered how Pierre had carried her across the beach to the car, tender and loving in a way he had never been before. She could feel his arms holding her and remembered how it had been to have her head on his shoulder. It had felt as if he loved her back. After all the horrors, that touch of kindness had been the best thing that had ever happened to her. She would never ever forget it. Yet all the time he had held her so close he had known he was going to leave her. At the thought the hot tears flowed again until at last she fitfully slept.

The morning didn't help the misery. She bundled the torn dress at the back of the closet where no one would see it. Grimly she went through the morning chaos of getting to work. Her mother left before any of them and her father shouted from his bed to get Kevin off to school. Her father always stayed in bed until they had all left. Getting to work meant boiling kettles on the inadequate oil stove that served as both oven and heating for the house when they could afford the oil. It meant fighting for space over the sink and out in the privy, but by the same miracle that happened every morning, she managed to get herself out of the house and down the road for the journey into town.

She loved her work at Jordan Marsh, ill-paid though it was, but she was a good salesgirl and commission brought up her basic $8.00 to something more healthy. And she was allowed a staff discount. For a girl who liked clothes as much as Feathers did this was a considerable bonus. She wanted to be the head salesgirl in the department, but the boyfriend of the girl who held the job kept shilly-shallying as to whether or not he would marry her. They had been courting for a year now, and Feathers' prayers were as fervent as the head salesgirl's that he would make up his mind soon.

Fortunately, the morning was busy. Feathers sold yards of

ribbons, liking the feel of the satin on her fingers, and at least half a dozen of the pretty lace collars that were the rage. In spite of her troubles, she was well on target for her sales figures and did her best not to think about Pierre. It wasn't easy. He was there in her mind and wouldn't go away. And he still hadn't gone away from her thoughts and she was still weepy a full week after the half-dreadful, half-wonderful night on Lynn beach.

It was Friday, always a busy day. Just after the lunch break the manager of the department, a stuffy sort of individual, came bustling across to her counter, glaring through his half-glasses. He was carrying a large gold-wrapped parcel.

'Miss O'Flanagan,' he said crossly, 'I'll thank you to have your packages delivered at home.'

'A parcel for me, Mr Donovan?' She was astonished.

'A parcel for you, and I'll have to be giving you a special pass to get you through the staff exit with it. It's Jordan Marsh merchandise.'

In the normal way Mr Donovan had a soft spot for Feathers because she was a good worker and never caused any trouble. But it was more because she was so pretty and her blue eyes, round face and dark hair reminded him of a girl he once knew and loved long ago in County Kerry.

She knew this well, and as her eager hands came out for the parcel, she smiled her most beguiling smile and said: 'But where did it come from, Mr Donovan?'

'A young man has just left it with me, Miss O'Flanagan. And I hope that you are behaving yourself,' he added sternly.

'But indeed I am,' she said, weighing the beautifully wrapped parcel in her hands. She knew what it was. It was a new dress to replace the one he had torn. But what sort of new dress?

'Please, Mr Donovan, may I open it?' she asked humbly.

'You may not,' he said, her smile failing to move him. 'There are customers to serve.'

There were no customers, but it was best not to argue with the manager of the department when you wanted to be the head salesgirl. It would be his word that did it.

She lowered her eyes. 'Of course, Mr Donovan,' she said meekly.

'I shall take it to the staff door for you,' he said relenting a little, 'and tell them you may have it at going home time.'

'Oh, thank you, Mr Donovan.' She made her voice fervent, though she would have liked to have snatched off his silly little glasses and stamped on them in her hidden impatience to see what was under the gold paper. 'You are so kind.'

Full of righteousness, he removed the parcel from her hands and set off, his back rigid, towards the lifts. She grimaced to herself, and settled back behind the counter, but annoyingly he had been right. There was a woman waiting, inspecting the display, just round the other side where she could not easily be seen.

'Yes, madam,' Feathers said, advancing armed with her salesgirl smile. 'Can I help you . . .'

With the parcel locked up in the office at the staff exit, the afternoon seemed interminably long. And then, once she was released and through the staff door with the gold-wrapped package in her hands, Feathers did not know where to go to open it. She could hardly stand there in the middle of Washington Street tearing off the paper and seeing what was inside. After some thought she decided to walk down to the Common. There she sat herself down under the verdigrised statue of some long dead hero, now reduced to having pigeons perched on his head, and savoured the pleasure of being given a surprise present.

She put the parcel on her lap and stroked the shiny paper. Now the moment had come to open it, she wanted to delay the pleasure, make it last longer because her foolish heart was hoping that he wanted to see her again and if he didn't want to see her again, she didn't want to find out too soon. But maybe this was a peace offering and everything would be back the way it was. Maybe there was a letter inside saying he loved her. Maybe, maybe, please sweet Jesus. She took a deep breath and carefully untied the ribbon that held the paper in place, rolling it into a small ball and putting it in her purse. That she would keep for ever.

Then off came the paper which she carefully folded and put beside her. Underneath was the Jordan Marsh box; she lifted the lid and just took a peep inside. All she could see was tissue paper. She lifted the lid right off and delicately folded back the tissue. The colour of what was inside looked familiar. It was familiar. He had found exactly the same dress as the one he had torn. She looked at it in amazement, astonished that he should go to so much trouble. And then, in the folds of crepe, she found the envelope. A surprisingly heavy envelope.

She tore it open and a pair of keys dropped out into her lap and with them was a $20 bill. She ignored the money and picked up the keys, wondering, half-hopeful, half-fearful, if he was going to set her up in her own apartment like Bridget Halloran's rich boyfriend had done. Bridget had accepted in spite of all the gossip in the neighbourhood when she came back wearing furs and no wedding ring. But Feathers' mother had sighed and said: 'Who can blame her?'

There was a letter with the keys and money, and cautiously, as if it might bite, she opened it.

Dear Feathers,

I heard you scream and I am devastated. I don't think I had ever believed what you told me about your father before I heard you scream. Having heard that I know what a dreadful situation I put you in.

Feeling as I do about settling down, there is little I can do for you in the way of recompense. The dress at least will replace the one I ruined. The money may be helpful.

The keys are the keys to my apartment. I leave for New York and eventually France this afternoon. I expect to be away for at least two months. The rent is paid for six months in advance and I am offering it to you so that you can escape from your home background for a while. I have told the janitor that you may be moving in, and that he is to help you in any way he can.

But I must stress that I do not think we should see each other again. I will send you a cablegram to warn you when I will be home, and I would be grateful if you could then leave. Until I return you are welcome to stay there, but I am trusting you to be gone when I get back to Boston. And I am certain that you will do nothing to cause problems with my landlords.

There will be no additional expenses for you to find. All the charges for the time I am away have already been covered.

Whether or not this is a good idea from your point of view, I cannot tell. It is up to you to do what you wish. If you prefer not to use the apartment, I would be grateful if you would mail the keys back there. I have another set of my own.

All I can wish you is happiness and a better life.
Sincerely, Pierre

She sat stunned, staring at the letter and fingering the key. Then hardly thinking what she was doing in her astonishment, she made the long walk up Commonwealth Avenue and let herself into the apartment where she had lost her virginity and been so happy. It still smelt of him; a man's smell. She tried to shut the scent from her nostrils as she walked woodenly into his bedroom. There, in his depleted closet, she hung her new dress and carefully placed the gold wrapping paper on the shelf above. Then she sat in his living room, staring down at the street and remembering him.

And at eight o'clock she plumped the cushion where she had sat, took one long breath of the smell of him, and made her way home to South Boston.

Chapter Four

'Oh, Lizzie, darling. How marvellous. Everything looks just the same.'

Rosie looked around Lizzie's little parlour and sighed a sigh of sheer pleasure at coming back again to a place she had always liked so much and where she felt so at home.

Lizzie, pretty as ever, though her yellow curls were now faded to a near platinum and her fine skin was beginning to show tiny faint lines, laughed.

'Not quite the same, Rosie. But Mr Webster so hates change he insists that when we decorate or refurbish, things are done in much the way they were before. I long to be more modern, but he simply will not have it.'

'The old-fashioned things are best,' Rosie said with a sigh as she sank into the same deep plush armchair she had always chosen since she first came to the Websters' mansion on Park Avenue when she was eighteen years old.

She and Lizzie were alone. Jim Webster had led Philippe away to his own den, singing the praises of his bootlegger and promising Philippe a cocktail to revive him from the ardours of the sea voyage.

'And besides, you girls will want to talk,' he declared as he took Philippe firmly by the arm and through the wide hallway with the sweeping staircase towards the back of the house.

'It's just like when we first met on the train,' Lizzie said, with a little giggle. 'Do you remember how Jim used to go to the club bar to drink with the men on the pretext of leaving us to get to know each other?'

'And when he came back he'd pay for my lunch,' Rosie said. 'You can't imagine what a relief to me that was, I was so worried about my money holding out on the journey. A dollar for lunch was a lot. My, we were young then.'

They were all older now, she thought. With forty only two months off, her own hair was becoming gently touched with grey. Philippe's face showed pain and suffering, and Jim Webster, who would now be over sixty, had become corpulent and red of face. But otherwise, nothing had changed. Lizzie was loving and garrulous as ever, still childlike in her middle forties. Her chatter washed over one like warm, scented water, soothing and restful.

'It was a relief for me to have someone so nice to talk to for all that long journey,' Lizzie said. She jumped up from her chair and came to give Rosie an impulsive kiss on the cheek. 'So many years,' she sighed, 'and so long since we last saw each other. Just think, it was before the war. But when you came here with Philippe that time for the wine congress, I knew you loved him. You couldn't fool me. You watched him all the time with such loving eyes, and your face simply lit up when he came into the room. And now you are to be married.'

'Yes, we are to be married,' Rosie smiled, content and happy.

Remembering her Christian principles, Lizzie said quickly: 'It was so sad about poor Clovis.' And then forgetting them again, added: 'But he was never really right for you.'

'I was never right for him either,' Rosie said, 'and he knew it at the end.'

They were both silent for a moment, then Lizzie said: 'Jim has been making all the arrangements for the wedding. We thought it would be nice to have it right here in the house, if you agree, of course. The minister will come, and you can appear on the staircase looking the most beautiful bride ever, and I'd love it if Jenny was your bridesmaid, please? If Philippe has no one to stand up for him, Jim would be honoured.'

'I'd love Jenny to be my bridesmaid,' Rosie said. She had a soft spot for Lizzie's no-nonsense daughter but she doubted if Jenny would be enchanted at the idea of being a bridesmaid. Jenny and frills did not mix. 'And I think it's Philippe who would be honoured if Mr Webster would stand up for him. But is it possible to get married in a house? I had no idea.'

'Oh, yes. I guess it goes back to frontier days when there weren't too many churches,' Lizzie explained. 'And we thought it would be something different for you.'

'I think it's a lovely idea,' Rosie said, though she would have married Philippe standing on a raft in the middle of the Hudson River if no other location had been available. 'I'm sure Philippe will, too.'

'Have you made plans for your honeymoon?' Lizzie wanted to know.

'You'll be surprised,' Rosie said. 'We're going to California to see my old home and stay with my brother. He was coming to New York for the wedding but he cabled just before we left to say he had changed his mind.'

'What a shame. He could have stayed here,' declared Lizzie.

'That would have been a kindness since I think he has financial problems since Prohibition. Maybe he was anxious about the price of his fare.'

'Everyone in the wine and liquor trade has troubles,' Lizzie said. 'Jim says Prohibition is the most stupid law ever. It has caused people to drink twice as much and twice as fast as they did before. And it's all so vulgar. Hip flasks full of bathtub gin and furtive drinking in nasty dark little dens they call speakeasies. And not wine or champagne any more. Just horrible cocktails and nasty whiskey made in someone's back kitchen – unless of course you have a good bootlegger with connections in Canada. Jim has. I don't like him buying it since it's all illegal, but everyone else does so I suppose it's silly to worry.'

'It's made a big difference to Philippe's business,' Rosie said. 'He used to export an enormous amount of wine here. Les Hérissons is affected, too, but we're selling more to Germany again now the war is over which makes up for it to some extent. Philippe has a theory that even if Prohibition is ever repealed it will be years before America is a good wine market again.'

'He's probably right,' Lizzie said. 'Everyone does seem to drink spirits these days. But Mr Webster will know.' Then she asked diffidently as if it might be rude to enquire: 'How is Philippe coping with his blindness?'

'He does very well. He never complains, but it's hard for him sometimes to run his business. He has to depend on other people's eyes, and that means giving his employees a lot of trust.'

'I think he's wonderful,' Lizzie said. 'I can see why you love him.'

'I loved him from the moment I set eyes on him,' Rosie said simply, finding it a relief at last to be open and honest with someone about her feelings. 'But by then it was too late. I was to be married to Clovis. There was nothing to be done about it. But even all through that marriage Philippe was all I ever wanted. With him I can be weak and he supports me. I shall never love anyone else.'

'You won't need to,' Lizzie said. 'Oh, I do like happy endings.'

'Yes, they're rare.' Rosie was silent again thinking how long this happy ending had taken, and then she asked: 'How is Alexander?'

Lizzie gave her a sharp look.

'I can see the way your mind is working. No happy ending there, I'm afraid. I don't think he has ever forgotten Allie. He brings a girl home occasionally, but I can tell there's nothing to it. He has his own house now in Gramercy Park. His father did help him a little, but he earns a great deal of money of his own. He's become really quite a famous journalist. He'll be in New York for your wedding. He's just come back from the South where he's been investigating the Ku-Klux-Klan.' She shook her head. 'Dreadful, wicked people, they are, and so dangerous. Jim says they're getting out of hand. Blacks, Jews, Catholics – they murder anyone they fancy and call themselves Christians. I worry about Alexander all the time.' She shook her head mournfully. 'He's always doing something dangerous.'

'But *you're* happy?' Rosie asked, remembering a time when Lizzie had been anything but.

'Oh, yes. Jim and I get along pretty well. He's stick-in-the-mud for these times but I guess at heart I am too. Though,' she added a trifle defiantly, 'I'd like to be a little more adventurous before I get too old.'

'In what sort of way?' Rosie asked, laughing.

'I know it's silly, but I don't even know what sort of way. Life is so different since the war. The city is growing taller all the time, and women drink and smoke now and go into speakeasies.'

'You want to drink, smoke and go into speakeasies?' Rosie teased.

'Of course not. But everything has changed. People even talk about sex now. Remember how embarrassed we were? Jenny's always going on about how necessary a fulfilled sex life is and, believe me, I want to cover my ears. She says all our generation's troubles are due to sexual frustration. I never heard such nonsense!' She shook her head and said with growing indignation: 'They pet in automobiles, they drink too much, they have no appreciation of money. Even older people. Not as old as me, but as old as you. Sometimes I don't recognise the world I live in. And I worry so about Jenny. Could she be having this awful fulfilled sex life? I do hope not. She hardly ever comes home before dawn. But at twenty-four we can't treat her like a baby. I do wish she'd get married. None of them are happy, you know.'

'Maybe the new thinking is less hypocritical,' Rosie suggested, her mind flickering back over her own past.

'Well, maybe. Maybe I'm just envious because I don't know what a fulfilled sex life is,' Lizzie said, laughing at herself. 'But most of my life I've been happy. Still, none of all this new thinking will seem so surprising to you, I guess. I thought when we visited Les Hérissons that attitudes were different in Europe even before the war. Jim says that's what's caused it here. All our young men and women going over there in the war. They've come back thinking different. They just want to live for the day.'

'War makes you like that,' Rosie murmured.

'It must have been terrible.'

'It was.' Rosie dismissed the subject. 'I want you to see my wedding dress. Will the maid have unpacked?'

'Surely,' Lizzie said. 'Oh, I want to see it. Do you know, I have my outfit already. I do hope you like it. Things in France are so much nicer. But I've got this marvellous little dressmaker now. I need someone good since I've gotten fatter. Come on, let's go upstairs and I'll show you my dress, too.'

After an orgy of tissue paper and trying on, they were back in the parlour, drinking tea. The men had gone off to Mr Webster's club where he had promised to introduce Philippe to some valuable contacts. Lizzie was explaining how Jenny was a volunteer nurse at St Vincent's in Greenwich Village when there was a tap on the door. A smiling face with thin, bony features, topped by tow-coloured hair, appeared round the door frame.

Rosie jumped to her feet.

'Alexander!' she cried. 'How wonderful to see you.'

She was delighted to see that his smile had not changed. It was a smile to melt stone, a smile that Sebastian long ago had said would take the young American through life on oiled wheels.

'It's good to see you, too,' Alexander said. 'How was the journey?'

'Marvellous,' she said. 'Lots of luxury, smooth crossing and your mother was waiting at the pier for us. We were whisked here like royalty.'

'You are royalty,' he said. And moving to his mother to kiss her on the cheek asked: 'Can I join you?'

'Of course,' Lizzie said. 'As a matter of fact you can keep Rosie company for a minute while I go and see chef about tomorrow's menus. I'll get some fresh tea sent in.'

She bustled out of the room, and Rosie grinned at Alexander. 'I presume she thought you wanted to be left alone with me.'

He grinned, too. 'No fooling you! I did ask her to leave us alone. I didn't expect her to disappear quite so quickly and obviously. But I've been longing to see you.'

'Because you're longing to hear about Allie?'

'All right.' He threw up his hands in defeat. 'Because I'm longing to hear about Allie. How is she?'

Rosie considered. 'I think perhaps a little better. But she is still not right.'

'Rosie, what is the matter with her? Please tell me because I don't understand. Is she mentally sick?'

Rosie chose her words carefully.

'Not really. Not enough to need being put in hospital or anything. She gets desperately depressed and she is very angry with the world and sometimes she takes that out on the rest of us. I don't help. I do my best, but she doesn't feel that I love her as much as I love Philippe. Her father adored her in a completely uncomplicated way, but now he's gone and she is desperate for every grain of everyone's love.'

99

'I wanted to give her every grain of mine,' he said passionately.

Rosie looked at him with pity. He was a man now, no longer a thin-faced boy. And still he did not understand. But why should he? He knew so little of the truth.

'Ah, but she's not ready to give any real love back,' Rosie explained. 'I think she's afraid to let herself go. All she wants is the kind of affection that a father gives a small daughter. Nothing more demanding. She's a child who is refusing to grow up. She was more grown-up at twelve than she is now.'

'I frightened her. I tried to kiss her,' he said, his voice low. 'Could it be my fault?'

'Absolutely not! She's easily frightened these days,' Rosie said briskly, 'and it's time she wasn't. She should be welcoming kisses. But slowly, slowly, things are improving.'

She wondered if she should tell him how well Allie had taken to both Luke and the dog and decided it was too complicated. Also the thought of Luke might frighten *him*.

'What happened in the war to make her like this?' he asked. 'It has to be the war. I fell in love with her the first time we met and she was only ten years old and so brave and happy. It was after the war that she changed so.'

Rosie hesitated. 'Alexander, a lot happened in the war. Her father came home shell-shocked and didn't recognise her. He didn't recognise me or his mother. The only person he recognised and wanted to be with was the Madame who runs the local brothel. We told Allie the woman was a dressmaker, but to this day I don't know if she knows the real truth.

'Then the Germans came and that . . . well, that wasn't good. But there are things that happened to Allie that I have no right to tell you. They are her secrets. One day, maybe she will tell you herself. But all I can say, Alexander, is try to forgive her for whatever she did to you. Try to remain her friend because she needs friends more than most of us.'

'She didn't do anything that bad to me. She just gave me hope and then took it away. It was my own fault because I misunderstood. But I shall never love anyone else,' he said in a matter-of-fact voice. 'It couldn't happen. I still hope that one day she will love me.'

Rosie sighed. 'But you ought not to tie yourself to her,' she said. 'She may never grow up.'

'I'll take that chance,' he said. 'I intend to go back to France as soon as I can. I'm going to start courting her all over again and do it right this time.'

It could work, Rosie thought. And how wonderful if it did.

'It's worth a try if you feel so strongly,' she said, and not caring if she sounded as if she was sermonising added: 'You get little in life without fighting for it. I hope for all our sakes that this is a battle that you'll win.'

With perfect timing the maid came in with a tray of fresh tea. When she had set it down, Alexander said: 'Thanks, Ellie. You can tell Mrs Webster that it's safe to come back now.'

His mood had lightened. He looked at Rosie and grinned.

'Tea?' she asked demurely, pouring him a cup.

'Now you can describe it all to me,' Philippe said. 'Just how beautiful did you look?'

Rosie's high-heeled, little flapper's shoes were kicked off, her legs stretched along the seat of their private compartment, her head on Philippe's lap as he sat in the corner seat of the carriage. It was ten minutes since the train had pulled out of Grand Central Station in a flurry of rice, confetti, and good wishes. The happy couple had left behind a messy reminder of their wedding that would have enraged the station staff if it hadn't been for the fact, as Philippe remarked, that Mr Webster paid a large chunk of their wages.

'I looked delectable!' said Rosie, who had drunk quite a lot of her own Les Hérissons champagne from the hoarded supply in Mr Webster's cellars. She giggled. 'I think my dress shocked them a bit. They haven't seen anything like it here.'

'Well, I haven't seen it, either,' he said. 'Describe, please.'

'Pink, a tight sheath of pink. Very figure-revealing, and over it another dress of transparent pink chiffon over different width hoops to hold it from the body.'

'That's why I couldn't get hold of you properly,' he grumbled.

'It moves most amazingly when you walk in it,' she said indignantly.

'It sounds ghastly. Sometimes I'm glad I can't see,' he said cheerfully.

'I'm not!' She was not laughing any more. 'But at least you'll never see me old and grey. You'll always remember me as I was when I was young.'

'Stop being morbid on our wedding day.' He put his arm round her and hugged her. 'Go on about the wedding.'

'Well, I came down the stairs with Jenny clod-hopping behind. Bless her, she's not grown up very graceful, and there were you at the bottom in the hall. You were standing under an arbour made of some sort of trellis all covered with roses with artificial bluebirds tucked in among them. There was a silver bell hanging from the middle and it was missing your head by about two inches. I kept expecting you to hit it and make it ring.'

'Sounds a bit excessive,' he said mildly.

'It was, but Lizzie was thrilled with it all. She hadn't let me go downstairs all morning so I'd be surprised. And surprised I was!' she said with a small giggle. 'Anyway, the minister was standing next to you. He was about five foot nothing. Even I towered over him, but as you could probably tell, he was adorable.

'Everyone standing behind the trellis was *très chic*. You've never seen such a forest of hats and a flurry of feathers. Pity we didn't know anyone under them, but Mr Webster was determined that we weren't going to celebrate alone.'

'It seemed like a lot of people,' he said. 'But I enjoyed it. Mr Webster was introducing me to people who used to be in the wine trade. They were all saying they're having a bad time.'

'Well, they weren't having a bad time this morning. There was an awful lot of our champagne flowing, considering it's illegal. And I've never seen so much caviare and foie gras outside of Fouchard's. The wedding breakfast was just beautiful; all set out on a huge table, decorated with lovely bright yellow ribbons and bright yellow flowers. The waitresses were all in buttercup yellow dresses to match.' She gave a little sigh of pure pleasure. 'Everyone was able to sit down and eat. They had those little tables and chairs in gold that leave funny marks on your bottom. You know, like those at fashion houses. Did you get to eat at all?'

'I did. Lizzie took me away and almost force-fed me,' he said, laughing. 'I think she realised caviare is not easy for a blind man to eat.'

'Isn't she kind? Wasn't it all delicious?' she sighed.

'Yes, my little sybarite, it was.'

'The best bit was when Jenny's cat shot through everyone in the middle of the service. The little minister was quite unnerved. Did you hear a kind of rustle and gasp? That was Felix making his presence felt. Since he's a black cat, I suppose it must mean good luck.'

'My good luck, to have you at last,' he said, leaning to kiss her. 'I just hope it's all legal.'

'If it's not, we'll just do it all over again in France one day,' she said. 'But isn't it exciting to be going West like this? You are a dear to let me spend our honeymoon on a train.'

Rosie was thrilled at the prospect of the train journey across America. Twenty years had passed since she had run away from her home and all alone, full of trepidation for the future, made this same journey, but from West to East. Lizzie and Mr Webster had saved her on that first journey, giving her comfort, confidence and, most important under the circumstances, financial help. Now she was returning to her childhood home a wealthy woman, with trunks full of beautiful clothes and in the company of a husband she loved and who loved her.

She was changing for dinner the first evening while Philippe, already in a dinner jacket, sat quietly waiting for her. She stood in her stockings and nothing else, rummaging through her luggage, enjoying an orgy of nostalgia: 'Do you know, when I came to Europe I had just two dresses for the entire journey? They were lovely dresses I bought in San Francisco, but they weren't enough. If Lizzie hadn't given me some of her clothes for the boat, I don't know how I would have managed. But I was so ignorant, straight from the backwoods, that I really thought two dresses would do.'

She had found what she was looking for. A black lace-trimmed corselet with a few diamantés scattered over the right breast.

She put it into his hands.

'Remember this?' she asked.

His fingers found the lace, the diamantés and the hooks which fastened the garment. He smiled.

'I remember it well,' he said. 'You wore it the first time we made love, and you wore it when we made love after I was blinded.'

'And I'm going to wear it tonight, our wedding night,' she promised him. 'Though of course it will ruin the line of Madame Chanel's dress. Madame Chanel does not believe in bosoms.' She took it back from him and stood looking in the mirror to hook it into place, her eyes dreamy as she remembered. 'I bought it in San Francisco when I bought the dresses. Madame Claudine's Paris Modes, the shop was called. It was the most idiotic extravagance, but I couldn't resist it.'

'I'm glad you didn't,' he said, and added, 'I just wish you had bought it with me in mind.'

'I didn't even know you then,' she protested and added untruthfully: 'I don't think I bought it with anyone in mind. It was just that I couldn't resist it.'

'Come here, my little lying wife,' he said.

Obediently she moved to sit by him. His quick fingers found the curve of her breasts and hesitated as he found them covered. Then skilfully he unfastened the hooks that she had just secured. As her breasts sprang free his head bent to take her right nipple in his mouth. He bit gently and she closed her eyes and gave a little groan of pleasure.

'We'll be late for dinner,' she whispered.

'I'm not hungry for food.' Speaking gave him the opportunity to switch his mouth to her left breast. His hands were running down over her stomach and to the strong hair that shielded her mound of Venus. 'Anyway,' he said, lifting his head again. 'You're not even dressed yet.'

'But you are,' she told him.

'This is something just for you,' he said. 'You can make love to me later.' And lifting her he spread her along the length of the seat. He knelt before her, his hands parting her thighs to admit his mouth and tongue. He found her warm, musky, wet depths and she lay, sighing gently, her limbs abandoned, her red mouth wet and parted, and gave herself up to pleasure.

They had become adept at making love in the bunk beds of trains by the time they arrived in California. Though she could remember little of her original journey except mind-pictures of unfriendly mountains and endless plains of snow shrouding the Midwest, Rosie was aware that America had dramatically changed in the past twenty years. Now in August there was no snow, only endless fields of yellow wheat in a flat unvarying landscape. The mountains of the West with their summer foliage looked gentler in the haze of high summer. But the unspoilt landscape now had dramatic interruptions. Not only had New York grown taller and bigger, but Chicago had its own dizzy skyscrapers, and even the small towns through which the train rumbled were burgeoning with sprawling surburbs. When she had left for Europe there had been traces of the old West and the old ways. It seemed that they were vanishing. America was growing up.

There was no need to describe the journey to Philippe. It was one he had made many times in the past, and he assured her that since he had become blind his memory was like a personal picture book. He had instant recall of most the things he had seen in his life before he had lost his sight.

'And most particularly of you, my darling,' he said, his fingers tracing her still firm chin, and running gently over her eyelids.

They changed trains at Sacramento, but from here Philippe did not have his memory book to consult. He had never visited either the Napa Valley where Rosie's childhood had been spent, or the nearest small town, Calistoga. But Rosie's own memory came flooding back as she described for him the great oaks that lined the railroad track, the hovering pineclad mountains, and the patches of drifting low cloud that in the autumn would turn to fog floating in from off the San Pablo Bay.

'It is very beautiful,' she said wistfully. 'I had forgotten how beautiful. But it feels so strange to come back. I don't remember it all as well as I should.'

He was holding her hand as she looked out of the window.

'Twenty years is a long time,' he said. 'It must have changed.'

'I suppose so,' she said. 'The winery most certainly will have done. I don't expect I shall recognise it at all.'

'Don't be disappointed,' he warned.

'I'm too excited to be disappointed,' she told him.

Peter was to meet them at the station, but Peter was not there. They waited on the platform and then in order to get out of the blazing heat, in the station itself. There was no sign of him. Rosie kept darting into the street, ostensibly to look for Peter, but also because she wanted to see how much the town had changed.

'There's hardly a horse and carriage to be seen,' she reported back to Philippe, fanning her face with her hand, 'and there aren't any wagons at all. I don't think I would have recognised it, but it still feels like a nice little town. My, it's hot. Hotter than Cannes was.'

They waited half an hour but there was still no sign of Peter and Rosie could see that the heat was beginning to trouble Philippe. Sometimes the sun could give him one of his terrible headaches.

'I don't think he's coming. I hope he's all right,' she said anxiously.

'He's probably just forgotten or confused the day,' Philippe said. 'Why don't we take a cab and go there?'

'We'll have to.' It was the only thing to do. 'You stay here and I'll find one.'

All the way out of town on the same hot, dusty road, now widened, that she had taken as a girl in the old wagon with Castor and Pollux's heavy hooves heaving it along, Rosie's head was craned out of the car window looking for landmarks and anything at all that she remembered. There was little. There were new homes but not much prosperity along the way. Some of the smaller vineyards had been let go and the buildings were already beginning to decay.

The cab at last reached her old home. The wooden winery gates that had always hung drunkenly open had gone. Now the entrance to the land was barred by a solid stone wall and imposing wrought-iron gates decorated with a motif of crossed champagne bottles. She did not describe the gates to Philippe knowing they were something else that he would judge excessive. The gates were not locked, and there was no sign of any gateman. The cab driver asked if it was all right to go in, and on Rosie's say-so, they drove up the old route to the house.

'This was just a dirt road when I left,' Rosie told Philippe, 'now it's been replaced by tarmacadam. It looks so different. Some of the trees have been cut down and there are gardens and small vineyards planted in their place. It's not at all like it used to be. It's so grand, and it used to be so shabby.'

As the cab rounded the corner bringing the house into view, Rosie gasped. The old stone house where she had been born was still in place, but two vast wings had been built on either side. A drive curved round in front of the house, and gardens had been planted in the centre. But there was something wrong. Once they were nearer she could see that the flowers were unattended and dying – in desperate need of water. From the house, dark, unfriendly windows looked down on them, curtains drawn. There was an ominous stillness about the entire place.

'Don't look like there's anybody home to me,' the cab driver ventured as he pulled up. 'They're letting a lot of these old wine places go now. Folks ain't got the money to keep 'em up.'

Full of anxiety, Rosie did not reply. She concentrated on helping Philippe from the cab as the driver unloaded their bags on to the front step.

'Want me to stick around?' he asked, 'just in case you need to go back.'

'It's okay,' Rosie said, paying him off hurriedly. 'I expect they're round the back.'

'Maybe,' the driver said, and shrugged. 'I'll be off then.'

She stood, her hand in Philippe's, watching as the cab disappeared round the bend, wondering if it had been wise to send him away. The place felt deserted. Leaving the baggage where it was, she began the not inconsiderable walk to the back of the house. As they rounded the right-hand wing, the first thing she saw was a huge swimming pool set between the two new wings and facing the old house. The water was turning green, and a coating of leaves covered the surface. From somewhere in its depths some small fish lived, making bubbles on the surface. The expensive poolside furniture had once been white and blue, now it was dirty and covered in bird droppings.

'There's a swimming pool here.' For some reason she was whispering. 'But it's all completely neglected. Everything's neglected. We'll try what used to be the kitchen door.'

What used to be the kitchen door was now all sliding glass, opening onto a room which seemed to consist of the entire ground floor of the old house. One side of the glass door was slightly open, and gently, nervous about what she would find, Rosie pushed it back.

'We'll go in,' she said, her voice low. 'Careful, there's a little step.'

She stepped into a superb room furnished with a vast desk, huge black leather sofas and a white carpet with a deep pile. There were some erotic pictures of nude women and men on the walls, and statues of naked women elegantly supporting light globes. As chic, modern and expensive as it all was, the room felt hostile and even cold, in spite of the heat outside.

'It's very modern and not really very nice,' she said to Philippe who was holding tight to her arm. He disliked being in unfamiliar rooms.

'Shouldn't you call out?' he asked. 'Aren't there any servants?'

'There isn't a soul about. Do you want to sit down here while I go through the house? It'll take a while. It's huge. Three times the size of when I lived here.'

'I'll come with you,' he said. Relieved that she would have his company in the unnerving silence, she squeezed her arm against his.

The big modern kitchen was in the left-hand wing of the house. A burnt saucepan sat on the gas oven. No fire burned in the oil range. There was some washing-up in the sink, a cup was growing mould. Everywhere was dusty and unkempt.

'I don't like it, Philippe,' she said, whispering again. 'Something's wrong, I'm sure of it. It looks as if no one has been in here for ages. Where can Peter be?'

They found a smaller living room, less exotically furnished and with a wall crammed with books on wine. Another room was an unused office, another appeared to be a library. There was a child's room with expensive old-fashioned, neatly stored toys. In none of the six or seven luxuriously furnished bedrooms upstairs was there evidence of the recent presence of people. In one of the three bathrooms a tap ran unchecked, water dismally staining the porcelain of the sink. The magnificent but unloved house belonged in a Hollywood movie. It was deserted and forlorn as if the movie was over and the stars gone home.

Rosie knew she was right. No one had lived here for some time, yet in what appeared to be Peter's bedroom, clothes were neatly hung up, the bed was made, his slippers and dressing gown in place ready for some morning he had missed. She drew a finger through the dust on his dressing table, and the pale wood surface beneath showed up brighter.

'Maybe he's gone to meet us and missed us?' Philippe suggested. His voice was a touch impatient, and Rosie understood the frustration that his blindness was causing him. Without sight he could not help her.

'It just doesn't seem like that somehow,' she said. 'I don't think anyone has been here in a long time. Let's look in the vineyard.'

It was a relief to get out of the sullen atmosphere of the house and into the bright sunshine of the day. A flicker was tap-tap-tapping with his beak at the wood of a tree or maybe the shingles of the house. A gentle breeze blew, and there to the left, hidden by the new wing but where it had always stood, was the old barn, astonishingly untouched, looking almost exactly the same as it had when she left home twenty years before.

More memories, she thought as she looked at the shabby tumbledown building incongruous among all the new splendour. In that building in the room above the wine vats she had slept with her first lover, terrified that her father would catch her. And it was there she had found her little brother, Peter, in bed with her lover. Events that had changed her life.

Bemused, she led Philippe towards the big wooden building. 'The only thing that looks the same is the old barn where we used to keep the pressing equipment and the barrels,' she told him as they walked along a paved path. 'It had a room upstairs where we put all the old bits and pieces of furniture we didn't want any more. The hired hand used to sleep there.' She could not bring herself to say that the hired hand had been Jean Paul Dupuis. 'I can't imagine why it wasn't modernised or pulled down like everything else has been.'

She pushed open the big wooden doorway. The half-forgotten smell of heady red wine still lingered, musty and heavy in the air. She had a sudden sense of someone's presence. If Peter was anywhere, he was here. She was convinced of it. But to find out meant climbing the ladder to the upstairs room. That would be difficult for Philippe to do, and yet she felt afraid to go alone.

Telling herself not to be a baby, she said to him: 'Darling, there's a ladder here that goes up to the room. I think it will be awkward for you. Just wait here for one minute and I'll be back.'

He sighed and she knew he was distressed that he could not go for her, but there was nothing to be done about it.

Swiftly she mounted the rungs, her apprehension growing. As her head came through to the ground level of the room she felt the draught that was blowing in from a broken window. There was a strange chemical smell and her eye was caught by several empty bottles lying on their sides on an old tattered rag rug that her mother had made long, long ago. She pulled herself upright and saw that the bottles led to an overturned, empty glass that had spread a wet stain across the rug. Above the glass hung a limp hand and arm. They belonged, she realised, to her brother. He was sprawled face down across the old broken-down brass bed.

She stared at the sight of the one dead white hand hanging down as if trying to reach the fallen glass. The draught from the window ruffled his hair slightly and the shock of the slow, ghostly movement was so great that Rosie did something she had never done in her life before. She screamed.

As the sound died away in the sun-streaked room she heard the scramble of Philippe's footsteps on the ladder below her.

'I'm coming,' he was shouting. 'Hold on. Are you all right?'

'It's all right,' she called back, 'don't come up.' But he was already there. She helped him to stand upright as his head appeared above the ladder and he took her in his arms to hug her close to him.

'What is it? What it is?' he was asking anxiously.

'It's Peter,' she said, her face buried in his shoulder. 'I think he's dead.'

She felt him tense. 'Where is he?' he asked.

'On the bed. He's been drinking. There are bottles all over the floor.'

'Take me to where he is.'

Shuddering, she led him the few paces towards the bed. He felt for the body, turned it over and listened for a heartbeat. Then he looked towards where she stood, his face grave. 'Rosie, I'm sorry, he's dead,' he said. 'He hasn't been dead long, but there is nothing to be done.'

She made a jerky dismissive movement with her hands as if she were brushing away the truth of what he had said, and then she covered her face as the sadness and the waste of it all washed over her. Her little brother, lost, found and now lost again. The last link with her youth had gone. She began to cry softly.

'We must call a doctor and the police,' Philippe was saying.

The thought of the police alerted her.

'You don't think he committed suicide?' she asked.

'I don't know. You say he's been drinking?'

'Yes.' She stooped to pick up one of the bottles and put it into his hand before picking up another.

He was smelling what was left of the contents and she did the same.

'It's some sort of alcohol, isn't it?' she said. 'It smells quite dreadful.'

'It's nothing but poison,' Philippe said, his voice angry. 'That's what killed him. Too much rotgut alcohol. How many bottles are there?'

'Four.'

'All empty?'

'All empty.'

'He wouldn't have stood a chance.'

Feeling a deep but somehow resigned sadness she moved to look down at her brother's face. In death it was peaceful. His eyes and mouth were decently closed. He looked gently relaxed, as if he were resting. But she noticed the grey that sprinkled his hair, and the deep shadows under his eyes. He had aged considerably in the three months since she had seen him. Now he was dead. Full of compassion, she put out her hand to stroke his cold brow.

'Poor, poor Peter,' she said gently.

There were two crumpled pieces of paper on the floor by the bed. She picked them up. A mouse had been nibbling at the corner of one, but the words were intact.

'He was writing a letter to Jean Paul's son, Pierre,' she said. 'It was on the floor by him. Shall I read it?'

'Why not?' he said. 'It might explain what happened.'

It felt wrong and intrusive to be reading a letter from the dead but there seemed nothing else to be done.

'He says he can understand why Pierre doesn't want to come back, but would he perhaps consider it,' she said hesitantly after reading the first two paragraphs. 'I think he must have been drunk when he started writing this. It's very incoherent. "I'm so lonely," ' she read out loud: ' "I've moved into the old barn because once long ago I was happy here with Jean Paul. It feels more like home than the house. I miss you both all the time. I just thought I'd stay here, and drink and drink and drink to forget him. I got the gin from a bootlegger, it makes me feel ill but I don't care . . . I couldn't move for a while but I didn't feel lonely any more. It kills the loneliness . . ." ' Her voice trailed away. 'That's all,' she said. 'There isn't any more, but he must have been replying to this letter from Pierre Dupuis.' She smoothed out the other piece of paper and started to read it silently. Then she gave a little gasp of astonishment. 'Listen to this,' she said. 'He says he's going to Les Hérissons to see if he likes France . . .' She read out loud again: ' "I am convinced that the thing to do is pack my bags, arrive at Les Hérissons and see what the place is like. I might as well claim my inheritance. And if the French relatives turn out to be hell, then I'd rather come home and get a job of work in Boston. I'm sorry, Uncle Peter, but I don't want to live in California ever again." '

She stood looking at the paper in her hand, the complications of Jean Paul's son arriving at Les Hérissons racing through her mind. 'Well!' she said. 'What about that! Oh, poor Peter. Left so alone.'

Philippe was still sitting on the edge of the bed beside Peter's body.

'I think the thing to do is to put those letters in your purse and forget that they ever existed,' he said. 'But for now we must get the authorities and try to sort out what is going to be the most terrible muddle. Young Pierre presumably has another inheritance here. It's all going to be very complicated, but first things first. Pull something over his face, my darling, don't cry any more and we'll leave him in peace.'

In spite of his brave front and comforting words to Rosie, Philippe was finding it difficult to control the feelings of anxiety that kept attacking him. He felt ridiculously afraid; a strange and uncomfortable feeling of naked fear had seated itself low in his stomach. He knew exactly what the reason was. He was unhappy in surroundings that were completely strange to him. Rooms and terrain that he could not begin to visualise left him defenceless against his blindness. He had no memory of Champagne D'Or and to him it was alien, dangerous territory. And then Rosie, his strong, undramatic Rosie had screamed. That had been the most terrible moment of his life. His one thought had been to protect her as in panic he had groped for the ladder and dragged himself up it, knowing that if something frightful had happened to her he would not be able to see whatever the horror was. He was ashamed that he had almost fainted with relief when she fell into his arms and he knew that she was safe and no harm had come to her.

Getting back down the ladder and walking back to the house was not so bad. He recognised when they were walking past the swimming pool by the change of sound. He heard the glass door roll back again, and knew they were going into the large sitting room. Rosie settled him on a sofa he could feel was made of leather. He was beginning to orientate himself, but the feeling of panic returned when she went to the telephone.

He sat quietly, breathing deeply, trying to quell his irrational fear and longing for her to come back. He could hear her voice explaining to the operator that they needed both doctor and police, and he cursed the blindness that meant she was having to cope with the things that he, as her husband and the man of the family, should deal with.

He heard her crisp footsteps crossing what sounded like a marble floor and then the softer thud as she walked on carpet. He could smell her perfume as she neared, and she sank down on the sofa where he sat, making it rise a little.

'They'll be here in ten minutes,' she sighed.

'Are you all right?' he asked, finding her hand to hold.

'Umm. I think so. I could do with a cognac.'

'Me, too,' he said and almost laughed at the absurdity of not being able to have one.

'We should never have let him come back,' she was saying. 'He could have stayed in France.'

'But he wanted to come back. He loathed France,' Philippe pointed out. He did not want Rosie blaming herself for this tragedy.

113

She squeezed his hand. 'We have to tell Pierre.'

'We can think about all those details when we have talked to the police and the doctor,' he said firmly.

They arrived in a wail of sirens in less than quarter of an hour. One man, the doctor, was small. His hand came up to meet Philippe's as they were introduced. The other man was big and heavy; Philippe could tell both by his footsteps and the way the furniture complained when he sat. Yet he had a small man's high breathy voice. Rosie introduced him as the sheriff.

'Ain't you Rosie Brunner?' the high voice asked.

'I was Rosie Brunner. Now I'm Rosie Lefevre.'

He noticed the touch of pleasure in her voice as she spoke his name.

'Well, I'll be doggone. We were at school together. In Calistoga. I'm Joe Oldham.'

'I remember!' He could tell she was wary. 'Of course. You don't look different at all.'

'Nor you, ma'am.' Philippe realised the man had turned his head to speak to him. 'Your wife was the best looking gal in the school,' he said. 'And head-in-the-air! Real class! No one got near Rosie. Guess we weren't good enough.' He chuckled. 'She always had something special about her. Yes sir!'

Rosie was embarrassed. She changed the subject as she always did when people embarrassed her.

'We've just come in from the East,' she said hurriedly. 'This is the first time I've been back. It's been over twenty years.'

'Whole town wanted to know where you'd gone that time,' Joe Oldham rambled on. He was a take-off of a sheriff, Philippe thought. Copying someone in the movies. 'Kept the ladies gossiping for weeks,' he was saying, his tone somehow suggestive. 'If it hadn't been that the station master remembered selling you that ticket East, sure as eggs we'd have thought old man Brunner got rid of you somehow.'

'He wouldn't have done that!' Rosie sounded shocked.

'Guess we knew things about him you didn't. Still, it's all a long time ago. It ain't much of a happy homecoming for you.' He paused, and then his voice dropped respectfully. 'Where will we find the body?' he asked.

'In the old barn,' Rosie said, her voice low. 'My husband thinks that what he had been drinking must have killed him.'

114

'Well, we'll just go and check it out.'

'Do you want me to come with you?' she asked, and Philippe knew that she was hoping they would say no.

'I guess you've had enough unpleasantness for one day. You stay right here with your husband and leave it all to us.' The breathy voice was unctuous. The chair groaned in relief as the sheriff stood and two pairs of footsteps crossed first the carpet and then the marble, fading away around the echoing pool.

She sat silently next to him and he took her hand again.

'He was a beastly little boy, Joe Oldham,' she said quietly. 'A bully. None of them liked us much and they used to beat Peter up because he was smaller and weaker than all of them. I had to protect him. If they hit him, they had to fight me. They were frightened of me.' Her voice faltered. 'Poor little Peter.'

He knew from the choked note that she was crying, and he pulled her to put her head on his shoulder. Sitting here, with no obstacles to navigate and Rosie by his side, his own confidence was slowly returning. They sat without speaking again until the footsteps sounded again in the distance.

'Guess you were right, Mr Lefevre.' It was the sheriff speaking. 'That rotgut killed him okay. Doc here thinks he's been unconscious for some days, but we reckon that times when he did come to for a while, he just drank some more. He ain't been dead that long. Pity you weren't here earlier. Might just have saved him.'

'We waited at the station for him for a good half hour,' Rosie said, her voice distressed.

'You'd have needed to be earlier than that,' the doctor said soothingly. 'And it's as well he died. His health would have been impaired for ever.'

The sheriff was walking round the room.

'Long time since I been up here,' he said. 'Where's that Jean Paul Dupuis these days? Ain't seen him around in a long time. Not since they smashed up his illegal vats. Word was he went back to France.'

'We don't know where he is,' Philippe said quickly. 'We had heard from Peter that he had disappeared, but we thought perhaps by the time we got here he would have turned up again.'

'Disappeared, you say?' The sheriff's voice was thoughtful. 'Disappeared from where?'

115

Philippe shrugged and opened his hands in a wide gesture.

'Who knows?' he said. 'Peter and he were visiting my wife in France, and he left suddenly. He said he was returning to the States, but it seems that he never got here.'

'France, eh? You live in France now, Rosie?'

'That's where I went when I left here.'

'You don't say?' The sheriff sounded impressed, then he added on an enquiring note: 'I heard Jean Paul had dealings with Gino Angelini.'

Philippe wanted to keep Rosie out of this conversation. 'I'm sorry, but I don't know who Gino Angelini is,' he said firmly.

'No, I guess a gentleman like you wouldn't. Nasty bit of work, Gino, but then so is Jean Paul. Make a great couple, they do. Now I just wonder where he's got hisself to.'

No one answered. He was walking around the room again, stopping here and there. Philippe judged he was looking at pictures.

'Quite a place this, ain't it? Bet you wouldn't have recognised it from the old days, eh, Rosie?'

'It has changed,' she admitted.

'Guess that boy Pierre's mother wouldn't recognise it either if she were alive to see it,' he said, and Philippe caught the sly note in his voice.

'I'm afraid I never knew Pierre's mother,' Rosie said coldly.

'Guess you didn't. Guess she came after you'd gone. Just as well you'd gone, too. Real slut of a serving girl from Russian River, she was. Not your style at all. She died when the boy was born. There were lots more sluts after her. He likes sluts, does Jean Paul. But I guess with him anything goes.'

Philippe felt Rosie stiffen. The silence lay heavy, and the sheriff's footsteps took another turn round the room.

'Gonna be complicated if he don't turn up, ain't it?' he suggested.

'Why?' Philippe asked.

'Well, what happens to this old place? Just you and that boy left if he don't turn up, ain't there, Rosie?'

'My wife and I have our own lives and our business in France,' Philippe said firmly. 'We want no claim here.'

'In my experience that's what folks always say – at first.' The sheriff chuckled. 'Where is the boy?' he asked abruptly.

'We have no idea,' Philippe said.

'Guess we'd better find out then. Tell him what's happened here.'

Philippe's brain was racing. Should he mention that Pierre was going to Les Hérissons? If he did, the sheriff would want to know why, and it would have to be explained that Rosie had once been married to Jean Paul's brother. Then if by any wild chance the sheriff knew anything about French law, he might start asking a lot more questions that would be difficult to answer. Philippe stayed silent and, to his relief, so did Rosie.

'We'll take the body down to the funeral parlour now, and you folks can make your own arrangements about the funeral. I guess you'll stay until the formalities are over.'

'Of course,' Philippe said. 'But not here. I think we'll move to a hotel in Calistoga.'

'Good idea. You could try Sam Brannan's old place. I'll send a cab back to get you. Here looks as if it needs a good clean up. That's the trouble with these big spreads. They need a lot of money to keep 'em going. Guess Jean Paul ran out of it.'

There was an unpleasant note of smug satisfaction in the man's voice. Neither Philippe nor Rosie answered him, and Philippe was relieved to hear his footsteps moving towards the door. Then they stopped and the man cleared his throat noisily as if he were about to spit and thought better of it.

'Say, Rosie, tell me – what did you have in that trunk that time you went away? Darn near broke the black porter's back getting it on the train.'

'Wild vine cuttings,' Rosie said.

'Well, I'll be doggone. Whole town swore for sure it was a body. Only problem, we couldn't figure out whose body it could be. We thought for a while there that it might be Jean Paul's. But then he turned up safe and sound with his pregnant slut.' He laughed loudly. 'Vine cuttings! Would you believe it! Just goes to show, don't it? Well, so long for now. I guess I'll find you in Sam Brannan's place if I need you.'

He left, the patter of the doctor's smaller feet following him. Philippe breathed a sigh of relief and pulled Rosie closer to him. 'That's the worst of it over,' he said consolingly.

She shivered. 'I'd forgotten how much they hated us,' she said quietly. 'And he still hates us. He made me feel dirty and

117

he made me feel guilty. I hated it all. I wish we were home. I was wrong to come back here. I should have left it in the past where it belongs.'

'Perhaps it was fate we came,' he said. 'What would have happened to your poor brother if we hadn't found him? It doesn't bear thinking about.'

'You're right, of course,' she said, taking his hand and kissing it. 'But it's a sad honeymoon for you.'

'And for you,' he said, and ruffled her hair, 'but then, we've always been star-crossed.'

'Only a little bit star-crossed. We've always managed to be together.'

'And the minute the funeral is over, we'll go home.'

'Oh, lovely,' she said on a sigh. Then added: 'But what shall we do about Pierre?'

'Nothing,' he said. 'Absolutely nothing. We're going to act as if we never read that letter. We'll let things take their course and sort everything out once we get back to France. Agreed?'

'Agreed,' she said and shuddered again. 'But I just wish I didn't feel so guilty.'

Les Hérissons, August 1920
'Miss, come for a walk.' It was Allie's voice and Allie's fingernails scratching insistently on her bedroom door. Emily Thoronson put down her fountain pen and pursed her lips. She did not want to go for a walk with Allie. She wanted to go for a walk with Luke West. And now, even if he asked her, she wouldn't be able to accept if she turned Allie down. She might as well go with Allie.

'Coming,' she said. 'I'll meet you in the hall in ten minutes.'

Emily Thoronson was not the same girl who had left Les Hérissons at the height of the war. She had been twenty-seven years old then, a quiet virgin who was beginning to feel that life was passing her by. So, having taken the dangerous trip over the Channel back to England, she had not returned to her country vicarage home. She had stayed in London, working as an ambulance driver.

It had changed her life. Emily had what she thought of as 'experiences', but then the experiences stopped. After the war, people tried to return to the old standards and everything seemed flat.

She took a post with a family in Scotland, but the remoteness of the estate and the rather dull little boy whom she was meant to teach bored her. When her parents had forwarded Rosie's brief letter asking if she would return to Les Hérissons it seemed like a small miracle.

She had been happy at Les Hérissons – until the dreadful incident at the end. The household had been easy-going and Allie a delight to teach; she learned so quickly. Emily was a little surprised to find that Madame Rosie had had another child so late in life but she put it down to M. Clovis's sudden return from the war. She wondered whether or not he had recovered his wits. As she re-read Madame Rosie's letter with a view of a bleak Highland moor outside her window she thought how marvellous it would be to go back and see what had happened to that remarkable family who had always been so kind to her. It might even lay a hovering ghost or two for her.

She accepted Madame Rosie's offer and in mid-August took the trains, packuet boat and train back to Champagne.

On arrival at Reims station something happened to make her think she might be even happier this time round in France. It wasn't old Henri who met her. It was a remarkably attractive (in a funny sort of way) man who was driving the Dupuis' ancient Léon Bollée. An Englishman, no less. He had introduced himself as Luke West, and said he was going to run Les Hérissons.

'But where is Madame Rosie?' she had asked.

'At Les Hérissons at the moment, but she's leaving soon for a visit to New York.'

Emily considered the news. 'She must be going to see her friends the Websters.'

'I think they are called Webster,' he said, his eyes on the road.

'They came here once. Before the war. They were nice. Madame Rosie had met them on a train when she was leaving her home in California and coming to France. They became friends and they've been friends ever since. It's a story Monsieur Clovis hates. He doesn't like to think that Madame is really an American.'

He had slowed a little and turned his head to look at her.

'Monsieur Clovis is dead,' he said. 'Didn't you know?'

She was genuinely shocked. M. Clovis was slow and daft as a brush, but he was kind and good and she had liked him.

'Was it the war?' she asked.

'I don't know. No one seems to talk about how he died.'

'How extraordinary,' she said. 'Tell me about other changes.'

He had laughed and said: 'How can I? I've barely been here a fortnight myself. But there's an English nanny called Nanny Shepherd who I suppose must be new.'

'Darn!' she said. 'Nannies can be a nuisance.'

'She seems okay,' he said easily. 'She's old, but very firm. They all seem pleased with her.'

They had then chatted about their respective backgrounds and he had carried her case into the house, picking it up as if it was full of feathers. He really was attractive, she was thinking as Allie, taller, thinner, with longer hair, flew down the steps to meet her.

'Miss!' she called out. 'How lovely!'

The warmth of the greeting had been flattering. They had given her a nicer room than last time, and old Madame Dupuis had received her kindly. Rosie had hugged and kissed her with genuine pleasure. As Emily unpacked her bags with Marie's help she congratulated herself on grasping the chance to come back.

But something, and it wasn't just Allie, was oppressing her. Since Madame Rosie had left, Allie sought her company all the time. The girl did not have enough to do, she needed other people to fill her life. It was probably all to do with that dreadful, dreadful day. Emily shuddered when she remembered it. If the girl had grown up a little odd, heaven knew there was reason. But much of the time Allie seemed content enough. She had a small, timid dog which slunk around after her wherever she went and her affection for it seemed excessive to Emily. As far as Emily was concerned it was rather an unrewarding dog. She was used to canines who liked having something to do and would settle for chasing sticks when they weren't picking up pheasants. This one seemed terrified of its own shadow.

She supposed that the walk Allie had suggested was to exercise this boring little animal who, to Marie's chagrin, was proving hard to house-train.

Allie was already in the hall when she got down.

'Off we go then,' she said gaily, and opened the door. Sure enough, the small dog was at her heels.

They set off down the drive and once they were away from the house Allie asked: 'How are you getting on with Rosanne?'

Emily laughed. 'She's not a bit like you were as a child. You were very good. Always dreaming, always reading, always making up stories. I'm afraid your sister is very naughty.'

'It's because we all spoilt her,' Allie said defensively. 'It's not her fault. We're not allowed to spoil her any more. Nanny Shepherd gets really angry if we do.'

'Thank goodness for Nanny Shepherd,' said Emily with feeling. 'Do you know what your naughty little sister did today?'

Allie shook her head.

'She emptied the ink pot over her head. So,' added Emily with some satisfaction, 'I smacked her bottom. She won't do it again.'

'She might,' said Allie in a tone of voice that indicated Rosanne didn't take too much notice of having her bottom smacked. Emily felt momentarily depressed and decided to change the subject.

'Where are we going?' she asked.

'Chigny?' Allie suggested.

'Couldn't we go through the vineyard and over the hill? I used to love to see the grapes when they were ripe.'

'I don't like walking that way. My father died walking that way. He fell down the Roman chalk pit.'

It was the first time that either of them had mentioned Clovis. Before she left for the States Madame Rosie had warned Emily that mention of Clovis upset Allie. But now she had brought the subject up on her own.

'Was it an accident?' Emily ventured.

'Of course it was an accident,' Allie said rudely. 'Why did you have your hair cut so short?'

'I'm sorry?' The turn of conversation was bewildering.

'I was wondering why you had your hair cut so short.' Allie's tone was milder.

'Because it's fashionable.' Emily decided to be abrupt herself.

121

'I liked it long,' said Allie. 'I don't like change. Not any kind of change.'

Emily shook her head. 'But things have to change, Allie. You can't go back again.'

And as she said it, she realised that was exactly what she had done herself.

Chapter Five

Pierre took a taxi from Reims station, and paid it off at the gates of Les Hérissons. His reasoning was that if the Dupuis did send him away, at least they would have to keep him on the premises while he called for another taxi – a small breathing space that might give them time to change their minds. He stood for a moment to compose himself while regarding the big iron gates to the house. They were open and in his anxious state of mind he decided that this was a good omen. Another good omen was that just inside the entrance was a small gatehouse which seemed to be unattended. He could not see the main house, but he felt there was no reason why he should not walk up to it since there was no one there to announce him.

He felt absurdly nervous. Already his lack of French had chipped away a little of his inbuilt natural confidence. It seemed ridiculous not to be able to understand people, and even more ridiculous when they did not understand his carefully prepared phrases. He had been so apprehensive about the whole adventure that he had cut himself shaving in the shabby bathroom of the Paris hotel where he had stayed the previous night. Now his whole face was sore. He knew the cuts and the redness made him look like a boy with a new beard and he had wanted to look sophisticated and grown-up for these new relatives.

Even though the gatehouse was unattended he decided to leave his heavy suitcases inside rather than carry them up the drive. It was a hot day and he was perspiring in his Brooks Brothers suit. He didn't want to arrive with a scarlet face and smelling of sweat.

The drive was a long one but shaded by trees at either side. He wondered where the grapes were; there was no sign of any

123

here though he had been through miles and miles of carefully tended vineyards on the road from Reims. He trudged on and rounding a bend in the pathway saw before him the house.

It was nowhere near as grand as Champagne D'Or, but it had the old-fashioned turreted look of one of the mysterious Edgar Allan Poe houses that he had once seen in Los Angeles. It was certainly big, with steps up to the front door and a big porch overlooking the drive. He liked the look of it – a solid, proper home.

The front door had a shining knocker made in the shape of a bunch of grapes. He lifted it and let it fall as gently as he could. He did not want to appear to be banging for attention. There was a brief pause, and then the door was opened by a plump but pretty middle-aged woman in a black dress over which she wore a small white apron.

'*Oui, monsieur?*' she said and as she looked at him he could see her eyes widening in surprise.

'*Madame Dupuis, s'il vous plaît,*' he said making himself speak slowly.

She said something in a gabble of French and he shut his eyes trying to work it out. Then she gave an impatient little sigh and said '*Entrez*', followed by more gabbling French.

He moved into the hallway, and someone called from the room at the side of where he stood: 'Who is it, Marie?' and he was thrilled that he understood the words.

'It's a young man, Madame,' the maid said, opening the door to the room. The tall elderly woman who was standing inside came towards him. She had a thin beaky nose and grey hair that escaped in little springing tendrils from her old-fashioned bun. Her eyes were very bright, and her expression alert though she moved slowly as if her bones ached.

'Good afternoon, Madame,' he managed. 'I am looking for Madame Dupuis.'

'I am Madame Dupuis,' she said. She was staring at him, and to his astonishment he saw that her eyes were filling with tears.

'Are you Pierre?' she asked, one hand coming forward to touch him.

He nodded, and delivered his carefully prepared sentence. 'I am your grandson, the son of Jean Paul. But you must excuse me, Madame, my French is very bad.'

She gave a little choking cry, and moved to take him into her arms. She hugged him to her, and to his amazement he found that his own eyes were full of tears as he hugged her in return. Then she stood back, and holding his arms looked at him long and hard. She said something, her voice full of emotion. He thought that maybe she was saying that he looked just like his father.

She then spoke urgently to the hovering maid, who hurried from the room.

'Sit down,' she said, and nodded approvingly when he understood and did so. 'You are welcome,' she told him, pronouncing each syllable carefully. 'I do not speak English, *hélas*.'

'But I am learning French, Madame . . .'

'Please, not Madame,' she said, raising one hand. 'Grandmother. I am your grandmother.'

It was a comforting thought, and they both smiled at each other without speaking.

He could hear other footsteps coming down the hallway. The door that the maid had closed burst open and a young girl clattered impatiently into the room, banging the door behind her. The sight of her was a shock. He caught his breath and felt a surge of excitement as he saw her face. She was wearing an ordinary skirt and blouse and he could see that though she was slight of build her figure was good. But it was her face that so bewitched him. She could have been his own sister. Her eyes were the same deep blue as his own; she shared his long-fringed eyelashes. Like his, her eyebrows stood in two points above the eyes, her nose might just have been a fraction finer than his own, and the chin not quite so pronounced, but they both shared the same full, well-shaped mouth that turned down at the corners giving an expression of melancholy to beauty. He was attracted to her as to his own image.

Madame Dupuis was speaking rapidly to the girl, but so enchanted was he with this feminine vision of himself that he made no attempt to understand what she was saying. The girl listened, her glance downcast. Then she looked up and at him and the hostility in her eyes startled him.

'You are Jean Paul's son?' she said in perfect English.

He nodded.

'My grandmother wants me to welcome you, and tell you

125

how happy she is that you have come to Les Hérissons.' Her tone was flat as she repeated the message, and then she added, her voice suspicious, 'Why have you come to Les Hérissons?'

'To find my family,' he said.

'Your father is not here. He left months ago.'

'I know that. I did not come to find him. I came to find my family.'

'I see.' She turned and repeated what he had said to the elderly woman.

'Who are you?' he asked. 'We must be related. We look so alike.'

'You look exactly like your father,' she said disdainfully. 'I am his brother's daughter. My name is Rosalie. Everyone calls me Allie.'

'Your mother must be Rosie.'

'Yes.'

There was no friendliness in her, and he could see that the grandmother's expression was becoming anxious. She spoke again. The girl listened, her mouth pursed.

'Grandmama is asking if you will stay so that she can get to know you. She wants to know if you have any baggage?'

'I left it at the lodge at the gate.'

The girl nodded. 'We will ask Henri to fetch it,' she said. 'And do you intend to stay?'

'If I may,' he said simply. 'Would you tell your grandmother that I am happy she has welcomed me so kindly. Since my father has disappeared and our business in America no longer exists, I have been uncertain what to do with my life.'

'So you thought you would come for your inheritance here?' the girl said her voice cynical. 'Just as your father did.'

'Yes.' There seemed no point in denying it. Then he added a question: 'You don't like my father?'

She flushed, looked a little ashamed and shook her head.

'I don't like him, either,' he said cheerfully. 'So we do have something in common.' He was smiling at her, willing her to like him, to accept him. 'My father is not a likeable man. But my Uncle Peter, who is, sends you his best wishes.'

She was smiling almost despite herself. 'I liked our Uncle Peter, too,' she told him, and her use of the word 'our' lifted his heart.

126

Madame Dupuis looked relieved as she spoke again. This time he tried to understand, and some of the phrases did come through the Gallic fog, but his new-found cousin was translating as her grandmother spoke.

'She hopes you will stay for as long as you wish. She is sad that my mother, your Aunt Rosie, is not here. She is in America, visiting your own home and Uncle Peter. She says it is astonishing for perhaps you even passed each other mid-Atlantic. She says you are to be given the best room we can find, and then I am to show you Les Hérissons, and that words will not suffice to tell you how happy she is to have her beloved Jean Paul's son under her roof at last.' She made a sharp little jerk of her head to indicate the speech was over.

'Aunt Rosie at Champagne D'Or?' he asked, surprised by the news. 'Uncle Peter will be pleased. He was so lonely there.'

'Why didn't you go there with him?' she asked, her voice inferring that he should have done.

He sighed. 'I hated the house. I didn't want to go back.' It was not the moment for involved explanations.

'I see,' she said, making it clear she didn't see. 'If you are staying,' and she sounded as if she would prefer he did not, 'would you like to look at your room while Henri gets your bags? You can wash and then I'll show you Les Hérissons.'

'I would like that,' he said, meaning it.

She opened the door and as she did so a small brindle bundle, almost crawling on its stomach, came through the door.

'Jessica!' she said, bending to pat the animal. 'Did I shut you out? How rotten of me!'

He could see Jessica was not much more than a puppy; a very timid puppy. He moved to stand next to the girl and bent to scratch between the animal's ears.

'Is she yours?' he asked as the dog wriggled ingratiatingly close to him. 'Why is she so frightened? Who has ill-treated her?' He couldn't control the accusing note in his voice as he bent to pick up the puppy and stroke her. The bitch relaxed in his arms as animals, wild or tame, had always done since he was a small boy, and put her long muzzle along his shoulder.

The room had gone very quiet. He looked up to see that both Madame Dupuis and Allie were looking at him with the strangest expressions on their faces.

127

'What's the matter?' he asked.

'Jessica is frightened of men,' Allie said slowly. 'She runs and hides when she sees men. She tries to bite them. And she makes puddles.'

'Then men must have ill-treated her,' he said. 'Do you know who?'

'No. My mother found her wandering and brought her home. But why isn't she afraid of you?'

'Me?' It seemed a silly question. No animal was afraid of him. 'Why should she be?'

'Because you're a man,' she said irritably.

'Oh, I see.' He laughed. 'Animals and I get along. We always have.' He sat back down on the sofa with the dog on his lap. 'Let's have a look at you, old girl, and see nothing's wrong.'

He carefully felt the dog's body, feeling along the backbone and turning her over to press the soft pink stomach. He then gently tugged on each of her legs. He examined the pads of her paws and finally he looked at her teeth and eyes before putting her back on the floor. 'She's fit enough,' he pronounced. 'She'll get less timid in time.'

Jessica, who had patiently endured his probing, stretched, yawned and curled up in a furry circle at his feet.

'It's amazing,' Allie said softly, looking at him as if he had performed a miracle. 'I suppose you couldn't house-train her?'

'Easily.' He couldn't help sounding confident.

'Marie will be pleased,' the girl said dryly, and he sensed that somehow her attitude to him had completely changed.

It took him three days to house-train Jessica, and Allie said that since he had come, the puppy's personality had gradually changed. She had become more confident; more friendly and even tolerated Henri, Robert and Luke, which came as a relief to all three men.

After a week Pierre realised he was happy. And it dawned on him that he had never been properly happy before in his whole life. When he sat down to meals there was Madame Dupuis, Allie, Miss Emily, who flirted a little with him, and Luke West who was pleased to have another man about the house. He was part of the group and the conversation and it was like belonging to a real family.

Madame Dupuis doted on him, and spoilt him. She had

insisted on giving him a generous allowance though he had nothing to spend it on. He found that he felt young – again for the first time in his life. He was aware of the pleasure of being only twenty and immature enough to be petted and cosseted. Madame insisted that he spent an hour with her every morning in her little parlour while they spoke French. He had to speak French to the staff, and Allie was stern about letting him lapse into English. He found that his ability in the language was growing apace.

'It reminds me of years ago,' Madame Dupuis said the morning a postcard from Rosie arrived from New York. 'When your Aunt Rosie first came from the States she spoke very little French, but as her mother had been a Frenchwoman, from Paris I believe, she had an advantage over you. We used to sit here each day talking, just as you and I do now. And, of course, today she is totally bilingual. It's disgraceful your father didn't teach you your own language.'

'Why did Aunt Rosie come here?' he asked.

'Why?' Madame's voice went drifting off vaguely. 'I don't really remember. She married Clovis of course, and never went away again.'

'But it's such a coincidence that she should come here and my father should go to her old home.'

'Yes, it is, isn't it?' Madame said. 'Maybe they passed like ships in the night as you and Rosie must have passed this time.' She flapped the postcard at him, laughed lightly and added: 'It's amazing the things one forgets as one gets old.'

'Or one chooses to forget,' he said in English.

She gave him a sharp look. 'What was that, *chéri*?'

He shook his head.

'Nothing,' he told her.

Allie couldn't explain this amazing coincidence either.

'I didn't know about anything until your father and Uncle Peter turned up here,' she said when he questioned her one day. They had taken Jessica for a walk and were sitting high on the hill in her favourite place overlooking the wide spread of Les Hérissons. 'I remember Mama once mentioned that she had a brother, and she said he wasn't anything like her. No one here ever talked about your father, though I sort of knew he existed. One night after he and Uncle Peter came when they

129

were having a frightful row I did gather that Mama had known him in America. They'd forgotten I was there and said all sorts of things I didn't understand. But why she came here, I don't know. No one will talk about it. I never even thought about it until your father came. My papa always pretended that Mama was born and bred here. He didn't like the idea of her being an American. I thought it was rather interesting and exciting and that it made me a bit different having an American mother.'

'So she did know him in America,' Pierre said, then asked: 'But why were they having a row?'

She was momentarily silent. 'I can't remember now. Something silly.'

It was, he thought, amazing what bad memories everyone at Les Hérissons had.

'Where do you think my father went?' he asked abruptly.

For a second she had the same trapped, cringing look that came over Jessica when a strange man appeared.

'I have no idea,' she said. 'He just went from here and we were all pleased to see the back of him. My! That reminds me. His Hispano-Suiza is still in the garage. You ought to have it. It's beautiful. Bright yellow.'

Later, he realised that she had deflected him brilliantly from the subject of his father's whereabouts by mention of the highly desirable Hispano-Suiza. It became more and more difficult to ask again. It was blindingly obvious that they were hiding something from him; no one seemed to want to talk about his father. But he didn't particularly want to talk about his father either.

He was learning all the time that there were taboo subjects at Les Hérissons. No one cared to mention the war, and that he could understand. No one had ever said how Allie's father had died and the subject of Jean Paul was partially forbidden. His grandmother told him endless stories of his father as a little boy, but nothing about when he was older. And she declared that she had no idea where he could have vanished to either.

'Of course,' she would excuse herself when Pierre pressed, 'he went to America when he was very young. About your age. I didn't hear from him for many, many years. But he was the most beautiful little boy. Much brighter than his twin. Though Clovis was a kind, hard-working fellow, your father was the clever one with all the charm.'

130

Pierre never told her that he had seen through his father's charm when he was seven years old. And in spite of himself, he enjoyed her stories for they were the stuff of his own roots.

He felt as if he were falling in love with life. He loved the permanence of Les Hérissons with the vines and the cultivated land that went back for generations. He loved the mellow house itself – a house in which generations had been born and died. Everything about it pleased him. The old, comfortable furniture. The stiff portraits and photographs. The good, spicy cooking smells wafting from the kitchen. The way the staff were near to being family friends, but the miraculous way in which everyone kept in their rightful place with not so much as a totter in the wrong direction. There was no pretence at being modern and smart here. This was a home, with an enchanting five-year-old in the nursery who came and sat on his lap at tea time, and whose starchy English nanny saw that she behaved. He loved Madame Dupuis and woke up amazed every day that he had a grandmother who appeared to adore him and who actively sought his company. He liked Luke West who was making him perceive that wine was a wonderful, living thing, and champagne perhaps the most wonderful of all. A perception that his father had never been able to instil in him.

And most of all he loved Allie, his new companion, someone of his age, someone so sensitive and who herself seemed to be relaxed and more content in his company than anyone else's. And when she announced over supper one evening that it was time he saw more of France, he diffidently asked her if she would go to Paris with him.

She was excited by the idea.

'We can stay at Philippe's house on the Ile de la Cité,' she said. 'He wouldn't mind at all. What fun. I shall buy some clothes. Mimi – can I have some money to buy some clothes?'

Their grandmother looked at the ceiling, pained. 'I am for ever giving this child money for clothes and she comes home with books. Will you see that she visits a dress shop this time, Pierre?'

'I will,' he said.

'And don't stay away too long. I shall miss you both.'

The trip was planned with enthusiasm, and once they were on the train he asked her the question that had been troubling him. 'Why,' he said, 'did you hate me so much the day I arrived at Les Hérissons?'

'Because I looked at you, and I saw your father,' she said promptly.

'How odd. I looked at you, and saw myself. It was the strangest feeling.'

She put her head to one side and looked at him thoughtfully.

'Now I only see you,' she said. 'But we are alike. And you're really more like my father. His expression was kinder than Jean Paul's.'

'No one could call my father kind.'

'No. That's true.'

He leaned his head back on the seat.

'You can't imagine how I hated him,' he said softly. 'I was terrified of him when I was little, but then I discovered that as long as I was good and did what he said and acted the little angel I could have anything I wanted. I was the best behaved child you ever saw . . . on the surface. It was worth it just so that I never had to see his terrible smile that was not a smile when he was angry.'

'I remember that smile,' she said. 'It was more like a snarl. A vicious snarl.'

'Yes. But really I was very bad and he never knew it. I always got my own back on him without him knowing. He once poisoned a family of wild cats that I had adopted. They were in his way. They were living in one of his barns. So once he had killed them, I burned down the barn. He never knew it was me. I was too angelic to do things like that. I think the servants suspected, but he never did and they never said because they hated him as much as I did.

'And he had these mistresses. I made their life misery. I'd put snakes in their bed, mice in their hats, and bats in their bedroom. They knew it was me, but they didn't dare tell him because he would never have believed them.' He shook his head in wonderment. 'Apart from the fact that I was his prize possession to be wheeled out and shown off when he had important company, my father was basically uninterested in me. He never even realised I had a sort of power over animals. I wasn't frightened of anything – poisonous snakes, huge spiders, anything. Funnily, he hated snakes and insects. I knew it,

132

and that's why I told him I was going to become an entomologist. He didn't even know what it was.'

'And didn't you really want to be?'

'Yes, I did. At the time. But I think it was because I knew it would annoy him as well. Now it doesn't seem to matter.' He thought about what he was saying and then added: 'Actually, I think I'd rather be a vet.'

'Mimi hopes you'll take over the business eventually,' she said.

And he surprised himself by saying: 'And I might even do that.'

They were silent for a moment, and he saw that she had her eyes closed.

'Are you asleep?' he asked.

'No,' she said. 'Just waiting for you to go on telling me the story of your life. Tell me about your mother.'

'I don't know anything about her. You know she died when I was born. Or at least that's what my father said. Peter said it, too, so maybe it's true. When I was little I used to long to have a mother, but it was a long time before it occurred to me that it was unusual to be brought up by two men. There was always a woman about, a nanny or governess, but they never stayed long. It wasn't a happy house. Peter would never talk about my mother. His face went all tight and strange if I so much as mentioned her, and my father would never answer questions either. Then when I was older and first went to Harvard I began to be less frightened of him. So, I asked some questions about my mother.' He laughed. 'I might as well not have bothered. I asked him what she was like. He said she was an angel, beautiful and gentle and that her parents were schoolteachers from Philadelphia. I didn't believe of word of it. My father wasn't interested in women who were angels.'

'It might be true,' she said comfortingly.

'No. I knew when he was telling lies.'

She took his hand. 'Poor you,' she said. 'It must be awful not to know your mother. I was so lucky with my parents. Not everyone is so fortunate. Tell me some more.'

'There's not much more to tell. Once I got older my father sent me East to school. It got me away from Champagne D'Or, and since then I've been trying to eradicate every trace of my father that's in me. I don't want to burn down any more barns. I don't want to hurt anyone ever again. But there's a lot of him in me still, and I want it out.'

'There can't be,' she said sleepily. 'Jessie would know if there was. So would I. I'm like her. I don't like men much either.'

'Who ill treated you then?' he asked.

She seemed to be thinking about the question. Then she sighed and said: 'No one.' And added: 'I'm going to doze now. Why don't you?'

Pierre had been gone two weeks when Feathers knew for sure that she was being punished for the dreadful wicked lies she had told about being pregnant. She was pretty sure that she *was* pregnant. And there was a prophetic inevitability about it that left her almost resigned to her fate.

She'd worked it out time and time again. After she had told him that she thought she was pregnant, he hadn't been near her until she left him the wicked, lying note. That was one week. Then he started seeing her again, and they made love three times in a fortnight. Then he'd frightened her by staying away for four days before the episode on the beach, but they hadn't made love that night. And she hadn't seen him since. So, that night at Lynn, it was three and a bit weeks since they made love. Then she had not heard from him until the parcel arrived on the Friday – call it another week – and now he had been away for two weeks. It made six weeks since she had seen her period.

She kept telling herself that he had said that sometimes girls were late, and that was probably all it was. It would be too cruel if she were pregnant because no one was going to marry her. If she'd got herself in the family way with an Irish boy from South Boston, like her mother had done, the families would have seen to it that they were decently wed. But no one would be able to force Pierre, and anyway he wasn't here to force.

There wasn't anyone she could tell or talk it over with. Her sisters were too young, and she'd only be a bad example for them. Her mother would sympathise but wouldn't be able to do anything, and her father would kill her.

Every night as she puzzled it out, she went to Pierre's

apartment and sat there quietly, reading a book or just looking out down on to the street below. One night, she opened a bottle of his champagne from the icebox and drank a glass, corking it carefully so that she could have a single glass every night when she came. She did not know why she did it, but it made her feel better.

The apartment became a haven. She hadn't the courage to stay the night because how could she explain where she had been? But she began to leave there later and later.It didn't seem to matter. These days her father never said anything no matter what time she came in. She constantly toyed with the idea of staying at the apartment until Pierre came back as he had suggested. Her quiet evenings there emphasised the squalor of her home. It seemed madness to go back to the South Boston slum every night when she could stay in the peace, elegance and comfort of Pierre's home.

Then when she realised that she must be pregnant, that punishment had struck, and all the prayers in the world wouldn't change a thing, she began to think seriously about leaving home. She couldn't stay there getting fatter and fatter. Her father would guess and what he would do didn't bear thinking about. Her mother had said she should get away and now she had the chance. If she wasn't contributing at home, and not paying rent for a while, she could really save hard. Pierre wasn't coming back yet. Not for at least six weeks, and six weeks seemed a long time in the future to Feathers, aged seventeen. In six weeks anything could happen.

She made no decisions until the night she came home from his apartment to find Kevin in her place in the big bed and Eileen, who was beside him, sobbing quietly. Kathleen, hard against the wall, slept on.

'What are you doing in there?' she asked fiercely, grabbing the boy by the neck of his worn pyjamas and pulling him out of the bed.

'Nothing,' he whined. 'It's just you wake us all up when you come in, so I left you my bed so you could sleep there.'

She didn't believe him.

'Why are you crying, Eileen? What's he done?'

'He kept touching me, Mary. In bad places. He wouldn't stop, and he wanted me to do dirty things to him. He said if I

135

told Dada he'd hurt me more. He's always trying to do it when no one's looking.'

Feathers' hand landed around her brother's ear with all the force she could muster. He began to let out a roar, but her hand clapped over his mouth to silence him.

'You filthy little beast! I shall tell Dada and he'll beat you black and blue,' she hissed.

He was shaking his head, his eyes wide and frightened. She took her hand from his mouth.

'Don't tell Dada, please don't tell Dada,' he begged. 'I swear I'll never do it again.'

Kathleen had woken up.

'What's going on?' she asked sleepily.

'Our brother has been doing dirty things to Eileen,' Feathers whispered. 'Why did you let him in the bed?'

Kathleen was sitting up.

'Mary, Mother of God,' she said. 'He hasn't! He said it was so you could sleep in his bed and not disturb us. Why the sneaky, dirty little —'

'Shh!' Feathers whispered. 'Keep your voice down. Dada would kill him, really kill him. Kathleen, don't you ever let him near Eileen again. And if he touches you, Eileen – scream.'

'I won't do it again,' the boy was whimpering. 'I don't know what made me do it. I'm sorry.'

'You'll be sorrier if you ever do it again,' Feathers said fiercely. 'If Dada doesn't kill you, I will.'

'I won't! I won't!' he protested as she bundled him towards his own truckle bed.

With everyone quiet again and Eileen, still sniffling, at her side, Feathers brooded on the conditions they lived in. Kevin was a filthy little beast, but it wasn't right that a boy of fifteen should be sleeping in a room with his three sisters. It was all wrong, but her parents would never be able to change it. And her coming in so late was what had given him the excuse. There was no point being angry with Kathleen for letting it happen. She herself wouldn't have suspected what was in Kevin's mind if he had suggested to her that he slept in the big bed, leaving his free for her.

She stifled a sigh. At least the two girls were warned now what sort of lad he was growing to be. Together they could deal

136

with him. And if she was not coming home at nights at all there would be no excuse for Kevin to get into the big bed.

She wondered whether she should tell her mother, and decided against it. Her mother had enough troubles. Besides, who was she to tell tales about her brother and call him a filthy little beast when she was pregnant by a man who didn't want her?

But the sordid incident had done one thing. It had made her mind up about leaving home. There wasn't enough room for all of them here, and if she truly was pregnant she would have to leave anyway. Her family could never bear the disgrace.

She had a roof until Pierre came home. A free roof. And when he came back she would have to think again about what she was going to do. But there was always the chance that he would love her as she loved him. She remembered her head on his shoulder that dreadful night on the beach. It felt as if he loved her then. Maybe everything would be all right. It had to be all right somehow, or there would be nothing left to do but kill herself.

If Pierre was happy, Allie was too. The depression which hung over her like a storm cloud seemed to be receding. Her life was suddenly so full of interest that she was neglecting her writing. Pierre's growing fascination with the creating of champagne had revived hers. He and she, along with Luke and Robert, worked together both on the land and in the barns and cellars helping with the various processes which gave the wine its life. It was a beautiful summer, sunny, but cool with a sky full of skudding clouds. The countryside and trees stayed green and bright poppies flecked the cornfields on the other side of the mountain where grapes did not grow. Robert was convinced it would be a vintage year.

The best times were when she, Luke and Pierre spent giggly hours in Rosie's tasting room working half seriously and half tipsily to make their own blends of champagne.

'You're supposed to spit it out when you taste,' Luke, who was the best at blending, would protest. But Pierre, who for a beginner had a surprisingly good 'nose', insisted this was a waste and that swallowing the wine did not impair his taste-buds in the slightest.

'Of course it does,' Luke told him. 'You have a real talent for tasting and blending. You shouldn't let it go to waste.'

Pierre grinned and said: 'If I have it's not surprising. I've been drinking the stuff since I was five years old. By the time I was eight I was in trouble with my father if I couldn't tell the difference between an ordinary Moët and a Dom Perignon. And by the time I was ten I had to be able to spot which was the Bollinger and which was the Krug and know their vintages. I was a great champagne imbiber from a very early age. I liked the taste, so I learned. Also I was terrified of my father.'

'Well, you learned well,' Luke said approvingly. 'I've been in wine all my life and, I can tell you, you're a natural.'

'I suppose it's in the blood,' Pierre said wryly. 'My father would be delighted if he knew that all his efforts had borne fruit.'

Allie hated it when Pierre talked about his father. Any mention of the odious Jean Paul left her awash with guilt. Faced with a conversation that alarmed her, she changed the subject.

'Pierre and I drank a 1906 Taittinger when we were in Paris,' she told Luke. 'We went to the Tour D'Argent and polished off the bottle before we had the duck. We were rather drunk at the end.'

'Paris was fun?' Luke asked.

'Paris was fun,' Allie said, nodding vigorously.

Paris *had* been fun. She had shown Pierre all the tourist musts and he had been impressed by the age and grandeur of the city. They had eaten and drunk well and been royally treated by Philippe's staff at the house on the Ile de la Cité. She had even been persuaded to leave Jessica behind, and with Pierre for company, had not missed her. The weekend reminded her of the times in the past when she had been young and happy in the company of Sebastian.

It was when they were dining at the Tour D'Argent with the romantic view of the Seine curling round the Notre Dame below that she surprised herself by saying as much to Pierre.

'And who is Sebastian?' he asked.

She answered him in her old open, impulsive manner which seemed to be coming back these days: 'He was the son of my mother's lover. He was older than me. He was killed in the war. I adored him, but he liked my mother better than me. Everyone

138

likes my mother better than me. Even you will when she comes home.'

He had put down his fork and was laughing.

'Dear me! Why should I like your mother better than you? I can't think of anyone I could possibly like better than you.'

She looked up at him, amazed.

'Really?' she said.

The laughter had gone, and there was an unnerving look in his eyes as he said: 'Yes. Really.'

She felt herself colour, and quickly went back to cutting up the duck on her plate.

'You haven't met Mama yet,' she said. 'My mother is very special. Very hard to live up to.'

'Then why try?' His voice was casual. 'You don't have to be her or anyone else. You just have to be yourself.'

'I suppose that works if you know who you are,' she said with what even she knew was a theatrical sigh.

'For heaven's sake! You are Allie Dupuis. You have had a lot of tragedy in your life but you will use all that so that one day you will be a famous writer. You are fun to be with, quite, quite beautiful and for some unknown reason you are jealous of your mother.'

'I am not!'

'Oh yes you are. It's obvious every time you mention her. It must be very difficult for her, because it's also obvious that she loves you very much.'

'How can you tell when you've never even met her?' She was aware of sounding petulant and childish. She was also aware there was truth in what he was saying.

'Again from everything you say about her. You love her, too, don't you, when you're not busy being jealous?'

She sighed and capitulated. 'You're right. It's just that she's so effortlessly all the things I want to be. She's beautiful, elegant, clever, enchanting and people just fall in love with her. If the German general in the war hadn't been in love with her —' she stopped short. She was straying onto dangerous ground.

'What would have happened?'

'Oh,' she said hurriedly. 'Everything would have been much more difficult. Even Luke was captivated the minute he saw her and he's years younger than she is, so why shouldn't you feel the same way?'

139

'Would you really mind if I did?' His dark brows, so like her own, were raised into question marks and his face was serious. She felt a strange little sensation in the pit of her stomach as he looked at her.

'I should be used to it,' she said with a nervous little laugh.

'That's not an answer.'

'Of course I should mind,' she said crossly. 'It's so nice to have a friend of my own after all this time.'

He laughed.

'All right,' he said. 'That'll do for the moment.'

Since then they had become almost inseparable. He had taken to calling her 'cousin' in a slightly mocking but affectionate way. She called him cousin in return, and she was to realise in days to come that they were using the word as a defence against what was happening to them.

He sparked an interest in clothes in her when he refused to go out with her one afternoon if she wore one of her old-fashioned dresses that still came down over her ankles.

'You look like someone's grandma,' he complained. 'I am not going into Reims with someone's grandma.'

Amazed at herself for taking any notice, she went back to her room and changed into one of the suits that she had bought in Paris. He had chosen it for her at the Galeries La Fayette. It was a deep blue that brought out the blue of her eyes, and it showed a daring amount of leg. He had said her legs were pretty, better than many he had seen, and the mention of other women's legs made her wonder about his life in Boston. He never spoke of his life in Boston.

Henri dropped them at Rilly station and they went into Reims by train. She wanted to see how the restoration of the city was getting on, and she was wondering whether or not to tell him of the time she and her mother hid in the cellars of Mumm to escape the shelling of the town and for other reasons she tried not to think about. But then he would ask why they had left Les Hérissons and it would all get too complicated. As much as she longed to tell him so many things it was better not to say a word. But she sighed to herself at the secrets she had to keep from him. She felt as if she was tricking him in some way.

He was appalled when he saw the extent of the destruction of the town.

140

'Do you know,' she told him, 'before the war there were nearly fourteen thousand houses in Reims? Guess how many escaped the shelling unscathed?'

They were in the Cours Langlet where huge boulders still littered the street, the battered cathedral forming a backdrop. He looked around him and shook his head.

'Not many,' he said. 'But I can't guess.'

'Twenty-one. Just twenty-one,' she told him solemnly and he whistled gently through his teeth as he looked around at the tottering buildings and huge yawning gaps around him.

'Some American major is replanning the city,' she told him. 'People don't like the idea much. Others say he is doing a good job. One of the Reimois architects says it's only fair since it was a French army officer, Major Lenfant, who was in charge of the construction of your Washington.'

He smiled.

'Is that so?' he said. 'Well, you learn something every day. Come on, let's sit down for a while and talk. I'll buy you a pâtisserie if you like.'

They found a *salon de thé* open on the Rue Gambetta where she drank tea and he asked for a cognac.

'Do you like France?' she asked, intent on stirring her tea. It was a question she had wanted to ask for a long time and she did not want to look at him while he replied, the answer was too important.

'I like it very much,' he said.

'Do you think you'd like to stay?'

'If your grandmother will have me, I would like to very much.'

'What about Harvard and your degree?'

'I could apply for a scholarship to a university here,' he said. 'If I got it, maybe I could go to the Sorbonne.'

'What, to be an entomologist?'

He smiled. 'I don't think so. It's maddening, but I'm beginning to understand my father's fascination with wine. I'm pretty sure he's dead, so I don't need to spite him by being something he doesn't understand.'

Her insides did a flip-flop at what he was saying, but she thought it best to leave well alone.

'Then why don't you go to the School of Oenology in

141

Épernay?' she suggested. 'Mama went there when she came from America. You have to learn all about the insects that attack the vine as well as how to make wine and all the newest methods of improving it. Anyway, you don't need to win a scholarship any more. Grandma will pay for anything you want.'

'But I couldn't expect that.'

'Why not? You are her only grandson. And your father was her favourite.' She couldn't control the note of bitterness in her voice at the thought of Jean Paul.

'Well, that's not my fault,' he said, smiling and taking her hand across the table. 'You mustn't blame me for my father.'

'I don't,' she said. 'Most of the time I forget he is your father.'

'That's good news,' he said, kissing her palm and replacing her hand on the table. Her hand seemed to be tingling, but she said nothing as he took a sip of his cognac.

'I'm happy here, Allie,' he said eventually. 'It's good to have a real family, to feel you belong somewhere. If only Uncle Peter were happy, everything would be perfect.'

'I wouldn't think you'd have the slightest difficulty in persuading Grandmother to let him come here to live,' she told him. 'She'd give you anything.'

Having said it, she had a quick moment of panic. If Uncle Peter came, would that spoil her closeness with Pierre?

'I don't think he'd come,' he said. 'But it would be nice for him to know that he could.'

'As long as *you* stay,' she said impulsively.

'I'll stay – as long as it's all right with your mother.'

'Grandma always has the last word,' Allie told him, 'and anyway, Mama will be back next week.'

'And, of course, I shall fall madly in love with her?' he suggested.

'Of course you will,' she laughed, confident that he would do nothing of the kind.

He called for the bill as she drank the last of her tea. Then he said: 'But I will have to go back and clear things up in Boston. Get rid of the apartment and bring all my things over if I'm going to stay here. Fortunately it's rented, so I don't have any furniture to deal with.'

Again a little moment of panic. Was there anything or anyone in Boston to keep him there when he went back?

'Do you have a girl in Boston?' she asked casually.

'No. No one. No real friends. Nothing to say goodbye to. I was lonely there.'

'And I was lonely here,' she said.

'And now we have each other,' he said, his expression droll, making a joke of the sentiment, but he squeezed her hand as he said it.

She dozed with her head on his shoulder for the short train journey back to Rilly-la-Montagne. She felt safe, content and loved. She wondered what she would do if he tried to kiss her. Would she panic? Or would she be pleased? The thought was too difficult to deal with. She pushed it aside.

Henri was waiting for them at the station, and a little light rain began to fall as they drove the few kilometres back to Les Hérissons. Henri was proceeding up the drive in his usual ponderous fashion and Marie was already at the open door when the accident happened.

Down the steps, frantic with excitement, came Jessica, barking, her fluffy tail waving welcome. She shot along the left side of the car to jump up where Allie sat but where Henri could not see her. As he stopped, he pulled the left-hand side of the car round, and from beneath it came an anguished squealing – and then dreadful silence.

Both Pierre and Allie were instantly out of the car, Pierre flat on his stomach under the machine. It seemed an eternity to Allie before he gently pulled out a limp bundle of brindle fur. Allie, kneeling beside him, clasped her hands in terror, her eyes full of tears. She was moaning gently. Henri, white-faced and shaking, was standing beside them, stammering apologies which neither heard.

'Is she dead?' Allie gasped, her hands now over her mouth.

'Just wait.' Pierre's voice was authoritative. 'Be calm.' He carried the dog to the steps and sat down. His hands were running over the furry body as they had the day he arrived. 'She's breathing,' he said. 'The wheel must have knocked her unconscious.' He touched one of the legs and grunted to himself as Jessica's inert body suddenly twitched. 'And she's broken a leg,' he added. 'Thank God Henri wasn't driving fast.'

'She's all right?' Allie asked frantically. 'She's going to be all right?'

'She's going to be fine, and you can have the vapours once you've brought me one of Cook's wooden spoons and her thickest, strongest kitchen string,' he said, still calm.

So great was Allie's faith in him that she did not even ask what he wanted them for. Marie, hearing his instructions from her vantage point in the hall, ran down towards the kitchen, and Cook was already handing her a ball of string and a wooden spoon by the time Allie came into the kitchen.

She heard a little squeak of pain from Jessica as she made her way back out again.

He was stroking the dog's head gently. 'It's all right,' he said. 'I was just setting her leg. It's fine now. Just give me the spoon and have the string ready.'

With the kitchen equipment he made a rough and ready splint for the broken leg. 'It'll do for the minute,' he said, 'but we'll have to get some plaster.'

Henri, who was still hovering anxious and white-faced, said: 'I'll go to the pharmacy at Chigny right now, Monsieur Dupuis.'

He didn't wait for an answer but hurried back to where the Léon Bollée was parked and set off.

She and Pierre were alone on the steps in the light drizzle. He looked at her and grinned. 'You can have hysterics now if you want,' he said.

'I think I will in a minute,' she said, but now she felt more exhausted than hysterical. 'But how did you know how to do that?'

He shrugged. 'I don't know really. I've always been able to mend animals. Even birds. I used to like birds and animals better than people.'

She was beginning to shake uncontrollably.

'Maybe I will have hysterics,' she said. 'I thought she was dead. I thought I'd lost her. It would have been so awful.'

'Stop shaking and hold her,' he said abruptly, putting the dog into her arms with tender care. 'Sit still and just stroke her. She's still in shock. Marie,' he shouted. 'Can you bring me a large pillow?'

'The one from the dog's bed?' the maid called back.

'That'll do.'

Marie came back with the big square pillow that lay at the bottom of Allie's bed and he carefully lifted Jessica onto it.

'We'll have to stay with her because she mustn't move until we get some plaster over that splint,' he said. 'But she'll be fine. Don't worry.'

Allie couldn't stop the shaking as she looked at him across the pillow. She felt she was bursting with gratitude simply for his presence.

'You are the most amazing man,' she said. 'What would I have done if you hadn't been here?'

'Taken her to the vet,' he said. 'Now relax. It's all over.'

They were both kneeling, their faces the width of the pillow away. She looked at the features so like her own and felt she could drown in the depth of his blue eyes. Imperceptibly she felt herself swaying gently towards him. She wasn't sure if she was going to faint or if she was going to kiss him. And then it seemed that he was swaying towards her. Inevitably their lips met and joined. His hands came to hold her shoulders and pull her nearer to him. And the touching of mouths became a proper kiss that filled her with the strangest, inexplicable longings. It was he who pulled away first, his face grave as he sank back on his heels and looked at her. She remained upright, wondering at the strength of the feelings that were engulfing her. And as they stared at each other, Allie's eye caught the slightest flick of the front parlour curtain. Her grandmother, she realised, had witnessed their kiss.

'It was a very strange honeymoon,' Rosie said, sunk in her usual armchair in Lizzie's little sitting room, her shoes off and her legs outstretched, a glass of champagne in her hand. 'Philippe was marvellous. I don't know what I'd have done without him.'

'I did very little,' he protested. 'In fact, I felt extremely helpless.'

'It was the support that mattered,' she said.

It had taken them ten days to sort out the formalities of Peter's sudden death, and then Philippe had insisted they return to the Websters and New York since Calistoga held little for them.

'The funeral was dreadful,' Rosie sighed. 'We thought we

145

would be the only two there, but the church was crowded. It looked like half the town had turned out. They were whispering and pointing and just horrible. Ghouls!'

'They'd come to get a look at Rosie,' Philippe explained. 'Just curiosity, really.'

'Small town mentality,' Jim Webster said as he refilled their champagne glasses. 'No one would give a toss in New York.' He perched himself on the arm of Lizzie's settee and asked: 'So what are you going to do about the property?'

'We've had it boarded up and made safe,' Philippe said. 'But we can't do anything until we've talked to Jean Paul's son.'

'And, can you imagine!' Rosie added. 'He's gone to Les Hérissons. Apparently to find his grandmother. The complications!'

'Whose property is Champagne D'Or?' Jim Webster, ever the businessman, wanted to know.

'Peter doesn't appear to have made a will, but the lawyer had documents that prove half the house and the original land belonged to Jean Paul, to revert to Peter on his death. If Peter died first, Jean Paul inherited the lot. I was astonished. The documents were made out late in 1899 – just about the time I got to France.' She turned to Jim Webster. 'I suppose Lizzie finally told you that I'd gone off to France looking for Jean Paul? We kept it a secret from you when we met on the train that time.'

'She told me,' he said, nodding.

'Well, Jean Paul must have gone away from our winery for only a short time and come back not long after I left. I guess Pa died in the meantime because the house and land all seemed to belong to Peter then. At least it was Peter who had agreed to signing over half of it to Jean Paul. But I don't want the property anyway. What would I do with it?'

'Sell it,' said Jim Webster promptly, 'and bank the money.'

'Not so simple,' said Philippe. 'If Jean Paul is dead and died before Peter it all belongs to Rosie, and if Jean Paul isn't dead, it's still his.'

'It is the most terrible muddle,' Rosie said. 'You see,' she paused and moved her hands in a little gesture of defeat, 'Jean Paul *is* dead but we can't really tell anybody.'

'He is?' Lizzie said, blue eyes round and questioning.

'He is,' Rosie said, her voice resigned. 'I never told you – or anyone else come to that – because the less people who knew, the better.'

'But how?' Lizzie asked.

As Rosie hesitated, Philippe took over.

'He and Rosie's brother came back to Les Hérissons when Prohibition wiped out their business here. Jean Paul snatched the Les Hérissons business from his brother and Rosie. He had some right to do so. In French law, as a child of the house, he could not be disinherited.'

'It was dreadful,' Rosie murmured. 'He humiliated poor Clovis.'

'And Clovis, who had never been right in the head after the war, killed him,' Philippe said flatly.

'Killed him!' Lizzie obviously couldn't believe her ears. 'Poor simple Clovis killed him. Well, I declare!'

'Clovis caught his brother assaulting Rosie and he lost his head,' Philippe explained. Then added without drama: 'He just picked him up and strangled him.'

Mr Webster was listening, fascinated.

'So how did you get rid of the body?' he asked with the air of a man who accepted that this was the only sensible thing to have done.

'We buried it in the little vineyard where the vine cuttings I had brought from California all those years ago were growing. Jean Paul had been about to tear them up. It seemed appropriate somehow,' Rosie said.

'And what about the police?'

'We never called them,' she said miserably. 'None of us could bear Clovis having to suffer more. We sent all Jean Paul's things back to California, and said he'd gone home. Then we just said that he seemed to have disappeared. We persuaded my poor brother to go along with it.' Rosie got to her feet and began to pace up and down the room. 'It sounds so awful and callous as I tell it now,' she said distractedly, 'but at the time, it seemed the only thing to be done. The tragedy was that just a few weeks after, Clovis died too. I think he committed suicide by throwing himself down a Roman chalk pit on our land. Maybe it was an accident, but in my heart I don't think he could live with the guilt of having killed his brother.' She sat down again, slumped

147

in the chair. 'The whole thing was a nightmare. And now with Peter dead – and all because of what happened in France – the complications just pile up.'

'We have reported Jean Paul missing, presumed dead,' Philippe said. 'The police didn't seem too interested. They knew he was in business with someone called Angelino —'

'Was he now?' interrupted Jim Webster. 'That sounds like your get-out to me.'

'And now Rosie wants to hand the whole lot over to Jean Paul's son,' Philippe said.

'Madness!' said Mr Webster. 'You were probably tricked out of your inheritance in the first place. Why give it away now?'

'For a start, I don't want it,' Rosie said, 'and more practically, if I keep it I have to prove that Jean Paul died before Peter, and that means explaining to the authorities what happened. I wouldn't want Madame Dupuis to have the shame of it being known that Clovis killed his brother. And worse, I'd have to tell Jean Paul's son what really happened to his father. It's best just to let the boy have the California property.'

'Umm.' Mr Webster looked thoughtful. 'But have you thought that if what you say about French law is correct, and Jean Paul was legally entitled to half Les Hérissons, his half should now go to his son? You may find the young man has turned up not to find his grandmother but to lay claim to his inheritance. And that could take a great chunk out of your provisions for your daughters. If you keep your right to the American property, that would become theirs.'

Rosie groaned. 'What do you think, Philippe?'

'I think you need a good lawyer,' he said ruefully.

'And so do I,' said Jim Webster. 'I can fix you up with a first class man in San Francisco.'

Rosie was silent, thinking what did it matter about the property when so many people had died? The property was the least important thing. She wan't going to waste another moment anguishing about bricks and mortar and a leaf-filled mucky green swimming pool. She bent down and put her shoes on. She tucked her feet under the chair and sat, her back straight, her hands in her lap. She was in control of herself and the situation again.

'Nothing needs to be done right now,' she said firmly. 'I

won't make any decisions for a while. And certainly not until we've met Pierre Dupuis. He may have some thoughts on the subject himself.'

'Same old Rosie,' Jim Webster grinned, moving to the ice bucket. 'Here, have a refill and then we'll go on in and have some lunch.'

'Good idea,' she said, proffering her glass. 'I'm hungry,'

Alexander joined them for lunch. He suddenly appeared in the dining room just as they had finished the soup.

Lizzie, who was always complaining that she hardly saw her children now they were grown, gave a little exclamation of pleasure as his fair head came round the door.

'Alexander!' she said, getting up to kiss him. 'How nice to see you. To what do we owe this unexpected visit? I suppose you've come to see Rosie.'

'Just ring the bell for another place to be set,' Mr Webster instructed his wife. 'And sit down, son.'

Alexander looked pleased with life. He kissed Rosie on the cheek and shook Philippe's hand before settling himself beside his mother.

'I have good news.' he said. 'Marvellous news.'

'They're making you the editor?' his father said dryly.

'Not yet, unfortunately. But they are sending me back to France. I told you, Rosie, I was looking for an excuse. I've found one. And not just to France. Actually to Reims itself. Isn't that swell?'

'Good heavens!' Rosie said. 'What's of interest there?'

'Well,' Alexander explained, shaking out the linen napkin that a prompt maid had put before him. 'You remember when I came over as a war correspondent and went through the trenches to the front line? I've never forgotten the destruction and how unbelievable and terrible it was. I'm going back to see how the restorations are going. My editor fell for the idea because it's an American army officer in charge of the rebuilding and replanning.'

'Major Ford?' Rosie said.

'That's right. You know about him?'

'Everyone in Reims knows about him,' Rosie said. 'There's a lot of argument about what he's planning and doing.'

'Exactly,' said Alexander. 'And since Andrew Carnegie is

endowing the new library and Rockefeller's paying for most of the restoration of the cathedral, there's a lot of American interest in what's going on in Reims.'

'You'll find that not everyone thinks the cathedral should be restored,' Rosie said. 'They feel it wouldn't be the real cathedral any more. There's plenty of controversy there for you.'

'That's what I thought,' Alexander said, 'so, I've got a whole three weeks to do the job, and then I propose to take some vacation that I'm owed. If you don't mind, I thought I would travel over with you two.'

'Alexander! Really!' Lizzie said. 'Rosie and Philippe are on honeymoon.'

'It would be a great pleasure for us to have Alexander with us,' Philippe said firmly.

'And of course you'll stay at Les Hérissons,' Rosie said. 'This is marvellous news.'

She could see that Lizzie was pleased. Lizzie still harboured a dream that one day Alexander would get his heart's desire and his heart's desire was Allie. It was a dream that Rosie was happy to go along with, though in her heart she feared that Allie might never permit herself to have a normal relationship with a loving man.

Alexander was pleased, too. As the maid left the room after serving them with fillet steak, he looked straight across the table at Rosie, holding her attention from everyone else.

'Should we tell her I'm coming with you?' he asked earnestly.

Rosie considered it for a moment.

'No,' she said, 'let it be a lovely surprise.'

And she said it, hoping against hope that a lovely surprise was what it would be.

Chapter Six

Pierre was not sure what was happening to him. The slow, delicate kiss he had exchanged with Allie had left him in tumult. In the moment when their lips had met she reminded him of some wild creature – a bird, perhaps – yielding to him. He could not get the kiss out of his mind. And when he remembered it, his loins tightened with the old familiar desire, but a desire that was more complicated than the simple lust he was used to. He felt tenderness, perhaps even love. And these were emotions that for him had been preserved for the creatures of nature – never for a woman.

Pierre at twenty was more sexually experienced than most young men of his age. Throughout his childhood, Champagne D'Or had been a temporary home for the many women that his father took as mistresses. None of them lasted long. They were only permitted in the house when Peter was not at home. When Peter went travelling to sell Champagne D'Or, some new 'Auntie', as Pierre was instructed to call his father's mistresses, would move in. When Peter returned, she disappeared never to be seen again or indeed heard of again. Pierre was not permitted to mention any of these women after they had left. Most particularly not to Uncle Peter. But he intuitively understood from a young age why the women were there. As he grew older, disturbing yet somehow exciting sounds from his father's bedroom confirmed his instincts.

When he was sixteen and home for the vacation from his first Eastern school, Jean Paul arranged for his son to lose his virginity.

The 'auntie' that time was young and blonde. Probably no more than twenty. She was a bone-thin girl with a nervous giggle and a common voice. She was terrified of Jean Paul and therefore slavishly followed his every command. His command one August night was to seduce the young Pierre.

Pierre had been sound asleep when she slipped into his bedroom. He woke to find her in his bed, her clenched hand gently moving up and down his penis. At first he was bewildered, but then the pleasure of what she was doing left no room for anything other than enjoyment. When he was near to exploding she threw back the bedclothes and, kneeling over him, lowered herself slowly onto his erection. With one hand she switched on the bedside light before she began to raise herself gently up and down on him. He found within seconds that his own hips and thighs were making convulsive upward movements, straining to get deeper into her. Then, without losing him, she swivelled round so that her back with its thin row of vertebrae was towards him and their bodies were fused to even greater depth. She rode him, hard, whispering words of encouragement that he could not believe he was hearing, until with a great cry, he came.

'Well done, son!' Shamingly, it was his father's voice. Now Pierre understood why the girl had switched on the light. His father had wished to see whether or not his son performed adequately. His father had wanted to watch.

'I'm proud of you, my boy,' he was saying when he caught sight of Pierre's horrified and embarrassed face. Then he laughed. 'She's yours any time you want her – providing I'm not using her,' he said and strode out of the room.

The girl was still kneeling over him. The shock of seeing his father had killed his erection, and humbly the girl took the hem of the shift she was wearing and wiped him dry. Then she turned round and he saw that she was crying.

'What's the matter?' he stammered. 'Did I hurt you?'

She shook her head, tears streaking her powdered face.

'No, but he did. He can't love me, can he, if he watches me with you?'

'He doesn't love anybody,' he said bitterly. 'Only himself.'

'He loves you.'

'Because he thinks I'm his possession.'

'I wouldn't mind being his possession,' she said sadly, 'if it meant I could stay here for ever.' And he realised she wanted

152

his father's love not for the man but for the wealth and the home that went with him.

His confusion over Allie had made him recall the girl. He hadn't thought about her for years. He couldn't even remember her name. At first he had been angry with both her and his father. Then he stopped being angry with her. He used her, as his father had suggested, for the three weeks she was in the house. But always with his bedroom door locked. He wasn't going to be a peep-show for his father. But it was she who taught him that girls could also get pleasure from lovemaking. She would beg him to do things to her in her breathless little voice. 'Touch my nipples . . . pull them a little. Yes, bite me, bite me . . .' Suddenly he remembered it all. All those early experiments in love. Then she was sent on her way with $300, a generous $100 per week, like all the others were given. There were occasions when his father liked to shower money, claiming it oiled the wheels of life. But before she left, she confessed to Pierre that she liked going with him more than with his father.

'It's better with you,' she said. 'With you it feels like love. With him, when he wants it, I reckon he'd be content with a hole in a barn door. You don't feel like a woman when you go with him, you feel like a hole in a barn door.'

He was mildly shocked by her crudity, but felt a sweep of male triumph that at sixteen years old he was a better lover than his father. And he told himself then that he'd never treat women in the way his father did. Ever since, though love had never got in the way of lust, he prided himself that no woman who had slept with him would guess that he felt nothing for her. And this rejection of his father's methods had given a bonus. Women – his father's whores, who were always on loan when he was home, or those he found for himself – gave themselves to him with affection.

That girl had perhaps come from the same squalid background as Feathers. Remembering Mary O'Flanagan, he felt a pang of shame. He had been untrue to himself the night he had tried to force Feathers. He still felt bad about it even though he had done his best to make it up to her. The loan of his apartment could, with luck, change her life and that would absolve his conscience. Being still only twenty, he had not thought his gesture through to the point of realising that the offer could prove to be no more than a short stay of execution. He wondered if she had moved in. If she had, he reminded himself, she would have to be told when he was coming home.

But for now, all he really wanted was to be with Allie. He thought about her all the time. He kept himself from sleep by concocting fantasies of them together in erotic and romantic situations. In the mornings he tried to laugh away his youthful dreams. He was, he feared, in love. But since he suspected that the feeling might be reciprocated his only real problem was finding the courage to kiss her again. He was amazed at himself. He, the master of so many conquests, was afraid to kiss his own cousin in case it spoilt what was growing between them.

They spent most of their days sitting with Jessica who appeared to be mending well. Pierre had insisted that the local vet check his work, and the vet had been gratifyingly impressed. Five days after that magic kiss, he suggested that Allie came for a walk with him. The dog was sleeping deeply in a basket on the porch. She nodded without speaking, looked anxiously at her pet and, finger on lips, tiptoed down the steps to the drive.

'Don't wake her,' she whispered.

They had eaten supper, but it was still light. Gnats buzzed in the trees around the house, and already it was a hot, humid night. All day the sun had blazed. According to Robert, the heat had come just at the right time to hurry the *vendange* along.

They slid into the woods and without any discussion made their way to Allie's favourite place at the top of the hill. There they sat down and silently regarded the view.

'It is beautiful, isn't it?' she said dreamily. He did not reply. No reply seemed needed. She was lying on her stomach, resting on her elbows, her chin in her hands. He sat beside her, his arms round his knees. He could see the curve of her breast beneath the open neck of the dress she wore. He longed to touch her, but was afraid.

'I suppose Mama will be home in a few days,' she said. 'You know, I wouldn't be at all surprised if she's married Philippe while she was away.'

'Without telling you?'

'Well, none of us was very nice about her marrying him

when she told us. It was so soon after Papa died.' She was silent for a moment, staring down to the vineyard below. 'Perhaps we weren't fair. I found out afterwards that he had a mistress. It was the local brothel keeper. She's fat and pink and awful. It upset me terribly. Particularly when she told me she'd seen him the day he died. She made me sit with her in a *salon de thé* in Épernay, and she said such strange things. I was so upset I didn't ask her enough questions. I wish now I had. I didn't understand a lot of what she was saying.' She paused, rolled over to sit up and then blurted out: 'If I went to see her again, would you come with me?'

'Of course I would,' he said.

'I can tell you. I can talk to you about it because you're family. I couldn't tell anyone else. I keep thinking about it. I hate the idea of him being with that woman. Mama must have hated it, too.'

'My father had dozens of mistresses,' he volunteered.

'Didn't you hate it? I hate it.'

'I didn't really care one way or the other. Some of them were nice to me when I got older.'

'How do you mean "nice"?' she asked in a tone of deep suspicion.

He laughed. 'Just kind,' he said, lying. 'Why, would you mind?' He had reached to take her hand.

'It wouldn't be my business,' she said with a touch of her old, stiff manner.

'Wouldn't it?' He was making small circles with his finger on the palm of her hand.

'No,' she said, but her voice was uncertain.

He lifted her hand to his mouth and kissed the palm, and then he gently bit her index finger.

'You have very pretty little hands,' he said, 'and a beautiful face.'

'You said it was just like yours,' she told him, attempting light-heartedness, but her voice was not altogether under control.

The yearning was becoming stronger. If he didn't kiss her, he felt he would die, but some instinct told him to do nothing rash. It was as if she was fluttering like an uncertain bird; afraid to stay with him and yet not wanting to go.

155

'Did you mind me kissing you the other day?' he asked.

She shook her head. 'No, but I think Grandma saw us.'

He thought about the implications of that. 'Did she say anything?'

'No, but it seems to me that she watches us now.'

He nodded slowly, thinking they would have to be careful.

'Have you ever been kissed before?' he asked, wanting desperately to know.

'Someone tried once, but I didn't like it.'

'Sebastian?'

'No. I was still only a little girl when he died.'

'Who?'

'It doesn't matter.'

He could tell by her tone that she was not going to tell him.

'Did you like it when I kissed you?'

To his delight she turned to look straight at him, her blue eyes candid. 'I liked it very much,' she said simply. 'But perhaps I shouldn't tell you.'

He groaned and wrapped his arms round her, gently pulling her close to him.

'Allie, I want to kiss you again,' he said. 'I want to very much.'

'Then why don't you?' she whispered.

He breathed a long sigh, and pushing her backwards so that her head was on the grass, he very carefully placed his mouth over hers. At first he gave her tiny little kisses, and when her mouth clung to his he gently tried to part it with his tongue. She instantly stiffened.

'It's all right,' he whispered. 'I won't do anything you don't like.'

They lay together on the grass, while he indulged her with long clinging kisses. He could feel her breath was coming faster and she was pressing closer to him. He began to worry that she would feel how aroused he was and that it would frighten her.

In a while, with delicate care, he let his hand slide up over her waist until he was cupping one of her full breasts. She stirred uneasily but did not push him away until he let the palm of his hand make small circles on her breast. Her nipple was standing upright and hard, but she moaned and pulled away.

'Oh, Pierre.' She had closed her own hands over her breasts. 'I feel so strange. I want to let you do what you like, but I'm frightened. I think I'll always be frightened.'

'You mustn't be frightened of me,' he said urgently.

'It's not you. It's men. It's all this . . .' her hands opened to throw away his lovemaking.

'Allie, darling, what is all this about men?' he asked, stroking her hair.

'I can't tell you.' Her voice was muffled.

'If you can't tell me, I can't help you.'

'Do you want to help me?'

'More than anything in the world.'

She suddenly clung to him, her arms tight round his neck.

'Oh, Pierre, I've needed help for such a long time. Everyone's tried to do their best, but nothing worked, I felt so much anger, so much hatred until you came. Because you don't know what happened, you didn't humour me. You made me see how mean I am about my mother. You've made me see so many things. But you won't want me if you know the truth about me. Nobody could possibly want me.'

'I suppose you're trying to tell me that you're not a virgin,' he said, keeping his voice calm though the disappointment was hard to bear.

'I'm not a virgin.' Her voice was dismal.

'A girl who's not a virgin but never been kissed.'

'Yes.'

'I don't really understand. And it doesn't matter if you're not a virgin. It's just hard to think that you've loved someone before.'

'I've never loved anyone in a grown-up way,' she said indignantly. 'Oh, Pierre, I can't tell you. I really can't tell you. It would kill me to tell you.'

She had begun to cry stormily, and he held her close.

'Tell me when you're ready,' he said, amazed at his own patience. 'And now we'll go for a walk and we won't talk about it any more.'

He found his handkerchief and gave it to her. She blew her nose and sniffed a couple of times which made him smile, and then she said: 'I've thought of a way to tell you, but you'll have to be patient. Is that all right?'

157

'That's fine,' he said. 'Now come on, we'll walk a bit further before it gets dark.'

He took her arm and she let her head fall on his shoulder as they walked. He wanted her but there was no way he could bring himself to pressurise her. His uneasy feeling that he loved her grew. Was it permitted to love a cousin? He didn't know. What he did know was that he felt the most awful blinding hatred for the man who had taken her virginity without even kissing her.

Luke West had been watching the romance between Allie and Pierre grow with an amused and tolerant eye. The boy had been at Les Hérissons only a short time and yet he had completely changed the girl. Now there were only rare flashes of sullenness and suspicion. She had become light-hearted and he could see what Miss meant about the young girl she had been.

Miss had spotted it, too. She thought it was lovely and sighed romantic sighs as she watched them. Everyone watched them but they didn't seem to notice.

'Can cousins marry in France?' Miss asked him.

Luke didn't know. 'But it's a bit early to be planning the wedding,' he said.

'I'll bet you five francs that they do marry,' she said confidently. 'They are obviously dotty about each other.'

'He's still only a kid. A bit young for marriage.'

'A very grown-up kid,' Miss remarked, sounding as if she wouldn't mind some dalliance there herself.

Luke liked the boy. He was remarkably sensitive for a twenty-year-old, much more sensitive that he himself had been, Luke thought ruefully. Pierre was also extremely bright. His education had taken, and privately Luke thought it a great shame that the boy was making no plans to go back to university. He seemed besotted with not only Allie, but Les Hérissons and all its inhabitants. He must have had a lousy childhood to become so enamoured of a completely strange and foreign family so quickly.

It seemed that Madame Dupuis had also been watching her two grandchildren. One night after supper when the young couple were on the porch of the house with the wounded Jessica, Madame asked Luke if he would sit with her for a while.

She asked how the work was going and then said: 'My

158

daughter-in-law will be back sometime in the next few days. I'm not sure exactly when. But she promised to be in time for the *vendange*.'

'It's getting near time,' he said.

'I know. If she doesn't return, could you manage?'

Her words alarmed him.

'You mean she might not come back?' He had to try not to sound anxious.

'Oh no, she'll be back,' Madame said, 'but I'm never surprised if Rosie doesn't turn up when she says she will. She does things on impulse. But she'll let us know. She always does. And, of course, once she marries Philippe Lefevre we shall have to get used to her not being around the place.'

'Marries Philippe Lefevre?' he said, astonished.

'Yes. They are to marry soon and set up their own establishment.'

So that was why Rosie was moving from Les Hérissons. He had to adjust to the news. He felt winded, as if a boulder had fallen on his stomach muscles.

'I see,' was all he managed.

'It won't make any difference to you,' she said kindly. 'In fact, the house is getting rather too crowded. We'll all be more comfortable once Rosie gets her own home. Also I shall insist that Allie goes with her.'

He was surprised again. Madame so obviously adored Allie that his guess would have been that she would have fought to keep her at Les Hérissons.

'Is it your impression,' she went on, 'that my two grandchildren are getting a little too fond of each other?'

'They seem very content in each other's company,' he said cautiously.

'I should be glad, Mr West, if you would try to keep them occupied apart from each other.'

'That would be very difficult, Madame,' he protested, one part of his mind still on the news that Rosie was to marry Philippe Lefevre.

'Why?' she asked in her calm, autocratic way.

'Because what they do is nothing to do with me.'

'Take him under your wing. Teach him the business. Keep him occupied.'

'I'll try, but I can't promise. Aren't you happy about their friendship?'

'If it is a friendship, I am delighted. If it is anything more, it must stop.'

Her vehemence puzzled him.

'Is it not legal for cousins to marry in France?'

'I have no idea. But these cousins are most certainly not marrying. I will not have it. Enough of that. I am sure you will do your best to help the situation. Now tell me when you think the *vendange* will begin.'

He excused himself at about nine thirty and went onto the porch to smoke a last pipe. Jessica was asleep in her bed and there was no sign of the young ones, as he thought of them. He had already made up his mind that he would not interfere in that situation. For now he wanted to examine his reactions to the idea of Rosie marrying Philippe. It wasn't right, he felt. A woman of her vitality and attraction shouldn't be married to a blind man, albeit a charming blind man. She needed more support than Philippe could give her. And then it occurred to him that Rosie was quite capable of providing her own support. Perhaps she preferred someone who needed her.

It seemed that his fantasies would not come true. But he wouldn't let go of them that easily. Something might happen. Perhaps he could make something happen. He had a surge of pure lust thinking of Rosie, her mouth, her scent, her eyes and her seductive body. But it wasn't only lust that troubled him. Sometimes Luke ached for love lost, ached to fill the gap in his life. He had half hoped that Rosie would be the woman to fill that gap. In the growing darkness he shrugged and blew smoke up into the clear night, telling himself that in matters of the heart he never got it right.

For now, he could hear the governess's crisp footsteps coming down the hall towards the porch. She was undoubtedly going for her habitual walk down to the gates before she went to bed. He thought he might join her. He thought he might take up the invitations that she had been throwing out with a great lack of subtlety. He might even join her in bed. After all, any port in a storm, he thought.

In the short time they had known each other, he and Miss had formed an easy kind of friendship. They were much of an age and background, and both were socially adept. It was a friendship that he realised Emily hoped might develop. She was thirty-two. It was time she settled down. And he, Luke West, was available. For that reason he had been careful to ignore the signals that she had been giving him. But maybe this warm, scented August night he would change his mind.

He went back into the house just as she was coming towards the front door. She stopped, and reddened slightly at the sight of him.

'Going for a walk?' he asked.

She nodded.

'Can I join you?'

She smiled and nodded again, and he thought that she really was an attractive enough woman. He took her arm, and remembering the stone seat set among the vines, said: 'Let's go out the back way.' They were a little old for courting on the grass, he thought, amused by the idea.

She hesitated for a moment, almost seemed to pull away; then she said, her voice low: 'If you like.'

He led her out through the back door of the house and into the courtyard, and he noted that she gave an uncontrollable little shudder as they crossed it before walking straight across to the gravel path at the side of the grapes.

'I've not been this way since I came back,' she muttered as if talking to herself.

She was definitely ill at ease, and it wasn't his presence causing her nervousness. He said nothing until they came to the carved stone seat at the end of the gravel path, then asked: 'Want to sit for a minute?'

'Yes, please,' she said, looking around nervously. It was obvious that this was not perhaps the moment to try to kiss her. Putting the thought from his mind, he took his pipe from his pocket, stuffed it full of tobacco and, once it was lit, contentedly blew smoke into the still air.

'Do you like it here?' he asked her idly.

'It's not the same as last time,' she began cautiously.

'Things never are. What was it like last time?'

She thought about it. 'Sort of happier in a way. You're a happy person, aren't you? It's lucky you're here. You make it happier.'

161

'I decided a long time ago there wasn't any bonus in being miserable. It's the easiest thing in the world to be miserable. I supposed I've trained myself out of it.'

She nodded.

'I'm not often miserable,' she said, 'I sort of *talk* myself out of it. Do you think it's being English? We're not a very dramatic lot, are we?'

'Not us middle-class stiff-upper-lip types,' he said with a chuckle. 'But the working classes love a bit of drama. Breaks the monotony. They could do with a bit of drama around here.'

She shivered.

'I think they perhaps had enough to last them for life in the war,' she said. She paused, and then added: 'That's probably why Allie's so difficult.'

She was sitting still and tense in the darkness. There was definitely something on her mind. Luke, by nature a sympathetic man, had a strong instinct that she needed to talk.

'What happened?' he asked gently, his pipe smoke drifting into the night. 'Do you want to talk about it?'

She hesitated. 'I don't know whether I should talk about it, but it's been most terribly on my mind since I've been back here,' she said slowly. 'I think perhaps I need to talk about it, but it's so many people's secret . . . not just mine . . . we were all involved . . .'

He said nothing, not wanting to pressurise her. It was best to let her make her own decisions; at heart, he would anyway just as soon not be burdened with other people's secrets.

Eventually she made her decision, sighed deeply, and then said, her voice so low that he had to strain to hear: 'It was September 1915 when it happened. The Germans came. They took over this house. There was a general who wasn't a bad old buffer, but he had a lieutenant who was strange and frightening. He was very blond with light blue eyes and horrible red mouth. You could see there was something wrong about him.'

She stopped.

He waited, letting smoke drift into the air.

'We all knew he was after Allie, and none of us ever left her alone for a minute. We didn't plan it or do it consciously, but we all knew instinctively that we musn't let him be alone with her. He tried to take little girls in the village, but the village knew about him, too. Everyone was frightened for their children.

'Then one day, it was the twelfth of September, I was in the house and I heard a terrible scream. I rushed out from the schoolroom and was at the top of the stairs when I saw Madame Dupuis and Madame Rosie running through the hall. I don't know why, but I didn't do anything. I just went downstairs and through to the kitchen. I think I was frightened. I should have done something, but I didn't.' She was speaking faster now, and shivering. 'I just stood there pretending I didn't know what to do. I suppose I didn't know what to do. Cook was in her big larder and hadn't heard anything. Then Madame Dupuis came back with Allie. She was only just fifteen. Her clothes were torn and she had blood all down her legs and she was sobbing hysterically. Cook came out from the larder to see what was going on, and Madame Dupuis told us to get out to the shed in the courtyard. Help was needed. She said not to rush in case the Germans saw us and realised something was wrong.

'I didn't have any idea of what I was going to see but when we got in the shed, it was horrible.' She was crying softly, and he moved to take her hand in his as he listened. 'The lieutenant was dead. He had a pitchfork stuck in his back. Madame Rosie had killed him.' She faltered and then said painfully: 'Perhaps I shouldn't tell you, but he had been raping Allie.'

She stopped to catch her breath. He said nothing but sat in the darkness with the gentle scent of the vines around them, holding her hand and thinking about what he had heard. Rosie, gallant Rosie, had killed her daughter's ravisher. He felt a sort of satisfied triumph. It was exactly what he would have expected her to have done. She had dealt out instant, unequivocal justice. 'Serve the bastard right!' he found himself thinking savagely and yet with pleasure.

'I was dreadfully sick and so ashamed to be so weak, but I couldn't help it,' Emily went on. 'Cook was fine. She just pulled the pitchfork out of his back and said there wasn't any point wasting it. She'd clean it up. I was nearly sick again.

'I knew that the Germans would shoot us all if they found he was dead. I pulled myself together. I remember thinking that I was British and I mustn't let the French be braver than me. I suggested that we put his body in a wine barrel to hide him.

163

Then Cook said something about getting him into her kitchen and she'd cut him in pieces and get rid of his head so that no one would ever recognise him. It was barbaric. Madame Rosie was white as a sheet, but very calm. The three of us somehow stuffed him into a barrel. God knows how we did it, but we did. Cook wouldn't let us use a clean barrel, I remember. I kept feeling we ought to put him in a clean barrel.

'And then I said something awful and cruel. I offered to wash the blood off the floor. "It's a dead giveaway," I said and when I'd said it I wanted to laugh. I suppose I was nearly hysterical.' She sat quietly for a moment. 'That was it really. Cook chopped up his body and Henri took the pieces up the hill for the foxes. The general looked for him, but not very hard. They pulled out that night. The French drove them back.' Her voice trailed away. 'I've never talked about it, ever. But being back here made me remember it all. Not that I've ever forgotten it, just buried it at the back of my mind. He was very young, the lieutenant.'

'Better men died,' Luke said, his voice sombre. His pipe had gone out and he relit it carefully thinking with awe of the courage of women. 'You were all very brave.'

'I suppose we were, really. Four woman faced with the reality of war. But it was Cook who upset me most in the end,' she said, painfully remembering. 'I kept thinking of her chopping up that young German, as beastly as he was, in our kitchen and I couldn't eat anything that came from there. I kept thinking it would be tainted with his blood. So I abandoned Allie. I went home. But I told myself I was going back to do more for the war effort, and I guess I did in the end. But I've always thought I should have stayed with her.'

'Can you eat here now?' he asked gently.

'It's odd, I had no appetite for the first couple of days I was here. I told myself it was the change of food. But I suppose that's what it was. Yes, I can eat now. It's over now.' She sighed a long, quavering sigh and rubbed her knuckles under her eyes. 'I don't know if I should have told you all that. It's everyone's secret really. And yet we never ever mentioned it. It was as if it never happened.' She was silent for a moment, and then said: 'I don't know why I told you. Perhaps because you're English.'

'You told me because you needed to tell someone. You'll feel

164

better about it now you have. And it does explain much about Allie.'

She sighed. 'I've wanted to ask her about it so many times. I think she should talk about it, too. But she won't. There's such a wall around her. I can't get through to her any more. If you'd known her when she was young, before it all happened, she was such a delight. She's another casualty of that dreadful war.'

'And she's not the only one who hasn't come to terms with its effects,' he said. 'Maybe young Pierre will help her,' he added, but wondering privately if a boy that young could himself come to terms with the knowledge of the rape of the girl he loved.

Emily was silent again for a moment as she thought about what he had said. And then he kissed her, but only like a brother, on her forehead.

She sighed.

'Do you know,' she said. 'I think you're right. I think I feel happier already.'

'Good,' he said, playing the hearty Englishman. 'Now, let's have this walk.'

As he helped her to her feet and handed her his handkerchief, he smiled to himself. It was not the moment for seduction, and perhaps, all things considered, it was just as well. It probably hadn't been a good idea in the first place.

Allie did not make him wait long. That night, just five minutes after they had parted with chaste kisses on the cheek, there was a soft rap on his bedroom door. Allie was outside looking white and scared. She held a school exercise book in her hand.

'I want you to have this and read it,' she said without any preliminaries. 'Don't read the beginning – it's all little girl stuff. But there are some pages stuck together at the edges. Open them. It's from there I want you to read. Then you'll understand.'

She thrust the book into his hand and hurried away from him back in the direction of her own room.

He shut the door and went to sit at the desk by the window. He looked at the exercise book. Written on the cover in the most careful of childish ornate lettering was 'MY DIARY, by Mademoiselle Rosalie Marie Dupuis, Les Hérissons, Chigny-les-Roses, Champagne, France, The World, The Universe'. The words made him smile.

In spite of her instructions he read from the beginning. She had started her diary on board a ship bound for America, and it seemed had almost caught her legendary mother in bed with Philippe Lefevre. He smiled again. The significance of the incident had escaped the fourteen-year-old Allie, though it had disturbed her. It would not have escaped him at the same age. He had caught his father too often in compromising situations.

Her diary was charming. Her impressions of her first visit to New York were fresh and observant, her descriptions of people droll. He could understand why she wanted to be a writer. When he came to the pages describing the effect of the war on their lives, he found himself moved by her word pictures of the carnage in the champagne fields and the humiliation of having the Germans take over her home. As he read, he realised that she had given him her life, set down in this child's exercise book.

The pages that were stuck together were not easy to open. He finally achieved it by gently rolling a thin pencil between them. The paper tore at the edges as they separated, but the words were still readable and here, he noticed, her handwriting changed dramatically. Elsewhere the book had been written with the same care as the words on the cover. Now the writing degenerated into a spiky, angry scrawl. And what followed shocked him profoundly.

She had written little about what she had not been able to bring herself to tell him. It seemed she could not bear to write of it either. All she had set down was: 'The filthy, odious lieutenant did something so dreadful and disgusting to me today that I shall never, never in my whole life forget it. Mama killed him with a pitchfork while he was on top of me. I'm glad he is dead. He will never do it to anyone again.'

There followed pages and pages of her pain and grief and terror of life. Fears for a ruined future. 'Mama explained that love is not like that,' she wrote, 'but how can I believe her? What else can she say? Men are revolting. The German has made me as filthy as he was himself. I am soiled, right through. There is no part of me that is clean any more, and no way that I can ever be washed clean of the stain that he has left deep in me. I am dirty and no one will ever want to touch me if they know the truth.'

He found his eyes were full of tears as he read her words. He was also wishing passionately that Rosie had not killed the man. If the man were not dead, he would have found him and destroyed him himself. But as he raged at the thought of the violation of his Allie, there was a worm of conscience stirring in him that grew to a seering guilt for man's inhumanity to woman. He knew too much of it. His father's cruelties – indeed, his own. He had been so near to raping Feathers. But Feathers was not Allie. Whatever had happened to Allie, however much she was hurt and disturbed, she, he knew, was chaste and untouched, and he would, he *must*, convince her of this. What had happened was nothing to do with her. She had no part of it. And when he and she made love when they were married – because that was what he wanted – he would be the first man she knew, the *true* first and he would wipe away all her grief and fears with his love.

He read on, aching at how she had bottled up feelings, unable to share her misery with anyone. Small things touched him and brought tears to his eyes again.

'Miss is going home. She helped get rid of his body. She has never said a word, but she knows and is kind and I shall miss her so much. If only Papa remembered me it would help. He knows nothing of it. Mama and Mimi are so strong. I need someone weak and silly who will cry with me.'

Then later: 'I find I cannot cry.'

The shock came a few pages on where the diary ended. As he turned the last page, he realised that she had torn out the remainder of the exercise book. All that was left for him to read were the shattering words: 'The most unbelievably dreadful thing has happened. I am going to have a baby.'

And then there was no more.

As the shock waves subsided, he closed the book and leaned on the desk, his head in his hands, thinking. A baby? Then where was the baby? Had she got rid of it? What had happened? If she wanted him to know everything, why had she torn out the rest of the pages? Did he mind if she had a baby, tangible evidence of the terrible thing that had happened to her? And if he was to accept the rape as none of her responsibility, where did this leave his emotions, knowing that there was a child?

He knew there was no way he could possibly wait until the

morning to console Allie and, more pressing, to learn the end of this tragic story. Sleep would be impossible, and he was convinced that she would be lying awake also, wondering what his reactions to her scribbled revelations would be.

He was still dressed, so any movement about the house would look normal enough. He quietly let himself out of his room and took the landing passage to where Allie slept. As he had guessed, a light burned round the edges of her door, and he tapped as gently as he could. Her mother's empty room was beside hers and it was fortunate, he thought, that their grandmother slept in another part of the house.

The door opened instantly, and she was standing there wrapped in a lightweight blue robe, her face anxious.

'Can I come in?' he whispered.

She nodded, and as he slipped through the doorway she shut it behind him.

He had never been in her room before. It was like a child's room, cluttered with soft toys and treasures: a pot of dying poppies sat on her desk; photographs of her father – physically so like his own – were stuck in her mirror frame; and there were books piled everywhere. Jessica opened a sleepy eye from her basket at the foot of the bed as he came in, decided he was friend not foe, and slept again.

Without speaking he gave her back her book. She took it, her hand shaking a little.

'Well,' she said, 'do you understand now?' Her head was bowed, and she had turned away from him. He thought she might be crying. 'I don't want to talk about it, you know. There's no need for that. Now you know and that's enough.'

'If you don't want to talk about it we won't, but I want you to understand that I love you very much,' he said roughly, suddenly terrified of saying the wrong thing. 'You'll think me wicked and cruel, but I could not help being glad that when we make love I would be the first man in your life. I had feared that you loved someone else once. And I want to be the only man you've ever really loved. I want to be the only man ever to touch you and kiss you and hold you.'

'It's too late for that now,' she said miserably, her face still averted.

'Did he kiss you?' he asked her, and stepped forward to take her in his arms. 'Did he kiss you like this?'

He smothered her face with gentle, loving kisses, stroking her hair and holding her close while he did so.

'Well, did he?' he asked, drawing back.

She shook her head, her face serious.

'And did he hold you in his arms and tell you he loved you? Did he worship the way your eyes shine, and the curve of your beautiful breasts?'

'No,' she said, her voice low.

'What he did was nothing to do with love.' He was trying not to shout. He wanted to shout. 'You were assaulted as surely as if he had shot you or beaten you. It had nothing to do with love between two people, Allie. Why do you blame yourself? Why do you think yourself unclean? You are chaste. Truly pure. What you don't understand is that for a man who loves you as I do, the knowledge you've given me only makes for terrible anger. I wanted to kill him. I wished your mother hadn't already done it. I wanted vengeance for you. But I still wanted you.'

She did not speak, but she was relaxed against him as he stood with his arms round her; all tension gone.

'The trouble with you,' he said lightly, feeling it was time for the mood to change, 'is that you see things in black and white, as if you're writing one of your stories. It's true, men can be cruel. Millions of women have been raped over the years, Allie, but my guess is that most of them don't let it ruin their lives.'

'But how could anyone ever forget it?' she whispered, shuddering.

'Why try to forget it? Just try to live with it. Though,' he added tenderly, 'I do have plans to make you forget it.'

She rested her head on his shoulder.

'You are wise,' she sighed.

He did not reply, just held her close and let her cry a little. Was he wise? Perhaps life with his father had taught him more than he realised. Perhaps the experience had not been all bad.

He manoeuvred her gently towards the bed, sat her down and then sat himself in her armchair.

'And now you have to fill in the end of the story,' he said. 'Why did you tear out the rest of the pages?'

She looked very beautiful and very young, he thought, her

eyes still glistening with tears, the soft blue shapeless robe pulled round her, her bare feet on the bedside carpet.

'Because if you went away, or stopped loving me because of *that*, I didn't want you to know the rest. It wouldn't have been fair.'

'Fair on who?'

'Mama and Rosanne.'

Light was painfully dawning. 'Do you mean that Rosanne is your daughter?'

She nodded. 'Mimi and Mother said the only thing to do was to pretend she was Mama's. So Mama and I went away and lived in the champagne cellars in Reims until she was born. Then we came back again and Mama told everyone the baby was hers.'

'Did you mind?' he asked, trying to analyse if he himself minded. Now he knew the truth it seemed so obvious. But obvious or not, for Rosanne to be Allie's child was hard to accept.

'Mind!' she said passionately. 'I mind every day of my life. At first I could have torn it out of me. I was terrified it would be like the lieutenant. He was so horrible. I just couldn't stop thinking it would be like him . . . blonde, blue-eyed and with that horrible horrible red mouth. I just wanted to die without seeing it. I hoped it would die when it was born. I tried to kill it when it was born. I wouldn't help, I wouldn't feed it. I wouldn't do anything. I thought I'd die myself from the pain. But then she came. So pretty, and Mama said she looked just like me. And she was a girl and not a boy, and she was dark and not blonde, and she was just my baby and nothing to do with all that filth and dreadfulness. But I wasn't allowed to have her. I'll never be allowed to have her. She loves me, but it's Mama she loves best. It's Mama she calls Mama. And now I can never tell her she's mine because it wouldn't be fair and because it's too late.'

She was crying softly again, and he moved to sit beside her.

'Grandma said there was no reason why sisters can't show each other lots of affection, but I could never get it right somehow. I wanted so much to shout that she was mine, and because I couldn't, I just sort of ignored her when anyone was about. I know Mama and Grandmother think I'm awful, but I couldn't

170

help it. Mama understands how I feel, but she can't help taking over Rosanne. She adores her, and she's lucky, she can show it. But Rosanne isn't hers. She's mine, mine, mine . . .' She beat at her breast with her fist. 'Mine, and no one knows it.

'I do now,' he said.

His voice seemed to calm her.

'Yes.' She thought and then asked: 'Do you mind?'

'I don't know,' he said honestly. 'But I do know that I love you and I want to marry you.'

'I love you, too,' she said. 'But marriage? I don't expect I'll be cured and right again all at once. I'm not always easy to be with, Pierre. I'm just so glad you didn't see how I was before you came. I wasn't very nice.'

'But then you weren't you,' he said gently.

'Who knows?' She turned to look him full in the face and asked: 'Are you always kind like this?'

It was a difficult question.

'No.' Again he felt only honesty would do. 'I can be cruel. But I don't think I'll ever be cruel to you.'

She sighed.

'Pierre,' she said, sounding about fifteen. 'Suddenly I'm so tired. I wish I could go to sleep in your arms, but I think perhaps we should talk some more tomorrow. If Grandma caught us together, she'd kill us.'

The thought of her sleeping in his arms created that familiar tightening of the loins, but he himself now needed time to think. The idea of leaving her room came as a kind of relief. He needed to be alone just as she did. There was too much for both of them to take in; the emotions weighed too heavy. Without argument, he rose to his feet and leaned to kiss the top of her head.

'Sleep tight,' he said, and went quietly back to his own room where he did not sleep at all.

Allie lay flat on her back, staring into the dark above her head. She could hear Jessica's gentle breathing and the soft rustle of a light wind in the trees outside. She felt very strange. Purged. Exhausted, but as if at last some light was falling on her life. But above everything else that was going on in her head was that Pierre had said he wanted to marry her. Was it true? And if he had meant it, would she accept? Marriage – living with a man and sharing his bed – had not been one of Allie's priorities.

Yet pictures of Pierre, with his smile so like her own and her father's, persisted. She thought of his dogged attempts to speak French, the way he listened to her so quietly, dark blue eyes fixed on her mouth as she spoke. And most of all, the way it felt when his arms went round her. There was safety in that and no fear. With him, she thought, all the fear might go away.

But now her feelings were confused. When he kissed her and held her she wanted to respond; her body urged it. When he had touched her breast it was the most beautiful feeling she had ever experienced, and her body wanted him to do it again. It was her mind that was the problem. Her mind whispered that he was a man, too, and if she let him, he would invade her as the German had done. And where would the difference be? Indeed, it would be worse; the betrayal would be greater and the stain deeper if a man she believed loved her left her or did not really love her at all. It was safer not to submit.

Yet her body clamoured hotly that it was ready for love and insisted it was different when the decision to let a man inside her was hers. Her mind said coldly her body was hers alone, and why did the woman have to be the vessel for a man? Why did women have to bear the penetration and violation, for surely that was what it was?

About six months after Rosanne had been born, her mother had tried to talk to her about these things. 'It seems a little late in the day to tell you the facts of life,' she had said, 'but I'm so anxious that you shouldn't believe that love with a man is anything like you have experienced . . .'

She could tell that her mother was ill at ease – something her mother rarely was. But of course it was ridiculous even to be attempting to discuss such things.

'I don't want to talk about it,' Allie had said rudely. 'I shall never be interested in *that*, so I don't need to know.'

'You feel that way at the moment,' her mother persisted. 'But one day – I only want to say that when you do love, don't give yourself too easily because —'

'I shall never give myself at all,' Allie interrupted, feeling herself flushing scarlet with embarrassment, 'so the question doesn't arise.' And she had stalked off.

Now her mind was cautioning her as her mother had cautioned her – but would she be able to heed the advice? She thought again of him touching her; felt the warm glow in the depth of somewhere vital inside her and slid her hand between her legs to guard what lay burning between. Even Pierre, love him as she did, would not take that with ease. She would need to be very, very sure indeed. Even if they were married. She could not believe that a few words, a bit of paper and a prayer was enough to give a man that right. There must be something more for him to prove. And if he truly loved her, surely he would understand that.

Rosie came home mid-morning the next day to find Les Hérissons somnolent and deserted in the heat of the sun. She had taken a taxi from Épernay, not wanting to disturb old Henri, and besides, a taxi was speedier. She had decided to arrive unexpectedly because she was not exactly looking forward to the homecoming. With great reluctance she had left Philippe behind in Paris with Alexander. It seemed wrong. But Philippe had persuaded her that it was better to break the news of their marriage without his being present.

'Coward!' she accused him lightly.

'No, just sensible,' he said.

And then there was the other matter. If Jean Paul's son had arrived at Les Hérissons, she faced the unpleasant task of telling him that his uncle was dead. All in all, she would be glad when the next few hours were over.

Alexander planned to follow her the next morning and had volunteered to bring her luggage with him. Unencumbered, she ran up the steps to the porch. She was pleased to find that the front door was open and the hallway deserted. She popped her head round the door of Madame's little sitting room. Madame had pulled the blinds down to shut out the sun and with a crumpled newspaper neglected on her lap, dozed gently. Rosie was about to tiptoe away when the old woman woke. One sharp eye opened and then the other.

'Rosie!' she said, instantly alert. 'You're back. Why didn't you let us know?'

'I thought I'd surprise you.' It seemed like the best thing to say.

'Well, you have.' Madame was pulling herself onto stiff feet to move towards her for a kiss on the cheek. 'How did you get here?'

'Taxi. Is all well?'

'All is very well,' Madame said and she moved to ring the bell for Marie. 'Good things have happened since you went away.'

'What sort of good things?' Rosie asked, unpinning her hat and dropping her gloves on Madame's little sofa.

'Well, your Luke West is a great success and such a charmer. He and Miss seem to be good friends. I have hopes of it. But the most exciting news of all you will never guess.' The face she turned to Rosie was wreathed in smiles. 'Jean Paul's son is here.'

Rosie sat down heavily beside her gloves.

'I had thought he might be,' she said. 'Oh dear.'

'He is a delightful boy,' Madame Dupuis said indignantly. 'He has his father's charm with Clovis's kind nature. I assure you, you will like him. But why,' she asked, suddenly suspicious, 'should you think that he would be here?'

Before Rosie could answer, Marie came into the room and Madame asked that she bring a bottle of champagne.

'As you see, Madame Rosie is back,' she said. 'We must celebrate.'

'Welcome home,' volunteered Marie with her usual perfunctory bob. 'May I ask if your trip was successful, Madame?'

'It was, Marie, but it's good to be back.'

'We'll all be pleased to see you back for sure,' Marie said.

'Now,' Madame said when the maid had bustled off. 'Tell me why you thought Pierre would be here.'

'Because I read a letter from him, written to my brother and saying that he was coming to Les Hérissons,' Rosie said. 'You see, Peter is dead . . .'

'Indeed!' Madame was startled but obviously not distressed. 'How on earth did he die?'

Rosie explained her arrival at Champagne D'Or, careful to leave out much of the detail. Then she said: 'Pierre will be very much alone now, I'm afraid.'

'Not in the least,' Madame said imperiously, then falling

silent as Marie came in with the bottle and two glasses. They both waited without speakng until the cork was drawn and the glasses filled, then, when they were alone again, Madame said: 'He is to stay here. He is happy here. And I am happy to have him.'

'I see.' Rosie was not entirely surprised. 'Does he know about his father?'

'No, and he never shall while I can prevent it,' Madame said. 'Everyone has been told not even to talk about him in front of the boy.'

Rosie wondered about the wisdom of this, but made no comment.

'I shall have to tell him as soon as possible about his uncle,' she said. 'I decided that I would wait until I saw him rather than send cablegrams. There was nothing he could have done.'

'The American estate will be his now,' Madame said thoughtfully. 'You don't suppose he will want to go back?'

'No,' Rosie said. 'I don't think that he will want to go back.'

Madame held up her glass and said 'Welcome' in an absent-minded way before taking a long sip.

'There is one problem,' she said slowly. 'He and Allie are getting too close.'

'Too close? What do you mean too close?' Alarm bells were ringing.

'There is only one way of becoming too close,' Madame said with a little sigh. 'I have longed for this for Allie, but of course any relationship with Pierre is impossible.'

Rosie was dismayed, but asked: 'Is she happier?'

'She is a changed girl.'

'Oh dear! And I have brought Alexander from America with me. He still feels the same way about her.'

Decisive as ever, Madame said: 'Now that is more good news. I presume that you and Philippe married while you were away?'

Rosie felt herself blush.

'How did you guess?' she asked, trying to hide her hot cheeks.

'My dear, I'm not a fool even if I am old,' Madame Dupuis said, but her voice was gentle. 'It's time you had a little happiness. And now you will presumably live in Paris.'

'Just for the time being,' Rosie told her. 'We have been looking for a house nearby here in the country and we want a small apartment in Reims.' She could not resist adding defiantly: 'As it happened, Philippe didn't want to live here anyway.'

'A man of good sense. And you will take Allie with you?'

'If she will come.'

'She must come. I fear that she and young Pierre must be separated for their own good.'

'Is it really necessary, Mama, if she is happy?' Rosie murmured. 'She is so young.'

'Of course it is necessary,' Madame said sharply. 'And hopefully young Alexander will take her mind off her cousin.' She put considerable emphasis into the word 'cousin', and Rosie winced and remembered how young she had been when she conceived Allie. 'How very fortuitous,' Madame continued with a thin little smile. 'Here they come now.'

From just below the lowered blind Rosie could see her daughter coming up the drive, hand in hand with a boy so like her he could have been her twin. She was wearing a pretty floral dress and there were poppies woven in her dark hair. The boy, who was just a little taller, was watching her as she chattered away, her face bright, her manner more animated than it had been for years.

'Where's Jessica?' Rosie asked abruptly. If Allie had abandoned Jessica for this boy, then maybe Madame was right.

'Broken her leg. Pierre set it. The dog adores him.'

'Good heavens,' Rosie said faintly.

As they came into the hall, Madame called out to them. Allie came into the parlour first, the boy close behind her. She saw her mother and her eyes lit up.

'Mama! How wonderful, you're home.' She flung herself into Rosie's arms as she had done when she was a child and it was so unexpected that Rosie felt tears beginning as she hugged her daughter close.

Allie released herself and turned to the boy.

'Pierre,' she said, 'this is my mother.' And there was a note of pride in her voice that made Madame and Rosie exchange a quick glance.

The young man came forward, his hand outstretched.

'*Enchanté*, Madame,' he said in careful French, 'but you are my aunt, no? My Aunt Rosie.'

'I am indeed,' Rosie said, taking his hand. 'Welcome.'

She found herself suddenly uneasy. Pierre Dupuis not only looked like his father but the timbre of the voice was the same. His body movements and his charm were disconcertingly reminiscent of the young Jean Paul Dupuis. Was his character similar, too? Rosie wondered with a spurt of alarm. Looking into those familiar quizzical blue eyes, the years flooded away and she remembered with devastating clarity the day she fell in love for the first time.

Madame was right, she decided in that split second. For more reasons than one, Allie must be separated from this remarkably handsome, and no doubt dangerous, young man.

Afterwards Pierre believed that he had known that Rosie Dupuis had come home instantly he and Allie had walked in through the front door. There was something indefinably different about the house. As if some kind of force had taken over. He recognised the source of that force when he saw Rosie with her thick, curling hair that was not as black Allie's, her aware amber eyes and the extraordinary aura of vitality that emanated from her even though she was standing quite still.

In fact, she was standing ominously still as she was introduced to him, and he found himself wishing that her face was less expressive. As she looked at him, her features fleetingly mirrored surprise, anxiety, pain and finally suspicion. It was the suspicion that remained in her watching eyes.

'Welcome,' she said, but her look was not welcoming.

He knew the problem. She was not seeing him. She was seeing his father. Just as Allie had. He wondered exactly what it was that his father had done to this household.

'I am very happy to be here,' he said in his careful French. 'Allie has been telling me about you. You've been away in the States?'

She nodded but she seemed uneasy.

'You went to Champagne D'Or? How was Uncle Peter?' He was smiling, hoping to charm her. It was important that Allie's mother liked him, but his smiles were wasted; she still seemed hostile.

'Yes,' she said. 'I went to Champagne D'Or.' Then she took a deep breath and seemed to square her shoulders. 'Pierre, please sit down. I'm sorry, but I have some bad news for you. There is no point in waiting any longer to tell you.'

He felt himself tense and remained standing. Allie's hand slid into his.

'My father . . .?' he began.

'No, not your father. There is no news of your father. I'm afraid it's your Uncle Peter.'

'Uncle Peter? He's all right?' He was aware he was stammering and sounded frightened.

Impulsively Rosie stepped forward to take his other hand in both of hers. The suspicion in her eyes had been replaced by a mist of emotion.

'No, he's not. He's dead, Pierre.'

He couldn't believe it. Through a blur he could hear Rosie's calm, kind voice explaining how it had been a dreadful accident, how loved Peter must have been, how crowded the funeral was and how he mustn't be sad.

'You have us now,' he heard Madame Dupuis say and then, convulsed with grief, he turned and pulled Allie to him, burying his head on her shoulder so that he could weep and be comforted.

'He was the only person who has ever been close to me,' he managed to choke out.

'Not any more,' he could hear Allie saying as she held him tight and made him sit on the small sofa. 'Not any more. You've got all of us.'

He managed to pull himself together, astonished at how much emotion he had been feeling in the last few days. He had hardly wept at all in his life. Now he felt as if he was being peeled like an onion. All the thick defensive layers that had grown over a lonely and frightened little boy were gradually being torn away. And the little boy was emerging.

Allie was rocking him, and he saw she was tearful too as he gently pushed her away and straightened up to find Madame Dupuis handing him a goblet of Marc de Champagne.

'Drink that,' she said. 'It'll do you good.'

He took a gulp and it did indeed make him feel better. Then he put down the glass and looked at Rosie.

'Uncle Peter was your brother, wasn't he?' he managed to say.

178

She nodded. 'But we hadn't seen each other for many years until he and your father came here.'

'What did happen to my father here?' he asked abruptly. It had unexpectedly become important to know in case, as he suspected, Uncle Peter had killed him and then killed himself. His instinct told him that Rosie Dupuis would tell him the truth.

'We don't know . . .' his grandmother began, but Rosie, her voice unemotional, interrupted. 'My husband, Clovis, killed him,' she said baldly. She waited for Pierre to react but he merely murmured: 'I see.'

'We never informed the police. But it's time you knew the truth.'

He could hear that Madame was making angry, distressed little noises, but Rosie was looking straight at him, her eyes direct and expressionless, waiting for his reaction.

'I won't ask why. I can guess why,' he said slowly. 'Did Uncle Peter know this?'

'He did. I suppose he didn't want to hurt you by telling you. But it's better you understand why. Your father tried to take over this estate. He humiliated Clovis in a hundred ways. Clovis had lost his mind in the war. he had been badly shell-shocked. He wasn't mentally stable. Your father went too far one day, and Clovis snapped – and killed him.'

'It sounds an inadequate reason,' Pierre said quietly.

Rosie hesitated. 'There were other reasons . . .'

'I am not surprised. But you must understand one thing, Aunt Rosie. I had no love for my father. He was bad. What you tell me about him causes me no pain. But I feel for Uncle Peter who loved him. Even my father's death brought misery, to your husband, to Peter, and therefore, because of Peter, to me.' He sat quietly for a moment thinking of the implications. What he had been told was no shock. He was only pleased that Peter was innocent of murder. In his heart he had believed all along that Peter had killed his father. 'It's going to be very complicated to sort out, isn't it?' he asked.

Rosie nodded.

'And it's up to me to sort it out now?'

She nodded again.

'I shall have to go back to California.'

'I'm afraid so. Monsieur Lefevre and I have had the house closed up,' Rosie said, 'but there are legal things that we couldn't do.'

He sighed. 'I was happy here,' he said.

'But you will come back,' protested Madame Dupuis, and he heard an anxious little breath from Allie.

'May I?' he asked, looking straight at Rosie.

She hesitated, and the suspicion was back in her eyes. And then suddenly she smiled.

'Of course you may come back,' she said, adding demurely, 'if your grandmother is agreeable.'

'This is your home,' Madame Dupuis protested, all emphasis on the word *your*.

'You want me to come back, Allie?' he asked.

'Oh, yes.' Her voice was fervent.

'I ask,' he said, turning again to Rosie, 'because, you see, I would like to marry your daughter.'

Rosie turned ashen pale and sank to sit on the nearest chair. His grandmother let out her breath with a hiss.

'This is no time to talk about that,' she said firmly. 'We will discuss it when you return from the States.'

'But, Mimi . . .' Allie began.

Madame Dupuis lifted an imperious hand.

'Not now, Allie,' she said. 'This is the wrong time. One does not talk about death and marriage in the same breath.'

She began to speak of Pierre's departure for America, and listening to her, Pierre had a strong presentiment that as far as Madame Dupuis was concerned, there was never going to be a right time for Allie and him to wed.

Chapter Seven

Arrangements were made with lightning speed for Pierre to return to America. He just wanted to get the whole thing over and done with, sort out the problem, return to France, settle down with his new-found family and marry Allie. They had calculated that he would be away for at least two months and Allie had said it would be the longest two months of her life. It would take a fortnight to get to Calistoga, and heaven knew how long to settle things there. Then he had to get himself back to Boston and dispose of his apartment. There would be much to pack both in California and Massachusetts. He had decided to ship to France the best of his own furniture and books ready for when he and Allie were married and had their own home.

He confided this to her on the train to Paris the morning after Rosie came home. He had packed as lightly as possible, and intended to take the first possible boat from Le Havre. Allie had elected to travel with him as far as Paris to help him make arrangements.

'His French is perfectly adequate to make his own arrangements,' Madame Dupuis grumbled when Allie suggested it but Allie ignored her.

She was full of restored confidence. Before Rosie had come home and broken the dreadful news about Uncle Peter, she and Pierre had walked and talked endlessly about themselves to each other. They had kissed and lain on the hillside, holding each other tight, but he had attempted nothing more than gentle caresses. He made it clear that he loved her and wished to marry her, and that he would expect nothing from her until she was his wife. Allie had found she was able to tell him more about the death of the lieutenant and her feelings about Rosanne. She was opening up like a flower in the sunshine.

'I shall formally ask your grandmother for your hand in marriage as soon as I get the opportunity,' he had said.

'And Mama will have to be asked, too,' Allie said a little doubtfully.

'I shall ask her when she comes home,' he promised.

Now, snug in a first-class apartment that blissfully they had all to themselves, Allie, holding his hand, her head on his shoulder, said dreamily: 'Our own house? Where shall it be?'

And they spent a delightful ten minutes discussing, as lovers do, their future. Then Allie said:'Grandma didn't seem too pleased that we want to marry. I hope she's not going to be difficult.'

'I suppose it's because we're cousins,' Pierre suggested. 'Maybe it's illegal for cousins to marry here. If it is, we'll just go back to the States and get wed there.'

'That would be fun,' Allie said chirping up. 'But I wonder why they both looked so dismayed when you said about us marrying. It can't really matter, being cousins, can it?'

'Of course not,' he assured her. 'Though a lot of old-fashioned people are against it.'

While they travelled and planned their lives, Rosie was instructing Marie and Henri to prepare for Alexander's arrival that afternoon. Alexander in his railway carriage would probably pass the couple in theirs, she thought, hoping that bringing the young American back with her had not been a terrible mistake. But then she consoled herself with the thought that he was really in France to do a job – not to court Allie.

She longed to talk to Allie, but she knew that her daughter was avoiding being alone with her and would not forgive her easily for marrying Philippe. When Rosie broke the news she said nothing, but her face showed deep disgust. Now she had gone off to Paris, there was no chance to explain about Alexander and, more important, probe her feelings regarding Pierre. Perhaps when she returned, without Pierre, there would be the possibility of some conversation.

All in all Rosie was not having a good day. Madame was angry with her, and the atmosphere over lunch was frosty.

'I would like an explanation as to why you told that boy about his father's death,' Madame said haughtily after they had been served their lamb cutlets.

'He's not a boy, he's a man,' Rosie said firmly. 'He asked for the truth, he wanted the truth and I wasn't going to lie to him any more. There have been enough lies already.'

'And supposing he had insisted on going straight to the police?'

'It would have been almost a relief to have the truth out,' Rosie said with a shrug.

'Truth!' Madame snorted. 'And do you propose to tell him the truth about Allie?'

Rosie mentally groaned. 'No.'

'Then do you propose to tell your daughter the truth about herself?'

'No.'

'Those lies are permissible, are they?'

Rosie decided to turn the questions round. 'Do you think she should be told? Will you tell her?'

'Most certainly not.' Madame was outraged. 'I have nothing against a comforting, sensible lie.'

'But if he wants to marry her . . .'

'He cannot.'

'It may not be as simple at that.'

'She is not twenty-one until June of next year. A lot can happen in that time.'

'But if he's living here . . .'

'And she is living with you away from him . . .'

'We won't be that far away, Mama. It would have been better if he had stayed in America or went back there now for good.'

The older woman sighed and put down her knife and fork. 'You are right, but I could not bear to part with him. I have lost both my sons. It is as if God has given me a replacement. Pierre has the best qualities of them both . . .'

'He has?' Rosie interrupted, her voice doubtful.

'Don't judge him because he looks so like Jean Paul.'

'It's hard not to, particularly as it seems he's more important to you than Allie, just as Jean Pierre was more important than poor Clovis,' Rosie said bitterly.

'No, that is not true. You know my love for Allie. But it is better that a man takes over this business one day and it is better that it is a man of the family rather than Luke West, charming and capable though he is. You yourself know that Allie shows no interest in wine. She is barely interested in drinking it.'

'Mama, we both know Allie. We both know all the problems she has had. If you insist she comes with me, and Pierre is here, she will be convinced that you are rejecting her in favour of him. She will also be convinced that I am deliberately parting her from the one man she has ever loved. You know how her mind works as well as I do. She is so much better and happier at the moment. She is her old self again. We can't throw away all that progress by autocratic handling of this situation. Please, Mama, let things drift for a while. Pierre will be away for two months. Alexander arrives today. Maybe the problem will go away. Maybe we will be spared ultimatums if we just don't do anything. Except perhaps pray . . .'

'I shall certainly pray,' Madame said stiffly. 'I have prayed for Allie every day since she was born. But please do not encourage her to think that there is the slightest possibility that she will be able to marry Pierre.'

Rosie sighed.

'All right, Mama,' she said, while privately thinking that if it would make Allie happy, she really didn't give a damn.

The other thing that was on her mind was the welcome that Alexander would receive from Allie. She was fairly certain that having waved Pierre goodbye for two months, Allie would arrive home in a flood of tears and in no mood to be charming to another young man. Two months was going to seem an eternity to her daughter, and the vivid imagination would be working overtime as to what could go wrong while he was away. Rosie gave a mental groan. It was all so complicated. A terrible tangled web. But she didn't want Alexander to be made miserable on his arrival. She decided to tell him that Allie would not be home until very late. She would then suggest that he and she took the Hispano-Suiza and went into Reims and wandered around so he could get the feel of what was happening in the city. Then she would take him to dinner at the Florence Restaurant. By the time they returned Allie, with luck, would be crying herself to sleep in bed. Perhaps, with more luck, by the morning she would be sunnier.

Rosie enjoyed her evening with Alexander. At twenty-six he was remarkably good-looking with his blond hair, bony face and startling blue eyes. He was very much a man of the world, well travelled and with much to talk about. The smile was as heart-shattering as ever, and he had a gentle, diffident charm that made Rosie wish with all her heart that Allie would look at him with fresh eyes.

'Why are you keeping me away from Allie?' he asked gently as the waiter poured a sweet champagne to drink with their dessert of raspberries. 'Hasn't she forgiven me for New York?'

'I don't know about New York,' Rosie said. 'What exactly happened?'

'I rushed her. I asked her to marry me, and the thought of it frightened her to death. She said she was never going to marry anyone – and then she came home.'

'Ummm,' she said thoughtfully.

He was looking at her quizzically. 'Is something wrong?'

She put down her spoon.

'Not wrong,' she said, deciding to grasp the nettle. 'Just complicated. I'm afraid you have some competition.'

He grimaced. 'I'm not surprised. Who is it?'

'Her cousin, Pierre. Jean Paul's son.'

'I see.' He accepted her statement mechanically, and then suddenly looked startled. 'But . . .'

It seemed Lizzie had been talking. Rosie looked down at her plate while she recovered her composure and then straight into his eyes.

'There's no question that she will marry him. Madame is adamant. She says it is wrong for cousins to marry. Particularly cousins by twin brothers.'

'She wants to marry him?'

Rosie nodded.

He had gone very white. He pushed his plate away and ran his hand through his hair.

'It's that serious?'

'At the moment. But she has known him only five minutes and at twenty it's natural to fall in and out of love.'

'For some, maybe,' he said, his voice low. 'Not me, alas. So there's no chance?'

'Alexander, I don't know. Pierre has gone away for two months to try to sort out the Californian estate. Then he is coming back here to live. He has nowhere else to go. In two months anything could happen. And you are here and he is not.'

185

'I see,' he said. Then he smiled his wonderful smile and raised his glass. 'Where there's life . . .' he said. 'Let's drink to hope.'

Rosie had been right. Her daughter had cried herself to sleep – the swollen eyes over the breakfast cups proved it, but it seemed she had put away her tears and was gratifyingly delighted to see Alexander. She was warm and natural as she had been as a child when she had gathered him to her as her special friend. Her happiness seemed to have wiped away all her hostility and suspicion. She even volunteered to translate for him when he was interviewing the Reimois and the planners who were rebuilding the city.

'Your French isn't bad,' she said magnanimously, 'but mine's better.'

'And so it should be,' he said mock indignantly.

She giggled. 'Well, it will be fun to find out how a journalist works,' she said.

Within days they had fallen back into their old companionship, the disaster of their American encounter never mentioned. Rosie noted how stoically he listened to her chatter about Pierre and how he never strayed a millimetre from warmth and friendship in his attitude towards her. And it helped that Jessica didn't instantly try to bite him!

She knew Allie was writing to Pierre every day – Henri had to take the letters to the Bureau de Poste and grumbled about it, but she said no more about marriage. And besides, with the *vendange* now in full swing in the most glorious early autumn sunshine, there wasn't much time for anything except work. It was a good harvest but everyone was exhausted once the grapes were gathered in and the crush finished. Rosie was more tired than anyone with her journeys back and forth to Paris to see Philippe and in between, looking at apartments and houses.

In spite of Allie's cheerfulness, there was an odd atmosphere at Les Hérissons. It was an uneasy time when no one spoke what was in their hearts. Allie said little about Pierre to her mother and grandmother, Alexander stifled his feelings for Allie, Rosie longed to be with Philippe, and had she known it, Luke West lusted for her while Miss Emily lusted for him.

And even Madame, with all passion spent, worried secretly about what effect what must happen in the future would have on Allie.

The cauldron of emotions began to bubble when Rosie came home one evening in early October highly pleased with herself. Alexander was working in Reims, but the rest of the household sat down to dinner as usual at eight thirty. It was a perfectly routine meal until, as they drank their after-dinner coffee, Rosie announced that she had found the perfect house for Philippe and herself.

'It's right in the country, on a hillside on the other side of the mountain and not far from Champillon,' she said. 'It's big and rambling. It has the most lovely walled garden that has all gone to seed but can be restored. There are stone floors and huge fireplaces. It's quite a bit older than this house and very run-down, it wants a lot doing to it. But we can move in while it's being restored to make sure we get it absolutely right.' She did not add that she had reached the stage where she would have moved into her own home had it been roofless just to be with Philippe.

'And Allie and Rosanne will be coming with you, of course,' Madame said.

Everyone at the table held their breath. Miss looked anxiously at Rosie. She had no desire to leave Les Hérissons, not while Luke West stayed there. Luke West tried to contain his disappointment and Rosie waited, full of trepidation, to see what Allie would say and do.

'Oh, no, I shan't go,' she said blithely. 'Mama and Philippe will want to be alone for a while. And besides, this is my home. Always has been, always will be.'

'It would be better if you went with your mother,' Madame said. 'The house is becoming very overcrowded.'

'That's hardly my fault,' Allie said hotly.

'When Pierre returns, if he is here permanently, he will need better living accommodation.'

'He can have Mama's room.'

'I was thinking of yours,' Madame said calmly.

Allie stared at her grandmother, appalled. Then she burst out with: 'Because he's a boy! Because he's a grandson – you want him more than me. You'll get rid of me to make room for him.'

Rosie groaned. All was happening exactly as she had predicted.

Luke West and Miss had both downed the rest of their coffee in one gulp and were excusing themselves.

'Time for my walk,' said Miss, her voice bright, and despite her anxiety Rosie had to smile at the tact and diplomacy of the English. No Frenchman or woman would have missed what was to come for the world.

When they had gone, Madame continued where she had left off.

'Your mother thinks it would be better if you were away from Pierre,' she said.

Rosie gasped at this barefaced duplicity on Madame's part.

'And I agree,' Madame continued smoothly. 'We feel that being so close to him here, you may become carried away. And marriages between cousins are a dreadful mistake.'

Allie glared at her mother, her face hostile in a way it had not been for weeks.

'Are you saying that I cannot marry Pierre?' she asked coldly.

'I'm not saying anything,' said Rosie feebly, wishing she was not involved in this dispute.

'You can't stop me,' Allie said.

'Oh yes we can,' said Madame. 'You are not twenty-one yet.'

'Then we'll wait until I am twenty-one,' Allie said defiantly. 'It's only nine months away. And in the meantime we shall be engaged.'

'There will be no engagement,' Madame said fiercely.

'Why not?' asked Allie, her blue eyes black with anger.

'Because you are cousins.'

'It's not that. I know it isn't that. It's because Mama hated Jean Paul, isn't it? Well, Pierre's not like Jean Paul. Nothing like him. How can you judge when you only saw him just that one evening?' She was glaring at Rosie, her cheeks scarlet, the old dislike re-etched on her face.

'It's nothing to do with his father,' Rosie said, hating to find herself having to lie yet again. 'You're both so young. You've had so little experience of life, darling . . .'

'I would have said I'd had enough to last me a lifetime!'

'That's enough.' Madame had risen to her feet. 'There'll be no more talk about this tonight. I am going to bed.'

She made her way slowly to the door and Rosie felt a pang at her slow, stiff movements. She would move easier with a stick, but the very suggestion affronted her. Rosie and Allie watched, knowing that in this mood help would be rejected. She was becoming more autocratic as the years went on, Rosie thought regretfully, and old age had made her sometimes mischievous and often unreasonable.

'Goodnight,' Madame said firmly as she grabbed the door handle with relief and used it to help herself out of the room.

Once she had gone, Allie rounded on her mother.

'It's all your fault, isn't it? You just want to spoil everything for me again. I love him, Mother. He's good and he's kind. He knows what happened and he knows about Rosanne and he still wants to marry me. But you'd stop that, wouldn't you? It's not fair. You've got your Philippe now, and I've got no one. Only Pierre, and he really loves me and cares for me and just because he's my cousin and because you all hate his father, my happiness is to be taken away from me again.'

Things were really serious if Allie had told him about the lieutenant and Rosanne. Rosie began to feel as if she was being suffocated, but she said, searching for the right words: 'Please, please, Allie – listen to me. Come and sit next to me, please. Don't fight me all the time. It makes me so unhappy.'

She patted the chair next to her, and reluctantly Allie moved into it. Rosie took her daughter's hand, and turned to face her.

'Your grandmother is worried because you are such close cousins and your fathers were twins,' she said. 'It could mean that there would be something wrong with any children you have.'

'Then we won't have any children,' Allie said.

'But maybe Pierre would like children.'

'Then we'll chance it.'

'I am worried because you don't know each other very well. Marriage is difficult enough, Allie, especially if you fall out of love. And at twenty it is very easy to fall in and out of love. I know.'

'I shan't fall out of love. And it's just that you think he's like his father.' She was trying to avoid her mother's eyes.

'I don't know if he's like his father. You're quite right when you say I've only known him for that one evening, and he impressed me. I did expect him to be like Jean Paul. I was suspicious at first, but things he did and said – his feelings for Peter – made me like him. But I don't really know him, any more than you do. It's only an instinct. Courtships should be longer because no one really sees straight when they first fall in love. So can I make a suggestion?'

Allie nodded grudgingly.

'Why don't you be secretly engaged so as not to upset Mimi, and then we'll talk about it again in June when you're twenty-one? Everyone might be thinking quite differently about everything by then. But it's always best not to rush these things.' She was blurring the issue and playing for time. It was a feeble way to deal with the situation but she could think of no other.

'We can be secretly engaged?'

'I don't see why not, as long as you really keep it secret.'

'Oh, Mama.' Allie was hugging her, and Rosie felt the guilty tears welling. 'How happy you have made me.'

'Well, that's all right then,' Rosie said briskly, giving her daughter a last impulsive hug. 'Now come along, it's time we both went to bed. And for heaven's sake don't tell your grandmother about this conversation. She'll murder me.'

Rosie rarely prayed, but that night she did. She prayed for a way out of this impasse in which they were all trapped. She couldn't think of any simple solution because Madame was right. Marriage between Pierre and Allie was impossible. So she prayed, hoping that with luck, God would come up with something, because sure as He made the earth in seven days, she couldn't think of a thing.

'Well, that was embarrassing,' Miss said as she and Luke West escaped through the front door and down to the driveway. 'And not good news, either. I don't particularly want to leave Les Hérissons and presumably Madame Rosie will certainly take Rosanne with her.'

'This house won't be the same without her,' Luke said. 'It's she who brings it alive.'

He could sense rather than see Miss's quick sideways look at him. And he wondered if she perhaps suspected the attraction he felt for Rosie Dupuis.

'There must be a terrible row going on in there,' Miss said. 'I'd love to have stayed, but of course one couldn't. I'd have guessed that Madame would have wanted Allie to stay, but obviously the young man has really taken her fancy.'

'I think she wants to separate them,' Luke suggested. 'She doesn't approve of the romance.'

'Why ever not? Oh, because they're cousins, I suppose. Some people really don't approve of marriage between cousins. My father doesn't.'

They had begun to walk slowly down the drive towards the gatehouse. The air was cool and Luke thought how swiftly the nights were beginning to draw in. He had been here since early summer but it felt much longer. He was happy at Les Hérissons but what would it be like when Rosie was gone for good?

'Families!' Miss was sighing. 'Why is there always so much trouble between families?'

'Is there trouble with yours?' Luke asked lightly.

'Father is a vicar, so of course we all had to be terribly good when we were young. Both of my parents are darlings, but they are dreadfully old fashioned. I'm afraid I could never live at home again. That spell in France before the war left me awfully Frenchified in my habits and they don't understand me any more. My young sisters have broken away, too. I worry about them being on their own sometimes.' She sighed. 'But one has to lead one's own life, doesn't one?'

'One does,' he agreed solemnly.

They walked in silence for a few moments, and then she asked: 'Do you have family?'

'In Spain.'

'Were you brought up there?'

'Yes, in Jerez.'

'I've never been to Spain. What's it like? Is it very different from here?'

'Very. Dustier, hotter, poorer, more colourful, more passionate. Jerez is beautiful. A secret little town. Full of tall whitewashed walls and heavy black wooden doors that seem to hide secret places. Life there is somehow more private than here. Not many cafés, but there are dozens of deep dark *bodegas*, like caves, where sunburned men drink a great deal of sherry away from the heat of the day.' He stopped abruptly, aware of sounding over-poetical.

191

'You make it sound wonderful. Why did you leave?'

'There wasn't enough there for me to do. My elder brothers and my father run the business. I was sent to school in England when I was very young. I never really went back properly.'

He was silent again, not wanting to talk about that part of his life. He did not like to remember the wrench it had been going to the grey school with little grey schoolboys in little grey suits, where it never seemed to stop raining. And the excitement of coming home for the holidays to the warmth and beauty of the Spanish countryside. In his head he could still see the mountains with their snow-capped peaks and hear the creaking of the cicadas and the clicking of the crickets under the skies. Sounds of sun and summer. He missed them.

'Of course it's the bullfight that puts the English off,' Miss was saying thoughtfully. 'It seems so dreadful.'

He laughed. 'Some of the English are mad keen *aficionados*,' he told her. 'And a bullfight can be a very moving experience.'

'I wouldn't want to see one,' she said with a sniff.

The thought had been in his mind to seduce this English miss tonight to assuage his disappointment at Rosie's departure, but the turn of the conversation was causing him to change his mind again. He doubted there would be much passion in her. Now, Rosie – there would be passion there! He felt a sudden blinding regret that he would never experience it. Once, long ago, he had experienced such passion that now nothing less would do. Without that burning brand that ignited all that was vital in a man, what point was there in making love? He deliberately and with a conscious effort turned his mind from that.

'You wouldn't go home if Allie goes with Madame Rosie?' he asked.

'Would you mind if I did?' she asked archly.

'I should miss your company very much.'

'And I yours,' she said, her voice low.

He felt a pang of sympathy for her loneliness, and in the misty dusk he slid his arm round her waist and gave her a gentle squeeze.

'Cheer up,' he said as if he were speaking to a four-year-old. 'I expect we'll both still be around here for donkey's years.'

'I almost hope we will,' she said. 'Unless you get married or something.'

'I am not the marrying kind,' he said firmly, glad of the opportunity to say it.

'Nor me,' she said with a kind of exaggerated fervency, but she had let her head rest on his shoulder.

It seemed expected of him, so he kissed her, and as his hand crept to find her breast he thought again, as he had thought before: Well, why not? Any port in a storm.

Autumn came early in Champagne. The rain fell with deadly monotony, and the vine leaves turned rusty brown against the green of the hillsides above. Mist shrouded the trees around the house in the early mornings, but Allie was happy because now it could not be much more than another month before Pierre came home again.

She had received a letter from him sent from California saying that he would have to stay there longer than he had intended. The good news was that with amazingly little effort he had managed to have his father declared dead from the time of his non-appearance at Champagne D'Or. Writing to Allie, he explained that in these days of Prohibition, gangsters and bootleggers, many people did just disappear. Since his father had been involved with one of the most notorious gangsters in America it had been taken for granted by the Calistoga police that Jean Paul Dupuis had met some unpleasant fate at the hands of the mob.

Allie shared the bits that weren't personal with her mother. 'He says that since you are Uncle Peter's only kin, you now legally own Champagne D'Or, for what it is worth. "This does not disturb me as I want no part of it," ' she read out loud, ' "I see my future in France with you, Mimi and your mother. Assuming that she won't mind, I intend to ship back to France my own personal things and some of the books and furniture from the house. I'm afraid Aunt Rosie will have to deal with the rest herself. Another week and I shall be on my way to Boston and I think that a week or ten days there will see me through all that I have to do. I've written to the Master at Harvard explaining my situation and asking if there is any chance that I can sit for the French scholarship that is on offer – just in case. I would be happier not to be entirely dependent on Mimi." '

Her mother groaned on hearing this news of her inheritance.

'Now there's a complication!' she said. 'How on earth will we deal with the house and the estate from this distance? Best just to leave the house boarded up and worry about it later. I suppose eventually we might as well sell it and split the money between you and Pierre.'

'Pierre says he has had it made secure,' Allie told her.

'Thank heavens for that,' sighed Rosie. 'But I feel we should wait before we do anything. One day he may regret surrendering it so casually. The house itself must be worth something and if we were to buy back some of the land, one day we might be able to . . .'

Allie burst out laughing. 'Mama, you are funny,' she said. 'You're already thinking what could be done with it, aren't you? But Pierre doesn't want it, and neither do you. Why don't you just sell it?'

'Things change,' her mother pronounced rather mysteriously and said no more.

The day after receiving the letter, Allie woke to see a thin sun struggling to shine and once breakfast was over she made the decision to drive into Épernay to buy some new winter clothes. She wanted to look her best when Pierre returned. It would be better to go to Paris, really, and she thought that perhaps she might do that when Alexander had time to come with her. Paris was no fun on your own. But for the time being she felt like getting away from Les Hérissons for a little while. When her good companion, Alexander, was in Reims, time hung heavy, but he assured her that he was nearly through with the work and then he proposed to take his vacation. This would be the time to go to Paris.

Alexander had taught her to drive. She had learned easily and he told her that she was a natural. Now she loved the sense of freedom that came from getting into the Hispano-Suiza or the Léon Bollée and taking herself where she wanted to be. Few women drove in Champagne, and the newly acquired skill made her feel a touch superior and rather pleased with herself, particularly when men stared enviously at the Hispano.

In Épernay, she parked the car outside the station, leaving Jessica, who loved to ride in the car, on the back seat. She then set off to wander through the town. Épernay had not had an easy time in the war but its problems were small compared to those of Reims. Much of the damage that the Germans had inflicted on Épernay was already restored.

She took her usual route, skirting the Avenue de Champagne and heading for the shopping streets. She found herself passing the *salon de thé* where she had encountered Madame Claudette in the early summer of the year. Casually she looked in, and there was the brothel keeper, plump and powdered and wearing pink, sitting alone at the same table as before.

Allie had often thought back on that curious conversation with the woman and regretted having left so precipitously. Not just because there might have been more information about her father to be gleaned but because, regardless of the woman's profession, she had been so kind to Clovis when shell shock had caused him to lose his mind in the early days of the war. Her original bitterness towards the woman had faded.

On impulse Allie went into the pale green-painted salon and stood in front of the table where the older woman was sitting.

'Good morning, Madame Claudette,' she said. 'How nice to see you. May I join you?'

The woman looked up, saw Allie and for an instant looked flustered. Then she recovered herself.

'Of course. Please sit down,' she said, with the air of a hostess. 'Will you have some tea?'

'Yes, please,' Allie said and as Madame Claudette made signals to the waitress, added: 'I wanted to apologise for rushing out and leaving you the last time we met. It was rude of me, particularly as you were so kind to my father.'

'It was a pleasure to help your father in any way I could. He was a good man.' The woman was stating a conviction, and Allie fell silent for a moment. Then without meaning to, she asked: 'Did you love him?'

'Love him!' The question had unnerved Madame Claudette. Allie saw her eyes mist over, but she was saved from replying by the arrival of the waitress with another cup and saucer and more tea.

Neither spoke until the waitress had gone.

'Madame, in my profession . . .' Madame Claudette began and then broke off, flustered again.

'I do know now that you're not a dressmaker, madame,' Allie volunteered gently.

195

The woman flushed. 'You shouldn't be sitting with me,' she muttered. 'Clovis would be angry.'

'I don't think he would.'

'Maybe not.' She smiled a small, almost shy smile and leaned forward, creating a little atmosphere of intimacy about them. 'I suppose I did love him as far as it was possible for me to love anyone,' she confided. 'And he was very fond of me, even though I'm not very clever and these days not very pretty. But I was pretty when I was young and we first met. I knew him long before your mother came and he married her. It was only her he loved, but he was very fond of me. Does that shock you?'

Allie shook her head. 'It makes me happy, because he had little love in his life.'

'That was because Jean Paul took everything from him. Always. His mother's love, your mother's love.' The woman's round face was sad and her hands trembled a little as she poured tea for Allie. 'He always had to accept second best all his life and I was far from being the best. That last time we met he said how he had never had anything of his own. He said it so sadly it broke my heart. Nothing belonged to him. Not his wife, not your little daughter and not even you. But he didn't mind. He loved both you girls just as if you had been his own. You must always remember that when you think of him. He was so proud of you and he loved you so much. But it was because of what he said that day that I was afraid he had killed himself and that there might have been something I could have done to stop it.'

The woman was speaking very fast, her voice low, saying what had been bottled up in her heart, things that should not have been said. With a dawning sense of horror, Allie began to comprehend exactly what it was she was saying, and panic was rising in her. This woman knew that Rosanne was her child and not Clovis's child, and that was most certainly true. She also seemed to be saying that she, Allie, was not Clovis's child either. Her stomach began to tie itself in knots and she felt perspiration spring out on her forehead. The woman had fallen silent, looking into her cup as if she was trying to read the tea leaves, her face pensive and curiously innocent looking.

Allie could not find her voice, but eventually she managed to blurt out: 'But if I am not his child, whose child am I?'

'Why, Jean Paul's, of course.' And having delivered the

blow, Madame Claudette's hand flew to cover her mouth, knocking over her teacup as she did so. Her round eyes became saucer-like as she said, her voice full of dismay, 'Oh, my God! You didn't know!'

Allie did not reply. She sat watching the tan stain of tea spread across the white linen tablecloth. She felt as if she had been paralysed as the implications of this dreadful truth sunk in. So much was suddenly explained. Madame Claudette was babbling apologies, her face distressed. Allie did not respond, and then from somewhere she found the effort of will to get to her feet.

'I just wanted to thank you for your kindness to my —' she faltered, then managed, 'I must go now. Goodbye.'

As if she was made of wood she walked to the door and quietly let herself out of the tearoom and walked on down through the crowded street. She bought herself a coat and a new hat in a trance. By the time she reached Les Hérissons it was mid-afternoon and she could not remember their colour or style, nor could she remember one kilometre of the drive home. She had no idea where she had been. Automatically she put the car away and was just leaving the garage when Alexander drove up in the Léon Bollée Rosie had lent him.

He jumped out of the car when he saw her standing on the gravel path, holding her packages, Jessica, ears back, at her side.

'Allie, what is it?' In a second he had his arms round her holding her close. 'What's the matter? What's happened?'

She sagged against him, grateful for his presence, grateful for a friend she could tell the awful truth.

'Jean Paul was my father,' she said baldly.

She felt him stiffen.

'Ah,' he said, 'and who told you that?'

She drew back and looked at him. His light blue eyes were full of sympathy as he looked down at her, but they were not full of surprise.

'You knew,' she said accusingly. 'How did you know?'

'Your mother was pregnant with you when she first came to our house in New York,' he said gently. 'She was on her way to France to look for Jean Paul. He had been working in her father's winery and then disappeared. She thought he had come back here.'

'If you know, who else knows?' Her voice was a wail of outraged anguish.

'My mother and father, maybe Jenny, my sister, but I don't think so, your mother and your grandmother. Only people who love you.'

'Oh, my God,' she whispered. 'Do you realise, it means Pierre is my half-brother?'

He said nothing.

'That's why Grandmother and Mother ... Oh God, oh God. I can't marry him. They'll never let me marry him. It's my mother, my mother again.' She clenched her fists and let scalding anger wash over her. 'It's all her fault. How could she get pregnant like that! She's a slut. It was the same with Philippe. I hate her! Oh God, what am I going to do?'

'You're going to come inside,' he said firmly, 'drink your grandmother's cure for shock, a Marc de Champagne, and then you're going to stop blaming your mother and tell her what you have found out.'

'I don't want to speak to her.'

'Then I shall tell her what you've found out,' he said decisively. 'This is not something that you can bury. It must be aired, Allie, or you'll never have any relationship with your mother again.'

'I don't want one,' she said fiercely.

'Not at this moment, but you will. Now come inside.'

The anger was subsiding and the paralysis coming back. She let him lead her into the house and meekly drank the Marc that he poured from the bottle in her grandmother's cabinet. The shock of its fierceness restored her spirit a little.

'Now,' he said, 'we must find your mother.'

She sat down in her grandmother's chair feeling totally exhausted.

'I can't, Alexander,' she said. 'I can't face anything at the moment. I need to be alone. You've been very kind, but now I must go to my room and think. It's so complicated, you see. I have to take in the fact that my father was not my father and that man I hated so, was. And Pierre is my half-brother . . .'

She heard her voice trail away on a sob. She got to her feet more weary than she could ever remember. She felt she needed to sleep and maybe she would wake and find it was all a bad dream.

But it wasn't a dream, and she knew it as she dragged her way up the stairs to her room, holding Jessica in her arms. The happiness that had been so near was snatched away again. She was doomed, it seemed, to be for ever alone.

Rosie had been working in her blending room and she was at the sink washing out the glasses she had used when there was a gentle tap at the door.

'Come in,' she called, and Alexander's head appeared round the door jamb.

'Ah, you're there,' he said, and he sounded relieved. 'Have you got a minute?'

'Several,' she said cheerfully. 'What is it?'

He hesitated and then said: 'I think you'd better brace yourself for a shock.'

'Oh?' She stood looking at him, eyebrows raised, looking anxious, a drying up-cloth in her hand. 'Is something wrong?'

He nodded gloomily. 'I'm afraid so. It's Allie. She knows that Jean Paul was her father.'

The drying-cloth fluttered to the floor as Rosie felt the blood drain away from her face.

'She can't. How could she possibly know? Surely Mimi hasn't . . .? For God's sake – who told her?'

'I don't know,' Alexander said. 'I found her standing in the drive with parcels in her hand, looking as if someone had dropped dead in front of her. I think she must have come back from shopping. She'd just put the car away. She was in a state of shock.'

Trying to ignore her own embarrassment that she and Alexander were having this conversation, Rosie sank down onto a wooden chair, hands in her lap, head drooped.

'I don't understand it. You didn't tell her?' She looked up at him accusingly. 'You knew. I realised you knew the other night.'

'Mother told me,' he said. 'Yes, I knew. But I didn't tell Allie.'

It never occurred to her to disbelieve him.

'Then it has to be her grandmother. There's no one else in the world who knows.'

Almost glad that there was someone she could be angry with other than herself, Rosie was on her feet again, pulling off her white overall. 'The interfering old . . . I'm going to confront her with this. It's too bad . . . the poor child . . . And I suppose Allie is blaming me.'

'Sort of,' Alexander said cautiously.

'Well, it is my fault,' Rosie said grimly. 'It's taken twenty years for my sins to catch up with me, and now they well and truly have. You just come with me.'

She stormed her way out of the blending room and up the stairs to the bedroom where Madame Dupuis would be taking her afternoon nap. Without bothering to knock she pushed her way in, blazing with anger that Madame could have been so cruel, so thoughtless. The old lady was dozing on her bed, fully clothed and covered by a cashmere shawl, but she jerked awake at Rosie's abrupt entrance.

'Dear me,' she said, 'is anything wrong?'

'There is,' Rosie said grimly. 'Why did you tell Allie that Jean Paul was her father?'

'Why did I do what?' Madame, still not quite awake, was puzzled.

'Tell Allie that Jean Paul was her father.'

'I did no such thing,' Madame said indignantly. 'Really, Rosie, you barge in here, wake me up, accuse me of things . . .'

Rosie was stopped in her tracks. 'If you didn't tell her, I apologise.'

'Of course I didn't tell her.'

'Then who did?'

Rosie turned to see an embarrassed Alexander hovering by the door.

'She told Alexander that she knew.'

'Is this true, Alexander?'

'I'm afraid so.'

Madame carefully swung her stockinged feet over the side of the bed and heaved herself up.

'But there *is* no one else who knows.'

'Exactly,' Rosie said.

'Then we must ask the child herself,' Madame said calmly. 'Perhaps it's no bad thing that she knows the truth. She will understand now why we could not give her permission to marry.'

Madame had a habit of being devastatingly right at the wrong time.

'Could you leave it for a little while?' Alexander suggested tentatively. 'Allie wanted to be alone. She's gone to her room. I don't think she's ready for any cross-examining.'

'I'm sure Alexander is right, Mama,' Rosie said. 'Remember how she does need to be alone when things go wrong for her. Let her work it out for herself for a while, and then we'll talk to her.'

'You talk to her,' Madame said firmly. 'But it is the most extraordinary, and perhaps fortuitous thing to happen. Perhaps we should have told her ourselves.'

'I'd rather she'd never found out. She will never forgive me.' Rosie said sadly.

'Oh, in time she will, in time.' Madame's voice was airy and Rosie resented it as she turned away to go back downstairs. Suddenly she longed to be away from Les Hérissons and her difficult children, and with her new husband. If Allie was all right tomorrow, she promised herself she would go to Paris and she would stay there for a few days. She needed the soothing presence of Philippe.

Allie did not appear for dinner so Marie took a tray up to her room. It was put back outside the door later, virtually untouched. Rosie decided it was time for some action.

She knocked on her daughter's bedroom door and without waiting for a reply, walked in. Allie was on her bed, fully dressed, lying on her back and staring at the ceiling.

Without beating about the bush Rosie said, 'Alexander has told me that you know.'

The girl did not respond.

'Who told you, Allie?'

'Does it matter?'

'It does. I had thought that there were only four people in the world who knew.'

'Well, there was another.'

'Who?'

'Madame Claudette.'

'Madame Claudette!'

'Yes. She told me. She didn't realise I didn't know.'

It was blindingly obvious now. Clovis had told the brothel keeper.

'Can we talk about it?' Rosie asked. 'We should talk about it.'

201

'There isn't much to say, really, is there? I'm not angry any more. I was angry with you at first. Now I just don't care. I loved him very much and of course he wasn't my papa at all.'

'Oh yes he was,' Rosie said fiercely. 'I won't let you say that. It would break his heart. He married me, knowing I didn't love him, to give you a proper future. I was desperate. I thought I'd ruined my life. I didn't want to marry him, but I had no choice. He took me on, and he took you on. You were his from the first day he saw you. You loved him and you were Papa's girl. When you were little he carried you everywhere. You'd sit on his shoulders while he walked around the estate, and he called you his flying angel. He taught you all the things that gave you pleasure when you were little. You were his companion, his daughter, no one else's and you gave him all the love that he had missed in his life. Of course he was your papa! Who else do you think was? Who got up in the night when you cried, even though you had a nanny? He couldn't bear it if you cried. Your father wasn't as tough as I am. If I'd told you the truth, it would have broken his heart. They say you should tell children the best of their natural parents, but what could I have told you about Jean Paul? There wasn't any best to tell. I won't have you saying that Clovis was not your papa. It's simply not true. He was the best and most loving father that any child could have had.'

Rosie stopped to draw breath and to calm herself. While she had been speaking Allie had at least turned her head to look at her, but the girl's expression had not softened.

'But you didn't want to marry him?' she finally asked.

Rosie thought there was no choice now but absolute honesty.

'No, I still thought I was in love with Jean Paul. I was so convinced that he would come back to France and that if only I could wait long enough it would be all right. I was very young, Allie. Younger than you are now, and it wasn't until I began to learn about Jean Paul and what sort of man he was that I was able to see clearly and realise that I'd had a lucky escape. And then when he came here, I just couldn't believe it was happening. For him to come and spoil all our happiness so long after . . . When all our lives were mended . . . It was terrible.'

'Did he know I was his daughter?'

'I don't really know. He inferred things sometimes . . .'

Allie was sitting up. Her apathy seemed to have gone but an alarming intensity had taken its place.

'If he inferred things, he had guessed,' she said. 'Yet he even tried to touch me once or twice,' she dropped her voice, 'that way you know, and yet he knew all the time I was his daughter. How do you think it feels to have a man like him for a father?'

'Allie, I have told you. We are not necessarily like our parents. You're not like me. You're nicer.' She managed a little laugh.

Allie got up off the bed and walked to the window. She stood looking out, her back to her mother.

'You must have been very frightened when you came all that way expecting me,' she was saying but her voice was indifferent.

'I wasn't that frightened. I wanted a father for you. And I had so much help. Lizzie and Mr Webster were wonderful. I was sick a lot, though.' Again she tried a little laugh. This conversation desperately needed humour.

'I wasn't sick with Rosanne,' Allie said absently. 'Madame Claudette knew about that, too. But I don't think she'll tell anyone. She said she loved Papa.'

'I know. They would have been right for each other if circumstances had been different.'

Allie came across the room and Rosie saw that her eyes were full of contempt.

'Poor brave Mama,' she said sarcastically. 'And now poor Allie. I can't marry Pierre, can I?'

She sounded too calm. Rosie shook her head.

'I love him very much. He made me so happy.' She seemed to be talking to herself. 'What do you think I should tell him?'

'The truth?' Rosie suggested humbly.

'But won't that make you look like – a slut?'

Rosie winced and then shrugged. 'I don't mind. Alexander knows, why shouldn't Pierre?'

'Aunt Lizzie should never have told Alexander,' Allie said fiercely.

'She probably didn't mean to. You know how she rattles on. Maybe she thought he should know since he wanted to marry you.'

'I wonder if he still does,' Allie said. 'It's a pity I don't love him.'

'But you do,' Rosie reassured her, 'just in a different way.'

'I suppose I do really,' Allie said thoughtfully. 'I suppose I always have, really. In a way.'

As they sat in the darkening room as far apart as they had ever been, Rosie thought with despair that now she had lost her daughter for ever. Truth could be too cathartic, she thought. Truth was best, but truth could destroy. Madame's comfortable lies were the answer.

Then Allie turned and said coldly.

'Mama,' she said. 'I want to be alone now. I want to think. Will you leave me on my own?'

'If that's what you want, 'Rosie said, leaning to kiss Allie's forehead. 'You know where I am if you want me.'

And closing the door quietly behind her she left her daughter's room. Her head was high and her eyes dry, but inside she was crying.

Chapter Eight

Pierre climbed off the train at South Street station feeling that if he never saw the inside of a railway carriage again it would not be long enough. His impatience to get back to France and Allie had made the journey across the States and back interminable. Unable to bear another minute in a rocking train, he had decided to stop over for a night or two in New York to recover his land legs before taking the train up to Boston.

There was another and more pressing reason for the delay. It was as the train was pulling into Grand Central station that he had suddenly remembered Feathers. With everything that had been going on in his life she had been wiped completely from his thoughts as if she had not existed. He was furious with himself when he remembered that he had meant to send her a telegram. Now the chances were that he would get to his apartment in Boston to find her installed there. He didn't want that to happen. He didn't want to see her ever again and yet he could hardly give her just a few hours' notice to pack and go. An abrupt request to depart would give her far too good an excuse still to be there when he arrived. He now saw in retrospect that it had been an idiotic gesture to give her the keys to his apartment. Cursing his own stupidity he had sent the telegram that he should have remembered to send from California. It informed her that he would be home on the Thursday afternoon, in two days' time.

Once in Boston he left most of his baggage at the depository at South Street station. There was no point in carrying cases when he had a whole wardrobe full of clothes and everything he needed at his apartment. He was looking forward to a change of clothes. Those he was wearing needed sponging and pressing and they were not really warm enough. Outside in South Street

205

it was cold after the warmth of California and the sky was leaden and grey as if it might snow. He turned up the collar of his coat and pulled his trilby hat more firmly onto his head as he waited for a cab to take him to Commonwealth Avenue.

His apartment block looked exactly the same. And why shouldn't it? he asked himself as he took out his keys. There was no sign of life behind the windows of his rooms, and with luck the place would be all his. He felt a small pang that he was going to have to lose this first home of his own. He had been happy there. But lonely, he reminded himself. Now he need never be lonely again.

He ran up the stairs, whistling softly, already planning which pieces of furniture would go to France and which would have to be sold. He thought how anxious he had been when he left here nearly five months ago and now he was back, a pocket full of money, courtesy of his grandmother, and not a worry in the world.

But worry, in the shape of Feathers, was waiting. As he came into his living room he stopped dead. She was sitting there in his armchair at the side of the fireplace, facing the door, her arms hugged protectively across her body.

'Feathers!' he said, exasperated. 'Didn't you get my telegram?'

She nodded without speaking.

'Then what are you doing here?' He was amazed he wasn't shouting.

She got to her feet and then he saw that her shape had changed dramatically. The wide Irish eyes were beautiful as ever, her skin seemed even creamier and her dark hair glowed with health. But her shape was different. Feathers, he realised with horror, was pregnant.

'I had nowhere to go,' she said quietly. 'I'm sorry but you see they laid me off last week. They found out that I am pregnant. I hadn't planned on that. I didn't think they'd get rid of me. I thought they liked me. I always worked hard. But it didn't make any difference. They fired me. If they hadn't fired me I'd have gone from here. But I didn't know what to do. I felt like a whore . . .' her voice had dropped very low.

He flung his hat on a chair, closed his eyes and gave a deep long sigh.

'Feathers, I told you that if you got pregnant I wouldn't do a thing about it. I meant it. I lent you this apartment so that you could sort yourself out – get away from South Boston. You've let me down by still being here. That wasn't in the deal.'

'Only you made the deal,' she said, her great eyes staring at him. 'I see now and you should see too that it wasn't a good deal. Where was I to go from here?'

'I don't know,' he said impatiently. 'Wherever girls who leave home go and live. A YWCA or something.'

'They don't want to know if you're pregnant.'

He gave a long, dramatic sigh. 'Feathers, I have no responsibility in this. I told you.'

'How can you have no responsibility when you are the father?'

He glared at her. 'Nobody made you go to bed with me.'

'I went out of love.'

'And there was a hell of a lot of lust there, too,' he said, suddenly remembering how abandoned she could be. It wasn't decent, though. Not when he remembered Allie's reticence and fear.

She hung her head. Silent.

'Now you make me feel like a whore,' she said sadly.

'Well . . .'

The cruel little word hung in the air between them. She flushed scarlet.

'I suppose you want money?' he asked contemptuously.

'I want help and advice. I don't know what to do.'

'Go home?' he suggested.

She put her hands protectively over her stomach. 'And have my father kick your baby out of me?'

'Don't call it my baby!' he shouted.

'It's no one else's,' she said angrily. 'Do you think I enjoy standing and listening to you say these things? Don't you understand that I'm fighting for my life and this baby's life – your baby's life, whether you like it or not?'

'Aren't there organisations for fallen women?' he asked, cruel again.

'Maybe, but I need help to find them. Losing my job . . . It upset me. I'd been all right until then. But they said they couldn't have me in the store – as if I'd be a bad influence or something. It's left me helpless, losing my job. I wasn't planning on that.'

She seemed to be talking to herself again, and with an angry gesture that threw the whole problem back at her, he stamped from the room into the kitchen. He needed a drink.

'I'm leaving for France as soon as I can. I'm going to live there,' he shouted to her. 'I'm getting married.'

He opened his drinks cupboard. It was bare. He let out a roar of rage.

'Have you been drinking my champagne?' he demanded, striding back into the living room.

'I had a glass every night. It made me feel better. I hadn't meant to drink it all, but it went.'

The missing champagne gave him something to focus his anger on. Something about which he had no need to feel guilt.

'That's stealing, you little thief,' he hissed at her. 'Just robbery.'

'I didn't think you'd mind.' Her anger had gone, and tears were falling slowly down her face. 'You're going to France. You're getting married. I can't bear it.'

Her tears calmed him a little.

'Feathers, you're going to have to get used to the idea. I'm not going to marry you. Can't you have an abortion or something?'

She looked totally horrified and crossed herself.

'It's a terrible, terrible sin,' she said.

'So was getting pregnant,' he said crudely. 'My God! You Catholics! The hypocrisy!'

But his anger was subsiding, too. Wearily he sat down, telling himself he must try to be reasonable.

'Now listen, let's talk this over. I'm packing up this apartment and going to France. The rent is paid here for about another month. If you don't mind living in it half-furnished, you can keep it until the rent runs out. Then you can sell what bits and pieces of furniture I've left here. And I'll give you some money as well. But you'll have to get out while I'm here. I'll pay for a hotel for a few nights. It's the best I can offer.' He wasn't sure if he was making a mistake, but something had to be suggested and it didn't look as if she was going to volunteer to disappear.

'You're very kind,' she said and the awful thing was that she was so crushed that she meant it. He felt a pang of pity for her and cursed unkind fate.

'That's it, then,' he said, getting to his feet. 'I'll stay in a hotel tonight while you get yourself packed and ready to go. I'll come back in the morning and help you move.'

He picked up his hat, trying to ignore her tears, and with unseemly haste made his way back into the hall. There was a pile of letters waiting for him. He picked them up and shoved them in his pocket and fled.

'See you tomorrow, then,' he shouted and left, slamming the door behind him. But as he ran down the stairs he could not blot out the sight of her stricken face.

He was back in the street again when the unbidden thought came that it was strange to think that he had fathered a child. Feathers was telling the truth when she said it was his child, of that he was sure. He didn't want a child. What would he do with a child at this stage of life? He couldn't as much as admit responsibility for it. Admitting responsibility meant some commitment and that he didn't want. And if Allie ever found out that he had got a girl pregnant she would think that he was his father all over again, just as she had at first feared. There was no way he could explain it to Allie.

He felt a moment of panic that maybe Feathers out of desperation would try to blackmail him in some way. It would be terrible if Allie ever found out. Absolutely terrible.

It was cold in the street and he was angry with himself for not picking up a warmer overcoat. Also, if he was going to stay in a hotel, he'd have to go back to South Street station and gather up some of his luggage. Feathers had totally ruined his return to Boston. What a mess! he muttered to himself.

To get out of the cold and to work out a plan of campaign he turned into a café and ordered himself a coffee. He sat there at the table staring gloomily out at the street and the rag-bag of people who passed. Black, white, yellow and brown. It wasn't like France where everyone looked French which, in a way, caused life to be simpler. He longed to be there.

And then he remembered the letters that he had picked up. There were about half a dozen. A couple he recognised as tailor's bills. There was a communication from the college which would probably be about his application to take the French scholarship. There were some booksellers' circulars which he tore up. The only interesting letter was from France and addressed in Allie's handwriting. He sighed a deep sigh of pleasure. Word from her could not have come at a better time. Word from her would give him the strength to cope with the tiresome situation that he was in.

He split open the envelope eagerly. Allie always wrote long, vivid letters, but this seemed rather short by her standards. Leaving his coffee to cool, and expecting a love letter, he settled back in his chair to enjoy what she had to say. But the first paragraph dispelled his complacency.

My darling, darling Pierre,

Something so terrible has happened that I do not know how to begin to tell you. But tell you I must. I have been trying and trying to think of a way of breaking this to you gently, but there is no way. The bald fact is that we can never marry. There will be no happy future for us. Grandmother had her reasons for being so strange about our love because she knew it would never be permitted for us to marry. Oh, Pierre, it is so dreadful. We both share the same father. Jean Paul was my father as well as yours.

Do you remember I told you about the brothel keeper woman? We were going to see her together, remember? I met her by chance in Épernay today and it was she who told me the truth. My mother met your father – *our* father – when he worked for her father's winery in California. She fell in love with him, and became pregnant. She has been brazen enough actually to admit it to me. The mystery of how our parents knew each other is solved. She came to France to find Jean Paul – and Clovis, who I believed to be my father, married her to give me a name.

I cannot tell you what contempt I feel for my mother. She left this room five minutes ago as proud as ever in spite of her past. She does not know what shame is. I shall never be close to her again as long as I live. It is unthinkable that she could have become pregnant with me without being married. She is nothing but a whore. At least

210

my troubles were not of my own making. And then to marry poor Clovis without caring for him in the very least, just for the security of Les Hérissons, is too horrible. For her it all came right even though she never made my father happy. She never loved him. She has always done exactly what she wants to do and I think she broke my father's heart and drove him to visit that *poule*.

He will always be my father in my eyes for the wonderful childhood he gave me. He was the only father I ever knew. At least she had the grace to admit that. But her! For years she cuckolded him with Philippe Lefevre, and now she has married him. My father's death was most convenient, was it not? She is a whore, a whore, a whore!

It is all her fault that we cannot marry. We are half-brother and sister, Pierre. God will not permit us to be lovers. I do not think I can bear it. With you I found happiness and now it has been snatched away.

Truly are the sins of the fathers visited on the children . . .

Her furious, angry scrawl, the same scrawl as in her diary, had filled a page. He had to stop reading. He felt sick with dismay in a shock. It could not be possible. There must be some mistake. But if Aunt Rosie had admitted it . . . Did it matter? he asked himself on a ray of sudden hope. If he brought Allie to Boston and they married here, no one would know. There would be no one to stand up and declare just cause and impediment. That was the answer. He would bring her here, away from the family and they would marry and live happily ever after and worry about how to live when it was done. He turned the page and read on.

I wondered if it would be all right if we ran away somewhere together where no one knew us and married there. But Pierre, I am frightened to do that. It would be wrong in the sight of God and suppose something terrible happened to our children? Then our sins would be visited on them. And how would we live? What would we do? How star-crossed we are!

What I am going to say now will hurt you terribly, but

211

I can think of nothing else. I feel I do not wish to be on the same continent as my mother. I don't want to be near her. I want no part of her life, and that, of course, means no part of Les Hérissons. At first I thought I would kill myself but that would only be punishing myself to punish her. Instead, with heavy heart, I have decided to go to New York. As you know, Alexander is staying here and he is kind to me and he loves me. He has always loved me. Once he asked me to marry him. I don't think he would ever be demanding. I have not quite decided, but I think I might marry him, Pierre. If I can't have you, it doesn't matter who I have. I don't care. And marrying him will give me a new life in the New World. It will get me away from here.

Please try to understand. I don't love him, I love only you. You unlocked me. I only wish that we had made real love that night; I wish I had not been so fearful. I shall tell Alexander that I may never be a real wife to him, but if he wishes to marry me knowing that, then I think that I will.

I have to think of you as well. Now your future is at Les Hérissons. Grandmother wants you to take it all over one day. She loves you very much – more than she loves me – but then you are more lovable than I. I could not bear to be there with you so close, nor, I feel, could you bear to be there with me. We have to separate, and this is the best way to do it.

I shall be gone when you come back. Alexander has a week's vacation and then he is travelling back to New York. I shall go with him.

Oh, Pierre, never doubt I love you. This is all for the best. It is the only way.

> Goodbye my darling one, for ever,
> Allie

Stunned, he put the letter down on the table. He felt the most terrible frustration. He wanted to be in France and hold her tight in her arms and tell her that nothing would separate them, ever. How could she even consider marrying anyone else when they were made for each other? They loved each other. But . . . but . . . the inescapable fact was that they were half-brother and sister. Marriage was taboo.

Dazed, he paid for his coffee. He needed something stronger. He asked the waiter if there was a speakeasy nearby. There was. The waiter directed him and told him to say that Jim had sent him. He tipped the waiter heavily.

In the dark of the speakeasy he looked neither to left nor right. He simply concentrated on getting as drunk as possible as quickly as possible. It didn't take long. Pierre was not used to hard liquor. When he could only just stagger he got to his feet.

'Where you going, buddy?' asked the barman.

'Home,' he said thickly.

'Where's home?'

Automatically he gave the address of the apartment on Commonwealth Avenue. Someone helped him into a cab, and at the end of the ride the driver took his key and let him in the main door of the building. He managed to stagger up the stairs muttering 'taboo, taboo, taboo' over and over again. With difficulty he put the key in the lock of his own door and as he fumbled to turn it, through the mists of rough alcohol he thought he could smell something strange. He could. As he came into the hallway the acrid yet sweet smell of gas enveloped him. Fear sobered him a little. Leaving the front door open, choking, his handkerchief over his mouth, he staggered through to the source of the smell – the kitchen. The oven door was open and a body lay before it. With difficulty he turned out the gas. He tried to open the window but his unco-ordinated hands could not manage it. He picked up a heavy iron frying pan and swung it to break the glass. Fresh air flooded in. But not enough. Pierre's knees quietly gave way and he sank to join Feathers' body where it lay on the floor.

The bitter cold blowing through the broken window and the fact that he needed to vomit woke him. He managed to get to his feet and stagger to the bathroom where he was violently sick. Instantly he felt better and he went back to the kitchen and tried to turn his attention to Feathers who lay inert, her face blue but he saw with relief, breathing harshly. Even so, she looked near to death. The smell of gas still lingered and he opened more windows. The apartment was freezing now. Somehow he managed to pick her up. There was no life in her. She was a dead weight and it seemed to him that her breathing was fading. He dragged her nearer to the window, and then wondered what on earth to do next. Ambulance. Get her to hospital or she would die. If she wasn't dead already.

'Don't die, Feathers! Don't die!' he kept whispering as he went shakily to the telephone and called for help.

It seemed an eternity before the ambulance came. He covered her with a blanket and sat rubbing her hands in his. All he could think of was how could he explain it all if she was dead? Once they arrived, the ambulance men showed no interest in him. Other than asking his name and telling him that they were going to take her to the Boston City Hospital, they ignored him while quickly and efficiently they got her out of the house.

'Is she going to be all right?' he asked once she was on a stretcher.

'She don't look too good to me,' one of the men said laconically. 'Pregnant?'

Pierre nodded.

'Poor little bitch,' the man said. 'I expect the police'll be round. You'd better stay here.'

Then they were gone and she was gone. He couldn't believe that it was still not dark. Outside, the street lights were just beginning to splutter into flame and the warm glow of lamps appeared in the windows opposite. He realised that the whole dreadful episode from the time he had rushed out of the apartment had taken less than two hours. Maybe she would survive if she hadn't turned on the gas immediately he had left. How long did gas take to kill? He didn't know the answer, and he felt too exhausted even to think about it. He sat down in the armchair by the fireplace where she had been sitting and closed his eyes. Just for a second, he thought. But when he woke again he was sitting in darkness, numb with cold and someone was knocking insistently at the door. His head hurt and he felt sick. Unsteadily he got to his feet and made his way down the hall.

There were two policemen with big, beefy Irish faces standing outside with belligerent stance, their nightsticks hanging from their belts.

'We've had a report of an attempted suicide here,' one of them said.

'You'd better come in,' Pierre said.

It wasn't as bad as he thought it would be. He said she was

the maid and in spite of their obvious disbelief, he insisted that it must have been an accident. She had obviously left the oven on without lighting the gas.

'After all,' he said, 'she would hardly have tried to kill herself when she knew I would be back at any moment, now would she?'

They listened and made notes.

'Is she alive?' he asked when the questions were over, dreading the answer.

'No idea,' the policeman who seemed to do the talking said. 'You'll have to call the hospital.'

'Will she be prosecuted?'

'Not if she's dead.' The policeman delivered this news with a grim chuckle. He was putting away his notebook and hitching his uniform into place. 'You want to shut some windows here,' he said as they both moved towards the door, 'or you'll freeze to death yourself.'

It was gone seven now. He looked up the number of the Boston City Hospital and rang casualty. Mary O'Flanagan was not dead but she was gravely ill and on the danger list. It would be better if he rang again in the morning.

He hung up the receiver feeling as if he had been beaten in battle. He took the policeman's advice and shut all the windows. And then he went to bed.

He woke ridiculously early to the grey light of a late dawn. For a moment he lay in bed staring at the ceiling remembering all the dreadful events of the day before. He wished he had slept longer so he did not have to face the possibility that Feathers was dead and the fact that he and Allie could not be together.

Reluctantly he got out of bed and made himself bathe and shave. There seemed to be no food in the house and a cold wind blew through the broken window. On the kitchen table he found a scrappy piece of paper that Feathers had left, presumably before she put her head in the oven.

'I am sorry to do this to you in your apartment, but I have nowhere else to go to do it.'

That was all. Twenty-one stark little words. Nowhere else to go to die. Shame washed over him. For a man who did not wish to be like his father, he wasn't doing very well.

He decided to get out of the apartment and retrieved his

winter overcoat from the closet. A long walk would clear his head.

In Commonwealth Avenue the trees were nearly bare and the wind blew up the broad street with icy intent. He walked briskly along until he reached Massachusetts Avenue and turned left into its length. Somewhere at the end towards South Boston was the City Hospital. Pierre had not made up his mind but he thought that was where he would go. He stopped for some breakfast at the first open café he saw. He needed a strong cup of coffee and he needed to read Allie's letter again.

He finished drinking the first cup of coffee and reading the letter at much the same moment. He called for another cup, folded the letter and put it back in his pocket.

She was undoubtedly hysterical when she had written it and his heart bled for her continuing misfortunes. Yet her bitter harangue against her mother left him uneasy. He found himself reluctantly thinking that this new piece of knowledge had become the excuse for Allie to spill out years of jealousy of her mother. She now had what she could see as genuine reason for her erstwhile buried resentment of the glamorous Rosie. And yet it did not seem to him to be logical entirely to blame Rosie Dupuis for what had happened. Allie did not give her mother any credit for so much that had been good. To marry a man you did not love to give a child a name seemed to him to be something of a sacrifice. Surely the true villain of the piece was his father who had abandoned Rosie in the first place?

Just as he had abandoned Feathers O'Flanagan? It was a chilling thought and he hastily pushed it aside.

He read the letter again and was filled with a resentment of his own. How could she contemplate marrying Alexander merely as a passport to another life? How could she! It was cruel and wicked when she knew that he loved her. He felt she should have waited until they could talk. He felt her gesture offering him Les Hérissons rang false. She was not running away from Les Hérissons because he might return there but to get away from her mother and her old life and old memories. She was prepared to shed him – and Rosanne – on the way. Maybe she had never really loved him anyway. Maybe she had been playing a game. And again that touch of envy and jealousy came through when she said that her grandmother liked him best. That was not true. He tried to tell himself that Allie had been writing when she was in a state of shock, and this was not the real Allie. But the impression of self-interest lingered on.

He groaned. He could hardly bear to think that she might not have loved him. Did he want to go back to Les Hérissons if she was not there? The answer was that he did. It would be most desperately painful at first, but it would be much worse here in Boston on his own without anyone at all. He had directed his entire life to being in France. He had been happy at Les Hérissons, even before he realised he loved Allie. Warmth, family and a normal life were there. Having tasted that life, he wanted it to go on. He had no doubt that his grandmother would welcome him with open arms. He was not so sure about Aunt Rosie, but his impression was that she was just.

The grey skies reflected his mood as he walked along Massachusetts Avenue, his head full of pictures of Allie. Her decision to marry Alexander had squeezed his heart yet, loving her as he did, he was already forgiving her for the selfish note in her letter, telling himself how much she had suffered in life already. Marrying Alexander must be better than killing herself. Remembering Feather's ghastly white face and lifeless body, he shuddered at the thought of Allie, his Allie, in the same condition. To die for love had a nobility about it, but how would he feel if Feathers died?

The hospital was a long way down the avenue and he was becoming nervous about what he would find when he arrived. If Feathers had survived he wanted to see her so he could tell her what he had told the police. If she did live, it would be too terrible for her to be prosecuted for attempted suicide as well as facing all her other troubles. He had probably saved her life by coming home drunk, and then he asked himself gloomily what he had saved it for?

'Are you the father?' the matron said with a sniff when he asked for Mary O'Flanagan. He pretended he did not know what she was talking about and she gave him a dubious look. But she had not mentioned death.

'Can I see her?' he asked, praying he would not be shown a corpse.

'If you wish,' she said, her tone making it clear she would

217

rather have sent him away. 'She's in the bed just inside the ward door.'

'She's going to be all right?' he asked.

'She'll be out of here tomorrow,' the matron said and swished away.

The ward was long and grey. A charity ward. He was glad he did not have to walk its length. She was lying on the high ugly bed, her hands folded across the greyish sheets. Her eyes were closed. She was still pale but the awful green colour had gone and she looked peaceful and very beautiful.

'Feathers –' he whispered.

The long dark lashes lifted from her cheeks and her blue eyes widened as she saw him standing there.

'You came,' she said wonderingly.

'Only to see you're all right,' he warned quickly.

'I'm all right.' She sounded as if it was a matter of complete indifference. 'Who found me?'

'I did.'

'You did?' She looked startled. 'Why did you come back?'

'I'd forgotten something,' he lied.

'I wish you hadn't.'

'You'd be dead if I hadn't.'

'That's right,' she said.

They were both silent and then she said: 'There is a place for fallen women, as you put it. They're going to send me there. They think the baby will be all right.'

'You would have killed that too,' he said accusingly, aware that it was his baby.

'Well, it would have been better for everyone. Now it will have to be adopted. I shall never see how it grows up.' She shut her eyes and tears squeezed from under her lashes. 'I hope it's a boy. The world is a better place for boys.'

He didn't want to think about its being a boy or being adopted or anything. It would be a child, like Allie, who never knew who its real father was. He brushed the thought aside and said quickly: 'Listen – I told the police that you're my maid and that it was all an accident. You forgot to light the gas. They prosecute people who attempt suicide.'

'I've already told the priest the truth.'

'Well, don't tell the police the truth.'

'I don't expect they'll bother anyway. Why should they care whether I'm alive or dead?'

'I suppose it's all about money. I shall pay for the ambulance and give the hospital something for their trouble, then maybe the police won't do anything about it.'

'Just as you like,' she said and closed her eyes again.

Awkwardly he got to his feet and stood looking down at her. He didn't know what to do next.

'Well,' he said, 'since you're all right, I'll be on my way. I'll put your things together so all you have to do is pick them up.'

She barely nodded.

'Well, goodbye then,' he said. She said nothing. He didn't know whether to take her hand, wish her luck, what to do. In the end he just turned and walked towards the door.

Outside he stopped by the kitchens where a nurse was busy heating up some milk. He found he was sweating and he felt dreadfully ill and confused. Feathers' face kept merging in his mind with Allie's. He was doing to her what his father had done to Rosie. No, it wasn't quite like that but the result would be the same. He thought of Allie's words: 'If I can't have you, it doesn't matter who I have. I don't care.' If she could reason like that, why shouldn't he? He turned and quickly, before he could change his mind, went back to the bed where Feathers lay. She had not moved and he did not touch her. He just blurted out, rather too loudly: 'I think we had better get married. As long as you're prepared to live in France, that is,' he added.

She opened her amazing eyes and stared at him. Then she closed them again and sighed a long, slow, relieved sigh. She stretched to take his hand.

'Anywhere,' she said. 'Anywhere in the world you like.'

Rosie was sitting alone in the small parlour at Les Hérissons. The house was quiet and still. Madame Dupuis had gone to evening Mass and Allie had gone to America the day before in company with Alexander and Jessica. This time Allie had made it clear that she was going for good. There had been no farewell kisses, barely a goodbye for Rosie. She lavished more affection on Marie than on her mother. Alexander had been dreadfully embarrassed and done his best to smooth things over, but it was plain that Allie was not yet ready to forgive and maybe never would be.

Rosie sighed. She had been feeling desperately depressed all day as she finished packing Allie's things – her childhood cuddly toys which she wanted to keep, her books, the pictures of Clovis. It had hurt Rosie almost unbearably when she found pictures of herself torn into small pieces at the bottom of Allie's wastepaper basket. She had let them run through her fingers, feeling utter dismay, then resolutely piled other rubbish on top to hide them. But in spite of everything, she could not resist putting in a little loving note before she sealed the trunk and addressed it to Lizzie Webster in New York. It was important that Allie knew she was loved. Tomorrow she would take the trunk on the train with her to Paris and Georges could despatch it from there, as he had once despatched another trunk, and with its departure Allie would truly have gone from her life.

Of course it was all her fault, Rosie thought as she sat in the gathering gloom, the lamps unlit. But she could not help feeling that the bitterness and anger that Allie spewed out were excessive. Apart from the accident of birth, Rosie felt she had nothing to reproach herself with in her conduct towards her daughter. She had always been a loving mother. What Allie could not forgive was that she had not always been a loving wife.

There was nothing she could do about that now. It was far too late. Rosie gave herself a small brief lecture, telling herself that the time had come to get on with her own life. Life with Philippe. Tonight she might just take a bicycle and go and see their new home near Champillon by moonlight. The exercise and the night air would invigorate her and being out of Les Hérissons would cheer her up. She would not continue to be miserable and sad, she instructed herself. What was the point?

She was just about to go out when she heard the telephone ringing in the house and Marie answering it. In a few seconds the maid was knocking on the parlour door.

'It's young Master Pierre calling from America, Madame Rosie,' she said. 'He wants to speak to you.'

Rosie's heart sank. Was she going to have to explain to Pierre that Allie had gone off to America with Alexander? She had no idea whether or not Allie had written to the lad. Since the day after her daughter had learned of their half-brother/half-sister relationship she had not so much as mentioned Pierre's name,

She went quickly to the telephone.

'Aunt Rosie?' Pierre's voice was not very clear. 'Is that you?'

'Yes, Pierre.' She was having to shout above a strange crackling noise. 'I'm sorry but your grandmother has gone to Mass.'

'It doesn't matter,' he said. 'I really wanted to talk to you.'

'Are you coming back?' she asked.

'Yes, but not for a week or two until I've got things settled here.' He paused. 'I heard from Allie.'

'You know then that she's left for the States?'

'I guessed she would have gone by now. She obviously didn't want to see me again.'

He sounded so desolate over the crackling line that she wished he was nearer so she could comfort him.

'Pierre, I'm so sorry. Why it had to turn out like this . . . It's all my fault.'

'It's not. It isn't anyone's fault really except perhaps my father's,' he said. 'He did so much damage. I pray every day that I am not like him. I try so hard not to be like him.' She heard his sigh from three thousand miles away and then he said: 'Grandma does still want me to come back?' His voice was anxious.

'We all want you to come back,' Rosie told him firmly.

'Only you see . . .' he stopped and for a moment Rosie thought they had lost the connection. Then he said: 'Will it be all right if I bring a wife back with me?'

The question winded Rosie.

'A wife?' she said unbelievingly.

'Yes.' He sounded apologetic. 'She's pregnant, you see. I'm glad I'm talking to you because you'll understand. It happened before I left here and since Allie's going to marry Alexander —'

'She is?' Rosie asked, astonished. 'She never told us that.'

'She said in her letter that's what she thought she would do. Oh God, do you think she was making it up?'

'Not necessarily,' Rosie said. 'She wasn't speaking very much to any of us before she left. She wasn't speaking to me at all.'

'Well, she said that since we couldn't be together, it didn't matter who she married. She didn't care. I suppose I think the same.'

'Oh Pierre, do be careful,' Rosie said, alarmed by the conversation. 'Marriage lasts an awfully long time. Please be sure you're doing the right thing. Don't leap into anything. You're so young.'

'She's pregnant,' he said stubbornly. 'It's my baby. And I don't want to be like my father. Look at all the trouble it's caused. And anyway, I've promised her now.'

'Is she a nice girl, Pierre?'

'She's not a bad girl, just an ordinary girl and she loves me.'

There didn't seem to be anything more to say.

'Then marry her and bring her back to France,' Rosie said briskly. 'We'll all look after her and the baby. It will be history repeating itself in a way.'

'That's what I thought,' he said.

But Rosie was anxious as she hung up the telephone. It seemed as if both young people were being driven into situations they might regret – and very soon. She was pleased when she heard the car coming slowly up the drive. Madame was home. Rosie needed to share this news.

Once Madame had her hat and coat off and her early evening glass of champagne in her hand, she listened to Rosie's report of the telephone call.

'Umm,' she said when Rosie had finished speaking. 'Marry in haste, repent at leisure. But Allie could do far worse than marry young Alexander, and if Pierre has made this girl pregnant, I suppose he's doing the right thing. Though it always seems like a very bad reason for a marriage to me. I hope she's not some little trollop.'

'I don't think he'd bring anyone like that here.'

'No, maybe not. For a young man he has quite a lot of sense. Just as his father had.'

Rosie bit her tongue. Madame's memory was sometimes a little too selective for comfort when it came to her precious Jean Paul.

'Do you realise,' Madame said smugly, 'that I shall be a greatgrandmother?'

'You are already,' Rosie pointed out and for an instant Madame looked startled.

'Of course,' she said, 'how stupid of me. I always think of Rosanne as yours.'

'And that is probably another reason why Allie will never forgive me for anything,' Rosie's voice was sad. 'Ah, well.

What's done is done.' She stirred restlessly in her chair and then said: 'I think I might go out for a while before supper, Mama, if you don't mind.'

'Not at all,' said Madame, her tone surprisingly gentle. 'Don't be late back. It's guinea fowl. Your favourite. I ordered it especially.'

It was now too late to cycle over to Champillon. Instead by the light of a watery winter moon, Rosie walked through the estate and up the hill to the high ground that had always been Clovis and Allie's favourite place. She sat there not troubling about the dampness of the grass, her knees under chin, her arms round her legs, staring down at the valley below. In the distance she could see the lights of Reims and, nearer, those of Chigny and Ludes. Les Hérissons, the estate that she had built up and made prosper, had faded into the darkness. All that glowed was the light in the tower room. Luke West's room. She wondered idly what he was doing.

Next month she would be forty – more than halfway through her three score years and ten. She had Philippe's love and she had the success of Les Hérissons to show for her life and, she thought, she had been neglecting them both recently. There was, thank God, still more to be done. She needed something to do. Something to do healed all disappointments. There was Rosanne to bring up and hopefully Rosanne would love her as Allie never quite had. Facing the truth, Rosie forced herself to accept that even as a small child Allie had always shown a trace of resentment in her relationship with her. As if she had known from the womb of her misbegetting. So, there was Allie to mourn. One day, Rosie promised herself, she would make Allie understand. One day they would be close as a mother and daughter should be.

But for now it was time to start a new life with Philippe in their own home. The house would be habitable in a few days' time. As she thought of him, a wave of desire concentrated itself somewhere vital inside. The appetite for love that Jean Paul had told her she possessed long, long ago had never been sated. Her desire and need for Philippe was the strongest thing in her life. How lucky she was to have him! A man who loved her, excited her and forgave her trespasses. What more could a woman want?

y

From her vantage point she saw the dining room light go on in the house below. Marie and Henri would be laying the table, Madame would be completing the toilette she always made before dinner, and Cook would be bad tempered, shouting at the little kitchen maid, as she put the finishing touches to the meal.

The light went out in Luke West's room. He was on his way downstairs. It was time she went back. With her own home almost ready, she would take few suppers at Les Hérissons in the future.

But Madame had said not to be late. She got to her feet, brushing leaves and damp from her skirt. She stretched, as if it was morning and she was starting a new day. And then she hurried back down the hill towards the house that had sheltered her for so long.

It was guinea fowl tonight. Her favourite.

BOOK TWO

BOOK TWO

Chapter Nine

'Well,' Rosie asked, 'when do we start picking?'

It was mid-October and the sun was low in the early evening sky. She stood on the roadside by one of the high fields which looked down to the River Vesle, her arms folded, head turned enquiringly. Luke West, Robert and Pierre were grouped around her. Pierre hung back a little. His degree at the Sorbonne won, it was his first involvement in the *vendange*. Soon he was to go to the School of Oenology at Épernay, but for the present he stood respectfully two paces behind while the experts solemnly inspected the clusters of dark red Pinot grapes that hung like huge black rubies on the vines.

It had been a bad year. Heavy frosts in April had destroyed one third of the crop. Flowering had come late and now the *vendange* was late. Rosie looked anxiously at the sky – a late *vendange* could mean cold miserable weather for the picking and the shortness of the days lengthened the work.

Luke pulled a single globe of grape away from the stalk. He squeezed the stalk for texture, looked at the fragment of pulp that was attached and then gently squeezed the fruit to test its elasticity. Then he carefully tasted the juice before spreading the pips on his hand to check their size and colour.

'A couple more days,' he said.

Rosie felt a sudden, quite irrational sense of loss that Clovis was not there. Clovis had always known, just as if Bacchus himself had given him a nod and a wink, exactly when the grapes were ready.

'Longer?' she said uneasily. 'If it rains they could rot. And the skins could taint the juice with red if they get too ripe.'

'Neither will happen,' Luke said confidently. 'What do you think, Robert?'

Robert's methods of divination were more in harmony with those of Clovis.

'Yes, two more days,' he said firmly. 'The vines flowered late and in two days it will be one hundred days since they were in full bloom.'

'And I suppose the lilies flowered ninety days ago?' Luke asked with a grin.

'That's right,' said Robert stolidly.

Robert believed, as Clovis once had, that nature rarely made a mistake. A grape, like a woman, had its own period of gestation. And that was a hundred days after the vine was in full flower. There were also those who believed that the harvest was ready ninety days after the lilies flowered. This time the scientific and the instinctive had come to the same conclusion.

'Are you sure? Look.' Rosie pointed to the sky where a black-bird lurched in dizzy circles. 'The poor thing's drunk! Some of the grapes must be ripe and fermenting!'

'Only the split ones,' Luke said firmly.

After inspection of other fields where the grapes were fat, glossy green and fragile-skinned, it was decided that these, the Chardonnays, would be harvested three days after the red Pinots. Rosie sighed with the relief of decisions made as the four of them mounted the bicycles that they used to cover the miles of vineyard. Robert rode as easily as any of them, holding the handlebars dead centre with his one arm.

'Will the *vendangeurs* be here in time?' she asked him in a sudden panic, appalled at the thought of all those grapes and no one to pick them.

'The first of them are arriving tomorrow. The rest come later,' Robert said. 'The *vendangeoirs* are all ready and Cook is starting to organise the food.'

It was Robert's job to make sure that there was enough casual labour from the towns to the north and east to pick the grapes and that their accommodation – huts like bunk houses built on the property – were clean and ready for them.

'That was good timing,' she told him. 'I suppose you were working on your hundred days theory.'

'Of course,' he said as if surprised she had mentioned it.

They pedalled in thoughtful silence for a while along the rough lanes between the orderly rows of laden vines.

'Let's hope it's a better crop than last year' Rosie said, still worrying as she worried every year at this time. 'Last year was a disaster.'

'Stop fussing. This year everything will be better,' Luke promised. 'Ten days' hard work and you can relax knowing that you have a harvest that will make some really fine wine. The grapes may not be too plentiful, but they're perfect.'

'That's good news,' she said and meant it.

It was becoming increasingly important that Les Hérissons did well financially. The business had to feed a lot of mouths. Madame still left all the handling of the money, both personal and business, to Rosie but in her old age she had become suspicious of any demands on her personal purse. Rosie sometimes thought that the old lady was saving as if she planned to live for ever. It had made sense to merge Philippe's company into Les Hérissons, but in the last six months his headaches had been plaguing him to the extent that often he could not work and the sales of her champagne depended on his efforts. There was no doubt that his business required more time spent on it, she thought anxiously. It was not as profitable or as efficient as it had once been, but Philippe resisted the idea of a full business partner. She no longer had total control. Philippe had insisted that if the businesses were merged, everything should be done legally and correctly. Now the import/export business, Les Hérissons champagne, the machinery and the outbuildings were hers and Philippe's. The house, the land and the vineyards remained the family's.

Times had been hard. For a year their English sales had been cut in half by a monstrously high tax which the British Chancellor of the Exchequer, Winston Churchill, had levied on champagne. The Germans and the Austro-Hungarian empire, struggling to recover from the war, were in no mood for celebration. The Russian market, which once had taken ten per cent of Rosie's output, no longer existed since the October 1917 revolution. Worse, Prohibition had wiped out the best market of all – the Americans. And now even the Scandinavians were trifling with the idea of prohibition.

They ought to be selling more of their wine in France, she told herself, wondering how that could be achieved. Her wine had a fine reputation. She had never lost a customer other than through historical circumstances. But they needed more customers as an incentive to increasing production.

Still, thank God, they were certainly not poor. They kept up the Paris house on the Ile de la Cité – indeed, Pierre and Feathers and their small son, Patric, had lived there while Pierre took his degree. Madame paid some of Pierre's bills from her own purse, but his family's everyday living expenses came from Les Hérissons earnings. There was also the generous allowance that went into Allie's New York bank every month. It wasn't necessary. Allie was well provided for but she never wrote home, and Rosie hoped the money would act as an assurance that she was still loved. Rosie bore the heavy expense of running the family home itself with all the bills and wages. Then there was the maintenance of her own home, Les Coquelicots, named for the field poppies she loved. She was also responsible for the small apartment in Reims which was used as part office and part *pied-à-terre*. She was even paying for a caretaker for the house in California. Philippe was right. They should sell that at least. It was an expense she could do without.

'Are you coming back to Les Hérissons?' Pierre, who was cycling beside her, asked, interrupting her thoughts.

'Just to get the car,' she told him. 'Then I must get back to Les Coquelicots. Philippe will be waiting.'

'It's just that Feathers wanted to have a word with you,' he said.

'Oh,' she turned to look at him, but he was resolutely looking ahead. 'Is something wrong?'

'No, no,' he said. 'She'll tell you about it.'

'As long as she is well.'

'She's fine.' He sounded indifferent.

She sneaked a sideways look at him, but his face gave nothing away. He was twenty-three now and growing to look more and more like the late Dupuis brothers every day. With his French haircut and his French clothes he could have been Clovis at that age, but where Clovis had been dull and heavy, Pierre was quick and bright with only occasional flashes of his father's cruelty. Those flashes when they sparked out like a swiftly drawn sword were reserved for Feathers, poor, lovable, frivolous Feathers who after nearly three years in Europe still struggled to speak French.

Madame was impatient with her new granddaughter-in-law, irritated that they could not chat together. She was also a touch resentful that the girl was married to Pierre since Pierre and little Patric were now the recipients of all the spoiling and love that she had once lavished on Pierre's father.

But Rosie had liked the girl from the minute she had come into Madame's parlour at Les Hérissons, so beautiful and young, so heavily pregnant, scared out of her wits but damned if she was going to show it. She remembered herself at much the same age, equally pregnant and facing the formidable Madame Dupuis – and in some ways Madame had grown more formidable.

Feather's relief when she found that Rosie spoke English was blindingly visible and her dismay equally so when she realised that Rosie did not live at Les Hérissons.

'You can always talk to Luke,' Rosie had said consolingly. 'And you will have to learn the language.'

But somehow the girl had never been able to master it. Nothing had been easy for her. A few days after her arrival, Feathers had been full of questions until Rosie asked, laughing, if Pierre had told her anything about France at all?

Feathers had turned her beautiful face away.

'He doesn't talk to me a lot,' she said sadly. 'He didn't really want to marry me, you know. He was going to marry someone else. I don't know what happened, but he suddenly said he would marry me. I suppose because I was pregnant and desperate.'

'I see,' said Rosie, feeling it was best to pretend she knew nothing.

'Do you know who it was he wanted to marry?'

Rosie dodged the question. 'He was only here for one day before I went to the States so I really didn't know him very well until you both came here.'

'It must have been a French girl,' Feathers muttered. 'It was after he'd been here for all that time. When he came back to Boston he told me about it.'

'Well, maybe he just changed his mind when he saw you again,' Rosie soothed. Feathers looked unconvinced.

Apart from her difficulties with the language, France, and in particular Paris, had suited the girl very well. She proved to have good taste in wine, food and, above all, clothes. At first Rosie's wardrobe had filled her with awe and wonder. Now her own was as good. At just twenty she was chic and elegant with a gift for discovering promising new designers. She used feathers as her trademark. She adored feathered hats, boas and trimmings and it was her good fortune that they were *à la mode*. She also adored her small son and since Pierre had insisted on a French nanny, at two and a half the boy was bilingual and already translating for her. Thank God, Rosie thought, he was not another saturnine, dark, bushy-browed little Dupuis. Though his hair was dark and his eyes were blue, his skin was fair and his face round and freckled with a small squashy nose. Luke West had laughed out loud when he first saw him.

'That child's face is a map of old Ireland!' he said.

But Rosie was aware that Feathers constantly bruised herself against her husband's indifference, and there was no sign of more babies. It was sad. Neither of them were truly happy though Feathers was painfully anxious to please and Pierre seemed to be trying to make the best of the situation. He was devoted to his son but barely involved himself in the boy's upbringing.

'Little children should be brought up by women,' he insisted and Rosie remembered he had had no mother of his own.

Feathers was hovering on the porch as the four of them pedalled up the driveway. When she saw them, she waved and ran towards them, smiling, her dark hair lifting in the breeze. She was really remarkably beautiful, Rosie thought, looking to see if Pierre was moved by his wife's glamour. He was not even looking at her but talking to Luke, asking what it was he had expected to learn from the grape pips. Rosie sighed. A man of his age should find a beautiful woman more interesting than the pips of a grape.

'Did Pierre tell you I wanted to talk to you?' Feathers asked as she drew level. 'Is it all right? Do you have time?'

'*Bonjour*, Feathers,' Rosie said gently as a reminder. One of the things that drove Madame mad was that Feathers never remembered to say *bonjour*, rarely remembered the compulsory kiss on the cheek, and was lacking when it came to saying *s'il vous plaît*. Feathers protested Americans weren't that formal, but it cut no ice with Madame.

'Can we walk?' Feathers asked, clutching her arm. 'The house oppresses me.'

'If you wish,' Rosie said, leaning her bicycle against the porch; someone would no doubt remove it and put it away for her. 'Where do you want to walk?'

'To the top of the hill, where the view you like is.'

'In those shoes?' Feathers was wearing little pink lightweight shoes that picked out the pink in the pattern of her summer dress.

'I've worn them a lot. It won't matter.'

The two women set off through the trees and towards the path up the hill. The men had vanished to the back of the house, Luke West wheeling Rosie's bicycle along with his own.

'Can we talk when we get there?' Feathers asked. 'I've such a lot to say.'

'Oh dear!' Rosie said lightly.

'But I won't keep you long, I promise.'

'You can keep me as long as you like,' Rosie assured her, but with an inward sigh, thinking of Philippe in his endless darkness waiting for her at Les Coquelicots.

They walked in silence. At the top of the hill they settled themselves on the grass looking down at the view below. It was spectacular at this time of evening with the sun throwing long shadows across the vines and the house itself softened by the coming darkness.

'Now, what is it?' Rosie asked.

'I want something to do.' Feathers turned her pansy face to Rosie, her expression pleading, then added abruptly. 'Will you lend me the money to start a dress shop?'

'Heavens above!' she said faintly. This was not what she had expected.

'I think I'd be good at it. I think I'd make it work, but I haven't any money of my own.'

'What does Pierre think of the idea?'

'He doesn't care what I do. He said why didn't I talk it over with you.'

'And what about Patric?'

'With nannies and servants, I hardly get to see him. It's all so strange to me, Rosie. You can't imagine what my own home was like. Four of us in one bedroom, three of them girls and one boy.

I never saw much of my mother either, but that was because she worked all the hours God sent to keep us fed. I wrote to tell them I was safe and well, but I don't want contact with them. Not yet. Maybe one day.' She paused momentarily before saying that sometimes when she could she sent her mother money. Then she went on hurriedly: 'But I had a job when I left school. I worked for Jordan Marsh in the drapery. If I hadn't got pregnant, I'd have been assistant head of department. I might even have been a buyer one day. I liked it and I was real good at it. Everyone said I was a great salesgirl and that I had a flair for fashion.'

She spoke with pride, and Rosie was aware how isolated and unsure of her own worth she must have been since she arrived in France.

'I think I'd get the hang of French if I was working,' she went on. 'In Paris there was no one for me to talk to at all. I wasn't sure whether I was allowed to talk to the staff and anyway they didn't talk to me. Pierre was studying when he did come home, and I was really lonely. He didn't come home all that much. He got friendly with another American student called Jack somebody, Patterson I think, and he was always out with him. I did try to learn and you may have noticed that I can do things like order a meal and buy something, but there was no one to talk to. Here Madame gets so impatient when I don't know the word or get it wrong that I'm frightened to try. Nanny doesn't like me around, so I'm always looking for poor Luke to talk to. I should speak French to him – and to you – but it's such a relief to be able to say anything at all.'

'Won't Pierre help you?' Rosie asked.

Feathers grimaced. 'Not really. We don't talk much.' Her eyes were filling with tears. 'I love him so much, Rosie, and he's always so pleasant and nice to me, but only as he would be to a friend or even a stranger. We don't even – well, do much, any more, if you know what I mean, and I miss it.' Her cheeks had reddened, and she looked embarrassed. 'Is that awful of me?'

'No, it's not,' Rosie said firmly, remembering her own youthful appetites.

'You see, I think he thinks I trapped him into marriage. I'd been staying in his apartment while he was over here and I tried to gas myself. He came back and found me. But I honestly had no

234

idea he was coming back. He wasn't meant to come back until the next day. But he did come back for some reason or other. He said he'd forgotten something. I don't know what, but it saved my life. We've never talked about it since.' She had been speaking very fast as if she wanted to get the explanations over. Rosie took her hand and said quietly: 'Oh my dear!' But Feathers just shook her head violently and went on with her story. 'It was when I was in hospital that he said he'd marry me. I was so happy.' She breathed out hard and shook her head. 'You can't imagine what it's like for a Catholic girl in Boston to get pregnant. I would have had to kill myself or go on the streets.'

'I *can* imagine,' Rosie murmured, remembering when she had been a seventeen-year-old girl in California with the same problem.

'You can? Well, not many people would understand, I can tell you. Of course I'm so unbelievably lucky. It's like heaven here. A husband I love, my lovely Patric, all the clothes I want, people to do the work. I only wish I'd been married in Church. I feel as if I'm sinning all the time. But even so, sometimes I can't believe my good fortune. But I must have something of my own. Some life of my own. Do you understand?'

Rosie felt a temptation to tell her own story in a way she could never tell it to Allie. Feathers would understand as Allie never had or could. But it wasn't the moment. All Rosie said was: 'I was the same when I came here, but I put my energies into Les Hérissons. Do you think it's being American that does it?' She laughed and squeezed Feather's hand. 'Where do you want this dress shop?'

'I thought in Reims. There's not much competition and I've seen some premises that could be just right.'

'Not on the rue St Honoré in Paris?' Rosie teased.

'Only if I make a success of it in Reims. If I do, why not on the rue St Honoré next?'

Rosie's laughter rang out over the valley.

'Why not indeed,' she said, and leaned to give Feathers a hug. 'Why not indeed! But Madame will have a fit!'

She drove herself home swiftly and competently after Henri cranked the car. She had learned how two years before when Henri had been retired from driving, and the old Léon Bolleé had finally given up. She had bought a new modern Salmson which was a pleasure to drive and she loved the freedom that the car gave her in her busy life.

It was becoming dark as she drove through the opened iron gates into Les Coquelicots. Michel, the young houseman who was some sort of cousin of Marie's, instantly appeared to put the car away.

She ran into the house, the sabots she had worn for inspecting the vines clattering on the black and white tiles of the hallway. It was so late that Nanny Shepherd would have put Rosanne to bed. The house was silent and the living room in darkness and she had to switch on the newly installed electric light as she came in. Philippe was sitting in his usual armchair beside the big stone fireplace, his head leaning on the back of the wing chair.

'Oh, darling,' she said as she moved across the expanse of room to kiss him. 'They've left you in the dark.'

'It hardly matters, does it?' His voice was flat, without life.

'I think it matters,' she said firmly, knowing he could distinguish between total darkness and light. 'It means they're not looking after you.'

'I told them to leave me alone,' he said.

She sat on the arm of his chair and stroked the fair hair that had barely changed colour.

'Does your head hurt?' she asked.

'Not with your hand on it.'

'But it has been hurting?'

'Yes.'

She tried not to sigh. Philippe was in almost constant pain, and she felt helpless, not knowing what to do to help him. She had insisted that he went to the best Parisian doctors but it seemed nothing could be done. The pain came from the same wartime injuries that had caused his blindness. One doctor had prescribed laudanum, which did wipe away the pain. But Philippe feared becoming addicted to it, and complained that it made him sleepy and out of control. He would rather bear the pain, he declared.

'I'm glad you're home,' he said, moving to lean his head against her waist. 'I've missed you. What made you late?'

She felt a pang of guilt. Philippe should really come first, before Feathers. Philippe should come before everything, but somehow life always got in the way.

236

'Feathers,' she said, rising to ring for the maid. They always had a glass of champagne when she came home as an aperitif before dinner. 'She wants me to lend her the money to open a dress shop.'

'A dress shop!' He sounded as scandalised as if she had said that Feathers wanted to open a brothel. 'Whatever did you say?'

'I said yes.' She was surprised by his reaction. 'Why? Don't you think it's a good idea?'

'No. And neither will Madame. She'll be appalled at the thought of one of her family going into trade.'

'A dress shop is hardly trade,' Rosie protested.

'What else is it?'

'Well—' she thought about it briefly and decided he was right. It was trade. But none the worse for that.

'She needs something to do. Something to fill her life,' she said firmly.

'She seemed perfectly happy going shopping. From the bills, she hasn't done anything else since she's been here.'

'Oh, Philippe! That's not fair. Anyway,' she added, deliberately frivolous, 'at least she'll get her clothes at cost price.'

They lapsed into silence as Suzette, the maid who was yet another relative of Marie's, knocked and brought in the champagne on a small silver tray. Without speaking she pulled the cork and carefully poured two glasses.

'That will be all, Suzette,' Philippe said as he heard the girl put down the bottle.

As the door closed quietly behind her, Rosie said a touch defiantly: 'I suppose Americans see things differently. We don't see anything wrong with any kind of work that earns a decent living. Feathers always had to earn her own living and she misses it. I can understand. I've always earned mine. I needed something to do, too, when I was caught up in a bad marriage.'

'But you created champagne which is rather different from running a dress shop,' he said and she was sad to hear that he sounded disdainful.

'It's still trading. Rather grand trading, but I think Feathers intends to have a rather grand shop.' She gently ruffled his hair. 'Don't be so stuffy,' she said lightly. 'It's not like you.'

He sighed and found her hand which he squeezed in his.

'I'm sorry,' he said. 'I seem to feel so scratchy and out of sorts all the time now. It can't be much pleasure living with me.'

She dropped onto her knees so she could bury her head in his lap and wrap her arms round his waist.

'I love living with you,' she said. 'I thank God every day that I have you. It's the pain you suffer that's the problem. Pain is causing it. It breaks my heart I can't help.'

'But you can and you do,' he said. 'Now at this moment I have no pain. Not now you're here.'

'But I can't be here all the time,' she said miserably. 'I get worried about where all the money is going to come from for everything. I really can't let up at the moment.'

'And I let you down,' he said, 'by not pulling my weight.'

She leaned back, sitting on her heels. It seemed like an opportunity to say what was on her mind.

'I don't want you to do anything except *be*,' she assured him. 'Be with me. I don't want you to worry about anything. And I do think that perhaps we should think about getting someone in to help run your company so that you can relax in peace.'

'Then I might as well rest in peace,' he said bitterly.

'Oh, Philippe! Please. Don't say things like that. There is no need for you to run that company almost singlehanded.'

'Someone else would do it better, you mean? Your champagne isn't selling as well as it should.'

'No one's champagne is selling as well as it should,' she said, ignoring his anger. 'The overseas market has slumped. We have to start thinking about selling in France. We need someone who knows the French market.'

She got to her feet and crossed the room to pick up the two glasses of champagne. She handed him one and said: 'Here's to us, my darling.'

He ignored the toast and sat, the glass loose in his hand, champagne slopping over the side. She let it happen, not wanting to say or do anything that would accentuate his own knowledge of his blindness.

'Rosie, you don't understand,' he began, his voice so low she had to strain to hear. 'The business is all I have left. Blindness has taken my manhood from me. I now rely on you instead of you relying on me, which is not how it should be.'

'But it's not my nature to rely on anyone,' she protested. 'Not even you.'

'Shh. That may be. I would never mind you relying on yourself if I was capable. It's different when I am forced to do so, as I am now. Don't push me concerning my own business, Rosie. I can't bear it. It's the only territory I have left.'

She put down her glass and shut her eyes in anguish at her own insensitivity.

'Forgive me,' she said quietly.

He stood and opened his arms for her.

'There's nothing to forgive,' he said, 'as long as you still love me.'

'How could you doubt it?' she asked reproachfully as his arms folded round her.

They stood gently rocking, close together, and then she pulled back.

'Let's drink our champagne and go in for dinner,' she said. 'The cook will be having hysterics I was so late.'

It was after their somewhat overcooked meal but while they were still at the dining table drinking coffee that Philippe asked: 'Can you afford to lend Feathers the money for this dress shop?'

With food and wine, both their moods had lightened. They had finished off the bottle of champagne, and Rosie, faintly tipsy, had been giggling at the thought of Madame's face when she heard about Feathers' ambitions.

'She will be absolutely furious, you know,' Philippe warned. 'Your trouble is that even after all these years you still don't understand us French.'

She laughed and said he was probably right. Now she contemplated his question.

'Afford it? Not really,' she said. 'But I'll find the money somehow. Anyway, what's money? All my life it's turned up when needed. It'll turn up again. Sometimes I think it's better to let oneself get broke. That way forces action.'

'It does from you,' Philippe said. 'Most people lose heart.'

'No point in that,' she said briskly. 'The harvest is small, but good. Luke assures me it will make fine champagne. In fact, considering what a terrible spring it was, it's a bit of a miracle. Therefore, I was thinking that we might give a *cochelet* for the *vendangeurs* and our own workers. It will be fun for Pierre and Feathers, Cook will grumble but be in her element and it will remind Madame of the old days. She's always complaining that the *vendange* isn't as amusing as it once was.'

'What,' asked Philippe, putting down his fork, 'is a *cochelet*? You're going to give everyone a cockerel?'

Rosie professed amazement. 'You don't know? That's the trouble with you sophisticated Parisians. You're not aware of your own country's traditions.'

'*Touché*!' he said. 'Nevertheless, what is a *cochelet*?'

'A feast. A meal that's meant to be of cockerel, and then an open-air dance. We'll invite all the *vendangeurs* and our own workers and we'll hold it in the courtyard at Les Hérissons or in one of the big barns if it rains. I was planning it as I drove home. We used to have them every year when I first came here, but the war stopped everything that was fun. Somehow, what with one thing and another, we haven't got around to holding one again. But since it's Pierre's first year at the *vendange*, we might as well introduce him to some of the old traditions. You and I can dance together. We never get a chance to dance together. I shall flirt with you outrageously, and we can creep away and do what the young people do.'

He laughed. 'What do the young people do?'

'They make love. *Cochelets* make work for the priest – a lot of weddings and christenings follow.'

'Rosie, you *are* outrageous,' he said tenderly. 'You never change.'

'Why should I?' she asked, tossing back her short, bobbed hair. 'Not when just being near you still makes me think of bed. Poor Feathers. She said today that Pierre never touches her and she loves him. What pain that must be.'

'You like her, don't you?'

Without hesitation Rosie said: 'Yes. It's disloyal and dreadful but sometimes she seems more of a daughter to me than Allie has done for years. And I wish you could see how beautiful she is.'

'More beautiful than you?'

'Philippe, darling, of course! She is only twenty and I was never as good-looking as that, even at twenty.'

'If I could see, I have no doubt I would disagree,' he said. 'You were the most exciting woman in the world at twenty – and at thirty and at forty. You will be for ever.'

He spoke with great seriousness as he felt for her hand across the table. She found her eyes had filled with tears, but said lightly: 'Then it's lucky for me you can't see! And lucky for me that you can still feel, touch, kiss . . . Oh, Philippe,' she finished on a little gasp. 'Do let's go to bed.'

He did not respond as quickly as she expected. He was silent for moment.

'There's something I must tell you,' he said eventually. 'Your speaking of Allie reminded me. I've heard from Lorraine.'

'Lorraine?' Rosie was startled. She had not thought of Lorraine for years. Lorraine had once been Philippe's wife but, unable to cope with his blindness, she had left him at the end of the war taking their small daughter with her to a new marriage. 'What does she want?'

'She wants me to take Françoise "off her hands" as she puts it. She says that Françoise and her husband do not get on and the child is disrupting her and Didier's marriage. And apparently she has a new baby. She says Didier has been given a marvellous diplomatic post in the Caribbean and that it is no place for a child.'

'I see.' Rosie, uncertain how to react to the idea of another responsibility and such an emotional one, played for time by working out how old Françoise would be now. 'She's a little older than Rosanne, isn't she?' she asked and added cautiously: 'How do you feel about it?'

'She's eleven. She will be twelve next April,' he said and hesitated. 'Rosie, this may hurt you, but there is never a day that goes past that I don't think about my daughter. I wonder how she is, what she thinks of me, what her mother has told her about me. I lost Sebastian and I believed I had lost Françoise. I cannot deny myself the chance to have her with me.'

She hugged him, moved by the emotion in his voice. 'You should have told me how you felt,' she said. 'We could have done something about it.'

'What could we have done? Rosie, can we have her? Do you agree that she can come here? There's Nanny Shepherd and Miss already part of the household. It would give me such pleasure.'

'Of course she can come here,' Rosie said enthusiastically. 'It will be marvellous for us all. And think what company she will be for Rosanne.'

His face was bright as he groped to find her hand across the table.

'Rosie, you're wonderful. You've made me very happy.'

241

'Don't be silly,' she said lightly as she squeezed his hand. 'There's nothing wonderful about it. You know I have a vested interest in your happiness. And now can we go to bed, please!'

As they went hand in hand up the curving stairs to their bedroom, she thought that perhaps the arrival of this child could even enhance their happiness. Françoise could give him an added interest and make him less dependent on her. But she could not help wondering why Françoise did not get on with her stepfather. Was it his fault or hers? Because *she* was Françoise's stepmother, and at the thought she unconsciously crossed the fingers of her free hand.

The *vendangeurs* began to arrive the following morning, straggling up the driveway to Les Hérissons. Robert's foreman waited to direct them to the *vendangeoirs* where they were to be housed. Feathers watched their arrival, fascinated. They came from the east and north, whole families piled on ancient carts pulled by even older horses and mules. A modern few had broken-down cars and vans which coughed and spluttered like bronchitics as they achieved the last leg of the journey. The people were grey of skin, mostly badly but colourfully clothed and many coughed as raucously as their cars. Their children ran free and ragged beside whatever transport had carried them. Among them were gypsies riding gaily painted horsedrawn carriages. Their dark skins and bright eyes glowed in telling contrast with those others who had come to pick.

Luke West joined Feathers where she stood on the porch watching the procession; the women in sunbonnets or battered straw hats with daisies stuck round the brim, the men in their *salopettes*, bib and braces in place ready to work.

'It's like a tramps' fashion parade,' she said to Luke in awe. 'Where do they all come from?'

He grinned at her. Feathers amused him without attracting him in the slightest. Three years at Les Hérissons had done nothing to quell his urge for Rosie. In fact proximity and her refusal to be aware of his interest had, if anything, increased his feelings. He dreamed of her often, and in his dreams they were always making love. Miss took care of his sexual needs on the rare occasions they became too pressing and he saw Feathers as a friend. He liked her courage, felt for her lack of education and was impressed by how she strove to better herself. When she first came to Les Hérissons, she had singled him out for friendship and he felt it was more than just that she could speak to him in her own tongue. His sensitive eye told him that all was not well with her marriage, and her inability to grasp the language left her isolated most of the time. She needed a friend.

He echoed her question. "Where do they come from? All over the place. Industrial towns to the north and east mainly. They're mostly factory workers or miners. It's the only holiday they get and their only chance to be in the open air. We feed them like kings, and pay them a few sous for their day's work, and we make them work like hell. But for them it's the best ten days of the year. And it does them good. Particularly the miners. They get some decent, clean air in their lungs for a change. According to Robert, some of the families have been coming to Les Hérissons for the past twenty years – except for during the war, of course.'

'But how do you find them all?' she wanted to know.

'We recruit in the industrial towns. All the champagne houses and the growers do the same. These people are absolutely essential at the *vendange* so we look after them well. They probably get more to eat here than they ever get at home.'

'What do they get?' Feathers asked as she watched four burly men pushing a battered van the last few yards of the drive.

'Coffee and cheese for breakfast —'

'Cheese for breakfast!'

'Terrible stuff,' Luke told her cheerfully. 'Maroilles, made in Reims. It stinks to high heaven, but they seem to like it. The smell puts me off. Then they get proper breakfast in the vineyard. Soup, cold meat, vegetables, more coffee and more cheese and a swig of Marc to finish. Lunch consists of much the same except for plenty of rough red wine. At mid-afternoon there's a little snack of bread, coffee and more Maroilles. Then there's an enormous supper when they get back to the *vendangeoir* in the evening. Breaks for eating are the only ones allowed. The rest of the time they work and they never stop. Believe me, picking grapes is hard, back-breaking work.'

'It sounds awful,' Feathers murmured.

'It's not. There's a great spirit and every evening's a party when they get back to the *vendangeoirs*. You wait until we have the *cochelet* on the last night. Then you'll be seeing a bit of real

France that few people, even Frenchmen, see.'

'Umm,' she said. He realised she was hardly listening to him. Her glance had caught someone who commanded attention in among the motley crowd drifting up the driveway.

'Look at that fellow,' she said. 'He doesn't seem to belong with the rest.'

She pointed towards the man who had caught her eye. He was on horseback. He rode with easy confidence, his head arrogantly high, his back straight. He wore a full-sleeved white shirt with a black waistcoat and a black shallow-crowned, narrow-brimmed hat. His skin was sunburned and he had a thin highbridged nose under light eyes. He was young, about Feathers' age, and very good-looking. His linen was grubby and he could have been a gypsy, but his manner was too aristocratic.

Luke took all this in as he peered across at the horseman, eyes narrowed against the sunlight.

'He must be Spanish,' he said. 'That's a Spanish saddle and an Arab mare he's riding. He's almost certainly from the south. What on earth is he doing picking grapes in Champagne?'

They both watched in silence as the foreman waved the man to stop. He reined in the mare and looked down haughtily at the Frenchman without bending either his back or his neck. Then he said something that Luke could not hear.

The Frenchman looked uncertain and then he pointed towards the porch where Feathers and Luke stood. Luke had the impression that the foreman was pointing him out.

'What's going on?' Feathers said, almost whispering.

'I don't know.' Luke was aware of being uneasy himself.

The man on the horse turned his head and looked towards the porch. He looked long and hard, the light eyes raking the older man. His glance then flitted quickly over Feathers before returning for a second, longer look. Then he threw them both a mocking little salute, wheeled his horse round and set off in the direction of the *vendangeoirs*.

'Now what was that all about?' Luke muttered, beckoning the foreman who was looking towards the porch with a worried air. The man immediately hurried over.

'What did the Spaniard want?' Luke asked as he neared.

'He wanted to know where he would find you,' the foreman said, adding anxiously, 'was it all right I told him?'

'Of course,' Luke said. 'But what exactly did he say?'

'He just said where would he find Luke West. And then when I pointed you out, he rode away.'

Luke shrugged.

'He must know my family,' he said to Feathers. 'We'll find out eventually.'

But there had been something in that searching look from the horseman that was unnerving. Luke decided he might even seek him out later, just to see what it was all about.

'He was very handsome,' Feathers was saying thoughtfully.

'A fairly average Spanish type.' Luke did not want to encourage her.

She looked at him mischievously. 'Perhaps I should go to Spain one day.'

He laughed. 'You just remember you're a married woman.'

'I'm glad you reminded me,' she said, and there was a note of bitterness in her voice that made him put his arm round her shoulders.

'Tell me what's happened about this dress shop, young Feathers,' he said, thinking it politic to change the subject.

Her face lit up. 'Rosie says I can.'

'And Madame?'

She grimaced. 'I haven't mentioned it. I hoped Rosie would tell her.'

'Coward!'

'I know. But I'd never find the right words.'

'And you want to run a business!' he said dryly.

'I'm going to take proper French lessons.'

'You've said that before.'

'But this time I will. I've a real reason to learn now.'

Luke shook his head. 'Really, Feathers, living in a country is the best possible reason for learning its language.'

'You don't understand,' she said. 'I've never felt permanent here. I always thought Pierre would send me back, or Madame would get fed up with me. I never felt I'd stay. But if I have my own shop . . .'

He laughed. 'I see. I thought Rosie would encourage you. But I think you ought to tell Madame yourself.' He cocked his head to listen, 'I think I can hear her coming down the stairs. Now's your moment.'

'Oh, no it isn't,' Feathers said, registering horror. 'I'm off.'

She scuttled down the stairs to the driveway, hesitated and then looked around for her getaway before rushing round the corner of the house.

He genuinely had heard Madame's heavy, hesitant tread on the stairs and not particularly wanting a conversation with her himself, he, too, went down to the drive but followed where the *vendangeurs* went. The young Spaniard was on his mind.

It was quite a way to the nearest *vendangeoir* and as he walked through the scented vineyard where the grapes hung waiting to be picked, he imagined the scene as it would be the next morning when the picking began. The people would be lying flat on stomach or back, or crouched double trying to find a comfortable position as they carefully clipped the bunches of grapes from the vine. It was a back-breaking job, and one that had to be done with care, particularly when cutting the delicate-skinned green Chardonnays. Damaged grapes could spoil the wine. The *vendangeurs* picked in pairs, one man or woman each side of the vine, putting the grapes into small wooden baskets. Another member of the team would be watching and waiting to take away full baskets and hand over an empty one. Donkeys, muzzled to stop them enjoying the fruit, were used for all the heavy carrying. All the while the overseer, a Les Hérissons employee, watched with eagle eye to see that no one slacked for as much as a second.

Luke reached the first of the *vendangeoirs* and saw that the pretty little Arab mare had been tied up at a railing. The young Spaniard had put his pack on the ground and was taking off the heavy saddle. He saw Luke walking towards him, nodded an acknowledgement and got on with what he was doing. The animal skittered a little as the buckles were undone. Luke waited quietly until the saddle was off, and then said, speaking Spanish: 'Did you want to see me?'

'I did.' There was a note of insolence that Luke found unattractive.

'About what?' he asked quietly.

The younger man pursed his lips and then said: 'I thought it was time that we met.'

'Is there some reason why we should meet?'

The boy looked straight at him and shrugged. 'Since I am Carlos, your son, there is reason enough.'

Luke heard the gasp that his own breath made. And yet curiously, after the words had sunk in, they were not the shock that they should have been. He felt as if he had known what the boy was going to say from the moment he had seen those grey eyes, so like his own, watching him from the driveway. He stroked the mare's pale flank before replying. He was aware that some dramatic response was called for, but did not know exactly what as he registered the fact that this was his son standing in front of him part defiant, part insolent and part, he felt, pleading for recognition.

'You should not be here,' he said, making a gesture that took in the vineyards and the wooden *vendangeoir*. The straw mattresses of the *vendangeoirs* were invariably flea-ridden. 'Why didn't you come straight to me?'

His son gave a scornful little snort of laughter.

'Why should I believe that you would welcome me when you have shown no interest in me or my mother from the day I was born? And incidentally, my mother does not know I am here. She would kill me if she knew.'

At the mention of the boy's mother, a half-forgotten pain flooded back. Luke dismissed it.

'And does *my* mother know that you are here?' he asked sharply. 'She has kept me informed of your wellbeing ever since you were born. My family has fulfilled its obligations to both you and your mother. You have just left school in England, I believe.'

The boy laughed again.

'It is true I have just left the school that my grandmother paid for, but how could she know that I am here? Her obligations are over now that I have been educated as an English gentleman. Besides, I have never had the pleasure of meeting her, or my grandfather, any more than I have had the pleasure of meeting you, my father. My mother's dealings have always been with your family lawyer. And as for "obligations", it was my mother who fought for all that I have had of my birthright.'

Luke looked at the boy and tried to think what to do next. He felt helpless in the face of such bitterness. He did not have the temperament to cope with Latin dramatics or talk of birthrights. He ought to be handling it better, he thought, as he stood in the hot sunshine confronted with the consequences of a mistake perpetrated twenty years before. Here he was talking to the son he

247

had never met and they were on the verge of quarrelling. He ought to have hugged the boy. He ought to have said something emotional and full of meaning, but that wasn't his temperament either.

'How is your mother?' he asked abruptly.

'Do you care?' Again the scorn in the boy's voice.

'I do.'

'You would not want her now. She is fat and careworn. She has lived only for me.'

Isabella fat and careworn! He thought of the tiny vivid streak of girl that she had been; the hair like a fall of black silk, the tiny face that was all great brown eyes. Above all, with a shiver he remembered the passion they had shared. Passion that had conceived this angry boy. Fat and careworn! He shut his eyes against the pain of the thought.

'Carlos,' he said abruptly. 'You cannot stay here. You must come to my *casa*.'

'I prefer to stay here.'

'I prefer that you do not.'

'It is too late for you to play the father.'

'I think not,' Luke said firmly, 'otherwise you would not have sought me out.'

'I shall be nothing but an embarrassment to you.'

'This is France, not Catholic Spain or prim England. You will not be an embarrassment to me or to anyone else. And you will not like the *vendangeoir*. It is very primitive.'

'Like the boy's school in England?'

'Exactly!' Luke said, finding he could laugh. He put out his hand. 'Come,' he said. 'We have to get to know each other. There's much I have to ask you.'

The boy stood hesitant but Luke picked up the saddle from the ground and put it on his shoulder.

'We'll put your mare in the Les Hérissons stables,' he said, taking the mare's bridle. 'And we'll find you somewhere to stay.'

He found Rosie in one of the big barns where she had been inspecting the vats to ensure that they were spotlessly clean for the coming new wine. She was wrapped in a white overall and her hair was tied back into a white scarf but she still somehow managed to look desirable.

'Luke,' she said as she saw him. 'How's it all going your end?'

'All set to start picking in the morning,' he told her. 'And the weather looks settled.'

'I think so, too,' she said, and held out two grubby, crossed fingers towards him. 'Please, please God – no rain.'

'It won't rain,' he said confidently, then added, 'I've been looking for you. I want to talk to you.'

She gave him a sharp look and he knew she understood that he had something important to say.

'Right,' she said briskly. 'I'm finished here. Is it too early for a glass of champagne?'

'It's never too early for a glass of champagne,' he said.

'Come on then.' She put her finger to her lips and whispered: 'We'll go to my tasting room where no one will see us.'

They went back into the house through the kitchen and Rosie stopped to take a bottle of champagne from the icebox in Cook's cold room.

In her tasting room she washed her hands while he opened the bottle, then she found two tasting glasses and they sat facing each other across the scrubbed table.

'You are not leaving us or anything dreadful, are you?' she asked.

He laughed, pleased that she should want him to stay.

'It's something more complicated,' he said. 'My son has surprised me by arriving here today.'

'Your son!' She seemed more surprised than he himself had been. 'I didn't know you had a son.'

'This is the first time I've seen him. He's twenty,' he said. 'You see—' He hesitated.

'You don't have to tell me anything you don't want to,' she said quickly.

'It's better you know.' He took a long swallow of the champagne. 'His mother was a gypsy girl. We were madly in love. She was sixteen and I was seventeen, home in Jerez for the school holidays. We met at a flamenco festival. She was dancing. When my parents found out – well, let's just say they weren't very happy.' He paused, remembering the scenes, the dramas, the tears all those years ago. 'They forbade me to see her, but of course I took no notice. Then she got pregnant and we were about to elope, but her father jumped the gun. He turned up at my parents' house saying I had despoiled his daughter and insisting that we marry. I was packed off back to England and my parents paid the father off. They've been paying one way or the other ever since. But my mother insisted that regardless of the circumstances Carlos was her grandchild. She would never receive him but she insisted that he must be properly educated. So this half-gypsy boy was sent to a very minor public school in England. Certainly not the one I went to. My mother considers her obligations are finished now that he is educated. So, not knowing what to do with his education he got on a horse and came and found me.'

'How do you feel about him turning up?' He was glad to see that her amber eyes were compassionate, not judging him.

'I don't know. Not really surprised, I suppose. He was bound to turn up one day. He'd have no problem finding me. Jerez is such a small town. One of my mother's servants probably told him where I am and what I'm doing. The *vendange* provided a good excuse. It's just what to do with him now he is here. I can't leave him in the *vendangeoir*. It doesn't seem right.'

'What's he like?' Rosie asked.

'He seems sophisticated enough. He's very good-looking, but arrogant and bitter. I think he's going to be a handful. He keeps going on about his birthright.' He was aware of sounding irritable, and aware, too, that irritability was hardly the right reaction when a long-lost son reappeared. 'And he doesn't speak much French. Schoolboy stuff, that's all.' He hesitated, feeling a need to explain himself. 'Rosie, do I sound callous? I probably am callous, but I was eighteen when he was born. I suppose I've thought about him once a year ever since. All I ever mourned was the girl, Isabella. I mourned her for years and I suppose I blamed the baby for breaking us up. If she hadn't been pregnant we might have worked something out. When he told me out there in the vines that I was his father, I felt nothing. Absolutely nothing. I couldn't have kissed him or hugged him to save my life.'

He stopped, thinking he was saying too much and not wanting her to judge him harshly. But he should have known better. Rosie was not judging, Rosie was thinking what to do.

'Where is he now?' she asked.

'In my room.'

'One of the tower rooms is empty. He could have that. Servants quarters, I'm afraid, but there isn't anything else. The question is – what shall we tell Madame?'

'I'd just as soon say he's my son,' Luke said, thinking that anything else would be another rejection for the boy.

'Quite right. Truth's best even if it does cause problems,' Rosie said. 'Just leave it to me. I'll sort it all out. Don't worry. Let me talk to Madame and I'll come and find you and you can introduce me to the boy.'

She was already leaving the room, her champagne untouched on the table. He heaved a deep sigh of relief. He had offered her his problem and she had taken it on without the slightest hesitation. But then, of course, he had known that she would.

He finished his own champagne, and after a moment's thought, picked hers up, too. It wasn't often that twenty-year-old sons appeared out of the blue. He made a silent toast before he drained the glass. And it was the young flamelike flamenco dancer, not the sad, fat and careworn Isabella, to whom he solemnly drank.

Feathers was in the kitchen trying to talk to Cook who had quite enough to do without being distracted by Feathers. Rosie could hear the girl's excruciating accent as she went past the kitchen and through to the front of the house. Poor Feathers had so little to occupy her, the dress shop had to be good idea. But how best to tackle Madame in order to get the right answer to both Feathers' needs and Luke's? she wondered. It would not be easy. It was absurd in a way that Madame even had to be consulted but that was the way things were done at Les Hérissons and Rosie, sometimes reluctantly, went along with it.

At the moment Madame would be in her little parlour nodding over the newspaper. It was 11.45 by the hall clock – just about ten minutes after the time Madame came down from her bedroom. These days the old lady did not always come downstairs early. She had her breakfast brought to her in bed, needing time to stretch her stiff limbs back into working order at the start of each day. The doctor had diagnosed that the pains and aches that troubled her were arthritic. She rarely complained but her temper was short and she was inclined to be contradictory if not downright contrary and cantankerous most of the time. And she saved most of her *mauvaise humeur* for Rosie. Since Rosie had moved to Les Coquelicots, Madame had taken to making tart remarks about being 'deserted', forgetting that it was she who had barred Philippe from the house. And she took out her resentment of Rosie's escape and continuing authority in the vineyard by continual sniping at whatever decisions her daughter-in-law made.

Rosie wondered exactly how old Madame was. In the twenty-three years they had known each other her mother-in-law had never given the slightest inkling of her years. She had to be seventy, if not a good deal older, but her face was still youthful and she was still particular about her appearance. It was just her style, long dresses and long hair which had barely changed over the years, that gave away her age.

Madame was indeed in her parlour, but wide awake and Rosie was not sure whether this was a good or bad thing. At times, when the old lady had been dozing, she paid little attention to what was said to her and forgot what had been discussed. She then complained that no one told her anything. Today Rosie felt it might be better if she did remember what had been said. But it was important to know exactly what sort of mood Madame was in before attempting anything.

'Good morning, Mama,' Rosie said as she came into the room and kissed Madame's surprisingly smooth cheek. 'Can I join you for a moment? I feel so exasperated and cross that I need some sensible company.'

The old lady looked up from her newspaper and gave Rosie a sharp look. Rosie registered that her face was pinched, the nose even narrower; signs that showed pain and its by-product – bad temper.

'What's troubling you?' Madame asked in a slightly belligerent fashion as Rosie collapsed on to the little sofa by the window.

Rosie sighed. 'There are offspring appearing all over the place and at this, the busiest time of year. Philippe wants to bring his daughter to live with us for a while, and of course I cannot refuse. And now, would you believe, Luke West has just announced that *his* son has arrived out of the blue. He was going to ask you if the lad could stay here, but naturally I told him that was quite impossible and that he wasn't to bother you with such things. Then to add to the problems plaguing me, Feathers said she wanted to talk to you about getting herself some little boutique in Reims. She's on about needing something to do. I told her it was absolutely out of the question, and if she wanted something to do she should learn French. I said categorically that I would not allow it.'

Rosie saw Madame quiver, her back straighten and her thin nose tilt upwards as if sniffing for blood.

'Really, Rosie,' she said, 'I will thank you not to make decisions for me in my own home. You should really understand who is the mistress here after all this time. I will decide what is to be done.'

'But Mama, those are both preposterous suggestions. Such impertinence of Luke . . .'

Madame adored Luke.

'Luke West hasn't an impertinent bone in his body,' she said sharply. 'What is this about a son? I never knew he had a son.'

'Illegitimate.' Rosie made her voice scornful. 'He had him when he was just eighteen by some girl his parents would not countenance. The boy has turned up looking for his father and Luke seriously thinks he can foist him on us.'

'That sounds remarkably like the pot calling the kettle black, remembering your own circumstances,' Madame said, dripping acid. 'You should have more understanding. Of course the boy can stay here if he is Luke's son. Where else would he go, indeed! You will find Luke and tell him that the boy is welcome here. I've no doubt that Marie will find somewhere to put him. And he can bring him to meet me here this evening before dinner.'

Rosie made her shrug a touch insolent knowing that Madame had a beady eye trained on her reactions.

'Just as you wish,' she said. 'But I can't believe you would approve of this crazy boutique idea of Feathers.'

'One must allow the girl has a way with clothes.' Madame's voice was thoughtful. 'It is a frivolous idea, but then she is a frivolous person. She is so bored most of the time that I suspect she troubles poor, dear Pierre who has his studies to think about.' She pursed her lips and sat staring into the small fire that always burned in her parlour. 'No one in my family has ever been in trade, but one must move with the times. Really, Rosie, you should not have discouraged her so unkindly. Send her to see me before we have lunch so that she can be reassured.'

'Before lunch today! Shouldn't you at least think about it?'

Madame made a regal, commanding gesture. 'Now. Without delay.'

'Very well, Mama.' Rosie flounced to the door, flinging back over her shoulder, 'But I still think you are making a mistake.'

The door was shut behind her before Madame could reply and Rosie, hardly able to conceal triumphant giggles, headed towards the kitchen where she knew she would find Feathers.

Cook's relief as she came in was palpable.

'Come along, Feathers,' Rosie said crisply, 'Madame wants to see you.'

'Oh, my! What about?' Feathers asked, rolling her eyes, but rising from the hard-backed chair where she had been seated.

Rosie grinned.

'She's all in favour of your dress shop, she is annoyed with me for discouraging you, and wants to tell you so herself.'

Feathers clasped her hands under her chin, her eyes shining.

'She said okay?'

'She said okay. But remember, I am supposed to disapprove. Don't mention money and just keep saying how wise and kind she is and thanking her. And for heaven's sake don't forget to say *bonjour* and kiss her when you go in.'

'Oh, Lordie! I shan't understand a word she says.'

'Then just keep smiling and saying *merci mille fois*. Tell her she's *très gentille*. That'll do.'

'Thanks Rosie – you're a marvel!'

Feathers left the kitchen crashing the door behind her. Cook looked to the heavens and muttered some imprecation as Rosie laughed and went out herself, closing the door more quietly.

It had all worked. She blessed Madame's predictability, but she felt surprisingly tired as she went to find Luke.

Chapter Ten

Carlos was dozing on his father's bed. He had bathed and not wanting to put back on his travel-stained clothes had wrapped himself in a large white towelling bathrobe that Luke had found for him. Clean again but weary he stretched out on his back, his arms under his head, staring at the ceiling of the big, old-fashioned room while he waited to see what would happen next.

He was almost asleep when the door opened and his father came in accompanied by a woman. Embarrassed, he pulled the robe tightly round him and stood up.

'It's all right,' the woman said in faintly accented English. 'I'm sorry we woke you up. I'm Rosie Dupuis. Welcome to Les Hérissons.'

He shook the hand she had thrust towards him and his father who remained near the door said: 'Madame Dupuis is my boss.'

'Madame wouldn't like to hear you say that.' She gave a small, mischievous giggle and then his father laughed too as if they shared a secret.

He felt uncomfortable standing there in the bathrobe, and he was aware that the woman's tawny coloured eyes were regarding him with curiosity. But it was friendly curiosity, he decided. Her smile was encouraging. The smile made him feel that she was on his side – that he had found an ally.

'You're tired,' she said, and it was a statement rather than a question. 'We've found a place for you. It's a room rather high up in the house, I'm afraid, but it's comfortable enough. Henri will fetch your things, and if you sort out your laundry, Marie will deal with it. I expect you'd like some clean clothes.' She looked him up and down. 'You're about Pierre's size. We'll borrow from him.'

None of these names meant anything, but he was too tired to ask questions. He just nodded, glad that he was being taken over and happy not to have to think.

'Would you like to come and see your room?' she was asking.

He made a little gesture towards the bathrobe.

'That doesn't matter,' she said cheerfully. 'Everyone's out working. No one will see you.' She turned to his father. 'In fact, Luke, you ought to be getting on. I'll look after Carlos now. You can get to know each other this evening.' She clicked her fingers. 'That reminds me, how's your French, Carlos? The *important* Madame Dupuis, my mother-in-law, wants to meet you before dinner this evening. As the *vendange* begins tomorrow, we're dining formally. You'll no doubt get a glass of our champagne but Madame speaks no English.'

'My French is poor,' he muttered.

'No matter. We'll all be there to help translate,' she told him. 'Now let's go upstairs.'

The three of them left the room together. Luke went down to the ground floor, Rosie Dupuis led the way upstairs. She was chattering cheerfully as he followed her remarkably pretty legs.

She wasn't young, he thought, looking at the legs, but she was warm and she was certainly kind. His nervousness at the enormity of what he had done began to wane a little. Maybe it would be all right if everyone here was like her.

She led him to a small room at the top of the house that looked spacious since it was so light and bright. There were windows on all four sides, and he realised that this must be the tower room he had noticed when he was riding up the driveway.

'Will my mare be all right?' he asked abruptly.

'She'll be fine. When you're organised, ask Henri to show you where the stables are. Then you can see for yourself.' She fussed briefly, checking the bed for clean linen and pulling out drawers to make sure they were empty, and then she straightened and said: 'I'll have to go now, but I'll see your things are sent up right away. There's no formal lunch today because there's so much to do, but Marie will bring you food and your father will collect you for dinner this evening. In the meantime, make yourself at home. Wander about as much as you like and I shall see you later.'

She had gone, light-footed and leaving behind the scent of some perfume that he was sure must be expensive.

Within a few minutes an elderly man and a middle-aged woman arrived in the room. The man carried some clothing on hangers along with the leather bag that had travelled all the way from Jerez on Sable's back. It held his few clothes and possessions. The woman carried a tray holding something covered with a linen cloth which she put down on a rickety table. She then set about emptying his bag, putting away what was clean and making a pile of what needed to be washed. He felt embarrassed by a stranger going through his clothing, but she worked efficiently and quickly. Neither of them spoke or showed any emotion. The man, who he assumed must be Henri, hung some clean shirts and a pair of trousers in the wardrobe – clothing that presumably belonged to the mysterious Pierre.

'Is there anything else, sir?' Henri asked.

When Carlos shook his head the two servants left, quietly closing the door and taking his dirty linen with them.

Alone, he ate and drank the bread, pâté and cheese that the maid had left along with a small jug of wine. He gulped it all down hungrily, and then he fell back onto the narrow, creaky bed and slept.

When he awoke the big round watch that his mother had saved so hard to buy him before he went to school in England told him it was four o'clock. Outside, the sun was flooding his eyrie with light. The room was shabbily furnished and he guessed it had been intended for servants. A wave of resentment washed over him. Why should he be put in a servant's room? It was another slight because of his illegitimacy. His anger against his father was fuelled again.

He tried on the trousers that hung in the wardrobe. They were far from new but had been expensive, he thought, as he felt the material through finger and thumb. The shirt was of fine English cotton and both garments fitted tolerably well. He looked at himself in the long cheval glass and was not displeased with what he saw. After combing his thick, straight black hair, he set out to explore.

The house was silent except for the rooms at the back on the ground floor where he realised the kitchens must be. A great deal of work seemed to be going on there and, standing listening

257

in the hallway, he could hear the odd angry outburst always from the same voice.

The front door was shut and bolted – probably against unwelcome visits from the *vendangeurs*, so he walked down towards the kitchens where he found another door that opened and led into a courtyard outside. He was standing by a small walled vineyard where the grapes had not been pruned as drastically as elsewhere. They grew wild, but were heavily laden. He opened the iron gate and went in among the vines, wandering through the fragrant rows, enjoying the silence.

As he reached the far wall and turned into the last row he came upon the girl he had seen standing with his father earlier that morning. She was sitting on a small chair out of the sun, a book on her lap, and she appeared to be asleep. She was remarkably pretty, he thought, as he stood covertly studying her. Her hair was as dark as his, but waved about her head in an unruly manner, falling into a fringe over her broad forehead. Her skin made him think of thick, heavy sweet cream, and the eyelashes that rested on her cheeks were long. Her cheeks were childishly rounded, but it was the woman's red mouth, broad, beautifully shaped, and just slightly open, revealing small very white teeth, that attracted him the most. She wore a simple white middy blouse and a plain skirt. Both looked as if they might be very expensive. Everyone had money, he thought resentfully. Everyone except him.

He stood still, uncertain what to do. Leave her to sleep, he decided, and cautiously took a step backwards. Immediately her eyelids flew open, she clasped her hands to her breast and leapt to her feet in fright, her book falling to the ground.

'Monsieur! Vous frightened moi!'

'I didn't mean to frighten you,' he said apologetically, once he had translated this mixture of two languages.

'You speak English?' she said as he bent to pick up her book. As he handed it to her, her huge velvet blue eyes opened in wonderment. 'Luke thought you must be Spanish.'

'I am. Half,' he told her. 'And you speak English, too.'

'I'm an American,' she said with a touch of pride. 'But what are you doing here? The *vendangeoir* is –'

'I am not staying in the *vendangeoir*,' he interrupted. 'I am staying in the house.'

'This house?' She gestured towards Les Hérissons.

'Yes.'

'You're a guest?'

'Yes.'

Her features widened into the most marvellous smile.

'How terrific!' she said. 'But why?'

'Because Luke West is my father.'

She sank back into her seat. 'I didn't know he had a son.'

'He has not been quick to tell people.' He knew his voice was angry but he couldn't control it.

She was looking at him consideringly. 'But I'm sure he didn't recognise you this morning. Luke's the most honest of men. He never pretends or lies.'

'He has never seen me before today.'

'My! You lost each other?'

'Not exactly.' He decided to say no more for the moment. 'But tell me, what are you, an American girl, doing here?'

She looked for an instant as if she did not want to tell him, and then she said: 'I'm married to Pierre Dupuis, the son of the house.'

Married! He felt a quite unreasonable sense of disappointment.

'He is Rosie Dupuis' son?' he asked.

She shook her head.

'She's his aunt. It's all a bit complicated. Aunt Rosie sort of runs the place, with your father, and Pierre's been taking a degree at the Sorbonne and now he's going to learn about the champagne business. He's American, too. But it's his grandma, Madame Dupuis, who is the head of the household. She's formidable. She terrifies me.'

'I have to meet her tonight.'

'Poor old you. Though I think,' she said thoughtfully, 'that she likes men best.' She got to her feet again. 'Look, this is silly, you standing there while we talk. Shall I show you round a bit? Would that help?'

'It would help a great a deal,' he said gravely, 'and it would help even more if you told me your name.'

'It's Feathers. What's yours?'

It suited her, he thought. He took a deep breath and told her his own name.

'Carlos. Carlos Ortega.'

259

She looked as if she was about to say something but then stopped. Instead she said: 'Come on then, Carlos. Let's have a look at Les Hérissons. Frankly, I think it's pretty boring.'

She whizzed him round vats, cellars, caves and barns in double quick time, and finished by walking him through the vineyard nearest the house to where there was a long stone seat at the end of one of the alleys of grapes.

'Now let's sit down for a bit,' she said. 'I'm so glad you've come here. It's lovely to have someone to talk to. My French is hopeless. Your poor father has to put up with me most of the time and he's got better things to do.' She sank down and sighed. '*Vendange* time can be awful. Everyone's far too busy to talk or do anything. And they're all in such a state of nerves in case anything goes wrong. All they worry about is the weather, as if they could do anything about it.' She stopped abruptly, then asked: 'How old are you?'

'Twenty,' he told her.

'Me too! When will you be twenty-one?'

'Next month. The fifth of October.'

'You're four months older than me. I'll be twenty-one in January.'

He was bursting to ask her a million questions about herself but then he would have to answer questions about himself. He found himself fascinated by her. Carlos was no virgin. His dark good looks had chalked up conquests enough amongst the housemaids at his school in England, and he had even managed to seduce one or two Spanish girls who worked for his grandfather's *bodega*. Everyone there knew that he was the illegitimate grandson of the *Patrone* and it gave him an added glamour. But this girl, Feathers, was something quite different. She was, he decided, truly glamorous. She must be the daughter of some rich American and he wondered what her husband would be like.

She was looking at her wristwatch.

'Oh, my!' she said. 'I'll have to go. It's time for tea with my son.'

'Your son?'

'Yes,' she sounded almost apologetic. 'He's nearly three. He's called Patric. Nanny allows me to have tea with him. I get so little time with him that I can't bear to miss any opportunity.

Do you mind if I leave you? Will you be able to find your way back?' She was standing, flustered, her feet almost pawing the ground just as his mare's did when she wanted to be off.

'I'll be fine,' he said. 'You go.'

He watched her hurrying down the gravel path and to assuage his disappointment noted that she was a little broad in the beam and that her legs were not a patch on those belonging to the woman called Rosie. But even so, it was a pity about the husband and the child. A very great pity indeed, he decided.

Pierre was half-dressed for dinner when Feathers left the nursery and went back into their big, sunny bedroom at the back of the house. He was sitting at the desk, writing a letter, wearing a clean white shirt and dark trousers. His dinner jacket and bow tie were carefully laid out on the bed.

Feathers gave him a quick kiss which he accepted with an absent smile.

'Patric was adorable,' she said. 'I could hardly bear to leave him. I wish we didn't have to have a nanny.'

'Madame insists,' he said.

'I know.' She moved towards the small bathroom that Madame had added to their room after their arrival in France. 'Madame's word is law. But she has agreed to my having the shop. She was even encouraging about it – I think,' she added doubtfully, having failed to grasp most of what Madame had said.

'That's good,' he said not looking up from his writing paper.

She looked at him despairingly. He wasn't interested. If only she could get some reaction from him. Abandoning the idea of running her bath she went and perched herself on the corner of his desk. This time she was determined to be heard.

'Pierre, I want to talk to you,' she said firmly.

'What is it?' he asked, putting down his fountain pen.

'Do you think we could ever have a house of our own? Where we could be alone together more?'

It was something that had been on her mind for a long time. In a home of her own maybe she would not have to have a nanny, or if she did, at least she would be in control and could make the rules. She felt that her marriage would stand more chance if he and she were alone. He rarely took her out and since they had come to live permanently at Les Hérissons they had not had one single meal alone together.

In some ways she had been happier in Paris. It had been lonelier, but at least there were occasions when she had her husband to herself.

'Feathers!' He sounded concerned. 'Aren't you happy here?'

'Not very,' she said. 'I don't have you to myself enough. I don't feel I belong here.'

'That's because you won't learn the language.'

'It's more than that.' She made a gesture that took in the whole of Les Hérissons. 'The house is so big and old, and I don't feel it's a home. Certainly not my home. I know you do, but then you're family.'

'Would you rather be back with your family in Boston?'

'Oh Pierre, you know I wouldn't.' She buried the quick surge of guilt comparing her good fortune with the life she had left behind.

'Isn't this better than that?'

She sighed, thinking how quickly one got used to luxury.

'You're deliberately misunderstanding,' she said. 'I'd like a home of my own. I wouldn't care about all the things there are here, like servants and baths and electricity and things. I just want a home of my own,' she repeated stubbornly.

'And what would we do for money to buy it?'

'Madame would give it to you. She gives you everything you want.'

'But I doubt if she'd give me freedom.' His voice was sombre. 'Feathers, she pays for things, or Rosie does, and the allowance is generous as you know—' he pointed towards her wardrobes. 'But the price of all that is being under her roof.'

He sounded sad and she wondered if perhaps he was as unhappy as she sometimes was. He was always going to Paris for the day as if he needed to get away. Sometimes he stayed overnight, and that worried her. But she told herself that maybe it was because he really did not like it here. Sorry for him, she leaned to give his unresponsive shoulders a hug.

'Never mind,' she said. 'You just wait until I make a fortune from my dress shop.'

He laughed and got to his feet. He put his hands on her

shoulders and held her away from him to look into her face.

'Poor little Feathers,' he said. 'Did we make a terrible mistake? Would you like to go back to the States?'

'With you?' she asked eagerly.

'No. This is my home now. If you went back I would see you were well looked after.'

She felt tears beginning to trickle down her cheeks.

'You don't understand,' she said, scrubbing them away with her fists. 'You sound as if you want me to go. I didn't make a terrible mistake. I love you and want to be with you. I just want us to be closer and happier, but you never give me a chance. Other people like me. Why can't you?'

He put his arms round her gently. There was no passion in the gesture, only comfort.

'I do like you, Feathers. I like you very much. I always have.'

'You don't love me.'

'I do. In a way. I do my best, I promise you. If you can settle for my best, maybe we'll rub along well enough together.'

'But you never even so much as kiss me.'

He took his arms away from her and walked across the room to look out of the window onto the courtyard below. She waited, her hands trembling but tears gone, to see what he would say. He was silent. Then he went to the bed and picked up his jacket and tie and put them on.

'It's time you ran your bath,' he said. 'We mustn't be late for dinner. Aunt Rosie and Uncle Philippe are here for dinner as it's the first night of the *vendange*, and Grandmama tells me we have another guest.'

Defeated, she went towards the bathroom.

'You mean Luke's son. I've met him. He's nice. Very handsome. We went for a walk.'

He raised his eyebrows.

'He doesn't speak French, either. Only English – and Spanish, I suppose.'

'That's nice,' he said lightly. 'He can be a friend to you.'

Standing in the doorway of the bathroom, she turned to stare at him defiantly. 'Yes, that's what I thought,' she said. 'I think he might make a good friend.' And aware of sounding childish she added: 'He liked me. I could tell.'

'Good,' he said absently. He had gone back to his desk and

263

was writing again. She wondered to whom. 'You need more company,' he said.

He just didn't care at all, she thought despairingly as she made her preparations for dinner. Still, she told herself, as she looked at her face in the mirror and noted how the corners of her mouth were beginning to turn down, there was the shop to think about. That might make all the difference. And Carlos. She wondered how long he would stay, and saw how, at the thought of him, the corners of her mouth had curved upwards into an anticipatory smile.

She wore her new Schiaparelli dress for dinner that night. It was black, simple and sleeveless with a deep V neck at the back and the front. The dress emphasised her breasts and creamy skin but skated kindly over her hips and legs. But the real reason that she had spent a fortune of Les Hérissons' money was because the gown came with an extravagant cock feather boa – half white and half black. It was the most dramatic dress she had ever had and she was determined to look her best at this unusual opportunity to dress up – even if she overdressed. She fluffed up the small fringe she wore and let the rest of her hair fall into a soft pageboy, Greta Garbo style. Garbo was Feathers' idol. She plucked her eyebrows in the Garbo way and used her lipstick to make her upper lip into a Garbo bow, but even liberal applications of Vaseline on her eyelids could not give her that hollowed, deep-set hungry look that made Garbo so romantic. Her own face was so well-fed and *Irish*, she thought as she applied powder to her round cheeks. It was such a shame that Patric had inherited her looks instead of Pierre's thinner, more aristocratic features.

She was a few minutes late for the pre-dinner glass of champagne in Madame's parlour. She was usually late and it irritated Madame. Tonight she did not care if Madame was annoyed. Her arrival in the beautiful, elegant dress was an entrance. Everyone turned to look at her, even Pierre. Carlos didn't seem to be able to stop looking at her. But it was Luke who came across to take her hand and give her support.

'You look the tops!' he whispered.

'Thank you,' she whispered back. 'Like it?'

'It's great,' he said.

Rosie was coming to greet her.

'Feathers!' she said. 'What a beautiful dress.'

Feathers debated whether or not to say it was a Schiaparelli and decided against it. At the end of the day she was aware that it was Rosie who paid for her extravagances, though Rosie never seemed to mind.

So all she said was: 'I'm glad you like it.'

'It's a Schiaparelli, surely?'

'Yes, and yours is a Grès.' Rosie was wearing a beautifully draped Grecian gown in flame red chiffon. Feathers had seen one not dissimilar photographed in French *Vogue*.

'Quite right,' Rosie laughed. 'You'll be fine in your dress shop, Feathers. Now go and kiss Grandmama and Philippe.'

Dutifully she did so. She was aware that neither Grandmama nor Philippe truly approved of her but she couldn't understand why in Philippe's case. She wondered if he was jealous because Rosie was always so kind to her.

Carlos was struggling to talk to Madame and Feathers' heart went out to him. He wore the same full-sleeved shirt and waistcoat that she had first seen him in that morning, but now the clothes were washed, sponged and pressed. He wore a black bow tie with the shirt, and the outfit, though not proper evening dress, looked dashing and romantic.

She was pleased to find that he had been seated on her right at dinner. Philippe was on her left and Madame, as always, was at the head of the table with Pierre and Philippe each side of her. Rosie was between Pierre and Luke.

As far as she could work out everyone was talking about the *vendange* and the price of champagne. French was always spoken at dinner, which normally made it the most miserable meal for her. But tonight, with Carlos at her side, she had every excuse to chatter in English since he could not understand the general conversation. Luke gave her a grin of encouragement from the other side of the table and she whispered to Carlos: 'It sounds silly, but what do you think of your father? It must be so strange to have met him for the first time. But you're lucky. He really is a great guy.'

Carlos seemed to be thinking about her question.

'That has never been my impression,' he said finally.

Feathers was somewhat taken aback by such frankness. 'Because he didn't see you when you were a baby?'

'Because he abandoned my mother.'

Feathers thought how nearly she had been abandoned herself and imagined Patric seeking out his father in the same way in years to come.

'I understand,' she said, and decided that was enough of this dangerous subject, with Luke sitting only three feet away. 'Tell me,' she said, 'how did you get here? Surely not on that horse.'

He nodded gravely. 'Sable? Yes, she carried me here from Jerez.'

'It must have taken for ever.'

'Six weeks.'

He wasn't as easy to talk to as Luke. A bit monosyllabic. Maybe he was shy.

'And how come that you speak such good English?'

'I was sent to school in England.'

'Did you like it?'

'Not really.'

He was nervously pushing his food around the plate and had hardly eaten anything.

'Don't you like it?' she whispered, wondering how anyone could dislike a good gigot of lamb. 'Don't worry. Just leave it. No one will mind.'

He turned to look straight at her, his light grey eyes vivid against his dark skin.

'I am not hungry.' Then he said abruptly, 'You are so beautiful. I have never seen anyone so beautiful.'

She felt herself redden and threw an anxious look around the table to see if anyone had heard, but the gabble of French had drowned his words. Pierre was engrossed talking to his grandmother. Rosie was quietly and unobtrusively helping Philippe with his meal while chatting to Luke. Luke's entire attention was on Rosie, but then Feathers had noticed that his entire attention was always on Rosie.

Satisfied that no one had heard, she stammered: 'Thank you.'

'You need not thank me for the truth,' he said. 'I do not lie. And I will never lie to you.'

He made it sound as if he was going to be in her life for a long time. Feathers felt a little stirring, a warmth that she had not felt for a long time. Knowing her cheeks were red, she applied herself to her gigot.

'I'm sure you won't,' she muttered, and added, knowing that

266

it was a perfectly inane thing to say, 'I guess you take after your father. He's always truthful, too.'

'It was a lovely evening, wasn't it?' Feathers said much later to Pierre. He was already in bed reading while she sat at her dressing table taking off her make-up. She wore a pretty pink satin peignoir and her dramatic dress was safely hung in the wardrobe.

'You had someone to talk to,' he said.

'Yes.' She wasn't sure how much to say about Carlos.

'You were right. He does like you.'

She thrilled. He had noticed.

'I like him,' she said, making her voice casual. 'He's pleasant, but he doesn't say a lot.'

'It's an awkward situation for him. And it must have been a great shock for Luke.'

'I suppose he's illegitimate.'

'Apparently.'

She sighed. 'Wouldn't it have been awful if Patric had been illegitimate?'

It was the wrong thing to say. The rare conversation they had been having faltered. He reapplied himself to his book.

'The gigot was really great,' she remarked brightly as she flung her peignoir over a chair, revealing a pretty matching nightgown below.

'Yes, it was.' Then as if he had made a decision he straightened himself, put down his book and said abruptly: 'I've been meaning to tell you. I'm going up to Paris for a few days.'

'Can I come this time?' she asked eagerly.

'Not really. It's all business. People to see, and things to sort out at the Sorbonne. I'll only be gone for about a week. I won't bother them at the house on the Ile de la Cité. I shall stay in a hotel.'

She suddenly felt very depressed. The pleasure of the evening had evaporated.

'I'd like to come,' she told him. 'You never let me go anywhere with you.'

'Really, there's no point, Feathers.' He had picked up his book again.

'When are you going?'

'In three days' time.'

'But you'll miss all the *vendange* and the *cochelet*. Won't Rosie mind? Shouldn't you be here?'

'Well, it can't be helped. I have to go.' He had put the book down again and was leaning to turn out his bedside light. She stood there beside the bed, feeling helpless. As she climbed in, pulling the sheets and blankets over her, she felt his involuntary little move away from her.

She turned her own light out and lay there in the darkness until she was certain he was asleep. And then she let herself cry.

Pierre caught the early morning train to Paris with time to spare. He wanted to get away from Feathers and, more particularly, he wanted to get away from Les Hérissons. He needed a little fun of the type a young man of his age should be able to indulge in and he had things to do. The sort of fun that his friend, Jack Patterson, enjoyed. But Jack was free – unencumbered by wife, child or family.

Pierre was a disappointed man. He was haunted by the memory of Allie and what might have been. He was fond enough of Feathers – it would have been difficult not to be fond of her since she tried so hard to please him and everyone else. But he did not love her. He did love the son she had given him and if he was doomed to live with a woman he did not love, things could have been worse. He was at least genuinely fond of her.

But he felt life had trapped him. He was twenty-three years old, caught by marriage and a child. He had his degree in zoology and now he was going to learn the family champagne business. But once he had learned it, what would they let him do? He wanted more responsibility, more control over his life. Les Hérissons had not proved to be the haven he expected. It was a luxurious shelter most certainly, but with a formidable string attached. The string – no, the ring through his nose – was Madame Dupuis whose generosity ruled his life. His grandmother gave him everything and nothing. He had all the money he needed but no precious freedom. He was making this longer trip without her knowledge and consent and he knew that she would be angry. She was like the legendary bees, he thought, ruling their territory, insisting that they were told all, and if they were not told, buzzing with anger and indiscriminately stinging the bee-keeper and all who neared the hive. How Rosie handled her whims and her sharp tongue with such tolerance never ceased to amaze him.

Madame was for ever telling him that Les Hérissons would be his, but he did not believe that this could be. Surely part of the estate was Allie's and Rosanne's? Rosie and Philippe owned the champagne company and, as far as he could gather, the actual stock of wine, much of the wine-making machinery and the newer outbuildings. The house, the land and the vines were his and Rosie's children's, but they could do little with them while Madame, the mother Dupuis, and Rosie, the widow Dupuis, lived.

If he was to learn the champagne business, and he had every intention of doing so, he wanted Les Hérissons and the champagne company for himself. He had ideas how things could be improved. The sales side was in a bad way. They were only just selling what they produced. He felt Rosie had deliberately slowed down on the production because her husband was no longer capable of running the business end. He was convinced he could do better.

When his train pulled into the Gare de l'Est he took a taxi to the rue Caumartin, close to the Madeleine where there was a discreet house that he had begun to visit after he and Feathers had ceased to make love.

A manservant opened the large double doors to his knock and quickly shut them again once Pierre was inside. Then he took Pierre's hat and coat and led him into a small, elegantly furnished room.

'Will you take something to drink, sir?' he murmured.

'A half bottle of Krug,' Pierre said, wondering if it would be possible to sell Les Hérissons' wine here.

He settled himself in a comfortable chair and waited. Within a minute the Madame, a tall, grey-haired woman, thin as a governess's hatpin and with the manner to match, arrived. She was followed by the manservant who carried a small silver tray holding a full bottle of champagne in ice and two glasses. He placed it on a table and left.

Pierre rose to his feet and bowed.

'Monsieur Dupuis, welcome,' she said. 'I took the liberty of joining you since we have not seen you for a while.'

'It will be my pleasure, Madame Beauregard,' he told her.

As she busied herself with the cork and glasses, she asked: 'You are well, Monsieur Dupuis?'

He knew she was anxious that he might have found another place to visit for forbidden fruit. As she handed him a brimming glass, he said: 'I am living in the country now, Madame. In Champagne. My opportunities to visit Paris are rare. But today I have made a special journey to see you and your charming young ladies.'

She smiled. 'The countryside has not changed your tastes, monsieur?'

'On the contrary,' he said. 'The enforced abstinence has heightened them.'

'Then we shall have to find you something very special today. But is there no such establishment as mine nearby your country home?'

'Indeed there is. But when one is used to the Ritz . . .'

'Of course.' She allowed herself to preen a little. 'Now, it is to be the usual arrangement?'

'If you please.'

'And was there anyone in particular that you had in mind?'

It was a question she always asked and she always received the same reply.

'No. Providing the girls are truly fond of each other.'

She knitted her brows and then nodded. 'I know just the pair. Charming girls. You have not met Francine. She has only been here a few weeks. But the poor dear girl was so homesick at first that Charlotte comforted her, and you know how it is – how these things begin?'

A reply did not seem necessary since Madame Beauregard was finishing her champagne with obvious enjoyment. When it was gone, she sighed faintly and regretfully put down the empty glass. 'I seem to recall that you met Charlotte perhaps a year ago. She was satisfactory?'

Pierre quite deliberately never remembered the names of Madame's girls. It was important to him that the entire transaction was totally impersonal. He disliked having the same girl twice, but sometimes it could not be helped.

He nodded again, and Madame Beauregard moved in her stately way towards the door.

270

'I shall send Charlotte to find you. Francine is still a little shy.'

The thought that one of the girls was shy excited him.

'Then perhaps both ladies would come and we could enjoy a glass of Krug together before we go upstairs,' he suggested.

'But, of course,' Madame Beauregard said. 'I shall send them both to you.'

The two girls appeared so quickly, accompanied by a maid with two more champagne glasses, that Pierre was certain that Madame had assessed his needs and warned them to be ready from the moment he had walked into the house. He recognised Charlotte; a buxom, dark girl with bold brown eyes. Her hair was unfashionably long, falling to her shoulders, and she wore a smart little tea gown made of red chiffon. He could not remember what she had been like in bed. Francine was small but beautifully rounded, he noted. She had huge frightened blue eyes, and soft smooth blonde hair which, like Feathers, she wore in a pageboy style. Her gown was of black chiffon and he could see just a hint of the pink of her small nipples beneath the fabric.

'Ladies,' he said, rising to his feet and moving to pour them some wine. Francine looked uneasy as she took her glass as if she wished he would just get on with what he had come for. Charlotte, more the trained courtesan, was able to make the drawing-room conversation that Pierre needed. It was important to him that these encounters began in an air of normality.

When all three glasses were empty, Charlotte led the way up the fine staircase to the girls' rooms. She had already informed him that she and Francine shared a room.

'Madame thought you would like to come to our personal boudoir,' Charlotte said. 'She felt you would find it more intimate.'

He doubted very much if the room they took him to was their personal boudoir. He suspected that their personal quarters were somewhere in the attics or in the basement. He could not see Madame Beauregard allowing her employees such luxury. The huge four-poster bed was draped in midnight blue satin, and spread with blue satin sheets. Soft blue carpets and walls with heavy blue velvet curtains at the windows gave the atmosphere of a cloister. The lighting was discreet, and mirrors strategically placed all round the room reflected the bed. Indeed, the underside of the bed's canopy consisted of one large sheet of mirrored glass. A comfortable armchair was placed facing the foot of the bed. One large teddy bear and a lifesize china baby doll with staring round blue eyes, dressed in frilly clothes, lay against the satin pillows. There were family photographs on each of the bedside tables. A formal chair held some carelessly thrown white and black underwear, and a jumble of perfume bottles and cosmetics were set out on a dressing table.

Charlotte took off his jacket and fussed him into the chair facing the bed. Standing behind him, she took off his tie while Francine, from the front, undid the neck of his shirt. She was so close to him he could see the soft, white down of facial hair on her upper lip. One small tooth was biting her lipsticked mouth as she struggled with the buttons. She was very young, perhaps only seventeen, and he felt a pang of compassion as she unbuttoned his trousers and slid them down his legs. Charlotte had removed his shirt and was standing, waiting, with a dressing gown. He stood, stepped out of his remaining clothes and put it on.

Then the girls left him. Francine flung herself on the bed and took the teddy bear in her arms, kissing it open-mouthed and hugging it, pushing it against her breasts. Charlotte stood watching her, her expression intense, until she went to sit on the edge of bed. Roughly, as if she were jealous, she took the bear from the other girl's arms and threw it on the floor. Then with her little finger she wiped the lipstick from Francine's lips before covering the girl's face with small, delicate kisses, gently biting at her lips until the kiss changed to a deep, thrusting one. Francine opened her mouth to receive the other girl's tongue, gasping all the while, her slender arms pulling Charlotte close to her.

Their play-acting was ending. This was for real, and watching he felt his arousal begin.

Charlotte began to undress the younger girl. Slowly and provocatively she undid the front of the black chiffon dress, folding it away so that Francine's small, pink-tipped breasts were revealed. Her nipples were already hard little columns, and as Charlotte uncovered her flat, white stomach and found the lightly downed mound of Venus, Francine began to moan as with her own fingers she tormented her nipples until their colour darkened and the columns grew taller.

Kneeling, her head bent, Charlotte's long dark hair was entwined with the yellow down as her tongue traced from stomach down to the dark line between soft full lips that faced Pierre. She had placed herself so that her body did not obstruct his view. Her tongue made the entrance and she swung round and parted her legs so that her own secret lips were poised above Francine's mouth. Then slowly she lowered herself until Francine's pink flickering tongue was probing between dark hair as she supported her partner's thighs.

They had forgotten him now. They were totally engrossed in themselves and what they were doing to each other.

They used every inch of the bed, moving from one side to the other, a series of beautiful erotic pictures made of curves and colour and light and shade. Charlotte's heavy, black-nippled breasts dropped like ripe fruit swinging into Francine's mouth. Charlotte suckled Francine. They lay on their sides, legs entwined, one rubbing against the other as they moaned with pleasure. He watched, enchanted, aroused and deeply moved. Their lovemaking was so much gentler than that between man and woman; a mutual pleasing and unselfish. It gave him joy to watch.

And then Charlotte's bold eyes were signalling him from where her head lay on Francine's waist. She sat up and spread the other girl's legs apart to reveal the glistening, engorged entrance waiting for him.

'We need you,' she whispered.

He stood and took off his dressing gown and walked to the bed. He entered Francine where she lay, hardly touching her body as he did so. Holding himself up on his arms, he rode her with long, slow, deep movements. Then the movements speeded and he was gasping until he climaxed. He fell back onto the pillows panting while the two girls idly played with each other again. Francine tried to touch him, but he pushed her away and waited until he was ready again. It was Charlotte's turn. He made her stand and lean over the bed so that there was no need to touch her. Then he straddled her and rode her. This time it took longer, but eventually, with a cry, he came.

And that was the end of it. It was over. He did not wish to sleep beside them. He wanted to leave. He would not have been able to bring himself to caress either of them. To have kissed them would have been impossible.

He washed and dressed in the bathroom next door while the two girls, limbs tumbled, slept naked on the bed. He did not wake them as he left. He was satisfied both physically and emotionally. He had completed the act for them both. He had provided the tool that they did not have.

He reasoned as he always reasoned that since he had not touched them with his hands or his mouth, what he had done was no more disloyal to his wife than masturbation would have been. And perhaps less dangerous. Pierre remembered the strictures of his tutors. Masturbation was a sin and could make you go blind. Pierre had never believed it, but a lingering doubt remained and he denied himself the relief it gave. He used Madame Beauregard's girls instead. He felt there was something pure and clean about love between two women. Watching excited him but it also filled him with a kind of awe and left him feeling omnipotent when he, the man, gave them the final satisfaction in a way they could not achieve for themselves.

Remembering his father's callous use of women, he told himself that they had used him as much as he had used them. Not any one of the three of them expected anything lasting from the encounter. It was no more than a question of fleeting pleasure and some cold hard cash. He did not have to pretend he loved them, or they him.

Downstairs Madame Beauregard kept him company while he finished the bottle of champagne. He paid her discreetly and left. There was just time for a little lunch with his friend, Jack Patterson, before they got on with the real business of the day.

Chapter Eleven

'But I didn't even know that Papa Philippe had a daughter,' Rosanne was saying, her expression mutinous.

'Well, he does. She's a little older than you,' Rosie told her firmly.

Rosanne let out a great theatrical sigh. 'Does she have to come, Mama?' she asked.

Rosie sighed herself. The arrival of Françoise was causing problems. Neither Miss nor Nanny Shepherd were happy at taking on an eleven-year-old who would no doubt be miserable at losing both her own nanny and her mother in one fell swoop. Rosie had bribed them with extra pay. Now Rosanne was rebellious at the very idea.

'Of course she must come,' Rosie said patiently. 'Her own mother has to go and live abroad in a place that isn't suitable for children. Philippe is her father. She has nowhere else to go. And it will someone for you to play with.'

'I don't need anyone to play with.'

It was true. Rosanne, as Allie had done as a child, lived in a fantasy world. The difference was that where Allie had day-dreamed and written down her dreams, turning them into stories, Rosanne acted hers out.

Rosie would find her dressed in clothes from the boxes in which Rosie put her old dresses, using any kind of household bits and pieces for her props, acting out some play that existed in her imagination. She was perfectly content on her own. For a while she had enjoyed the company of imaginary playmates. 'Do be careful, Mama,' she had once said, startling Rosie. 'You very nearly trod on a fairy.' But that phase seemed to have passed.

She was also much easier to handle than when she had been

little. Rosie hated to admit it, but the child had definitely calmed down after Allie left. She seemed more secure somehow and happier. But then Rosie also had to admit that she found herself happier without the disapproving presence of her daughter.

'Well, darling, there's nothing to be done about it,' Rosie said. 'She will be here the day after tomorrow, and I want you to be very kind and nice to her. She'll be lonely for her own mother and very homesick. So don't do anything to make her unhappy.'

Rosanne let out another theatrical sigh.

'Oh, all right. If she's got to come she's got to come, I suppose. But I bet she's awful.'

Remembering Françoise's silly, shallow mother, Rosie had an alarming moment of misgiving, but she said: 'Nonsense! Can you imagine Papa Philippe having a little girl who is awful?'

Rosie felt she had made a strong point since Rosanne loved Philippe as if he were her real father.

'You're a lovely mama and my papa was a lovely papa but Allie was awful a lot of the time and so was I when I was little,' Rosanne pointed out with logic beyond her eight years. 'And I bet this Françoise won't want to share Papa Philippe with me. And I don't much want to share him with her.'

'Really, Rosanne. If you had a little sister or brother you'd have to share him.' Rosie was beginning to get exasperated.

'Ah,' said Rosanne, 'but they'd be *my* brother or sister, wouldn't they? She isn't.'

Rosie gave up.

Philippe was openly happy at the thought of his daughter arriving, and Rosie, determined that the girl would feel welcome, went to a lot of trouble to make her room pretty and cosy. Philippe had said that even as a toddler Françoise had been a very feminine little girl so the room was furnished in pink and white with big white bows to hold back the curtains and fluffy rugs on the floor.

'Ugh!' said Rosanne when she inspected it. But then Rosanne had positive ideas about anything she felt was 'soppy'. However, when the décor was described to Philippe he said it sounded just right.

Françoise's arrival at the same time as the *vendange* was an added chore for Rosie at what was a feverishly busy time.

Happily, there was Luke to make sure everything went well at Les Hérissons. Rosie was aware that she had grown to depend more and more on the Englishman. Just thinking about him gave her a feeling of security. She could trust him to see that the pressing of the picked grapes was properly conducted and she had felt easy telling him that she would not be able to come to Les Hérissons at all the day Françoise arrived. She knew he would understand, and at the news he grinned and said: 'Kids are turning up all over the place, aren't they?'

'They are indeed,' she said, then asked: 'How's Carlos working out?'

Luke shook his head.

'I haven't had much time to really talk to him,' he said. 'When the *vendange* is over I'll have to find out what he wants to do. I just don't know what to do with him or say to him. It's a ridiculous situation. He can't stay here for ever. But where can he go?'

'Is he helping with the *vendange*?' Rosie asked. 'We could pay him if he is.'

'Is he hell!' Luke exploded. 'A bit of hard work seems to be beneath his dignity!' Then he tutted in annoyance at himself. 'Sorry to swear. It's that school my mother sent him to. If she was going to send him to a public school she might at least have said to hell with the cost and chosen a decent one where they beat some sense into them and send them out as gentlemen. Now he's behaving as if the world owes him a living just because he's had five minutes of inferior education in the company of a lot of *nouveau riche* kids. He thinks he's a guest here. All he's doing is running around the estate with Feathers who is delighted to have someone to talk to. You'd have thought anyone who likes to talk as much as she does would have learned the language, wouldn't you?'

'She swears she's going to.'

Luke, who seemed generally out of sorts, just grunted and muttered something that sounded like 'That'll be the day!'

Rosie, driving herself back to Les Coquelicots, reflected that, generally speaking, offspring only brought trouble.

Françoise Lefevre arrived from Paris sharp at eleven on the Wednesday morning. She sat in splendour in the back of a large black chauffeur-driven car surrounded by a great deal of luggage. Though the weather was still warm she wore a fur-trimmed coat and hat with shoes that would have been more suitable on an adult.

She was tall, almost as tall as Rosie, blonde like her mother and father and extremely pretty in a rosebud kind of way. She was also disconcertingly adult for her age.

Young Rosanne did her best. She was there, smiling, with her mother and Philippe ready to greet the new arrival as she was helped from the car. But Françoise ignored both Rosie and Rosanne and with a delicate little ballet dancer's flounce half-ran to her father.

'Papa!' she said, flinging her arms round him. 'Papa, it is I. Your daughter. Françoise! Oh, it is heaven to see you.'

Rosie and Rosanne looked at each other, both startled by the theatrical greeting, but Philippe's face was alight with love and pleasure as he hugged the child to him.

'You do remember me?' he asked, and Rosie could see there were tears in his eyes.

'Of course,' she cried. 'How could I forget you? I've missed you so much!'

Then why did she never write? Rosie asked herself.

Philippe hugged his daughter again, and then said: 'You must meet your stepmother and sister. They've been so looking forward to your coming.'

Françoise turned reluctantly to where Rosie and Rosanne stood, close together for mutual support. Her look was disdainful but her voice rang out with the sweetness of a silver bell.

'Oh, it's so kind of you to have me with you,' she trilled, but her expression indicated that it was Rosie and her daughter who should feel honoured.

'You're very welcome,' Rosie said, making her smile as warm as she could. 'Come inside. You must be tired after your journey.'

'Not really,' the girl said, pulling off her gloves finger by finger. 'The Rolls is very comfortable, and Alexi drives very well.'

Turning her back on Rosie and Rosanne, she took her father's hand and said: 'Show me the way in, Papa.' Beaming with pleasure, Philippe did so. Once in the hallway the girl looked around as she if were inspecting the lobby of a hotel where she did not wish to stay, and then waited for help removing her coat. Suzette who hovering close by leapt to oblige and was left holding the garment without so much as a thank you.

Heart beginning to sink, Rosie in a slightly pointed fashion said: 'Thank you, Suzette,' before asking if Françoise would like to be taken to her room.

'Can't dear Papa take me?' Françoise said with a pout.

Rosie hesitated. Philippe was not at ease in the areas of the house that he never used. He would not want to stumble in front of his new-found daughter.

'I think it's better if we take you,' she said. 'Your father will wait for you down here.'

'Is that all right, Papa?' Françoise asked.

Rosie he could see that he was torn. Then he said jovially: 'Rooms are women's work. You go with your stepmother and Rosanne.'

But once upstairs it was quite obvious that Françoise was not impressed with her room.

'I suppose this was yours when you were little,' she said to Rosanne, nose definitely turned up at the white and the pink. 'My room at home is black and white. Mama says that black and white are quite the smartest furnishing colours.'

'Well, yes,' Rosie said quickly, aware of Rosanne's wrathful expression. 'Do you want to wash or anything, or do you want to go straight back downstairs?'

'Oh, downstairs,' Françoise said in a slightly drawling voice. 'Back to Papa, please. He and I have so much to say to each other. All those years to catch up with.'

'Yes, of course,' Rosie murmured, apprehension growing.

They found Philippe settled in his usual chair in the sitting room. Françoise ran across the polished floor towards him, jumping on his lap and twining her arms round his neck.

'My room is beautiful!' she told him. 'It's so wonderful to be here with you. We've so much to talk about. I want us to get to know each other all over again.'

'We will, my dear, we will.' Philippe was hugging her to him, his face bright with happiness. Françoise looked towards where Rosie and Rosanne stood, her face cold and her pale blue eyes glittering. 'Off you go,' her expression said as clearly as if she had spoken.

Suppressing her anger, Rosie said lightly: 'Well, we'll leave you two together then,' and taking Rosanne gently by the arm, led her back into the big hallway, carefully shutting the door behind them.

'Told you so!' said Rosanne laughing and giggling as she scampered back upstairs to tell Miss the latest.

But somehow Rosie did not think that Françoise would prove a laughing matter.

As the *vendangeurs* worked their way across the vineyards and the year's crop was rushed to the vats for pressing, Rosie had little time to worry about Françoise. The girl didn't bother Rosanne who acted as if she wasn't there. Since in the schoolroom they were working on totally different subjects, there was little need for communication. Miss, agreeably surprised, had reported to Rosie that Françoise was bright and well educated and though rather superior in her manner she was reasonably polite and well behaved. But she had not warmed to the girl, Rosie was sure of that. Françoise was also courteous with Nanny Shepherd. It was only with the servants and with Rosie and Rosanne that the girl was downright unpleasant.

'She is unbelievably cunning,' Rosie said gloomily to Luke when he asked if Françoise was settling in well. 'She will be saying the most charming things that Philippe can hear, but at the same time her expressions, which he cannot see, are insolent. She's downright rude when her father's not about. But he thinks that she is delightful. He has no reason not to. He's so happy to have her with us that I can't bring myself to tell him what's going on. To tell you the truth, it would give me the greatest of pleasure to smack her smug little pretty face and send her back to her awful mother. But the fact that I even want to appals me. For heaven's sake, she's a child! She's only eleven years old and she's getting under my skin. But there's not much of the child about her. I have to think of some way of dealing with it.'

'You wouldn't like to think of a way of dealing with Carlos while you're at it, would you?' Luke said, equally gloomy. 'He seems to think he ought to be treated like an English milord. He wants an allowance, which I suppose I shall have to give him, and now he's complaining that I've put him in a servant's room. I think he thinks he ought to have my room. It's my mother's fault. Educating him above his station and I don't doubt his mother waited on him hand and foot. Spanish mothers do.'

Rosie couldn't help smiling.

'*You* didn't put him in that room. I did. Shall we try and find something else?'

'There isn't anywhere else. And the room is perfectly all right. He's lucky to have anywhere, turning up like that. It's no good, I can't get used to thinking he's my son. I don't even like him much.'

Rosie took his hand and squeezed it comfortingly.

'We're a fine pair,' she said, 'letting ourselves get upset by a pair of adolescents. We'll sort it all out after the *vendange*.'

'He's twenty. That can't be adolescent.'

'It is when they act like it,' Rosie told him.

It was dusk and Luke had come into the courtyard to crank the car for her journey home. Standing there, the smoke from his pipe blending into the evening mist, she felt curiously reluctant to leave. Les Hérissons seemed so peaceful and Luke was so solid and dependable. There was one more day of picking to be done and the work had gone well. Robert was at the vats, supervising the pressing, for it had to be done quickly before the grapes fermented. Those who had picked the grapes were back in their rough and ready quarters. The cheerful noise of an accordion floated on the evening air, and from another *vendangeoir* came the sound of voices singing.

'They sound happy enough,' Luke remarked.

'They'll be happier tomorrow at the *cochelet*.' She squinted at the sky. 'I hope it stays fine. Is Cook still grumbling?'

'Never stops,' he said cheerfully, 'but she's got half the village to help her and she's really thoroughly enjoying herself.'

'That's all right then,' she said absently, and yawned. 'I suppose I'd better get going.' She turned to kiss him on the cheek. 'Goodnight, Luke. Thanks for everything.'

'Anything for a beautiful lady.' He put his hands on her shoulders and held her away to look at her. 'You're tired. Get some sleep.' Then he added abruptly, as if it was important, 'Will you dance with me tomorrow?'

She laughed.

'If you ask me,' she said. 'It's impolite to say no.'

281

Before he could reply she slid into the driving seat of the Salmson and he shut the door for her.

'See you tomorrow,' she called as she drove off down the gravel drive.

She was a little late leaving and she drove swiftly through the gathering darkness. The roads were empty, but she could see the lights and hear the music from other winegrowers' *vendangeoirs*. Champagne was *en fête* tonight. The fairgrounds in the villages would be full of the *vendangeurs* squandering the few sous they had earned. At home Philippe would be waiting for her and she drove a little faster at the thought.

It was dark by the time she reached Les Coquelicots and Suzette opened the door before she could find her key to let herself into the house. Rosie hurried into the sitting room where Philippe always sat patiently waiting for her until she came home. But the room was empty. She felt a quite unreasonable wave of disappointment as if she had been abandoned.

'Suzette,' she called, 'where is Monsieur?'

Suzette who had been on her way to the kitchen returned.

'Monsieur and Madamoiselle Lefevre went for a walk about an hour ago, Madame,' she said. 'He said they would be back in time for supper.'

'But it's dark. Where can they be?' Rosie went to the front door and opened it, looking anxiously into the night. 'We should look for them. Something must have happened.'

'Shall I ask Michel to go, Madame?'

'Please, Suzette. As quickly as possible. Do you have any idea where they went?'

Suzette had no idea, and after she had gone to find Michel, Rosie paced the living room anxiously. A blind man wandering in an area he did not know and a young girl who had only been in the house a few days. Both of them in the dark. What on earth had possessed them to go out so late in the day?

But even before Suzette returned with Michel, Rosie heard laughter, Philippe's rare and therefore treasured laughter, and the lighter, girlish contrived giggle that passed for amusement with Françoise.

She rushed to the front door and opened it as they stepped onto the front porch.

'Rosie?' Philippe said tentatively as the light from the hall flooded into his face.

She moved forward to put her arms round him.

'Where have you been?' she asked. 'I was frightened.'

He kissed her, then extricated himself and shrugged off his overcoat.

'I'll take it, Papa,' Françoise trilled.

'We got lost for a while,' he said. 'I had intended to be back before you. But we were perfectly all right.'

'But why did you go out so late and in the dark?' Rosie scolded.

'It was perfectly all right,' Françoise said, echoing her father. 'And besides, I had Papa to look after me.'

She was standing very close to him, and he patted her shoulder.

'Yes, don't fuss, Rosie,' he said, and she noticed the slight flush of pleasure on his cheeks at the girl's words. The girl noticed it too and was looking at Rosie, naked triumph in her eyes. Rosie swallowed hard.

'As long as you're both safe,' she managed. 'Now come and sit down, Philippe.'

'Yes, we'll rest,' he said. 'Come and join us, Françoise.'

'Of course, Papa,' Françoise said, and deliberately handed her coat to Rosie before walking straight into the living room. Standing in her own hall holding the fur-trimmed coat, Rosie shut her eyes and silently counted to ten. Then she hung the coat in the hall cupboard and, boiling with rage, followed her husband and his daughter into her living room.

In the short time she had been in the house, Françoise had been limpet-like in her attachment to Philippe. She never moved far from his side except when she was in the schoolroom. Philippe was beginning to neglect his work but his headaches seemed to be less severe so Rosie said nothing. The girl even sat with them at dinner. She had told her father that she always joined her mother and stepfather for dinner and would like to do the same here. She insisted that she had been finished with the nursery routine for ages.

'It will be a pleasure to have you with us,' Philippe said fondly.

Rosie had not been alone with her husband, apart from at bedtime, since the girl arrived. She told herself that things would get back to normal once Françoise was truly settled in. But she was beginning to think that this would not be.

The night before, after she and Françoise had left the dining room to leave Philippe to his cigar, they had been seated in the drawing room for a minute or two before the girl said: 'It's so nice for me to be in Papa's home. I used to be so afraid that I would never see him again after you took him away from us. But he still loves me best, doesn't he?'

The crude thrust was delivered in the guise of childish innocence, but this time Philippe was not nearby. Tired of biting her tongue, Rosie said coldly: 'I think you should understand, Françoise that I did not take your father from you. Perhaps you should ask him the truth of what happened and then perhaps you might feel inclined to mind your manners while you are in my home.'

She received a blistering look of sheer hatred, but Suzette's timely arrival to pour the coffee ended further conversation, and a few seconds later Philippe joined them.

Curled into Philippe's warm, sleeping body later that night in their bed, Rosie told herself she was not handling the situation very well. She had little choice but to put up with Françoise since her presence made Philippe so happy. To tell him what the girl was doing would distress him; he might not even believe it as he had no evidence of eyes. And Françoise was so careful to make her voice warm and loving, regardless of what her eyes and face were doing. The girl wanted revenge for the childhood loss of her father, and she was doing a good job of getting it.

She stroked his head as she always did before she went to sleep. He said it helped his headaches. He stirred and turned to hold her close to him.

'Did Françoise look pretty tonight?' he asked sleepily.

'Very. She was wearing a blue dress that suited her very well.'

'And she looks like me?'

'She has your colouring and she's very like you in her looks.' It wasn't entirely true, but it pleased him to hear it.

'She looked more like her mother when she was a baby.'

'Well, there's still a touch of Lorraine about her, but everyone would know that she's your daughter.'

He sighed contentedly. 'Do you know why she wanted to go out in the dark tonight?'

'No,' Rosie said cautiously.

'She wanted us to be in the dark together. She wanted to see what it was like for me. I was so touched.'

Remembering how once, long ago, she had blindfolded herself for the same reason, Rosie felt a pang of guilt. Maybe the girl did truly love her father. Maybe the mother had put all the blame onto her, Rosie. She resolved to try to win over this unlovable stepdaughter.

'She doesn't really want to go to the *cochelet* tomorrow,' he was saying. 'She says her mother would be angry with her for going. I suppose we shouldn't let her do anything that Lorraine would disapprove of.'

'But why would her mother disapprove?' Rosie asked.

He shifted uncomfortably. 'Lorraine's a bit of a snob. Apparently Françoise was never allowed to have anything to do with the servants, other than her nanny and governess.'

'And this party is for the servants and the workers. I see.' Rosie could not suppress her irritation. 'Well, Rosanne's going. She's looking forward to it. And Miss and Nanny Shepherd have been promised they can go. One of them will have to stay with Françoise. They'll be so disappointed.'

'I know. That's why I thought I'd stay at home and keep her company.'

'You!'

'It's not that interesting for me, darling. Just a lot of noise and people I can't see.'

'But I love you to be with me. You were going to dance with me.' She could not rid her voice of the note of protest.

'I told Françoise I'd promised to go with you, but she pointed out that she's been deprived of her father for a long time. It makes me feel so guilty when she says things like that, Rosie, I feel I can't refuse her anything.'

'It shouldn't. Lorraine left you for Didier. Lorraine had different plans after the war once you were . . .' she stopped.

'Blinded?' he said. 'That's true. But she knew I loved you, and she knew I had always loved you. She knew we were lovers. I should never have married her. The guilt is mine.'

'Well, if you hadn't married her, the wretched girl wouldn't be here today,' Rosie said angrily.

'Shhh!' He put his fingers over her lips. 'There'll be other *vendanges* and *cochelets*, my darling. Just let me get to know her again, and please don't call her "wretched". She is, you must admit, a most charming child. And it's hard for her to be so uprooted.'

Rosie swallowed hard, reflecting that she seemed to be doing rather a lot of that lately.

'I'm sorry,' she said, putting her arms round him. 'It was just that I was looking forward to being with you.'

'Well, don't work so hard and then you can be with me more. You're not often here, darling.'

Now who had been putting those thoughts in his head? she wondered, and this time she could not hold back.

'Are you sure I wouldn't be in the way?' she said crossly as she heaved herself onto her other side, her back to him. 'Good-night.' She made the word two separate bad-tempered syllables. She heard his sigh but he said nothing and she realised with dismay that they were quarrelling. The first quarrel since they had married. She heaved herself back over again and buried her head in his chest.

'I'm sorry, darling,' she said.

His hand found her breast.

'So am I,' he whispered before he began to kiss her.

She let her lips open in response and as he pressed against her, she felt how aroused he was. Her hand slid over his lean stomach to hold and rub him and she sighed with pleasure.

At least Françoise could not take that away from her.

Feathers had hugged what she knew was a rather mean inner pleasure when she realised that Aunt Rosie was more than a little irritated by Pierre's departure to Paris.

'I thought he was supposed to be learning about wine-making,' Rosie said when she was told. 'This is one of the most important times of the year. And he's gone to Paris?'

'Apparently it was business,' Feathers said.

Aunt Rosie raised her dark eyebrows.

'Oh, really?' Her tone was dry, inferring 'what business?' but she said no more. It was Feathers' impression that Rosie was no more convinced by the excuse than she had been herself.

Pierre's departure had dismayed her. She was beset by nagging doubts about what exactly he was doing. She feared there was another woman, and yet, in a way, she found herself relieved by his absence. She did not have to strive to please him all the time because he was not there to please. She felt surprisingly free – almost light-headed as if a path of eggshells had been temporarily removed from her life. And there was no time to mope since she had someone to keep her company and to talk to – Carlos.

It was on the last day of the *vendange* that she was taken by the urge to go and see what she thought of as 'her shop'. The Dupuis family lawyers were already in negotiation with the owners and Carlos, hankering for city streets, had asked if they could go to Reims together. It was a perfect excuse to get away, and they cycled to Rilly and then took the mid-morning train. As well as her shop she wanted to show him the city. The three years since she had first seen it had made a big difference to Reims. Now it was partially rebuilt, though the cathedral still needed much work. She tried to describe to him how terribly badly damaged the city had been, but she realised he had no concept of war any more than she had had before she came to France. He told her that Spain had not been affected and Jerez was so far south that what happened in northern Europe was of little consequence. The conflict had been almost over by the time he went to his British public school. His English schooling had not begun until he was nearly fifteen because his mother would not let him go when she heard that the Zeppelins were bombing England.

'My mother is very protective towards me,' he said proudly.

'That's nice,' Feathers murmured, feeling some comment was required but thinking that for a grown man he seemed to talk a great deal about his mother.

But he duly admired the shop premises just off the Cours Langlet and agreed they were in exactly the right part of town. They wandered around, chatting, stopping for lunch and tea, and eventually, when they were both bored with window-shopping, they took the train back to Rilly. The day had not been an unqualified success. The atmosphere had been strange. He said little. She had had to make most of the conversation and she kept catching him staring at her. His look was so intense that it made her uncomfortable. It also made her very aware of him and she found that she was flirting a little and enjoying his response.

Cycling home they found themselves caught up in among the

wagons returning from the vineyards to the *vendangeoirs*. The *vendangeurs* were singing bawdy songs as the rickety wagons trundled along, each cart decorated with bunches of wild flowers, the girls wearing poppies in their hair.

'Tonight is the *cochelet*,' Feathers said. 'I'm so looking forward to it.'

'Surely it's just for the workers?' he asked.

'Yes, but we all go.'

'So my father said.' He raised a cynical eyebrow and said in his sibilant accent: 'It is very odd.'

'Why is it odd?' She did not understand why he was being so unenthusiastic. 'It'll be fun. You will come, won't you?'

'If you go I shall be there,' he promised.

The family's instructions were to meet in Madame's parlour half an hour before the *invités* arrived. Madame proposed to give everyone a glass of champagne because only still wine – and a very ordinary one at that – would be served throughout the evening. About a hundred people were coming, and the courtyard at the back of the house had been laid out with four long linen-covered tables. They were set for twenty-four people, with a place at the head for a member of the family. Feathers had been told that she would have to deputise for Pierre, but she wheedled Rosie into agreeing that Carlos could sit beside her to give her support. Feathers knew it was a little more than just support. She wanted to know him better. He was a bit like an itch that needed scratching, she thought, irritating and yet so satisfying when scratched.

Aunt Rosie had arranged things so that Madame's table held her own Les Hérissons' staff. She, Luke and Feathers had the *vendangeurs* to deal with, and to enable Marie, Henri and the rest of the household staff simply to enjoy themselves, Rosie had brought her own servants from Les Coquelicots to do the work of serving and clearing. They were already in the courtyard, putting the finishing touches to the tables. Opened bottles of wine, white and red, ranged their length, along with baskets of roughly cut bread. Sturdy white china and basic knives and forks were set before every place. The meal – a steaming, fragrant coq au vin, would be served from oversized tureens.

When Marie announced that the guests were gathering, the family left Madame's parlour and trooped through the back of

288

the house. A touch self-consciously they filed into the dusky blue of the early evening, Madame leading the way. Some of the guests had already seated themselves; others were in groups talking. The courtyard was so full of brightly, if shabbily, dressed people that it looked as if it were home to a public meeting. But everyone seemed happy and Feathers noticed how much fitter the *vendangeurs* looked for their ten days in the fields.

As Madame, her arm held by Luke, appeared there was a sudden hush before a spontaneous burst of clapping burst out. And then an enchantingly pretty girl with long black hair and bare feet hurried forward to present Madame Dupuis with a huge bunch of wild flowers. As she handed it over she bobbed in such a way that it looked almost like a curtsy. Madame accepted these tributes as her due.

'It's awfully crowded,' Carlos, who was standing with Feathers, whispered. His elbows were tight to his side as if he was afraid of being jostled. He seemed to be trying to make himself thinner.

'Yes, isn't it fun!' she said, but he did not answer.

Once they were seated, Feathers did her best to communicate with the people at her table with smiles and gestures. Eventually she gave up. Everyone was enjoying themselves without encouragement from her. The wine and food on the table vanished rapidly but Rosie's servants replenished both as fast as they disappeared.

Feathers was aware that Carlos was staring at her again and she twitched at her neckline, wondering if it was too low. Because he was Spanish she had decided to wear a low-necked white blouse with a frill that pulled down over the shoulders. She teamed it with a full black taffeta skirt with another frill round the hem. The outfit was not fashionable; almost like a fancy dress, but it seemed to have a Spanish look, was rural and seemed just right for a *cochelet*.

He leaned over to fill her glass with the rough wine and whispered: 'You look like a gypsy girl tonight.'

She pouted. 'I meant to look Spanish.'

He smiled, pleased.

'A Spanish gypsy girl,' he said. 'Like my mother.'

'Your mother is a gypsy?'

He nodded. 'She was the best flamenco dancer in all of Jerez and Cadiz.'

'And she fell in love with Luke?'

'And he betrayed her.'

He was pouring himself more wine and his attitude and expression were deeply melancholy. Melancholy he might be, but this blunt criticism of Luke embarrassed her.

'They must have been very young,' she murmured. 'Younger than we are now.'

'Before him, my mother was innocent.'

She was tempted to shock him by saying that before Pierre, she too had been innocent, that everyone was innocent before someone came into their lives. Anyway, she thought, what was so great about innocence? Innocence only got girls into trouble.

Looking for an excuse to change the subject she downed her wine and asked if he would pour her more. He leaned his arm against hers as he did so. It made her jump and tingle. It felt as if he had burned her.

The courtyard, lit by the soft light of oil lamps, was full of noise and laughter. Someone had taken out a mouth organ and a little group were singing to the music as they ate. Rosie's servants were red-faced and breathless as they brought more wine, served from the tureens and offered bread and cheese. The barefoot girl who had presented the bouquet was dancing on the table, and already those who had finished eating had found a spot in which to dance cheek to cheek.

'Soon everyone will be dancing,' she told him. 'There's going to be music. Proper music. Fiddles, a guitar and an accordion. Aunt Rosie arranged it all.'

'Will you dance with me?' he asked, fixing her with that intense stare that both made her nervous and turned her stomach over at the same time.

'Of course. Can you dance flamenco?'

'I can.'

'Will you?'

He pursed his lips. 'For you, yes.'

The tables were gradually being cleared, white cloths folded, and the men were encouraged to carry the trestles into one of the barns. Just one table was left to hold bottles of wines and Marc, along with more bread and cheese. Feathers stood looking around, not certain what to do next. Madame had disappeared inside taking Rosanne with her, but Luke, Miss and Aunt Rosie had settled themselves at a small table near to the larger table. Rosie beckoned for Feathers and Carlos to join them.

'The musicians are just arriving,' she said as they sat down. 'I've told them to start with a fast waltz to get everyone moving. Do you think it's going all right?'

'I think it's marvellous!' Feathers told her.

Once the little orchestra had tuned up, within seconds the courtyard was full of whirling figures as the men swung their women around the cobbles.

'Are we allowed to dance?' Feathers asked. 'Or do we have to sit and watch?'

'We can dance. Go on, off you go.' She turned to Luke and said, laughing: 'Come on, Luke, dance with me. You know it's rude to refuse.'

He got to his feet grinning as if they were sharing a secret and Carlos put his hand out to Feathers.

'Come,' he said.

She staggered a little when she got to her feet and realised that she had drunk rather too much of the wine. She giggled as she clung to his arm for support.

'That wine has gone to my head,' she told him.

He shrugged shoulders. 'Is it possible? It is like water. Wait until you taste the sherry from Jerez. That is a wine with strength and body.'

'Maybe I'd better not if water does this to me,' she said and giggled again.

Once they danced, the cool night air fanned her face and she began to feel steadier. The light touched his face, deepening the sockets of his dark eyes and making his hair shine as if it had been polished. He was very handsome, she thought, even more handsome than Pierre, and she had always thought that no one could be more handsome than her husband. Carlos was very foreign in some respects, what with his funny way of pronouncing English words. He held himself proud and upright, his head back as they swooped and swayed across the rough courtyard. He moved more as if he were killing a bull than waltzing with a girl. People were singing as they danced and though she did not know the words and they were not the songs she heard on her new wireless she tried to hum the tunes. She felt content, almost drowsy with contentment, and as they danced she let her head rest on his shoulder.

His arm tightened round her and she could feel his breath on her hair.

'You are very beautiful.' He was whispering again and she felt warm and comforted by the words. She couldn't quite remember if anyone had ever said she was beautiful before, but she didn't think anyone had.

'You think so?' she whispered back.

'I know so,' and she felt a kiss brush her hair and again there was that tingling feeling, as if he had burned her.

They danced on and on. The music did not stop and it seemed to Feathers that the stars were whirling in the sky in a dance of their own. It was a beautiful night, scented and warm; she let her body sway to his rhythm and the music's rhythm until she had a feeling of abandonment and release.

'I used to love to dance when I lived in America,' she said dreamily. 'It's good to dance. I knew all the new dances. I could do them all. Do they have the new dances in Spain?'

'No,' he said. 'Only the old ones, like these where you can hold your girl close.'

'Umm,' she said. She was aware that even if the wine was not more than water to him, he, too, was a little drunk. They were supporting each other. His arm was tightly round her waist and she felt as if she was melting into him. She ought to pull away. Madame and Aunt Rosie might be watching but somehow she couldn't find the strength or the willpower. It was nice being held.

She did not notice at first that he was dancing her further and further away from the music. It was not until she felt the crunch of gravel under her feet that she realised they had left the courtyard. He was dancing her down the path through the vines which led to the stone seat where they had sat and talked the first day they met.

'Where are you going?' she asked, alarmed and pulling away from him in the sudden darkness. 'Aunt Rosie will see we've gone.'

'Madame Rosie is too busy dancing with my father to notice

what we are doing.' He was stroking her bare arm.

'Oh, that's all right then,' she said rather feebly, finding herself leaning onto him as he put his arm round her waist again.

He led her towards the stone seat. Gradually her eyes adjusted to the light from a thin sliver of moon and the stars. At her side she could see his carved profile, and behind she could hear the music and the singing and the sound of dancing feet on cobbles. Now and then a rustle and a giggle came from the rows of vines each side of them. She found herself excited at the thought of people making love all around them in the darkness.

They had not even reached the seat when he abruptly turned and took her into his arms.

'I cannot wait one moment longer to kiss you,' he said theatrically. His mouth came down over hers and he crushed her to him so that she could hardly breathe. It was so long since she had been kissed, all her young instinct for love had been so repressed, that her blood rose to match his desire. She clung to him and kissed him back.

'Feathers, Feathers, beautiful Feathers,' he was murmuring, kissing her eyes, her forehead, her neck, biting at her ears and nibbling her lips. 'I have wanted to do this since the moment I saw you.'

He gave her no opportunity to reply, occupying her mouth with his. The hand that had been on her shoulder was pushing down the neckline of her blouse, and had found her breast. He was rolling her nipple between urgent fingers, hurting her a little, and she heard herself groaning half in pain and half with desire. His other hand had slid between her legs and was rubbing her through the taffeta of her skirt. He tried to push her to the ground and she wanted to let him. She felt she wanted to tear off her clothes, open her body to him, let him fill her. But the cold wind of commonsense blew. What was she doing? she asked herself. With these same feelings and importunate desires she had made trouble for herself once before. But that time she had at least been in love and that was sin enough. This time there was no love – only lust, and that was too big a sin.

She pulled away.

'Stop,' she said. 'We mustn't.'

His hands continued their frantic work. 'Why not? Why not?' He was panting, biting at her throat.

'Please, Carlos, stop,' she begged. He took no notice but pulled her blouse off her shoulders. She heard the sound of tearing fabric and felt the cooler air of the night blowing on her bare breasts.

'Carlos!' she cried again. He had her in an iron grip now and was forcing her backwards, down to the ground. She was suddenly aware of how much taller and stronger than her he was. Suddenly she was sober and frightened, and hearing his incoherent mumblings as he pulled at her clothing, she realised just how drunk he was. She thought she should scream, but then remembered those other lovers in the vines who might come running and see the daughter of the house in this compromising position. She remembered that she had encouraged him, flirted with him, led him to believe . . .

What was happening was all her own fault.

'Please, Carlos,' she said frantically. 'Please stop or I shall scream.'

She was on the ground, the gravel digging into her bare back. He was on top of her, and she could feel how hard and aroused he was. He pushed his mouth down onto hers so that she could feel his teeth grinding into her, preventing her from speaking, let alone screaming. She could hardly breathe. She beat at his back with her fists, scratched at his face and tried to bring her knees up, but his weight was pinning her to the ground. He pulled up her skirt, dragged aside her underclothes and he was in her, muttering urgent words she could not understand. The stupid thing, she thought frantically as he heaved up and down on her, was that she was ready for him. She had wanted him, and the worst thing was that as he neared his climax she found herself responding to his rhythm as she had responded to the rhythm of the dance.

'Oh God! Oh God! Oh God!' she kept saying as she lay there, one hand covering her eyes as if it would shut out the horror and guilty pleasure at what was happening.

Then he gave a deep shuddering moan and it was finished. He rolled off her, one arm still over her body.

'Oh, you beautiful girl,' he whispered.

'I told you to stop! I said no,' she said hysterically, trying to get to her feet.

He sat up, his back straight with indignation.

'Don't pretend.' His voice was full of contempt, and she remembered her own frenzied movements at the end and understood why.

'Oh, heaven help me! Oh Mary Mother of God help me!' she sobbed and dragged herself to her feet, trying to rearrange her clothing. Her back hurt from the gravel, her blouse was torn, and lipstick would be all over her face. She must look a sight. 'Why does it happen to me?' she cried out in anguish, remembering a time before. 'What is it I do wrong?'

He was standing too, and she could see he was looking down at her from his superior height.

'Be quiet,' he said coldly. 'Just shut up. You wanted it too.'

His words were what was needed. Hysteria left and anger took over. Her tears stopped and her right hand came from low down with all the strength she had to hit him across the face. The blow made a crack like a pistol shot, and its force reeled him back.

'Bastard, *cochon*, swine!' she hissed and hit him again with equal force. He stood stunned, his hand on his cheek. Then she said with deadly meaning: 'Tomorrow you'd better be gone from here or I shall tell the police you raped me. There'll be trouble such as you've never known! Your mother won't get you out of this one. I never want to see you again and you should think yourself lucky I'm giving you the chance to go. And when you've gone, if you ever tell a single soul what you did to me I'll kill you. I swear it, I'll kill you.'

Trembling with rage she turned her back on him, wondering just for a moment if he would hit her. He did nothing. Her head high, she walked towards the house holding her blouse together and telling herself that all she had to do now was be calm and work out how she could get inside and into her bedroom without anyone seeing her. For the moment, that was the most important thing in the world.

She achieved it by skirting the dancers who, only interested in themselves, were oblivious of her. She scampered past what was known as Rosie's vineyard, where the vines Rosie had brought from America grew, and crept along the side of the house. Mercifully the door that led past the blending room and the kitchen was open. There was a great clatter from the kitchen but no one saw her as she slipped past. Then she ran upstairs on tiptoe in case Madame appeared and gained the sanctuary of her bedroom.

She assessed the damage in her long mirror. Her blouse was torn and would have to be thrown away. Her skirt was dusty and stained but would wash. Looking at the stains she realised she would have to wash it herself. Her lip was bleeding where he had kissed her so violently, and bruise marks were appearing on her shoulders and throat. Her back was bruised and scratched from the gravel. She could not let anyone see her like this. Tomorrow she would have to be indisposed. The cut lip and the bruises would be a giveaway. And it would be terrible for Luke if people knew what his son had done. Luke had always been kind to her. He must be protected.

She ran a bath and climbed into it with relief. Soaking in the warm water she faced the fact that, like all her troubles in the past, she had brought this upon herself. She had encouraged Carlos. Right until the last moment she had tempted him. What had happened was basically all her own fault. But when she said stop, he should have stopped. Even Pierre had once stopped when she said no.

She sighed deeply and soaped and scrubbed between her legs as if she was filthy there. The only thing to do now was to pray that Carlos went away and then make sure that no one in the world, most particularly Pierre, ever knew what had happened. And when she went to confession, she would be sure to seek out the old priest who understood no English at all.

'Stop! Stop!' Rosie said. 'I'm dizzy. I'm thirsty and I'm worn out! It's all right for you young ones!'

Reluctant to take his arm from her waist, Luke led her into a few more whirling steps and then, looking down into her laughing face, capitulated and began to walk her back to the table.

'You may be worn out but you look happier now,' he said. 'You looked really down when you arrived this morning.'

'It's amazing what a few glasses of wine will do,' she said dryly. 'Even this rough stuff we've been drinking tonight. Actually, I was low. I was disappointed that Philippe couldn't come here with me. It's so long since we've done something that was fun together. But apparently Françoise's mother would have a fit if she thought her daughter was at a party with the servants and the *vendangeurs*. As I'd promised Miss and Nanny Shepherd they could come, Philippe volunteered to stay at home with the child.'

'She sounds like Carlos.' Luke felt gloomy at the very thought of his son. 'He didn't approve of the *cochelet* at all. I'm surprised he came.'

'I suppose Feathers talked him into it,' Rosie said. 'My God, the French can be the most awful snobs.'

'He's not French,' Luke pointed out. 'He's just acquired the worst snobbisms of the middle-class English. The Spanish are not snobs. Every man is judged a gentleman – a *caballero* – on his own merits.'

They had reached the table where the Les Hérissons household staff sat with Miss and Nanny Shepherd. He saw how Miss's face brightened at his return and hoped that Rosie hadn't noticed. He did not wish to think about Miss at the moment, not with his nostrils full of Rosie's scent and his fingers still remembering how it felt to hold her close to him as they danced. She was graceful and light on her feet. For a big, clumsy man he danced well himself. His Spanish governess had seen to that when he was very small but not since he danced with Isabella twenty years ago had he so enjoyed waltzing with a woman.

'I'd love to dance, Luke,' Miss said, half rising to her feet. He had already danced with her once, and now he just wanted to sit beside Rosie. Rosie's mischievous eye, glinting in the lamplight, was on him; he knew she was tempted to say: 'It's rude to refuse,' so rather than give her the opportunity he held out his hand for Miss to join him.

But before she had edged her way round the table there was a diversion. He felt a tap on his arm and turned to see Carlos, his face swollen and scratched and his eyes wild and distraught.

'Carlos! Whatever is the matter?' he said, shocked by the boy's appearance. 'Have you been in a fight?'

Carlos shook his head. 'I must speak to you,' he muttered.

Luke hesitated and then turned to Miss and excused himself. Her face dropped into disappointed lines but then she nodded and tried to smile.

He took the boy's arm and led him round the side of the house to the front door. Neither spoke but Luke was aware that Carlos was breathing strangely. Luke diagnosed that he was frightened to death of something.

It was dark and quiet at the front of the house; the music sounded far away and it seemed cooler.

'Do you want to go inside?' Luke asked.

He saw the movement of the boy shaking his head in the starlight. 'No, let's stay here,' he said.

'All right.' Luke sat down on the steps that led up into the house. He patted the space beside him. 'Come and sit here.'

Carlos sat down. His breathing had quietened a little, but he smelt strongly of sweat.

'Now, what is it?' Luke asked gently and was astonished when the boy burst into noisy sobs.

'She says I've got to get out of here,' he blurted out. 'She says that if I'm not gone by the morning she'll tell the police I raped her.'

Luke could hardly believe what he was hearing.

'Who will?' he asked bewildered.

'Feathers.'

'Feathers!'

'Yes. But it was all her fault. She led me on. I thought she wanted it. She did want it. I could tell, and then she suddenly wanted to stop. I didn't take any notice. Girls do that, don't they? They pretend they don't want to when they do so that they can say afterwards it wasn't their fault. And they cry but all the time they really like it.'

Luke drew a deep anxious breath. 'Carlos, are you telling me that you have raped Feathers?'

'I didn't rape her.' The boy's voice was hysterical and he was crying even harder. 'She let me do all sorts of things and even when I was doing it, really doing it, she liked it. I know she liked it.'

'Was it Feathers who scratched your face?'

'Yes, the bitch, when she was telling me to stop . . .'

He himself stopped, no doubt aware that he had said the wrong thing. Luke was trying to keep calm, though furious anger was boiling inside. His son. His misbegotten son raping a girl. Raping Feathers. He could not believe it.

'She was telling you to stop?' He made his voice patient.

'Yes,' Carlos said sullenly.

'And you took no notice?'

'I didn't think she meant it.'

'No from a woman should always mean no to a man, Carlos.'

'Well, it never has before.'

'Am I to understand that you go around raping women all the time?'

The boy shifted uneasily in the darkness.

'Of course not,' he said defiantly.

'But if Feathers asked you to stop, if she was scratching you – and presumably hitting you by the look of your face . . .'

'That was after.'

'That was after, was it?' The wrathful note was creeping through.

'Yes.' Suddenly the boy straightened himself. 'Father, you don't understand. She is the most beautiful thing I have ever seen. Girls like that have never taken any notice of me. She was nice to me. I was beginning to feel that she felt the same way about me as I did about her. She danced with me, she put her head on my shoulder, she rubbed herself against me. And when I kissed her, she kissed me back. Properly. I know she's a married woman but her husband has gone away and I thought she wanted it. And I wanted her. I've never wanted anything like I wanted her. I was a bit drunk and so was she, and once it started I couldn't stop. I just had to go on, it was as if something was forcing me like I was forcing her. But I honestly believed that she wanted it.'

His voice faltered and he put his head in his hands. Luke sat with his eyes shut in despair. He could see it all. The provocative, frivolous Feathers, not realising that her warm kittenlike friendship could be misconstrued. He had watched them dancing that night and they danced like lovers. Two young sexually hungry people in a romantic setting, a conflagration that started with a kiss – and then Feathers realising she was making a mistake. Realising it too late. Carlos, with the hot blood and the urgent needs of a young man and the added arrogance of the Spanish male, had refused to stop. Luke groaned to himself. What was to be done about it now?

'Will I have to go, Father?'

Twice in the last two minutes his son had called him father.

'I think you will,' Luke said slowly.

'But where shall I go? What shall I do? Can you give me money to live?'

'Carlos, I will give you what I can, but you must understand that I am not a rich man. I have only what I earn.'

'But your family are rich.'

'By your standards, yes. But I left Spain because there was not enough work for all three of us brothers. The business is successful, but it is nothing to do with me.'

Carlos gave a start of surprise. 'Mama said you left to get away from us.'

'No, I did not do that. I loved your mother very much. If her father had not intervened we would have run away together and perhaps we would have worked something out. But as it was, I was sent back to school, and that was that. The money my mother paid for your school fees came from her own purse. I have paid your mother a small sum every month for many years now.'

There was silence in the darkness. 'Is that how Mother was able to leave the encampment?'

'I don't know. We have had no contact since you were born.'

'Mama left her family because she said that I was the son of a *patrone* and should not be brought up on the encampment. Perhaps it would have been better if I had been,' Carlos said, his voice bitter. 'Where can I go, and what can I do now?'

Luke was thinking, pushing the problem of Feathers to the back of his mind. That could be dealt with later.

'Would you be happy in England?' he asked.

'It's better than Jerez where everyone knows who I am.'

'I have friends in the wine business in London. I think one of them might give you a job as a salesman.'

'I don't want to be a salesman.' Carlos's voice was sullen again.

Luke sighed and thought it was time for some plain speaking.

'Carlos, you see yourself as a gentleman, but none of us who need to earn a living can afford to see ourselves that way – except in our relationships towards others. What you did to Feathers tonight was not the behaviour of a gentleman. Even if she did tempt you, it was unforgivable. No means no. Your snobbery is not the mark of a gentleman, nor your unwillingness to work. I am not going to find you a job unless you tackle

300

it with a good heart. You must accept the truth. You have to work if you want to eat, just as I have to work. The life your mother dreamed of for you is not possible.'

'I understand.' Now the boy's voice was resigned.

'Where is Feathers now?'

'I don't know. She just ran back towards the house.'

'I'd better go and see if she's all right.'

Carlos panicked. 'No, don't. She said if I ever told a soul what happened she would kill me. And she sounded as if she meant it.'

Luke nodded. It made sense that she would not want anyone to know.

'Get yourself packed and I'll take you to Reims in the morning and put you on the first train. Go to London. I'll give you what money I have available here and telephone my friends and say that you're coming to see them. I'll give you the addresses. Then you will have to make your own mark. Sell yourself. You're a handsome lad. If you work, you'll do well.'

Carlos's head nodded in the darkness. Then he said: 'What about Sable?'

'We'll keep her for you, or if you wish I'll send her back to Jerez.'

'No, keep her. Maybe one day I'll be able to have her back.' The boy sighed a long wavering sigh. 'I've made a mess of it all, haven't I?'

'No, not really. Not at twenty. There's all the time in the world to recover.'

Carlos nodded, and then tentatively put his hand out.

'I needed to get to know you, you know,' he said. 'I had to come.'

'And I'm glad you did,' Luke said – and realised to his own surprise that there was truth in it.

He was back at Les Hérissons in time for breakfast after driving Carlos to the Paris train. He and the boy had left the house while the Champagne countryside, blurred by an autumn mist, was still asleep. Luke was sure that no one had seen them go. All was silent as they went out quietly through the front door. It was equally silent when he returned alone three quarters of an hour later. Les Hérissons had not yet stirred, exhausted by the

301

eating, drinking and dancing of the night before.

Carlos had been subdued; his arrogance gone. Luke feared the improvement would not last. Yet he could not help feel some compassion as the boy's miserable face vanished from view when the near-empty Paris train drew out of the station. It was a pity that they had only begun to talk to each other when it was too late. He resolved he would go to London if Carlos did settle there and try again to achieve some rapport with his son. Perhaps he could do something towards undoing the damage that had been done by Isabella's – and his own mother's – pretensions for the boy.

His problem was what to do about Feathers? Should he pretend to know absolutely nothing? Should he go as far as pretending that Carlos had left Les Hérissons without his knowledge? Should he admit to taking Carlos to the train? And if he did that, would Feathers suspect that he knew more than he was saying?

He could well understand that if the boy had raped her after a petting session that had got out of hand she would be happier if no one knew. Luke felt a surge of fresh anger towards his son who had been brought up to believe that what he wanted he could take.

And suppose Feathers became pregnant? Luke went cold at the thought and hastily pushed it to the back of his mind.

Breakfast was quiet. Madame came down just after Luke had poured his coffee but there was no sign of Feathers.

'Marie tells me that Feathers is indisposed this morning,' Madame explained as she lavished *confiture* on her croissant. 'And where is your son?'

Luke made a split-second decision.

'Still in bed, I suppose.'

'I trust they are not in bed together,' Madame said and gave a short, snorting laugh. Obviously she had seen them dancing the night before and she was nearer the truth than was comfortable.

'Wouldn't you think it more likely that they both have hangovers?' he suggested. 'That wine was pretty rough.'

'Quite good enough for a *cochelet*. Personally, I thought the whole thing was a great success.'

'It was,' he said. 'It would be good to have one every year.'

'Ah, but at one time we did,' she said, and launched into a description of *cochelets* of long ago – from which he escaped as soon as he decently could.

Marie confirmed that Feathers had taken to her bed and wanted to see nobody.

'She's all right?' he asked anxiously.

Marie gave him a wink.

'Hangover, I reckon,' she said.

What troubled him was that Carlos might have hurt her. This morning the boy's face had not been a pretty sight. He had a black eye and streaks of red scratches. Had he hit Feathers back? Was she having to hide away? He was going to have to find out. He could not spend the day worrying.

Mid-morning when Marie was in the kitchen gossiping with Cook he went to Feathers' bedroom door and knocked.

'Who is it?' she called, her voice sounding perfectly normal.

'Luke,' he said. 'Can I come in?'

'I'm in bed.' A pause. 'What did you want?'

'Just to see if you're all right and if you've had any word from Carlos this morning. He didn't come down to breakfast. I wondered if he'd said anything to you, or told you what he planned to do.'

He felt idiotic standing shouting lies through a closed door, and for a long moment there was silence.

'I've no idea.' Feathers sounded dismissive. 'No idea at all.'

'Well, I don't know what he's up to. Are you all right?'

'Hung over,' she said firmly.

He went back downstairs none the wiser but confident that Feathers would believe he knew nothing about it. And it might be best, he told himself, if he now tried to forget all about it. Just as presumably she would do too.

Rosie was late arriving at Les Hérissons that day. It was well gone mid-morning when she appeared. He found her in the barn that held the vats, checking that the pressed grapes were beginning to ferment.

She looked, saw him and grinned.

'How's the head?' she asked.

'Fine. Yours?'

'Could be better.'

'Feathers is still in bed. Hung over. Apparently she's not putting in an appearance today.'

Rosie laughed. 'And what was the matter with Carlos?'

He remembered then. Rosie had seen the boy wild-eyed,

scratched and swollen-faced. So had Miss and all the staff. He rapidly improvised.

'Apparently he got into a fight with one of the *vendangeurs*. He was frightened that a whole gang of them might come after him.'

'And where is he this morning?'

'No sign of him yet.'

She frowned. 'Perhaps we should go and see if he's all right? He looked in a bad way to me last night.'

Luke was quick to agree. It was a fortuitous suggestion. Rosie and he could discover together that the lad had gone.

They made their way to the top of the house and there they found the door to the tower room open, the bed unmade but no Carlos. Luke went in and began opening cupboards and drawers.

'How extraordinary,' he said. 'It looks as if he's gone. None of his things are here.'

Rosie opened a couple of drawers, found them empty and sat down on the bed.

'I suppose he's all right?' she said.

'The bed's unmade. He's obviously slept in it. It looks as if he must have gone very early this morning.' He made his tone casual but Rosie gave him a quick, suspicious look. He wasn't good at lying.

'It's most odd,' she said. 'Why would he suddenly go like that?'

'Just my good luck, I guess,' Luke said flippantly.

But he was aware that she sensed something was not quite right.

Feathers reappeared at breakfast the next day, wearing a high-necked frock and rather a lot of make-up. Pierre came home from his trip and apologised for missing most of the *vendange*. There was a small flutter of curiosity as to where Carlos could have got to, but his impact on the household had been so slight that within a week everyone seemed to have forgotten him. Luke made Sable his own responsibility, riding the mare every morning. Then, when he received word from London that his son was working as a trainee salesman for a small wine shipper, he breathed a sigh of relief.

All was well that ended well.

He thought.

Chapter Twelve

New York, December 1923

Allie Webster tossed the letter across the breakfast table to her husband.

'Do we need money?' she asked.

Alexander looked up from his newspaper.

'Not particularly,' he said, 'but a little extra would never come amiss. Why?'

'Some man called Patterson says he's acting on behalf of someone who wants to buy Les Hérissons. He wants to know if I'll sell my share. Nothing would give me greater pleasure, but it's apparently dependent on my half-brother agreeing. This man says he's approaching him as well. I can't see Grandma letting it happen. And *she* won't be very keen either.'

Alexander picked up the letter and read it. It was brief and to the point. Someone did want to buy Les Hérissons. He nodded and made no comment. He never interfered in anything that had to do with either her career or her money, though she was aware he would have been far happier if she were more financially dependent on him.

'You ought to get good advice before you do anything,' was all he said. 'Why don't you ask Father?'

'Wouldn't he tell *her*?' Allie never mentioned either her mother or Pierre by name.

'Not if you asked him not to. He's very fond of Rosie but you are his daughter-in-law.'

She grimaced.

'I'm also me,' she said.

He sighed and half-grinned, throwing up his hands in mock surrender. 'I know. I know,' he said.

She read the letter again thoughtfully then folded it and put it back in its envelope.

'How long will you be away?' she asked.

'About a fortnight. Not sure – however long it takes.' He was involved in researching an in-depth series of features on the effect of Prohibition on American crime. That afternoon he was leaving for Chicago where he had tentative plans to talk to mobsters. Then he would go on to the Canadian border where the bootleggers operated. She was not sad to see him go. She was happier on her own working at her typewriter in her study at the top of the Gramercy Park house. In her heart she knew she should never have married him, but it seemed the right thing to do at the time and the arrangement suited her perfectly. He was the one who suffered, though he had long ago accepted that their marriage was in name only. She frequently told herself there were worse marriages. Theirs worked because they were good companions. She never let herself wonder if he missed and needed physical love because he knew that in her own way she loved him. And she was very sure that he loved her. Besides, thinking of those things of which he was deprived did not make for a clear conscience.

She finished her coffee and walked round the table to kiss him on the cheek.

'Have a good trip,' she said. 'Is there anything you want me to do?'

'Just be here when I get back,' he said lightly, and she was moved to give him a quick hug.

'I'm going to my room to get dressed,' she said. 'I'll say goodbye now. See you in two weeks. I'll take your advice about going to see your father.'

'He'll be home today if you want to go over there.'

'I might just do that.'

With a small backward wave she left him and went to her own bedroom, Jessica padding behind her. His room was the other side, with a shared bathroom in between. It had his and her washbasins with a shower for him and a tub for her. The nearest they ever came to intimacy was cleaning their teeth, standing side by side and sharing the same large mirror.

She dressed quickly, putting a mink coat over a plain wool knee-length dress. Looking out of the window she decided to

306

walk uptown to her in-laws' Park Avenue home and perhaps do some Christmas shopping on the way. It was one of those magic winter New York days, bitterly cold but with the palest bright blue sky and a sun that shone with an icy glitter – a day for enjoying. She pulled a mink hat over her ears to keep out the bone-chilling cold, and set off up Fifth Avenue.

As she walked, her brain was busy, formulating sentences and conversations, unaware of the fairy lights and the shop windows dressed for Christmas. She was in the middle of a short story for *True-Story* magazine which she had titled 'Secret Kisses'. She liked writing for *True-Story*. It had the largest circulation of any magazine in the country and therefore she felt her work was being read, which was important to her. But better still, since all the stories were written in the first person, she could be anybody and anything could happen. She could be a betrayed waitress, a betraying chorus girl, an intrepid journalist, a lady of high fashion or even a whore. The publishers of *True-Story* demanded that the fiction they published aroused the reader but the ending must be moral. No good must come of any hanky-panky. Hypocrisy, she thought, was not dead.

Allie was content when she was writing. All her inhibitions disappeared when she was creating her scarlet stories scattered with sexual innuendoes. Her heroines were passionate, yearning for love, quite unable to control their urges. But how they suffered for surrendering to the enemy – men!

She wrote more thoughtful stories for *Ladies Home Journal* and *Schribners*, and bitter little pieces for *The New Yorker* which just occasionally were published. Mostly they came back with a polite rejection slip but she went on trying. The pulp fiction, hacked out, poured out in an afternoon, was never rejected. She found this the simplest and, in a curious way, the most rewarding to write. The medium permitted her to release all that she had repressed in herself. And the bonus was that since the stories were supposedly true, the author's name was never printed. No one would ever know who had written 'Secret Kisses' except the magazine's staff and herself.

Lizzie Webster greeted her with a kiss when she arrived at the mansion on Park Avenue and told her that Mr Webster was in his den. Allie left her hat and coat with the butler and went straight to the big study overlooking the garden. She liked Jim Webster and he liked her, perhaps more than his wife did. Lizzie's maternal eye had long since spotted that her beloved son was not as happy as she would have wished. And there were no signs of grandchildren which distressed her. Allie was bored with being asked when they were going to start a family.

Jim Webster, rising from the big chair where he had been reading his *Wall Street Journal* gave her a paternal kiss.

'What can I do for you, young lady?' he asked.

Allie sat in the chair opposite him and thought that he was getting old. His hair and moustache were quite white and his face was red. He was heavily built, and she noticed as he went to get himself a cigar and bring her a cigarette that he moved stiffly.

'You'll get me into trouble with Mrs Webster,' she said as she drew the smoke down to her lungs.

'We won't tell her,' he chuckled. 'Now, what is it? You haven't come all this way just to say hello.'

She opened her purse and handed him the letter.

He grunted as he read it. 'Does Rosie know about this?' he asked.

'I wouldn't have thought so, and I'd rather she didn't know.'

He pursed his mouth and looked at her from under heavy white brows.

'Do you want to sell?'

'I never want to go back there. My home is here.'

'Where does your income come from? Les Hérissons or the business?'

'I don't honestly know. The cheque just arrives.'

'Are the business and Les Hérissons one and the same?'

'I don't think so. The business belongs to her and Philippe. I think they own most of the machinery and the outbuildings. She spent a lot of her own money on it after the war. And I think she put in some money when she first went there before I was born. But that wouldn't count, would it? That would be regarded as my father's money.'

He shook his head. 'Depends if she put it in before or after she married your father, I guess. I wouldn't know about that, but it seems that Les Hérissons without the wine business is just another vineyard.'

308

'A very big vineyard,' she said. 'But I don't know if selling would be as simple as that letter makes it out to be. Rosanne, my little sister, owns a third, and *she* would have power of attorney as far as Rosanne's concerned. That could stop it all. The trouble is that I don't really understand the law. It's just so odd that anyone would want the place and take the trouble to find me here. It must be someone who knows us.'

He handed her back the letter.

'If you want to sell, it's your decision, but you'll probably break your mother's heart.' He paused, but she stayed obdurately silent and he sighed. 'You'd better find a lawyer who understands French law and see what the position is. If your allowance is generous, you might be better off just letting that go on, particularly if the property has to be split three ways. It really all depends how much you can get for it.'

She put the letter away again, her face thoughtful.

'I'd just like to know who wants it,' she said. 'It's all so very peculiar. I'll think about it later. Personally, I can't see it ever happening.'

Jim Webster insisted that she stay for lunch and since it would have seemed churlish to say no, she agreed. She would rather have been back at her typewriter enjoying the make-believe world of 'Secret Kisses'. Still, she had to eat and there was always the afternoon to indulge in the voluptuous pleasure of writing.

'Be prepared, though,' Jim Webster warned her when she said she would stay. 'Mrs Webster is in a rare state of excitement. Quite apart from Christmas and all the preparations, Jenny's coming home at the beginning of next week.'

'Really. That's great,' she said, making herself sound enthusiastic. The truth was she didn't care much for Jenny and hadn't from the first time they met. Jenny was blunt and forthright and had clear, penetrating eyes that saw through pretence. She had no time for anything she considered nonsense. And Jenny, who was fiercely protective of her more gentle brother, had never believed that Allie treated Alexander right. She had come home from Africa, or wherever it was she worked, for Allie's wedding. When she kissed Allie goodbye before she and Alexander left for the honeymoon she said: 'Now, you be good to him.' And it sounded remarkably like a threat. She had gone back to Africa by the time the newlyweds returned from the Bahamas and they had not met since.

Mrs Webster was indeed beside herself, planning a huge party. Jenny had been working abroad for nearly four years and her only trip home had been for the wedding.

'She may not want a party,' Mr Webster warned. 'Quakers may not approve of parties.'

'Well, we're having one,' Mrs Webster said firmly.

To everyone's surprise Jenny had become a Quaker four years before. Her reasons were that she believed the Quakers practised the only religion that had common sense but no mumbo-jumbo. Since she had no need to work for money, she had taken her nursing skills, learned at St Vincent's Hospital, to North Africa with a working party of fellow Quakers.

Mrs Webster had never quite come to terms with all this, nor could she grasp what the religion was all about.

'She's a sort of modern Quaker,' she explained to Allie as they ate their fried chicken. 'She doesn't say thee and thou or wear those funny clothes. She's just like anyone else. I said to her when she first told me she was going to Algeria that I supposed she'd be some sort of missionary. She was quite shocked. "Good heavens, no!" she said. "The people are Muslims, they've got a perfectly good religion of their own. Why should we try to change it?" '

'Good thinking,' grunted Mr Webster.

'Well, I don't know. I don't know anything about Muslims but I can't help feeling that it must be better to be a Christian,' Mrs Webster said. 'But these Quakers that Jenny is with just seem to try to help the black people. Teach them things. Show them how to look after their babies and make crops grow better. Things like that. I suppose it's all very nice and kind, but do I wish she'd stayed at St Vincent's.'

'How long is she home for?' Allie asked.

'Oh, quite a while. I don't think she's going back. It will be lovely to have her with us again.'

Allie was thinking that maybe Algeria would be a good place to set one of her stories. Maybe Jenny would tell her about it. Locations where it was hot all the time and passions ran high were always good backgrounds but she did like to get the details right.

They talked for a while about Alexander's latest project and as soon as it was decently possible, Allie said her farewells. She walked home for the exercise but the wind had become so chill she was glad to get indoors. The maid took her coat and she called Jessica and went straight up the stairs of the tall, thin house to her study, sighing with pleasure as she took the cover from her typewiter.

Within minutes she was engrossed in her story, Les Hérissons, Alexander, Jenny, all forgotten.

Allie was where she was happiest – in the malleable fictional world of her own creating.

'Give me a cigarette, darling.'

He leaned up on one elbow and took a packet of Lucky Strikes from the bedside table. He placed one into her open, waiting crimson lips and lit it before lighting one for himself.

They lay side by side, two heads on one pillow, saying nothing as they puffed smoke spirals towards the ceiling. The curtains were drawn, but a grey light from off the lake outside found its way into the big, ornately furnished hotel room.

'That was wonderful, Alex,' she said softly, her hand moving to scratch gently at his pubic hair.

'Good,' he said drowsily.

'Was it good for you?'

'Perfect.'

'Do you still think I shouldn't have come here with you?'

'Not at this moment, but I probably will later.'

'No one will ever know.'

'Let's hope so.'

She sat up abruptly, pale blonde hair swinging to fall across her eyes.

'Would it be so terrible if anyone did find out? Damn it, it's nearly 1924. Queen Victoria is dead.'

'Even in 1924 people will still get hurt,' he said quietly. 'I wouldn't want Allie to know, and you shouldn't want Walter to know.'

She stubbed out the cigarette, twisting it into an ugly brown mess on the ashtray.

'I was going to tell you. I'm leaving Walter.'

He was shocked into sitting upright himself. 'But why?' he asked.

'That's a damn fool question,' she said, leaning across him to help herself to another cigarette. 'Because I love you, of course. I can't go on living a lie. On the rare occasions that guy lays a hand on me these days, I freeze. The only hand I want to bite is yours. I guess it's just swell for you, having two of us, but it isn't for me. But it's different for you. You don't love me.'

'That's not true,' he protested.

'Okay, you love me, but you love her better.'

He was silent.

'You see! I'm right!' she said almost triumphantly. 'Anyway, leaving you out of it, I need Walter like a dose of the black plague. I earn more than him, I can keep myself. We fight all the time, he's always drunk as a skunk and he reckons he's straining his ticker if we have sex more than twice a month. At least there's that to be thankful for. The truth is I'm sick to death of going home to him nights, let alone going to bed with him at night.' She gave a bitter laugh. 'Don't you panic, though. I'm not expecting any great dramatic gestures from you. We go on just as we are – if you want to. I guess the arrangement suits us both. As far as I'm concerned my career and you are enough to cope with.'

Naked, she stood and stretched. The sight of her raised arms, full, lifted breasts and taut ribs and stomach should have stirred desire in him, but he was thinking about what she had said.

'Shall we do it again or shall we shower and get ourselves some lunch?' she asked, turning to look at him. Her bony, elegant face was mocking and her pale blue eyes glittered almost maliciously.

'You've shocked me into impotence,' he said lightly. 'Perhaps we'd better grab some lunch.'

'That's okay by me,' she said. 'You know sex makes me hungry.'

She turned and padded in her loose-limbed, feline way into the bathroom.

'Under the circumstances I suppose I shower alone?' she called just before the water began to run.

'I'll come and scrub your back in a minute,' he promised her.

But he sat quietly without moving, drawing on his cigarette.

312

The arrangement had suited them both but if Beth Rogan, hard-boiled New York girl reporter, successful in a job few women aspired to, was going to start talking of love and of leaving her husband, perhaps the arrangement would have to end. Maybe Beth was not as hard-boiled as she pretended. He had begun to suspect as much. And his suspicions had deepened when she insisted on taking her vacation time to come with him to Chicago. She said she had always wanted to go to Chicago, and besides, they would be able to spend the nights together instead of his rushing off back to Gramercy Park. The added bonus, she had said blithely, was that maybe he could use a legwoman.

He had reluctantly agreed; reluctant because he was aware it was dangerous, but agreeing because the thought of unfettered sex appealed to him as much as it did to her.

They had met two years before when she joined *The Times*. She was a year younger than he was, twenty-seven, and dazzlingly attractive in a Nordic way. They had covered one or two assignments together and a good, warm friendship had developed. One night after work they went for a drink at Jack Bleeck's Artists and Writers Club, a speakeasy on West Fortieth. The conversation was good and one drink turned into two, two into three and then they lost count. Beth said she was hungry, and they tottered arm in arm to West Forty-ninth to Jack and Charlie's Puncheon Club, a speakeasy where the liquor was the finest and the chef was paid $20,000 a year.

They ate and drank like kings, and the conversation did not stop. He paid a monumental bill and then insisted on taking her home. She and her husband had an elegant apartment nearby in Columbus Circle, overlooking the park. She insisted he came in for a nightcap. Her husband, who was even more drunk than Alexander, was already in bed, out cold. Alexander ended the evening's entertainment by making love to his blonde lady colleague on her husband's large leather sofa in front of a dying fire. He enjoyed it very much. It was the first satisfactory sex that he had had in a long time. Married to Allie, the eternal virgin, he had been forced into snatching one-night stands on occasions when he had been working out of town. With Beth that night there had been companionship, then laughter, and after he had come, panting and sweating while she clung to him, moaning, there was laughter again as they tried to stifle their giggles when she slid off the sofa and onto the Persian carpet below. Alexander noted tipsily that Mr Rogan might be a drunk, but he sure had good taste.

The following morning he had been embarrassed at the thought of what had happened, but Beth just grinned and said 'Good morning' when, a little late, he walked into *The Times* offices.

She acted as if nothing had happened, and in a curious way that made him want it to happen again. And, of course, it did, about a week later. Having tasted the fruit again, he wanted more. Since both of them were married, it was difficult to find places to make love, particularly as Alexander insisted that he must return to Gramercy Park every night unless he was legitimately away. And when he was legitimately away, Beth was not there to make love with.

Eventually he took a room in a building on West Fifty-seventh Street where they could be alone. But they only used it in the lunch hours and the occasional early evening. The affair was entirely sexual as far as he was concerned, but it was better than the casual encounters of before. In New York sex was no longer a sin but Alexander, who had echoes of the old order in him, felt that if casual sex was not a sin, it meant that sex was no longer important. It had lost all meaning. With Beth there was some meaning, and he did care about her. He was content to be faithful to her in body, and to Allie in spirit.

Beth made it absolutely clear why she was prepared to sleep with him. She explained that Shakespeare would have understood her husband's drinking. Wine or whisky or whatever he drank increased the desire in Walter Rogan but impeded the performance. In fact, most of the time he was incapable.

'Or,' she said, 'he goes grinding on and on until I could scream. He can't complete. Now you might think this a good thing and maybe in the first throes of an affair it is. Believe me, now all I pray for is for him to get off me.'

He never spoke to her of what went on between himself and Allie, mostly because there was nothing to say. He could not tell Beth that they had no sex life of any kind; he felt it diminished him in some way. But he did make it clear that he loved his wife and had no intention of leaving her. If Beth was ever

314

curious about why he needed an affair, she asked no questions.

Now he wondered if it would all have to end. Without a hus-band, Beth might want more than sex from him. And he could give no more, for Alexander's foolish heart was still Allie's and he feared it would always be.

He scrubbed her back, and they dressed in uneasy silence.

'Maybe I shouldn't have come,' she said when they were ready to go downstairs. She was standing very straight by the bed, her pale blue eyes questioning him. She did not look very happy.

'Beth, I'm glad you're here,' he told her. 'I wanted to be alone with you, too. Come downstairs, we'll talk it out over dinner.'

'I could do with a drink,' she said.

'We should have brought some with us. Maybe the waiter can do something. Or we'll find a speakeasy after we've eaten.'

'Swell,' she said, sounding a little happier.

Once they were settled at the table and had ordered she said: 'I've got something to ask you.'

'Shoot,' he said.

'I am going to leave Walter – very soon. Can I take our room for a while until I sort myself out an apartment? Anyway, if we do go on, once I've found an apartment, you won't need to carry on paying for the room.'

'Sure,' he said. 'But I've kind of got used to us being there. I might keep it on anyway.'

'You prefer it if it seems illicit?'

'Maybe.' She was making him uneasy again. But he didn't want to explain that he feared sleeping with her at her own place would make it all seem more permanent to her.

She laughed. 'Maybe it is more fun that way.'

They were both silent while the waiter served them a dozen oysters each and then she asked: 'Alex, tell me about your wife. You never say anything about her, you know. But I reckon there must be something wrong or what are you doing with me?'

She was watching him with steady eyes. He sighed. He did not want to talk about Allie, but after two years maybe he owed Beth some explanations.

'Okay.' He knew he sounded reluctant. 'But maybe you won't like some of it.'

'Try me,' she said.

'She's French,' he said. 'Well, half French. I met her in

315

Champagne when she was ten years old. She was enchanting – full of spirit, beautiful and brave. She and her mother faced a mob who had come to wreck their vineyards and burn down the house. They had those men simply eating out of their hands within minutes.' He shook his head in wonder, remembering. 'I was seventeen, and I just fell in love with her then and there. I knew I'd marry her. I didn't think I'd ever want anyone else, and that has never changed.

'But then came the war. Champagne was overrun by the Germans. Troops moved into their home. Something happened to Allie at that time, something that no one ever talks about. When we met again she had grown up and she had changed. The sparkle had gone. She wasn't a happy person any more. But she was so pleased to see me I thought perhaps she felt the same way I did. I tried to kiss her and I terrified her. She just ran away from me in a panic and I could have killed myself for being so insensitive. Then she came to New York for a while and stayed with my family. It wasn't a success. She was suffering from the most terrible depressions. None of us could do anything for her and she seemed to take out her anger on me. Truthfully, she made me miserable but it didn't change how I felt about her. I guess I'm just a masochist,' he added half-laughing, but wondering if that were true.

'Eventually she went home again and a few years later I got the chance to go back to France. I went hoping to court her all over again, but she was in love with someone else. It's all terribly complicated and would take too long to explain, but the hell of it was I knew this man she loved was her half-brother but she didn't know it and neither did he. No one wanted to tell her the truth. But then, by mistake, someone let the cat out of the bag. It was then that Allie agreed to marry me. I couldn't believe my luck. I thought it was my chance to make her happy again – to bring back the ten-year-old Allie. Lay all her ghosts, love her and cherish her.' He heard Beth sigh but continued relentlessly. 'I've done my best to do that. She is happy. She doesn't get depressed. She writes stories all the time, and she's successful. We get on well. But we have no sex life. Allie made it clear that if we married our marriage would have to be celibate. She can't bear the thought of a man touching her. Not even me.'

316

Neither of them had begun to eat. Now he picked up his fork and looked at it as if wondering what to do with it.

'And what about the half-brother? Did he make love to her?' Beth asked, ever the journalist, getting straight to the heart of the matter.

'She says not. The night she told me she would marry me if I still wanted her, she sobbed in my arms. She said she wished she had let him make love to her because maybe it would have cured her. But she didn't. He wanted to wait until they married. But she has never let me touch her.'

'Hence me?' Beth suggested.

'Hence you.' There seemed no point in denying it.

She reached across the table to touch his hand.

'Poor old you,' she said. 'You are amazing to put up with it.'

'I've no choice. And you came along to save me.'

She had picked up her fork and was eating her oysters. She seemed remarkably content.

'You know,' she said thoughtfully, 'the worst thing about being a mistress is imagining your lover going home and making love to his wife. To think I've been worrying about that all this time.'

He couldn't think of anything to say. Her reaction was so unexpected.

'I wonder what happened in the war?' She considered the question and then said: 'I reckon she got raped by a German. How old would she have been?'

He found himself aghast at her clinical manner. 'In her early teens.'

'Yeah. I bet that's it. She was raped. At that age I guess it would put you off for life. Poor kid. Poor you. If I didn't want to keep you for myself that way, I'd suggest you sent her to a psychiatrist – but he might cure her.' She pushed her empty plate away. 'They were good,' she said, wiping her lips with her napkin.

Mechanically he finished his own food. He was stunned by her words because they made such blinding sense. She must be right. That must have been what changed his happy, spirited Allie. His palms were sweating but he accepted the knowledge. She had been raped. By a German. Sitting at the table in the cathedral calm of the restaurant he was suddenly incandescent with a rage he had never felt before. He wanted to kill.

Beth was lighting a cigarette.

'Put that out,' he said.

She looked at him, thin arcs of eyebrows raised.

'I want to go upstairs,' he said. 'Put it out.'

'In the middle of dinner?'

'We can come back. Put it out.'

Obediently she stubbed out the cigarette. He was already standing. The rage had turned to an uncontrollable urge for violent angry sex. He strode across the restaurant ahead of her.

'We'll be back,' he told the surprised head waiter. 'We have to make a phone call.'

He was silent in the elevator, but once inside their bedroom, he turned to Beth, taking her into his arms and kissing her savagely, knowing he must be bruising her mouth. He forced her back downwards until she was on the carpet, and then without kisses, without caresses, he pushed away her clothing, pulling aside the French knickers that she wore. He undid his trousers and grinding her into the floor took her hard and fast.

When it was over he lay panting on her slim body, feeling sanity returning and, with it, shame.

'I'm sorry, Beth,' he muttered.

For a moment she was still, and then, pushing him gently away from her, she said with a little laugh: 'I know what they say about oysters, but I never knew they took that quickly.'

He tried to laugh, but only a sob came out.

'It's okay,' she said. 'Honestly, it's okay. I understand.'

And she held him very tight while he wept pent-up tears into her warm shoulder.

Much to Allie's disgust the day before Jenny came home she began to feel a cold coming on. Since she had been in New York, Allie had become subject to monstrous attacks of the grippe, when her eyes ran constantly, her throat was sore and her nose so stuffed up that breathing became a miserable chore. She put it down to too much central heating.

When a cold of these dimensions struck, there was only one thing to do – retire to bed for four or five days with a pile of books, a chest rub and a constant supply of hot lemonade and aspirin and indulge in feeling sorry for herself.

The attack was at its height when Jenny came to visit her. It was not a welcome visit as far as Allie was concerned. She liked being left alone, but Jenny telephoned to say she was coming and arrive she did.

She came into the room bringing a breath of rude good health with her. She was very brown and her hair was cut like a boy's, just long enough at the back to touch the collar of a poncho-like garment. She wore no make-up and did not need it. Her brown eyes were very bright, her teeth predatory white against the tan. She had an air of confidence and command. She made Allie feel even more pallid and weepy-eyed than she was.

'Gosh! You do look poorly,' was her greeting.

'I don't feel so hot,' Allie admitted.

A cool firm hand was laid on her forehead.

'You need some aspirin. You've got a fever. Have you had the doctor?'

'It's only a cold,' Allie, who hated doctors, protested.

'Nevertheless . . .' Jenny said, and rummaged in her purse. 'Good. I thought I had some.' She produced a packet of aspirin, took out two tablets and handed them to Allie with a glass of lemonade.

'Swallow those,' she said, 'and keep the rest for later.'

'You were always bossy,' Allie grumbled, but did as she was told.

Jenny sat in the armchair across from the bed. Her bright eyes ranged the room and Allie was uncomfortably aware that she must be noting the single bed, and would be registering that Alexander did not sleep here.

She was right.

'Where does Alexander sleep?' Jenny asked abruptly.

Allie wanted to say: None of your damn business.

'He has his room the other side of our bathroom,' she said stiffly and changed the subject, not caring if Jenny realised what she was doing. 'It was nice of you to come. I hope you don't catch it.'

'I never catch colds.' Allie could believe it. Jenny looked like an advertisement for health and fitness.

'I suppose it was too hot in Algeria for the sneezes.'

'It's not hot all the time,' Jenny said. 'I was in the Atlas Mountains. It can get very cold in the winter.'

'What exactly were you doing?' Allie asked.

'Making myself useful more than anything. Teaching mothers to wean their babies – they go on breast-feeding for years when food is short. It's bad for them and the child. Trying to bring down the infant mortality rate. Trying to persuade them not to have so many babies when they haven't the means to feed them. Give them ideas about birth control. Teach them a bit of hygiene. That sort of thing.'

'Sounds like the sort of help they need in the Bowery,' Allie remarked, deliberately flippant. She was finding the conversation rather embarrassing. She did not feel that breast-feeding and birth control were subjects for afternoon chat.

'You're right.' Jenny took the remark seriously. 'But can you imagine what sort of a welcome we'd get if we tried to do the same work there?'

'Well, the welcome mat certainly wouldn't be out.'

'That's Catholicism for you,' Jenny sighed, and Allie who hadn't been to Mass in years felt herself bristle.

'You think being a Quaker is better?' she asked, aware of a slight note of aggression in her voice.

'Frankly, I think anything is better,' Jenny said. 'But I'm not particularly interested in religion as such. I've been so privileged myself I just wanted to do something useful in the world. This group of Quakers I work with have the same idea.'

'Sort of missionary work?'

It was Jenny's turn to bristle. 'Certainly not. It's a dreadful impertinence to try to change other people's religions. We wouldn't dream of attempting any such thing.'

Not displeased to have annoyed her sister-in-law, Allie created a diversion by blowing her nose. Jenny got up and wandered around the room.

'Talking of babies,' she said, 'Mama is longing for you and Alexander to have some.'

'I'd noticed,' Allie said with a sniff.

'Is there some medical problem?'

'No.'

'Then?'

'Really, Jenny,' Allie was outraged, 'surely that is Alexander's and my business?'

'Family business,' Jenny said tersely.

320

'Well, that may be your opinion, but I think it's nothing to do with anyone.'

'I just happen to know that Alexander always wanted a big family. I can't imagine that he's changed his mind.'

'Well, he's never mentioned that to me.' She could feel herself getting hotter and angrier.

'Oh, well,' said Jenny, 'I can ask him myself when he comes home.' She made a chopping movement with her hand as if dismissing the subject. 'Do you think we could have some tea?' she asked. 'Then I must go and let you sleep.'

'Of course.' Allie rang the bell and deliberately made herself calm down. 'Do tell me more about Algeria,' she said. 'The Atlas Mountains sound so romantic.'

Jenny told her about the Atlas Mountains and their people in vivid detail over two cups of tea and the atmosphere slithered back to normal. But after she had gone, Allie thought about what Jenny had said. The gut-aching guilt hit her for an instant as she wondered if it were true that Alexander wanted children. But even if it were true, she was not prepared to do anything about it.

She exorcised the guilt from her mind by thinking about the Atlas Mountains. She began to concoct a story set in their dizzy, inhospitable heights. And she decided a touch spitefully that the hero would be a Catholic missionary who out of Christian charity married a Quaker teacher who had got herself pregnant by an Arab. It was a pity that Jenny was unlikely ever to get to read it.

Alexander was away for nearly three weeks. On his return, Allie's cold was better and as usual she was up in her study writing, Jessica at her feet. She greeted him absently which meant that whatever she was working on was going well. She hated to be interrupted when the words flowed. Sometimes Alexander wondered if it were possible to cite a typewriter in a divorce case.

He was a troubled man. Beth's explanation of Allie's frigidity made sense. He had tried to convince himself that it was her journalist brain working overtime, but he feared she had struck upon the truth. And if she had, he was angry that Allie had never confided in him. It would have all been much less painful if he had known. He would not have felt that he himself was lacking in some way. On the long train ride home from the Canadian border he told himself that it was time there was a bit more honesty in their marriage; that he had been too soft by far. The problem was that it was not in his nature to be hard.

He left Allie to her work and took a cab to Park Avenue. He wanted to see his parents. Finding Jenny there was an added bonus.

'Didn't Allie tell you I was here?' she asked after they had hugged and kissed.

'She was busy writing. You know what she's like when she's writing,' Alexander said defensively.

'I don't know. I've been away for four years, remember?'

'Well, she's sort of miles away. Somewhere else. Anyway, let me look at you.' He held her by the shoulders and drew back. 'You look marvellous. God! It's good to see you again.'

Jenny was giving him searching looks in return.

'You don't look so great,' she said. 'Tough trip?'

'It was a bit.' He could hardly tell her that he had been working all day and evening, and making love to Beth most of the night. 'But it worked out well.'

'Good,' she said briskly. 'Do you want a drink?'

'Has Father still got some of that Scotch?'

'I think so. I'll join you.'

'I thought Quakers didn't drink.'

She grinned. 'Not a lot. But I do break some of the rules.'

She poured them both a Scotch from the drinks cabinet and they sat down each side of the fire. He stretched his legs towards the flames.

'This is good,' he said.

'And what isn't good?' she asked.

He looked at her, startled. 'What do you mean?'

She threw up her hands. 'Alexander, you are my brother. We grew up together. I know you better than any other human being, and something is on your mind. Is it your work or your marriage?'

He hesitated.

'Okay, I'll tell you,' she said. 'It's your marriage. Separate bedrooms, separate lives.'

322

He shook his head. 'You don't change, do you, Jenny? Straight for the jugular.'

'I want you to be happy.'

'Happiness isn't that easy. And you're not fair to Allie. You've never really liked her much, have you?'

'Nope. I always thought she was a pain.'

He put down the whisky glass. 'Jenny, you never knew her when she all right. When I first met her she was different.'

'She was ten years old,' Jenny pointed out. 'People change when they grow up. Not necessarily for the better.'

'I believe people only change for the worse if something makes them.' He hesitated again. 'Jenny, I'd like to talk to you about it if you'll promise me to listen with an open mind. If you've pre-judged her completely there isn't any point in the conversation. I need to talk it out with someone and I'd like it to be you.'

She looked at him, her brown eyes compassionate.

'I'll try and be objective,' she said. 'But nothing is going to stop me being on your side.'

'It's not a question of sides. It's a question of trying to work out what to do. Since you brought up the separate bedrooms, what you are undoubtedly thinking is correct. We don't have any kind of sex life. I've never touched her.' He stopped, embarrassed at talking of such things to his sister, but Jenny merely nodded as if she was pleased to be proved right.

'No babies?' was all she said.

'No babies,' he agreed. 'It's not Allie's fault. She told me when she said she would marry me that there would never be anything like that. She gave me the option to go. I love her so much – always have, always will – I accepted her conditions. And I admit it's not been easy.

'But now I think I know why she's like she is. Jenny, I believe she was raped by a German in the war. I reckon that's the reason. It would explain why she was so changed by the war. It explains everything. I asked Rosie once why Allie was so different, what had happened to her, and all she would say was that it was Allie's secret. It was up to Allie to tell me herself if she wanted to.'

'And she never has?'

'No. Do you think I ought to make her talk about it or would that make things worse?'

Jenny shrugged. 'I'm no new-fangled analyst, but in my

experience most things in life are better out in the open. Yes, if you want my opinion, I think you ought to make her talk about it.'

'It does explain things, doesn't it?' he heard himself asking eagerly.

'I guess so. But just because something rotten happens I see no reason to make the rest of the human race suffer. Well, maybe the rest of the human race, but not you. She is totally self-absorbed. Perhaps you ought to take her to a psychiatrist.'

'You're the second person that's said that,' he muttered.

'Ah, you've been confiding in someone else?'

Annoyed with himself he just nodded.

'Anyone special?'

'Oh, Jenny. Let's just say it was someone who consoles me now and then.'

'Oh, a mistress. How very sensible.'

He laughed ruefully. 'I'm glad you approve.'

'I don't know if I approve, but I can see the sense of it. I happen to think it would be better if you were sleeping with your own wife but if you do have a mistress, your wife has no one to blame but herself.'

'I doubt if she'd care,' he said miserably.

'Don't kid yourself, Alexander. Those babies want everything for themselves. She'd go madder than she is if she thought someone else had a claim on you.'

'Well, I don't propose to let her know,' he said. 'I wouldn't want to hurt her any more than she's been hurt already.'

'And how about your hurt?'

'You said you'd be objective,' he said reproachfully.

'Okay,' she threw up her hands in a gesture of surrender. 'Subject closed. But we're agreed you get her to talk about it.'

But how to get her to talk about it? he wondered as he walked home to Gramercy Park. He knew now that they were going to have to talk. He'd burst if he didn't. There was anger growing in him that she hadn't confided in him. Unless they talked, his feelings would fester.

As it happened the subject was raised without any manoeuvring from him. While they were eating dinner together that night he told her that he had seen Jenny.

'And I suppose she wanted to know why we haven't any

children?' Allie burst out. 'She is the most interfering, nosy —'

'Whoa!' Alexander said. 'That's my sister you're talking about.'

'Well, she is interfering and nosy,' Allie said sullenly. 'I was right, wasn't I? She was asking about children?'

'She put two and two together,' Alexander said.

'And made fourteen, I suppose.'

'No, she got it just about right. Separate bedrooms, separate lives and no babies.'

Allie went deep crimson and then white.

He took a deep breath. 'What caused it, Allie?' he asked quietly. 'Were you raped? In the war? By a German?'

She let out a strange little moan that was halfway to a scream.

'How dare you ask! How dare you!' she cried, her fists beating the lace tablecloth.

He mentally stiffened his spine.

'Well, were you?'

'You mustn't ask me things like that. Not ever.'

'Why not? I'm your husband. Aren't I entitled to know? Do you think it would make the slightest difference to how I feel about you? Well, it wouldn't. It would just make me want to love and cherish you more.'

She looked around the room wildly. 'Just shut up! I'm going to bed. I don't want to talk about it ever, ever, ever, ever, ever.'

He rose and swiftly went to lock the dining room door, slipping the key into his pocket.

'You're not going to bed. For once we're going to have a proper, honest conversation. We're going to face up to this marriage of ours before it goes bust.'

She was shaking, half standing, clinging to the edge of the table for support, her face deathly white.

'Why would it go bust?' she demanded.

If he wanted honesty from her, perhaps she should have some honesty from him, he thought. All cards on the table; air cleared.

'I could have a mistress,' he said.

She looked at him, her deep blue eyes wide with horror. 'You wouldn't? You wouldn't betray me?'

'What do you expect me to do?'

'Not betray me. Not that way. Not that horrible disgusting way.'

He pressed on. 'It's not horrible and disgusting. Not when you love someone.'

'Then you love her?'

'I never said any such thing.' He was beginning to panic. 'I never even said I had a mistress.'

'You do. You love her. You want to abandon me. You said you loved me when we married. I thought you loved me more than just for horrible sex. I was safe with you. You understood. But you're like all men. It's all sex in the end. That's all any of you want. It's disgusting! Vile! Obscene!'

Her eyes were wild, rolling back in her head. Foam had formed at the corners of her mouth and her voice was a shriek which turned into a scream. She screamed and screamed, her hands over her ears as if to block out the terrible sounds she was making.

He rushed to take her in his arms and try and calm her, but she fought him off, fists flailing. He tried slapping her face, but the hysteria did not stop. The screams went on. He ran to open the dining room door. Their butler was standing outside, his face horrified.

'Quick,' Alexander shouted above the frightening noise. 'Call Dr Goddard.'

Alexander had never seen Johnson move so fast as he went for the telephone. He ran back into the room and picked Allie up. Her hands were back over her ears. She kept them there while she continued to scream as he carried her up the stairs to her bedroom. She was still screaming long after he went downstairs to wait for the doctor's arrival.

He sat in the hall, his head in his hands. It was all his fault, he thought despairingly. All he had done in an effort to right their marriage was to send her into hysteria. And now he was terrified that she might have lost the small hold on sanity that she had.

It was much later that night when Alexander started on the frustrating task of ringing Rosie in Champagne. Uncertain how long it would take to get through, he put in the call at midnight. The house was deathly quiet and he felt a deep melancholy as he waited by the downstairs telephone for the operator to ring him back. It was gone two when the call came and he heard the noise of a French phone ringing. It must be about seven in the morning in France, he figured. Rosie would probably just be thinking about getting up.

Her voice was delighted when she heard him through the crackling wires.

'Alexander! How lovely!' she said.

'It's not good news, Rosie,' he warned.

He heard her little gasp from three thousand miles away.

'What's happened?' she asked. 'Is it Allie?'

He hesitated, his carefully prepared speech lost.

'She's not dead?' Rosie's voice was anguished.

'No, no,' he said. The thought of death made what had happened seem trivial. 'She's just had a mental breakdown. Can you talk now? I need to ask you some questions and you might not want others to hear.'

'I'm in my bedroom. It's all right. What sort of nervous breakdown? Do you want me to come over?'

'I don't think that would help.'

'She's still angry with me?' Rosie's voice broke a little.

'I'm afraid so. But I think it's all part of what's happened. She's had to be taken to a clinic, I'm afraid.'

'I see.' A silence. 'I think it's been coming on for years.'

'That's what I wanted to ask you,' he said. 'It's hard to say all this on the telephone, but she and I have never had . . .' He paused.

'A sex life?'

'That's right.'

'I'm not really surprised.'

'Well, tonight I took a chance and asked her if the problem was because she had been raped by a German soldier.'

Another gasp came from over three thousand miles. 'You didn't know? She never told you?'

'No. She told me nothing except that our marriage would have to be celibate. I just guessed in the end. It wasn't hard to work out once I thought about it.' It was a lie but this was no time for the truth.

'And?'

'She began screaming and couldn't stop. Rosie, we need to know what happened. The doctor says that the people treating her will need to know. Was I right? Was that what happened?'

'You were right.' Rosie's voice was weary. 'Absolutely right. But I think it would be better if I wrote to you with all the details.'

'What happened to the man?'

'The German? I killed him.'

'You killed him?' He could not believe what he was hearing.

'Yes. But I was too late ... Alexander, there's worse. Rosanne —'

'Your daughter?'

'Is not my daughter. She is Allie's. Rosanne was the result of the rape.'

'Oh, my God.' He was dizzy with shock.

'Listen,' her voice was urgent. 'I'd rather write it all down. But what has happened to Allie was predictable. Don't blame yourself. She's been holding on to sanity for years. All those terrible depressions. Perhaps it's better that she has let go. She was too brave when it happened, too silent when it was over. Perhaps now she has let go she can purge it all and begin again.'

'Rosie,' he was crying and could not stop. 'I love her so. I can't bear to think that she has had all this pain and suffered it alone. If only she had told me.'

'Alexander, try to understand. If she didn't talk about it, she could pretend it never happened. Be of good heart. Maybe this is the breakthrough that we have all prayed for.'

'She's very sick, Rosie.'

'She's also very strong. Look what she survived. Alexander, you must go to bed. It must be terribly late there. Go and get some sleep and tomorrow we can talk again. I'll ring you around midday my time. But for now you need sleep.'

He was exhausted. He hung up the phone and could barely make the steps up to his bedroom. But he felt better for talking to Rosie. She would be right. She was always right. And he put his head on the pillow and slept.

There was a strange little humming noise that she could not place and the muffled sound of someone walking in soft shoes. Who was walking outside her bedroom in soft shoes?

Cautiously she opened her eyes and realised with a rush of panic that this was not her bedroom. She was somewhere else. The bed was narrow and white-covered, the room clinical with polished wooden floors. White net curtains waved in a small breeze from long, slightly opened windows, but the room was still too hot.

Blinking as she looked around her, it all came back. Alexander asking her those dreadful question; telling her about his mistress. She could still hear her own hysterical screaming echoing in her ears but after that she remembered nothing. She sat up cautiously and looked around. As the curtain blew back she saw that the windows had iron bars across them. This must be a hospital room. Why was she in this starched white gown that tied at the back? And why was she in hospital at all? There was nothing wrong with her.

There was a bell push beside the bed. Allie prodded at it angrily. She would have got out of bed if there had been a robe to put on but there was nothing of the kind in the room and she was sure that the gown would gape open at the back in an undignified fashion.

Within a few seconds the door opened and a white-clad blonde nurse came into the room, a determined smile on her face.

'Awake then, are we?' she said, 'My, we've had a good sleep.'

Who the hell was this 'we', Allie wondered and didn't bother to reply.

'We've even missed Christmas and New Year,' the nurse said archly while ferociously shaking a thermometer.

Missed Christmas and New Year?

'What do you mean, missed Christmas and New Year?' Allie demanded.

'Slept right through them,' said the nurse, popping the thermometer into Allie's mouth.

Allie took it out again. 'Are you telling me that I've been asleep for nearly three weeks?'

'With a little help from us, yes.' The nurse retrieved the thermometer and pushed it back into Allie's mouth. Rendered speechless, Allie slid back down in the bed and stared at the ceiling. Grey memory was beginning to return, recollections of moments of twilight wakening and drifting back into sleep. But nearly three weeks!

The nurse removed the thermometer, peered at it, made a note on a clip-file at the bottom of the bed, swung starchily towards the door and said: 'I'll get you some lunch brought in.'

The mention of lunch made Allie realise that she was ravenously hungry. Uncertain what to do next, she decided that she would make all decisions, like getting out of here and going home, after she had eaten. But before any food appeared there was a gentle knock on the door. To her dismay Alexander came in, accompanied by a man with slicked back black hair and a heavy black moustache. He was bigger and a little older than Alex, with dark eyes and a large, thin, high-bridged nose. Allie slid even further down the bed, tempted to put her head under the bedclothes. She was not ready to confront Alexander or anyone else. Not yet.

As he came towards her Alexander was smiling his wonderful smile that never failed to touch her. But coinciding with the rush of uncontrollable affection came the memory that she had lost him to another woman. She burst into tears.

She was gratified to see his smile fade. She wanted to hurt him. He hurried to take her in his arms, rocking her, crooning, telling her not to cry, while the other man stood watching.

Eventually she pushed him away.

'Don't touch me,' she said angrily. 'You just go to your mistress. I suppose you've put me in here to get me out of the way.'

His face crumpled in distress and he looked helplessly towards the other man.

'Allie,' he said, 'this is Doctor Ziegman. He wants to talk to you.'

'What about?' Allie said rudely. She knew she was behaving badly, but why shouldn't she?

'You,' the doctor said. 'I want to talk to you about you.' He had a strong foreign accent. It sounded German.

'Well, I don't want to talk about me. I want to get out of here.'

Dr Ziegman sat down on one of the hard-backed wooden chairs. He motioned for Alexander to take the armchair that stood by the window.

'Very well. Where do you want to go?' the doctor asked calmly.

'Home,' Allie said, and burst into tears again as she realised that home meant going with Alexander. 'I don't know. Anywhere but here.'

'I see. Back to France?'

France meant her mother.

'No. And get him out of here.' She pointed a vicious finger at Alexander.

'Perhaps you should go for the moment, Mr Webster,' Dr Ziegman murmured. 'Then your wife and I can have a little chat.'

Allie sat glowering from the bed as her husband left the room. She had a feeling of power. Being rude got results. Bad behaviour gave you control of the situation. Alexander closed the door behind him.

'And now you can go,' she said belligerently to the doctor. 'Send that china-doll nurse in here with my clothes and I'll be off. I have work to do.'

'Certainly,' the doctor said mildly. 'But we haven't yet established where you are going.'

Since she did not know the answer to that she decided on further attack. 'Are you German?'

'I was born in Germany.'

'Then I don't wish to speak to you.'

'Ah, yes, of course. You had a very bad time with the Germans in the war, did you not?'

She stiffened. 'If you speak of that I shall start screaming again.'

'If you wish,' he said. 'We are used to people who scream in here, Mrs Webster.'

She looked around her. The bars on the windows were suddenly sinister.

'Where am I?' she asked fearfully.

'You are safe. You are in a clinic to be made well again.'

'I'm not ill,' she protested.

'You don't think so?'

'I've no pains. Nothing's wrong.'

'I am aware you have no physical pains.'

The fear came back. 'Are you saying I'm mad?'

'Why should I say that?'

'I am not mad.'

'I did not say that you were.'

'Then why do I need to be made well again?'

'Because you are disturbed. I know the burdens that you carry, Mrs Webster, those burdens that you hide from us all. It is hiding them that turns them into burdens. You could be free of them for ever if you would only face the truth.'

She stared at him, hating him, and said nothing.

'Some of your burdens are of your own making. Your conviction that your husband has a mistress, for example.'

'He told me he did,' she hissed.

'Did he?'

'Yes.'

'You are certain of this?'

She hesitated.

'Is it not true to say that his words to you were: "I could have a mistress"?'

'I don't remember.'

'A pity, for that is what he said. But of course if you did misunderstand him it is to be expected. No doubt in your heart you are aware that that is the only possibility for him if he is to lead a normal life. You fear it, of course, but expect it. Therefore you choose to believe that he said he had a mistress.'

'I never even thought of such a thing,' she said angrily.

'As you never even think of Lieutenant Schmidt?' She put up her hand as if to ward off a blow. Schmidt, name of horror, name that must not be spoken. 'No,' he said warningly, 'you may scream when I am gone if you wish. What I have to say to you is that Lieutenant Schmidt was real and is dead. Your husband's mistress is not real and does not live. Yet both are burdens with which you have laden yourself.'

He had said the name again. She should scream to blot it out, but she was silent. If it didn't matter if she screamed, there wasn't much point. And maybe he was trying to make her scream again, in which case she would do no such thing. Her mind seemed to be in fragments and needed putting back together again. To help herself she mentally reburied Lieutenant Schmidt and concentrated on that which was the most urgent. 'You are saying that my husband does not have a mistress?'

He nodded his head.

'Under the circumstances you are very fortunate,' he said and rose to his feet. 'Now I shall send your husband back to you and lunch will be served to you both. I shall return to see you later today.'

She watched him leave with relief and as she lay waiting for

Alexander, some degree of a sense of security was returning. If Alexander had not done that ugly thing with another woman, she could continue to be his wife. Life could go on as it had been. She had a sudden longing to be at her typewriter in her study. All of this would make a story. She had so much she wanted to write and here she was wasting time in this sterile room designed for mad people. Alexander must take her away immediately. She had no doubt that he would. She sighed. The thing about – sometimes the trouble with – Alexander was that he always did exactly what she wanted.

Before Dr Ziegman reappeared Alexander had started and immediately stubbed out three cigarettes. He was waiting in the doctor's office – a room which bore little resemblance to a work place. It was furnished like a comfortable sitting room with one large couch and two big armchairs and the usual small tables and knick-knacks of any upper-middle-class drawing room. The paintings on the walls were all of serene landscapes that could have been the English countryside.

He stood up as the doctor walked into the room.

'What do you think?' he asked anxiously.

Dr Ziegman grinned in a remarkably boyish way. 'It would be accurate to say that her depression has turned to aggression.'

'Is that good or bad?'

'I would say that aggression is a much healthier attitude. Much more positive. A fighting attitude.'

'Can I take her home?'

'You can do exactly as you wish. But I would recommend that if you can convince her to stay in our care for, say, a month or two it might be possible to enrich her life – and yours.'

'And how can you do that?' Alexander felt a touch of hope.

The doctor pursed his rather full lips. 'By making her accept all the tragedies in her life instead of trying to bury them. By making her face the truth.'

'As simply as that?' Alexander said, knowing that he sounded disbelieving.

'No, not as simply as that. It will take a long time, but it would be better if we could begin the psychiatry while she is with us. Obviously we will remove her from the hospital wing. I would suggest that we take her to our clinic in the Catskills. It is more like a luxurious hotel than a clinic. And she can have a typewriter and continue with her work if she wishes. I should be interested to see what she writes.'

'If she'll show you. She never lets me see anything unless it's printed.'

'We shall see.'

'And she'll want her dog with her.'

'That might be possible.'

'I don't know . . .' Alexander said. He could not conceive of any way that Allie would agree to going to a clinic.

The doctor was silent, taking a pipe from his pocket and stuffing it with tobacco. Alexander realised he was being given time to think.

'What if she refuses to stay?' he asked.

'We cannot hold her here by force.'

'You mean I have to persuade her.'

'You do not have to do anything.'

'I appreciate that,' Alexander said, a little irritated. 'But what do you really think you can do for her?'

Dr Ziegman drew slowly on his pipe. 'What changes would you like to see in her?'

'That's easy,' Alexander said. 'I'd like to see her lose her suspicion of men, her fear of sex, her hatred of her mother and her general distrust of the human race. I'd like her to be happy again, warm and open as she was when she was a child.'

'Would you say she has reason for all the quirks in her character?'

'Good God, man! I've told you her history. Of course she has reason.'

'Then there is hope. It is the meaningless, groundless fears that are the hardest to change. When there are real reasons, those reasons can be faced. Yet I can promise nothing. This science of the mind is in its infancy, but we can try.'

'If I can persuade her?'

The doctor nodded and smiled. 'If she can persuade herself. You may tell her that this bloody Boche will not be working with her. We have a well-qualified woman psychiatrist at our Catskill clinic. She is a Viennese which perhaps will be more acceptable to your wife.'

Slightly embarrassed, Alexander just nodded.

'Well,' Dr Ziegman stood up and stretched. 'We can do nothing until we find out her reaction. I will take you back to her and I wish you luck.'

He led the way to the door of Allie's room and when he reached it turned and said: 'By the way, Mr Webster. Your wife is now convinced that you do not have a mistress – because she wished to be convinced. Should it be the case that you do have another lady in your life I would suggest that you take every possible precaution to make sure that Mrs Webster does not find out.'

The doctor's eyes were twinkling and there was no trace of judgment in them, but nevertheless Alexander felt himself go scarlet.

'I understand,' he muttered.

'Good,' said Dr Ziegman briskly. 'Now, why don't you go in?'

Allie did not move when he came back into the room. She was flat on her back again, staring at the ceiling.

'When are you taking me home?' she asked belligerently from her supine position without looking at him.

'Not yet,' he said.

She sat up. 'Why not?'

'Shall we talk about it?' he asked gently.

'There's nothing to talk about.'

'There is, Allie. You know there is as well as I do. We have our marriage to talk about.'

'You'll make me ill again.'

'Hysterical, you mean? It doesn't matter here. They'll just put you to sleep again for a while until you're calm and rested again.'

She was silent and slid back down under the bedclothes.

'The doctor was right when he said you carried burdens. I know about them all now. I know about the lieutenant and how brave you were. I know about Rosanne and how much the loss of her hurt you. There's nothing now that I don't know about you, Allie. All the secrets are gone. Everything is in the open. And I understand everything so much better. You see, all this time I thought there was something lacking in me that meant you couldn't love me fully. To find and face the truth has lifted a terrible weight from my shoulders. I want to lift that weight from yours. I love you so much. Nothing that has happened to you or to me can change that.'

335

Allie's face was set in obdurate lines. 'Who told you? I suppose she did. That wicked bitch.'

'The doctors needed to know. I needed to know.'

'But they were my secrets.' Her voice was a wail of anguish.

'It sounds as if you treasured them. What you need is to shed them. These people can help you do that. Dr Ziegman suggests that you go to a sort of luxury hotel they run in the Catskill Mountains. You can have a typewriter and work and you can have Jessica with you. It will be like a holiday, just talking to a doctor and resting and enjoying yourself.'

'I'm not talking to any German.'

'You will be in the care of a woman – a Viennese.'

She was silent. Then she said: 'I'm not going to change, you know. I am the way I am but I am not mad. There's nothing to be done about the person I am. It's what you're all suggesting that is real madness.'

'Maybe, but it's worth a try.'

'I don't think so.'

He sighed. 'Allie, do you care for me at all?'

'I love you,' she said rather crossly. 'I've always loved you, but not in that horrible way.'

'Then if you love me, will you try for me? If it doesn't help you – well, at least I can feel that you did something you didn't want to do for me.'

He held his breath and waited.

'If I don't go, would you take a mistress?'

He took the chance. 'I might if I felt you didn't even want to do something for us both.'

She pursed her lips and thought. 'If I do do it, will you promise me something?'

'Yes,' he said cautiously.

'If I do it and it doesn't work, will you swear to me that you'll never take a mistress?'

Without hesitation he said: 'Yes.'

'On the Bible?'

He nodded.

'Say you'll swear on the Bible,' she demanded.

'I swear on the Bible,' he said, heart sinking and fingers surreptitiously crossed.

'I can have Jessica with me?'

336

'Yes.'

'And a typewriter?'

'Yes.'

'And I just have to talk to this woman about myself?'

'Yes.'

'All right, I'll do it. As long as I can write and I've got Jessica, it doesn't much matter where I am.'

'And me?'

'Oh, you!' she said, her voice indifferent.

He turned for the door. He didn't want any lunch. He felt as if she had knifed him. She obviously could not be bothered to kiss him. Her mind had no doubt gone back into her fantasy world. How could she love him and be so cruel? he asked himself as he left the room. How could she!

Hurt and angry he came out into the chill of a New York winter. It was just into New Year. What sort of new year would 1924 be for him? he wondered. Remembering her words – it didn't matter where she was as long as she had her dog and a typewriter, he felt that there was no real place for him in her life. And he was sure of one thing. He wasn't giving up Beth Rogan.

Champagne, February 1924

Rosie had spent the last two weeks of January in her little laboratory tasting and blending the various still wines that would come together to compose her *cuvée* for the year. While she worked, the young wine pressed at the time of the *vendange* in October rested in the vats of Les Hérissons. While the wine slept, Luke and Robert directed the laying of the manures and fertilisers around every vine on the estate to ensure a good healthy vintage in the autumn.

Hers was the loneliest job, working in concentrated silence in the clinical little room at the back of the house where she had always blended since she first learned how. Pierre had joined her on a few occasions and she had shown him the routine. She had taught him that the wine must be consistent in taste and quality from one year to the next and she let him test his palate on some blendings of his own. He was avid to learn. She thought he might have the gift and flair that would make a fine

337

chef de cave one day, but he still made her uneasy – as he had made her uneasy from the day he arrived at Les Hérissons.

She was glad to be kept busy with the exacting work. Away from the peace of the blending room her life was not particularly happy. She worried constantly about Allie. Alexander had written to say that she was receiving psychiatric treatment for her depressions at a clinic in the Catskill Mountains. He added, rather despairingly, that she seemed so content there that she showed no signs of wanting to come home. Rosie, who knew little about this new science of the mind, was deeply concerned that dabbling in people's psyche could do more harm than good, but there was nothing she could do to intervene from so far away. At Les Coquelicots Françoise continued to be a thorn in her side, ensnaring Philippe with charm and sweetness and showering insolence elsewhere. Rosie longed to be rid of the girl but while Philippe was so besotted she saw no hope. At Les Hérissons Madame Dupuis became more eccentric daily. She was deeply suspicious of every move that Rosie made, sarcastic and sometimes cruel to Feathers. But Pierre could do no wrong. Rosie sometimes feared that the old lady's mind was going. The light of Rosie's life at this difficult time was Rosanne who was funny, lively, sailed through life and was always warm and loving.

Feathers was causing Rosie the most concern. She had been busy working towards the opening of her dress shop and it would be ready very soon, but the girl still seemed deeply depressed and unhappy. Pierre was at the School of Oenology in Épernay, but he frequently went to Paris at the weekends, leaving Feathers at the mercy of his grandmother. No wonder the girl was downcast, Rosie thought.

She was parking her car in the driveway outside Les Hérissons on a chilly, grey morning in the second week of February when Feathers came flying out of the front door and down the steps.

'Rosie,' she said, holding her hand to her side as if she had a stitch, 'can I talk to you?'

'You certainly can,' Rosie said cheerfully, hoping that maybe she would now learn what it was that ailed Feathers. 'Where shall we go?'

'Your blending room? We won't be interrupted there.'

338

'Okay, but you can't smoke.' Feathers had taken to smoking quite heavily (something else that annoyed Madame), and smoking, even the wearing of perfume, was not permitted in the blending room since any strong smell affected the 'nose' of the wine.

The girl grimaced. 'I suppose I'll survive without one.'

'I'll give you a taste of what I think will be this year's blend instead,' Rosie told her.

Once they were in the blending room Feathers seemed to be having difficulty in coming out with what she wanted to say. She sat at the table, twisting the stem of her glass and staring into the champagne as if it might tell her her fortune.

'What is it?' Rosie asked gently. 'Madame or Pierre? Which one's getting you down?'

'Both of them, but they're not the problem.' To Rosie's dismay, slow tears began to spill over Feathers' rounded cheeks. Then she said, almost defiantly: 'The trouble is that I'm pregnant.'

Rosie's instant reaction was delight.

'Well, what's so terrible about that?' she said.

'What's terrible is that the baby isn't Pierre's.' And Feathers' tears flowed faster.

There was silence while Rosie digested this unwelcome piece of information.

'Not Pierre's?' she finally said for want of something better.

Feathers shook her head miserably. 'No.'

'Will he think it's his?' Rosie asked cautiously, but guessed this was unlikely since it wasn't long since Feathers had confessed that she and Pierre had no intimate life.

'No. He hasn't touched me for about a year.'

Rosie remembered herself in the early days of her own marriage when, fearful of becoming pregnant by Philippe, she had forced herself to make love with Clovis – just in case. This girl did not have the same guile or perhaps the opportunity.

'How pregnant are you?' she asked.

'It happened during the *vendange*.'

Rosie did a rapid calculation.

'More than three months.'

'That's right,' Feathers said listlessly.

'Perhaps we could do something . . .' Rosie began to say, but Feathers held up a commanding hand.

'I'm going to have the baby,' she said. 'I've sinned enough in my life without doing anything like that.'

Rosie felt a spurt of impatience. It was a bit late to be worrying about sinning.

'I suppose it's Carlos's baby?' she volunteered.

Feathers' cheeks reddened. 'It doesn't matter whose baby it is. If I say, it will only cause more trouble. It wasn't my fault. I was raped. But Pierre will never believe that.'

Rosie wasn't sure that she believed it herself.

'Raped?'

'Yes. I let this man kiss me and it just got out of hand. He wouldn't stop.'

It was Carlos's baby all right, Rosie thought, remembering the night of the *cochelet* and how Feathers had blatantly flirted with the lad and how totally smitten he had been by her. She pictured him scratched and distraught wanting to speak to his father, recalled his disappearance and Feathers' non-appearance the next day. It all added up.

'So what are you going to do?' she asked gently.

'I don't know. It's a lot to ask, but I wondered if you would tell Pierre for me. I just wouldn't know what to say. I'm so frightened. Do you think he'll throw me out? Where would I go? What would I do?'

Feathers was crying dismally, her nose beginning to run and redden, her lips quivering. Rosie took her hand and squeezed it hard.

'If he did such a thing you would come to Les Coquelicots,' she said firmly, 'so stop worrying about that.' But what a mess! she was thinking as she added: 'If you think it will help, I'll tell him, but you'll have to talk to him yourself in the end, you know.'

'As long as I don't have to break it to him . . .'

'All right, I'll break it to him,' Rosie said, not relishing the task, but realising that Feathers was not capable of facing up to doing any such thing herself.

They sat in silence, looking at each other across the table. There didn't seem to be a great deal more to discuss. But Feathers blew her nose loudly and said: 'Rosie, why does it happen to me? That's twice, and I'm not a bad girl. I don't mean these things to happen. God must be punishing me for something. Do you think it could be because of having Patric – not being married when I got pregnant?'

'No, I don't,' Rosie said firmly. 'It's a funny sort of God you believe in.'

'But He lets so many terrible things happen. There must be a reason.'

Rosie, whose hold on faith was fragile at the best of times, grunted and said: 'I've always thought that even if there is a God, the devil's the one in charge.'

'Rosie!' Feathers was scandalised.

'Listen.' Rosie leaned to hold the girl's hands again. 'You are not a bad girl. You are one of the nicest people I have ever met. But you're a human being with feelings and needs like anyone else. You've been deprived of an outlet for those feelings. And you've been unlucky. I was once deprived like you, and Philippe became my lover. I was lucky. I never got pregnant. You're not wicked, Feathers. God doesn't need to punish you for anything since He presumably gave you the urges that gave you Patric. The only one who might punish you is Pierre, and if you want him to believe you, it would be better to say who the man who raped you is.'

'No,' Feathers said stubbornly. 'It will only make more trouble and what good would it do? This way it will just be my baby. Maybe they'll let me love this one properly if it's not really a Dupuis.'

'Oh, Feathers!' Rosie felt her own eyes mist over. 'We haven't made you very happy, have we?'

'*You* have,' Feathers said, her voice muffled. 'If it hadn't been for you I don't know what I would have done.'

'Well, be of good heart,' Rosie said, kissing her on the cheek. 'I'll do the best for you that I can.'

Vega, Catskill Mountains, February 1924

Allie was at her typewriter, staring out of the big picture window of her room at the view of gentle snow-covered mountains beyond. After three years in New York she could not get used to the quiet. At first it had left her a little fearful in the night while she slept alone, but now the silence acted like a soporific. She found she could sit dreamily watching the mountains changing colour from greyish white to ice blue when the sun shone, while Jessie snorted and snuffled in sleep at her feet or on her lap. She was content to be where she was and most of the time, when the waves of depression were absent, was at peace with herself.

She was writing, but not fiction. She was recording her day to day experiences in the clinic. And writing down what was happening to her was helpful. The conversations with Dr Anna Weingott, her therapist, followed by recording them in her diary were making her understand much about herself that she had buried for far too long. It had not been easy. At first she had been as rude and belligerent to Anna as she had been to Dr Ziegman. But Anna was a woman and therefore more to be trusted. She even looked trustworthy. She was thin-faced and dark-haired and she dressed in simple dark clothes. She wore her hair in an old-fashioned bun, and though she was not that much older than Allie, she had a motherly quality about her. Her voice was very soft, she said little, but just listened with attentive grey eyes as if every word were of the utmost importance.

It had taken Allie a long time before she began to open up to Anna, and still there were things that she did not wish to talk about. For weeks she had regaled Anna Weingott with trivia; describing her grandmother, life at Les Hérissons, talk of her early writings. She had said nothing significant. Anna had listened patiently. But she looked forward to the psychiatrist's morning and afternoon visits. Being listened to made her feel important in some curious way and it was beginning to dawn on her that she had never really felt important; always a little inferior and as if she had no worth.

They had just spent an hour together and the psychiatrist had gone off to see another of her clients. Allie knew that this session had changed everything. She had begun to open up. With Anna gone the room felt bigger and emptier. Allie put Jessie on her lap for compensation and sat idly stroking the little dog's soft head and watching the purple evening light on the mountain tops. Then she sighed, put the dog down on the floor and went to where her typewriter waited on a neat and tidy desk.

She slid in a sheet of paper and began to type.

Today we talked about my childhood. Anna wanted to know if it had been a happy one. I enjoyed telling her about Les Hérissons and Papa, and how we used to tour the estate together, and our favourite place high on the hill where we could look down at Les Hérissons, laid below like a patchwork quilt of vineyards. It made me remember how the poppies used to bloom in the verges and in the cornfields on the side of the mountain where the grapes did not grow, and how much my mother loved them for their brave, bright colour.

Anna wanted to know what my mother was like when I was little. I told her how much I had adored her and worshipped her, but how she was always away. For ever in Paris or somewhere, coming home like a wonderful exciting apparition, smelling marvellous and looking so beautiful and then fading away out of my life again for what seemed like for ever, though I suppose it was only a few days really.

'Didn't she love you?' she wanted to know.

I had to think about that, and I knew that it was mean of me to do so, because I was always aware that she loved me very much. I was sure of that even if she did keep leaving me.

But thinking about it turned out to be a good thing because it made me remember what I'd been frightened of. I'd always been frightened that one day she would never come back.

'She did love me,' I told Anna, 'but I understand now that in my heart I always knew she loved someone else more than she loved me or Papa or Mimi. I used to feel even when she was at Les Hérissons, putting me to bed, kissing me goodnight, telling me stories, anything, that she was really absent. That she was in another place in her mind and in her spirit. I knew she wanted to be somewhere else, and it frightened me that one day she wouldn't come back at all and then we would all have been lost. Papa, Mimi, all of us. We needed her more than she needed us. And, of course, I was right. Many

343

years later I found out that she had been having an affair with Philippe Lefevre, the man she's married to now. She'd been unfaithful to my father almost from the day that they married. And yet everyone went on loving her. She got away with it. Everyone forgave her.

'Now I'm an adult it seems wrong that she got away with it. She ought to have been punished, but she never was. Papa died and she lived and she got what she wanted. She married Philippe and moved away from Les Hérissons and left everyone behind.'

I waited for Anna to say something, but she was silent. I should know by now that she hardly ever makes any comment, which in a way makes it so easy to talk to her. Because she's silent you have to think it out for yourself. This time, when she saw I wasn't going to say any more about my mother, she just asked me what my father was like.

I was glad to talk about Papa.

'He was big and strong and dependable,' I told her. 'He loved me very much. He was never absent. I knew he was with me in every way. He wasn't very clever. My mother was much smarter, and she used to get impatient with him because he was slow and couldn't think fast like she could. I suppose she used to try to be nice to him, but I always knew she didn't love him like he deserved. And later I found out the truth of that, too. She had never loved him at all.'

I thought I'd said too much. I didn't want to tell her the truth of that, because it was disloyal to Papa, but she didn't say anything, she just sat there waiting for me to go on, her mouth curling upwards into a gentle smile. And thinking about Papa and everything that happened and how cruel it all was, I started to cry. I just sat there crying, remembering it all, and still she didn't say anything. She just took a clean handkerchief out of her pocket and handed it to me and waited.

I needed to tell her how awful it had been, and I heard myself saying: 'You see, he wasn't my papa at all. He was my uncle really, and he'd married my mother because he loved her from the moment he saw her and because she

344

needed a father for the baby she was going to have – me. She had got herself pregnant without being married and she came to France looking for a father for the baby. I suppose my mother was always a slut. And it was that that ruined my life.'

'In what way?' Anna asked, but I wasn't going to explain about Pierre. I just went on talking about Mama. 'Papa married her when most men would have turned the other way,' I said. 'He saved her from Madame Frédéric's brothel . . .'

'You think she would have gone there?'

'What else could she have done?'

'What do you think she would have done? Gone to the brothel?'

I thought about it and I had to concede to myself that it was unlikely that my mother would have agreed to go to a brothel. She would have found someone else to marry her, or she'd have done something to make money and bring me up.

'I don't know,' I said, feeling cross and scratchy, 'but if she had gone to the brothel she'd have been running it within weeks. She takes over everything from everyone. But Papa saved her from that. He did all that for her and he was the kindest, most wonderful father you can ever imagine, and still she cheated on him. I wouldn't have minded as much if it was because she'd never stopped loving my real father. She hated my real father.'

'Why was that?' Anna asked me.

It was an easy question to answer, because my real father was hateful, so hateful I could never understand why my mother had ever gone with him in the first place. I explained to Anna how he'd come to Les Hérissons and how wicked he'd been, trying to take over our vineyards because he'd lost his own in America when Prohibition came. I didn't tell her any more. I didn't want to tell her how Papa had killed him. That was Papa's secret. She just said: 'So you think your mother had reason to dislike your real father?'

I don't like to admit anything good about my mother,

but I did have to agree that maybe she had some right on her side about that.

'She would have been very young when you were born, I suppose,' Anna sort of murmured. 'Much younger than you are now.'

'Nineteen,' I said and it occurred to me how young it was.

'And you think she was cruel to her husband?'

'She cheated on him!' It was annoying me that she didn't seem to think this was very important.

'Did he know?'

'She was too smart for that. None of us knew. But she was always making my father look small. It was as if she was the man. He was more like a mother to me than she was, and she was more like a father. Doing the masculine protective things . . .'

I stopped to think about that, and she just sat there gently smiling and saying nothing, waiting again for me to go on.

'It wasn't Papa's fault. Everything always went wrong for him. He was never there at the right time. Poor Papa sort of blundered through life. But even he . . .' I didn't want to tell her about Madame Claudette because that gave my mother an excuse for her own behaviour. Even now I still wonder which of them was unfaithful first. Rather than get into all that, I thought it would be better to tell her something else. 'When I was little,' I said hurriedly, 'I used to make up stories. They were very romantic, and I was always the beautiful heroine and some wonderful man would rescue me from an awful fate.'

'Why did you need refuge in fiction even then?' she asked thoughtfully.

'It wasn't refuge, it was just something I liked doing,' I said, feeling a bit mad that she should think that even that had a deeper meaning. 'I'd send myself to sleep with my stories, and anytime I was bored I'd make them up in my head. I made one up the first time I met Alexander, my husband. I sort of half fell in love with him because he was gentle and nice. He and his mother had come to

346

France to see my mother. They were old friends. It was an exciting day for me because Sebastian was at Les Hérissons, too . . .'

Anna interrupted to know who Sebastian was, so I explained that he was Philippe Lefevre's son who had been killed in the war, but that he didn't know any more than I did that his father and my mother were lovers.

'I hero-worshipped Sebastian, but I got this fancy for Alexander when he came to Les Hérissons.' Remembering made me feel quite nostalgic. 'I was ten and thought I was in love with both of them. I was having this daydream while we were all having dinner. Sebastian and Alexander were rescuing me from the Boche. Grandmama was always on about the Boche and how they ravished people. I didn't really know what being ravished meant but in my story the Boche rushed into our dining room and tried to take me away to ravish me. But of course Alexander and Sebastian rescued me.

'It was that night that all the *vignerons* – the growers of grapes – came to our house to burn it down. They had a grievance against the champagne makers because they didn't think they were getting the right money for their grapes and they thought people like my mother were using grapes from the south because they were cheaper. They burned down most of the little town of Ay that night, and Papa who had heard that something dreadful was going to happen had gone to guard our fields on the Marne. So there was no man in the house when this mob came up our drive, all shouting and waving burning brands.

'Mama never panicked for a minute. She went out onto the porch and faced them and I stood with her. She made Marie and Henri and Madame and all of us give them glasses of our best champagne. She made a speech and then we and those men all drank a toast to *la belle Champagne*. Then they went away sad and beaten. It was terribly exciting – just like my story, in a way. It was Mama who rescued us but what was horrible about it was that she just took all the pride and dignity out of those men doing it. She made them look small. She robbed

347

them of their manhood, and when Papa came home because nothing had happened to our fields and he'd caught a cold staying out all night, he looked small, too, and as if he wasn't the man. She was stronger in spirit than any of them, and when my story came true . . .'

Damn her listening eyes, I thought. I had nearly blundered into telling her about the lieutenant. I knew she knew about the lieutenant because treacherous Mama had told her, but I didn't want to talk about it.

'Yes, of course, you were ravished,' she said. 'What a strange old-fashioned word that is. But a good strong word that says what it means. Your mother rescued you again. What was it she did exactly?'

'I don't remember,' I said and I knew I sounded sullen.

She laughed, and it was the first time I felt I didn't like her.

'I can't believe you've forgotten that,' she said. 'Have you?'

I didn't say anything. I just sat there looking out at the view and she didn't say anything either. Then I thought I might as well get it over with.

'She killed him,' I said. 'With a pitchfork.'

'Did Alexander and Sebastian kill the Germans in your story?'

I just nodded.

'What did they use?'

I thought back all those years and remembered the dining room at Les Hérissons, with Mrs Webster and Alexander sitting at the table, Alexander so fair and serious and handsome while Sebastian showed off his English which was never as good as mine. I remembered how in my story they had grabbed the carving knives when the Germans came in. And then Grandmama had called for me to pay attention because I was daydreaming again.

'Carving knives,' I said.

'So when real trouble came, your Papa or Alexander or Sebastian were never there to save you?'

'Only Mama,' I said reluctantly. 'Papa was shell-shocked, Alexander in America and Sebastian was dead.'

'Do you feel they'd all deserted you – except your mother, of course?'

'It was just that she was there. She was always there.'

'You just said she wasn't always there.'

The woman was confusing me. I didn't want to talk about it any more. I decided to ignore that.

'What you don't understand is that Papa loved her best, so did Sebastian. So does Rosanne now.' I was aware I sounded jealous.

'Ah, Rosanne,' she said thoughtfully.

And I was definitely not talking about Rosanne.

'Would you say that your mother stole Rosanne from you?' she asked, not taking any notice of my silence.

'Of course,' I muttered.

She nodded as if she agreed with me. 'What would have been another way, I wonder? I suppose your baby could have gone to a children's home.'

I remembered the agony of having her. The disappointment that she wasn't a boy and therefore couldn't bring the dead Sebastian's spirit back into the world. The awful shame of it all. The fear she might be like her father. I'd rejected her for all those reasons. But a children's home, where I'd never see her again? Oh, no! That wouldn't have done at all. I had to admit it had been a good question from Anna. What would have been another way? Particularly as Rosanne had grown up so like me, but so much nicer than me.

'I'm tired,' I said.

She instantly stood up and stretched and I couldn't help noticing that under her drab clothes she was a very good-looking woman.

'Me, too,' she said. She looked at me very seriously. 'Your mother sounds like a remarkable woman, but a lot to live up to,' she said. 'Someone like that could be enough to make you feel that you were a bit second rate, wouldn't you say? But without any real reason, of course. That would be nonsense. We all have our own strengths and we must learn to respect them. There's no need to envy other people's.' She smiled at me with her kind grey eyes all twinkly. 'It's funny about relatives, even mothers,' she said. 'We can't choose them like we choose our friends, and sometimes they're hard to love. Personally I've never thought it was necessary to love relatives, even mothers, if you can't. It's good to respect them, if you can. And I would say that your mother merits your respect even if you can't give her your love. I'd say that was the truth of the matter.'

She gave a brisk little nod and headed for the door.

'See you tomorrow,' she said.

When she had gone I found that her words had left me with the most tremendous sense of relief. I had been told it wasn't obligatory to love my mother unquestioningly. I wasn't wicked because I couldn't quite manage it. Someone else, someone sensible and qualified like Anna Weingott, had said that the remarkable Rosie Dupuis could be hard to live up to. The relief was indescribable. Anna was right. My mother did merit my respect. If I could get used to the idea of that, maybe one day I would even be able to give her my love as I had when I was a child.

Allie stopped typing. The words had poured out, half composed like the first draft of one of her stories, but totally the truth. She was suddenly exhausted but very calm. She thought she might go to bed early and sleep. The quietness, she was sure, would only cradle her.

Pierre returned from Épernay in the late afternoon. Rosie had waited for him with some trepidation. She had always understood why the Greeks slew the bearers of bad news. She wished she got on with Pierre better, but there was a coolness between them which she knew was her own fault. It was because he was his father's son, and that wasn't fair. But somehow she could not warm to him. And had he not come to Les Hérissons, she might not have lost Allie.

She cornered him in the hallway at the foot of the stairs as he was going up to the rooms he shared with Feathers. He looked alarmed when she said she wanted to speak to him, and then his expression became set and bland.

'What about?' he asked.

'Feathers,' she said, and thought she saw a flicker of relief before he raised his eyebrows enquiringly.

'Not here. Your grandmother won't be down for a while, we'll talk in her parlour,' she suggested, and then remembered it was there she had told Madame, many years ago, that she was pregnant by Pierre's father.

'As you wish,' he said and opened the door for her.

Neither of them sat, and Rosie said abruptly: 'Feathers is pregnant.' There seemed no point in beating about the bush.

He looked winded.

'Pregnant!' he said, astonished. 'But she can't be.'

'I'm afraid she can,' Rosie said.

He sat down heavily on the small sofa. 'I don't understand . . .'

It was Rosie's turn to raise her eyebrows.

'You mean there's been another man?' He was beginning to sound angry.

'Not exactly,' Rosie said cautiously. 'She was raped.'

'Raped?' His face flushed scarlet. 'Do you think I'm a fool, Aunt Rosie?'

'No, I don't think you're a fool and I think she is telling the truth.'

'Then who raped her?' She could see he was fighting to keep control, but his anger wasn't for the man who had raped his wife. His anger was for Feathers. She began to get angry herself.

'She won't say.'

'And you believe her?'

'Don't sound so scornful. I do believe her. It was during the *vendange*. Probably at the *cochelet* when you were in Paris.' She saw his eyes move shiftily in his head. Pierre, it seemed, did not wish to be reminded of Paris in this context. She added: 'She let someone kiss her and it got out of hand.'

'Let someone kiss her?' He was outraged. 'What was she doing letting someone kiss her?'

'Perhaps she was seeking affection,' she suggested tartly. 'She gets little enough.'

He stared at her, then shut his eyes and sighed deeply.

'And how would you know that?' he asked disdainfully.

'Pierre, if things were right between you and Feathers your

351

reaction to the fact that your wife is pregnant would not be that it is impossible and that it must be another man.'

He was silent.

'What do you expect her to do when she has no love in her life?' Rosie demanded.

'Stay chaste,' he said firmly. 'Not get pregnant by other men. Accept that I do love her in my own way. However, this, of course, is the end of the marriage.'

Rosie could have hit him. She advanced two paces and said: 'Stay chaste indeed. Men! What the hell do you get up to on your little trips to Paris on your own? Are you staying chaste while you neglect your wife? Not likely! Do you think I'm a fool, or that your wife is a fool? Business in Paris! What business? A mistress more like it. Your wife is a truly beautiful and delightful young woman. What's sauce for the goose is sauce for the gander. You may find it difficult to accept but she has the same appetites as you do. She wouldn't have let herself get pregnant if she hadn't. As a Dupuis and your father's son, you should know that.'

She paused for breath and he said coldly: 'I am very aware of my wife's appetites. I remember them well. Which is why I do not think that she was raped.'

Rosie snorted. 'She was just mad enough to fall in love with you. She's no slut and you know it. Okay, you made the great generous gesture of marrying her because she was pregnant. But would you have done that if you'd been able to marry Allie? Of course you wouldn't. Feathers would be struggling to bring up her Patric in some Boston slum and you'd never have given her or your baby another thought. But having married her, have you given her a minute's real happiness since she's been here? I wouldn't have said so.'

His hands had begun to shake at the mention of Allie.

'I am very fond of Feathers,' he said stiffly. 'I do my best and I do not care to think of her being pregnant by another man. Who is it that's supposed to have raped her? Tell me.'

'She won't say.'

'If she was raped, she would say.' He smashed his fist on to the arm of the sofa. 'I know,' he said, his voice intense. 'It was Carlos. She was having an affair with Carlos. She made it obvious she was attracted to him. She flaunted it, she wanted me to know, and now she has done this.'

'Oh, for God's sake.' Suddenly weary, Rosie sank down into Madame's chair. 'Can't you just think how she is feeling for a moment? You're kind to her but you treat her with complete indifference. Madame is downright cruel to her. Luke is the only one at Les Hérissons who is halfway decent to her. If it was Carlos who raped her she's too nice a person to make trouble for his father, the one person in this place who is on her side. Luke's position would be intolerable if his son was responsible. You understand nothing. You once said to me that you wanted to be a different man from your father. My God! You've still got a long way to go.'

He looked at her and then dropped his head into his hands.

'I shouldn't have married her,' he said. 'But I never thought she'd be unfaithful.'

Rosie sighed. 'She hasn't been unfaithful. And why shouldn't you have married her? Allie's my daughter, but I can tell you, you got the better bargain. Allie would have broken your heart. She breaks hearts wholesale. Instead, you're breaking Feathers'.'

He was hardly listening to her. He was muttering to himself: 'I need to know whose child it is. I need to know the truth. It's Carlos. I know it's Carlos.'

He stood up, his fists clenched.

'It's intolerable! Intolerable!' he said. 'I have to know.'

His face set and his eyes staring he strode to the door. He opened it and went out, slamming it behind him. She heard his footsteps thudding down the hall. Alone again, Rosie sat down and stared into the small fire that burned in the grate. She felt deeply depressed. She hadn't handled it right. She'd done it all wrong. She'd lost her temper and let her dislike of his father show through. She had let Feathers down. She heard the front door slam and was relieved that at least he wasn't running to Feathers' room. It would be better if he had calmed down before he spoke to his wife.

Then sitting in the sudden quiet of the room it dawned on her where he was going. He would be looking for Luke, and the question was, once he had found him, what would he do?

Pierre ran Luke to earth in the coldest of the cellars where the storage vats were kept and where the resting wine would be taken after it had been cleansed. Luke looked up in surprise as he heard

Pierre's footsteps clattering across the stone floors.

'Good afternoon,' he said cheerfully, but Pierre was in no mood for the niceties.

'Where is your son?' he asked abruptly.

'Why?' Luke sounded cautious.

'Never mind why. Where is he?'

Luke leaned his back against one of the vats. 'He's in London as far as I know.'

'What's his address?'

Luke scratched his head. 'What is all this about, Pierre?'

'What this is all about,' Pierre said through clenched teeth, 'is that your son had an affair with my wife and made her pregnant. I wish to inform him so that he can take on the baby. I'm not going to. I shall send her to join him wherever he is.'

Luke smote his forehead with his fist. 'Ah! That is the most terrible news,' he groaned. 'Terrible.'

'It will be terrible for him if I get my hands on him,' Pierre said. He was aware of a confusion. He wasn't sure what he wanted to do. What he would have liked best would be to kill both his wife and her lover. He felt hurt and betrayed. He had done his best for Feathers – and now this. And he had guessed correctly. His instincts were right. It was Carlos who was to blame. Luke's reaction proved it.

'What does Feathers say about this?' Luke was asking.

'I haven't spoken to her yet. Rosie told me the glad tidings,' Pierre said, his voice bitter.

'Not glad tidings, Pierre.' Luke took a long breath as if screwing up his courage. He was looking at the ground like a man shamed. His voice was so low that Pierre had to strain to hear. 'Didn't Rosie tell you that Carlos raped Feathers?'

Pierre's instant reaction to this information was that Rosie and Feathers had cooked up the story between them.

'Is that what they told you, too?' he asked contemptuously.

Luke looked up sharply. 'Neither of them told me anything. That is what my son told me.'

'He told you?' Pierre could not believe it.

'Yes. It happened on the night of the *cochelet*. They had been dancing together. They were both a little drunk. Carlos misunderstood . . .' his voice trailed away. 'He came to me badly scratched and with his face damaged. She had tried to fight him off but he had refused to stop. He hurt her, too. She had to stay in her room the next day.

'She told him to get out. To leave Les Hérissons and never come back or she would tell what had happened. He had to come to me because he had no money to go. He told me the truth. The worst of it was that he didn't seem to understand that he had done anything wrong. He seemed to feel that women were meant to be treated like that.' He turned his back and leaned his face against the barrel as if he could not face Pierre. His voice was sad in the chill of the cellar. 'I never told Feathers I knew. I thought she would be more comfortable if she thought no one knew. But to think that she has been suffering this ever since then. Oh, God! The poor child. And what makes it worse is that I've always suspected that she stayed quiet because he is my son.'

Pierre stood uncertain of what to do or say. He was suddenly aware of the cold and he shivered. His anger had gone and like Luke he felt only an overwhelming sadness. Poor Feathers. Nothing went right for her and nothing, he thought with a rush of self-pity, went right for him, either.

Awkwardly he moved towards Luke and put his hand on his shoulder.

'Please,' he said. 'You mustn't blame yourself.'

Luke turned. 'It's hard not to. The sins of the fathers . . .'

The words struck a chord.

'Yes,' Pierre said thoughtfully. 'The sins of the fathers.' He made a despairing little gesture. 'I must go and talk to Feathers,' he said. 'Thank you for telling me the truth.'

'I am very fond of Feathers.' Luke shook his head, his eyes closed. 'It will always be my shame that my son has done her such damage. She deserves better than she gets from this place.'

'And than she has had from me. I did not believe the truth when I was told it.' Pierre put his hand on Luke's shoulder again, and without looking back walked leaden-footed to the cellar steps and up into the grey mist of the evening.

Feathers was in the little sitting room off their bedroom. Seeing her there, wearing a wrap-around dressing gown and stretched out on the chaise longue, it occurred to him that for the past few months she had spent most of her time in this room. If she was not in Reims she was hidden here. She rarely went downstairs these days except for meals and he recalled that sometimes she had even eaten supper in this room.

She looked up anxiously as he came in but said nothing.

'Rosie has told me,' he said abruptly.

She shut her eyes in relief. 'I'm sorry, Pierre.'

He wanted to expurge all guilt. 'I didn't believe that you had been raped.'

Her head jerked defiantly upwards. 'Well, it's true.'

'I know. Luke told me.'

'Luke!' He could see she was shocked. 'How did he know?'

'Carlos confessed to him. He needed money to get away from here.'

Her head drooped as she looked down at her hands. 'Poor Luke,' she said softly. 'How dreadful for him to know. He never said a word to me.'

'He thought you would be happier if he didn't know.'

'He was right. But I'm glad he knew if he convinced you.'

She put down the book she had been reading and stood up, pulling her gown tight round her. Then she walked to the window and stood with her back to him.

'It was partly my fault,' she said. 'Carlos liked me, and I could see he found me attractive. It was so long since anyone had made me feel attractive . . . I suppose I gave him the wrong idea.' She turned to face him. 'I'm not putting any blame on you, Pierre, but I'm like anyone else. I need love and affection. I suppose I was vulnerable. So it was a bit my fault. But he's a savage in a way, that man. He thinks he can take anything he wants. He wanted me and I couldn't stop him.'

'Some blame is mine,' he protested and realised that he meant it. 'Rosie told me a few home truths today. What she said was right. I haven't treated you well.' He realised, with considerable dismay, that his treatment of Feathers had been no better in its own way than that his father would have meted out. The old Adam had not yet been expelled. 'We'll try again,' he said eagerly. 'I have a plan that will make Les Hérissons ours. It will be your home – the home of your own that you wanted. We'll be a proper family as we should have been from the beginning. We'll make it all work for Patric and this new baby.'

She looked at him round-eyed. 'You'll bring up this baby?'

'Someone has to.' He said it lightly though the idea filled him with more dismay.

'Oh, Pierre!' Impulsively she walked to put her arms round him and nuzzle her face into his neck. He could feel the dampness of her tears.

'Hey! Hey!' he said, and lifted her head. He had been playacting, but looking into the depths of her violet eyes and seeing how her full mouth trembled, what he felt was not false. He bent to kiss her tenderly, affectionately, but as she clung to him, he kissed her again, differently. He was remembering as he felt her breasts pressed against him and smelt the scent of her hair the nights they had shared in Boston before she had become pregnant and before Allie had come into his life. She had excited him then, and she was exciting him now. And in a strange and curious way the brutality of the rape excited him, too. The thought of another man invading her body made him want to love her gently and sweetly – as his whores loved each other. That would wipe away the memory of Carlos for both of them.

He kissed her again, more deeply, and she was clinging to him, panting little sighs. Gently he stroked her hair, then her eyes, kissing her eyelids, his hands doing soft and tender things. Remembering exactly how his whores did it, he carefully untied the strings of her dressing gown and drew it back. Then he gently steered her into their bedroom, kissing her face and lips as they moved. Carefully he arranged her on their bed and began to lick her nipples and then down over her rounded belly to the soft hair and soft wetness below, causing her to sigh and moan. He pretended that it was not his tongue that was causing those convulsive little movements of her hips or his fingers that had strengthened her nipples to dark red, pointed sentries. He imagined that it was another woman who was doing these tender, loving things to his wife, and that when the time for gentleness was over, it would be his male strength that would engulf her and complete her pleasure, superceding and wiping out the brutal strength that had entered her last.

She lay there, wide open for him, begging him with her huge, glistening eyes to take her. Her hands slid down her body and her legs parted wider and she opened a tempting, shining entrance for him with her fingers. Conscious of his maleness he

357

stood and let her see the hardness of his erection. Her free hand tentatively stroked him as she watched his face. Then he lowered himself between the fingers that gave him passageway and he was riding her as she clung to him, her small teeth biting into his shoulder while he did the one final thing that only a man could do to a woman.

Afterwards neither of them spoke. She looked at him as if something unbelievable had happened. He was thankful for her silence as he let her rest her head on his shoulder before she slept.

Rosie wanted to go home to Philippe but she also wanted to see Luke. She felt it was not a good idea to go looking for him. It would be better if they met naturally. She sat quietly, listening for what seemed a very long time. After about ten minutes she heard Pierre return and run upstairs, and then silence. A few minutes later she recognised Luke's footsteps coming down the hallway and she slipped from Madame's parlour, bracing herself for the encounter.

He stopped in his tracks when he saw her and she noted that he looked tired and defeated. His shoulders were slumped, and his boxer's face was grey.

'Ah, Rosie,' he said abruptly. 'Well met. I want to talk to you.'

'And I want to talk to you.' She grinned at him cheerfully to make it clear that she had nothing ominous to say. 'Come on. Let's get away from here. We'll go for a drive.'

He just nodded and moved to open the front door for her and they walked together down the steps to where her car was parked.

'Here.' She handed him the keys. 'You drive.'

'Where to?' he asked as if making decisions was beyond him.

'We'll go to that Bar Tabac in Ludes and speak English so no one understands,' she said. 'I don't know about you, but I could do with something stronger than champagne.'

She grinned at him again but received no answering smile. His expression was grim as he cranked the car and settled himself behind the wheel before driving off rather faster than she enjoyed.

Neither spoke until they were seated in the gloomy little bar, a glass of Marc de Champagne in front of each of them. The customers, agricultural workers with mud on their boots, glanced at them furtively and then looked away.

'Madame always insisted on a glass of this after any kind of shock,' Rosie said, tentatively swirling the alcohol round in her glass. 'And I had a bit of a shock today.'

'I know,' he said. 'Pierre told me.'

'I guessed he'd gone to look for you. He did find you then?'

'Yes. He did.'

She touched him lightly on the arm. 'I'm sorry, Luke. Did he tell you the whole story?'

His grey eyes were bleak. 'You mean about the rape.'

'Yes. It must have been a terrible shock for you.'

'Not really. I knew.'

'You knew!' Rosie stared at him, astonished.

'Carlos told me the night it happened. Feathers had told him to get out. He wanted money from me. I gave him money and took him to the station and sent him on his way.'

She felt bewildered and a little betrayed. 'But you and I . . .'

'. . . went to his bedroom and found him gone. That's right. I was acting, Rosie. I thought it better if I pretended to know nothing about it. I thought Feathers would be happier if I knew nothing about it. I thought I was protecting her. The only good thing in the whole mess is that I was at least able to convince Pierre that Feathers was telling the truth and that Carlos did rape her.'

She sighed with relief. 'Thank God for that. He didn't believe me, and I doubt if he would have believed Feathers. What happened? Do you know what he's going to do?'

He shook his head. 'He went off to find Feathers. His whole mood had changed. I have a feeling it's going to be as right as it can be.'

She clasped her hands as if she were about to applaud. 'You think he'll accept the baby?'

'I don't know.' He was silent for a moment. 'It's going to be my grandchild, Rosie.' His leaned his elbow on the table, hid his head in his hand and said, his voice full of despair, 'I feel so responsible. I feel terrible. My son comes out of the blue into our lives. He was only here a few days before he went out of our lives again, but God Almighty, what destruction, what havoc those few days have caused. It crossed my mind that this could happen when he told me what he had done, but I rejected the very idea as too impossible, too unfair. But I suppose nothing is too impossible and unfair in life.'

'Not for poor Feathers. Maybe she's doomed to be a victim,' Rosie said sadly. 'Life is unfair to her, but there is no reason why you should feel responsible.'

'Don't be silly, Rosie,' he said impatiently. 'He's my son. A rapist.'

'Feathers has to take some responsibility, too,' she said, trying to console him. 'I watched her dancing with him. She led him on.'

'But no means no. She told him to stop. He admitted it.'

'True. But she was playing with fire. I love her very much but she's no judge of character.'

'And my son's a bad character.'

'Maybe,' she said calmly, thinking it pointless to protest otherwise. 'But he's got a long time to improve. Like I said once before, he's an adolescent.'

'A dangerous one,' he said angrily and sat up straight, downed the Marc in one and then coughed until his eyes ran.

'A bit strong?' she asked, unable to keep the mischief out of her voice as he struggled for breath.

'Not as smooth as we make. Anyway, I shall have to leave Les Hérissons,' he said grimly. 'I'll get out tomorrow.'

'What!' She picked up her own glass and downed it, then spluttering said: 'That's the worst shock of the day, Luke. You can't go. I need you. Please don't even think about it. Don't frighten me like that.'

She knew there was a pleading note in her voice, but she didn't care. At that moment she could think of nothing worse than Luke West going away.

'But how can I stay?' he said patiently, as if explaining something to a backward child. 'Every day of their lives when Feathers and Pierre see me they will remember what my son did. There's no chance of either of them forgetting while I'm about.'

'What makes you think they'll forget it if you're not about?' Rosie said sharply. 'I don't care about Pierre and Feathers. Damn them. They must grow up and settle their own differences. We've all done the best we can for them. But now I'm thinking of myself. I don't want you to go. I won't let you go.'

He was looking at her with the most curious expression on his face.

'Why don't you want me to go, Rosie?' he asked.

'Because I need you. I lean on you. I feel safe when you're around. I know that I can rely on you. There isn't anybody else.'

'Philippe?' he asked softly.

She was overcome with a wave of guilt at her disloyalty to Philippe, but what she had said was true.

She folded her hands as if in prayer and held them to her mouth, looking down to hide the tears in her eyes. 'Luke, I have loved Philippe for most of my life, but it is not easy at this moment. Françoise is destroying our marriage, slowly but surely, and it is killing me to sit helpless and watch her do it. She makes Philippe happy. He feels fulfilled in that he has a child of his own to love. And she has most cleverly cut me out of his life. She is his priority now. I can't break his heart by telling him what she's doing. How can I describe to him the insolence to me that he can't see; the way she gloats over her triumphs. She's not even twelve but she's wicked and clever. She's also taking him from what work he is able to do. The sales side of the business is in a terrible mess. We haven't had a new client for six months. His agents are getting desperate from lack of direction. The stocks are getting too high and the turnover too low. Somehow I have to do something to save it. I can't let it go. It's been my life's work. But it's all too much for one person. And Philippe can't bear to hand over to anyone else. It would finish him if he felt that he wasn't in control.

'I am telling you all this to prove how much I need you. While you are running the vineyards and overseeing the making of the wine, I know that there is one area where I have no worries. I feel safe with you here. You are very important to me, Luke. Not only in a business way. You've become a dear and loved friend.'

He had been listening with his head resting on his hand again. He looked up when she finished speaking, and she was startled by the unconcealed longing in his eyes.

'You're important to me, too, Rosie. You have been since the

361

first time I saw you,' he said, his voice intense.

She had always sensed his attraction for her but dismissed the sexual invitation that he discreetly left open. Suddenly that invitation was more pressing, and instead of dismissiveness she felt that hot pleasurable churning inside that once only Philippe had been able to arouse. She knew her own eyes had widened in surprise and that her colour had heightened. His steady gaze never left her face, and the heat within grew. He knew what he was doing to her. She knew he knew it.

'I must go home,' she said abruptly, pushing her chair away from the table. 'I'll drive you back.'

'No,' he said. 'I'll walk.'

It was a relief. She did not want to be close to him in the intimacy of the car – not until she had cooled down a little.

She nodded and when they were outside and he had opened the car door for her, she carefully put her hand on his arm. 'You will stay?' Her voice sounded uncharacteristically timid.

'I'll stay.' He hesitated as if he was about to say more, then gave her a sort of salute and quickly turned to walk back in the direction of Les Hérissons.

She sat quietly in the car for a while to compose herself. Thinking over the conversation she realised that it had helped her to voice her anxieties about Françoise. Something was going to have to be done about the girl. She had been feeble and let the situation get out of hand. She had no positive idea of what to do, but at least she could start working on it. And she would take the first step this evening. She had a lot to say to Philippe – she wanted to tell him this latest Les Hérissons news, and it was time they talked about the business. Tonight Françoise would take her supper in the nursery. It would be a battle to make her do so, but this time it was a battle that Rosie was going to win.

Rosanne had been given a puppet theatre for a Christmas present and she was contentedly playing with it in the nursery while waiting for her supper. She had just arranged all the puppets for a performance of Cinderella when the door opened with a bang. Françoise stomped in, her pretty face contorted by bad temper.

Rosanne was not used to seeing Françoise at this time. She was usually downstairs with the grown-ups – an arrangement which suited Rosanne very well. In the three months that the girl had been at Les Hérissons, Rosanne had managed to have very little to do with her. They had certainly not become friends.

'What's the matter with you?' she asked, deliberately cheeky since she was irritated that the disagreeable Françoise had appeared in the nursery at all.

The older girl did not answer but flung herself into Nanny Shepherd's chair. She threw her legs over the arm and sat scowling, kicking her patent leather shoes against the chair's upholstered side.

'Nanny will give you socks if she catches you doing that,' Rosanne pointed out.

'She wouldn't dare.'

'She might,' Rosanne said, but privately conceded that Françoise was probably right. Since it was obvious that Papa Philippe was besotted with his beastly daughter, all the staff were wary of her. And she could get extremely unpleasant if she was thwarted in any way.

'Not eating downstairs then?' asked Rosanne mockingly. She had neither fear of nor interest in the older girl and rather enjoyed baiting her. 'Did Mama get rid of you?'

'Your Mama will be sorry,' Françoise said viciously.

'Oh, really? What will you do to make her sorry?' Rosanne was registering how ugly a pretty face could become in temper. She decided that even though Françoise was a blonde and blue-eyed beauty she would be perfect casting for the wicked witch.

'Never you mind,' Françoise said, her voice furious. 'And don't be insolent to me. Or I'll do to you what I did to my baby brother.'

Rosanne regarded her with interest. 'What did you do?'

'Something,' Françoise said darkly.

'Tried to kill him?' said Rosanne, hazarding a guess.

Françoise stopped kicking the chair and looked round furtively. 'How did you know?' she whispered.

Rosanne was fascinated with the turn of the conversation. 'Because when you're bad-tempered you look as if you could go around killing babies,' she said. 'Did you kill him?'

'No.'

'How did you try to do it?'

'With a pillow,' Françoise said sullenly.

'Didn't it work or did you get frightened?'

'I'm never frightened of anything,' Françoise said defiantly. 'I would have done it but my stepfather came in and stopped me.'

'Gosh!' Rosanne was impressed despite herself. 'Perhaps it was just as well. You could have been sent to the guillotine.'

'I got sent here instead.' She made it sound as if the guillotine would have been preferable.

Rosanne digested this information, aware it could be useful. But Françoise was obviously beginning to regret having mentioned the subject.

'If you tell your mother,' she said, 'I'll do it to you.'

'I'm too big. I'd kick you. Anyway, my mother knows,' Rosanne said airily as insurance since she had every intention of telling her mother.

'How do you know she knows?'

Rosanne improvised. 'Just something I heard her saying to Nanny about watching you with pillows and wasn't it lucky we didn't have any babies.'

'Does Papa know?'

'Probably.'

Françoise was silent, then said 'It's all very well for you. You're with your own family and your mother didn't send you off when she married someone else. Nor did she have another baby. My mother was sickening over that baby. Cooing and talking awful baby talk to it. She didn't want to know about me any more. My stepfather always hated me, and you'd got my own papa. I didn't have anyone. And I haven't got anyone here except my papa. The rest of you hate me.'

'Well, you are pretty hateful, Françoise,' Rosanne said with her usual devastating logic.

'I am not. I am only hateful to people who hate me. Like your mother. And I hate her.'

'I'd noticed. But you didn't give her much chance to like you, did you?'

'I don't want her to like me. She stole my papa. Everything's been her fault. I'm going to make her sorry and you can tell her that if you like.'

'I don't need to tell her. My mama is very clever and she knows what you're doing.'

'Not clever enough,' grunted Françoise.

'We shall see,' said Rosanne, thinking if not the wicked witch, certainly one of the ugly stepsisters. Ugliness wasn't always just in someone's face, she thought, as she began to rearrange the stage of her little theatre. She didn't want to talk to Françoise any more, and anyway, soon it would be suppertime, and she was hungry.

But Françoise had not finished.

'I don't know how you can stand living here,' she said, kicking the chair again. 'It's so dreadfully boring and provincial.'

Rosanne wasn't sure what provincial meant, but she understood boring, and Les Hérissons wasn't boring.

'What's boring about it?' she asked.

'No shops, no life, nothing to do, just a load of grapes and boring people. I want to go back to Paris to live.'

'Then why don't you?'

Françoise threw her a vicious look.

'Oh, of course, they don't want you back, do they?' Rosanne said cheerfully. 'Well, that's too bad. You'll just have to put up with all us boring people.'

That night when her mother came in and sat on her bed to kiss her goodnight, Rosanne wrapped her arms round Rosie's neck and said into her scented dark hair: 'I've got something to tell you, Mama.'

'What's that, darling?'

'I'm going to whisper it.'

Her mother laughed. 'Okay,' she said and leaned her ear towards Rosanne's mouth.

'I know why Françoise was sent here.'

'So do I,' her mother said cheerfully. 'Because her parents were going away.'

'No,' Rosanne whispered. 'Because she tried to kill her baby brother. With a cushion. Her stepfather caught her and stopped her or she'd have been guillotined, wouldn't she? They sent her to us instead.'

Her mother sat bolt upright.

'Rosanne, what are you saying!' Her voice was shocked. 'You mustn't make up these terrible stories.'

'I'm not making it up.' Rosanne was aggrieved. 'She told me herself. She was furious because she had to have supper in the nursery.'

'I know,' her mother said. 'Now tell me exactly what she said.'

Rosanne repeated the conversation as verbatim as she could remember while her mother listened.

'I pretended you knew already because she said she'd do it to me if I told.'

'Did she now!' Rosie said, her voice grim. 'And they sent her here after that.'

'That's right.' Rosanne decided she wouldn't repeat the bit about Françoise hating her mother in case her mother was hurt by it. 'She says Papa is the only one here who likes her.'

'She's right,' Rosie sighed.

'That's because she's ugly. You can be ugly and pretty at the same time, can't you, Mama?'

'You can indeed.' Her mother was sitting thinking in the soft light from the bedside lamp, her eyes downcast. She, thought Rosanne, really was beautiful. Then Rosie sighed, smiled a determined sort of smile, took Rosanne into her arms and hugged her. 'But, darling, I don't want you ever to mention this to Papa Philippe, will you? It would really hurt him very much, so it's a secret that you and I will keep just for us. Okay?'

'If you like,' Rosanne said cautiously. 'But what if she tries to do it to me?'

'She won't. You're too big,' her mother said, refusing to be serious and tickling Rosanne until she was giggling. 'And I don't expect she was telling the truth anyway. She was probably making it all up.'

'Maybe,' said Rosanne, getting ready to say her prayers. But she knew in her heart that Françoise hadn't been making it up. Still, if her mother wanted to think that, why not? But it was silly not to tell Papa Philippe, she thought, as she snuggled down and squeezed her eyes shut ready for sleep, but if that was the way her mama wanted it, that was the way it would be.

Pierre felt very strange the next morning when he woke to find Feathers curled closer to him than she had ever been since they came to Les Hérissons.

She was sound asleep, her hair tousled, mouth faintly parted to show her small white teeth. And she was, he conceded, very beautiful. But he wasn't entirely sure what he felt about her.

Yesterday his feelings had been nearer to love than in the entire time they had known each other. In fact, he had experienced a sense of something very deep and serious for her that surely was love. Almost what he had felt for Allie. But could he hold on to the feeling? Would it drift away? Looking at her now he felt the stirrings of desire again. He could make love to her now, but how much more wonderful it would be with another girl as well. To make love to her and Allie at the same time would be the ultimate experience. To watch them undressing each other, playing languidly together, arousing each other, tasting each other's flesh, opening each other – for him . . .

He felt himself spring into stiffness and reached for her, sliding his hand inside the silk of her nightgown. With a little cry of contentment she woke and turned to him, soft and feminine, wanting him, and letting him do whatever he wanted . . .

He had even contemplated taking her to Paris with him. In the light of Rosie's strictures of the day before, it was a little unfortunate that he had an appointment in Paris. And it truly was a business appointment. He had planned to visit Madame Beauregard as well but that would not now be necessary. Not because he was sexually sated. As much as Feathers had pleasured him, he had no doubts that he would be able to fill two of the Beauregard girls to his and their satisfaction. But in future it might be wiser just to keep Madame Beauregard's *maison* for the occasional treat as long as this renewed sexual interest in his wife lasted. Since there were suspicions at Les Hérissons about his visits to Paris, it would be better if this interest could be sustained. He dwelled fleetingly on how much more permanent his interest would be if he could introduce a second girl into the marital bed. Somehow he could not imagine Feathers agreeing to that, no matter how much she deferred to him in every other way.

Today he took a taxi to an anonymous building behind the Bourse where a lawyer, Maître Bousquet, had his offices and where Jack Patterson had his. Jack, a fellow Bostonian, had been taking a crash course in French when Pierre encountered him at the Sorbonne. Lanky, loose-limbed and Boston top-drawer, Patterson was the first male friend that Pierre had ever had. Circumstances – the fact that they were both from Boston and knew no one else – had pushed them together. Jack was wild and wealthy; the only son of a stockbroker who had decided that for the sake of the family reputation it would be better if his son stayed abroad for a while. Unfortunately Jack had been careless enough to make the daughter of one of his father's wealthier clients pregnant and then refused to do the decent thing and marry the girl. He was quite content to remain in Paris while a healthy remittance was paid into his bank each month. He also dabbled gently in import/export without letting *les affaires* spoil his playtime. Paris in the twenties suited Jack Patterson's style. He had introduced Pierre to the Moulin Rouge, the erotic appeal of Josephine Baker, the jazz clubs of Montparnasse, and also to Madame Beauregard's establishment. In return, Pierre had fired his new friend with an enthusiasm for champagne and fine wine. It was a taste that the young Patterson would have acquired earlier had it not been for Prohibition. So, in the three years that Feathers waited lonely at the house on the Ile de la Cité, her husband and his new friend played at being *les bon vivants* around the brothels and the cabarets of the Champs Élysées and the Latin Quarter.

It was to Jack that Pierre had confided his dissatisfaction with the situation at Les Hérissons. And it was Jack who had said airily: 'Why don't we buy the place? I'll sell the product and you can make it. We could go into the bootlegging business. There's a huge market in the States. All you have to do is drop it in cases offshore and they come and pick it up. You get paid even if it sinks.'

'Jack, making champagne is a serious business,' Pierre had said. 'If you were exporting my product, I'd fire you if you didn't come up with the goods.'

Jack snorted his amusement. 'Since you haven't the money to buy the place, my dear Pierre, and you would be borrowing mine, believe me I would sell your champagne so that you could pay me back and with interest.' He gazed at himself admiringly in one of the mirrors of the Deux Magot where they were drinking, and added cheerfully: 'Quite a lot of interest.'

'I don't know if it would be that easy,' Pierre said. 'French law is very different from ours. I don't think I could do a thing unless Allie and Rosanne were willing to sell. I'm sure they're entitled to a share.'

368

'The elder one lives in the States, doesn't she?'

Pierre nodded.

'Ask her then. If she has no plans to return, what does she want with a vineyard in France?'

'It's impossible for me to ask her,' Pierre said, his voice positive.

'Why?'

'It just is.'

'Okay, I'll ask her. No harm done, and it must give us some bargaining power if she's prepared to sell. What's her address?'

Swept along on Jack's persuasion, Pierre gave him the address. But Jack had received no reply from his letter. Fired with the idea of dealing in champagne, which was, he said, a pursuit worthy of a gentleman, he suggested that perhaps they had better see a French lawyer to find out exactly what the position was.

Maître Bousquet, the advocat, a small, block-shaped man with smooth black hair and a matching small black moustache was waiting with Jack in a room full of dusty books and piles of red-tied bundles of paper. The introductions over, Maître Bousquet impatiently shuffled the papers on the cluttered desk before him like a man with no time to waste. Pierre was made aware he had been five minutes late.

'Now, gentlemen,' the lawyer said, but addressing himself to Pierre. 'The situation is that you wish to acquire the property Les Hérissons for yourselves? Is that not correct?'

Pierre nodded.

'You must understand, gentlemen, that French law is very different from yours in America. Here we follow the Code Napoléon which is very precise on the subject of property and inheritance. You, Monsieur Dupuis, will in God's good time certainly inherit a portion of this property if you are prepared to wait for your grandmother's demise. However, in the meantime, since the property is hers, there is nothing to stop your grandmother selling it to you or to anyone else. I personally consider it most unlikely that she will do so.' He nodded sagely. 'In my experience, landowners, and particularly landowners in wine-growing areas, never sell land or property. But there is no reason why you or anyone else should not approach her, including Monsieur Patterson here.

369

'I have made enquiries and have ascertained that the house and the land are hers unentailed. I gather that she married,' he coughed delicately, 'beneath her. There was a pre-marriage contract drawn up so that in the event of her being deceased before her husband and without issue, the property would revert to her own family.

'As it is, the property remains entirely hers, but you should understand that on her death, legally she can only bequeath it in either two portions or three.' He paused and picked up a pair of spectacles which he put on his nose. 'I am right in thinking that there are two young women with a claim on the property?' he asked.

'Yes,' Pierre said, 'my Aunt Rosie's two daughters.' He wondered if he should mention that in fact Allie was his half-sister and Rosanne was in reality Allie's child and then decided not to unless it was absolutely necessary.

'*Donc*,' said Maître Bousquet. 'If your grandmother shares her property two ways, it will be apportioned half to you and the other half to your Aunt's daughters. This comes about from the fact that had your respective fathers lived, they would have received fifty per cent each on their mother's death. Since neither has survived, you and these two girls now stand in their shoes. Each of you can only receive what would have legally gone to your respective fathers had they lived. However, if your grandmother chooses, she can split her property three ways and bequeath to her daughter-in-law one third, leaving one third for you and one third to her granddaughters.'

'What about my own child?' Pierre asked. 'Does he have any claim?'

'Your child, on your death, will be entitled to your share of the property, be it a half or a third. Should either of your cousins produce issue, these children must share their mother's portion. This is the law and it cannot be changed. We do not disinherit our children or their children in France.'

Pierre thought over what had been said.

'So my only hope is that Grandmother will agree to sell, or that, when she dies, she doesn't leave anything to my aunt and I can persuade Allie and Rosanne to sell?'

'That is about it, Monsieur Dupuis. Inheritance laws here in France are very rigid. No Frenchman or woman likes to see property leave the family. But then, you are family. Perhaps you can persuade your grandmother to sell to you and indirectly to Monsieur Patterson since he has the finance.'

'The problem is,' Pierre said slowly, 'that Rosanne is really Allie's daughter but she is registered as my Aunt Rosie's child. Would her legal mother have power of attorney?'

It did not seem necessary to mention his relationship to Allie.

'If she is under age, yes. And if she is registered as your aunt's child it would be a complicated court case if you wished to challenge the inheritance.'

Rosie would block it, he thought, and he knew he could never put Allie through the shame of such a court case.

'Then the only hope is getting my grandmother to sell it to me since my aunt never will,' he said. 'But in any case I wouldn't do anything unless Allie agreed. Whatever happens, she must have her share.'

'A very commendable attitude, Monsieur Dupuis, but Monsieur Patterson tells me that this young woman has not replied to his letter.'

'I believe she has been ill,' Pierre said. Allie was rarely mentioned at Les Hérissons and never in front of him. But he had overheard Rosie speaking to Madame, and though he had not grasped exactly what was the matter, he had heard the word clinic mentioned.

'Your grandmother is in good health?' enquired the lawyer suggestively, his fingers knitted under his chin, his eyes to heaven.

'Very good, thank you,' Pierre said, guilt at what he was trying to do suddenly attacking him.

'His grandmother is crazy about him,' Jack put in. 'I reckon he'll be able to persuade her.'

'Ah, that could be a help if that is true, Monsieur Dupuis.'

'She has been very kind to me.'

'Then it would seem there is little problem. Ask her.'

'Only if Allie agrees,' Pierre said stubbornly.

The lawyer shrugged and shuffled his papers, this time back into his briefcase.

'And, of course,' he added, 'there is the problem of your aunt. As you thought, the wine business and the artefacts are her and her husband's property. It would seem that the two businesses are interdependent. Do you have scruples about approaching Monsieur and Madame Lefevre?'

'Absolutely none,' said Pierre firmly, feeling the familiar spurt of resentment as he remembered Rosie's obvious distrust of him, 'but it might be better if that were done through you and Monsieur Patterson. I have no influence with her.'

The lawyer gave him a sharp, knowing look.

'But let's get the land first,' Jack said eagerly, twitching at his Celluloid collar as if it were choking him. 'Wouldn't you think that would be the best way?'

'Perhaps you should write to your cousin yourself, Monsieur Dupuis,' Maître Bousquet suggested. 'She might be more inclined to reply to you.'

Pierre thought about it and then sighed. He yearned for and at the same time feared contact with Allie.

'She may not even reply to me,' he warned.

'You have quarrelled?' asked the lawyer.

'No, not at all.'

'Then there can be no harm in writing.'

'I suppose not,' Pierre said slowly. 'All right. I'll contact her, and then we'll have to see.'

Chapter Thirteen

Allie had created a comfortable routine for herself at the Ziegman Clinic. When her breakfast was brought in at 8 a.m. one of the staff took Jessica out briefly while Allie ate waffles, drank coffee and read the morning paper.

A leisurely bath and casual dressing was followed by a brisk walk around the well-kept grounds with Jessica, girl and dog's breath steaming in the cold of the mountain air. Twenty minutes later they were back in the imposing entrance hall of the mansion that housed the clinic.

Allie returned to her room with smarting red cheeks and nipped fingers and toes. She warmed up by the open fire in her room, and then carefully applied her make-up and waited for Anna Weingott to appear. They generally talked for an hour or so before Allie was left to her typewriter or a session in the health and beauty gym that the clinic ran for its clientele. Allie never went to the gym. It meant she had to make conversation with other people and after a session with Anna she felt all talked out.

This morning, after yesterday's conversation about her mother, she was concerned that maybe she had said too much. A lingering feeling that her life was none of the psychiatrist's business remained. She could not quite convince herself that all that was happening in this cosy womb of a place was not sheer nonsense. She had always parried Anna's questions, but then the psychiatrist had been trying delicately to ask about her sexual attitudes and she found this embarrassing. Talking about her mother was different. And after yesterday's conversation, she awoke seeing her mother in a new light.

Walking through the frosty gardens with Jessica, she was realising that she had not always been fair to her mother. Her anger regarding Rosanne was unfounded. What else could Mimi and her mother have done? And it was her own fault in that she had not let herself love Rosanne when she was little. As her grandmother had said when Rosanne was just a baby, someone had to love the child, and it had been Rosie who had done it. With this reluctantly acquired new-found honesty, Allie was starting to accept that at first she had had no love to give Rosanne. She had seen her daughter as the irrefutable evidence of what had happened. Once she had begun to care about the child it had been too late to play the little mother.

But she most certainly did not feel that she had been unfair about her mother being pregnant without being married. That showed no moral standards – and look at what the consequences had been for her and Pierre. She felt her resentment of her mother's affair with Philippe was also justified. She only wished her father had not been with that dreadful Madame Claudette. But it might have been that her father was driven to it, and anyway, it was different for men.

And then came the alarming thought that perhaps she was driving Alexander to 'it' – and if it was different for men, did that apply to him as well?

Back in her room, her anxieties about what she had revealed to the psychiatrist grew. To reassure herself she unlocked the drawer of her desk and took out the pages she had typed the night before and sat down to read them through. As she read, a sense of dismay grew. When she had finished reading, she laid the type-written sheets on the desk, closed her eyes and sank her head in her hands. The words were certainly revealing but not in the way she had expected. What she had written spoke more about her than about her mother or the encounter with the psychiatrist. Her outpourings proved that she was a childish, whining young woman who had made no effort to grow up and face life. She was appalled at how selfish she sounded in her own words; appalled at how selfish she was.

Angry, she was about to tear up the incriminating pages when there was a gentle knock on the door of her room. Thinking that it was Anna she called for her to come in.

But it was not Anna. To Allie's surprise it was Jenny, breezing through the door, exuding that same rude health and appearing warmer in her manner than she had ever been before.

374

'Do you mind me coming?' she asked as she kissed Allie on the cheek. 'I wanted to see you but I thought if I asked you'd say no.'

'Why would I do that?' Allie asked, a little coolly.

'Because I haven't been very sympathetic to you in the past.'

'I hadn't noticed,' said Allie, lying.

'Well, I'm glad about that.' She looked around the big, comfortably furnished room and at the fire burning in the grate and moved to warm her hands. 'It's a lovely room. What a wonderful, peaceful view. Are you happy here?'

'Very,' said Allie, appreciating that she was. 'Do sit down.'

Jenny murmured thanks and sat on one of the hard-backed chairs, leaving the sofa for Allie.

'Alexander sends his love,' she said, 'and he's sad you don't want to see him.' She paused enquiringly.

'Not just yet,' Allie told her firmly and Jenny gave a little sigh.

'I came because I needed to tell you that it was all my fault that this happened.'

Allie raised her eyebrows. She felt surprisingly in control of the situation.

'Yes, my fault. I told Alexander to tackle you with . . . well, you know what. I thought it was best brought out into the open. I suppose I'm a very good nurse but I don't know much about dealing with the mind. No one does, except these new-fangled Freudians. Are they Freudians here?'

'I've no idea,' Allie said. 'Just rather unusual doctors. They only ever seem to listen.'

'Alexander says they're Germans and Austrians, so I guess they are Freudians.' Jenny shook her head doubtfully. 'I suppose it works, but I can't help feeling that we have to pick up the pieces of our lives ourselves – though you've had rather a lot of pieces to deal with, haven't you?'

She must have caught sight of Allie's set face, because she went on quickly: 'Alexander told me everything. Please don't be angry with him. He needed someone to talk to, just as they say you do. He is my brother, and you and I are sisters-in-law and I'd like us to be closer. I've always thought it would have been nice to have a sister, particularly such a beautiful sister.'

Allie found herself warming to Jenny, and she noticed for the first time that Jenny had clear grey eyes that were not unlike those of Anna Weingott. And her expression was soft and a little sad. She was not particularly good-looking; her features were too heavy, but her face was pleasant. Now she stood up and came to take Allie's hand, surprisingly kneeling on the floor to do so.

'Since Alexander showed me your mother's letter, I've thought so much about what you've been through. Not so much that German – he's dead and punished and though it must have been horrible and disgusting it was only a physical thing. I believe that in time I could live with that. I could wash it away as you must. But the baby is a different matter. Not to be called mother by your own child must be the saddest thing that can happen to a woman. To watch it growing up and never be able to say 'you're mine'. Oh Allie, I know it's possible to live without the love of a man, but it must hurt most terribly to live without the love of your own child.' She paused and added diffidently and without much conviction: 'If only you loved Alexander, there could be another.'

Suppressing her anger at the thought of Jenny reading all those secret things that her mother had revealed, Allie asked herself if Jenny had come to plead for Alexander. If she had, it was no good. Allie had hardly given Alexander a thought since she had been in this safe and sheltered place.

'Jenny,' Allie said, 'there won't be any more babies. I don't think that I shall ever love a man in that way. Not even Alexander.'

'Nor I,' said Jenny intensely.

Allie frowned in concentration. 'I don't understand.'

'I could never love a man in that way which means that I shall never have a child,' Jenny said. 'It is a loss I feel keenly, and therefore I can understand your loss.'

'But have you reason to feel as I do about men?' Allie asked, puzzled.

'No.'

'Then why can't you love one?'

'Because I know that nature made me differently.' She dropped her eyes and then looked up full into Allie's face. 'I know your secrets,' she said. 'It's only fair that you know mine.'

'I see,' said Allie. But she did not see. She was grasping to understand what Jenny meant, and anyway, she didn't particularly want to know her secrets.

'You're not shocked?'

Allie shook her head. 'No. No more than I am by myself.'

It was Jenny's turn to look puzzled. 'You mean it wasn't the lieutenant that made you this way? It was nature?'

'Well, it was something,' Allie said, still uncertain what the conversation was all about, but pleased to find that the mention of the lieutenant did not cause an icy hand to squeeze her heart as the very thought of him once had.

'You have been very brave.' To Allie's relief, Jenny got off her knees and went back to her chair. 'Mama and Papa are very anxious about you,' she volunteered. 'They asked me to ask if they could come and see you.'

'Not yet,' Allie said quickly.

'Can I come again?'

Allie considered. 'As long as you are not really coming for Alexander.'

'He doesn't even know I'm here,' Jenny protested. 'But I can't pretend that I don't want him to be happy.'

'So do I,' Allie said quietly, looking into the grey eyes that were so like Anna Weingott's. 'I love him but I should never have married him. But it seemed the only thing for me to do. What else do girls do but get married? And he wanted to marry me.'

'There are other things for girls to do these days,' Jenny protested. 'You earn money writing. I do my work with the Quakers. Men are not necessary. Only for babies.'

'And companionship?' Allie suggested.

'Women are better companions.'

Allie considered what she had said.

'I don't know,' she said. 'I have never had a woman companion. I never even had a girlfriend when I was young. I suppose my governess was the nearest to one, but she was so much older than me.'

'It was because you are an only child and never went to school,' Jenny said, explaining for her.

'I went to school for a bit after Miss went home, but then when they found I was pregnant we had to go and live in the cellars at Reims and pretend to be someone else. I was just with my mother then.'

Jenny nodded sympathetically. 'It must have been terrible.'

'It was and it wasn't.' Allie was letting herself remember again. This changed new Jenny was, like Anna, so easy to talk to. 'There was so much spirit and kindness in those cellars while the Germans shelled us above. If I hadn't been so angry, so eaten up with the terrible thing that had happened to me, if I'd been the young girl I was before the lieutenant, I would have enjoyed it all. As it was, I was too bitter to see anything good about anything or anybody.' She made a little gesture that threw the whole episode away. 'But that's long ago. It's all over now.'

They sat in silence for a few seconds, a silence that was broken by another tap on the door.

'That will be Dr Weingott,' Allie said apologetically. It seemed rude to send Jenny away after she had travelled so far. 'She comes to see me every morning.'

Jenny jumped to her feet, all energy again.

'I shall go now,' she said, 'but I might just stay up here for a few days. It's beautiful in the mountains. So much more peaceful than New York.' She grinned. 'You know I like mountains. Can I come back tomorrow?'

'Please do,' Allie said and meant it, thinking it was nice to have a friend, but how extraordinary that the friend should be the prickly Jenny.

The prickly Jenny kissed her gently on the cheek as Dr Weingott came into the room. 'I shall be thinking of you,' she said, and first stopping to shake hands with the doctor and murmur who she was, she hurried from the room as if afraid of being in the way.

'Your sister-in-law?' Dr Weingott asked, settling herself in the chair that Jenny had just vacated. More grey eyes regarding her, Allie thought, but both pairs were kind and caring.

'Yes,' she said. 'I was surprised to see her.'

'Oh?'

'Well, we never got on very well. She didn't approve of me.'

'Why do you think that was?'

'She thought I was unkind to her brother.'

'Do you think she was right?'

'Yes, I suppose I do. I was just telling her that I should never have married him.'

Anna Weingott nodded as if something had pleased her. 'What do you think you should have done?'

'Picked up the pieces on my own.' She realised she was using the same words that Jenny had used, but in a subtly different way. 'Relied on myself more,' she added.

'And you were relying on Alexander?'

That was exactly what she had been doing. There seemed no point in denying it any more.

'He was a crutch,' she said simply.

'You felt you were lame?' It was a question, not a statement.

Allie hesitated. 'I felt I was worthless. My mother made me feel . . .' she sought for the right word. 'Feeble, I guess. The lieutenant had made me feel dirty. I couldn't conceive that anyone would love me after that. But Alexander did. Pierre did, too, but because of my mother that was no good.'

'It was your mother's fault?'

'Well, she should have told me he was my half-brother.'

'But wouldn't that have meant telling you other things?'

'Like the truth?' Allie said angrily.

'Ah, yes, of course. The truth that the man you loathed was really your father and not the father you loved. She should have told you. It was wrong of her to hold back. Truth is always the best way to face anything.'

Allie glowered at the doctor who sat quietly, hands folded in her lap, gently smiling. She knew exactly what Anna was getting at. The truth was better but she, Allie, had never had the courage to face it. It was better talking to Jenny. Jenny was all sympathy.

She played her trump card. 'But she shouldn't have got herself pregnant in the first place.'

'She was wrong to fall in love?'

'It's not wrong to love,' Allie protested. 'It's wrong to give in. I loved Pierre, but I didn't give in. I loved Alexander but I didn't give in.'

'Nor,' said Anna Weingott flatly, 'did you give.'

'But it's wrong to give like that,' Allie shouted. 'All right, I could have done it after I married Alexander, but I told him from the start that was out. I was honest with him,' she said virtuously.

'So,' Anna nodded backwards and forwards in her chair like an old lady, her lips pursed. 'Would you think that perhaps you were punishing him instead of the lieutenant? Your mother had taken the pleasure of punishing the lieutenant away, but here was another man to punish, maybe. Never letting him have what the lieutenant had taken?'

'That's not fair,' Allie protested. 'I never wanted to punish Pierre and he's a man, too.'

'I wonder if he felt that your getting married so quickly to Alexander was a punishment for his being your half-brother?' The soft, relentless voice went on. 'Do you think he might have thought that you could have waited for a while?'

'He got married, too.'

Anna was nodding again. 'That is true. But maybe no one told you – and why should they – that he was so hurt that you said so swiftly that it didn't matter who you married that he decided to follow the same path.'

Allie was silent for a moment.

'I did that girl a good turn. She must have been pregnant,' she muttered.

'Yes. He had slept with her, but what do you think would have happened if you and he hadn't been half-brother and sister?'

'He would have married me,' Allie said promptly. 'But what's the point of talking about it since it could never be?'

'It's interesting to speculate how events could be different without the hand of fate,' Anna said. 'So, you think he would have married you?'

'I know it.'

'And that girl he has now married would have been in a difficult position, wouldn't she?'

'The same position I was in.' Allie decided on defiance.

'And I suppose your mother was.'

Allie was silent.

'And,' said Anna relentlessly, 'that would have made Pierre as bad as your real father who abandoned your mother and left her to do the best she could for you and herself.'

'It was their own fault,' Allie shouted again. 'They shouldn't have given in.'

'That is what Christian morality says,' Anna agreed, adding: 'It's amazing how recent that sort of thinking is in history.

Morality put about by the Church to guard property and inheritance basically, but not a lot to do with our natural instincts. Our instincts are to mate. However, tell me something. What happened at the end of all your stories that you made up when you were a little girl? When the man had rescued you, did you make love in your daydreams?'

Allie was quite shocked by the question.

'I didn't know what making love was,' she said. 'He might have kissed me, but nothing else.'

'And you had no instinctive, misty concept of what love might entail?'

'None.' Allie's voice was firm.

'And you never pleasured yourself – never found those secret places to touch which give warm pleasure while you were daydreaming?'

Allie felt her cheeks go scarlet.

'I don't know what you're talking about,' she said, hoping that the lie did not show.

'How unusual,' Dr Weingott said, her voice surprised. 'Everyone else does.' She was beginning to gather up the notebook that she never used. 'I have to go,' she said. 'That's all for this morning.'

Allie was still savouring the relief of knowing that everyone did those things, even though she could hardly believe it. She wanted the conversation to go on.

'Can you tell me something?' she asked, putting out her hand to keep the doctor with her for a moment longer.

'I'll try.' The grey eyes were smiling.

'My sister-in-law just said something very strange. She said that like me, she could never love a man that way because nature had made her differently. She said she knew my secrets because her brother had told her them and it was only fair that I should know hers. I didn't understand what she meant.'

'You had no idea?'

'Well, I couldn't believe . . .' Allie wriggled on a pin of her own making. 'That couldn't be, could it?'

'That she would give her love sexually to a woman? Is that what you thought it might be?'

'Well, yes and no.'

'I would imagine that is what she meant. Many people do

love their own sex and have no sexual interest in the other. It is called homosexuality between men – from the Greek "homo", same, and lesbianism when the love is between women. We are just beginning to understand it a little better.'

'I've never heard of it,' Allie muttered.

'Most people haven't. Those who are attracted to their own sex do not speak of it since many people consider it wicked.'

'Is it wicked?'

'We do not consider it so. We consider it is another form of sexuality and of love. Something that is not to be judged. It was brave of her to tell you.'

Allie was trying to digest all this new information and understand it. It didn't seem so terrible to her, she decided. Looking at Anna Weingott she could understand why a woman might love another woman like that.

'Are you like that?' she asked abruptly, almost rudely.

Anna was standing in the doorway. She laughed. 'I'm the one who is supposed to be asking the questions. But the answer is no. Are you?'

She did not wait for a reply. She just smiled and was gone.

It was at the end of the first week of March when Pierre found a letter with a New York postmark and a typewritten address waiting beside his plate at the breakfast table. He felt his heart begin to beat very fast, realising that this must be the reply to his letter to Allie.

He felt absurdly nervous. He had not seen or heard of Allie for three years and yet he still thought about her at least once a day. He could not expel her from his thoughts. He longed to see her handwriting and read her words, but at the same time feared their effect on him. All the pain could return. The letter would also give him her answer as to whether or not she would agree to selling her share of Les Hérissons. He feared she would say no. He looked at the innocent-looking envelope and picked it up as if it might explode. Hurriedly he slid it into his pocket hoping that no one else had seen it. The chances were that no one who mattered had since neither Feathers nor Madame were down. He wouldn't have wished to explain a letter from New York to either of them.

The envelope was burning a hole in his pocket but he waited

until he was on the road to Épernay before he opened it. Inside, the words were handwritten and he did not recognise the writing. It was certainly not Allie's. Disappointed, he looked quickly to see who it was from. The signature was that of Alexander Webster.

Was that good news or bad? he asked himself as he turned back to the beginning.

Dear Monsieur Dupuis,

Forgive me for both opening and replying to your letter to my wife regarding the sale of her property in France.

The situation at the moment is that Allie has had a kind of nervous breakdown and she is in the care of a clinic in the Catskill Mountains. Her doctors want her to have absolute peace and quiet for a while, and for her not to be burdened with any decisions of any kind. Therefore, I am sure you will understand that they have asked me not to show her your letter for the time being.

You are in fact the second person to write about this matter. The first was an American in Paris called Jack Patterson. We have never replied to his letter since at the time it arrived my wife was taken ill.

But I detect a note of urgency in your letter and therefore I am taking it upon myself to tell you that in my opinion my wife will be willing to sell. On the arrival of Mr Patterson's letter she stated categorically that she had no wish to return to France and had no interest in Les Hérissons.

I think I should point out to you that on her grand-mother's death, she will own only the house and the land. The actual business belongs to her mother.

I must confess to an interest in this matter. As I am sure you will understand I would prefer that my wife regarded America as her home. Personally I feel it would be a good thing if she broke all ties with the past.

If, therefore, she should ask my advice, I shall suggest to her that she sells either to you or Mr Patterson, who-ever offers the better price or is prepared to meet hers.

I think you can safely assume that her portion of Les

Hérissons will be on the market at some time in the future, and either I or my wife will be in touch with you when that time comes.

Yours faithfully,
Alexander Webster

Pierre read the letter through twice and then folded it and put it back in his pocket. Alexander Webster was an unexpected ally. Alexander did not want Allie ever to come home again. And if he were Alexander, he would not want her to either. Tomorrow he would go to Paris to see Jack. It was time to write to Rosie and Philippe, and time to speak to his grandmother.

He drove on down towards Épernay wondering why he suddenly felt as if his spirits had trickled out through the soles of his shoes. What is the matter? he asked himself, knowing that he should have felt elated at the possibility of his scheme working.

Elated he was not and he forced himself to face the reason. What hurt so badly was Alexander Webster's constant references to Allie as his wife. Four separate references along with one 'we'. It made Allie sound such a part of this other man that he had never met.

He stopped the car and took the letter from his pocket and tore it into small shreds. He flung the remains out of the car window. The March wind caught the flakes of paper and whirled them high and away just as Allie had been whirled away out of his life.

And his eyes were full of tears as he grimly drove on to the School of Oenology.

Madame sat dozing in her little parlour. The fire had been stoked up by Henri who was almost as stiff and arthritic as she was. None of them were getting any younger, she thought, enjoying the way the flames warmed her toes while a heavy shawl kept the draught from her back. It irked her that she could no longer do her petit point. Her fingers, like her legs and feet, were too swollen and painful. But she managed most things. There was life in the old girl yet, she told herself as she told herself every morning while she waited for the night's stiffness in her bones to disappear. At Les Hérissons she was still in charge, still head of her family; a family which, in spite of the death of her sons, the good Lord had let her live to see expanding. Another grandchild on the way, she thought contentedly as she sat, her hands relaxed on her lap. Another boy would be nice. Of course it would be hopeless to ask Pierre if it could be called after Jean Paul. Pierre's face froze at even a mention of his father. She sighed. Jean Paul had been bad, but she still missed him and knew that she always would. He had been such a charming baby. So bright and intelligent. Where had it all gone wrong?

A gentle tap on the door roused her from her reverie.

'Enter,' she called, glad to think that here might be some company and even more glad when she saw that her visitor was Pierre.

'Do you have a moment, Mimi?' he said, his head round the door jamb, hovering as if she might send him away.

'Of course,' she said. 'Come in.'

He came in cautiously, and her shrewd old eyes looking at his nervous face told her that he had something serious on his mind.

'Sit down,' she said. 'Do you want tea?'

'No, just to talk.'

She looked at him consideringly. 'What about?'

'Les Hérissons.'

'Ah.' For one worrying moment she feared he was going to say that he was leaving her.

'You're happy here?' she asked.

'I could be happier.'

He had ranged himself on her little sofa and his long legs looked homeless.

'And what would make you happier?' she asked, knowing her voice was indulgent.

'To own it,' he said baldly.

She looked at him startled and dismayed, unable to believe what she was hearing, all her suspicions and hackles rising.

'No one will ever own Les Hérissons other than me in my lifetime,' she said firmly, shocked that he should even think of such a thing.

'It wouldn't change a thing if you let me buy it. It would still be your home.'

'Buy it! And what are you going to use for money? Mine?' she asked sarcastically.

He flushed. 'I can find the money, Mimi.'

'By what means?'

'Let's talk about that later.' He was evading the question. 'Please don't dismiss the idea out of hand. Please let's discuss it.'

'Why do you want to buy it?' she asked. He looked more uncomfortable than ever on her little sofa and she felt a pang of pity for him. The traces of his wicked father were there no matter how he tried to suppress them. But if it were his father sitting there, trying to deprive Allie and Rosanne of their inheritance, he would have been so much more at ease, smiling, cajoling, persuading – and she would have given in. Or would she? Maybe not. Not any more.

'Because I think I can make a bigger success of it,' he said eagerly. 'I want to run it my way, and while Aunt Rosie is in charge I'll never be able to do that.'

'Rosie is not in charge,' she said outraged. 'I am, and always have been.'

'Oh Mimi, you know she does things behind your back. You knows she does exactly what she wants in the end.'

She looked at him. This was more like the underhand style of his father, but Pierre was sweating where his father would have been smiling. And Rosie? Did she do exactly what she wanted in the end? Madame conceded that most of the time she did but with tact and charm. Rosie was interfering in many ways but she always deferred and left no sense of having won any battles. Rosie never crowed.

'And how do you think you can run it better?'

'The sales side is going to pieces. Philippe is not up to it,' he said with the cruelty of youth. 'I know someone who can bring all that up to strength again. Our champagne is good, but it could be better. We could be a name ourselves. We needn't just make for the rich who want to show off with their name on our bottles, pretending it was made specially for them.'

Madame had never quite approved of Rosie's sales methods, though the snob in her had to admit that the people whose names were on Les Hérissons' bottles were very fine names indeed. But she had wished over the years that Les Hérissons'

386

champagne had become as famous as Bollinger or Krug or any one of the great Champagne houses. It would have been an honour to her husband's memory.

'I can do it, I know I can do it,' he was saying eagerly, twenty-four years old and with the fool's gold of over-confidence driving him on.

'If I were to *give* you Les Hérissons,' she said, 'it would make no difference to the sales or to the wine. That part is Rosie and Philippe's. It is nothing to do with me.'

'But the one is dependent on the other. I think my friend could persuade them to sell if the house and the vineyards were no longer under Aunt Rosie's control.'

'And who is this friend?'

He hung his head. 'An American I know in Paris.'

'And he will lend you the money you need?'

'Yes.'

'So Les Hérissons will become his?'

'Well,' he wriggled uneasily. 'Only for a while until I've paid him back.'

'Pierre! Pierre!' The suggestion filled her with horror. 'You really think that I would hand over Les Hérissons to an American?'

'It would be to me.'

'It would be to an American.'

'Well, you could give the estate to me and then he needn't be involved,' he said, suddenly cocky.

She could see he was holding his breath at the audacity of what he was saying. She looked at him and shook her head.

'And what about Allie and Rosanne?'

'Allie doesn't want it. I've been in touch with her. She would be quite agreeable selling her portion to me. I wouldn't have asked you if she hadn't agreed.'

'And Rosanne?'

'Rosanne is not my half-sister. We're not even related.' His face was sullen. He knew he should not be saying such things, and she knew he was ashamed.

'You might find yourself in some difficulty if you said such a thing,' she said, and made her voice threatening. It was insupportable that he should speak of this.

'Not if Allie backed me.'

'I don't know what you are talking about,' she said dismissively but wondering if it could be true that the erratic, unpredictable Allie would do such a terrible thing.

He shrugged. 'I could always tell Rosanne the truth myself.'

'What truth?' she asked coldly.

'Grandmother, Allie told me about the lieutenant and Rosanne. I know she's not Aunt Rosie's daughter. And I'd be quite capable of telling Rosanne the truth – if I don't get Les Hérissons.'

But her still keen ears detected the sound of misery. His heart was not in this cruel, cheap blackmail.

'And if you do tell Rosanne,' she said quietly, 'I shall sell Les Hérissons to Rosie and Philippe and your inheritance will be gone, except for your share of what money I leave. But I will never sell to an American. You will have to wait, Pierre. Be patient. When I die you will receive your portion exactly as the law decrees and then you can do as you wish.'

He went white and then red. 'And Aunt Rosie? Will she receive a portion?'

'That is no business of yours, Pierre,' she said firmly as if speaking to a small child. 'I think you'd better be on your way now. There is nothing more to say.'

He got to his feet awkwardly and went towards the door. There he hesitated and turned.

'I wouldn't really have told Rosanne,' he muttered. 'But that's what my father would have done, isn't it?'

She looked at him and smiled. He was so young and she was so glad that he was part of her life. But impatient youth must be taught to wait.

'Yes, your father would have done it, but I knew that you would not,' she said gently. 'Now run along, there's a good boy.'

She heard his footsteps hesitate outside her door and then go upstairs. She sat staring into the fire. Thank God he was not quite his father's son. There was something kinder in him than had ever been in Jean Paul. Did it come from his mother? she wondered, realising she had no idea who his mother had been. It could have come from her father who had been a good man. And her husband had been the kindest of men in spite of his fierce moustaches. And she herself was not cruel. Perhaps the

388

real question was from whom did Jean Paul inherit his wick-edness?

She sighed. And now Jean Paul's son wanted to rob Rosie and Philippe of their share of Les Hérissons. She did not care about Philippe. She had never forgiven him for the affair with Rosie while her son was still alive. She had not forgiven Rosie completely, but even so she loved her – though perhaps no one would have suspected it. She knew she was not always kind to Rosie, but when you were old and your bones ached and all the old appetites had gone it was those you loved the best that felt the brunt of the frustrations of age.

But in her will Rosie had been left her rightful portion – one third of all the property. Remembering the many years that Rosie had been loyal to Les Hérissons, Madame knew that never, never for anyone in the world, even Jean Paul's son, would she change that.

Alexander brought Allie home from the Ziegman Clinic in mid-March. He was nervous and ill at ease on his arrival since she had refused to see him the entire time she had been away. He had no idea what kind of Allie he was going to find. His only reassurance had come from his sister. Amazingly, Jenny and Allie had become close friends and Jenny had told him that there was nothing to worry about. Allie was calm, collected and facing up to life in a way that she never had before. She had even started writing a novel.

'Is she cured?' he had asked.

Jenny gave him a funny look. 'You mean . . .?'

'Yes.'

'I don't know. We don't talk about that,' she said dismissively.

Most of the two months that Allie had been away he had spent with Beth Rogan and his concern was that he was becoming far too fond of the girl. She was so blissfully uncomplicated. A healthy, easy-going modern girl who had shed an unsuitable husband without making a big deal of it. She swore the divorce was going to be amicable, but he woke sweating in the night that Walter Rogan might just cite him. Then what would he say to Allie? But he couldn't give Beth up. Not yet. Beth loved cocktails, jazz, the movies, speakeasies, clothes and conversation. She didn't care if she got a little high. She liked all the things that Allie despised. The big difference between them was that Beth was fun to be with. Since Allie had been away, instead of sitting alone at nights, listening to the wireless crackle or reading a good book while his wife sat in her study writing, Alexander had been enjoying New York. He had been experimenting a little with life. He and Beth had become part of a floating crowd of wealthy young people who worked and played hard, drifting from one restaurant and speakeasy to another, going to bed at dawn unless they had some urgent sex to attend to. He got a little drunk most nights, made a lot of love and was enjoying what he called a swell time.

He knew he still loved Allie and always would. She was the challenge in his life. But somewhat to his dismay he hadn't actually missed her. In fact, her absence, the removal of her brooding presence, had been something of a relief.

But there was no brooding quality about the young woman who met him in the reception room of the Ziegman Clinic. Allie came briskly out of the elevator, chic in a velvet coat that she clutched round her in the approved *Vogue* manner. The coat was a wonderfully warm cherry colour and had matching fur all round the edges from neck to hem. With it she wore a little fur pull-on hat and her eyes, darkened with mascara and something else, peered mysteriously from beneath it. Behind her trotted Jessica, tethered on a bright red lead that seemed to be diamanté-studded.

'Alexander!' she said. 'How lovely to see you,' and her cool lips were kissing his cheeks and her small hand was sliding into his. 'I've said all my goodbyes to everyone here. We can go now. It's better if I don't see them again.'

Outside in the misty mountain air she fussed Jessica into the jump seat of his Bugatti and then herself into the deep leather seat in front, wriggling to make sure she was comfortable. Settled, she took off her hat and flung it into the back at the side of the dog and shook out her bobbed hair.

'You're the chauffeur today?' she asked.

'I thought it would be nice to be on our own after so long,' he said hoping it was the right thing to say. His nervousness was still making him tongue-tied and uncomfortable.

'Yes, it is a long time,' she said thoughtfully. 'I'm afraid they had to persuade me to go in the end. I'd become so cosy there and so close to Dr Weingott.' She chuckled. 'It was like being back in the womb. She said that was how it was supposed to be in a way. Starting out all over again. She's helped me a lot.' She gave a theatrical little sigh. 'Now I have to face the real world again.'

'Was it such a difficult world before?' he asked cautiously as he drove through the big iron gates of the clinic.

'You sound like them. Always asking questions,' she said. 'No, it wasn't a difficult world. You gave me a lovely world. But I was sort of hiding in it, I guess.'

He was afraid to say anything else. There were so many questions he wanted to ask, but it was all too soon, he thought. Better to wait.

'Jenny says you're writing a novel,' he volunteered.

'Yes. I'm trying. A serious one. Now I've got so much out of my system Dr Weingott says I won't need to write that pulp stuff any more. She says she thinks I can produce something with real meaning – perhaps based on my own problems now I understand them. She thinks I could be a famous novelist if I stopped being such a recluse and let myself go and found out a bit more about life.'

'Great,' he said cautiously. He didn't know what she meant by the pulp stuff, but he didn't want to ask any more questions.

'So, Alexander, you'll have to show me the big wide world.'

'Great,' he said again, his mind turning to the big wide world that he had been sharing with Beth.

'It's a lovely day.' Again the theatrical sigh and the wave of a cherry-red gloved hand that took in the mountains, the sun fighting its way through the mist and the dappling of dew that lay on the bare branches. 'A lovely day for a new beginning.'

A new beginning for whom?, he wondered. Both of them – or just her?

'Spring's coming,' he said, feeling fatuous. 'The snow's beginning to leave the mountains. The leaves will be green soon.'

'Salad days. How I wasted them.' She ran her fingers through her hair and tossed her head back. 'So much to make up for.'

Alexander began to feel distinctly uneasy as he drove steadily back to New York and this threatened new life. He did not recognise the affected young woman sitting next to him. This was a brand new Allie; neither the bright, lively child that had been lost, nor the introverted woman. Who was this Allie? And was he going to like her?

'How did it go?' Beth asked at the office the next morning. She sat on his desk, a cigarette touched with crimson in her manicured fingers, pretty legs swinging from beneath her blue mid-calf length dress. Her pale blue eyes regarded him sympathetically.

'Bewildering,' he said, pushing his typewriter further back on his desk.

'In what way?'

'Her personality has changed completely. It's most extraordinary. She's someone quite different.'

'A nicer person?' Beth tipped her chin back and blew smoke into the air, now avoiding his eyes.

'I don't know. I haven't had time to get to know this new person.'

'Tell me about it at lunchtime,' she said and wandered off back to her own desk, stopping to chat with others on the way.

He decided he wouldn't tell Beth too much about the night before. He had taken Allie out to dinner at the Ritz Carlton to celebrate her homecoming and she had surprised him again at how stunning she looked. She was wearing a pretty chiffon dress made in three layers of green and white stripes. Each layer was scalloped, as was the hem. The sleeves were no more than butterfly wings, held by her middle finger and leaving her arms bare. The olive skin on her shoulders and neck was smooth, and her dark blue eyes were alive. Allie was definitely different.

'That's a very pretty dress,' he said. 'I haven't seen it before, have I?'

'No.' She giggled. 'The clinic let me out once or twice. Jenny drove me down to New York and we went shopping. She said it was time I had some nicer clothes.'

'She helped you choose that coat you were wearing this morning?'

'Yes. Did you like it?'

'Very much,' he said.

392

'New life, new clothes,' she said. 'This dress is a copy of a Chanel. Mama used to love Chanel. Jenny has a little dressmaker who copies things from *Vogue*. She made this. It's hard to get the real thing here.'

He could hardly believe she was mentioning her mother so casually and easily.

'Your mother always dressed well,' he ventured.

'Yes. Jenny says I look just as good in clothes as she does. It's just that I never bothered.'

'Actually,' he said, 'you're prettier than your mother.'

'I know it. I guess I don't have her personality. But I'm working on it.'

'You feel better about her?' he asked cautiously.

She laughed. 'Oh, yes. Poor Mama. I've been terribly unkind to her.'

And he did not care for the condescending note in her voice.

'That reminds me,' he said, 'you remember that letter asking if you would like to sell Les Hérissons?'

'Gosh, yes,' she said, looking up from the menu which she had been studying as if it might tell her something important. 'Did we ever reply to that man?'

He shook his head. 'Events sort of took over and I forgot. But while you were away you received another letter . . .'

'Oh.' Her attention was back on the menu.

'They asked me not to show it to you.'

'Why was that?' she asked absently.

'Perhaps because it came from Pierre.'

'Oh.' She put the menu down, and looked at him. The colour rose in her face. 'Pierre! For heaven's sake! What did he want?'

'The same thing. He wanted you to sell your share of Les Hérissons. I replied for you.'

'Do you still have the letter?'

'I kept it. I thought you might want to see it. It's a nice letter.'

She sighed. 'I don't really think I want to see it. What's done is done. What did you tell him?'

'I said I thought you would sell and that we would be in touch. I mentioned the other letter and I said that if you did sell it would be to whoever met your price.'

'Can I have lobster?' she asked abruptly, startling him.

'You can have anything you like.'

393

'Lobster Thermidor. I don't know if I want to sell. There's Rosanne to consider. And, I suppose, Mama. It would make things very difficult for them. I'll have to think about it for a bit. I don't want to make any decisions right now. Not until I've decided exactly what I'm going to do with my life.'

They were ominous words, and as the meal wore on he became more and more nervous. She ate with greedy enjoyment and chattered on, telling him about Dr Weingott, almost as if she were speaking of a lover. She spoke a great deal about Jenny. He had not realised how much time his sister had spent with her, and he felt a small pang that Jenny, who had always been so close to him, had not seen fit to tell him about the times she had stayed in the Catskills for days at a stretch.

It was while they were drinking their coffee that she said: 'I told you I'm writing a novel.'

'Yes, a serious one.'

'It's about the war in France and its effect on a young girl. I guess it's autobiographical in a way, but then most of the best novels are. Dr Weingott thinks it will be good for me. The girl in the story gets raped, just as I did, and has a baby like I did. I think it might have more of a happy ending than my life. She gets her baby back in the end.'

He reached across the table for her hand. 'Maybe you will, too.'

'Oh, no,' she said. 'I remember too vividly the terrible shock of finding that Clovis was not my father and that the ghastly Jean Paul was. I'm not giving Rosanne those sort of shocks.'

'But you're not ghastly,' he protested. 'She might be delighted to find you were her mother.'

For a moment Allie looked sad. She shook her head: 'I'm not ghastly, but the truth is I'm not as nice as Mama. Mama isn't selfish. She wants everyone to be happy. I just want me to be happy, as you must well know.'

He was silent, and she laughed. 'See,' she said. 'It's true.'

But as he paid the bill what was really disturbing him was what would happen at bedtime. Her ghosts were laid, it seemed, but what effect would that have on their life together? The moment of truth was looming up and he was not sure how to handle it. Should he assume that they would sleep together at long last? Should he court her as if they had only just met? Or should he leave all the moves to her?

He decided on the last option, but by the time they had eaten and were strolling home along Fifth Avenue, he had become so anxious that his mouth was dry and his stomach churning. The walk was delaying all decisions. By the time they had reached the Rockefeller Plaza, Allie was complaining that her feet were hurting and that her fur wrap was insufficient to keep out the cold. He hailed a horse-drawn cab.

In the leather-scented darkness inside, he tentatively took her hand. To his relief she did not snatch it away, but let it rest in his. He began to hope and at the same time to panic that even if she was prepared to come to his bed, he would not be able to perform. His mind was full of the awful vision of finding Allie willing while he was totally impotent and unable to do anything about it.

In the event, his anxieties were wasted. When they reached the house in Gramercy Park she declined a nightcap.

'It's lovely to be home, darling,' she said with a huge yawn. 'But I think I'll just run up to bed now. See you in the morning.' She swayed across to him, her gown rippling around her pretty legs, kissed him lightly on the cheek, said: 'Thank you for a lovely evening,' and with a backward wave was gone.

Deeply depressed he sat downstairs alone in their elegant but sterile living room, furnished by some interior decorator his mother had recommended, and stared miserably into a glass of whiskey.

He wished he was with uncomplicated Beth. By now they would be kissing, and he would be helping her out of her clothes. The thought made his loins tighten and he made himself push the thought away. And once it had gone he realised that what was troubling him the most was that he didn't actually care a great deal whether Allie would sleep with him or not.

Chapter Fourteen

Champagne, 1 April 1924

'Everyone's coming, aren't they?' Feathers was laughing, excited, delighted, addressing the breakfast table at Les Hérissons. 'You can all forget your vines for the day and come and look at my shop. It's beautiful.' She rolled her blue, blue eyes and laughed out loud. 'You'll all be a-m-a-z-e-d!'

The bright clear morning sun had woken Madame early and she was making one of her rare appearances at breakfast time. The old lady spread *confiture* heavily on her croissant and said crossly: 'What is the girl saying?'

'Feathers, you're breaking the rules. Say it again in French for Madame Dupuis,' Luke instructed.

'Oh God!' Feathers rolled her eyes again, this time in dismay. 'I'll try.' She took a deep breath. '*Maintenant, tout le monde arrivera, n'est-ce pas? Oubliez-vous vos vins pour le jour et venez chez moi cette soir, à ma magasin. Il est très, très beau et vous sera a-m-a-z-e-d.*'

Pierre was laughing.

'Feathers,' he said, 'that was terrible, and there is no such word as amazed in French.'

'What is it, this amazed?' Madame was grumbling.

'Etonné,' suggested Luke.

'Stupéfait?' Pierre offered.

'Hah!' said Madame. 'I do not wish to be either. But have no fear. We shall all be there.'

'She says she's coming?' Feathers asked eagerly.

'She's coming,' Luke said.

Feathers leapt to her feet and ran round the table to kiss Madame's cheek. '*Merci, merci mille fois, Madame,*' she said. '*Je suis très, très heureuse. Vous êtes très gentille.*'

Madame bowed graciously under the kiss and delicately wiped her lips with her napkin.

'You say that the Mayoress is coming?' she asked.

'She is.' Luke could see that Feathers was congratulating herself on understanding.

'Of course, we know her family well,' Madame said. 'It is many years since I have seen her. It will be a pleasure.'

A look of anxiety was clouding Feathers' face. Her French was much improved, but Madame gave no quarter and spoke as fast as she wished, leaving Feathers to struggle.

'She knows the family well,' he whispered.

On cue, in what sounded like perfect French, Feathers said ingratiatingly: 'But of course.'

Madame preened under the compliment and Luke thought how the atmosphere at Les Hérissons had changed for the better in the last few weeks. Madame, who most certainly had not been told the truth, was delighted at the thought of another grandchild and, most important, Feathers was happy. She seemed to be blossoming in spirit as her waistline blossomed in girth. She had been working hard to get her shop ready and now there was to be a launch party with most of the notables of Reims attending. It was something of a triumph for an American girl who still spoke the most excruciating French but was managing to get herself understood and, more important, most of the time understanding others. There was a new rule at Les Hérissons. When Feathers spoke English, everyone ignored her. Since she loved to chatter, she was forced to chatter in French.

Luke was anxious about Pierre, wondering what went on in his head. He seemed more relaxed, happier, but he was quiet. But then he had always been quiet. The boy was certainly working hard at his studies, and he helped a lot around the estate, for ever asking questions about how things were done. For the past two weeks he had been almost ingratiating as if he were aiming for popularity, particularly with Madame Dupuis who seemed to have been treating him warily.

But it was his own state of mind that was really worrying Luke. He and Feathers had had no conversation about the baby's parentage, but he found himself tinglingly aware that the growing bulge she carried, almost defiantly, was his grandchild. He had watched her anxiously these past few months, noting every time she was tired and pale and trying to help if he could. He felt for her whenever she put her hand to the small of her back and stretched and he knew that she ached and that the burden was becoming heavy. He wondered if the baby would be a boy or a girl, if it would look like him, or if it would be black-haired like his son. It might even be another little Irish potato like Patric. The speculation brought about the most extraordinary feeling, almost of awe. A feeling that he had missed completely with Carlos. He and Isabella had never seen each other again once she was pregnant and he wondered if this was the reason that he had felt no affinity with his son. Now he was privileged to watch this beautiful girl, for whom he had always felt a deep warmth, go through a pregnancy carrying *his* grandchild. There was wonder and excitement about it and he wished there was someone with whom he could share these remarkable feelings.

He found himself lingering over the breakfast table. Normally he left before anyone else and set about his work but this morning he stayed while Madame dragged herself up on her tired, stiff feet and took herself back upstairs. Pierre left for the fifteen-minute drive to the School of Oenology, and he was alone with Feathers.

'Excited?' he asked her, speaking English. He wanted her to understand the conversation.

'Thrilled,' she said. 'The shop looks so pretty. I'm so proud of it.'

'And at last we're allowed to see it.' No one had been permitted to see what Feathers had been doing in Reims. Not even Rosie. 'You've done very well,' he said. 'And your French is improving.'

Her face lit up. 'Do you think so? I've been having lessons. I didn't tell anyone because it seems so silly after all this time.'

'Well, the lessons are working,' he told her. 'Are you feeling well? You're not doing too much?'

'I'm fine,' she said, and then added tentatively but still mischievously: 'Grandpa.'

He felt himself flush with pleasure. They smiled at each other in what he knew was a soppy kind of way but he didn't care. There was a lot he wanted to say, but he held back, choosing his words with care.

'You know if you want anything, if anything goes wrong . . . if I can be of help . . . I'm always here,' he said.

'I know. I've known that all along.'

'And—' the words came out in a rush – 'I know it's wrong of me, but I'm so proud. I won't ever speak of it again, but I wanted to tell you how glad I feel, even in spite of the circumstances. I couldn't think of anyone better . . . I think of you as a daughter. I've wanted to say so for a long time. As long as what happened doesn't harm you, or make you unhappy, I can't help feeling glad about it though I know I shouldn't under the circumstances . . .'

She was silent for a moment, her finger tracing the crumbs on the tablecloth into patterns.

'It was good of you to stay quiet at the beginning,' she said. 'It must have been hard on you to know that your son . . .' She broke off. 'And it was good of you to tell Pierre the truth. Not everyone would have done. And in the end it's helped us,' she said. 'It changed Pierre. It made him understand and see things differently. I know he'll try to love the baby as best he can. He's a good man really. Even when he tries to be hard, in the end he can't do it. Look how he married me. But whatever happens, this baby is going to be all right, because it's got two people loving it already. You and me.'

He felt an enormous relief.

'We'll never talk about it again. We'll just know how we both feel and keep it to ourselves,' he said awkwardly. 'And I'll always be here if you need me.'

She smiled.

'It'll be a beautiful baby and a lovely person if it's anything like you,' she said simply. She got to her feet, stretched with a grimace, and came round the table to kiss him. 'See you later, Grandpa,' she said lightly, and was gone.

Philippe made his way downstairs alone. He had mastered most of the house that was necessary for him to use; what he lacked was a picture of this new home. Rosie had described it to him from the big deep sofas that tied at the sides to the colours of the Oriental rugs she had spread over the black and white tiled floors. But he still felt more comfortable at the house on the Ile de la Cité and often wished that they could go back there to live. But Les Coquelicots was the first home that Rosie had ever owned. She had found the house and fallen in love with it, chosen every bit of decoration, and the results gave her great pleasure. She did her best to make it home for him. She described the view from their bedroom, looking down the hillsides and across to the pretty village of Hautvillers where Dom Perignon had discovered how to make champagne, and she had walked him high above the house and explained how from here it was possible to see, far below, the slender grey ribbon of the Marne winding its way to the Seine.

As he came carefully down the stairs on the morning of the first day of April, he was aware that she was not far in front of him, moving quickly and lightly. He sensed her presence and he knew that she hovered in case he should fall or come upon some unseen obstruction. Françoise reacted differently to his disability. Françoise took his arm and guided him with cooing words of encouragement. He found that he preferred this to Rosie's attempts to let him do things for himself. Yet if Rosie had for ever been taking his arm and leading him through life he would have resented it. Somehow, from a daughter, assistance was different. A daughter's support did not diminish him.

His head was aching very badly this morning, so badly that he had been tempted, but refrained, from taking some laudanum. He made his way into the breakfast room and Françoise's and Rosanne's young voices broke into a high, clear chorus of 'good morning'. Rosie had permitted them both to come down for family breakfast now that Françoise was about to be twelve. She insisted that Rosanne, now going on nine, should have the same privilege, though he sensed that Rosanne was indifferent about where or even when she ate her meals.

His head was pounding as he found his seat, lowered himself into it, carefully found his napkin and spread it on his lap. Any fast movement made the pain worse. Françoise was at his side, and she took his hand and guided it to his coffee cup. Rosie had always left him to find things for himself and he was aware he was beginning to rely on Françoise's assistance. Since the girls had started to come downstairs for breakfast, Rosie sat across the table from him . He could hear from the slight rustle that she was reading the newspaper.

'Any news?' he asked.

'Not a lot. They're starting to rebuild the Hôtel de Ville. They say it will be finished by 1927.'

'You mean it's still in ruins?'

'Yes. Unbelievable, isn't it?'

Another of his mental pictures gone for ever, he thought. He would never know what the new building looked like.

'There's a story here that's interesting,' she said. 'Someone is training dogs to lead people who can't see. It sounds marvellous. Apparently the dogs are taught to take people across roads, and to avoid obstacles. They're even taught to find the way home. They say it means that people without sight can go out alone and in much more safety.'

The thought of being led about by a dog depressed him unutterably. Françoise, her voice indignant, said: 'Why would Papa want one of those when he has me? I can lead him anywhere he wants to go better than a silly old dog.'

His heart lifted and he reached to find her hand and pat it.

There was that familiar half-beat of silence that always followed anything that Françoise said. A disapproving silence, he knew, and he could not understand why. Françoise was always so happy, so full of love, so eager to please, and yet he could not help but be aware that Rosie never responded to the child with the warmth that she showed everyone else. He meant to discuss it with her, but something always held him back.

'You can't be with your father all of the time,' Rosie said, and he detected a cold note in her voice. 'Anything that gives him independence —'

Françoise interrupted: 'You don't want to be independent from me, do you, Papa? And anyway, if I'm not here you can always look after him, Mama Rosie.' She laughed a happy little laugh. 'I give you my permission to be my deputy.'

There was a long silence which Philippe himself broke by asking if someone would pass him a croissant. Rosanne, from his left, did so. Françoise said: 'Let me put the *confiture* on for you, Papa,' and took it away from him again.

He could hear the clatter of knife on jam pot, and then Michel's footsteps, coming in with the mail as he came in with the mail every morning at this time.

'Thank you, Michel,' Rosie said, and he heard the whisper of paper, and then of paper being cut. There was silence for a moment, and then Rosie said: 'How extraordinary. Someone wants to buy our business. An American called Jack Patterson. He asks if we would be interested in selling everything – the machinery, the vats and the sales business.' He heard the sound of paper being decisively folded. 'Well, I'm sorry to have to disappoint him . . .'

Françoise had given a little squeal.

'We could all go back to Paris,' she said. 'Papa wouldn't have to do horrid work any more and we could all be happy and comfy in his house and go walking by the river every day.'

The silence again.

'We have to earn a living, Françoise,' Rosie said.

'Oh, I don't know,' he heard himself saying, and thinking of how day by day he lost more control of what was happening in his own business. 'I'm beginning to think that there's not a lot of sense in work for work's sake. We'd have enough to live very well . . .'

Françoise's small hands clapped, but he knew that Rosie has straightened herself. The atmosphere was suddenly tangibly tense.

'Philippe! You can't mean it!'

He shifted uneasily.

'Maybe it's worth considering,' he said defensively, feeling the pain in his head throb harder at the unusual hostility in her voice. 'We could all be together – more a family. You do have to work very hard, Rosie. It does keep you away from us a lot.'

There was a heavy silence. Then what he thought of as Rosie's tight-lipped voice saying: 'Why don't you two girls go up to the nursery? Miss will be waiting for you.'

'Very well, Mama Rosie,' Françoise's pretty voice rang out. 'Come along, Rosanne.'

He pictured her smiling at Rosie and holding her hand out for her stepsister. He wished he could see how pretty she was.

He heard the door close behind the girls and then Rosie asked: 'You think I'm away too much?'

'No. Not too much. I just wish you were here more.'

She was silent. 'It's the business that takes me away.'

'I know. And it's what I don't do that makes it worse. I'm beginning to feel that it would be better to give it up completely than do it half-heartedly. I haven't the energy any more, Rosie.

These pains . . .' he broke off, not wanting to complain and say that today the pain was very bad. 'But I couldn't bear to hand it all over to someone else while I was still involved. If it was gone, sold and finished with, that would be different. I think it might prove to be better if we just cut free of it. It's time you had a little relaxation and fun. We could go to Paris and forget Les Hérissons and let them get on with it themselves. It's obvious that Pierre is dying to get his hands on the place.'

'You think so?' She sounded surprised.

'Yes, can't you feel it?'

'I can't. But you're so much more perceptive than I am.'

'It's being blind that does it,' he said.

She sighed. 'Well, we'll think about it. I don't know . . . I think I might be lost without something to do. But if it's what you want.' He heard the note of desolation that she could not hide, but he did not respond. This was what he wanted, he realised. The letter from the unknown Jack Patterson seemed like a key to a new life. Suddenly he was aware of all the frustrations he had been feeling. If they sold they could be together as a proper family, and he'd make them all so happy that Rosie would soon get over any disappointments.

They sat quietly for a moment and he knew she was neither eating nor drinking.

'It's tonight that Feathers opens her shop, isn't it?' he asked, more to make conversation than out of interest.

'Yes. She's so excited. You will come, won't you?'

He had had no intention of going into Reims for a soirée where he would not even be able to see the shop that was being opened. But there was a note of resignation in Rosie's voice as if she knew that he would not come, a note that inferred that now he never did anything or went anywhere with her. He felt a flash of guilt. He had neglected her. Since Françoise arrived he had barely left the house. And if he wanted Rosie to give up the business, perhaps he should let her see that he still could be a companion. His head hurt with the effort of thinking it out, but he said: 'Of course I'm coming. I'm not letting you go to parties alone. Who knows what might happen.'

'You really will?' She sounded incredulous and delighted at the same time, and he thought again how neglectful he had been. 'That's lovely!' He heard her rise and felt her warm lips

403

pressing his cheek. 'That's the nicest thing I've heard for ages,' she said. 'And now, I'll have to get moving. We're transferring the blended wines to the bottling vats today. But I'll be home to get ready for the party and to help you with your bow tie.'

'Oh, don't worry. Françoise will do that,' he said and noted the silence and then a small, muffled sigh as without another word she left him alone.

He managed to pour himself another cup of coffee. As he sat, suffering the pain in his head and thinking about the offer for the business, he heard the door of the breakfast room open again.

'Hello, Papa Philippe,' a cheerful little voice said. 'Can I have another cup of coffee?'

He turned sightless eyes to where Rosanne would be standing.

'Aren't you supposed to be in the schoolroom?' he asked.

'No, I've been let free while Miss goes over something with Françoise. I thought I'd come and see you. I hardly ever see you now.'

He was neglecting her, too, for Françoise, he thought guiltily, surprised to find that she was pushing her way to sit on his lap.

'It's a long time since I've sat on your lap, too,' she said and added in a matter-of-fact way, 'I miss you.'

'I'm always here,' he protested.

'Of course you are!' She gave him a hug. 'But Françoise always beats me to it. It's a shame really that she's so much older me. She thinks I'm too small for her to play with. Not as small as her little brother of course, and that's just as well, I suppose.' He was wondering where this conversation was leading, when she added in a puzzled voice. 'I wonder why she did that?'

'Did what?' he asked.

'Tried to kill her baby brother with a cushion. It's a funny thing to do, isn't it?'

'Rosanne! What are you saying?' He was horrified.

'Didn't you know? I thought you must know. That's why they sent her to us.'

'Rosanne, this is one of your stories,' he said firmly, trying to push her off his lap, but she wound her arms round his neck and refused to budge.

'It's not a story,' she said indignantly, her breath warm on his cheek. 'It's true. She told me herself. I often wonder what would have happened if Didier hadn't caught her and stopped her. Papa Philippe,' she dropped her voice, 'would she have gone to the guillotine?'

'She was making it up,' Philippe said firmly.

'Oh, I don't think so. She explained that she was jealous of the baby – just like she's jealous of Mama. She said it wasn't fair. When the new baby came, no one took any notice of her and we'd got you, so she tried to kill it. I suppose Mama and I could feel the same way. You don't take much notice of us any more, but we wouldn't try to kill her because of it. She said she'd do it to me one day when she was cross, but I told her I was too big. I'd kick her. But I do feel a bit sorry for her. It must be horrid when no one loves you and wants you. But you love her, so that's enough. If only she'd be nice to Mama, I might get to like her, too. She is very pretty.'

'Rosanne, I don't want to hear any more of this,' Philippe began, and then heard himself saying: 'What do you mean she's not nice to your mama?'

'Maybe she doesn't mean it.' Rosanne sounded as if she doubted that. 'When she's saying loving things to you, you can't see her face but we can. And if looks could kill, Mama would have been dead and buried weeks ago. And she's very rude sometimes when you're not there. It's all because Mama's got you, and you're not with her mama. But perhaps you could tell her that we all understand about that and we want to make her happy, if she'll let us.'

Philippe was struggling to keep some composure. He didn't want to believe what he was hearing, but Rosanne never lied. And all those silences and Rosie's reticence with Françoise were being explained. Rosie had said he was perceptive. Only when it suited him, he thought.

'Does your mother know you're telling me this?'

'No,' the child said. 'She said I wasn't to.'

The pain in his head was so severe he thought he could easily scream. It felt so bad he was sure it was coloured vivid blood-red.

'Then why are you telling me?'

'Because I'm a bit fed up with it all, Papa Philippe. So is

405

Mama but she won't admit it. But mostly because I don't want to go and live with Françoise in Paris away from here, and I bet Mama doesn't either. Here's our home. But Mama will never tell you that. If you want to go, she'll go. She'll do anything you want. It's hard for us to tell you the truth sometimes and say things you don't want to hear because you're blind. We have to be careful with you.'

Her devastating honesty again. No one ever used the word blind in front of Philippe, though he sometimes used it himself. But Rosie had garnered a comfortable collection of euphemisms that made the hard little word redundant.

'Blind in more ways than one, Rosanne,' he said heavily.

'It's not your fault,' she said cheerfully, giving him a hug. 'That Françoise is very clever.' She slid off his lap but did not move away. 'As hateful as she is, I do feel sorry for her. It must be horrid to know that nobody wants you. Except you, of course.' She gave a big sigh. 'I'll have to tell Mama tonight that I've told you how we feel. She'll kill me!'

She gave him a rather sticky kiss on his cheek and he heard her half-running out of the room and back down the hallway. He felt only relief that she had gone. The pain in his head had made a red mist in front of his eyes. It hurt too much to think about anything. All he wanted to do was to get to his room and blot out pain and everything else with laudanum. He'd think about what Rosanne had told him when he'd slept. But he was already reassuring himself that it was all childish nonsense.

Along with her anxieties that Philippe really did want to sell their business, something else was nagging at Rosie. It was the name of the man who had written the letter. Jack Patterson. She was sure she had heard it somewhere before. But where? And why?

The pumping of the blended wine into the huge bottling vat, the *foudre de tirage*, down in the cellar beneath the house was going well. But it was chilly down there. She had never liked being in the cellars. The dim light gave the thick curtains of cobwebs and the curious dark fungus that grew on the stone walls a sinister aspect, like some old dungeons. By midday she was freezing in spite of gloves and a woolly hat and she could see that Luke's nose was turning red.

'I want something to eat,' she said. 'Let's go and have lunch.'

'Good idea,' he said, blowing on his fingers like a schoolboy. 'Hot soup would be welcome.'

Leaving the workmen to get on with it, she and Luke made their way to the Les Hérissons dining room. Madame was already seated at the head of the table, while Feathers, exuding impatience, had started to eat. She had to get back to her shop, she explained. She wanted to make sure all the last-minute details had been taken care of.

'I came back because I wanted to see you all,' she said. 'I've got a present for Aunt Rosie and Madame. Well,' she lost the French and said to Rosie, 'tell Madame it's sort of a present. There are strings attached. You have to wear it tonight.'

Feathers went running out into the hall and came back with four large boxes wrapped in gold paper. 'There's something for Rosanne and Françoise, too.' she said, speaking French again. 'Nothing for the men. I don't sell men's clothes.' She laughed and clapped her hands like an excited child. 'You're not to open them now. I know they'll fit. I got Marie to borrow one of your dresses and they're made exactly to size. Mimi,' she turned to Madame Dupuis. 'You don't have to wear it if you don't like it, but it would be lovely if all the family were dressed in clothes from my shop tonight. Do you mind?'

Madame was smiling and patting the parcel. 'As long as it's not too modern,' she said. Feathers rolled her eyes.

'I promise it is perfect for you,' she said, 'elegant, stylish and with great dignity. Just like its new owner.'

Madame went quite pink.

Rosie stood holding her three parcels. She was smiling, too. When Feathers was happy she had the trick of making the rest of the world happy with her.

'Now, since I'm supposed to be eating for two I'd better get on with it.' She grimaced and patted her bump. 'I just hope I'm not overdoing it.'

'Eat what you want,' Rosie said encouragingly. She put the boxes down and sat down, pushing the tureen of soup over towards Luke. Then she asked him: 'Have you ever heard of anyone called Jack Patterson?'

'Nope,' he said, tearing off a chunk from the bread Cook had made that morning. 'Who's he?'

'Oh, no one really.' Rosie felt it would be unwise to mention the letter to Luke, but Feathers was looking up from her plate.

'Jack Patterson?' she said. 'He's a friend of Pierre's. He's that American that Pierre goes to see in Paris all the time.'

'Ah!' The memory of Feathers mentioning the name returned. 'Of course. You talked about him once. I remember. What does he do?'

Feathers pushed her plate aside and stood up, groaning as she clasped her hands on her stomach over one of the floating, accordion-pleated dresses she had designed for her pregnancy.

'I don't know. I think he's very rich. Pierre never gives me any details. But I know he sees him all the time.'

Madame was alert and listening, her eyes darting round the table.

'American, you say?' she asked.

'Yes. A fellow Bostonian apparently. They met at the Sorbonne.' Feathers edged towards the door. 'Must go,' she said. 'I'll be back to change. Don't forget – everyone's to be on time.'

No one spoke for a moment, and then Madame said: 'Why did you want to know about this American, Rosie?'

The hooded eyes were bright with enquiry. Rosie felt convinced that the old woman knew something about whatever it was that was going on.

'No reason really.'

'Being a rich American, I just wondered if he might be interested in buying your business.'

Rosie couldn't help smiling. Madame did know something, but, unusually for her, her approach to find out more had been clumsy.

'My business is not for sale, Mimi,' she said. And knew as she said it that she was speaking the truth. She would not sell to Jack Patterson or anyone else. Somehow she would create the life Philippe wanted but not by selling her business. Not by losing all she had worked for since she first came to France. She couldn't let that happen.

'Good,' Madame said, lifting her wine glass, as if in a toast, a satisfied little smile on her face. She looked exactly as if she had heard what she wanted and expected to hear. But how did she know anything about it? That was the question. Rosie ate in silence thinking about the connection between Pierre and Jack Patterson. She also remembered uneasily that Philippe had said how interested Pierre was in the business. Was he involved in this offer? she wondered.

After they had finished lunch, Rosie had one quick look at the cellars and decided to go back to Les Coquelicots. The work for the day was now routine and Luke would take care of anything that went wrong. She would be better employed doing some paperwork with Philippe. The paperwork was always behind. She put Feathers' presents in the back of the car and drove home, her head buzzing with queries and problems. What was the link with Pierre, Madame and Jack Patterson? She had an uneasy feeling that something was afoot; something Madame wanted her to know about but wasn't going to tell. Madame was rarely as unsubtle as she had been today.

And Philippe. What was she going to do about Philippe? The sad truth was that he was not the same man she had married. He could not come to terms with his blindness even now. He was withdrawn, almost a recluse, and totally involved in his own troubles. They still loved each other, and their loving moments were as sweet as they had ever been but, alas, now few and far between. It seemed, she thought bitterly, he needed a hand-maiden daughter more than a wife.

She tried not to think about it, and made herself enjoy the sight of the baby green leaves sprouting from the vines, heralding spring and hopefully a good crop. Another year of wine was beginning with all the hopes and fears and triumphs. Madame had once said that a Champagne *vigneron* must be tough to fight the pests, the weather, nature herself, and must always live with hope. After so many years, Rosie believed herself to be tough, and never without hope. And if nature herself had never been able to make her give up, Jack Patterson, whoever he was, didn't stand a chance.

Les Coquelicots, standing mature and distinguished on the hill, was quiet in the weak sunshine of the mid-afternoon as she drove up to the double wooden front door. The girls would be in the room they used for their lessons and Philippe in his office. But he was not in his office. Worried she ran upstairs to their bedroom and found him there. He was fully dressed and fast asleep on the big bed. She stopped in her tracks, stood still and turned quietly, meaning to leave the room without waking him. But he had heard her. A useless reflex action opened his eyes.

'Rosie?' he said.

'Yes. I'm sorry, I didn't mean to wake you.'

He sat up. 'What time is it?'

'Gone two.'

'I've been dozing since this morning. I took some laudanum.'

'It was that bad?'

'It was very bad,' he said grimly. 'And your daughter didn't make it any better.'

He was swinging his legs over the side of the bed and sitting up. His face was set and she could feel his hostility. She was bewildered. Philippe was never hostile.

'Rosanne?' she said. 'What's she done?'

'Told me a lot of terrible lies about my daughter. I believed her at first. No wonder I had the worst headache I've ever known. I realise now it was just a lot of jealous rubbish.'

'What did she say?' Rosie asked quietly, heart sinking.

'Some nonsense about Françoise trying to kill her baby brother and being rude to you. She even said that my daughter was hateful. If I hadn't been in such pain I might have hit the little liar.'

Rosie's heart dropped to her boots. She drew a deep breath. She could have murdered Rosanne, but she was not going to let Philippe judge her a liar.

'Philippe, you know that Rosanne never lies.'

'Now you're defending her.'

'Yes. I am.'

She stood, her eyes closed, trying to control her temper and trying to think what to say next. Perhaps it was time for some truth around the place. The situation with Françoise couldn't go on indefinitely. Maybe it wasn't a bad thing that Rosanne, undoubtedly incensed by the breakfast conversation, had punctured the wall of pretence.

'I'm defending her,' she said levelly, 'because she is telling the truth.'

'You're both jealous.' His face was reddening.

'My darling, do you think that I have changed that much?

410

Have you ever known me jealous?' she asked quietly, trying to calm him.

'Yes. You were jealous when Françoise was born.'

'I was shocked when she was born. You hadn't even told me that your wife was pregnant. Remember?'

'You didn't want her here. I could tell.'

Rosie was beginning to get angry.

'I was uneasy, I admit,' she said through gritted teeth. 'But I did my best to make her welcome. I swear to you that I did. The fact that the child never responded in the slightest is not my fault. However, I'm sorry you've heard all this. I thought I had made Rosanne promise never to tell you what was going on.'

'She said that,' he said sullenly. 'She said you'd kill her. And I feel like killing her right now. Lies. It must be lies.'

'I doubt if she has told you one single lie. But what did she tell you?' Rosie asked, keeping her voice even.

'That Françoise had been sent here because she tried to smother her baby brother, or some such nonsense.'

'That is what Françoise told Rosanne. Maybe the girl was lying. Maybe she was making it up for some reason. But Rosanne was only repeating what had been said to her. If it is a lie, the lie is not Rosanne's. The lie, if it is one, originates with your daughter.'

'It's because Françoise is unhappy here that she makes up things like that.'

Rosie exploded. 'She's unhappy! She's managed to create the most terrible atmosphere in this house and for all your so-called perception you can't feel it. I suppose you don't want to feel it. She's charming to you but to everyone else she is rude, insufferable and insolent. We have all put up with it in silence for months. And you tell me that she is unhappy here! If that is the case it's because she is determined not to be happy and to make as much mischief as she possibly can.'

'Don't shout at me,' he said coldly. 'I may not be able to see but there is nothing the matter with my hearing.'

She felt a lot better for shouting at him, but she made herself count to ten, and then went and sat beside him on the bed. She took his hand, but he pulled it away.

'Darling, please.' She put her head on his shoulder. 'You must believe me. We have loved each other for so long, surely

411

you can't believe that I would deliberately set out to make your daughter unhappy. I have never told you what has been going on because I saw what comfort and happiness you found with her. It hurt a little, perhaps, but I was glad for you. But I was not glad for myself. She has truly been impossible.'

'But you couldn't tell me how you felt because I'm blind. Is that it? That's what Rosanne says.' His voice was bitter but the hostility was fading.

'Yes, that's why I didn't tell you. But I was wrong. The fact that you can't see . . .'

'That I'm blind!' He was shouting now.

'All right, that you're blind, shouldn't have stopped me. I was cosseting you by not speaking out, just as Françoise cossets you and stops you doing things for yourself.'

'Ah, that's it. She pays me too much attention.'

'Much too much, in that way.' Rosie was angry again. 'You may be blind, but you're still a young man and you don't need a nursemaid.'

He put his elbows on his knees and sank his head into his hands.

'All right,' he said wearily, 'What has been going on?'

'Nothing really dreadful.' She was picking her words carefully, trying to dodge any traps. 'Just hard to live with. Françoise has a tone of voice for you and facial expressions for the rest of us. Expressions she would certainly not wish you to see. She dislikes us all very much and deliberately shows it, but she loves you dearly. She feels that I stole you from her mother, and maybe she's right. She wants to punish me, and indirectly Rosanne, for that. I have tried to think what to do for weeks now. Everything she does is so subtle that it's difficult to pick upon any one incident that could start a discussion about it with her. Now you know what has been going on, since she does genuinely love you, perhaps you could persuade her to become more part of this family. She has made me unhappy in my own home, Philippe. And your response to her has made both Rosanne and me feel that we are no longer important in your life.'

'Jealous women!' he muttered, but there was not much conviction there.

She laughed. 'Honestly, not so much jealousy as anger. It's

412

as well that Rosanne took matters into her own hands. I was getting very close to clouting your daughter. Hard. I'm amazed I haven't.'

She wanted to add that if things did not improve, Françoise would have to go, whether the Caribbean climate was suitable or not and at whatever risk to the baby brother. But she held back. This was not the moment.

He took her hand.

'I suppose I suspected something,' he said slowly. 'I noticed your reticence with her, and I kept meaning to ask you about it, but I kept putting it off. I suppose instinctively I knew that I wouldn't like what I heard. All right. I'll talk to her. When we're all in Paris and living like a proper family, it'll be easier for all of us.'

Rosie had to stifle a groan. Nor was it the moment to say that she would never sell. One step at a time, she thought, and leaned to kiss him.

'And it would be nice if you and Rosanne really made an effort to get on with Françoise. She's really such a sweet girl and everything is six of one and half a dozen of the other.'

She could have hit him. Instead she gritted her teeth and said: 'Of course. And now we'd better start getting ready for this party.'

New York, 1 April 1924

Jenny had taken to coming round every afternoon at about three. She would join Allie in her study, Allie would put the cover over her typewriter and the two of them would sit and gossip. Sometimes, if the weather was fine, they would walk in Central Park. Jenny liked to watch the children playing around the Hans Christian Andersen statue. For Allie it was the best part of the day. She knew their meetings were important to Jenny as well. Nothing was ever said, but sometimes she would catch the other woman's eyes looking at her with a sad, almost lovelorn look. And when they went shopping, Jenny would never come into the trying-on room while Allie was undressing. For Allie it had become a game to make Jenny see her half undressed. She knew she was being provocative, but she could not seem to help herself. As the days went past, she could tell

413

she was becoming more and more dependent on Jenny's presence in her life, but this did not trouble her. There was time to see what her feelings meant. Time to work out what should be done. As it was, she had her work, she had a husband who loved her and she had Jenny.

Allie had been home for a fortnight when Jenny announced over the teacups that she would soon have to go back to work again. Probably in Algeria.

'I can't just sit around eating cream cakes and doing nothing else,' she said, helping herself to one from the plateful that the maid had brought in with the tea.

Allie was truly dismayed.

'But why?' she said. 'You don't need to work. You don't get paid for it.'

'I *do* need to work,' Jenny said. 'But not for money. I need something to occupy me.'

'But I need you,' Allie wailed. 'You can't go. I shall miss you so.'

'You'll be all right,' Jenny told her, avoiding her eye. 'Anyway, these afternoons with me keep you from your work.'

'It's not you that keeps me from my work,' Allie protested. 'It's going out in the evenings. Alexander always wants to go somewhere. The evenings were always my best time for writing. He's going to Washington for a week on some story. Thank goodness I'll be able to get on a bit.'

'And if I don't come every afternoon, you can get on even faster.'

'You help me with my work,' Allie protested. 'Talking to you clears my head. You're so like Dr Weingott . . .'

'Golly!' Jenny said. 'I've seen never myself as an analyst.'

'You listen in the same way. I can tell you things.'

'Right then,' Jenny said in her forthright way. 'Tell me how you're getting on with Alexander. Apart from all this social life, is it working out?'

Allie averted her face.

'Not really,' she said. 'I don't know how to behave with him. And I think he's totally puzzled by me. We go out a lot now. We go to the theatre and the movies and I enjoy it, but I guess the truth is I'd just as soon be with you as with him. In fact, I'd rather be with you. You can discuss things better with women.

414

I do love him, Jenny. I love him a lot, but as another human being. Not as a man and a husband.' She stopped. 'You asked me, so I'll tell you. But you're not to be angry with me because he's your brother. I've come to the conclusion that my reluctance about sex and all that is more than the rape. Or if it is the rape that caused it, it's incurable. I meant to be a proper wife when I came home from the clinic. I promised myself I would. And I guess that's why I stayed there so long. While I was there, I didn't have to be a proper wife. In fact, I fell in love . . .' She hesitated.

'With Dr Weingott?' Jenny asked, looking into her teacup.

'You guessed?'

'No, actually I didn't. But New York is littered with people who've fallen in love with their analysts. It seems to be a part of the cure, if there is one.'

Allie laughed. 'That's what she said. I got very brave and I told her I loved her one day. I was longing for her to kiss me, but all she said was that my reaction to her was perfectly normal and I'd get over it once I left the clinic. I felt so stupid having spoken out. I'll never do that again.'

'And did you get over it?' Allie noted the intensity in Jenny's voice.

'Yes, I guess so. I think about her all the time, but only figuring out what she would want me to do. I think she'd want me to sleep with Alexander, but I can't do it. I wonder if I'd have been able to if she had been a man? Do you think falling for a woman has kind of twisted things up?'

'I don't know.' Jenny spoke so quietly it was hard to hear her.

'I liked being in love. It's a good feeling, isn't it? It hurts and yet it's wonderful at the same time. You have a focus for all your emotions and there's an excuse for them. And even if the loved one doesn't love you back, you know you're alive, and you know you're feeling something and that there's blood in your veins and a heart pumping away there. That's another reason why I didn't want to leave. I was enjoying being in love. And once it goes, you miss it. Where does it go, I wonder? It just isn't there any more, until someone else comes along, of course . . .' She broke off. 'Have you ever been in love, Jenny?'

'Several times. But I've never dared speak of it.'

'With women?'

'Yes. Always with women.'

'Dr Weingott told me about it. She said it was brave of you to tell me.'

Jenny half-smiled and nodded.

'I asked her if she was like that. But she wasn't. She said there was nothing wrong with it, though.'

'Not many people would agree with her.'

'And she said when I left the clinic never to be afraid of my own sexuality.'

Jenny was not speaking, just staring into the fire.

'What do you think she meant by that?' Allie asked, her voice all innocence.

'Exactly what she said, I suppose.'

'Even if it's a love some people might think was wrong and wicked?'

'No love is wrong or wicked,' Jenny said firmly.

The atmosphere in the room was tense. Allie was not quite sure what she was doing; what game she was playing.

Something seemed to be pushing her on. She looked at Jenny where she sat, eyes downcast. Jenny was in no way beautiful, but she had the nicest face. Also she had Alexander's wonderful smile, though it shone only rarely. What Allie liked best about Jenny was that she was strong and sensible. Stronger than any man that Allie had ever met. Alexander was delightful, but he was not strong. Nor had her father been, or even Pierre. She had always known that she was stronger than any of them. She found strength attractive. She needed someone strong in her life since she had rejected her mother. A strong woman or a strong man, she thought? She wasn't sure. And she wouldn't know the answer until Jenny kissed her. She had to make Jenny kiss her.

Taking the initiative, she did the thing that Jenny had done when she came to the clinic for the first time. She went and knelt in front of her and took her hands.

'Jenny,' she said pleadingly, 'what am I to do about Alexander?'

'What do you want to do?' Jenny's hands rested passive.

'Let things go on the way they are, but it isn't fair. I understand that now.'

'And would you care if he had a mistress now?'

Allie sat back on her heels and thought about it.

416

'I don't think I'd care,' she said. 'Just as long as I wasn't aware of it, but I'd hate it if everyone but me knew.'

'You wouldn't care about him sleeping with someone else as long as he was discreet?'

'No, I wouldn't mind. Not if it meant I wasn't guilty about not sleeping with him. I do get most awfully guilty about it, you know.'

Jenny sighed a long sigh.

'Poor Alexander,' she said. 'And poor you.'

'No.' Allie leaned forward and laid her head on Jenny's lap. 'Not poor me.'

She felt the other woman stiffen, and then, slowly, a hand came to stroke her hair.

'Why not poor you?'

Allie breathed in Jenny's warm, womanly scent. 'Because I've got you. Haven't I?'

There was a long silence that seemed to go on for an eternity. Then Jenny's two hands were round her face, lifting it so that they were looking at each other.

'What do you want me for?' she asked, her grey eyes sad.

'A friend. More than a friend . . .'

'How much more?'

'A lover?' Allie suggested, and found she was not breathing as she waited for the answer.

Jenny took her hands away and stood up, leaving Allie kneeling. She moved to the window and looked out.

'You're my brother's wife,' she said. 'I mustn't think about this.'

'We have to think about it,' Allie said quietly. 'We know we do. We've known for weeks.'

'I've known for months,' Jenny said with her rare sudden smile. 'It's so strange. I never liked you, and then suddenly I loved you. I wanted to protect you from all the dreadful things. Men, and the things men do. But you're my brother's wife.'

Allie got to her feet and slowly walked towards where Jenny stood. She fixed her eyes on Jenny's mouth, and when she was close she wrapped her arms round the woman and laid her head on her shoulder.

'We can't help it, Jenny,' she whispered, still not sure if she was playing a cruel game.

'Of course we can help it!' Jenny's voice was anguished. 'I shouldn't have let it happen. It's my fault. I should have stayed away. But I wanted to be near you.'

'I could tell.'

'I didn't want you to know.'

Allie tightened her arms and lifted her face. Jenny groaned and very gently brought her lips down to meet Allie's. For a moment they just clung to each other, and then the kiss deepened. As she tasted Jenny's sweet mouth, Allie knew it wasn't a strong man or any other kind of man she wanted. Now, at this moment, she wanted Jenny.

Pierre was home early from Épernay and the house was silent, deep in afternoon slumber.

There was a letter with a New York postmark waiting for him the hall. He picked it up, and this time the handwriting was Allie's. Holding it, seeing her bold decisive script he felt a curious clenching of the heart.

The letter itself was of more importance than what she would say about his request to her to sell her share of Les Hérissons. The letter was contact with her. He knew he was a fool to want contact, but there was nothing he could do about that.

He took the letter up to his rooms, glad that there was no sign of Feathers. She would be at her shop, making sure that everything was all right before the party. He could savour this letter alone.

He slit it open carefully and spread the single sheet of paper on his desk. He found himself reluctant to read it.

Dear Pierre,

Thank you for your nice letter and you must forgive me for not having replied to you myself. Alexander told you that I was in a clinic. I had a sort of breakdown, but it's all over now and I am well again.

Unfortunately, Alexander may have misled you with his reply. I believe he said that I would be willing to sell.

Well, I have thought about it long and hard and now my mind is clearer I don't feel I wish to do that. You see, I must consider Rosanne. It's all very well for me, living in

New York, to sell out all interest in her home. I know you say that nothing will change if I do sell to you, but life is very uncertain and I would not want to feel that Rosanne did not have any rights to her own home. And Les Hérissons has always been a family place, belonging to all of us.

In any case, it is not mine to sell. It was kind of you not to mention it to Mimi until you knew how I felt, but I can't help feeling that the whole question is an academic one. Mimi would not sell. I am certain of that. I can just imagine her saying to you that you will have to wait until she dies. Then, in the French way, we will all get our portion. It is the way things are done in France.

I am sorry to disappoint you. But as I say, life is very uncertain. Maybe one day, when Rosanne is grown up, I shall change my mind.

I hope your family are well, and give my love to everyone.

Yours,
Allie

He put the letter down and sat for a moment with his head in his hands. The dream was dissolving. A refusal from Mimi, another from Allie. And he knew the chances of Rosie selling were slight. Would it be better to call the whole thing off?

In a rush of decisiveness, he picked up the phone and asked the operator to connect him with Jack Patterson in Paris. He sat fidgeting while he waited to get through, his resolve strengthening. Fortunately Jack was in and answered the call. Without preliminaries, Pierre said: 'It's no go, Jack. My half-sister won't sell, my grandmother won't sell, and I doubt very much if my aunt will sell. I think it's best to call it off.'

'Hang on, old boy,' Jack, who affected English manners, said. 'I haven't had a reply from my letter yet. She can only just have got it. And you never know your luck.'

'I don't want to do it any more,' Pierre said. 'Things have changed. It'll split the family. I must have been mad even to think about it. This is the only family I've ever had.'

There was a silence, and then Jack said silkily: 'Well, old chap, you may have changed your mind, but I haven't. I quite fancy the idea of owning a champagne house. I might even drive the old motor down there and have a word with your auntie myself.'

'Jack, forget it. You'll be wasting your time,' Pierre said, suddenly alarmed at what he might have started.

'I shall make them an offer they can't refuse.' The American was laughing, but it was no laughing matter.

'Jack, I'd rather you didn't do anything of the kind.'

'Let's talk about it.'

'There's nothing to talk about.'

'Tell you what, I can be down there in a couple of hours. Where can we meet?'

'We can't. My wife's having her shop opening tonight in Reims. I have to be there. All the family are going.'

'A shop!'

'A dress shop.'

'In the fashionable quarter, I trust.'

'Of course,' Pierre said testily. 'Jack, the whole thing was a crazy mistake. I wish I'd never started it. I'll come up to Paris in the next couple of days and we'll talk about it. But I'm not going to change my mind.'

'Neither am I,' Jack said cheerfully. 'Okay then, we'll leave it for now. Talk to you later in the week, eh?'

'Sure,' Pierre said, and hung up the receiver. He sat staring into space. It looked as if Jack was going to be difficult. But he was fairly convinced that Jack could be as difficult as he damn well liked. Rosie wouldn't sell. He'd stake his life on it.

What with one thing and another Rosie was nearly late for the party. The excitement of opening Feathers' presents had caused the delay. The dresses she had chosen were beautiful. Each box had a note inside that said: 'Please wear this for me tonight, and keep it as an expression of my thanks.'

Rosie's was vivid green; a simple dress of embroidered chiffon with a deep round neck and thin shoulder straps worn over a shorter, deeper green taffeta slip. The skirt of the chiffon tunic was cut to hang in a point which just touched the ground on the right side. A balancing pointed deep scarf floated from the left shoulder, held in place by a narrow band at the shoulder and another at the wrist. Every move of the left hand created a graceful flurry of vivid green. A dramatic flower made of pale green feathers marked the hip line where the dress softly folded. Feathers had even put in a pair of pretty, matching high-heeled green satin shoes with a lacy band across the instep and a pair of long drop jade earrings to complete the outfit.

The two girls had been given matching dresses which were perfect little copies of a grown-up party frock. Made in crepe they had deep square necklines, and a soft bodice which ended in a broad, inset waistband. The skirt below ended well above the ankle and was made in three layers. Both dresses had full slit shawl sleeves that floated free of their childish arms. Rosanne's was a deep raspberry pink, warm against her dark hair and skin. Françoise's was glacier-blue, perfect for her ice-maiden colouring. Both had matching little garlands of feathers for their hair.

Françoise was so thrilled and excited by all the dressing up that for once she was behaving like a normal little girl. And Rosanne couldn't get over herself when she looked in the mirror.

'Since you're to be mannequins,' Rosie said when Nanny Shepherd brought them dressed ready and pleased with themselves to her room, 'you may both have some powder on your noses.'

'And lipstick?' squealed Françoise.

'All right, just a touch,' Rosie said, and sat them in turn at her dressing table and gave them a light make-up. 'Your grandmother will kill me,' she said to Rosanne when she stepped back to examine her handiwork.

'You've done it so nicely, Mama, that Mimi will never notice.'

Looking at this suddenly grown-up Rosanne, Rosie felt a great wave of love. Rosanne was going to be beautiful in a way that she had never been. Allie was beautiful, but Rosanne was something special. She had the blue eyes and the black hair of the Dupuis but her nose was finer, her cheekbones more pronounced, her mouth fuller and perfectly shaped, the lower lip raised and rounded. And the violet eyes were fringed with an incredible profusion of black lashes. Her party finery released in the child all the promise of the woman to come. Impulsively Rosie picked her up and hugged her, not caring if she crushed the dress.

'You look beautiful, darling,' she said, and putting her down, turned to hug Françoise.

'And so do you,' she said, but Françoise dodged away.

The party was to begin at 7.30, and it was 7.25 when Rosie's group arrived. She had had the Salmson polished to mirror perfection and Michel was wearing the chauffeur's uniform they rarely bothered with. She and a quiet, rather pale Philippe sat in the back with Françoise between them. A thrilled Rosanne was allowed to sit in front with Michel.

Feathers' shop, revealed to the inhabitants of Reims now all the boarding was down, was as elegant as anything on the rue St Honoré. Above the huge windows and white wood work, the fascia read FEATHERS in beautifully scripted gold leaf. Inside, the floors were covered in thick white wool carpet, the walls mirrored with the glass placed in such a way that the customer was reflected in a series of diminishing images. The changing rooms and the clothes themselves were hidden by layers and layers of gauzy white curtains. Two huge white velvet sofas comprised the furniture and the only decorations were some nude figures in Lalique and tall white glass jars filled with peacock's feathers. Cleverest of all was the lighting. It was hidden in some way, but the room was bathed in a soft light. Rosie, seeing herself reflected in the mirrors, noted that it was kind to ladies of a certain age.

What it was all going to cost she shuddered to think, then pushed the thought away as being churlish.

Feathers was rushing to meet them.

'Did they fit? Were the shoes all right?' she was calling as she came across the thick carpet. 'I think you all look marvellous. And Philippe, too, so distinguished!'

She herself was wearing daring pyjama trousers, white ones in crepe with a boxy, deep turn-up. The turn-up swung clear above square-toed black patent leather shoes with small heels. The tunic was equally daring: black and full to cover her bulge, long sleeves widening at the wrists, and a huge collar which opened into a deep V neckline, showing the curve of her full breasts. The hem of the tunic and the collar were bordered with hundreds of tiny white feathers and a simple white bow on the hip distracted the eye from her bulk. Glowing with excitement, her dark hair in a curly fringe over her forehead, eyebrows plucked into the thinnest of thin lines and her mouth a perfect bow, Rosie thought she was quite as exotic – if not more exotic – as her idol, Garbo, and much more glamorous than most other film stars.

422

She told Feathers she looked beautiful, and that the outfit was absolutely perfect, adding: 'Honestly, that and these clothes you have given us are as fine as any couturier's. You are a clever girl! And the shop is superb.'

'You really like it? The clothes are couture in a way. I copy them from *Vogue* and change them a bit. I know you're not supposed to, and I won't when I get going. I've got plenty of ideas of my own. My outfit's a sort of Lanvin. They had a modesty bib in the tunic. I thought it was more dramatic to leave it out. And theirs was bordered with ribbon. I wanted feathers.'

'But of course,' Rosie said laughing, but aware that Philippe was clinging to her arm in a desperate kind of way.

'Papa, do you want to sit down?' she heard Françoise's voice say.

'Yes, please, my dear.' He detached himself, and Françoise led him away.

'Rosanne, I've got a job for you,' Feathers was saying. 'Will you keep winding the phonograph and be in charge of the music? I've brought lots of jazz records. It's going to be all American music. I'm an American and I speak rotten French so I'm going to capitalise on it.'

Rosanne was thrilled at the idea of being in charge of the music. She vanished with Feathers towards the phonograph where it sat square, horn gleaming brassily, in the corner of the salon. In a few moments the shop was full of music . . .

> *Ain't we got fun?*
> *Not much money, oh! but honey,*
> *Ain't we got fun?*
> *There's nothing surer,*
> *The rich get rich and the poor get – children.*
> *In the meantime, in between time,*
> *Ain't we got fun?*

It was just as Rosanne had put on the record that Madame Dupuis arrived accompanied by Luke West and Miss.

'I designed Mimi's dress myself,' Feathers whispered before she went to greet her mother-in-law. 'Is it all right?'

Madame's dress was beautiful. Cut like a nun's habit in two

layers, it flowed from the shoulders to the ground. The long sleeves were wide. It could not have been more simple; almost ordinary, except for the fabric which was soft and delicate and shimmered in a miraculous way with every move. It was perfectly correct for a woman of Madame's age, but glamorous in the most understated fashion, and from the way she was walking and the way her head was held, Madame knew it.

However, pleased as she was, it did not stop her asking: 'What is that terrible music?' as Feathers led her over to where Rosie stood.

'American music, Mimi, and we've got a Negro jazz band coming later. Do you like the shop? Isn't it a-m-a-z-i-n-g?'

Before Madame could reply she had fled away to greet an arriving guest. Waiters were emerging from the back of the shop with trays of champagne. Rosie took a glass and tasted it. Her own 1921 vintage, she noted.

Madame tasted hers and grunted approval.

'Our 'twenty-one?' she asked.

'Right,' said Rosie. 'Do you want to sit? Come and sit with Philippe.'

The shop was filling up when Pierre arrived, looking a little harassed. He stared around the room in wonder, and as Feathers came hurrying to greet him, his eyes widened more. Rosie watched as he kissed her, held her back to look at her properly, and saw the proud smile that he could not quite conceal. She sighed. Maybe that was going to be all right.

The guests were pouring in now; the cream of Champagne society, Rosie thought. Or maybe the champagne of Champagne society. Madame Jacques Bollinger, Compte Robert-Jean de Vogue from Moët, the Pommery family *en masse*. The Mayor and the Mayoress arrived, and Madame insisted on going with Feathers to greet them since they were old friends of the family.

Philippe was silent, and surprisingly Françoise was not sitting at his side.

'Are you all right?' she asked Philippe. 'Do you want Françoise with you?'

'No, you.' He said. 'I sent her off.'

'Is your head hurting?'

'Badly,' he said briefly. 'I've never felt it so bad.'

424

'Do you want to go home?' she asked, taking his hand. 'You should have told me. You needn't have come. We perhaps ought to call the doctor.'

'It's not that bad and it's time I went somewhere with you,' he said. 'This is important. I should be with you.'

'Well, we'll just sit quietly here and I'll tell you what's going on.'

'No, don't speak. The music is almost too much. Just hold my hand.'

Rosie tried to imagine what it must be like for him. The noise was growing. Rosanne was enthusiastically keeping the phonograph up to full strength and people were talking loudly above it. The salon was filling up so that there was standing room only. The waiters never let a glass remain empty and others were now bringing round a bite-sized selection of food. Rosie found herself worrying about the brand new carpet. She was finding the noise level pretty disturbing herself, and Feathers had said that there was a jazz band arriving later. Philippe would not be able to bear that. She wasn't sure she could bear it herself. When the band arrived, it would be better if he and she left.

As it was, she was content to sit beside him and watch. This was Feathers' night and she shone. As the girl struggled to speak to her guests, their expressions were of amused tolerance. They liked her, it was obvious. They didn't care about her atrocious accent.

Rosie could hear her explaining to a young pregnant woman that she intended to stock maternity frocks.

'This year even *Vogue* has started featuring maternity clothes,' she said. 'I think there's a real need. I had to make all my own. Otherwise they are so dull and boring. Most of my clothes will be made to measure, though. And look, all my family are wearing Feathers creations tonight and I think they all look wonderful, don't you?'

Rosie felt a grin spreading over her face. Feathers wasn't backward in coming forward. Rosie's own faith in the concept of the shop was growing apace. She saw that Luke had left Miss talking to a son of one of the champagne houses and that he was pushing his way through the crowd towards her. He looked faintly uncomfortable in his dinner jacket, as if the bow tie were strangling him.

He said good evening to them both, shaking Philippe's hand, and then sat down beside them on the sofa.

'Everyone looks great,' he said. 'A most distinguished gathering of the Dupuis family.'

His eyes were frankly admiring her and Rosie was almost relieved that Philippe could not see.

'The noise is rather too much for Philippe, though,' she said. 'I think we shall have to go when the jazz band arrives.'

'You're going to miss some good American jazz?' he teased.

'Since the band are all Negroes, wouldn't you call it African?' she said.

'Whatever it is, it's a good sound and I like it.'

'I might if it wasn't for these interminable headaches,' Philippe said. 'How are you getting on at Les Hérissons?'

'Everything going to schedule,' Luke said.

He was interrupted by Françoise who reappeared and slid her hand into her father's.

'I don't know anybody, Papa,' she whined, 'and Rosanne won't let me wind the phonograph. I'd rather be with you.'

Her father patted the seat beside him and as the child sat down he said: 'Rosie and I are thinking of selling up, Luke. Did Rosie tell you?'

Rosie felt the horror on her face. She looked straight at Luke, opened her eyes wide and shook her head violently.

'Why are you pulling that funny face and shaking your head at Luke, Mama Rosie?' Françoise asked honey-sweet. 'Don't you agree with Papa?'

As Rosie resisted the urge to do violence to her stepdaughter, Philippe stiffened and stared suspiciously towards where Rosie sat.

'I thought that was what Françoise was supposed to do,' he said sharply.

Luke stepped into the breach.

'As a matter of fact, Rosie has mentioned it,' he said smoothly. 'But she said nothing was settled yet.'

Rosie dared not throw him a grateful look in case that was relayed back as well. Françoise was too much!

'Well, my health isn't up to it,' Philippe said, 'and it's time Rosie had a rest. We should go back to Paris to live. Perhaps follow the sun. Amuse ourselves for a bit.'

Rosie tried desperately to keep dismay from clouding her features.

'Aren't you well, Mama Rosie?' Françoise piped up. 'You look all funny.'

'I'm fine, thank you,' Rosie said coldly. 'Don't you find it hot in here, Luke?'

'It is rather. Shall I ask Feathers if she has any fans?'

'I can't imagine she won't,' Rosie said lightly. 'Feather ones, of course.'

'I'll go and see what I can do,' he said.

She blessed his tact as he worked his way back through the crowd. Rosanne was winding vigorously for a rendering of 'Lady Be Good'. Sung by Fred Astaire it was a decibel or two down on what had been played before.

'You're not happy about selling, are you?' Philippe asked abruptly.

She cursed Françoise sitting there. 'I'm trying to get used to the idea,' she said lightly. 'But this is no time to discuss it.'

'It never will be the time if you have your way,' he said.

'Certainly now isn't the time. Anyway, brace yourself. Feathers is bringing someone over to meet us.'

Feathers was waving at them and making signs that she was coming over. She had in tow a tall, gangling young man with an unmistakably American look. Pierre was behind him, and Pierre did not look a happy man. Rosie watching them coming towards her began to get a strong feeling of foreboding.

'Rosie, darling. Philippe,' Feathers said. 'Here's the young man you were asking about today, Rosie. Jack Patterson himself. He heard I was having this party and drove down from Paris to give his support. He even found the shop all on his own. Wasn't that terrific? Now he insists on meeting you and Philippe. He says Pierre has told him so much about you both.'

As Feathers blew a kiss and hurried away to greet new arrivals, Philippe rose to his feet and pushed his hand out. The American took it and then half-bowed to Rosie.

'Delighted,' he murmured. 'And well met.'

'It was kind of you to make the journey.' Rosie was praying that Philippe had not made the connection between this morning's letter and the man standing in front of them. But her prayers went unanswered.

'Did we receive a letter from you this morning?' Philippe asked abruptly.

'Asking if I could buy your business. That's right. Jack Patterson, one and the same.'

Pierre looked more miserable by the minute. There was an awkward silence as Luke reappeared, holding a large feather fan.

'Here,' he said, pushing it into Rosie's hand. 'It suits you better than me.'

Agitated she opened it and fanned her hot face, leaving Philippe to perform the introductions.

'Jack Patterson?' said Luke. 'Really? Rosie was asking after you today. What a coincidence.'

'I'm going to buy her business.'

'Ah!' said Luke.

'And we're all going to live in Paris and be happy and never go back to the boring old country again,' Françoise said smugly. 'Aren't we, Papa?'

Papa did not answer. He had turned his head sidewards to where Rosie stood.

'No decisions are made yet,' she said firmly.

'Papa,' said Françoise, 'Mama Rosie is pulling those faces again.'

Mama Rosie was doing no such thing. Mama Rosie had been controlling herself brilliantly until that minute. But at that moment all control disappeared like a puff of smoke in a high wind.

'That will do, Françoise,' she said, and did the thing she had wanted to do for months. She slapped her stepdaughter's face as hard as she was able.

The girl staggered back and would have fallen but for the press of people. The crack of flesh on flesh had rung through those nearest to them, and heads were turned in curiosity as Françoise screamed: 'She hit me, Papa! She hit me!'

That's done it! Rosie thought as the screaming girl flung herself into her father's arms. That's really done it.

She looked dispassionately at Françoise. With a bit of luck the girl would have a black eye to remember her stepmother by. And she felt no remorse. Not the faintest, tiniest twinge. In fact she felt better than she had done for weeks.

'Stop screaming, Françoise,' she said briskly. 'Control yourself in public.'

'Really, Rosie,' Philippe protested, looking over the girl's head. 'Did you hit her?' Then his face went very red and then white. He clutched his hands to his temples.

'Oh, Christ! Oh Christ! Oh Christ!' he moaned, swaying on his feet. He put out a hand, feeling for support as he began to slump and it was Luke who leaped forward in time to catch him as he fell.

New York City, 2 April 1924

Alexander and Beth Rogan left their office in Times Square together. It was quarter to one on a blowy New York April morning with blue skies above and a sense of spring in the air.

They walked slightly apart. Alexander looked around for a cab. At his wave one drew up. They both quickly climbed in and Alexander murmured the address and they drove off.

Still neither spoke, but Alexander took her square, capable hand in his and squeezed it. She turned her blonde head to smile at him. They were heading for the small studio apartment that Alexander had insisted on keeping. Since she had left her husband Beth had had her own apartment on the West Side, but even so, their rendezvous still took place in the one room where their affair had taken root. Alexander preferred it. Though Beth swore that Walter Rogan would cause no problems, Alexander was still uneasy at the thought of maybe being cited in a divorce case. He had his suspicions that maybe Allie wouldn't care any more, but his parents would, and so would his clubs and maybe even his employers. Beth seemed indifferent, but she was bolstered by confidence that Walter Rogan would do nothing to make waves. He would be the guilty party.

'It's all fixed,' she said as they came into the studio room away from the ears of the cab driver. She threw her hat on the wide couch that doubled as a bed and kicked off her shoes. 'I'm divorcing Walter for adultery.'

'You are?' Alexander said.

'Yep! He feels he should do the gentlemanly thing and take the blame. Some lady, paid for her trouble, will be playing cards and drinking with him in a hotel bedroom one night this week. Or that's what he says they'll be doing. The hotel maid and the desk clerk will provide the evidence that Walter spent the night with this unnamed female committing adultery, and that will be that.'

'And how about your adultery?' Alexander asked cautiously.

'What adultery?' she asked with a grin, and moved to wrap her arms round him. 'He's a funny old-fashioned thing in his own way, is Walter. He accepts his drinking is to blame for things going wrong, but he says he'd rather drink than be married. So, he's prepared to take the blame.'

He stood, his arms round her, staring over her head and wondering what effect this divorce would have on their relationship. Would she want to marry him? The thought was almost tempting. Life with Beth would be so uncomplicated. Life with Beth would be fun, but there was no way he could abandon Allie.

As if she were reading his mind, she said: 'And don't worry. It won't make any difference to us,' and then added lightly, 'Unless of course, I find some guy who's free, white and over twenty-one.'

Was it a threat? He felt a stab of jealousy at the thought of her with another man.

Her fingers were loosening his tie and she was blowing small hot breaths into his ear. She brought her knee up to his groin experimentally and wriggled it a little. 'Ah, that's better,' she whispered as he sprang into life. 'That's what we came for.' He pushed himself hard against her and began to kiss her. Beth was a pleasure to kiss. Her soft lips, mobile tongue and warm breath approximated the deeper act of love. He tasted her for a minute or two as they stood in the silent room and then pushed her back towards the couch without breaking the contact of their mouths. Her tongue teased around his lips then plunged and then teased again. It had become imperative to get her clothes off.

Naked she was beautiful. She had a narrow waist and full breasts with small pink nipples that hardened quickly to crimson under his hands. Her stomach was flat and the mound of Venus rose gently from that flatness, covered with a light down of blonde hair. When he had fully aroused her she liked to open her legs and touch herself gently with her long fingers, eyes closed, mouth slightly open as she explored her own arousal.

Then she would whisper: 'I'm wet,' and her legs would open wider to let his fingers dabble in her warm, musky juices as first her fingers, then her strong positive hand curled round him, stroking, rubbing, until neither could wait any longer and she guided him into her rosy depths.

They began the act of love slowly, with gentle thrusting strokes, her long legs wrapped round his waist and grasping him tight to her. Then without uncoupling they rolled onto their sides, her leg slid between his as they scissored their movements and her deepest muscles clutched and sucked at him like a hungry mouth. She liked to ease him onto his back and ride him, her hands on his shoulders, her light blue eyes, glazed with the intensity of what they were doing to each other, on his face. Sometimes she would turn so that he watched her long, slender back with its delicate fishtail of vertebrae rippling up and down, back and forth as she swayed above him. Always she talked, breathlessly describing her feelings. 'That's it! That's it!' her voice strangled as he pushed deeper and deeper. 'Oh, beautiful. So beautiful!'

It was never quite the same with Beth. There were days when, light of heart, she turned their lovemaking into a game. Without intensity but with laughter and giggles she would make him take her in and on places that were hardly romantic but, for him, exciting. There was a small dining table in the room and she had discovered that this was just the right height for her to perch on, opened-legged, while he stood erect in front of her or on his knees to plunge his face into her secret, scented layers. Sometimes she would not let him undress until she had knelt before him where he sat in the studio's one armchair, nimble fingers unfastening until he sprang free and her mouth closed over him.

With her he had discovered that he was both erotic and sensual. A man who could please a passionate woman. It saddened him that Allie would never know it.

In their usual routine they showered when the lovemaking was over, soaping each other in the intimate places and laughing. Beth prepared a sandwich from the small amount of food they kept in the icebox and then after eating they would leave the apartment separately. Allie's return had changed the pattern of their lives together. Now Alexander went home each evening

431

if he was in New York. Beth went out with their friends. So far she had not complained. He was aware that one day she would, and that it was dangerous to leave her alone every evening and weekend, but there was little he could do about it.

'How is she?' Beth asked as they sat eating a pastrami sandwich. She rarely mentioned Allie's name.

'Quite a bit different really,' Alexander said. 'Less introvert, more reasonable and not so depressed. I think she enjoys going out, but . . .' he hesitated.

'She's still not coming up with the goods?'

'No.'

'Well, that's good news,' Beth said cheerfully and then caught sight of his face. 'Not good news for you, eh?' She put down her half-eaten sandwich and stood up abruptly. 'Listen,' she said, 'I've got to get out of here. I'm due at a reception.'

He made no move to stop her. She grabbed her light spring coat and shoulder bag and after running her fingers through her hair picked up her hat, jammed it on her head and was gone. 'See you later,' she shouted as the door slammed behind her.

He stayed on for about ten minutes more, tidying the rumpled couch and clearing the tiny kitchen. He had little appetite for his own sandwich and flung hers and his in the garbage pan. It was an idiotic situation, he thought. A mistress who pleased him, satisfied him, excited him, whom he did not love (or didn't think he did), and a wife who gave him nothing except a challenge. Human beings were just plain perverse, he decided, hoping Beth would not find someone free, white and over twenty-one.

There was no sign of her in the office when he returned. Maybe she really had been going to a reception. But there was a cablegram for him. He opened it casually, thinking it was merely something to do with his work. Then he saw it was signed Pierre Dupuis. Immediately he felt anxious. With some reluctance he read the terse message. The information was unembroidered:

PHILIPPE LEFEVRE DIED EARLY YESTERDAY MORNING STOP PLEASE BREAK IT GENTLY TO ALLIE AND YOUR FAMILY STOP LETTER FOLLOWS STOP.

He sat staring at the stark words, deeply shocked, his heart with Rosie, feeling her loss, aware of the pain of having waited so

432

long and having her husband for so short a time. He remembered their wedding day as if it had been yesterday. She had been truly radiant as she led her blind groom through his part in the ceremony. Now the brave and beautiful Rosie would be devastated. He read the words again and sighed, wondering what had happened to Philippe. An accident? Something to do with his war wounds? He would have liked to have been at the funeral to give Rosie his support. But there could be no possibility of any of the Websters attending. They would never get to France in time and there was nothing any of them could do except write or telephone to give their condolences.

Deeply saddened, he walked to the city desk where Charles Marcus, the city editor, was briefing a reporter.

'Got anything for me, Charlie?' he asked.

'Not right now.' Charlie lifted his balding head and his shrewd little eyes assessed Alexander. 'What is it? Want to go for a beer or something?' he asked.

'Some bad news. My wife's stepfather's died in France,' Alexander said. 'Mind if I go on home and tell her?'

'Feel free,' said Charlie. 'I'll get you at your place if I need you.'

Alexander decided to walk home through the gusty streets, delaying the moment when he would have to tell Allie what had happened. He wasn't certain whether or not she would be upset. Probably not, though her attitude to her mother had changed a lot since she had left the clinic. The bitterness seemed to have gone. He felt it would be a good thing if Allie could now grieve for her mother's loss. She might. Before the clinic she would have been more likely to rejoice in it.

The house was quiet when he let himself in. Allie would certainly be upstairs working at her novel. He bounded lightly up the thick carpeted stairs to the top of the house where the workroom was. He could not hear the sound of her typewriter and wondered perhaps if she had gone out. He gave a perfunctory knock on the door and without waiting for a reply, opened it.

'Allie?' he began. And stopped dead. Frozen in a dismayed tableau before him were his wife and his sister. They were both naked, entwined around each other on the heavy rug before the burning fire. Allie lay with her dark hair confused with the paler pubic hair of his sister. Jenny had lifted her head from Allie's thighs and was staring towards the door in horror.

'Oh, my God!' she said as Alexander escaped back out of the room and with exaggerated quietness closed the door behind him.

Chapter Fifteen

Philippe died at five o'clock on the morning of 2 April at the Reims City Hospital. He had been taken there from Feathers' party. Luke and Pierre had between them half-dragged, half-carried him to the door of the dress shop, believing that all he needed was some fresh air. Outside in the street Luke realised that Philippe was deeply unconscious, breathing strangely and that his colour had not returned. The two men had managed to get him into the back seat of the Salmson while Rosie watched terrified, her hands clasped in supplication. Then Luke drove while Rosie and Pierre sat one each side of Philippe's inert body, supporting him until they reached the hospital.

One of the most painful things, Rosie thought afterwards, was that most of the guests at the party had simply believed that Philippe was drunk and had politely looked the other way as he was carried out.

He never recovered consciousness. Rosie, sitting at the side of his hospital bed in the darkened ward, his hand in hers, knew from one convulsive little last movement that he had gone. His hand went limp and gradually very cold but she continued to hold it for a long time after, not wanting to face the end. Then she gathered her courage and kissed his peaceful face before going quietly to look for a nurse. There was nothing to be done. He had left her and gone on before.

Afterwards the doctor explained that it had been a tumour on the brain, caused by his war injuries.

'You must never reproach yourself,' he said. 'Nothing could have saved him, and, my dear, he must have been very difficult to live with. He must have suffered the most dreadful constant pain.'

'He did suffer,' Rosie said sadly. 'Maybe he was a little bit

435

difficult sometimes. Not often. But it didn't matter. Not to me.'

The days following were a nightmare. Feathers was full of guilt that she had not even noticed what had happened until after the party, the most successful in Reims since the war, it was said. Only when everyone had gone home did Pierre tell her that Rosie had gone and that Philippe had been taken to hospital. She was deeply distressed by his death, the first close person in her young life to die, and over-compensated for her guilt by fussing and trying to be helpful when all Rosie wanted was time to mourn on her own.

Rosanne, too, was full of guilt, convinced that her revelations had caused the fatal attack. And Françoise laid about her, blaming everyone, but most particularly Rosie. Her theory was that it was hearing the crack of Rosie's hand on her precious cheek that had been responsible for tipping her father into the valley of the shadow. The terrible thing was that she could have been right. Madame tried to be comforting, but Rosie knew that this deeply religious woman felt that it was God's judgment on the man who had cuckolded her son.

Pierre came to see her and she asked him if he would like to start to learn how to run the business end of Les Hérissons – gradually take over Philippe's role. He had flushed scarlet and stammered that he would like that very much. Then he added that he would have little time for the moment because of his studies at the School of Oenology.

Not really caring one way or the other, Rosie, letting her total indifference show, had said that he could start when he liked. Visibly embarrassed, he stayed a short while and, muttering apologies, left. Only Luke, as ever, was a pillar of strength. It was he who came to take her from the hospital and insisted that she spend the rest of the night at Les Hérissons, away from the children. It was he who dealt with all the awesome formalities of death and he who arranged the funeral which took place on a blustery, showery day at the Père Lachaise Cemetery in Paris where the Lefevres had a mausoleum. It was weeks later that she felt strong enough to go through Philippe's papers, and when she found his will she handed it to Luke to give to the lawyer. She could not even bring herself to read it. If she read it, then he would really be dead.

She let Luke do everything that was required. She felt weary unto death and yet somehow she stayed dry-eyed. She wanted to cry but she could not. And while her head told her that this terrible, tearing grief and sense of loss would subside in time, her heart said different. She would not let herself believe that he had gone for ever. All her adult life she had loved Philippe Lefevre. She had loved him through their youth when they were kept apart by her own sterile marriage. She had loved him through his blindness and the difficulties of their last years together. She had never ceased to love him for one moment in all that time – even when he had hurt her. And thinking about it, the only times he had ever hurt her were at the birth of Françoise and when the girl had arrived at Les Coquelicots. Only Françoise had ever come between them.

For the entire months of April, May and into June she hardly left her room at Les Coquelicots and let the life of the house flow on around her. A tear-stained Rosanne came to see her every morning and evening but Rosie had made it clear she did not wish to deal with Françoise who had been hysterical with grief for days. Not yet. The problem was what to do with Françoise. Even in her own misery, Rosie felt some pity for this girl that nobody wanted. She also accepted that almost certainly she would have to make the offer to let her stay on in Champagne unless by some happy chance her parents would take her back. It was unfair that nature made some people so unlovable, she thought, but nevertheless she did not want to see Françoise. Not until the worst of her depression passed. She had asked Luke to write to the girl's mother, Lorraine le Brune, but to her knowledge there had been no reply. Apart from Rosanne's presence, the only thing that had given her any comfort was a brief but loving and generous letter of condolence from Allie. The first since she left home. Reading it, Rosie thought how sad it was that it had taken Philippe's death to make her write.

Madame also made the most generous gesture imaginable and sent Marie to look after Rosie. Marie clucked and brought food, and tried to coax her charge with delicacies, chit-chat and tales of what a fine brave day it was and how the vines were in full flower and why didn't she get a breath of fresh air? But Rosie stayed in her room, sleeping away her misery and depression. There seemed nothing to get up and go out for. Nothing at all. Most days she wished she had died with him.

Then in the middle of June two things happened that gave her the impetus that she needed to begin living again.

The breakthrough began when Rosanne reminded her that Feathers' baby was due within the next two weeks or so. Rosie was spurred to some action. She had promised Feathers that she would pass on the prettiest of Rosanne's baby clothes – clothes that had been carefully put away for the next infant in the family. Some of the garments had been Allie's and there were also two fine christening robes, handmade long ago by Madame Dupuis for her twin boys. One had been worn by Allie and the other by Rosanne at their christenings. All of these had been stored in a trunk in the attic with other reminders of the past. Her own two wedding dresses were packed away in tissue paper along with the two outfits that she had brought with her from America all those years ago. But as she carefully lifted out the layers from the trunk, searching for the baby things, she realised there was one thing in the trunk that she had forgotten was there. Something glittering caught her eye, and then she remembered. Her hands began to tremble a little as she lifted out a black lace corselet with diamanté scattered over the right breast.

She looked at it lying in her hands and then clutched it to her, convulsively, as if it were a lover. It was the corselet that she had worn the first time she and Philippe made love and that she had worn again on their wedding night. Her head full of memories, she spread the garment on the lid of the trunk, tracing the design of the lace with her finger. It seemed unspoilt. The diamanté still shone; the lace was intact and soft, the hooks that fastened it in place untarnished. She remembered how Philippe's loving fingers had unravelled those hooks, even when he was blind, and remembering what happened after, the love that she so missed, her throat closed on a sob. She clutched the black lace to her again and at long last the stubborn tears came in healing profusion.

She stayed in the attic for a long time, sitting on the dusty floor in the light that crept in through the tiles, a smell of camphor in her nostrils, her back against the sturdy trunk, her past all around her. She let herself remember the happiness that she and Philippe had found and at last truly accepted that he was gone, buried but in peace and without pain. It was time for her to find some kind of new life again. She blew her nose heartily, got to her feet and shook herself like a dog shaking water from its coat. Then, her arms full of baby clothes, she went back down into the house. But she was not ready to visit Les Hérissons, not yet. She packed the clothes and left them ready for when Feathers called.

Two days later another letter came from the American, Jack Patterson. It offered his condolences and said that out of respect he had not approached her for a reply to his letter before. Now, would she be kind enough to give him a decision?

Rosie wrote him a brief reply, saying that she had no intention of selling, but thanking him for his condolences.

Ten days later another letter arrived. This one was from Didier le Brune's solicitor. In essence it said that Madame and Monsieur le Brune wished to remind Rosie that on the death of Françoise's father, his half of the Les Hérissons' champagne business, including the export business, had become the property of Mademoiselle Françoise Lefevre (subject to the formality of the agreement of the courts). Mademoiselle Lefevre had today received a substantial offer of half a million francs for her share of the business, and her family had decided that it was in the child's interests to sell. His question was: did Rosie wish to have the first opportunity to buy her stepdaughter out, on condition, of course, that she matched the offer that they had already received? And would Madame Lefevre please be kind enough to make arrangements as soon as it was convenient for Mademoiselle Lefevre to rejoin her parents, who happily were now returned to Paris.

The letter was a shock. The shock she needed. She sat bolt upright as she reread it. Her first reaction was that it was all nonsense. It couldn't be true. Philippe had assured her that he had arranged things in such a way that should anything happen to him the business would be entirely hers. But that, of course, was long before Françoise had come to live with them. She read the letter yet again, angry with herself for not having found out exactly what was in the will. In her grief she had ignored letters from the lawyers. Her mind had been concentrated on her loss, not financial matters. The le Brunes' minds were concentrated on their bank balance. No doubt they wanted Françoise back since the child was now worth a small fortune and they were welcome to her. But how long had they been back in Paris while Françoise was damaging the lives of everyone at Les Coquelicots? she wondered.

Anger was wiping away her depression. How could Philippe have done such a thing? If it were true, his mind must have been more affected by his illness than she had realised. As for the offer, that would be from Jack Patterson, and a well-advised Jack Patterson at that to have found Françoise's parents so quickly.

It was time she found out exactly what was in Philippe's will and time for a family conference.

She first telephoned Philippe's lawyer and was shocked by what he had to say. He explained that Philippe had visited him a few weeks before his death, accompanied by his daughter. Monsieur Lefevre had been anxious that she should be well provided for. He had changed his will then and there.

'But why didn't you warn me?' she protested.

He sighed. 'Madame, I have written you not once but twice and telephoned your home several times. I received no reply.'

She thought of those early twilight days after Philippe's death when she had thrown away official looking letters unopened, refused to come to the telephone and just slept and then slept more in her misery.

'I apologise,' she said.

Heavy-hearted she hung up the receiver and then rang the local switchboard again for a call to Les Hérissons to ask Madame if she could join the family for dinner that night. Madame was delighted. Rosie had not been near Les Hérissons since Philippe had died.

'Of course,' the old lady had said. 'My dear Rosie, we have been so concerned about you.'

'I'm feeling better, Mama,' Rosie told her. 'And something has happened that I want to talk to you all about. Something very serious.'

Madame had never really come to terms with the telephone.

'Then we will talk about it tonight,' she said firmly. 'It will be a great pleasure for all of us to see you.'

She spoke almost as if Rosie was a distant relative who visited but rarely. It puzzled Rosie until she realised that it had been well over two months since she had left Les Coquelicots.

Rosie instructed Miss to make the arrangements for Françoise's departure that very afternoon and as dusk fell she set off, driving herself to Les Hérissons. She was deliberately early since she wanted to see Feathers and give her the baby clothes. Marie opened the door and said Madame was sleeping and Feathers was resting in her own little sitting room upstairs – the room that had once been Rosie's. Rosie went straight there and was gratified by her welcome. Feathers' face lit up with pleasure and she lumbered from the chaise longue where she had been stretched out. She did her best to give Rosie a hug, but her girth got in the way.

'Only twenty more days or so,' she sighed, patting the bulge that even her clever floating dress could no longer hide. Rosie handed over the package of baby clothes. Feathers tore off the paper and looked at them with squeals of delight.

'They're so lovely!' she said. 'If I sold children's clothes I'd copy them all.'

'And how's the shop doing?' Rosie asked, sitting down and letting the familiarity of the room that had once been hers wrap itself round her.

Feathers' great violet eyes lit up.

'A-m-a-z-ing,' she said in English and then returned to French that had come on apace. 'I just go in in the mornings now as people seem to want to see me when they buy. I'm making a lot of money, Aunt Rosie. Everyone who is anyone buys their clothes from me now. I'm employing five seamstresses. Can you imagine! And I'm doing all the designing. People are asking me to make them something special, just for them. And they don't seem to mind what they pay.'

'Next stop rue St Honoré?' Rosie teased.

'I'm thinking about it.' Feathers was perfectly serious. 'After this baby's settled down and a bit older I might even do it. I've put away quite a lot of money to pay back what you lent me. And you might have noticed, I'm not so extravagant as I used to be.'

'I suppose you get your clothes at cost?' Rosie teased again, thinking she was going to need this money that Feathers had put aside.

Feathers giggled. 'True!' she said.

'And Pierre?'

The beautiful girl was suddenly serious. Her hands closed over her stomach protectively and she said simply: 'We're happy. He's been wonderful, Aunt Rosie. It's all different now.'

'Good.' Rosie squeezed her hand, thinking how strange life was and wondering exactly what it was that had changed Pierre. It seemed strange to mend a marriage when another man's baby was on the way. Strange, but extraordinarily generous-spirited. And yet remembering Pierre's friendship with Jack Patterson, she wondered how much he had really changed. Now her grief was lessening and she was thinking straight she had her suspicions about Jack Patterson and Pierre.

'Are you all right?' Feathers was asking.

Rosie nodded. 'The worst is over.'

Feathers' eyes filled with tears.

'I've thought about you so much. You're so good to everyone else. You've been so kind to me. Why should this happen to you?'

'Why should it happen to Philippe?' Rosie asked, then added: 'Shush now. No tears. You'll start me off. I'm going to get on with life again now. There are things to be done.'

Feathers took her hand. 'That sounds more like you.'

Luke was at dinner with them, but that was all right, Rosie thought. He had as much interest in what she was about to say as any of them. He had his share of the profits to think about and anyway his life was tied up in Les Hérissons. He had become part of the family and she relied on him completely.

She waited until everyone was finishing their dessert before she began.

'We have a problem that affects us all,' she said as Madame put down her fork after demolishing a large portion of apple tart. 'Philippe left Françoise his half share of the business in his will. Obviously she gets half of his personal property, but for some reason he left her the business as well. I thought it was sewn up so that it reverted to me. Apparently not, but at least, thank God, she can't touch my portion. The trouble is that now her parents want to sell her share of Les Hérissons' champagne.'

There was a clatter as Pierre dropped his spoon.

'You're saying that Philippe left part of our business to his

442

daughter?' Madame said angrily. 'That is outrageous!'

Rosie nodded. These explanations were like a knife in her heart.

'He was afraid Françoise wouldn't be properly provided for. And I don't expect he thought he would die as young as he did.'

'But how can she have a share of Les Hérissons?' Feathers asked, puzzled.

'Not the estate itself,' Rosie said. 'Only the part that Philippe and I own. She automatically inherits his personal property, though I keep an interest in it until my death. The law wouldn't let him disinherit her, of course, but I never thought he would leave her the business. He could have arranged that differently. He has left the house in Paris to us both but it reverts to her on my death. He says in the will that I already have Les Coquelicots and the apartment in Reims. Happily they are both mine. She can't touch them. I bought them with my own money in my own name. I suppose technically they are part of the Les Hérissons estate. Though the le Brunes have no claim on the estate itself, the complications of someone else in the manufacture and distribution of Les Hérissons' wine would make life very difficult for all of us.'

'Who wants to buy it?' Madame was asking.

'I don't know,' Rosie said. 'I suspect that it's Jack Patterson. He wrote to me again last week.'

She looked hard at Pierre and noted that he looked faintly sick.

'Jack Patterson?' Feathers said. 'But he's your friend, Pierre. He doesn't know anything about wine, does he? Why would he want to buy Les Hérissons?'

'Why indeed?' said Madame Dupuis looking straight at Pierre, her wrinkled eyes narrowed. 'Tell us, Pierre, why do you think he would want it?'

Madame knew something. Rosie was now certain of it. And if Pierre told the truth perhaps something could be done to give her time to raise some money. She waited, her eyes on his face, in the sudden silence of the room. The others were waiting, too. Pierre was going to have to speak.

'Come along, Pierre,' Madame said sternly. 'I think it's time you told us exactly what has been going on.'

*　　*　　*

With his grandmother's piercing eye fixed firmly on him, Pierre felt himself turn scarlet. He looked around the table for an escape. There was none. They were all looking at him. Luke, his expression quizzical, Feathers puzzled, Rosie waiting, and his grandmother challenging. He felt as miserable as he ever had been as he muttered the lie: 'I really don't know.'

He had been anxious for weeks, certain that Jack would do something now that he had the bit between his teeth. And his anxieties had been troubling him since he visited Rosie at Les Coquelicots just after Philippe's death. She had come downstairs to receive him and they had sat by the big open fireplace in her living room. He was shocked by her appearance. She seemed to have aged ten years. He noticed that there was a sprinkling of grey in her dark hair and her face was drawn. But what alarmed him most was that her electric energy and commanding presence were not there any more. It was as if someone had switched off the light. This was a tired, sad, lethargic woman.

She thanked him for coming to see her and an uncomfortable silence settled over them. She sat staring into the fire and he couldn't think of anything to say.

Then she had suggested he should start learning Philippe's end of the business. He had felt himself flush then, too. The thing that he had plotted for behind her back was being handed to him on a plate. He had felt like vermin and was also aware that if Jack persisted, this could be snatched from him.

Now she was sitting at the other side of the table from him, her amber eyes bright and watchful, her vitality restored, and he knew that she knew he was lying.

And so, of course, did his grandmother. 'Really?' she said on a rising note.

The silence was oppressive. No one was eating. They were all waiting for him to say something. He gulped.

'It's all my fault,' he heard himself blurt out. 'It was I who put the idea in Jack's head. I was bored and I wanted to take over the business. I thought I could do better than Philippe. I asked Grandmother to give it to me, but she said the business and the production end was yours, Aunt Rosie, and that she wouldn't give me the estate. It had to be shared among the family.' He looked round the table. No one moved, waiting for him to continue. 'Then things changed . . . I wasn't so miserable as I had been. Feathers and I . . .' He looked at his wife and she gave him a brilliant, encouraging smile. 'Well, we're a lot happier than we were. I've stopped being so impatient. The trouble was that Jack still wanted to go ahead. I couldn't stop him. I've deliberately stayed away from him for weeks, but he's got a very good lawyer. I expect that's how he contacted the le Brunes. The worst thing, Aunt Rosie, was that day at your house when you offered me the thing I'd been plotting to get. I felt real bad; I felt terrible.'

His voice trailed away miserably, almost a whimper. He wanted to explain himself properly. He wanted to tell them how his father's badness fought against the good in him all the time. He wanted to say that he thought that most of the time he was winning. He wanted these people who were his family to forgive him and expurge him of guilt and blame.

Rosie gave a deep sigh. She stared down at the tablecloth then picked up her glass of wine and took a long swallow.

'It wasn't such a terrible thing to do,' she said slowly. 'We're all impatient when we're young. And anyway, if it hadn't been your Jack Patterson, the le Brunes would have come up with someone else to buy Françoise's share. Since Philippe had altered his will, his death was bound to change things. I was just so occupied with losing him that I didn't think of anything else. The question is how to deal with it.'

He did not know what to say in the face of such generosity.

'How much do they want?' Madame asked.

'Half a million francs,' Rosie said. 'Do you think it's worth trying to stop them doing anything until my death? Fight them in court?'

'No,' said Madame firmly. 'Françoise's share of the property is hers to do what she likes with. Your money will merely line the lawyers' pockets. It's as well you had a proper business agreement about the division of the company or she could have claimed your share as well on your death.'

'It's my own fault,' Rosie said. 'If I hadn't insisted that Philippe and I made our two businesses into one, Françoise would only have got the distribution and shipping part – the part that was Philippe's originally. I would not have minded that. She is his daughter, and from our point of view it wouldn't have mattered. We could easily find another shipper. But for her to own half the business . . . I must get it back.'

'Half a million francs!' Feathers said, awed. 'Have you got it, Aunt Rosie?'

Rosie half laughed. 'No.'

'Is the business worth it?'

Rosie considered. 'It is too high because the distribution side is so badly run down, but if you include the stock, I suppose it's not too far out.'

'I can pay you back at least a thousand francs,' Feathers said eagerly. 'And now my business is successful I bet I could get a loan to pay you back the rest that I borrowed.'

'Feathers, it would be a drop in the bucket,' Pierre said impatiently, his wife's reaction twisting the knife of shame in him.

'Can you bargain with them?' Luke suggested. 'Could you give them your share of the house in Paris as part of the money?'

Pierre saw how Rosie's face saddened.

'I may have to,' she said. 'But they will probably reason that since Françoise will get it one day anyway, there isn't any point in taking it now. I love that house. It's full of wonderful memories for me. But I suppose they will want to keep it, or ask an inflated price for it. The only thing to do is to sell Les Coquelicots. I wondered if I could move back here, Mimi? Would you have me and Rosanne?'

'You know I never wanted you to go,' Madame said sternly and Pierre noticed how Rosie, even in her despair, had to hide a little smile.

'I could try to talk to Jack again,' he said, eager to make some practical contribution.

Rosie shook her head. 'If it's not him it will be someone else. They'll try to sell now. But in any case, we ought to buy it back for our own sakes. I don't care for the idea of Françoise as a partner, any more than I care for the idea of Jack Patterson or any other total stranger.'

'Can you help, Mimi?' Pierre forced himself to ask, remembering how she had rejected him.

'Only a very little. I am only a rich woman on paper, Pierre,' his grandmother said sternly. 'And we have all lived very extravagantly.'

He flushed scarlet yet again. He was aware that much of the

extravagance had been his and Feathers'. Nor had he earned a sou or contributed in any way since he had been in France. His grandmother's money – and Rosie's – had paid all his bills.

'Isn't Allie's husband's family very rich?' he suggested.

'Very,' Rosie said, 'but I'd never ask them for a loan.'

'Perhaps they'd buy it?' Feathers suggested.

'Impossible,' Rosie said firmly. 'I wouldn't want to push Mr Webster into buying something that he wouldn't want and is too far away to have any real interest in. And besides, there's the situation with Allie . . .'

'You were friends with her in-laws before she was born.' Feathers sounded indignant and Pierre wondered if she had ever guessed that Allie was the girl he had once been going to marry.

'Even so . . .' Rosie sighed and dismissed the thought. 'There is the house in California but I suspect it will be worth very little. But don't worry. Somehow we'll scrape the money together. I'll never let the business go. Never. It's family. It belongs to the Dupuis.'

Madame chuckled.

'You're becoming quite a Frenchwoman in your old age, Rosie!' she said. 'Let us hope that Pierre will soon become more of a Frenchman.'

She said it lightly, but the words hurt. He had let his family down, and now they all knew it.

Feathers went up to their rooms ahead of him. With the birth so imminent she tired quickly. He took coffee in the drawing room with Rosie and his grandmother. Luke, too, excused himself. Rosie and Mimi were both thoughtful but it seemed to him that Rosie made a special effort to be pleasant to him and he was grateful.

'Do you still want me to learn Philippe's work?' he eventually managed to bring himself to ask. He would not have been surprised if she had said no. But as it was, she said: 'Of course. If you would really like to.'

'I could still be involved with the vines?' he asked. It suddenly occurred to him that it was the vines and the land and the production of the wine that he liked best. He had a sudden doubt about himself as a salesman. What use would his degree and the work he was doing at the School of Oenology be to a salesman?

'I think you should be involved with the whole business,'

Madame said firmly. 'One day it will be shared among you, Allie and Rosanne. Allie may never come home and who knows what Rosanne will want to do with her life. It would be my wish that you ran it.'

'I'll try, Mimi,' he said, aware of the absurdity of saying that he was no longer certain what he wanted to do, not after all the plotting and planning that he had done.

'What about Luke?' Rosie's voice was abrupt. 'We're not going to abandon him, are we?'

'I'm talking about the future,' Mimi said, avoiding the question. Rosie did not look satisfied.

'We should make Luke's position clear,' she said. 'He's been wonderfully loyal to us all.'

Pierre's feelings towards Luke were ambivalent. Whenever he saw Luke he remembered Carlos. He wished Luke were not there.

'Luke is only a hired hand,' he said abruptly and saw how Rosie drew herself up, eyes suddenly cold.

'That will do, Pierre,' she said frostily, as if he were ten years old and making him feel six years old.

'I'm going to bed.' He got to his feet abruptly. 'It wakes Feathers if I go up too long after her.'

Rosie said a cool goodnight, but his contrary grandmother gave him an indulgent hug.

'Sleep well, my boy,' she said.

He was irritated as he walked upstairs. There were times when he came near to liking Aunt Rosie very much indeed, but then she did something that made him realise that she still saw his father in him. It wasn't fair. He wasn't his father. His father would never have told the truth to his own detriment as he had just done in front of them all. Even in front of Luke West. She had no right to be so authoritarian with him. Whatever she said, Luke was a hired hand. He was not a Dupuis. Pierre did not dislike Luke but he had no intention of sharing his inheritance with him. In fact, eventually Luke West would have to go. The Englishman knew too much about Feathers' and his lives. He didn't fancy having Feathers' baby's grandfather about the place. And there was the fact that Luke could prove to be a threat one day if Rosie continued to champion him. But still, he felt he ought to try to make amends for what he had caused. He decided that he would visit Jack as soon as he could and see if he could make him pull out. There was no harm in trying.

Feathers was already in their big bed, her bump making a hillock of the bedclothes. He felt cross and out of sorts and slammed the door behind him. He saw her give him a quick look.

'I thought you were very brave,' she told him as he angrily pulled at his bow tie.

'Why?' he grunted, feeling slightly soothed by the admiring tone in her voice.

'Confessing what you had done. But Aunt Rosie's right. It would have happened anyway.'

Damn Aunt Rosie who was always right! he thought. But he was calmer as he said: 'Even so I thought I'd go and talk to Jack. See if he'll forget it.'

'No harm in trying,' she said, heaving herself into a more comfortable position.

'That's what I thought.'

She lay on her back staring at the ceiling, and then said: 'Is that what you meant that time when you said you had plans to make Les Hérissons ours? And that it would be the home I wanted?'

He nodded.

'So you did it for me?'

He nodded again. He hadn't done it for her in the slightest at the time. At that time he had done it strictly for himself, but if it made her happy to think that she had been the cause of his treachery, if it took some of the guilt from him, let her think it.

Feathers sighed a happy sigh.

'We are happier these days. It was nice of you to say it in front of them all. I don't need a home of my own so much now. And I wouldn't have wanted it at Rosie's expense anyway. She's always been so good to us. But now it's all different. I'm not frightened of Madame any more. I'm not even frightened of Nanny.'

It was true. Feathers' success had given her confidence. She had changed. She was no longer frightened of him, either. Sometimes she argued with him and stood up to him in a way she would never have dared when they were first married. She no longer gave him anxious looks before she volunteered an opinion or expressed a thought. His disapproval no longer disturbed her, and he found he liked her better for it and rarely disapproved of her. Sometimes he even found himself jealous when she laughed and flirted a little with Luke and when he saw men look at her in the street when they were out together. She was extraordinarily beautiful and always so strikingly dressed, even while pregnant with this baby that was not his. The pregnancy had given her a radiance that she had not possessed when she was carrying Patric. Was that because he didn't love her then? he often wondered. He thought perhaps he was near to loving her now, but the memory of Allie would not go away. Mind pictures of her hovered at the corners of his consciousness. Never a day went by when he did not think of her. She intruded into his thoughts at the most unlikely moments.

'I want a cuddle,' Feathers was saying as he slid into bed. 'If, of course, you can get your arm round me.'

He laughed and tried, and as his hand rested on her side he felt the sudden kick of the baby.

'Ooops!' said Feathers as it kicked again and he had a sudden feeling of reverence for life and its beginning. Once born, this baby would be another little animal to be reared as he had reared so many small things when he was small himself. He missed his contact with nature these days, but here was nature under his hand, jumping to be freed. And when it was freed, the helpless arrival would be his responsibility. So did it really matter who the real father was? he asked himself as he pressed his face close to the back of his wife's warm and scented neck. And as he slid into sleep he told himself virtuously that he would definitely go to Paris to see Jack first thing tomorrow. The School of Oenology would have to do without him for the day.

Rosie and Madame talked quietly by the fire in Madame's parlour over cups of coffee once the obviously disgruntled Pierre had gone to bed. Rosie, content to be sitting in the chair on which she had always sat in this room, felt that she and her mother-in-law were closer than they had been for many years. It was sad that it had taken Philippe's death to bring the renewed warmth but Madame never had and never would forgive him for cuckolding her son. And he was still not forgiven in death. She did not mention him at all. It was Pierre and his future and the future of Les Hérissons of which Madame spoke. Her anxiety was that the estate and the business should be preserved for her grandchildren, particularly Pierre and Patric, her great-grandson, the remaining male Dupuis.

Nothing has changed, Rosie thought, listening with affection as the old woman went back over the years, remembering her long-dead husband, the dreadful days of the war and how Les Hérissons had come through it all.

'The land is stronger than all of us,' she said. 'But the land needs its champions. You, with Clovis, were its champion, my dear Rosie. Pray God that Pierre will take on your mantle.'

'Not yet, Mama,' Rosie warned. 'I need a life for myself again. Les Hérissons will occupy me. Pierre will have to wait. And besides, in spite of what I told him, at the moment I'm not all that certain I want him to have my part of the business.'

'Aren't you afraid I shall give him mine?' Madame's eyes were twinkling either with mischief or malice.

'No,' said Rosie. 'You wouldn't do that. Because it would not be fair to your other grandchildren. In any case, it is not Pierre's time here – not yet. Remember, I did ask him if he would like to start learning Philippe's end of the business, but he did nothing about it.'

Madame sighed. 'My fear is that he will never do anything properly. The dear boy is weak in many ways. He does not see things through.'

Rosie thought about what Madame had said. He own feelings towards Pierre were ambivalent but she did not think that Madame was being entirely fair to the lad.

'He's not weak,' she said slowly. 'He just starts off in the wrong direction and then strives more than most of us would to get back into the right one. There's something of his father in him that he's for ever trying to suppress.'

'His father had many good points,' Madame protested and Rosie looked at her lap to hide the smile she could not control. No, nothing changed.

Around ten thirty Madame's head began to nod and the old lady announced that it was past her time for bed. Rosie had stayed later than she intended, not relishing this first arrival back at Les Coquelicots with no Philippe waiting for her. Goodnights said, she hesitated on the outside porch. A three-quarter moon rode high, turning the land silver. The stars seemed dim against its sharp white light and there was a chill in the air. Shivering, she ran down the front steps to where her car was parked. As she did so a figure came out of the gloom, making her start.

'Only me,' said Luke's voice. 'Start your car, ma'am?'

'Luke! Would you?' Rosie said gratefully. She was for ever grazing her fingers on the handle when trying to crank the engine into life.

'Pleasure,' he said but did not move. 'Got time for a chat?' he asked.

'All the time in the world,' Rosie said, thinking with another pang that Philippe would not be sitting in his own pool of darkness, waiting for her. Talking to Luke would delay going back to a lonely house.

'Shall we walk or shall I drive you home?' he asked.

'Drive me home if you like, but how will you get back yourself?'

'In your car. I'll get Henri to drive it back tomorrow. Then your Michel can drive him back.'

'You've got it all worked out, haven't you?' she laughed, looking up at the square shape he made against the night sky.

'Yup,' he said. 'I've been wanting to talk to you for a long time, but I didn't want to intrude.'

'I'm glad you didn't,' she told him. 'It's not been a good time. It was better to get over it alone.'

'Better now?' he asked as he moved to crank the engine.

When the noise and the small explosions had died down and the engine was ticking gently, she slid into the passenger seat and said: 'Yes. Better now. I needed something to fight.'

'And you've got the le Brunes and Jack Patterson.'

'I've got the le Brunes and Jack Patterson. Tomorrow I shall write and tell the le Brunes' lawyer that I'll match his offer and then worry about where the money is coming from.'

'Is it really that bad?' he asked as he eased the car down the drive.

'It is, I'm afraid.' There seemed no point in lying. 'I don't have enough ready cash. One way and another it all drains out

452

as fast as it comes in. And for the past few months there's been precious little coming in. There's been no one really selling our champagne. The agents do their best, I suppose, but they need someone to drive them. That hasn't been happening. Once Françoise came, Philippe did very little. And his health deteriorated. I keep telling myself he wouldn't have done what he did in that will if his health hadn't been so bad. I truly think his mind must have been affected.' She stopped before she poured out to this listening, sympathetic man just how betrayed she felt by Philippe's actions.

'People do strange things where their offspring are concerned,' he said.

She sighed. 'Yes, I suppose the urge to protect one's own flesh and blood is strong. I'm really fighting now for Allie and Rosanne's inheritance as much as anything. I built it all up. I can't bear to let it go. And it makes me boil with rage that Françoise should benefit from my hard work over the years. I don't dislike many people, but I'll make an exception in her case.'

'Is there anything I can do?' She could see his bumpy profile in grey silhouette as he drove through the forests towards her home.

'Just go on letting me depend on you,' she said simply.

There was a silence.

'You know you can always do that,' he said and his voice sounded husky, almost uncertain.

She put her hand out to touch him and felt the hard springy hairs on the back of his hand. He jumped as if she had pricked him with a needle.

'I know.'

'I don't know that you do,' he said roughly.

She felt the same hot gut feeling that she had felt with him once before. It frightened her by its intensity and the feeling it brought of disloyalty to Philippe, in spite of Philippe's damaging disloyalty to her.

'Don't say any more. Please,' she said urgently.

'Never?'

'Not now. Not yet.'

He was silent. The car was too small for his size; too intimate for the two of them. She felt a wave of longing for love; to be

453

held and kissed and turned into a woman again. Oh, Philippe! Philippe! she thought, anguished, but made herself speak lightly.

'We'll save it. We'll pull through,' she said, deliberately returning to the subject of Les Hérissons.

'Rosie,' he said, turning his head from the road for one moment. 'Believe me, you will. I know you will. You can do anything you want, and have anything you want. You're that sort of woman and I . . . I admire you.'

'Gee, thanks,' she said lightly but was aware that her heart seemed to be beating much too fast.

He drove her to her front door and jumped out to let her out of the car. He shut the car door behind her and stood big and black against the sky; squarer, tougher, a different style of man from Philippe.

'You going to be all right?' he asked and she wondered if he had sensed her reluctance to enter the house that did not have Philippe inside.

'I'm going to be fine,' she said. 'Thanks for driving me home.'

He hesitated, and then he bent to take her face between his two hands. They felt rough on her skin. He leaned down and solemnly kissed her on her forehead.

'Take care, beautiful Rosie,' he said. 'I'll send your car back to you tomorrow.'

With a few long strides he was back to the driver's side and into the car, revving up to drive off. She watched the lights disappearing down her driveway. When the red gleam disappeared, she let herself into the house. She went straight to her room and quickly undressed. Shivering, she got into bed and lay curled into a tight ball, waiting to get warm. Philippe had always kept her warm. She tried not to think of how his death had left her in the cold in so many ways. Be optimistic, she told herself. Things were improving. Another hurdle had been jumped. She had left her cocoon and faced coming home alone. Without Luke it wouldn't have been so easy. But then, she thought, without Luke a great many things wouldn't be so easy.

Luke drove back to Les Hérissons slowly. He wanted to savour the clearness of the night and the scent of Rosie that still lingered in the car, intangible, ghostlike. She had told him once that it was

454

called L'Heure Bleu. He had a handkerchief in his desk drawer that he had soaked in the perfume just after she hid herself away from everyone. The scent of it whenever he opened the drawer invoked her for him.

He cursed himself for a fool as he drove. He was behaving like a lovesick schoolboy. After excusing himself from the dinner table that night, he had sat, uncomfortably perched on the bonnet of Rosie's car, smoking cigarette after cigarette. He wanted to drive her home. He wanted to be alone with her in the closed, dark interior of the car. He wanted her all to himself. And it had worked out just as he had planned. He had driven her home.

And now what?

It had taken all his self-control not to kiss her properly when they said goodnight. Thank God she had not appeared to be angered by the kiss on the forehead. He thought that she had been grateful for his company. He imagined her in bed, alone, and shut his eyes against the pain she must have felt entering the house knowing Philippe was not there. A worse pain than that he had felt when she left Les Hérissons for Les Coquelicots. For the first month after her departure, Les Hérissons had felt empty to him whenever he went inside. But he at least saw her every day. She would never see Philippe again.

He had not seen her since Philippe's death and tonight he thought that she looked a little older. Her face seemed to have became fine-drawn, but the spirit was there. Pierre had said she had lost her spirit and that had worried him more than anything. Without her spirit Rosie might as well be as dead as her husband.

Death was dreadful, he brooded as he idled along the moonlit road. But death might give him his chance. Maybe slowly, slowly he could win. She wasn't a woman to be without a man. But for now the most important thing was to find the money to buy Les Hérissons' champagne back. He had been shocked to hear just how bad things were financially, but it was not hard to understand why. Rosie's expenditure had been enormous for a long time. All the Les Hérissons' bills went to her. She supported so much, leaving little chance to save against a rainy day.

And it was all very well Madame wanting Pierre to take over the estate. Pierre did not pull his weight. Luke believed that

Pierre was the eternal student, all theory and no action. It was time that the lad got off his backside and did something to support his wife and child. As it was, Feathers had twice the go and spunk that her husband had. Pierre was not much of a man in Luke's eyes. Though he was relieved that Pierre appeared to have accepted Feathers' pregnancy, something atavistically male in him despised the younger man for doing so. But even if Pierre had not accepted the baby, Feathers wouldn't have needed him. Feathers was a success. She had become a well-known personage in Reims and if Pierre wasn't careful she would outgrow him. Luke sighed thinking of the baby that was on the way. His grandchild, but never to be acknowledged as such.

He knew three things as he pulled up in front of Les Hérissons. He wanted to marry Rosie, he wanted to see his grandchild grow up, and he wanted to keep some control over Les Hérissons. And if he was to get all those things, he told himself, he had better start doing something about it. And quickly.

Pierre caught an early train to Paris the next morning. He left his wife, rotund and sleepy, under the bedclothes, kissing her goodbye without waking her. He put his hand lightly on the highest point of the mound but disappointingly the baby was asleep as well.

He wanted to get to Paris early. Jack rarely set foot outside his apartment until near noon. After that, he could be drinking and lunching anywhere. It was best to catch him early.

'My dear fellow!' Jack's greeting was as effusive as ever. He drew back the door of his apartment to let Pierre in, pulled his silk paisley dressing grown, bought from Liberty's of London, closer round him and pattered in leather slippers through to his kitchen, Pierre following behind.

'Do you bring me news?' he asked Pierre.

There was no point beating about the bush. 'Yes and no,' Pierre said. 'Aunt Rosie won't sell. I suppose it's you who have offered to buy it from the le Brunes, but whoever it is, she won't sell.'

'Everyone has their price.'

'Not Aunt Rosie.'

Jack looked sceptical as he poured a cup of coffee from the pot on the stove.

'We shall see, my dear boy. We shall see. My estimable papa is so beside himself with delight that there is something I truly want to do that the sky has become the limit.'

'Jack,' Pierre said urgently, ignoring the coffee. 'I've come to ask you to stop. There isn't any need any more. Aunt Rosie has asked me to run Philippe's end of it, and I'll get the estate in time anyway. It was nice of you to offer to help, but it isn't necessary now. And it's all causing terrible trouble in the family. Aunt Rosie will have the greatest difficulty matching your offer but she'll do it and the le Brunes will be the only ones to benefit in the end.'

'Now that is good news,' Jack said cheerfully. 'If I just increase my offer a little . . .'

Pierre cursed himself for not thinking before he spoke.

'And besides, my dear Pierre, I dislike being thwarted. I have made up my mind to buy Les Hérissons for you, and I won't be content until I have done so.'

'But I don't want you to,' Pierre protested.

'But I want to.' Jack's voice was steely. 'You say your aunt has offered you the chance to run the business end?'

'Yes.'

'And is that what you are interested in doing?'

'I prefer the production, I suppose,' Pierre said reluctantly.

'That's exactly what I thought. You haven't considered it enough. You'll still be working for a woman, you won't have any freedom to do what you want. You've told me what a tight grip she keeps on things. You won't even be doing what you like doing. I don't see you as a salesman, Pierre. I'm the salesman in this team.' Jack nodded sagely and paused to sip at his coffee. Pierre found himself waiting for what was to come next, remembering Rosie snapping 'That will do, Pierre' as if he were a schoolboy.

'Has she offered you shares or given you part of it?' Jack asked.

Pierre shook his head. 'But she would if I asked her,' he muttered.

'Ah!' Jack looked scornful. 'You may think so, but you have no guarantee. The ideal thing is for me to buy it. You handle all the production without any interference from me, and see me put this champagne of yours on the map.'

'And will you give me part of it or offer me any shares? You may remember it was going to be in my name when we started all this. You were going to lend me the money.'

'Ah, but your grandmother didn't want to know, did she? That changed things.'

'All right. Things have changed. But will you give me a share of it?'

He stared at Jack challengingly. 'Depends.'

'On what?'

'How much I get it for. You really should persuade your auntie to sell. If I get it for the price I've offered, I shall sign fifteen per cent of it over to you.'

'Are you prepared to commit that to paper?'

'My dear fellow! Don't you trust me? In any case, if I didn't sign any of it over to you, you would still be better off with me than with your aunt. Do you really want to work for a woman? And eventually, when your aged grandma throws off these mortal coils and you get your share of the estate, you'll really have me over a barrel. I shall be forced to do a deal with you, won't I? With me, you can only win in the end.'

It was as full of holes as a butterfly net, Pierre thought. But with Jack he might get a share, and Jack was right. He didn't really fancy working for Rosie. Best perhaps to do and say nothing and let things take their course. But since he was in Paris, he might as well lunch with Jack, and afterwards he could visit Madame Beauregard's establishment. It was a long time since he had been there.

But thinking of how he had let down the family and remembering Madame's remark that maybe one day he would become a Frenchman with all the feeling for continuity of inheritance that implied, he decided to try for one last parting, hopefully delaying, shot.

'All right,' he said. 'I'm with you. But a bit of advice. Don't sign anything or give the lawyers any money until you're sure everything is cleared. Aunt Rosie thinks that the will isn't legal. And it would be a shame to lose any money over it. That wouldn't help either of us, would it?'

Jack looked thoughtful. 'Okay,' he said. 'Thanks for the tip.'

*   *   *

458

'Have you heard from her?' Beth asked. She and Alexander were eating filet mignon in a quiet corner of their favourite speakeasy just off Times Square. Since they had been going to bed together most nights for the last seven weeks they were now able to use their lunch break for its real purpose.

'Not a word,' Alexander said. Every day Beth asked him the question and every day the answer was the same. Beth then dropped the subject, seemingly accepting that Alexander didn't want to talk about it. In his shattered state he had told her briefly what had happened but given no details. Now he wished he had said nothing.

The afternoon he had found his wife and his sister making love had been the worst of his life. For the two people he loved best in the world to have betrayed him was intolerable and once he had shut the door on their obscene antics he went out and got extremely drunk.

He stayed at the studio flat that night and the next. Alone. Trying to think what to do. His emotions were a storm of anger, hurt, humiliation and sheer bewilderment. He knew that women could fall in love and have sexual contact, but he had never imagined that that was the problem with his wife. What hurt most was the picture that remained in his mind of Allie's ecstatic abandonment. He had never seen her naked before. The memory of her full breasts with dark red engorged nipples and her tumbled limbs and how her face had been buried in his sister's secret depths tormented him. He had dreamed of her mouth over him, his tongue searching where Jenny's had been. The dreams were unfulfilled, and he had accepted that there was no sensuality in Allie, that her experiences had killed it.

He saw now that her experiences had sent her on a different road. But with his sister? It was too much to bear.

When he was calm enough to return to his home to discuss what had happened, Allie was no longer there. The servants said that she had left for a vacation with Miss Webster and not said when she would be back.

He went to his parents' home. No Jenny. She had gone away for a few weeks, his mother said, fussing because he looked pale and tired.

He had escaped maternal attention and made his way back to

Gramercy Park in a gentle April shower. They couldn't face him, he thought, but as he had no real wish to face them he only felt relief.

Over the quiet weeks that followed, he and Beth returned to the routine they had shared when Allie had been in the clinic. Life was not unpleasant. He tried hard to come to terms with what he had seen. Then gradually he became impatient for something positive to happen. This limbo could not go on indefinitely. He even began to worry that something had happened to the two women. Could they have disappeared for ever? He began to think that perhaps he should go to the police.

'We ought to talk about it, you know,' Beth said, spearing a piece of sauté potato on her fork and staring at it as if it held the secrets of the universe. 'It's not good to bottle things up.'

She was trying to appear casual, but she could not hide the tension she felt. It showed in the way she sat and when she looked up, directly into his eyes, he could see her anxiety that she might have upset him by speaking out.

He put down his fork. 'I was beginning to think that I ought to go to the police. It's been two months.'

She considered. 'They'll have run away somewhere. Those women act more dramatic and romantic than us normal mortals. I don't think anything terrible will have happened, but it must be tough not knowing where they are.' She was stilted, being careful. 'More important, do you care where they are? How are you feeling about it now?'

It was his turn to consider.

'You know,' he said slowly, 'I'm realising I feel more humiliated than anything. It is humiliating to find that your sister can arouse your wife when you can't. Allie was enjoying it. Allie was doing everything I'd wanted from her. The room even smelt of sex. I reckon I'd have felt a sight better about it if she'd been with another man. I could have hit another man – done something. What am I going to do about my sister?'

She was silent in the dimly lit, noisy room while he pondered his own question. Beth had picked the right moment. He wanted to talk about it. The lack of light in their small corner created the atmosphere of a confessional and the two large highballs they had drunk had made him slightly drunk and relaxed.

460

'Apart from the humiliation and still some anger I don't feel too bad,' he said. 'After all, I've had you to take my mind off things. I can't imagine you going off with my sister or any other woman.'

She smiled and tossed her head in a deliberately feminine way and said: 'Can't see myself lusting after a woman.'

'And I don't lust after fellows,' he said. 'But I guess it takes all sorts, though why my wife and sister had to be among 'em . . .'

'Do you still love her?' Beth asked, looking straight at him.

'Yes.' He was certain that he did. 'But in a different way. I don't want her sexually any more. If I tried to make love to her, all I'd ever see was her, unrestrained on the floor, with Jenny. It made me sick to my stomach to see them like that. But I suppose I've gradually come to understand. I guess what happened to Allie made her like that. It's easy to see that she'd be put off men for life. I can understand why she turned to a woman for love. We all need love. I've begun to understand that her need for sex can't have just disappeared completely. It had to be dormant there somewhere, waiting for someone to get it going. It just wasn't me who was the one to do it.' He paused, and still Beth said nothing. 'It's Jenny that puzzles me. Why should she be like that? Nothing ever happened to her. Or not that I know about. I don't understand at all why Jenny should be homosexual and why she should pick on my wife. God damn it, there was a time when she hated Allie.'

'Love hate?' murmured Beth.

'Could be. I just wish I knew where they were so I could stop imagining them in some kind of suicide pact, dead in each other's arms somewhere or other.' She was shaking her head. 'It's no good you looking so doubtful,' he said. 'It could happen. I've always feared that Allie might do away with herself when she has one of her depressions. All that stuff could have come back, for all I know. She's fragile mentally. Me catching her like that . . .'

'My guess is that your wife has at last discovered herself and what she wants to be and do,' Beth said briskly. 'But if you're imagining all these things, perhaps you'd better go to the police. But it's going to be embarrassing explaining. Do you want everyone to know about her?'

461

'No. I don't.' Alexander was aware his ego couldn't deal with that. 'I just want to know she's safe.'

'And then?'

'God knows. We'll just have to sort it out when she turns up. If she turns up.'

'She will,' said Beth. 'She will.'

Two days later Alexander received a telephone call in the office. It was from Jenny.

'I'm at Gramercy Park,' she said abruptly. 'We ought to talk.'

'We should indeed,' he said dryly. 'I'll be home as soon as I can.'

She was waiting for him in the drawing room of his home. She looked brown and well and he noticed for the first time how masculine she was. Had she always worn such mannish suits and cut her hair so short, or was it that now she had a lover she was letting her real predilections show? The sight of her brought back the image of her naked and without clothes, totally feminine, her hands parting his wife below her rounded belly, and he was angry again.

He stood inside the doorway looking at her. Nervously she rose from the chair where she had been sitting.

'I'm sorry, Alex,' she said simply. 'It just happened.'

'So I saw,' he said grimly.

'Neither of us could help it. It's just the way we are. The way we were made.'

'Allie wasn't made like that,' he said furiously. 'It was circumstances . . .'

'She believes now that it wasn't the circumstances.'

'I suppose you persuaded her of that.' He walked across the room to the whiskey decanter. 'Want one?' he asked abruptly.

'Please.'

'A man-sized one, I presume?'

She shivered. 'Alex, don't hate me.'

He poured the whiskies, thinking about that.

'Oddly, I don't hate either of you,' he said as he handed her the glass. 'I find myself more angry and humiliated than anything. And what next?'

'We want to stay together,' she said, her voice low, and he could not believe that his forthright sister was being so humble.

462

'You're not suggesting that we all live together?' He found himself wondering if that would be tolerable and immediately dismissed it as impossible.

'No. It would be dreadful for you. But you do have your mistress . . .'

'Did you tell Allie about that?' he asked angrily.

'Only after we'd . . .' she hesitated, 'we'd discovered that we love each other. You do still have your mistress?'

He didn't see why he should make things easier for her and ignored the question.

'And what did Allie say when you gave her this good news?' he asked.

'She was relieved. She said that living with her must have been awful for you. I think she understands better how hard it must have been now that she knows . . .' she stopped.

'What love is all about?' he suggested bitterly.

'Yes. Alex, it's hard for all of us. I love you. You're my wonderful big brother, and I love Allie. You did love me and you did love Allie. It can't all have gone, has it?'

'It's diminished.'

'I'm sorry.' Her voice was desolate.

But the truth was that diminished or not he did still care about them. He sighed and sat down.

'I've been worried about you both,' he admitted. 'I was afraid you might have done something silly.'

'We've been to California,' Jenny said eagerly, obviously happy to be on less dangerous ground. 'Allie wanted to see her mother's old home and where Pierre was brought up.'

'I see,' he said, not sure where this was leading.

'Alex,' she said, putting down her glass and clasping her hands together. 'We want to go and live there. That's what we want to do and that's where we want to be. California is so beautiful, Alexander, you can't imagine. It's a new world out there, a golden land. The sun shines. It's soft and gentle. We don't want anything from you. No money or anything. I've got plenty and Allie's got her allowance from her mother and the money she earns from her writing. We both think it would be better for us to start again somewhere else. We shall say that we're sisters. We are in a kind of a way . . .' She laughed uneasily as his face told her that he considered the remark in bad taste.

463

'And what are we going to tell our parents?'

'I know. That's the difficult bit. We wondered . . .' She fidgeted nervously.

'Wondered what?'

'If you would let Allie divorce you for adultery and then we could just go off as friends in Mama and Papa's eyes.'

'I don't want a divorce,' he said angrily. 'Why should I take the blame? A divorce could wreck my life.'

'Well, you should have thought of that before you started committing adultery,' Jenny pointed out, her voice sanctimonious. 'Allie might just get one anyway, even if you do object.'

'That doesn't sound like Allie. That sounds like you.'

'Maybe it is. Maybe I'd make her do it. I don't want Mama and Papa to be hurt.'

'By knowing what you are?'

'By knowing what I am,' she said defiantly.

'And supposing I counter-petition on non-consummation and the fact that my wife is homosexual.'

'That would break Mama and Papa's heart. My way, they would be glad. They've never been sure about Allie, and they guess something's wrong because you don't have any children. You want children, Alex. If you divorce you could marry again and have them.'

He was silent.

'Look, I know it's all too much to think about at once. Allie and I are going away for a while. You could think about it until we come home. It'll be about six months. But we have to do something to tidy up this mess, Alex.' She was pleading with him and he didn't like it. It wasn't like Jenny to plead. 'We're both sorry it happened, but it's done now. We love each other and there's nothing to be done about it. But we love you, too. You see, loving me hasn't changed anything that Allie ever felt for you. She didn't love you as a man in the first place. She loved you as a friend and that hasn't changed. It's not as if she's found another man that she likes better sexually. She never liked you sexually.'

'Thanks for reminding me,' he said dryly.

'Well, if you think about it, it should help,' she said. 'You know me, I'm never good at putting things tactfully. But it's true.'

'I guess so,' he said, resigned.

'Can you forgive us?' she asked, a touch dramatically.

'For Christ's sake, Jenny! Of course I can't forgive you. I'll come to terms with it in time, I expect, but I'm not going to stand here and give you absolution if that's what you want. If the pair of you weren't so damn selfish, you'd both live in New York, get on with your affair as you were before I found out and let everything remain as it was.'

'That would be hypocritical,' she pointed out.

'There's nothing wrong with a sensible bit of hypocrisy,' he said. 'As it is, it's all going to be the most dreadful upheaval.'

'You agree then?' she said eagerly.

He sighed. 'I'll think about it.'

And as he made the concession, he was thinking of Beth. If he could get Jenny out of the house, there would still be time to see her tonight.

Chapter Sixteen

On 10 July Rosie received a telephone call from the le Brunes' lawyer. He rang to say that the offer the le Brunes had received for Les Hérissons' champagne had been raised to 600,000 francs. Clearing his throat he carefully reminded her that on the proving of Monsieur Lefevre's will the property would be instantly sold. He also reminded her that once the purchaser had paid ten per cent down, the deal would be irrevocable. He then suggested that perhaps she would be prepared to raise her offer to 650,000 francs and pay her ten per cent before the proving of the will. This would be a private arrangement that would secure her interest in the property

It was fortunate for her, he pointed out, that Monsieur le Brune's client was quite properly insisting that the will be proved before he paid over any money.

Having recovered from her instant outrage at the financial blackmail, Rosie's heart lifted as she took in the implications of what he was saying. Here was temporary salvation. The le Brunes, aided by their lawyer, were prepared to bend the rules and make a premature deal with Rosie. But why? It dawned on her without too much stretching of the mind. This way they would have over 60,000 francs in the bank, earning good interest, well before they could legally sell to an outside party. They had no guarantee that Jack Patterson would go higher than his offer. The business was simply not worth any more. The le Brunes obviously believed in a bird in the hand and Rosie blessed their bourgeois, greedy little hearts for giving her this opportunity. All she had to do was find 65,000 francs as a downpayment. The only problem was she did not have 65,000 liquid francs. She could raise a chunk of it, but not all of it.

Nevertheless she told the notaire that she would be at his

office in two days' time, at 11 a.m. sharp, with the money.

All her instincts told her not to mention what was happening to Madame, Feathers or Pierre. Both Feathers and Madame would tell Pierre, and she was not certain what Pierre was up to. For all his grovelling confession there was still an antagonism between them and she wondered about his trips to Paris. He could still be in Jack Patterson's pocket.

So she went to the bank in Reims alone. The bank manager was businesslike. By putting up her own home, the house in the States and some of the stock in the cellars as security, she received a loan without too much trouble and the promise of more when and if she needed it.

She came home from Paris exhausted. She had formally met fat-faced and embarrassed Didier le Brune and a triumphant Françoise whose expression shouted: 'He loved me best.' Sick at heart, she had to sign the papers committing her to buying what she thought of as her own property. She handed over her company cheque full of apprehension. Ninety per cent more to find. It was a fortune. It could take her the rest of her life to earn it back, the interest was horrendous and it was all Pierre's fault for bringing Jack Patterson into their lives. Without the American's intervention it was unlikely the price would have been so high. But Jack Patterson was not to be told that he was out of the running yet. Not until the will was proved. As the lawyer said, it was best that no one knew what had been arranged in order to give 'chère Madame Lefevre' this opportunity. 'As chère Madame will realise, it was a little unorthodox,' he added with a small, embarrassed cough.

'I understand,' said Rosie gravely, hiding her contempt for his grubby methods. 'You are very wise and you may be sure that I shall tell no one.'

Breathing space. That's all it was. A snatch of breathing space, she thought on the train back. Only 585,000 francs to go. A nightmare sum. But she had lived through worse nightmares before and survived.

As arranged, Michel was waiting for her at Rilly station. He bore a message that she was to go straight to Les Hérissons.

'Why?' she asked.

'Marie said to tell you,' he said, his solid face lightened by smiles. 'Madame Dupuis has had her baby. It was born at three o'clock this afternoon. A little girl, Marie says, and the young Madame wants to see you.'

Quarter of an hour later Rosie was in Feathers' bedroom. The girl looked exhausted but proud. Her face was properly made up without an eyebrow out of place, her dark hair bounced round her broad but beautiful face and she wore the most enchantingly pretty nightgown. The baby was in a beribboned crib at her bedside, and to Rosie's surprise, Pierre was sitting on the bed beside his wife, holding her hand, while Madame sat knitting by the fireplace.

'Isn't she beautiful, Aunt Rosie?' Feathers said, leaning to pull back the covers from the baby's face. Rosie peeked in. It was a pretty baby. Still a little red and battered but with delicate small features and surprisingly, a great tuft of gingery fair hair. The colour of Luke's hair.

'She has my colouring,' Madame said. 'My hair was just that shade when I was a young woman.'

How very fortuitous, Rosie thought as she offered her congratulations.

'She's smaller than Patric was,' Pierre said. 'She'll need a lot of care.'

'What are you going to call her?' Rosie asked, putting out a tentative finger to touch the baby's soft cheek.

'We're giving her English names. Hope, and her second name will be Joy, and Teresa for her saint's name.' Feathers said. 'Do you like them?'

Rosie smiled. Hope leading to Joy. They were good choices under the circumstances. 'But the French will never be able to say Hope,' she warned. 'She'll be 'ope all her life.'

'I don't care,' said Feathers stubbornly. 'That's what we want her to be called.'

We! Rosie looked enquiringly at Pierre.

'They're the perfect names for her,' he said solemnly with all the pride of a new papa and she thought again what a strange, contradictory young man he was.

There was a gentle tap on the door. It opened and Luke's head appeared round the jamb looking a little ill at ease.

'I've just come in. I've just heard,' he said. 'Can I see the baby?' And Rosie saw how Pierre's face set.

'Of course,' Feathers said, waving her hand towards the crib. 'She is very beautiful.'

Luke crossed the room awkwardly, looking large and out of place. Cautiously he peered into the crib and Rosie held back the soft pink blanket so he could see in.

'Gosh!' he said. 'She is beautiful.'

'And she's called Hope Joy,' Feathers said gently.

He stood upright and looked directly at Feathers, his expression questioning. The girl smiled at him encouragingly.

'Do you think they're good names?' she asked.

'I think they're perfect,' he said gruffly. 'Well, thanks for letting me see her.'

He made for the door as if it might imprison him if he didn't hurry. And Rosie noticed how Pierre, his expression resentful, stared after him. It wasn't going to be easy between those two, she thought. It wasn't going to be easy at all.

Excusing herself while Madame grumbled that she couldn't see why the baby couldn't have a good French saint's name like everyone else, Rosie slipped from the bedroom and ran down the stairs after Luke.

He heard her call his name and turned.

'Are you all right?' she asked as she caught up with him.

'I'm fine. I'm just glad Feathers and the baby are all right.'

'A beautiful baby,' she said.

'A beautiful baby,' he agreed.

'And would Grandpa like a glass of champagne to celebrate?'

He put his fingers over his lips, cautioning her.

'Grandpa would like that very much,' he whispered.

She grinned. 'Come on, we'll go to the blending room.'

It was there that she tentatively asked him if he would tell Carlos what had happened.

He shook his head. 'Better he knows nothing,' he said. 'And besides, he seems to be doing quite nicely in England. He might even be growing up.'

'It's the right decision not to say anything.' she said. 'Life's all decisions, isn't it?' She sighed, and told him what she had done that day and how the le Brunes' greed had temporarily saved her.

'And what about the other ninety per cent?' he asked.

'Les Coquelicots and the apartment in Reims are already on

the market, but no biters yet. I've arranged for the house in California to be sold, I'm looking for a new agent to move the stock, and when the time comes, I'll borrow from Madame, get my money back from Feathers and pull in every sou I can.'

'Will it be enough?' he asked.

'No,' she said. 'I'll have to borrow the rest. I'll be well short unless Madame helps and I don't think she has that much money these days. The bank will let me have more – at a price – but I'll worry about that when the time comes. I'm not letting Les Hérissons' champagne go. I just wish I hadn't been quite so spendthrift for so long.'

'It's not you,' he said indignantly. 'It's all of them. They all live off you.'

'Oh, I've done my share of spending,' she said cheerfully. 'And why not? It's fun spending. But now I've got to start earning again.'

He looked as if he was going to say something, but stopped and said instead: 'You'd better get back upstairs. They'll be wondering where you are.'

'Yes, I suppose I'd better.' She drained her glass. 'But not a word to anyone for the moment. I don't want it to get back to Jack Patterson, though it's too late for him to do anything now, unless, of course, I can't deliver come pay day.'

'You'll deliver,' he said with such confidence that her heart lifted and she began to believe it herself.

'I hope you're right,' she said.

It turned out to be a day of surprises. Back at Les Coquelicots a letter from Allie awaited her. She sat staring at the envelope, the familiar bold handwriting and the New York postmark anxiously. Her first thought was that something must be dreadfully wrong for Allie to be writing to her. Except for the letter at the time of Philippe's death, Allie had never written since she left for America.

Cautiously she tore open the envelope and two sheets of flimsy paper fell out.

My dear Mama,
   I'm coming home just for a little while and I can't wait to see you all again. Alexander and I are having a little break from each other. So, I'm coming to Europe with

Jenny and the two of us are going on to Algeria for a month or two when she's got all her papers together from the French Government to allow her to go back there.

She's a Quaker now and she works with the Berbers in the mountains, helping them. The idea is that I'm going with her to research background for a book. But we'll come to Les Hérissons first.

I have so much to tell you. My life is so much happier now. I've come to terms with so many things and realised that there was much that I was wrong about. I owe you a lot of apologies, Mama.

I have a great need to see Rosanne again. I have been away from her for too long. All those growing years that I've missed that can never be recovered. I don't want to do anything damaging – like declaring myself to her – but I think that now I can be with her without the pain I used to feel. I need to know her properly, Mama.

I suppose you could say that I've been trying to find myself for a long time now, and one of the things I did was to go to California and see your old home outside Calistoga. I wanted to see where I began. We found it okay. We couldn't get in because the caretaker wouldn't believe who I was. It was all boarded up, but we went round the outside and all through the grounds. Mama, it's all crumbling and needing love, but it could be fantastic. We fell in love with it, and, Mama, I want to live there. I want to start again in a new place, and being where your roots are and I was started feels kind of right. Can we have it and make something of it? I don't know what we'll do. Turn it into an orphanage, farm it, grow grapes again. Something positive and good that will make it all come alive again. You can stop my allowance if we go there. I don't need any money. We have plenty of money – though not enough to buy the house from you. You always said it would be mine if I ever wanted it, and it's better someone should live there than it should sit and moulder.

Will you think about it? We won't be long arriving after this letter. We plan to be in Europe by July the 21st. We'll telephone Les Hérissons from Paris and Henri can come and pick us up on the morning of the 22nd. How is dear Henri? He must be getting old.

We can talk about everything when I arrive. Will you prepare Pierre so that it's not too much of a shock? It'll be good to see him again, too.

Love to Rosanne, Mimi, Luke, Miss, Marie, Henri, everyone, and of course to you, my dear mama.
          Allie

Rosie put down the letter, stunned and full of consternation. After so long to receive such a warm, affectionate letter from Allie was like a miracle. She didn't know whether to laugh or to cry. In eleven days her daughter would be home. The fact that Allie would be with Jenny, that too was unexpected. Allie and Jenny had never got on all that well. She was astonished that Allie had been to Calistoga and who was the 'we' who went with her? Surely not Alexander? Surely Alexander would not want to give up his life and his job in New York? Or would he if it would make Allie happy?

Her asking for the old family homestead was shattering. Only two days before, Rosie had made arrangements to put it on the market. She needed to sell it. But the house would have been Allie's one day if she had kept it, and if Allie wanted it now, how could she sell? The thought briefly crossed her mind that perhaps all of this reconciliation was coming about because Allie wanted the house. Then she was annoyed with herself for thinking such a thing for even an instant. Allie was many things, but she was not conniving and she would not pretend to feelings she did not have for material gain.

Rosie reread the letter and then went upstairs to see Rosanne to tell her the news. Rosanne was working on the evening revision that Miss set her every night, sitting at the desk which had once been Allie's.

Rosie read out bits of the letter to her. 'And how about that for a birthday present?' she concluded. But Rosanne was not particularly excited by the idea of Allie's coming home.

'It's nice for you, Mama,' she said, 'just as long as she doesn't upset you like she used to when she was here before.'

'She was ill before,' Rosie protested.

'Maybe. But she was always funny. Hugging me and kissing

472

me one minute and acting as if I wasn't there the next. I think that was what made me so naughty.'

'Well, it'll all be different this time,' Rosie said, sad that Rosanne had so little affection for Allie. 'And anyway, she won't be staying long. She's going to Africa for a little while.'

'Good,' said Rosanne in positive tones before returning to her English grammar.

Rosie went to bed early that night. She ached for Philippe, wishing he was there to share the news. She needed someone who would understand how glad it had made her. But who? It did not seem the time to telephone Les Hérissons. All of them there, even Luke, had their own excitement to think about with the new baby. She'd have to tell everyone in the morning.

She slept, imagining Allie on the boat somewhere on the Atlantic, getting nearer and nearer. In just a few days they would be together. She felt warm and content as she lay there alone, happier than she had been for a long time. It was true that Allie had intensified the problem of money by wanting the house in Calistoga, and Rosie's heart still ached for Philippe, but at least one of her deep secret sadnesses had been wiped away.

Her daughter was coming home again.

Feathers liked being a mother again. Everyone fussed over her so and really the birth had been easy. Nowhere near as painful as when she had Patric. Even Pierre seemed enchanted by the baby – almost more than he had been over Patric. Patric himself had hung over the crib, dutifully given the baby a kiss and then scampered off back to his nursery. At four, Patric had better things to do than bother with baby sisters.

To her amazement, Pierre had said he would skip college and sit and chat with her for the day and he was comfortable in the bedroom armchair when, just before eleven, Madame came to visit. Feathers could tell from her stiff bearing and the gimlet look of her eyes that she was in one of other contrary moods.

'Your Aunt Rosie will be here soon,' she said as Pierre made way for her to take the chair. 'She's just gone out to the fields to find Luke for something or other. She has some wonderful news too . . .'

Madame, who liked to touch a drama, waited.

473

'What's happened then, Mimi?' Feathers, who had learned to play Madame's games, asked.

'Allie, her daughter, is coming home. The girl will be here on the twenty-second.'

The old woman's steely eyes were on Pierre. Following their direction, Feathers saw her husband turn quite white. The cigarette that he had been about to light dropped from between his fingers. With a muttered expletive he bent to pick it up.

'She has shown me the letter. A loving letter, thank goodness. It seems the child has returned to her senses. She says she is looking forward to seeing you, Pierre.'

There was something wrong about her tone and Feathers noted that Pierre was still white, his hands shaking. He murmured something that Feathers did not catch.

'Is Aunt Rosie pleased?' she asked, still watching her shaken husband.

'Delighted. They are not staying long. They are going to Algeria or somewhere to do good works.' Madame sniffed. 'There's plenty enough good works they could do right here.'

'She's coming with her husband?' Pierre's voice sounded strangled.

'No. Her husband's sister. He is staying behind in New York.' She shook her head. 'Allie has always been unwise.'

'Unwise?' Feathers asked.

'It is unwise to leave husbands on their own. They get into mischief.'

To Pierre's obvious relief there was a tap on the door and Rosie's smiling face appeared, murmuring good mornings.

'And how are you today?' she asked, advancing to give Feathers a kiss.

'Less tired, and the baby's less pink,' Feathers said, unwilling to admit that yesterday the baby had been downright crimson. Rosie peered into the crib.

'So she is,' she said.

'I've told them your news,' Madame announced.

'You have?' Rosie looked briefly dismayed as she glanced quickly at Pierre. 'Of course you haven't met my daughter, have you?' she said to Feathers. 'She's a bit older than you in years, but young for her age. Or she was. Maybe she's grown up now.' She turned to Pierre. 'Pierre,' she said coaxingly, 'why don't you go and get us a bottle of our best vintage? I'm sure Feathers would like a glass.'

'Marie will bring it perfectly well,' Madame said, her eyebrows raised at the idea of Pierre doing servants' work.

'No, Grandma, I'll go,' he said hastily, already making for the door. What on earth was the matter with him? Feathers wondered, but the baby gave a little cry, distracting her. She bent to pick her from the crib and croon her back to calm.

'I wanted the two of you on your own,' Rosie was saying. 'I hate to ask you this, Feathers, but do you think you can pay me back some of the money that you had for the shop?'

'Of course,' Feathers said, alarmed by Rosie's anxious look. 'Quite a lot of it. At least five thousand francs. And if you need more, I'll borrow some from the bank like I said I would.'

'I don't want you putting yourself in debt,' Rosie said, obviously hating every minute of the conversation. 'What you have will do. And Mama, could you make me any kind of loan? Just a temporary one of course.'

'What's happened?' Madame wanted to know.

'Jack Patterson topped my price. It's gone up to 650,000 francs now.'

'Good heavens!' Madame looked quite shocked. 'He must be mad.'

'He may be but the le Brunes aren't.'

Madame thought. 'I could let you have ten thousand francs,' she said. 'But Feathers, you will have to pay Pierre's bills until Rosie pays me back.'

'It's time Pierre started paying his own bills,' Feathers was surprised to hear herself saying. Her heart was bleeding for Rosie. Fifteen thousand francs between them. It wouldn't make the tiniest dent in 650,000 francs.

'Are you going to let Allie have the house in America?' Madame was asking.

'What else can I do? I promised it to her long ago. I don't want anything to happen to upset her homecoming. I'll find something else. Les Coquelicots will fetch a good sum. About twenty thousand francs. Then there's the apartment in Reims. I'll sell off as much stock as I can. Then I'll just have to borrow.'

'The interest will cripple you,' Madame said.

'Not for long. Once I get the business moving again . . . I've got an idea about making a lot more still wine with the grapes we don't use. It's good. I'm sure I could get Parisian restaurants to take it.'

'Rosie, Rosie!' Madame sighed. 'You never change.'

'I don't intend to,' Rosie said grimly.

Pierre was coming through the door with a bottle and glasses on a tray. He seemed to have recovered his composure. He looked round the room quickly and seemed reassured. Playing the waiter, the tray on his shoulder, a cloth over his arm, he moved to his desk where there was a clear space and put down the tray.

'Now,' he said, 'we'll drink to our new baby.'

Our baby! Feathers thrilled at the words. She waited misty-eyed until they were all served, and then holding up her glass so that the light shone through the bubbles said in her very best French, 'To our baby, and to us all.'

Rosie was just setting off for Les Hérissons on the morning of Allie's arrival when Suzette called her back from the drive where Michel was cranking the car. The le Brunes' lawyer was telephoning with what he called good news.

'The will has been proved, Madame, and after certain formalities we shall expect the remainder of the money,' he said. 'Shall we say a week? And then Les Hérissons' champagne and the Lefevre distribution company will be all yours. Of course, should you not be able to raise—'

'A week will be fine,' Rosie interrupted calmly, and hung up the receiver feeling slightly sick. Her insides churned at the thought of having nearly to bankrupt herself to buy back her own business.

It was happening so quickly. She cursed herself for those months of inactivity after Philippe's death when she uncharacteristically had let herself wallow in grief. She should have read the will and then the danger confronting her would have been obvious. She could have put Les Coquelicots and the apartment in Reims on the market long before. Everything had been left far too late. As it was, there was no a sign of either property selling and they most certainly would not within the next week. And then there was the small matter of explaining to the bank manager that the Californian house was now not for sale and could not be counted as collateral.

She groaned and went back out to the car, determined to wipe the problem from her mind for at least today. Today must be Allie's day, and nothing must spoil it. She'd worry about raising the money tomorrow. She had no doubts that in the end she would. It was the thought of the millstone of interest that frightened her. 'Think about it tomorrow,' she told herself as she drove along the quiet roads. At least it was a perfect day. Not too hot, the sun shining, the poppies nodding at the roadsides; all Champagne was looking its best to welcome Allie home.

Everyone at Les Hérissons was busy. Marie polishing everything in sight, Robert making sure that the driveway was swept and clear. There was champagne ready on ice in the drawing room and Cook had announced that she would surpass herself with the lunch. A little river trout to begin, she thought, after the soup of course, then a gigot with flageolet followed by one of her *Tarte Tatin*. Miss Allie had always liked her *Tarte Tatin*. Besides, it was well known that the food in America was absolutely frightful. Miss Allie's homecoming lunch must be one to remember.

The entire household appeared to be delighted that Miss Allie was coming home. The house was *en fête*. And Rosie thought how marvellous it was that all at Les Hérissons had understood Allie's problems and loved her still. But then, most of those at Les Hérissons had grim and bitter memories of the events that had created Allie's problems.

Henri insisted on meeting Miss Allie at Rilly-la-Montagne station. He had word that Miss Allie had specifically asked for him, and though he did not enjoy driving these days, nothing, not even if all the traffic in Paris had appeared on the quiet Champagne roads, would have stopped him going. He duly trundled off to meet her train after the call came from Paris to say what time she would be arriving.

Rosie agonised as to whether to go with him. She wanted to be at the station but she was afraid her emotions would overcome her at the first sight of her daughter. She did not want to make a great performance out of Allie's return. Perhaps best to keep it normal. But she had that same anxiety that whatever she did would be wrong. Just as whatever she had done in the past had always been wrong.

Instead she arrayed the entire family on the front porch. For fun she had Luke hang the Tricolour and the Stars and Stripes from the tower bedroom window and both blew bravely in a light summer breeze.

Allowing for Henri's funereal speed of driving, they all gathered on the porch with five minutes to spare. Miss dressed in her best, Rosie noted, standing with Rosanne. Allie would see a big difference in Rosanne. Feathers had not forgotten it was the child's ninth birthday back in June and had presented her with a charming simple frock with an all-round pleated skirt and a top with a big sailor collar over full puffed sleeves. It was deep crimson, Rosanne's favourite colour, and wearing it she looked very grown-up and self-possessed. Rosie had been uneasy about bringing Feathers, Pierre, the baby and Patric into the group on the porch. Would the sight of Pierre with his family distress Allie? But she told herself that Allie would have to face Pierre and his family at some point. Just as well to get it over with quickly while other people were around to take away the sting. It was Pierre who might find it the most difficult. Rosie had registered his stricken face at the news of Allie's homecoming, but there was nothing she could say or do to help.

She herself was wearing plain black. She had not been able to bring herself to wear colours yet. It was too soon. But everyone else had dressed to the nines. Old Tomas, Cook, Robert and Marie all waited with their mistress who sat, back like a board, on a high chair, her hands folded in her lap, a pleased smile on her face. Nanny Shepherd kept a weather-eye on Feathers, who had insisted on getting out of bed. She had been settled in a rocking chair, her baby, well wrapped up, on her lap. Pierre, looking white and uneasy, held Patric tight to him. Luke hung back, Miss at his side, and Rosie beckoned Rosanne beside her, centre stage, where they stood holding hands.

It was just striking noon when the familiar chug of the Salmson's engine was heard and everyone saw the faint rise of dust from the drive. Suddenly there was silence as if all Les Hérissons were holding its breath. Miss Allie was coming home.

Chapter Seventeen

'Nervous?' Jenny asked.

'A bit.' Allie had felt herself tense as the car entered the driveway of Les Hérissons and she held on closer to Jessica who, passive as ever, was curled on her lap. Apart from sheer nervousness she felt scratchy because her mother had not been at the station. And now there was no sign of old Tomas in the gatehouse. Was he still alive? she wondered, hoping that he was. Old Tomas was part of her childhood.

'Well, relaxez-vous,' Jenny said lightly. 'It's stupid to be nervous,' and added, 'what you have got to be nervous about?'

In her current frame of mind, Allie thought it a stupid question even if it was meant to be rhetorical. And she noted that Jenny's hands were tightly clenched in her lap. She, too, was not exactly at ease, so how could she be so insensitive?

'Of course I'm nervous,' Allie said crossly. 'About Rosanne. I've never written to her once since I left Les Hérissons. About Pierre. I don't know what I'll feel when I see him. About Mama, to whom I've been a bitch. I didn't exactly leave home with everyone loving me, Jenny. I should think that they were all glad to see the back of me. I'm not sure they'll be that delighted to see me home again.' She wanted to voice her anxieties that her mother had not been at the station. She wanted to expand on her fears at meeting Pierre again, but decided against both.

Jenny drew a long nervous breath.

'Do you think you still feel something for Pierre?' It was a question Allie was aware Jenny had been longing to ask. Until now Allie had been careful never to give her the opportunity, mainly because she didn't know the answer herself. Her worry was that nothing would have changed. But the question was so self-interested on Jenny's part. She seemed to have forgotten all about Rosanne – the most important person of all.

'Who knows?' she said, giving Jenny no comfort. 'But what does it matter if I do? There'd be nothing to be done about it.'

The other girl was silent and Allie said nothing. She had too many worries of her own to deal with anyone else's. Besides, Jenny was pushing her again. Ever since they had decided to go to France, Jenny had been pushing her for reassurances.

'Any minute now you'll see the house,' she said as Henri cautiously crept up the drive. She waited while they rounded the curve and as the turreted house came into view her nervousness was overtaken by excitement. 'Look, there it is! Exactly the same as it ever was. Except for the flags. Just look at those flags! They must be in our honour.'

Jenny craned forward to look.

'I hadn't imagined it as big,' she said. 'And it's old. There are an awful lot of people on the porch.'

Allie felt her eyes misting over and in that moment could not understand why on earth she had stayed away from home for so long.

'Mama's got everyone out there,' she said, her voice choked. 'Everyone. Oh, there's Tomas. He isn't dead. And Marie and Robert. Cook and Miss – the whole lot!'

'Which one is Pierre?' Jenny asked.

Allie had spotted him immediately and her stomach lurched at the sight of him. But where was Rosanne?

'The dark one standing by the dark woman. That must be his wife . . .'

'He looks just like you.' Jenny sounded astonished.

'Well, I told you he did,' Allie said impatiently, still looking for Rosanne. Then she spotted her. 'Gosh! Rosanne has changed. She's grown up so. I wouldn't have recognised her.'

Henri was swinging the car round so that Allie could get out on the side nearest to the porch. He then clambered creakily from the driving seat to open the car door for her.

'Welcome home, Miss Allie,' he said as he opened the door with a flourish.

A flood of people were coming down the steps towards her, led by her mother. At first glimpse her mother seemed older. Her hair did not shine as much as it had, and her face was thinner, but her arms were open and she was smiling.

But ahead of them all was Jessica who had leapt from the open door and bounded up the stairs to where Pierre stood. Her tail wagging frantically, she was uttering little yaps of joy as Pierre bent to pick her up.

It was the diversion that they all needed. Everyone watched, laughed, and then Allie let herself be hugged by her mother and did her share of hugging back. Madame, who looked exactly the same, had risen from her straight-backed chair and come to kiss her and inspect her. She was tut-tutting that Allie was too thin. 'But, Mimi, it's fashionable,' Allie protested, feeling that something profounder would have been more in order. Then the staff came to shake her hand, one by one. Miss, with tears in her eyes, hugged her in a most unBritish kind of way.

Allie found herself surprised and deeply moved by the warmth of her welcome. She hadn't expected it, particularly when only Henri had come to meet her. The only disappointment was that her daughter had hung back, but as the staff returned to their duties she feasted her eyes on Rosanne for a moment before going towards her. The girl was all of four inches taller and looking so pretty in her fashionable crimson dress. She stood slightly apart from the group, waiting at the side of the dark girl in the rocking chair who must be Pierre's wife.

'A belated happy birthday, Rosanne,' Allie said, as she kissed her child. 'Nine years old! My! Haven't you grown. And aren't you pretty?'

It was all desperately inadequate for what she was feeling. The years had faded away. She was back in the champagne cave at Reims reluctantly holding her newborn daughter. The daughter that to her great sorrow she had rejected and never managed to be close to.

Rosanne, who didn't know that, flushed.

'Hello, Allie,' she said shyly. 'Welcome home.'

Trying to control her emotions, Allie turned to the dark girl who had not risen from the rocking chair. 'And you must be Pierre's wife. With a new baby?'

'A very new baby. Forgive me for remaining seated,' the girl said in heavily accented French, then added: 'Welcome home.'

It was said with true warmth. She doesn't know! thought Allie. Thank heavens she doesn't know!

'It's great to be here,' Allie told her, and slowly, slowly forced herself to turn to where Pierre stood holding Jessica in his arms.

'Jessica still loves you,' Allie said, and realised that unwittingly she had put the slightest inflection on the word 'Jessica'.

'And I still love her,' said Pierre putting the same inflection on the word 'her'. They stood looking at each other gravely and searchingly and it seemed to Allie that in those few seconds they were in a pool of silence. Then they both laughed as if something comical had happened. Pierre put Jessica down. He moved to kiss Allie on both cheeks, his hands lightly on her shoulders. It was going to be all right.

'It's good to see you,' he said.

'And to see you,' she said, her eyes misting again. For a moment she was afraid she was going to cry, but happily Luke was coming towards her.

'You look quite wonderful, young Allie,' he said. 'Every inch the New Yorker.'

She felt herself blush with pleasure at the compliment. She smoothed the slim skirt of her navy-blue Mainbocher suit, remembering what a scruff she had been when she lived here at home. Then she turned to look for Jenny. Jenny had been left at the foot of the steps, forgotten in the excitement. But Rosie had taken care of the situation. Jenny was already up on the porch and being introduced to Madame. Her time in Algeria had given the American girl a smattering of French and Allie could see that her forthright friend was setting out to charm Madame.

'Ah, you've met my wonderful grandmother,' she said, taking Jenny's arm. 'Now come and meet my sister Rosanne and my cousin Pierre and the rest of the family.'

By the time they had gone inside, bottles of champagne had been cracked, presents exchanged, and some emotional, happy tears shed by both Allie and Rosie. Her old room had been prepared for her and Jenny had been given the nicest of the guest rooms. Jenny, she saw, was anxious. The conversation was in French and she could not keep up. And she kept throwing nervous glances at Pierre.

'They do look alike, don't they?' Allie heard Feathers say, speaking in English. 'I'm finding it disconcerting, too.'

482

Jenny muttered something about it being extraordinary, and Feathers patted the sofa next to her.

'Come and talk to me,' she said. 'I know just how you're feeling. It took me years to learn this impossible language and I'm still not that good at it.'

As Jenny gratefully went to sit beside Feathers, Allie noted how beautiful Pierre's wife was. She was like some Hollywood star in her glamour. But she appeared to be kind. Beautiful, kind and Pierre's wife and the mother of his children.

How do I feel about him and her and all of it? she asked herself, but the middle of a family party was not the time to examine her emotions.

After an enormous lunch at which Cook kept appearing to make sure all was well, Allie suddenly felt overwhelmed. She needed to be alone. She rose from the table and said, a little abruptly: 'I think I'll just take Jessie for a walk.'

'I'll come with you,' Jenny said eagerly from the other end of the table where she was sitting between Feathers and Luke.

'No, you stay where you are,' Allie said. Jenny sank back into her seat disappointed. Allie touched her lightly on the shoulder as she passed. 'I'll only be a little while,' she said quietly. 'I just need to be alone.'

'Okay,' Jenny said with a brave smile. 'I'm all right.'

Jessica pattered after her mistress down the porch steps and through the trees to the path up the hill. Allie wanted to see the spot where she and her father had always walked to look down over Les Hérissons. The spot where she and Pierre had fallen in love. But it was for her father and for Les Hérissons that she wanted to make the walk. She knew with complete certainty that Pierre was not important any more. Home and her childhood memories were what she wanted from her hilltop view.

It was a lovely hot sunny day with that special light that her father had always said was enhanced by the white chalk of Champagne. Below, the vines stood in orderly rows, peacefully guarding the house. The vines would have almost finished flowering, and she imagined that she could smell their agreeable scent blown to her on the wind. Her father would have been worrying if the pollination had taken place successfully. The crop depended on the pollination. Today the wind was right, but the sky too clear and high, she thought, casting a knowledgeable eye upwards. It needed to be overcast and warm; not dry and sunny. But at least there was no sign of a heavy rainfall to wipe the pollen away.

She sat on the ground, regardless of her Mainbocher skirt, Jessica at her side, as she took in the view. Tomorrow she would bring Jenny here, but today she needed to see it alone and let all the memories float free. She had needed time alone to accept the warmth of her welcome. Allie had not realised just how loved she was. No one in New York, not even Alexander, had made her feel loved in the same unquestioning, undemanding way as her family had this morning. Jenny was always so demanding of her affection. It was good to be with these people who had known her since she was a child, people who were aware of her past and all her secrets and loved her still.

Suddenly Jessica let out a small 'woof!' and bounded away back down the hillside. Allie felt herself tense. Jessica must have heard Pierre coming to find her. Jessica would not leave her mistress for anyone else. Allie was not certain that she was ready for a confrontation with Pierre but now it could not be avoided.

He came in sight, striding up the path, still in the formal suit that he had worn at lunchtime. They both looked ridiculous, she thought, so formally dressed on a Champagne hillside.

He sat himself down beside her and they were silent, staring at the house below as Jessica settled herself between them. Then he said: 'I wanted to make sure that you're happy. You look happy.'

She thought about it and then said as if it surprised her: 'I am happy now. And you?'

He nodded slowly. 'As happy as I'll ever be.'

'Your wife is beautiful.'

He nodded again. 'She's remarkable,' he said. 'She's strong and brave. She has the courage to do things.'

'And you knew her before you knew me?'

He turned to look her straight in the face. 'I'd been making love to her back in Boston. She was just another girl then. A girl who'd let me make love to her. She was in love with me. She came from a terrible background – I'll tell you the whole story one day. But when I got back from here and you wrote me that

484

letter, she was pregnant. You said you were going to marry Alexander since it didn't matter who you married if we couldn't be together, so I decided to do the same and marry her.' He paused and then began to speak faster as if he wanted to get it over with. 'It didn't work out immediately. I made her dreadfully unhappy, but she stuck it out. Then things happened, and I realised I admired her a lot. And that other people liked her a lot. I suppose I started to look at her properly. She started her own business, a dress shop, and it's a success. She's doing a lot more with her life than I am. She doesn't really need me, but I've discovered I need her.'

'You love her?' Allie knew she ought to be feeling pain, but she felt nothing more than interest in his story.

He examined the question.

'I suppose I do,' he said. 'Not the way I felt about you. But I can't imagine that ever happening again.'

'I think we fell in love with ourselves,' Allie said thoughtfully. 'It was like Narcissus. I looked at you, and once I no longer saw our father I saw myself. And you looked at me and saw yourself.'

'But it was real,' he protested.

'It was very real. It was the strongest emotion I've ever felt – other than hate for the lieutenant. But then self-love is probably the strongest emotion.'

'For most people,' he said. 'Feathers isn't like that.' He paused. 'And do you love Alexander?'

She shook her head. 'Not as a husband, only as a dear friend.' She suddenly knew that Pierre was perhaps the only person in the world that she could talk to freely. 'We've never made love the entire time we've been married. I wouldn't let him. I'll never make love with a man. Ever. I think it wouldn't even have happened with you.'

'Poor Alexander,' he said softly. 'And to think I was so jealous of him for so long.'

'Were you? You needn't have been. It must have been dreadful for him. He finally took a mistress and it was only when I had a breakdown and went away for treatment that I began to realise how cruel I had been to him.'

'And now?' he asked.

'We're divorcing. At least, I hope so. He hasn't agreed yet,

485

but I think he will. It would be better for us both.'

'And you'll be alone. I can't bear to think of you without love in your life, Allie.'

She decided to tell him the truth. She wanted to tell him the truth.

'But I do have love. I have Jenny.'

He gave her a sharp, searching look. 'You love Jenny?'

'Yes, and she loves me.'

His expression was very strange. There was something almost prurient in it.

'That way?'

She couldn't help smiling. 'Yes, that way. Are you shocked?'

'No. I think sexual love between two women is the most beautiful, tender thing.' His voice was full of passion. 'So much more loving and gentle than the love between men and women. It's the most erotic and sensual thing a man can see.'

'See?' she asked, shielding her eyes from the sun to look at him and wondering how on earth he could have seen such a thing.

He looked embarrassed for an instant, and then repeated: 'Yes, see. I have seen many women making love.'

How very strange, was her first reaction, then she asked: 'Where?' not sure if she really wanted to know.

'In an establishment,' he said, a little reluctantly.

'You mean like Madame Claudette's?'

He nodded.

'And the women make love to each other while you watch?'

He nodded again. She thought about it, imagining a man – Pierre? – watching her and Jenny in their most loving moments. The idea gave her a touch of hot excitement but she said: 'How strange. I shouldn't want Jenny and me to become a sideshow.'

Did he look disappointed for an instant? She wasn't sure.

'I shouldn't have told you,' he said. 'I'm sorry. I don't think the girls in the establishments love each other, really. They only do it for money.'

She wrinkled her face in distaste. 'That's almost worse.' But a thought struck her. 'Maybe they do love each other, though,' she suggested. 'They have no man to love and every day men use them. They might turn to a woman for love. A woman they

486

know, who has to do the same horrible thing with men every day of her life. I think that's why I turned to Jenny. Because of the lieutenant.'

'That's what I always feel about those women,' he said eagerly. 'Perhaps I shouldn't have told you, but I wanted to so you wouldn't think you'd shocked me about you and Jenny.'

'It doesn't hurt you?' she asked.

'No, I'll never love anyone like I loved you. There hasn't been a day when I haven't thought about you. But it's over, isn't it?'

She nodded.

'Now I just feel that you and I are bound in some way. I can tell you things. We can share each other's secrets. There's no one else in the world I could have told that I like to watch girls making love.' And then he added, his voice low: 'I needed to tell someone. Have I shocked you?'

'No,' she said thoughtfully. 'I guess I'm a lot more open-minded than I used to be. And besides, I couldn't have told anyone else about Jenny and me.' She put her hand on his knee. 'Shall we keep each other's secrets, Pierre?'

'I shall keep yours, sister.'

'And I yours, brother.'

They smiled at each other and he reached to take her hand.

'Perhaps we should go back,' he said. 'Jenny and Feathers will be wondering what has happened to us.'

'Yes,' she said. 'Perhaps we should.'

As they walked back down the hill in the sunshine while Jessica searched for old, forgotten smells, he took her hand in his. Neither of them spoke, but it was a shared silence, the comfortable silence of a brother and sister who were also good friends.

'She looks more like your twin than your cousin.' Feathers sounded as if she was accusing him of something.

'We are alike,' he grunted, wrestling with his bow tie.

Feathers was already dressed for dinner. She wore a white velvet bias cut dress with crystal shoulder straps and a long crystal necklace embroidered on it. The dress flared into hand-kerchief points that almost touched her ankles, and her high-heeled shoes had a strap of crystal beads. Long chandelier

487

earrings swung below her bobbed hair and crystal beads filled in the deep expanse of bare bosom and shoulders. A huge white soft floating feather fan completed the outfit.

'Aren't you a bit overdressed for dinner at home?' Pierre asked, as much to change the subject as anything.

Feathers bristled. 'I don't think so.'

'Okay then,' he said.

Neither spoke while he managed to get the tie to lie flat.

'I wanted to look good,' she said in a small voice.

'Oh?'

'Because of her.'

'Who?

'Your cousin.'

'Allie?'

'Yes.'

'That's not difficult. Allie doesn't dress very well, and anyway, she's not as good-looking as you.'

His instincts told him that was what she wanted to hear.

'I didn't think she was dressed badly today. That was a Mainbocher suit.'

Pierre didn't know who or what Mainbocher was.

'Well, all I can tell you is that when she lived here it was almost impossible to get her to dress up. She wasn't interested in clothes at all. Grandmother was always on at me to try to smarten her up.'

'Why you?'

He wasn't sure what to say. He could see trouble coming.

'Because we were friends, I suppose,' he said lamely.

'Good friends?'

'Yes, good friends,' he said, trying not to sound defensive.

She picked up her fan and flirted it across her face. It was so big it caused a draught.

'Did you follow her this afternoon after lunch?'

He tensed. 'Yes, I did.'

'Why?'

'Why not?'

She put down the fan with a slap and started to speak very quickly.

'It was her that you were in love with, wasn't it? I could tell from the way you looked at each other on the porch. And all that business with that boring little dog. Everyone knew. I could see them all looking at you both to see what would happen. It was humiliating. Awful. And then for you to go and follow her and stay out all that time . . .'

Her face was pink with indignation, her eyes full of tears and she looked quite remarkably beautiful.

'You're jealous!' he said.

She went pinker. 'I am not. I'm just upset. And why shouldn't I be? You should have told me. You should have prepared me.'

He sat down on the bed and said again: 'Feathers, you're jealous. I like it. The times I've been jealous of you . . .'

Her violet eyes widened. 'Jealous of me?' She sounded incredulous.

'Yes, jealous of you. I see the way men look at you. And you flirt, and I'm jealous.'

The gleam of tears intensified.

'Oh, Pierre,' she said, clasping her hands. 'How wonderful.'

'So, you see, you don't need to be jealous.'

'But there was something once? Between you and her?' she asked.

He hesitated. He should have worked out what to say if she guessed. Now he would have to improvise.

'Yes, there was. We thought we loved each other for a while, but as Allie said, it was Narcissistic. Because we looked so alike we were falling in love with ourselves.'

'But you wanted to marry her. When you came back to Boston you said you were going to marry her.'

'Well, I changed my mind. That was why I came back to the apartment that night.' He made a split second decision not to tell her the truth of it. If she learned that they could not marry because Allie was his half-sister, Feathers would feel second-best for ever.

'And saved my life. Is it true?' Her face was full of wonderment.

'Honestly,' he said firmly.

'Oh, Pierre!' She left her chair to wrap her arms round him. 'It wasn't just that I was pregnant?'

'You knew my views on that at the time. I'd never have married you just because of that. I tell you. I'd changed my

489

mind.' He said it doggedly, willing her to believe him.

'Yes.' She shivered a little at the memory. 'Did you love her very much?' she asked.

'I thought I did. But it was a combination of all sorts of things that caused it. She spoke English and I spoke no French. We were the same age. We were cousins and so no one ever took any notice when we were together a lot. And I was lonely here in France.'

'Did you ever . . .'

'Make love to her? No, I didn't. She wouldn't let me.'

She turned her head away. 'Not brazen, like me!'

'She isn't passionate like you. Allie is a little cold. It wasn't difficult for her to say no.'

'I see.' He saw she liked hearing that she was the more passionate. Then she asked, a little timidly: 'And how did you feel when you saw her again?'

'I didn't feel anything much,' he said.

'Then why did you go after her this afternoon?'

'Just to talk and lay ghosts. It had to be done, Feathers,' he said gently.

Almost every word he had said was true, though much had been left out. But he had told Allie he would keep her secrets and keep them he would.

She gave a great, relieved sigh.

'We ought to go down,' she said. 'Are you ready?'

'Yup.'

She brushed face powder from the shoulder of his dinner jacket.

'Can I ask just one thing?' she said, looking into his eyes.

'What's that?'

'Don't be alone with her again. Everyone must know that you loved her, and it hurts me.'

He kissed the tip of her nose.

'There's no need to be alone with her again,' he said reassuringly. 'No need at all.'

And that at least was absolutely true.

He picked up the ridiculous fan and handed it to her.

'Are you sure you need this?' he grumbled.

She laughed and took it from him, flirted her eyes at him over it and then put it down on her dressing table.

'No,' she said. 'I don't need it. I don't need to hide any more.'

Jenny stood it as long as she could in her charming bedroom in the free hour before dinner and then, dressed in her simple grey evening dress, she went looking for Allie. They had not been alone for a moment since they arrived at Rilly station and she was desperate to know what was going on in Allie's mind. She felt Allie was slipping away from her.

Jenny felt as if she had been wrenched away from security. She felt isolated and almost frightened. The house, the people were all so claustrophobic. There was an atmosphere about the place which bound all its inhabitants into a tight, tight group as if someone had wrapped an elastic band round them all. And Jenny was not part of that group.

She was reassured when Allie let her into her room and gave her a great hug and a kiss.

'I should have come and got you,' she said. 'Oh, but Jenny, it's all so emotional for me. They love me. They still love me. I never thought they would.'

'Don't forget I love you,' Jenny said gruffly.

'I know, I know.' Allie hugged her again. 'Just give me time to get over the excitement of it all. Isn't Rosanne lovely? She's going to be a beauty. If I can only get her to love me again I shall be happy beyond words. I thought I might give her Jessie to look after when we go to Algeria. She always wanted Jessie when she was little. She'd look after her now.'

'He followed you, didn't he?' Jenny asked, ignoring what Allie was saying and moving to look out of the window at the view of the drive below.

'Pierre?'

'Who else?'

'Yes, he did.'

Allie had returned to her dressing table and was fluffing out her hair.

'What did he want?'

'He didn't want anything, except to talk.'

'About what?' Jenny knew she was behaving like an inquisitor, but she couldn't help it.

'Oh really, Jenny!' Allie said, sounding thoroughly irritated. 'You sound like a police inspector.'

'What did he want to talk about?' Jenny persisted.

'How we don't love each other any more. How he loves his wife and I love you.'

'You told him?' She could not believe it was possible.

'I told him.'

Jenny went limp with relief. 'What did he say?'

'Only that he thought love between two women was better than love between a man and a woman. I guess he really was talking about sex. Not love.'

'What an extraordinary thing for a man to say!'

Allie shrugged. 'He's a very sensitive guy.'

'But you don't still love him?'

'I love him like a brother. Which he is.' She slammed her hairbrush down and gave an impatient sigh. 'Must we talk about it any more? It's all over. Finished. Okay? Don't keep asking me questions, Jenny.'

'Okay,' Jenny said hastily. 'His wife is nice.'

'His wife is beautiful. Apparently she owns a successful dress shop. Imagine! I can't think how Grandmama ever let that happen. I bet Mama fixed it.'

'Your mother looks older.' Jenny snatched at the new subject.

'And worried, I thought. I haven't had a moment alone with her yet. I guess we're both avoiding it.'

'Will you tell her about us?'

'Good heavens, no!' Allie looked quite horrified. 'You don't want your parents to know, why should I tell my mother?'

'I thought the French were more liberal about these things.' If Allie would tell her mother, Jenny knew she would be safe again.

'My mother is American,' Allie said shortly, 'and I reckon no one's that liberal when it comes to their own kids.'

Jenny was silent as Allie gathered up the shawl that went over her pleated turquoise dinner dress. She looked once more in the mirror and said: 'Shall we go down?'

'I suppose we should,' Jenny said meekly.

Again Feathers came to her rescue, speaking to her in English as the family gathered in the drawing room for champagne before dinner. Jenny asked her about her dress shop and was answered with such enthusiasm she almost wished she hadn't asked. Luke, the big Englishman who never seemed to take his eyes off Rosie, joined them, eyes twinkling, and managed to change the subject to Jenny's work in Algeria. Allie was talking to her grandmother and to Rosanne who, since it was Allie's homecoming, was joining them for dinner. Pierre stood alone for a while and then Jenny noticed that Rosie, stunning in a vivid green frock which Feathers said was one from her shop, seemed to be taking a lot of trouble with him.

When they moved into the dining room, Jenny found that she had been seated with Pierre on one side, Luke on the other.

'This is the English-speaking end of the table,' Luke said cheerfully, but somehow the two men kept drifting back into French and joining the mainstream of the conversation. Pierre seemed awkward and uncertain of how to talk to her. That was hardly surprising, Jenny thought grimly, since he knew that she and Allie were lovers.

It was when everyone had finished their dessert that Allie caught her eye and made a small signal that Jenny realised meant that she was to listen.

'Mama,' Allie said in English. 'Did you think any more about the house in California?' She looked down the table to where Pierre sat. 'Did Mama tell you that Jenny and I went to Calistoga? I wanted to see the house where she used to live. We fell in love with it and we'd like to go and live there. Put it all back to rights again. Make it beautiful. Would you mind, Pierre, since it was your house once?'

Everyone except Mimi, who obviously did not understand what was being said, looked shaken by Allie's words. Pierre didn't seem to know what to say. He looked at Rosie as if for guidance and then at his wife.

'I don't mind,' he finally said. 'It's Aunt Rosie's house, not mine.' Then he seemed to take a gulp of air. 'But don't you need to sell it, Aunt Rosie?'

Rosie looked dismayed for an instant. And then she said gaily: 'No, no. Not really.'

'Aunt Rosie, that's not true,' Feathers was saying. 'You know you do need to sell it.'

'No, really,' Rosie was saying quickly. 'There's another way. There's always another way. And besides, the house belongs to all you children.' And she was positively glaring at both Pierre and Feathers as she spoke.

There was something wrong here, Jenny thought, and asked: 'Why do you need to sell it, Rosie?'

'I don't,' Rosie said firmly.

Jenny looked across the table to Feathers and raised her eyebrows enquiringly.

Feathers, after a quick look at Rosie, just looked down at her plate.

'Of course you can have it, Allie,' Rosie was saying. 'It was always meant to be yours.'

Allie, who seemed to be oblivious of the anxieties her question had raised, clapped her hands saying: 'Oh, goodie!' and it was at that moment that an irritable Madame broke in, asking what everyone was talking about.

Rosie looked relieved at the opportunity to change the subject, but then Rosanne's childish treble cut across the other voices.

'Honestly, Allie, you're just the same,' she said in remarkably fluent English. 'You didn't even listen to what everyone said. You didn't want to hear because you want your own way. You have to have what you want. Mama does need to sell that house. She has to find a fortune to buy her own business back from Papa Philippe's daughter, but you've never worried about Mama's problems, have you? Only your own.'

'Rosanne!' Rosie said, almost shouting. Allie went white, putting down her knife and fork with a clatter. There was an unhappy silence as Rosanne stared defiantly at Allie and Allie looked back, almost pleadingly. She started to say something but the words would not come at first.

'But I didn't know!' she finally said before bursting into tears. 'How could I know? Oh, Rosanne! Rosanne! My little baby, please don't hate me,' she sobbed as everyone at the table sat in appalled silence.

'What is going on!' asked Madame in a voice of thunder.

Jenny could not stand it. She got to her feet and walked round the table to where Allie sat. Almost rudely she pushed Rosie, who had also moved towards the girl, out of her way.

'Come along,' she said in her schoolmistress voice to Allie. 'It's time you went to bed.'

Allie's tear-stained face looked up at her.

'Come on, Allie darling,' she said more gently. 'You're overtired. It's been a long day.'

Allie rose, and Jenny took her firmly by the hand.

'Goodnight, everyone,' she said, staring defiantly around the room. 'It's time Allie was in bed.'

'Will someone please tell me what is going on!' Madame demanded again. 'Rosanne, what did you say to upset your sister?'

Rosanne's small face was set in the stubborn lines that Rosie knew meant she would not back down one inch.

'I told her she was selfish, Mimi. She wants Mama's house in California, and when everyone told her Mama needed to sell it she took no notice.'

'That's enough, Rosanne,' Rosie said sharply. 'You've done enough damage. Go to your room.'

'All right.' Rosanne got to her feet and made for the door. But before she closed it behind her she turned and said: 'Whatever you say, I'm right. She is selfish.'

Rosie sank back into her chair.

'Oh, dear!' she said. 'This is dreadful!' The room was silent; the embarrassment was almost tangible. She threw down her napkin. 'Look, I'm going to go and see Allie. Will you all excuse me?'

There was a small murmur of agreement round the table and Luke smiled at her encouragingly as she headed for the door.

She sped up the stairs and along the passageway and without ceremony opened the door to Allie's room and walked in. She was confronted by the sight of Jenny holding Allie tightly in her arms and kissing her tear-streaked face. As Rosie stopped dead in her tracks, Jenny sprang back, releasing Allie. No one spoke, but Jenny's face was scarlet.

Something was wrong, Rosie thought, looking at the two hangdog young women standing before her. The atmosphere was electric, but since her mind was bent on reassuring her daughter she merely said: 'Would you mind leaving me alone with Allie, Jenny?'

'I'd like to stay,' Jenny said belligerently.

Rosie felt her eyebrows rise. 'Well, I'd prefer to talk to Allie on my own for a while,' she said coldly and held open the door for the girl to leave. Jenny hesitated, looked at Allie for support, but Allie had averted her face. Jenny then went to the door with obvious reluctance, turning back to say: 'You know where I am if you want me, Allie.'

Allie just nodded. The other girl looked as if she wanted to say something more, but then she closed the door, leaving Rosie and her daughter alone. Allie did not move. She stood where Jenny had left her in the same stance as when she had been in Jenny's arms, shoulders drooped, head bowed, arms at her side.

'I'm sorry, Allie,' Rosie said, uncertain what to do. 'So very sorry.'

Allie gave a little hiccup of a sob and stepped forward to bury her face in her mother's shoulder. Relieved that Rosanne had not destroyed the new closeness, Rosie hugged her tightly with one arm, stroking her dark hair with the other hand.

'But, Mama, Rosanne was right,' Allie said, her voice muffled. 'I didn't want to hear what you were all saying. I am selfish and Rosanne is the last person in the world I wanted to know it.'

Rosie's heart lifted. This unexpected confession seemed to prove conclusively that Allie was a different girl from the one who went away so full of hostility, hatred and self-pity.

'Come and sit down.' Rosie was manoeuvring them both back to the bed. 'Sit down here beside me and we'll talk.'

Allie sat and sighed heavily, wiping her eyes with the back of her knuckles.

'She hates me, Mama.' She sounded full of despair.

'She doesn't know you,' Rosie said firmly.

'She obviously knows me better than any of you.'

Rosie shook her head. 'She only knows the Allie from the time after her birth. The rest of us know the real Allie and we love her. You have to give Rosanne a chance to know you properly.'

'I think the real Allie has gone for ever.'

Rosie gave her daughter an impulsive hug. 'I think she's come back again. In fact I know she's come back again. I knew it the minute I touched you when you arrived this morning. When I put my arms round you, you were with me, you were soft and pliable and pleased to be held. Loving. The Allie who went away was stiff and unbending. Even when I kissed your cheek it was as if you were afraid I was going to bite it, you were so tense at the idea of me touching you. And look at you now, with your head on my shoulder, and how you were letting Jenny comfort you. After Rosanne was born you distanced yourself from everyone. Before you were so different. Do you remember how when you were little you always liked to snuggle up with your father and me if you had a bad dream in the night? After Rosanne was born, you never let me cuddle you again. But you're better, Allie. You're my Allie back again. But Rosanne doesn't know that yet.'

Allie was sitting up again, sniffing, and Rosie handed her the handkerchief that she kept tucked in her sleeve. Allie blew her nose loudly.

'When she was little I used to hug and kiss Rosanne a lot, but only when no one was looking,' she said. 'I ignored her when anyone was about and that used to upset her and make her cry. I did it because I didn't want you to see that I loved her. I was jealous of you because you'd got my baby and I wanted her for myself.'

Rosie felt her heart contract.

'Oh, Allie, what could I do?' she said sadly. 'I didn't want to take your baby, but someone had to love her, and you didn't seem to want to have anything to do with her.'

'I know. Mimi tried to tell me once that I could love her like a sister, but I was so full of resentment . . .'

'And your grandmother tried to tell me not to pay so much attention to Rosanne when you were about.' She hugged Allie again. 'If only we'd both listened to wise old Grandma.'

'I was too bitter to listen to anyone. I blamed everyone. Papa for not being there to save me from the lieutenant. You for doing what I felt should have been his job. I'd always been a bit jealous of you, Mama – you always took the limelight somehow. I know you didn't do it deliberately, but the sun always seemed to shine just on you. I wanted to be like you, and yet at the same time I told myself I didn't want to be like you. After you killed the lieutenant—' Rosie shuddered involuntarily and it was Allie's turn to hug her – 'I should have been so grateful to you, but I wasn't. I think I even felt that if you hadn't gone into the house and left me alone it wouldn't have happened and I wouldn't have been pregnant, so it was all your fault. I blamed you for everything. And when I couldn't marry Pierre . . .' she shook her head. 'Well, it was easy to blame you for that.'

'I did understand how you felt,' Rosie told her sadly.

'I must have hurt you.'

'Well, yes, but you were still my daughter.'

'I see things so much more clearly now. I didn't love Alexander in the right way when I married him and yet I berated you for marrying Papa when you didn't love him in the right way. I can see now why you needed Philippe. We all need love, of some kind or another.'

'We just got ourselves on the wrong track,' Rosie said, trying to be comforting but wondering what Allie meant by love of some kind or another. 'But we never stopped loving each other, did we?'

'You never stopped loving me. They made me see that at the clinic. They made me see a lot of things at the clinic. I think I have changed.'

Rosie smiled. 'You haven't changed from what you really were. You're just back home with yourself again,' she said. 'As a little girl you were always rushing into things. You were full of enthusiasms and full of love. Remember how you loved Sebastian and Alexander, too, when he first came here. It was the lieutenant who killed the love in you until Pierre came. When you fell in love with Pierre all the love came back for a little while and then circumstances destroyed it again. It's back again now, isn't it?' Allie nodded and squeezed her mother's hand as confirmation.

'And was it all right, seeing Pierre again?' Rosie's voice was tentative.

'It was strange,' Allie said thoughtfully. 'I wasn't sure if all that I'd felt for him would come back when I saw him, but it didn't. I was pleased to see him. But I really didn't feel anything. I looked at him and just remembered how once I'd been crazy about him and knew that I wasn't any more. Where does all that love go, Mama? How can it just disappear like that when once you thought you could die for someone?'

'Time takes it away. Growing up. Circumstances,' Rosie said sadly. 'It was the same with your real father. I thought I would die when he left me and yet when I met him again all those years after, I didn't even like him.'

'I still like Pierre. He's nice. Soft. He's not strong like Jenny.'

The words came out as if Allie had been speaking to herself, and as they hung in the air, she blushed scarlet. Rosie suddenly realised what had been wrong with the tableau when she came into Allie's room. Jenny had been holding Allie not as a sympathetic friend. The caresses and kisses were those of a lover. The scene had not been simply of comfort, but of burning sexuality.

Very carefully, fearing her words could harm this wonderfully restored rapport with her daughter, Rosie said: 'Give yourself time, Allie, don't rush into love again. It's such a rich brew, so intoxicating, that it's tempting to drink too deep of it. And since it was stolen from you for a while, finding it again will be heady stuff. Give yourself time to contemplate all the commitment that real love is before you give yours and accept someone else's.'

They sat in silence, holding hands in the room.

'It's all been a waste of years, hasn't it?' Allie said, then added abruptly: 'I'm going to divorce Alexander.'

Rosie, not surprised, simply nodded.

'It will be kinder to him. I'll never be a proper wife. Jenny wants to look after me.'

'You can't look after yourself?' Rosie asked the question very gently.

'I'm beginning to think that I can. Coming home has changed things in a way. I'd forgotten there were people who love me and who would always be there if I needed them.'

'Lots of people if you need them,' Rosie said cheerfully. It was time to lighten the mood.

'But not Rosanne.'

'I think Rosanne probably feels much the same way about you as you did about me. There's love there somewhere.'

'But she doesn't know I'm her mother? She won't have guessed from what I said?' Allie asked anxiously.

'I don't think so. You would be entitled to think of her as "your baby" – since she sees you as a much older sister.'

'I don't want her to know. Not yet.'

'Then if you want her to know one day, you'd better get to know her.'

'Yes, perhaps I'd better,' Allie said thoughtfully. 'And

Mama, I don't want the California house. I think I'm changing my mind about lots of things. Being home has made me see things so differently. New York's so brittle, all gloss and excitement and everyone being so modern and daring. I never really got involved with it all. I never felt safe there. I didn't really belong. I had to have someone to look after me. Maybe I will go to Algeria for a while and maybe I won't. I'll have to think about it. What I would like is to take Rosanne away with me somewhere.'

'With Jenny?' Rosie asked, apprehensive.

'No, just with me. We could go to the seaside. Could I do that?'

'If Rosanne wants to go, of course.'

'Do you think she will?'

'Once she gets to know you again.'

'But she was right about me,' Allie said sadly. 'I didn't realise when I asked for the house —'

'How could you know?' Rosie interrupted.

'Are things very bad?'

'Not very good,' Rosie admitted, and briefly told the sorry tale.

'How could Philippe have done such a thing!' Allie asked indignantly when her mother stopped speaking.

'He was ill. The tumour must have affected his thinking. And Françoise was very persuasive.'

'It's frightful!' Allie said. 'I've got some money, Mama. Quite a lot. I made it myself from my writing. I went on taking what you sent even though I didn't need it because I was so angry with you. You can have all that back. It's not my money, it's yours. It won't be anywhere near enough, but it will help. I'll telephone Papa Webster tonight and get him to arrange to transfer it to you.'

'I don't want to take your money, Allie,' Rosie said and made a desperate little gesture of rejection with her hands.

'It's not my money. I should never have taken it after I started to earn so much and was married to Alexander. And besides, this is my inheritance, too, isn't it? Won't Les Hérissons be mine and Rosanne's one day?'

'The business will. And the production company if I can manage to raise the money. You'll share Les Hérissons itself with Pierre and Rosanne.'

'Well, we don't want our livelihood to go to some stranger, do we?' Allie said, with a touch of her old sparkle.

'Allie, it's 650,000 francs I have to find.'

500

'Well, every little helps.' Allie was smiling. 'You will take it, won't you? It's about 50,000 francs.'

Rosie understood that it was important to Allie that she took the money. To refuse would be a kind of rejection.

'Yes, Allie, I will, and thank you,' she said, kissing her daughter on the cheek and hugging her hard. The money would be, as Allie said, only a little help, but it was the gesture that was so important and so moving. She took Allie's hand in hers. 'Come on,' she said. 'We'd better go and see Rosanne in case she's crying herself to sleep. It's time you two made friends.'

Rosanne was not crying herself to sleep, she was sitting up in her small bed in the nursery reading. She gave a quick scared look up as her mother and Allie came in and said, defiantly casual: 'Oh, hello.'

'Rosanne,' Rosie said quietly. 'You owe your sister an apology. She is going to give us some money to help save Les Hérissons.'

Rosanne put down her book.

'You are, Allie?' she said, eyes wide. 'That's terrific. But where did you get it from?'

'Writing stories,' Allie told her.

'Gosh! You write them well enough for people to pay for them?'

'That's right,' Allie said.

Rosanne was visibly impressed.

'Have you ever written a play?' she asked.

'Not yet.'

'When I'm an actress, will you write a play for me?'

'It's a deal,' Allie said. 'Funny, I wanted to be an actress when I was your age. I was going to call myself Blanche le Beau.'

'I thought I'd use my own name.'

'It's probably better.'

Neither of them noticed as Rosie slipped out of the room. It was going to be okay with those two, she thought thankfully as she went back downstairs. Now she could turn her mind to the immediate problem of money. In the morning she would have to go and visit the bank manager again and throw herself on his mercy.

Luke was hovering in the hall.

'Drive you home, ma'am?' he said, doffing an imaginary cap.

Rosie laughed. 'I'll have to buy you a chauffeur's cap if this goes on. Where is everyone?'

'All gone to bed in disarray. Is Allie all right?'

'She's fine. She's with Rosanne. Discussing the play she's going to write for Rosanne's debut as an actress.'

'Kids!' he said.

'Kids!' she echoed. 'But it's all so emotionally exhausting. Particularly now . . .'

'Ah, now,' he said. 'I wanted to talk to you about that.'

'Then let's go and steal some of Madame's Marc,' she said, 'and talk.'

They sat in Madame's little sitting room before a dying fire and Rosie thought how many of the most important moments of her life had happened in this room. Madame had not so much as changed a knick-knack. The fire that always burned, even in high summer, the little sofa, always re-upholstered when necessary in the same fabric. There was a continuity about the room that was comforting.

'So what's new?' Luke asked, twirling the amber Marc in the large goblet a little intently.

Rosie looked into the depth of her goblet and said baldly: 'I have ten days to find the rest of the money.'

He was silent. He sat on the sofa with his shoulders slumped, his hands dropping through his parted thighs.

'Rosie . . .'

She looked at him enquiringly. He seemed to be having trouble finding words.

'Listen,' he said suddenly resolute. 'How would you feel about having me as a partner?'

'You?' He had startled her.

'Yes, I didn't want to say anything before because I wasn't sure if I could pull if off. But my father's company would be interested in buying into Les Hérissons' champagne. Either just the distribution end, which honestly isn't worth a great deal since it's so run down, or buying the whole of Françoise's share, or a proportion of it. Whatever you think. My father feels that owning part of a champagne house would blend in well with his sherry business. They have their own distribution set-up, of course, but if they took over all Philippe's old contacts in the claret world it would work out very well for them.

My father says that if you have a team selling sherry, they might as well be selling other wines as well. They are ready to expand, and the truth is they've always felt a bit guilty about me. My father feels that if you were agreeable to the idea, it would give me a proper stake in Les Hérissons and what he calls a proper future.'

She just stared at him, not yet able fully to take in what he was saying. He took her silence as discouragement.

'Rosie, you don't have to say yes. I expect you're thinking about Allie and Rosanne. I'm thinking of Hope, too. Believe me, I'd make legally sure that if anything happened to me none of the Dupuis would lose out.'

'You're saying that you want to be my partner in the business and that your family firm will find the 650,000 francs?' Rosie asked slowly.

'Yes. Or just part of it, if you would prefer to retain some of Françoise's share.'

He sat there looking too big for the small sofa, staring at the floor. His bumpy forehead was creased into a frown. Then he looked up, almost shyly, and said quietly: 'I'd be a good partner for you, Rosie, because I love you very much.'

She sat looking at him, thinking what a good partner he already was. She had leaned on him shamelessly since he arrived at Les Hérissons. She had always been aware that he cared for her and in the last weeks his presence had begun to stir her. Even before Philippe had died it was to Luke that she went with her problems. He had always been her good friend. But his declaration of love she could not deal with. Not yet.

He didn't press. He said: 'It's time you had someone who helps you, Rosie. Someone who's on your side and who'll be tough for you when there's need to be. Your trouble is that you want everyone to be happy, often at your own expense. And I don't just mean financial expense.'

Suddenly she smiled. She could feel all the tensions of the past months draining away. Relief was setting in. Unexpectedly the burdens were to be lifted and in a perfect way.

'Luke, I can't think of anyone I would rather have as a partner than you,' she told him. 'I think it's a wonderful idea.'

His face lit up and he stood and came to take her hands in his. 'You do? Rosie, that's wonderful. But what will Madame say? Will she agree, do you think? She wanted it for Pierre.'

Madame would probably have a fit, but Rosie said: 'She's not going to get the chance to disagree. You've put as much love and labour into this place as anyone since you've been here. A darn sight more than Pierre ever has. But I think Pierre will work with you. He and I don't trust each other and he resents working with a woman. I think you'll get him on course. And Madame is very fond of you . . .'

'Not that fond,' he said ruefully.

She laughed. 'Well, it's not Les Hérissons itself we're talking about. What we're talking about is my business. Luke, I accept. I accept with gratitude.'

'And the fact that I love you?' His intent look stirred all the old, buried appetites.

She hesitated. Philippe had not been dead four months and yet looking at the man towering above her she could not control the urge to wonder how he kissed. It was shameful to feel that way. Disloyal. And she knew she should behave like a respectable widow and refuse to discuss his feelings.

But that would be neither fair nor honest.

'I know what you're thinking,' he said urgently. 'I know you very well, Rosie Lefevre. You're thinking that it's no time at all since Philippe died, and that you must go on mourning and that you cannot accept any declaration until that mourning time is over. But I need to know, Rosie. If you tell me honestly that you feel nothing for me, I'll never mention my feelings again. It won't make any difference to our professional association. But I think you do feel for me. And I think in your heart you want to tell me so. You're just being loyal to the dead. But the dead can't hold you in their arms, kiss you, and make you happy again. I can. I don't mind waiting. I've waited a hell of a long time already, but I need to know. I need some hope.'

She felt as if she were melting from the warmth of his words. She would have to be truthful. But an imp of mischief made her say: 'I'm too old for you.'

He made an angry, chopping movement with his hand.

'Don't be daft,' he said. 'That's idiotic and you know it. Rosie, stop messing about. Be honest with me. Is there any hope?'

'Oh, yes,' she said quietly. 'A great deal. But I'm not quite

ready yet, Luke. I have so many things to come to terms w
seems my life is calming. Allie home again, but there ar
problems there. I think she wants to stay. How will Pierre
Feathers react?'

'She's not going off with that Jenny?'

'I don't know. I don't think so.'

'That's a good thing.'

'You thought . . .' she hesitated.

'Yes, I thought. It's pretty obvious, isn't it? But under-standable. You can see why that kind of arrangement might attract Allie – for a while.'

'I suppose so,' Rosie said doubtfully. 'I admit to being shocked.'

'That's because she's your daughter.'

'I suppose so. But will you give me a little more time, Luke? Not long. I promise I'll sort myself out as quickly as I can.'

'You can have as much time as you like as long as it's not longer than six months,' he said gruffly.

'Agreed.' She stood up and kissed him on the forehead, pulling his head down so she could reach. 'And now, I want to go home. I want to be alone to think.'

'I'll drive you.'

She shook her head. 'Just crank the car for me, will you?'

'Anything you want.'

He looked as if he might kiss her and then drew back.

'I'll do it now,' he said and made for the door as if he had a train to catch.

They said quiet goodnights. For the moment no more need be said and he went back into the house.

Rosie drove her car to the lodge. She left it there and made her way back up the drive on foot. She wanted to climb to her high view over the estate. She wanted to sit there in the dark-ness and say her goodbyes to those whom she had loved who had gone.

Her footsteps were firm on the narrow path in the moonlight and as she came onto the crest of the hill, Les Hérissons was laid out below her, painted silver by the moon that rode high in a windy sky.

She sat on the dew-damp grass, her hands round her knees, looking down on the estate she had worked for all her adult

had been a long, long haul. In a few months' time she
be forty-four and for a while it had looked as if she
have to start all over again. The bitter hurt she felt that
Philippe could have done that to her rose again in her throat.
Luke would save her from the consequences of Philippe's
actions, but now she was going to have to share Les Hérissons'
champagne with Luke. It would no longer be wholly hers.

Then she thought with a lifting of the spirit that in time,
when she was ready, she would be sharing much more with
Luke. What was left of her life would be spent with him.

The life behind her had not turned out so badly after all.
Allie was home again. She and Rosanne would rediscover each
other and maybe that one remaining secret could be told.
Madame, thank God, still survived to boss them all and hold
them all together. Feathers had proved to be a real force for
good in their lives. Maybe she would one day inspire Pierre to
greater deeds. Les Hérissons would go on. The children would
grow and the vines would grow. The new generation would
take over one day and that was as it should be.

Suddenly tired, she stood up and stretched, throwing back
her head to look at the stars. Down below she could see the
shadowy outlines of the house. A light burned in Luke's turret
rooms, twinkling as bravely as any star in the darkness, a
beacon to guide her home.

She smiled to herself, imagining him thinking of her as she
was thinking of him. And then she set off back down the hill,
quietly content.

All was well.